yo

Marcia Crooker Cowles

SWING INN PUBLISHING

1440 Caton Rd.

Corning, NY 14830

Cover photo by Marcia Crooker Cowles

Special thanks to:

Harriett Harris, kindred spirit friend,

for your encouragement and lifesaving help;

Erin Wilson, granddaughter,

for your expertise in getting YO published;

Barbara Cowles my first reader;

Charlotte Cowles who wouldn't let me give up.

For Dick,

and all the roads we've traveled together.

.

1 Corinthians 13: 12

For now we see through a glass, darkly:

but then face to face:

now I know in part:

but then shall I know even as also I am known.

Chapter 1

When the bus pulled out of the station in Maplehurst, I felt a depth of emptiness so deep that in spirit I was dead. My heart lay beside Carrie's lifeless body. Her death was a wound that is impossible to articulate. Nothing that had ever happened to me cut as deeply or painfully. The wheels of the bus droned, "Dead, dead, dead, dead, dead." I covered my ears, and I could still feel it vibrating up though the bus floor through my soul, over and over, "dead, dead, dead." Why at the last minute hadn't I gone up on the mountain and taken my life? It would have been preferable to a walking death. Why had I thought the Wallaces could help me? Why had the thought of them kept me from traveling further into death? A pervasive paralyzing numbness kept the feel of my arms locked around Carrie's lifeless, oh-so-sweet, little body.

There was no way I could have stood by her coffin next to Porter as he went on and on about how his precious Carrie was in a better place. His precious Carrie, who he had said was pretending to be sick, who he would have dragged to the studio that terrible morning. He was more concerned about the cost of a hospital visit than he was about his grief. It was beyond my comprehension that he proposed God was using Carrie's death to get even with me for what he considered my sins; that God purposely let Carrie die because I had not prayed. I could never worship such a God! I would never have been able to endure his funeral sermon. To hear the wrathful words of his vengeful God spewed out into the very air I was breathing would have torn my heart to shreds.

I searched for a prayer and it was like a north wind blowing over frozen land. I had known God. My faith at one time had been important and part of everything I did. Where was it? I wanted to believe, but Porter had made faith false and irrelevant without reason. In my state of withdrawal my lack of confidence made everything I thought questionable, but I knew beyond a doubt, Porter would end Carrie's funeral sermon with an altar call, one aimed directly at me. That, in the midst of my consuming grief, would have been the final blow to any hope of ever returning to reality. Running away was the only way to keep from breaking apart and flying into a million pieces. In the process I would have hurt many people I loved in both Jackson Junction Free Methodist Church and Good Shepherd Evangelical Church. It was far better for everyone; I had rationalized, to run away. My heart and my faith were dead.

***

Once I arrived in the Binghamton bus station, I curled up on a bench with my few possessions clutched in my arms, sought oblivion, and slept. I had no thought that some lone fan from my singing tours could recognize me. I was a stranger to myself and so would be to anyone. When I climbed over the tailgate of Jimmy's truck unseen just hours ago all connection to that life was severed.

During the next days I changed into my old high school clothes, braided my hair into tight pigtails and washed away all makeup. Most of the time my mind was blank, but periodically strange fragments of thoughts or segments of a tune would flit across my consciousness.

When an elderly woman sitting next to me on the bus asked what my name was, I answered, "Rachel Reuben." The phrase, "Rachel, Rachel, I've been thinking what a strange world this would be, if the men were all transported far beyond the northern sea", had been going round and round in my brain. When I could again think rationally, I decided the name was a good choice because it fit my looks perfectly.

How far and where I traveled, I couldn't say. I only knew it must be north, away from condemnation, toward Bardo and the family whose name Ma had stolen and given to me. At a bus station I wandered by a newsstand and like a slap of reality, my smiling face stared back at me.

VANISHED WITHOUT A TRACE...Suicide?...neighbor Mildred Comb, "Millie", blames herself..."I should never have left Jo alone after what she suffered that terrible day."...

...bible in hand, a teary-eyed Rev. Porter Kent said, "I don't know how I can go on without my soul mate and vocal partner. She had the voice of an angel."...

Soul mate! Voice of an angel! More like devil! Did Porter ever tell the truth? It was the money my voice made that he would miss!

...house left undisturbed...door unlocked...purse with money and identification left on the kitchen table...speculate suicide...police very troubled...hunt for missing suicide note...volunteers refuse to give up and still search the mountain...

Horrified, Carrie's funeral was to be that day. My heart beat with such force I put my hand over it to hold it in as I ran into the restroom and threw up.

Once I was back on the bus, I put my head against the window and let the drone of the tires on the pavement jar my brains into mush until I fell into a troubled cops-and-robbers sleep. In my dream Carrie had been stolen, and all the villains wore black robes like the one Porter bought for preaching in his prestigious new Good Shepherd Evangelical Church. All the policemen had Porter's face. Finally, I was sobbing because I couldn't find Rev. Grey. Ma had hidden him.

The man sitting next to me gently touched my shoulder. "Young lady, are you all right?"

"Just a bad dream. Thank you for waking me."

He looked like an executive because he had an attaché case across his knees. He must have mistaken me for a student because he said, "My daughter was home recently on break. She struggled in the beginning but she's fine now." The bus was stopping, and he stood up. "Good luck. It'll work out OK. You'll see." I took note because how disturbed I felt must be alarmingly evident, but at least I passed as a student and not Josephine Kent, VANISHED WITHOUT A TRACE, run away minister's wife.

The next stop was Bardo, and summoning-up the dregs of my depleted courage, I left the bus and my neutral world behind, as I took my first step into an entirely new reality. I found the restroom and freshened up, stored my grocery bag of clothes in a locker and bought the BARDO MORNING NEWS. I had hardly eaten anything during my travels, and the morning Carrie died there had been no time to eat. Carrie's voice echoed in my head, "Fried egg, Mommy". I ordered an egg salad sandwich, and while scanning the paper for rooms to rent, I was able to wash it down with the aid of a coke.

There were two rooms available, and I decided to check out the one on First Street because it sounded closest to downtown Bardo which would be convenient. The room was small, but clean. I would share a bathroom with two other roomers. $25.00 per month paid in advance.

Mrs. Henley, my landlady asked me if I intended to apply for a Nursing Assistant job, as that was what most of her roomers did. She said Bardo Memorial Hospital was only a short walk, and the hospital was just starting an on-the-job nursing-aid training class. She was a real busybody and added that few stayed with the program. That was why she required a month's rent in advance. She had been stuck with unpaid rent once too often though she was sure I'd make a wonderful nurse's aid.

It worked out well because Bardo Memorial Hospital paid weekly, you wore their uniform and it was only a two-block walk to work. During my first week I went to my classes, studied my lesson hand-out and slept. I felt like I could sleep forever. If I were not involved in class or studying I wanted to be asleep. At the end of the second week I forced myself to do some shopping for clothes, and I started looking for the Wallace name in the phone book. There was only one listed in Bardo: R. Wallace, 4 Rainbow Drive.

Once my class was completed, I was given an afternoon shift from 3 to 11 which suited me because the evening's descending darkness was impossible to bear. It was lucky for me that I was assigned to the geriatric ward, which was as far from pediatrics as I could get. Seeing a sick child would have sent me into a fatal tailspin. My patients made me think of Aunt Carrie, and yes, Aunt Alma too, and were easy for me to care for. The work was purposeful and so demanding I had little time while at work to reflect on my troubles.

Away from work, I grieved. Anguish over the loss of Carrie consumed me. Her death left little room in my emotions for considering the feelings of those I had left behind. When unbidden contemplations did manage to crowd into my thoughts, I cringed at the untold pain I was responsible for with burning guilt. Strangely, Ma was seldom in my thoughts, but when she was, she was the disruptive emotional connecting-thread between the world of those I loved and Porter's world that was the source of an underlying anger that never left me.

Walking became the outlet for my anger and pain. Bardo was a beautiful town of aging trees, large manicured lawns and mostly posh mansion-size houses. I wondered where all the money came from that supported such a grand life style. The beauty of such opulence was smothering and made me feel insignificant. Porter's new parsonage, that I had thought too grand, was meager in comparison. The First Street neighborhood houses were smaller but still nicely maintained.

Finally, I asked one of the nurses for directions to Rainbow Drive. It was a short street close to the Bardo High School. That fit perfectly and told me I was on the right track because Ma had said the Wallaces lived near where she went to high school. I walked by 4 Rainbow Drive a dozen times, asking myself what I hoped to gain from the crazy notion that I must meet the family whose name Ma had given me. What was the secret of the "good life" they possessed that she had coveted? Why had its mystery kept me from climbing the mountain to oblivion? On my next day off, I would ring the doorbell and find out.

***

The musical tones of the doorbell surprised me. They were pleasant and probably the first indication of the good-life that Ma talked about. It took a long time for the door to open. There stood an elderly woman with white hair as abundant as mine, poorly pinned in a flyaway knot on top of her head. Her right arm was in a cast held to her chest by a triangular sling. She was tall and thin with bright eyes as dark as mine.

"Hello, I'm Rebecca Wallace, as I'm sure you already know." She stepped back for me to enter.

My mind whirled, spinning around; what was going on? I hesitated.

"Do come in. Marie said not to expect you until tomorrow but I'm so happy you're here. You can see the predicament I'm in."

I stepped into the house, evaluating what my response should be. Of all people, Aunt Alma and one of her sayings popped into my mind.

"What webs we weave when first we practice to deceive." In a split second, I decided to tell half-truths. "I'm afraid you've mistaken me for someone else, but I'd be more than happy to help out. I'm Rachel Rubin, and it's a long story."

"Well hello, Rachel. Tell me, what brings you to my door?"

I looked into those dark eyes and with a quiver in my voice, began my story. "I'll tell you right off I'm a runaway. I can't give you my real name because my husband's looking for me. And I can promise you, he's never gonna hurt me again." How to go on? "I'm not from around here as you probably guessed. We're country folk and our neighbor, my good friend Clara, said I should come to Bardo and find you. She said you helped her go to high school when she was a welfare girl."

I could see her mind was fishing for the right connection. "Clara? You must mean…could it possibly be Mary Louise Long? This is most unusual. Do come and sit down and tell me if it could possibly be our Mary Louise. We searched for her for months. Come."

She weaved slightly as if the shock was too much for her, and I took her arm. The house spoke of tasteful wealth. She led me past a room lined with books, and in the corner I could see a free standing beautiful globe of the world. I had the distinct impression Mr. Wallace had been a professor.

She led the way through open French doors. "What a lovely sunroom, Mrs. Wallace. Your gardens are magnificent. Makes me want'a get right out there and start digging in the soil. I'm a gardener at heart."

"Then you have mine. Please call me Rebecca."

The sunroom was decorated in spring-green and white, erasing the barrier to the lovely gardens outside. She directed me to an elegant white wicker sofa. I blinked away the image of the brown wicker sofa in the Jackson Junction parsonage that I had reupholstered with Millie's feed sacks.

"Now tell me, could your neighbor really be our Mary Louise? What happened to her?"

"I think she must be. She's blonde and very pretty. She loved you and said you treated her like one of the family."

"How is she? What happened? Why did she disappear without a word? John and I were frantic, as were our friends the Burns family, where she worked. They loved her too. The police were unable to find her. They searched for months. Our minds have never been at ease, fearing the worst." Rebecca's eyes filled with tears.

I swallowed guilt ridden bile that rose up in my throat. I must not let myself think of those I left behind. "Clara never talked about her past. She was ashamed because she was a welfare girl. I think she was an orphan or something. I don't know what I'd have done if I hadn't had her for a neighbor. I didn't know what I was getting into. I married when I was sixteen to get away from home. You can see what a big mistake that was."

She took my hand in hers, just as Rev. Grey had taken Ma's when she confided the story of her rape to him. But I couldn't tell Rebecca Wallace that, or that I was the product of that rape.

"You poor child. But why did Mary Louise run away? Something must have happened. We should have adopted her. I want very much to see her again."

"No...please don't ask me...I can't tell anyone...not yet. The only way I can be safe is to stay hidden. There's so much more to my story that I can't talk about. I've just finished the nursing-aid training session over at Bardo Memorial. And I've a room over on First Street, please help me keep my secret."

"I don't know quite what to say. I'm overwhelmed with relief to know Mary Louise is alright. She is alright, isn't she?"

"Oh yes. She married a farmer and has two wonderful stepsons, Matt and Mark." I left mean Luke out.

"Your safety is the most important consideration, but knowing how I felt when Mary Louise disappeared I can't help worrying about what those you left behind must be going through."

I had to lie. "There's no need. Clara understands where I am and my folks won't even miss me. If they wonder Clara'll explain." I hated to lie to Rebecca, but there was no way I could face all the terrible things I was running away from.

"Rachel, I do need a hair comb and if you'd like to get us lunch, I'd love to have you fill-in until I hear from Marie's replacement."

***

My nurse-aide training made it an easy task for me to take over Rebecca's care. I washed her hair and helped her with a bath, cleaned up the kitchen and cooked lunch and supper for the two of us. All of which was an immense pleasure because Rebecca was exactly the grandmother of my dreams. It was easy to see why Ma loved her so much. And working in her lovely home was a joy, evidence of the good life Ma talked about.

When she learned I didn't have to report to work until the following day at three o'clock, she invited me to spend the night. She confided, "Rose," who was Marie's niece, "is a country girl too. You'll be able to meet her, and I'll bet she'd like a shopping pal or someone to visit with besides an old lady. She's anxious to earn some money for her trousseau."

I would have given anything to be the one taking over her care, so I agreed. It occurred to me how trusting she was to invite a stranger to stay overnight. So many things were foreign to any experience I had ever had before, including calling a person old enough to be my grandmother by her first name. I could feel an awakening awareness of life happening around the edges of my withdrawal.

Next morning I rose early and slipped out to her flower garden and deadheaded her daffodils and tulips. Suddenly, I realized, spring was happening all around me, and for the first time in my life it had failed to warm my soul. Carrie and her beautiful little face full of wonder squeezed my heart so hard tears slipped down my cheeks. Before I could shut out that world I had left behind, I was sobbing for Carrie, something I had not allowed myself to do.

When Rebecca awoke, she came to the sunroom and waved to me through the slider. I dried my eyes on my shirt tail, and Rebecca pretended not to notice, which was further proof of her kindness. I fixed poached eggs on toast with a dish of fresh fruit for our breakfast. Visions of Carrie's animated little face as she asked, "Do yellow yolks turn into yellow chicks?" filled my mind before I could shut them out.

Our talk was light and mostly about our mutual love of gardening. I combed her hair again and helped her dress, and by lunch time, Rose arrived. It was obvious she would be a good caregiver, but to my disappointment, she couldn't wait to marry and move away from the farm. How I wish I had never left the Stanley farm, but I must not let myself go there! But at least she was a farm girl and that was enough to make her interesting. Her future husband was in the service and would be home in time for a June wedding.

As I was leaving, Rebecca invited me to come and work in her garden. "You're more than welcome anytime you feel the need to put your hands in the soil, and I'd love seeing you again."

"Thank you. It's therapy for me."

Her invitation was a caress; I felt she understood and that was the beginning of our friendship. She always came out to the garden with praise for my work and to sit awhile and chat. Often she invited me in to have tea with her and Rose. It became a natural and gradual transition for me to takeover Rose's duties when she left to go home to make final plans for her wedding.

When I was with Rebecca or working in her garden, I was a new person with no ties to the past. She had stopped asking about Mary Louise. I lived one day at a time, never looking backward at the past or to the future. When Marie decided to stay with her daughter indefinitely to help with the twins, Rebecca asked me if I'd continue with the schedule we had worked out. I was overjoyed, and that joy should have sounded an alarm; you can not live for the moment indefinitely. How many times had my life changed in a moment's time?

My head-in-the-sand world ended abruptly the day I accompanied Rebecca to the nursery. She wanted my help selecting annuals to spruce-up her beds. She explained that she was always at a loss to know what to buy, and she was sure I'd know exactly what was needed.

We arrived home from the nursery at noon, and I was full of excitement to get started with my planting. So after a quick lunch, I lost no time in getting out to the garden. I was sorting petunias according to color when Rebecca came out onto the patio accompanied by a lady I had never met.

"This is one of my dearest friends, Hilda Burns. She's anxious to meet you because she knew Mary Louise very well. Hilda, this is Rachel Ruben."

"Hello, Rachel, it's wonderful to know Mary Louise is alive and well. Rebecca and I both wanted to adopt her."

As Porter's wife I had learned to be a pretty good diplomat. "Sounds like a joint custody case to me."

Rebecca laughed. "That's about the way it was."

I don't think Mrs. Burns was aware of how little I had revealed of myself to Rebecca because she said, "I can hardly wait. When are we going to meet your friend? Whatever happened to Mary Louise?"

Rebecca answered for me. "I should have explained. Rachel is hiding from an abusive marriage. Her friend knows the situation and where she is."

Sympathy showed in Mrs. Burns' eyes. "I'm sorry, if I can help in any way let me know. I have a very close lawyer friend if you need one."

I needed more time to know my own wishes, but her kindness was gratifying and heartened me. "Thank you. I'll certainly keep that in mind."

Rebecca led Mrs. Burns around the garden as I continued with my planting. They sauntered along the winding paths that were much more beautiful than the ones I still remembered in the mural on Aunt Alma's Sweet Shop wall. Here and there, they'd stop to examine a particular arrangement of plants, and I could hear them praise my gardening skills.

Rebecca had begun to pay me, insisting, "You do a better job than my landscaper so you should be paid his wage. I never have to tell you what to do; you just know. Plus, I enjoy your company."

"But I'd pay you; that's how much I enjoy gardening. As I told you, gardening's my therapy."

They made a beautiful picture as they strolled side-by-side, two elderly white-haired, slim, well-dressed ladies. I thought, "Wouldn't it be wonderful if the world were really like this garden, this moment, with the sun's blessing shining down on all it touched?" I struggled for a moment to keep my thoughts from slipping back in time to the real world I couldn't face. They ended up on the patio again and waved to me as they disappeared inside to finish their visit. I liked Mrs. Burns. She had not pried or made me feel uncomfortable.

I was starting on the geraniums when I heard Mrs. Burns' car back out of the driveway. Her car had hardly had time to reach the street when a concerned Rebecca came back out to the garden. "Rachel, please come inside. I have to ask you some very distressful questions."

For a moment I closed my eyes. Fear prickled up my spine. I was in jeopardy. To give myself time, I put away my tools, and took off my shoes on the patio. I had to be calm, and at the same time keep myself alert. My first defensive impulse was to escape, to run. I must control it, keep my concern from showing.

Rebecca opened the slider, and I entered the sunroom. "Please sit down, Rachel. This pains me to have to quiz you, but Hilda was so excited about meeting you that as soon as we were alone inside, she began to ask me about you. And when she learned I really knew nothing about you and how little I actually knew about your neighbor, Clara, our Mary Louise, she grew troubled. I have to explain, Hilda just came back from visiting her son and daughter-in-law and her first grandson. They live down near the Pennsylvania boarder. She said there was something about your looks that kept trying to surface. She guessed Mary Louise had taken the Wallace name when she ran away because the papers were full of a missing person story with a mother named Clara...Clara caught our attention due to your neighbor." Her eyes were full of concern. "You are Josephine Kent, aren't you?'"

All the air went out of my lungs. I had made a fatal mistake. I had given Rebecca Ma's name. How stupid of me. I covered my face with my hands.

"I can see; you are Josephine Kent and Mary Louise is your mother. Oh, Rachel, I am so sorry about Carrie's death. Your grief must be overwhelming, but there has to be more to the story than Hilda read in the papers. Your picture is all over the newspapers in south central New York State. At first they thought that in your grief you had taken your own life, but the police have become involved and ruled it suspicious, and are investigating. Your husband is their primary suspect. Rev. Kent's parishioners said they thought you and Rev. Kent had a perfect marriage. According to Hilda you're a star, and all your fans love you and want to know where you are. She said your beautiful voice was on the radio all the time. Your mother, Clara Osborn, our Mary Louise, insisted you would never do anything that was irresponsible; something was amiss. A Mrs. Stanley said amnesia was the only explanation that made any sense. The police have a dragnet bulletin out for a possible dazed runaway while they continue their investigation for possible foul play." She reached out and took both my hands in hers. Her face and eyes were full of concern. "Rachel, can you talk to me about what happened?"

My heart began to beat so fast it was urging me, escape. Danger was all around me.

Rebecca said, "I can see the fear in your eyes. I promise to keep you safe. But to do that, you have to talk to me."

"I don't think I can, and I must get away. Mrs. Burns may be calling the police right now, and I will never go back."

"Hilda gave me her word she'd wait to hear from me."

I had no options; I had to say something, and it had to be the truth. "When I left the hospital that terrible day my only sane thought was that I had to get away, and that I had to come here. I should have joined Carrie and taken my own life. I don't know why I didn't. Many times when I was little, I wanted to die and join Aunt Carrie who had loved me and abandoned me when she died."

"Oh no, Josephine, you did exactly the right thing. I have thought these weeks that soon you'd feel comfortable enough to confide in me. Can you trust me?" I was quiet too long. "You must see that we have to let the authorities know you're safe."

"No, no...no. I cannot let Porter know where I am. I'm sorry for how unfair I've been to put you in this position." I pulled my hands free and started for the slider and my shoes. I had to get away. How and where could I go?

Rebecca stepped in front of me. "Please, Rachel, talk to me. We can figure this out. You'll have a better chance with my help . . . Come, sit back down . . . Is it just Porter that you're running from?"

"Yes. I don't ever want to see his face again, and I can't be sure Mrs. Burns won't tell where I am. I have to go."

"She has promised. She's waiting to hear from me, and I need to hear more from you."

"I don't know if I can . . . I didn't love Porter when I married him. He didn't ask me to, and he didn't love me. I thought it was a convenience marriage for a singing career . . . nothing more . . . I was only sixteen . . . this is very hard . . . Ma ran away because she was pregnant and didn't want you to know."

Rebecca shook her head. "Oh my, I never guessed."

"It's such a long story . . . she found a place to hide with Aunt Alma and Aunt Carrie in their Sweet Shop. She knew no one could find her there because she was more or less slave labor doing all the candy making and cooking...and she was able to pawn me off on Aunt Carrie until she died." I wasn't going to get into that! "Then Ma married Aunt Alma's son, Paul Osborn, and we moved to the country." Nor was I going to get into that! "It wasn't long and Ma farmed me out to the

15

Stanley family where my stepfather worked as hired man . . . So you see, when I told you Clara, Ma, was a neighbor, in truth she was always more of a neighbor than she was my mother." I could see the shock on her face, not the Mary Louise she knew. "The Stanleys had a son, Forrest, who was my hero, and when he came home from the service and married . . . I knew it was time for me to find a new place to live. I prayed to God and Jesus to send me a sign, and I was sure Porter was the answer to my prayer. He said we'd have a singing career. Singing was my only talent; everyone said I sang very well. I thought God had spoken . . . My faith was not good enough for Porter. I was continually badgered and humiliated because I wouldn't submit to his idea of being saved. Nine months later Carrie was born, and I had grown up a great deal. Our singing career did work out very well, and I had endeared myself to his congregation. Now I had a powerful weapon, and used it . . . no more sex . . . or babies without love. But, with my new persona and stardom, the battle was beginning again.

"I can't go back. When he finally came to the hospital when Carrie died, his comforting words to me as he looked at her lifeless, perfect, oh so sweet little body, were that her death was God's punishment to me for my sins and a lesson for me to repent. I hate him so much it scares me."

Rebecca was near tears and visibly emotionally shaken. "I'm overwhelmed; what you have suffered is beyond belief. I don't know how you've managed to hold yourself together. We'll get this figured out. I won't let anything more happen to you."

I felt cold and she seemed to know because she began to rub my arms like you do a child's after a cold swim. She said soothing things to me about how it was a very good thing that I had I come to her. There was an answer. Together we'd find it before the situation became even more difficult. I thought of Aunt Alma's saying, "It's always darkest before the dawn," and for once I hoped she was right. Then I thought, Mr. Stanley would say that too, and I knew I'd rather hear it from him than anyone. A feeling of homesickness swept over me so powerfully, I began to sob.

Rebecca said, "Crying is a good thing. You have to let yourself feel if we're to get this thing figured out properly. How about a nice warm bath? And get you out of your sweaty work clothes. I'll get you one of my robes."

I knew she figured that if I didn't have my clothes, I couldn't run away, and she could pretend she trusted me. But strangely, I did trust her, or I wouldn't have consented to a bath.

Though it was a little early for supper, when I came downstairs wrapped in her warm robe, she had a chicken salad attractively fixed in a star-cut tomato for each of us along with a large slice of cornbread.

"I've called Hilda and asked her to be patient. I think you need a little more time; I'll call her after we've eaten. We hurried through lunch so fast this noon . . . and, it may be a while before we get things straightened out. A little food in our stomachs will give us some much needed strength."

We ate in the sunroom with all the windows open so that it was like eating outside amongst the flowers I tended and loved. We sipped tall glasses of ice tea with lemon and talked about what to do. In the end there seemed to be no way around the fact that I felt vulnerable because I didn't completely trust that Mrs. Burns wouldn't call the police.

"Well, Rachel, I think we can clear that up with a phone call. You'll see that you can trust her."

The words "trust her" weighed heavily on my conscience because she was such a close friend of Rebecca's. My guilty feeling softened my reluctance, and I conceded that talking to her was a good idea.

It was nearly an hour before Mrs. Burns arrived, and during that time I told Rebecca all about what a wonderful little girl Carrie was. How I had been afraid I wouldn't be able to love her; and how much I loved her from the first moment. Mrs. Burns suddenly appeared coming around the corner, onto the patio and in through the slider.

After we exchanged greetings, Rebecca started to rise, and Mrs. Burns said, "Don't get up, Rebecca. I'll get myself a glass of ice tea."

Almost from that moment, I wondered why I hadn't trusted her, because her relationship with Rebecca matched the one I had with Millie, my neighbor on the farm next door to the parsonage, and how I missed her at that moment. My past was with me; I was beginning to feel again.

Mrs. Burns came back with her glass of tea. "Rachel, please call me Hilda. Children are the only ones who call me Mrs. I know you were brought up to think it was disrespectful because I'm an old lady, but I don't feel like one . . . so Hilda, please. Go on with your conversation. I'll catch up."

"Rachel was telling me about her little girl, Carrie."

"Oh, yes that was in the newspaper. I'm so sorry. I can identify with your loss because my eldest son died trying to save a life when he was a junior councilor at summer camp."

She did understand. "How terrible, he shouldn't have died. With my Carrie there was no hope."

"Yes. I felt that. One never forgets. But it will get easier, Rachel . . . can we call you Josephine?"

"Not just yet please. I must stay hidden."

"Rachel it is then. The two of you were saying?"

"Rachel was telling me how much she loved Carrie from the first moment she saw her."

I don't know what came over me, but I answered, "Yes. It was a surprise . . . because Ma didn't love me. I overheard Ma tell Rev. Grey that she couldn't love me because of what happened to her. She was raped where she worked as a maid, and that's why Ma ran away and why I was born."

Instantly, Rebecca's arm was around me. "That's dreadful for both of you."

I could see it was especially upsetting to Hilda as she agitatedly shifted about in her chair. "Imagine, a child learning such things in that manner. It's criminal what children have to endure, and poor Mary Louise. Rachel, I'm afraid this terrible thing happened to your mother while she lived in my home. I had no idea what she had suffered, or that she was pregnant. If only I had been more alert. If only I had known."

"She didn't want anyone to know because she was so ashamed, and she thought it was her fault because she hadn't locked her bedroom door. She learned that as a foster child."

"Who could have done such a thing...and in my house!"

I could see the alarm on her face and on Rebecca's. Did I again let something slip that I shouldn't have? And I quickly said, "It was someone your son brought home from college for a weekend visit. You couldn't have known. Ma's good at hiding her feelings. Life in foster homes taught her that skill too."

"A houseguest? Who?"

"I don't want to know. I hate him." The last thing in world I needed at that moment was to confront Ma's rapist. I couldn't even think of him as my father.

"But if he raped once, he could be still doing it. I feel I have to know."

Rebecca took my hand. "Be strong, Josephine. Think, can you recall any clues that might help Hilda figure out who he was? You don't ever have to meet him."

"He came and spent the weekend right after college started, and it was the only time he came when Ma was there. I'm not positive about that, but I think the way she felt about what happened she would have told Rev. Grey about it had he come again. She thought him nice because he was polite and handsome. That's all I know except that after the first night Ma locked her door so he couldn't get in, but he hid under her bed and forced her again."

"How awful," they both said in unison.

Hilda was beside herself. "Who did Ryan bring home that fall when Marry Louise was here?"

They talked back and forth about possible young men when suddenly Hilda declared, "I know who it was. I had nearly forgotten about him because the following year he was killed in an auto accident. As I recall, the police tried to pull him over because his driving was erratic, and a chase ensued. Come to find out, he was struggling with a girl in the car. Luckily, she recovered. There was never anymore in the paper. I'm sure his father saw to that."

My mouth fell open. "That's unbelievably weird. Ma made up a story when we moved to the country, and in it she said she had married a reckless kid who was killed in a car crash. And, that his parents didn't know about their marriage and wouldn't have believed her because she was a poor orphan welfare girl." Their concern radiated to me, but I felt nothing. "I was very confused about the idea that I had a father, one I didn't want or like, in heaven. Wasn't God, 'The Heavenly Father'?"

They both shook their heads in disbelief and sympathy. Hilda said, "You dear, dear girl. I daren't say a word. But I'm so glad to know you, and to know that Mary Louise is alright."

"Rachel," Rebecca hesitated, "do you think you can bear up a little longer? We have to come up with a plan. The police have got to be informed that you're safe."

Alarm resurfaced. "Only if they don't know where I am. I can never ever go back. If Porter learns where I am, he'll force me to come back because he needs the money our singing career makes. I shudder to think of how he's dealing with all this unwanted attention. But I realize I can't let the investigation go on. Can the police be told and still not know where I am? And the Stanleys, Millie and Jimmy must be worried sick . . . and Ma too . . . and Abbey and Allen. Abbey's the Stanleys' daughter. She was a sister to me."

***

After more tears and much back-and-forth discussion, I finally agreed to call Rev. Grey. I could confide in him; he'd befriended Ma and me when I was a child. But he'd have to be willing to keep my new identity a secret. Yes, he'd be the perfect go-between me, the police and the world.

Rebecca said, "We must call him at once. I'll get his number for you. You say he's now in the Buffalo area?"

Unbidden, the nightmare I had had on the bus flashed though my mind. For an instant, the distress I had felt at not being able to find Rev. Grey overwhelmed me. Just as quickly the assurance that I had chosen the right course of action flooded me with relief; I had found Rev. Grey

The operator dialed the number, the phone rang and I heard his voice. "Hello, Rev. Grey speaking."

"Hello Rev. Grey. This is Josephine."

"Josephine, thank heavens you're safe. The police have been here thinking you might have come to me. How sad I was to read of Carrie's death. Can I help you in any way? Have you called your mother and the Stanleys?"

Hearing his familiar voice was reassuring; it was a lifeline thrown to a drowning person. I hadn't known how much I needed to talk to someone who had known me before I met Porter, someone who could look at the situation objectively from a distance. I talked to him for nearly an hour, explaining my marriage, Carrie's death and my absolute need to have my whereabouts kept secret. After he talked to both Rebecca and Hilda, he agreed to contact the police and to keep my new identity a secret.

I had one more concern I had to get off my chest. "Rev. Grey, about Porter's congregation . . . they trusted me and were my friends. They didn't know I was not the person I pretended to be . . . and they genuinely love Porter and look to him for guidance. I don't want to destroy Porter's reputation as a minister. If he is unfit to be a pastor, his congregation should make that judgment by how he treats them. So, when you talk to the police, say I'm recovering from an emotional collapse due to Carrie's death, and that I am in seclusion to heal. Porter will not be easy to deal with. Tell him I have no wish to humiliate him publicly, but if he doesn't cooperate, I'll let the papers hear my story. Tell him there is no way he can force me to come back. I know how hard the task I'm asking of you is going to be."

"Not too hard. Of course I'll explain everything and do just as you ask."

"Thank you for the lifeline. Thank you."

"Bless you Josephine. You are most definitely very special and important to me. You have never disappointed me, my dear one. Bless you."

"Thank you for understanding and for the love you gave to me as a child. Good bye."

I purposely avoided talking to Rev. Grey about Ma or the Stanleys. I couldn't deal with the pain and anxiety I had caused them, or face what they must think of me.

***

Now that Rebecca and Hilda knew my true identity, the idea that I could be recognized suddenly became a new problem. They suggested I should get my hair cut very short.

"Don't you think it would make me look my age? I think my braids make me look too young to be Josephine Kent."

"Maybe you're right," Hilda said. "I didn't recognize you until I began to piece together all the clues."

I told them I wanted to keep my job, and they thought that was the right decision and would be good for me.

Rebecca said, "But I think you should give up your room and come and live with me. It'd be such a comfort to me, and I think you need to be where you're loved."

"What to say . . . I'm overwhelmed . . . of course I'd like to live here. But have you thought it through? Are you sure?"

"From that first day when I thought you were Rose, I rather wished it was you who were coming to stay."

"Not half as much as I wanted to stay."

"Wouldn't it be wonderful to be near the flower garden you love? It'll be such a nice change to have the excitement of a routine with your comings and goings. You can drive my car to work."

"Yes, wonderful, but I have to tell you, I don't have a license to drive."

"We'll get you one. Until then, I'll drive you to work. We'll look after each other."

With a happy smile, Hilda suggested, "And if you ever get tired of your hospital work, you could make an excellent living as a landscaper. I'd hire you in an instant . . . I must be on my way."

I remained seated as the two of them stood and hugged.

Hilda took both my hands. "This has been quite a day. Rachel, your secret is safe. Good bye."

Rebecca sat back down beside me. I didn't know what to say. I felt exposed, naked now that my true identity was known.

She started the conversation. "Rev. Grey is an amazing minister and friend. It didn't take him long to know how to manage the situation. No one will ever know where you have taken refuge...that is, until you're ready. Does sharing your secret make your burden lighter?"

Lighter? Now I would have to confront what I had done. There was no way around it. I had let everyone down. I could never make amends. "I'm sorry I lied to you . . . and I'm glad you know . . . I always let those I love down."

"Rachel . . . Rachel, you haven't let me down. Perhaps the world has let you down. You're welcome here as long as you want to stay. Don't you know what a joy it is to me to have you here?"

"It seems I'm always saying thank you, yet however many times I say it, it's never enough."

"You're more than welcome. It was past time to get things out in the open . . . between the two of us . . . no, the three of us. Hilda's in this too. Not only was she the one who recognized you, but she was very much a part of your mother's life."

"Yes, that's true, and I can see why Ma liked working for her."

"What puzzles me is why didn't I realize there was so much more to your story?"

"I've had a life of pretending. It's second nature."

"Maybe if I had known your husband was a clergyman."

"Preacher fits Porter better than clergyman, though he's a very beloved minister to many. He was ordained by his congregation with no formal ministerial training. To many people that makes him even more special because to them it means God laid His hands on him in a special calling. In Porter's doctrine there's only one narrow little door to salvation, and he holds one of the keys to that door." I think that stunned Rebecca because she made no response. "Did my mother go to church while she lived here?"

"Not at first, but she did get involved with the youth group in the Methodist Church, and she seemed to enjoy it very much."

"When we first moved to the country my stepfather said Ma was a heathen, and he was so worried that he asked Rev. Grey to talk to her. That was really a big step for Daddy because he said Methodists were watered-down Christians. Anyway, that's why Rev. Grey started coming to our house. It worried me that I liked watered-down Christians better . . . Are you a Methodist too?"

"No."

"Why didn't Ma go to your church?"

"Well, that's a bit of a story too. You see, I'm Jewish and John was a protestant. The welfare system likes to encourage their children to continue in their own faith."

"Really, I'm surprised. Did you go to John's church, or did you do like Ma, and not go to church? Sometimes I think that's the best way."

"Actually, John and I chose a church that allows for different faiths to worship together. You've had way too much to think about for one day. It's dinner time. What do you say I order us a pizza?"

By her change in the direction of our conversation, I wondered if I had asked something too personal. I quickly got in step.

"I've heard my friends back in Maplehurst talk about ordering a pizza. I've wondered what it would be like."

We curled up on the sofa in the TV room and ate our pizza as we watched the evening news and The Ed Sullivan Show. When the programs were over she said, "There's no time like the present . . . I can't bear to think of you going home to a cold boardinghouse room."

My heart skipped a beat. She did want me to live with her.

"You need love and warmth around you on a day such as you've had. No need to even go home to get pajamas. You'll swim in mine, but that'll be no problem. Come, we'll go up together and get your room ready. "

As she led the way upstairs, tugging at my emotions was the memory of how I had envied Rose that first day when I knocked on Rebecca's door, and she thought I was her new caregiver. Now Rebecca made it seem as if we were going to take care of each other. Caregiver was an area I was well acquainted with. Still, this was a strange and wholly new set of circumstances.

We cleared the closet, making it ready for my clothes. Then we made the bed with misty-green sheets trimmed with eyelet lace. When that was done, she went in search of pajamas and came back with white satin ones neatly folded, and also in her arms was a set of thick plush rose-colored towels with light pink flowers embroidered across their hems.

"You remember from that first night, your bathroom is just across the hall."

Imagine a bathroom all to myself, luxurious towels, fancy sheets and satin pajamas! I slipped out of Rebecca's robe and into the pajamas. Rebecca had invitingly turned back the corner of the bedcovers, and as I crept between the sheets, I felt an easing of tightness. My body was no longer poised to spring and run. A thought of Ma flashed across my mind. This was probably the very room she had slept in when she was a high school girl. Her presence filled the room, and it wasn't of the Ma that I knew. It was a happy presence, one full with hope. Was that the magnet that drew me here? Was that a reflection of what was possible for me?

There was a soft knock on my door, and Rebecca stepped into the room. She came over and sat down on the edge of my bed as if it were the most natural thing in the world, like a grandmother.

"Was this my mother's room?"

"Yes. She loved it and even after she went to work for Hilda she came back to it on all her days off. She was going to night school. Did you know she wanted to be a teacher?"

"No. I didn't know. She helped my stepbrothers and they're great students."

"What about you, Rachel?"

"As I said, I lived with the Stanleys. Forrest helped me learn to read. I wasn't a good student so it didn't bother me much to quit school. I never graduated."

"I can't imagine Mary Louise allowing that. You could go to night school and get your diploma."

"I'd have to work days."

"Why don't you think about putting your name on a waiting list for a daytime shift?"

"Maybe I'll do that."

27

"You must be exhausted. I'll let you sleep now." She kissed my forehead with my first kiss since Carrie's last sweet one. "Sleep-tight. You're safe now, and your identity and secret residence are safe. This is the first page of your new life."

I did feel safe for the first time in a very long time. I looked around the room in the dim filtered light that came in through the window from the streets lamps. What would my life have been like if Ma had confided her pregnancy to the Wallaces? They would have taken care of her. Maybe I'd have grown up here. A picture of Ma, loving and caring for me as Aunt Carrie had, filled my emotions.

I cried softly for Ma, for what might have been, and I cried for Carrie because I was a mother with empty arms. With my secret out, now I was able to grant myself the right to cry for her. For the first time since her death, I slept soundly, free from nightmares.

Chapter 2

Mrs. Henley hovered at my elbow. "Where did you say you were moving?"

"To Rainbow Drive."

"Didn't you find your room here satisfactory? I hate to lose a good boarder. I didn't think anyone over on Rainbow took in boarders, but I suppose anyone can run out of money."

"It's not like that. Your room's been fine."

"You still have your job?"

"Oh yes. I hope to work days soon." I didn't have much to pack, but my carpetbag was bulging as I pulled the handles together.

She decided that was all the news she was going to be able to pry out of me and said, "Well, good luck. Let me hear from you."

I hadn't felt like making up another false story. "Good bye. You'll have a new boarder soon. Another class is just starting."

I tossed my carpetbag into the back of Rebecca's Lincoln station wagon, as Mrs. Henley peeked out through the curtains. She'd have fun trying to figure it out.

The phone was ringing as Rebecca and I entered the house, and it was Rev. Grey.

We exchanged greetings and he asked, "Is this a good time to call?"

"Yes. It's always good to hear from you."

"I need to update you on how things stand. I've heard from Rev. Kent, and he's relentless. He's demanding I tell him where you are, and of course I'm not going to do that. Is it too soon to consider your future plans?"

"I guess it's time. I hate all the trouble I'm causing you and everyone."

"Helping you is a pleasure . . . I'm here when you're ready."

"Hilda said she had a lawyer friend if I needed one. I could ask her for his name?"

"I think that's an excellent idea. I'm certain she'd be glad to introduce you to him."

"I have to face my marriage . . . sometime . . . and Porter . . ."

"I'll be here for you no matter what you decide." He hesitated, weighing his words. "After talking to Rev. Kent, I can't imagine what you must have suffered."

I made no reply, I couldn't talk about that.

"Your mother was greatly relieved to know you're safe, and of course I didn't tell her where you are even though I knew how pleased she'd have been to know you're staying with Rebecca Wallace . . . I could hear Mark in the background saying, 'Yippee, she's safe' . . . it was good to hear your mother's voice again. I hadn't talked to her since Abbey's wedding, though we always correspond on holidays. I also phoned Matt . . . he's anxious to be of help in any way. May and Fred broke down and cried with happiness when I called them. And they said they'd be on the phone to Forrest and Abbey the minute we hung up. From our conversation the other day I knew how important Millie was to you, and I was able to get her phone number, and I called her too. What a wonderful friend you have in her. She's with you one hundred per cent."

"Thank you so much for calling her. I'm not up to it just yet."

"Of course, I understand . . . I called the police immediately, and they asked me to thank you for your cooperation in coming forward voluntarily . . . They accept my role as liaison. And there will be letters to forward on to you very soon."

Before we ended our conversation I asked him what he thought about an annulment. "I think you have grounds for one. That's definitely something you should consult the lawyer about."

"Rev. Grey, I don't feel as though I ever had a real marriage. I'd just like to make it disappear."

"In the true spirit of a marriage, I think you're right. I think the lawyer will be able to correct the record. You can count on me. We'll talk again soon. You're in my prayers and have my blessing."

***

During the following weeks, the pages of my new life began to unfold. Rebecca did her best to blend my past life into the rhythm of my new one. She seemed to know what troubled me even better than I did.

For example: at breakfast one morning she started a conversation with, "Rachel, what did you do for fun when you were a little girl?"

I thought that was a strange question to ask out of the blue, but it forced me to think about my old life even though I sat in her airy ruffle-curtained breakfast-nook. "Oh, I don't know. Matt and I were playmates in the early days when I lived with Ma in the tenant house. He was two years younger and so cute, but not pretty-cute like baby Mark with his golden ringlets . . . Little as Matt was, he used to protect me from Luke; he's my oldest step-brother . . . and Daddy's darling . . . and Forrest's friend. Matt and I played house a lot . . . while we looked after Mark."

"You never talk about Luke. What became of him?"

"He ran away from home when he was a senior in high school...he lived with his grandma . . . the infamous Aunt Alma . . . she was no fun! He works selling cars and is very successful."

"Let's see, Alma was Aunt Carrie's sister?"

"Yes, but they were different as night and day. Aunt Alma was hard as nails, Simon Lagree the slave driver. Aunt Carrie was soft and loving. She made everything fun, even staying out of Aunt Alma's way. When she died I felt like my world had come to an end."

Rebecca stopped eating and placed her hand over mine. "How old were you when she died?"

"I think four." I started to get up to refill Rebecca's cup. She always drank two cups of coffee for breakfast, her quota for the day.

She read my mind and gave my hand a squeeze. "Sit. I'll get my second cup in a minute. I should think it must have been very difficult for a four year old to know what was going on."

It was a moment before I could force my mind to travel back to that painful time. "Aunt Carrie looked asleep. The casket was a beautiful pink frilly special bed. Aunt Alma said she was in heaven with Jesus when that was plainly not true. Of course she went into great detail about sin and being saved. Ma said that was only Aunt Carrie's body, she was not sleeping . . . that the doctors couldn't make her well so her soul left her sick body and went to heaven. I just couldn't believe or make any sense of any of that, so when Ma and Aunt Alma weren't looking I climbed into the casket to find the hole the soul made when it came out! You can imagine the ruckus that caused. That was the only time Ma ever held me on her lap. She told me your soul was invisible like your breath."

Sorrow and disbelief swept Rebecca's face. "What a dreadful experience for a four year old. How did you manage without Aunt Carrie?"

"I used to talk everything over with her just like she was alive. You know . . . like an invisible friend. And I began to help Ma in the kitchen, and I'd crawl under the kitchen worktable to stay out of Aunt Alma's way. She was always praying to God about the naughty child who needed to be spanked."

"Was your stepfather like his mother?"

"I thought so but I learned too late that he really wasn't. If Ma had listened to him she would never have signed the papers allowing me to marry Porter."

Rebecca thought about that for a moment. "It would seem you were great pals with Matt and that you enjoyed taking care of cute little Mark. What about Luke; why did you need Matt's protection?"

"He hated me. The first day we came to the farm on Ma's wedding day, he stole my yoyo and broke the string. Forrest fixed it and that made Luke dislike me even more, and he nicknamed me Yoyo Jo. I guess he had never seen anyone like me before. And he called me Witch Face or Gypsy and made fun of my hair. To this day I'm Yo. Mrs. Stanley tried to make Forrest stop calling me that, but Luke was the ringleader in control of everything. It's a wonder Forrest liked me and took me under his wing. They grew up like brothers, and if Luke was on your side it was difficult to see his faults."

Rebecca looked troubled by my answer, and I could see she wasn't satisfied. "Matt must have been aware of Luke's meanness if he saw that you needed protection."

"Luke always made Matt look bad in Daddy's eyes." Luke's story was not for Rebecca or anyone.

She continued. "What could one so little do?"

"He kicked Luke in the legs and threatened to tell Daddy on him."

I felt she wanted to press on, but thought better of it. "What a brave little boy Matt must have been . . . didn't you live with the Stanleys?"

"Oh yes; I helped take care of Mrs. Stanley when she had her heart attack. That's how I got to live with them. That's where I learned to love gardening, and how to can . . . lots of things."

"What did you do that wasn't associated with work?"

"Let's see . . . Forrest gave me a cat, and I named her Snooks, after Baby Snooks. Oh how I miss that cat! And he took me on lots of walks and taught me all about plants and animals . . ."

"Forrest seems pretty important."

"Oh he most definitely was. I was convinced he knew everything."

"I see, a real hero. What else?"

"Abbey gave me her doll to play with, and she read to me and played games with me . . . Mrs. Stanley played tea-party with me . . . Mr. Stanley told me stories that made me feel good about being called a gypsy. And he told me witches were misunderstood and were falsely blamed when bad things happened."

"It's no fun to be made fun of. Luke must have thought you might get too much attention, and was jealous of you."

"That's just what Mr. Stanley said."

"I say, thank heavens for Mr. Stanley."

As my mind rehashed Mr. Stanley's idea about blame, Porter came rushing to the forefront of my thoughts. "You know, Rebecca, now that I think about it, that's what Porter was doing when he blamed me for Carrie's death. He had to put the blame somewhere. Naturally that had to be on me . . . the non-believing outsider who refused to say the words to be saved."

"Very perceptive. I'm afraid it's human nature to always lash out and blame, especially when things happen we have a hard time understanding and accepting, or even worse when we fear we might be partly responsible."

"And . . . a believer couldn't possibly be responsible, pretty good protection from blame. And he was surrounded by like believers to reinforce his beliefs, his proof he is right."

"You amaze me, Rachel. That's an army of protection. Hearing the same things over and over is a form of conditioning."

In my mind I could see Porter's congregation mesmerized, chanting Amen with rapture beaming from their faces as he thundered on and on about man's sinfulness and the way to salvation. "You mean sort'a like being hypnotized?"

"Perhaps. And if their message . . . belief . . . or dogma isn't received as the truth by someone, that person becomes an outsider. Being an outsider can be devastating."

A hundred ideas came storming into my brain. Porter thought he was commanding general of God's army. That's why everyone looked to him for their answers and why they loved singing "Onward Christian Soldiers". That's why the message was always the same. They were assuring each other they had the right answers. That amazed me, and I blurted out, "I never thought of that. Do you think that's always true with all religious people?"

"Most of us just go along . . . believe whatever our parents or our peer-group believe. We need acceptance and friendship."

"Yeah, Ma taught me to be a doubter, but I had the Stanleys to help me find a faith, but Porter battered me until he tore it down . . . now I question everything. Once you begin to think and question, you know God has to be bigger than any one belief system."

Rebecca smiled. "I certainly hope so."

"Hard as it was to be an outsider, I can't say I believe something that doesn't make sense. There are too many generals who say they have the only line to God . . . the Commander in Chief . . . and there are too many things that just don't add up."

"Thankfully we live in a country where we have the freedom to worship, or not, as our conscience dictates. And isn't it wonderful; our knowledge is continually growing, exposing new puzzles to be solved? Of course there are always rules of conduct we must obey, but you have nothing to worry about in that department. You're a very responsible person with a big heart."

"Thank you. I do worry about that because I can't control what makes sense to me, but I really want to be what God wants me to be."

"It seems to me, you try so hard you even try to purchase your acceptance with a lot of hard work."

"I never thought about that. That's Ma's way . . . mine too, I guess."

Rebecca was quickly on her feet and poured herself that second cup of coffee. Why hadn't I gone ahead and refilled her cup? I should have. She knew my thought and very subtly motioned to me that it was alright.

She replaced the coffeepot. "I don't think anyone should have to purchase their rights."

She had made me realize one of my core beliefs; one I didn't even know I had. I did feel I had to be of service in order to be granted the right to be alive, the right to enjoy life. I would never have allowed Carrie to feel that way. No one asked to be born. Everyone should have the same right to be alive, have fun...as well as work...and to believe what made sense to them. That was a lot to think about and my mind was absorbed.

Rebecca had to break the silence. "You know, Rachel, I think you should write a story about all the things that have happened to you, good and not so good. Tell your story. You're a survivor. It will help heal your wounded heart."

"You think so?"

"I know so."

"Aunt Carrie and I used to make up stories all the time. After she died I still told her stories."

"See, you're a natural story teller."

Something clicked in my brain and I asked, "Were you a nurse or something like that?"

"Why do you ask?"

"You sound like a medical person of some kind."

"I was a social worker. That's how I managed to have your mother come and live with us. I wanted to give a high school girl a chance at a better life. Mary Louise was such a bright promising young lady, and she was on her way. Sometimes life is very unfair." She stood up. "Time to get on with the day."

I started my journal story that very day. I never knew how much my story wanted to get out until my pencil touched the paper.

***

Evidence of how fast the tide was turning came shortly after I requested a day shift. The nursing office left word at my nursing station that I should stop by the office at my first opportunity.

"Rachel, the hospital applauds education. We'll see to it you have a day shift in time to enroll in the next GED course. You have an excellent work record. Good luck with night school."

That same day I found the courage to ask Hilda for the name of her lawyer friend.

"Attorney Abner Baruch. I'll make the appointment and introduce you. I think you'll like him."

I had taken the first two steps into the future as Rev. Grey advised. I felt good about my progress until the box of letters that Rev. Grey had promised arrived. The box of letters represented all the guilt I felt about the heartache I had caused so many people I loved. I was holding my past in my hands. How could I face what I had done?

As I carried the box of letters up to my room, it felt like a hot potato! The impulse to toss it away was strong. In it were words from some of those who had attended my precious Carrie's funeral, from those who had searched the mountain for my body. I closed my eyes in dread. Yes, and words from Mr. and Mrs. Stanley, from Forrest and Abbey, from Ma, Matt and Mark. I felt an overwhelming love for all of them. How I missed them. How unfair I had been to them, but they would have been compelled to tell Porter. How much I needed their love and forgiveness came stampeding into my heart.

I closed my door behind me, curled up on my bed and gritted my teeth in preparation for the onslaught of an emotional rollercoaster ride.

I chose Millie's letter first and began to read:

Dear Jo,

Thank heavens, you're alive. You're the daughter I never had. Jimmy and I have been going around here with our hearts dragging the ground. Now that we know you're alive our hearts are halfway up to where they ought'a be. I don't think mine'll ever get to its normal resting place without our dearest Carrie. She was my heart. Life's biggest mystery to me is how when hearts get down just as low as they can get, the sun keeps right on coming up and everything around us keeps right on going along on its merry way. The downs of life teach me that "merry way" is not the insult it feels like at the time, because eventually, I find myself getting swept right along too even though it's not so merrily. Life must go on my dearest, Jo. Don't you go beating yourself over the head with what your escape might have put us through. I only wish you could be with us now so we could love you back to health, but I understand why you can't come back to Jackson Junction. In my heart I'm for you every step of the way no matter where you are. I know you did the only thing you could do. You gave me little clues of how the land lay for you and I'm sorry I missed them. In hindsight they are clear as day. You helped me through the abyss that first year after Henry passed. You not only helped me pull the farm together, you gave me hope. I think probably it was your grit that saved the farm and my livelihood. The farm and Jimmy are doing good. Better than ever I dreamed. I'm sure Jimmy is working on a letter to you too. People here love you much more than I'm sure you are aware of. If you can, write and tell me how you're doing. I've never known anyone with more get-up-and-go. I know you're going to be all right. Jimmy and I are beginning to pick the first string-beans of the season. I know wherever you are nature is coaxing you to live again as am I.

 Your most loving friend, Millie

I wouldn't have survived without Millie. I wouldn't have been able to make it. She was my lifesaver. I closed my eyes and I could see the path at the foot of the mountain with the sun shining on Carrie's buckwheat hair as she scampered along ahead of me. I could see Millie scoop her up in her arms as she came down her back steps to meet us. I wished Millie could hug me at that very moment. They were arms that knew Carrie. There was a knot under my breastbone. Tears slid down my cheeks, consoling tears. I would be eternally thankful to Millie for sparing me the painful details of all that transpired during that awful time. If she had, those tears would have turned that knot under my breastbone into a knife-stabbing wound.

Rebecca was right. I did start out purchasing Millie's friendship, but in the end, our friendship was one of equals. I was sure I was right about that. Thanks to Rebecca and the thought process she initiated, I was able to recognize it, and how good that felt!

My hands searched the box for Jimmy's letter, and I began to read:

Dear Jo,

How can I tell you how sad losing Carrie makes me? Because I can't begin to find the right words for my own grief, I can't imagine how you are managing to keep going though I know you can because I never knew anyone like you. I'm glad you ran away even though I know I'll probably never see you again. Right from the first I wanted to punch handsome Porter (Rev. Kent, I should say!) in his fire-and-brimstone/ not so sweet mouth. I know I shouldn't say that about a minister. You will get well and find happiness. I know that for certain sure! Regardless of how impossible things were, and I knew they were, you sowed happiness everywhere you went, never a complaint. And you were mother to the sweetest little girl I ever knew.

Your friend, Jimmy

I smiled at the thought of Jimmy punching Porter in the mouth! I liked that picture! Jimmy was about my own age! In another world he could have been my school beau. With that thought, strange as it seemed, I could have liked Jimmy. He was really a nice person and a farmer. How many friendships like that had my love for Forrest kept me from? That was another new thought!

And with that thought, I had to read Forrest's letter next:

Dear Yo,

Thank you for being alive. When Dad told me Rev. Grey had called with the news that you were alive and safe, whew, what'a relief! None bigger! Jeffy began jumping up and down, and when I started out the door, I just had to go for a walk, he was at my heels, but I said not this time Jeffy. I walked over the lane where we walked so often. I ran my hand along the old rail fence. I shouted to your mossy stones, "She's alive! She's alive!" Yes, I thought the very worst. I thought I had lost you forever. I should have known better because even before Rev. Grey's call there were echoes of you everywhere I turned. You have left your print on our hearts and on this soil, this farm.

While I was away in the service, it was your letters that kept my world real, anchored me to reality, this same farm your stamp is upon. You made one season follow the next. No matter what was happening in the war-torn world and to me, the sun would always continue to come up, the world would heal. Because you made the world keep right on turning, so could I. Wondrously, you're alive, and today the land is here under my feet as ever it is. Everything around me smells of earth ripening. The apple tree branches are bending down with their abundance. Mom will be making her early-apple pie soon, and she always sends one down to us.

Forgive me for my inability to be the understanding big brother you needed when I came home from the service. I was pretty twisted-up myself and was unable to see your dilemma accurately. Dad tried to tell me. However, when you came home for Paul's funeral you appeared to have your life well in hand, and I could see how much Carrie meant to you. She stole my heart and will always occupy a corner of it. Maybe had I been more perceptive much of the tragedy in your life could have been avoided. However, I venture that a world without Carrie's short life would seem empty. I know there are no words to take away your sorrow. Is there anything I can do to help you cope? Thank you for being alive.

My love always, Forrest

No question, our souls were linked together in a special way. He could reach out and touch me as no one else could. My mind went flying over the lane, meadows and by the mossy fairy-stones. I ran through the apple orchard and climbed the old black cherry tree with its huge hanging-down branches.

It was painful to come down to earth because I knew I had to grow in a new direction without losing what Forrest and I shared.

Jeffy's letter was enclosed with Forrest's:

Dear Aunt Yo,

You almost scared us to death. I know how sad you are because I am very sad too. I was planning to marry Carrie because she was interested in farming and was so pretty. When are you coming to see us? My dad is happier now and Grandpa whistles when he comes to the barn. Grandma said she could breathe again. I don't know what she meant but she hugs a lot more and is cleaning her kitchen cupboards. I know it'd make her awful happy if you came to see her. Me too.

I love you, Jeffy

The day Mrs. Stanley boldly carried Jeffy into the tenant house and put him into his rightful grandfather's arms came flooding back to me along with all those rough days during the war when Linda pushed Jeffy away. How could anyone not love Jeffy? Linda thought it was Jeffy that kept Luke from coming home to her. My hero, my Forrest I thought, married to Linda to save her from disgrace. Jeffy was planning to marry Carrie! Luke's son, married to my daughter! That was a road better left unexplored. I began to weep.

When I had control of my emotions again, I went to the window, and let my mind drink in the beauty of Rebecca's garden. The bedding plants we bought the day Hilda came and changed everything, were doing beautifully. It was time to pinch-back the mums. I needed to go out and pick the dead blossoms from the petunias before I went to work.

With my courage back again, I picked up Mrs. Stanley's letter:

Dear Josephine,

You are a second daughter to me and I grieved for you as a mother, and because I'm a mother I have a small idea of what you are suffering. Carrie was like a granddaughter to me and my heart shares your sorrow. I fear for you at the same time I have confidence that you will overcome your sorrow in time. Our home is always open to you. It's your home.

My dearest Jo, I remember the wonderful care you gave me when I had my heart attack, and to think, you were just a little tyke yourself. Sometimes I look up and expect to see you coming to visit with your dolly in your arms to have our little tea party with your tea mostly milk. I'll never forget the look on your face when Forrest put Snooks in your arms. She's a very old cat now. We baby her because I don't think her hearing is very good, and she's content to sleep in the kitchen near me most of the time. When Jeffy comes up he gets a pretty good response out of her. I think because he puts her in mind of the little girl who loved her so well.

Abbey and Allen have been coming as often as they can which is a comfort to us. You stole Fred's heart in a very special way and he wants to add a line to my letter so I will close by saying how much you mean to me and let you know I share your sorrow, and I hope the love I'm sending will be of some comfort.

My love always, Mrs. Stanley

I unfolded Mr. Stanley's letter and read on:

Dear Jo,

I can't add much to May's letter except to let you read my hand spelling out that you are very special to me indeedy. No one but you sat on the banking with me. No one loves the crows like I do, except you. I loved the way your black braids swung to-and-fro as you hurried about always busy doing good things. You have the stuff to turn many a new page.

I feel so lucky to have been able to share in Carrie's short life. It meant a lot to her to take us over your well traveled path to the farm next door, and how I enjoyed seeing her shining face as she showed us her garden. It was a comfort to meet Millie and be able to know first hand what her farm and friendship meant to you and to Carrie.

As May said, this farm will always be your home, your home base. And I am your biggest fan. Be well again.

   My love, Mr. Stanley

Love came flooding into my heart with the force of a torrent. Remembering all those tranquil days soothed my troubled heart. I lay back on my pillows with my hands behind my head and closed my eyes. Scenes raced by. The perfection I always associated with those pictures had a minor flaw I'd never have realized had it not been for Rebecca. Even after all that time, I still thought of them as Mr. and Mrs. Stanley, not my equals, not quite family. I knew they were a product of their time, and they loved me as they said they did, but something very subtle was missing.

Ma's letter was in my hand. It should follow Mr. and Mrs. Stanley's. Somehow I felt reluctant to open it...I read:

Dear Josephine,

   Paul told me I was wrong when I signed the papers allowing you to marry. I now know what a grave mistake it was. I'm sorry. I've never wanted to hurt you. And I'm sorry I was unable to be the mother you needed and that every child has a right to expect. The hard part about that is that I'm afraid you have felt that the problem was you, as would any child, when the problem was with me. I'm proud of you and proud of the way you were able to love Carrie. She was the child of any grandmother's dreams, and I'm so sorry for her death. I'm glad you called Rev. Grey. He helped me.

   I wish you well, Ma

I should have felt reassured, but I felt a chill. I shouldn't have been surprised that she still couldn't bring herself to use the word love. I should have been used to Ma. She was the most honest person I knew.

Life's lessons were very concise and clear to her, and she would only say exactly what she felt. Thinking about that made me wonder if to question and have areas of gray was a necessary part of life if you were to grow in knowledge and understanding. Could that idea help with my feelings toward Ma? Did I love Ma? Did I need to? Would understanding her make room for love to grow? At that moment old hurts were running wild.

I needed the healing influence of Abbey. She was able to calm the Stanley's troubled household when Linda came to live with us. I wondered what insights she might lend. I opened her letter:

Dear Jo,

I'm holding you in my heart, little sister. I love you so much. As sister of my heart, I must start this letter by saying I am still hanging onto my belief in God. It's necessary to say that because it has been a huge struggle for me to keep it. Life is so unfair. I have done very little to deserve the privileged life that I have been blessed with while you have fought a valiant battle every step of way and deserve so much more than you have ever been given, and now you have been made to suffer the most devastating loss I can imagine. I think the only reason I've been able to keep my faith is for Louisa May and Jenny. How could I help them through their first terribly sad loss without it? I know you too must be struggling with your faith. I remember well the little girl I used to take to Sunday School. Pat answers would never do for her. You made us all think a little harder about what to believe. For me it all boils down to love. I don't care what it's called, and I know you are greatly loved by many and especially by the Stanley family. Love is the only thing I can think of to give you in this hour of your great need. You have always given your love so freely, and we are all blessed because of it. You have both my personal sisterly love and my portion of that greater universal love.

Even though I have only seen you three times since the day of your wedding, I feel we have remained very close through our correspondence. Each time I was at your home in Jackson Junction I was overwhelmed with the feeling that your life had been a series of situations where much was demanded of you while the give-back to you was far from what it should have been. I wish your life with us could have been the one place where that wasn't true. I feel even with us you were the greater giver. Partly it's because very few have the ability to give back the way you do. Our love for you was true and remains so. Despite all you did for us, I just bet you thought you were taking advantage of us because we gave you a home. You were a blessing to us, a very sweet dear blessing. Forrest has expressed similar feelings to me, and I'm sure he is writing to you.

Knowing Rev. Grey is in communication with you is such a comfort. He will always remain the minister that is the pastor of my heart, and I know you loved him too. We are sisters hooked together forever, and you can share anything with me, or not. I'm here to help in any way. I love you so much it hurts. And I hurt for the loss of Carrie. And yet thinking abut her is a joy at the same time.

You've had a tough life, but it's made you very strong. I'm glad you escaped. Stay hidden as long as you need to. Your strength to fight back gives me courage. Our home is always open to you.

Allen sends his love too, and the girls do too. We are so glad we didn't lose you, oh so very, very glad. Write to me when you can. I love you.

Your sister, Abbey

My tears were flowing before I finished Abbey's letter, and I gave over to my emotions and wept long and hard. No one ever had a sister more loving and true than Abbey. There was no pretense in her love and concern. I had to get my life back together. How could I not with the gift of so much love? I wished fervently that I could find the courage to write Louisa May and Jenny a letter, telling them how happy they made Carrie when they came to visit and when she went to visit them. But, I knew what little children really wanted was for someone to tell them she was in heaven with God, Jesus, and loving people like Aunt Carrie whom she was named for. I couldn't write that, and I cried some more.

When I could cry no more, I opened Matt's letter:

Dear Yo,

You are always in my thoughts and prayers, but ever so fervently these last months. We have been soul-mates since that first day when we joined hands and Abbey took us to the barn to see the new calf. That's almost my earliest memory, and probably because you are so important to me.

I wish I could have known Carrie better. What little bit I saw of her when Abbey brought her to the farm while I was helping with the haying, I could see what a winning little girl she was, very like her mother. How much we, and the world, will miss because she is no longer in it. All of us who love you share your devastating loss. I'm here to help in any way I can.

This may not be the time to tell you, but I want you to know I am aware that the love Ma gave to Mark and me was never complete because you were not included. Sometimes I felt like we stole it from you. However, I don't think in reality that is true. Ma should have had enough for all three of us. I fear that part of your healing therapy may involve dealing with some of those feelings from the past. That's the reason I'm mentioning it. If ever talking about it with me would help, let me know. Luke may figure into your healing process, and I'd be willing to help in anyway possible there also. I know how strong you are, and that your strength will stand you in good stead. If you can't write, but still need me in any way send word to me through Rev. Grey. It's a great comfort to me to know you sought his help as I have great respect for him and know how much he meant to you not so long ago. Plus he knows you very well.

Your loving brother, Matt

My heart swelled up with love for the brave little boy who kicked Luke in the legs and threatened to tell Daddy. What a wonderful minister he was going to make in the not too distant future, one like Rev. Grey. Maybe I could ask Matt to help me understand Ma. In time, things might come around right; how very much I needed to find peace.

There were dozens of cards from Jackson Junction and Maplehurst. I dug through them looking for a letter from Mark. I found Porter's letter in the process and laid it aside. I decided to confront his letter last.

Mark's letter turned out to be a note on a sympathy card:

Dear Yo,

Good for you! You outfoxed them all! Keep right on doing it and you'll be OK. You always have been more than OK in my book. Everyone should have a big sister like you! I'm glad you're free from Porter. You know me and religion! I am so sorry I never met Carrie. I'll always wish I had because from what I hear I missed something very special. I send you my love.

Your brother, Mark

Mark was more a child of Ma's than I ever was and more even than Matt too. The feelings I had that first day when Mrs. Stanley put Mark with his sunshine curls into Ma's arms came winging back to me. Yet I've loved him as I know he genuinely loves me. I felt a special warm fuzzy feeling for Ma when I closed my eyes and remembered her with baby Mark. Life was a mystery.

Melancholy swept over me, and I left my letter and card-strewn bed again and walked back to the window. I could feel the beauty of Rebecca's backyard beacon me. Millie's suggestion that nature would coax me back into the world again was true. How appropriate with Porter's letter waiting to be read; that was certain to jar me back into the real world. If I could survive the blast, I could lick anything. Even the loss of the child he fathered and I loved more than life itself.

At last, I returned to my task and opened his letter:

Josephine,

I pray God have mercy on your soul. Great is His wrath. Jesus is the way, the truth and the light. You must come home and repent and accept Jesus as your savior, at once. People here are very attached to you and will forgive you anything if you are contrite and pray for their forgiveness for the wrong you thrust upon them. That is to say nothing about the wrong you visited upon me. How could you run out on your daughter's funeral, leaving me to grieve alone and tend to all the formalities? How could you put us all through thinking you had taken your own life? That would have been an unforgivable sin against God. Faking it is just about as bad. I think if you are contrite we can keep the record company going and your fans will accept you back. Due to all the publicity, I think it may even enlarge our market reach and improve our business. The outpouring of love and concern expressed for your welfare is unbelievable. Nothing has been going as it should. You can not fathom the disruption you've caused. Let me know where you are immediately. I need to talk to you in person. Having to go through Rev. Grey is ridiculous. I don't like his attitude. After talking to him, I can see why you have the misconceptions you possess about your salvation. Let me hear from you at once. And I do mean at once, Josephine.

    Your HUSBAND, Porter

Being hit with a ball bat would have hurt less! I wanted to curl up and die. What, oh what, should I do? I could feel myself begin to

49

tremble inside. Tomorrow's appointment to see Hilda's lawyer friend, Abner Baruch, was no longer troubling. I was ready to talk to him.

Rebecca tapped lightly on my door. "Rachel, I've a snack ready." Her voice came to me from another world. "I'm afraid you've lost track of time."

"Oh my gosh . . . what'm I gonna do? I'll never make it to work on time."

Rebecca opened my door. I sat cross-legged in the middle of my bed, rocking back and forth with Porter's letter clutched in my fist.

She swept the letters aside, making room to sit down and took me in her arms. "My dear...you're cold and clammy. We have to warm you up." She released me and quickly grabbed the afghan from the reading chair by the window, wrapped it around me and held me tightly in her arms until my shaking stopped. "If it's all right with you, Rachel, I'm going out in the hall and phone the hospital to tell them you're unable to come to work this afternoon."

I couldn't answer her, and suddenly the tears started to flow again.

She gently released me. I could hear her in the hall explaining that Rachel Rubin, who was a guest in her home, had had a very bad shock and would be unable to come in to work that afternoon. By the tone of conversation that followed, I knew she was talking to someone she was acquainted with. She explained that, yes she thought I'd be able to keep my work schedule tomorrow, and that she was certain I'd be glad to fill in for whoever they could get to pinch-hit for me.

She came back and eased me from my perch on the bed, keeping the afghan around me as she guided me downstairs and into the sun-warmed cozy sunroom. We sat down together on the white wicker sofa with its squishy cushions. My letter from Porter was still clutched in my fist. She took no notice of it and began to massage the back and sides of my arms to stimulate the blood flow to them. When I began to relax, she asked, "Is it the letter in your hand? Can you tell me about it?"

Hesitantly, I answered. "I want to. I don't know if I can." Then on impulse, I thrust the letter from my hand into hers, and tears began to slide down my cheeks again.

Seeing my tears, Rebecca asked, "Is it too soon? Maybe we should wait a bit longer."

"No, please read it."

As she read, her face became troubled and very grave. Her eyes were moist as if she might join me in another good cry, but she held her tears back. "You've survived, Josephine, you escaped . . . remarkably, you have survived." She took both my hands in hers. "You're safe here, Rachel."

She was so upset, she wasn't aware she had slipped and called me Josephine. That was a graphic indication to me of how much the letter had upset her. That she was that horrified told me she understood, and words started pouring out of my mouth. "When Porter came to the hospital after Carrie died, there were no comforting words, no tears. He said it was my fault Carrie died. God was punishing me for my sins...that it was a lesson to repent."

Aghast, "Oh, my dear! You can't possibly believe that."

"Porter believes it. What kind of a God could kill an innocent child to teach anyone a lesson? No. I don't believe it."

"Nor do I, or anyone else in their right mind. It would seem to me from my talk with Rev. Grey, and from this letter, Porter is beyond reasoning with."

"He has all the answers." A sob shuddered through me. "I can't bring myself to talk about why Porter's and my relationship is so mixed up."

Gently, she asked, "Can you tell me about Carrie?"

I closed my eyes to gain my composure. I felt Carrie's little arms around my neck as she kissed me that last night as I put her to bed. "Millie said in her letter that Carrie was her heart. She was mine too. So when she died, my reason for living was gone. She was everything to me." I went on to tell Rebecca all about what an exceptional little girl she was; about her buckwheat honey-colored curls; about her gold-flecked snapping bright eyes; about her curiosity and all her questions, and how Millie bought a child's encyclopedia so we could answer her questions. I described her little garden and how she loved the chickens and Jimmy too. I explained how Jimmy had started out as Millie's high school helper and was now in charge of the farm. While I talked about Carrie, I warmed up and threw off the afghan.

Rebecca listened most earnestly. Love and compassion radiated from her face. "How heart wrenchingly sad to have to part with such a delightful child, such a lovely brilliant one. Oh, Rachel, I am so very sorry. Thank you for sharing Carrie's memory with me . . . Would it be too much to tell me how she died?"

I took a deep breath. "It was so sudden. She woke up with a headache and high fever. Porter refused to believe she was sick and left. Before his car was out of the driveway, I was on the phone to Millie. She drove us to the emergency room. It was meningitis and she died before noon."

Tears were on Rebecca's cheeks. "Way, way too much to bear. I'm so glad you came to me. Oh, so very, very glad."

During the sad silence that followed, my mind was busy trying to wish away Carrie's death. This was all a nightmare that I would awake from. God would never let something so tragic happen. Then it came to me suddenly, and I blurted out, "You know, I think God has to follow the same rules all nature follows. If there is a God, He would have saved Carrie if He could. That's why a lot of things don't add up."

She reached out and clasped my hands again. "You're wise beyond your years."

"I used to believe God answered prayer and was guiding my life. Porter and his wrathful God have made me look at things differently. I don't think God plays favorites. He lets the rain fall on the just and the unjust alike. That explains a lot. I've heard so many people say the Lord was watching over them when they were spared some tragedy, but never say God was asleep on the job when tragedy strikes. I've always wondered about that. Abbey, the Stanley's daughter, said in her letter that she remembered the little sister, me, who was not happy with pat answers. Even when I was a child I asked embarrassing questions that the Sunday School teacher couldn't answer. Abbey was worried about the struggle I might be having, and said that Carrie's death had shaken her faith, but helping her two little girls through losing their friend, helped her keep hers."

"Abbey sounds like a very nice person."

"She's one of the nicest people I know. She's always treated me like a sister. You can't believe how pretty and smart she is. You'd think she'd be stuck on herself. Things just seem to always work out for her. But really she's very unselfish and kind." I was quiet for some minutes and Rebecca waited for me to continue. "If there is a God, I don't think He's a superhuman, or anything like us. Do I shock you?"

"Not in the least. Each of us has to come to our own conclusions about matters of faith."

"Not many see it that way. Each of us thinks we have the one truth. How could we when we don't all have the same experiences or ability to reason."

"Maybe that's why all answers are not the same." She left it there, and a short silence followed before she changed the subject back to

Abbey. "Seems to me Abbey must have been a big comfort to you, and life with the Stanleys was good."

"Yes, she was the peacemaker. I'm so lucky in spite of everything. There's always been someone there to rescue me...first Aunt Carrie, then the Stanleys, and in Jackson Junction my neighbor Millie. Now here I am with another loving friend."

"That's nice. You're easy to love, Rachel."

Scenes I had written in my journal tumbled one over the other. Should I share my story with Rebecca? She would understand. The rest of the morning and as we ate lunch, I wrestled with my dilemma. I wanted her to read it; but could I take the chance? The torment of indecision plagued me every which way I turned. I must decide one way or the other and carry through. I must end the torment of indecision.

As I came down the stairs ready to go to work, I laid my journal beside her as she sat sipping her afternoon tea. I thought, "Fred would say, 'The dye is cast, for good or ill.'"

Rebecca looked up. "Thank you, Rachel. I know what it means to let someone into your secret place. I honor your trust."

I couldn't speak, but I gave her shoulder a caressing squeeze and left for work.

Chapter 3

MY JOURNAL

I was born in 1929, Josephine Louise Wallace. Yo became my nickname when Ma married my stepfather, and we went to live with him on the Stanley's farm. How clearly the day I learned about our impending move stands out in my mind . . .

***

"Josephine, come out from under that table . . . this instant . . . show some respect. Mr. Osborn's going to be your new step-daddy." Aunt Alma used her sharpest voice.

I grabbed hold of Ma; what had I done; what did Aunt Alma mean?

Her cheeks fluttered, "Clara, haven't you explained anything to that child?"

"There's time . . . a week's a long time when you're five."

Actually, I had just turned six, but without Aunt Carrie no one remembered my birthday, even me.

"Well, I never. You'd think . . . well . . . she's your child. You're the one who let Carrie spoil her. I warned you . . . but do as you see fit . . .

you will anyway."

Ma began to pry my clinging arms from around her legs as she explained, "Next Sunday we'll be moving to the country to live with Aunt Alma's son and his country family."

Live with Aunt Alma's PERFECT country family! My six year old heart froze in terror. Live with scary tall Mr. Osborn in the black rumpled suit, dark shadow on his face with his big hairy nostrils that matched the black hair on his huge grimy hands.

I escaped, ran upstairs as my mind flew away to heaven: *Aunt Carrie, I don't want'a move . . . would you know where I am? I miss you . . . no one hugs or kisses me anymore. Aunt Alma hates me. Do you know what a Billy Sunday is? Aunt Alma says her wonderfulest grandson, Luke, is going to be a second Billy Sunday. Sunday's the day Ma makes candy and she knows that. Is it anything like the Billy in the story Billy Goat Gruff and the mean troll under the bridge? So what if her SWEET little Mathew can dress himself. I can't ever remember when I couldn't dress myself. No one says anything about that, or that I could walk BEFORE I was a year old! What's died in childbirth? Luke and Mathew's ma died in childbirth. Jesus took their ma to heaven, and now Aunt Alma has a poor motherless baby grandson. What does that mean? Is Luke and Mathew's ma up in heaven with you?*

I fled up to my secret rooftop world where I often hid to avoid Aunt Alma's wrath. The honking clankity-rumble of the busy alley traffic contaminated the air around me, but I was oblivious of the assault and to the other world out there beyond my knowing. This was my outside world. The shopkeeper from Brown's Tobacco Store next door came out his backdoor to the garbage can. He always waved to the little head peering down at him from over the low wall that edged my rooftop world. His yappy little dog made a white streak past him in hot pursuit of the orange tabby cat that had been hiding in wait for a mouse. Garbage bags went flying as Mr. Brown's arms flew up in the air, and his thick glasses nearly slipped off his Jimmy Durante nose. He swore under his breath, called and whistled to his little white dog, and forgot to wave at me. Disappointed, I crept quietly back into the apartment to the front window where grand cars whizzed by on the bumpy brick street below. I watched a little boy skip happily along beside his father. I couldn't imagine Aunt Alma's perfect grandsons skipping along beside their scary dark gloomy father.

That night Ma must have known I was crying though I'm sure I made no sound where I lay curled up on the edge of the bed so as not to disturb her, because she comforted, "Josephine, you'll be in the country. You'll have a real family. It'll make all the difference. You'll see."

How could I be comforted? Aunt Carrie was gone and she was the one who had loved me and made me feel safe. I closed my eyes, squeezing the tears down my cheeks. I could almost feel her soft jowl pressed against my cheek. How I longed for her stout gentle arms that held me, oh so tightly, against her ample bosom, tightly, to keep me from slipping off her lap cut short by her jolly girth.

***

Before I was born, Ma had answered the "HELP WANTED" sign in the aunts' Sweet Shop window. They guessed her plight, knew she had no place to go and would be the good cheap help they had been praying for ever since, as Aunt Alma put it, "Since Carrie took poorly."

Actually, Aunt Alma was the praying aunt. She prayed often, or rather brayed loudly for ears other than God's, "God, help this UNGRATEFUL child keep her DIRTY hands OFF my glass cases," or, "God, help this ungrateful child make less noise," or, "God almighty, keep her out from under foot," always ending, "so's she doesn't have to be SPANKED," big sigh, at her rope's end, "in Jesus name, AMEN." There was no one around that I could see, so I concluded, Aunt Alma had imaginary friends too, only Aunt Carrie's and my imaginary friends were nice.

One time before Aunt Carried died, I heard one of the patrons in the lunchroom exclaim, "JEES-US CHRIST!" Aunt Alma gasped, "In here, we do not take the Lord's name in vain."

I spoke up: "Yes you do, Aunt Alma." Everyone laughed.

There was blood in her eyes as she started toward me. "Why you little liar."

Aunt Carrie's arm went protectively around me, "Sister, you know, you're always saying, 'in Jesus' name' at the end of your prayers."

Grudgingly, "Well...yes....yes, that is so...But you well know that's different."

Before Aunt Carrie died, Paul Osborn came every Sunday to fetch Aunt Alma for her Sunday visit with her "perfect country family". He hardly had time to reach the stairway before Aunt Alma came pecking her way down the squeaky steps. She and Aunt Carrie always wore the same style black leather laced up shoes with sturdy stacked heels. Their shoes and ankles fascinated me because Aunt Carrie's ankles were balloons, hanging over her shoe tops, and I wondered how she fitted her feet into such tiny shoes. Aunt Alma's ankles were sticks stuck down into shoes that looked so large I wondered how she kept them on her feet. From under the worktable, I listened to Aunt Alma's footfalls, making a double clickity-clack rhythm on the stairs as her shoes chucked up and down on her heels. I hoped that one day they'd defy her and fall off, but even her shoes obeyed.

Aunt Alma and her scary, tall, bony, rumpled son looked like a matched pair as they halted in the doorway while Aunt Alma, in her black fitted coat with brown fur trim and black hat with a brown feather, barked orders at Ma whose ankles were just right like everything of Baby Bear's in the "Three Bears" story. And, Ma's shoes fit her feet just right and danced as she worked.

Aunt Alma always ended her spiel, "Leave a tidy kitchen Clara," as if Ma ever left anything untidy.

When there were patrons in the shop Aunt Alma donned an effervescent personality, as if stepping on stage. She flitted and fluttered about gushing sweetly, "Oh yes, do try my chocolate kisses . . . . MY chocolate is PERFECTION . . . and my turtles!! You can't find turtles anywhere that can come close to these, I guarantee." There was just room enough for skinny Aunt Alma to slide behind the glass candy cases where all MA'S candies were displayed in MA'S mouthwatering PERFECTION. Just to walk by them set up a reaction in my mouth that only fear of Aunt Alma kept me from succumbing to temptation.

The outside door into the lunchroom was located right in front of Aunt Alma's candy cases. Three little round bells hung on the door knob, and their constant merry ring-ding-a-ling drove her crazy, but Aunt Carrie used to chuckle, "You can bet, if they ever stop ringing Alma will sing a different tune!"

The dining side of the room was filled with round tables covered with square red and white plaid oilcloths. The chairs were antique with plank bottoms discarded by the Episcopal Church Sunday School. Down the middle of the floor, a shiny aluminum ribbon patched together two widths of green and gray marble linoleum. In front of the candy counter, and along the edge of each floorboard, the green and gray marble pattern had worn away completely, exposing the linoleum's brickish-rose backing. I thought this made the floor much more interesting and pretty. Above the old-fashioned dark walnut wainscoting was a catsup and mustard spattered mural where hummingbirds hovered among pale-blue morning glories that twined in and out of the garden fence. A stone walkway led to a latticed arbor with a bench that beckoned, inviting me to come and sit a while. Still, faded and yellowed with age, it had strange and wonderful vistas for me to wander in.

It was a perfect setup: one of the aunt's long time friends, Mrs. Cameron, came in at noontime to be their waitress. Ma was in the kitchen sweat running down her brow; Aunt Alma selling candy or rushing about filling water glasses and offering second cups of coffee, and Aunt Carrie upstairs with me.

***

When Aunt Carrie died, I demanded to know where she had gone and when she was coming back. Aunt Carrie would never leave me.

In frustration Aunt Alma demanded, "Clara, you're going to have to explain heaven to that child."

Ma never looked up from her work at the big candy making table in the Sweet Shop kitchen, "What's to explain?"

"For the love of God, girl, about how all God's children are called to heaven one day," she stood in the doorway, hands on hips, skinny elbows jutting out, stabbing the air.

Ma's motions, as she stirred the dark luscious chocolate, were quick and annoyed as if it were the candy that offended her. "You tell her."

Aunt Alma flicked the end of her index finger at me, "Come here, Josephine," then with her whole hand, "come, come . . . come here."

I was leery. This was the first time Aunt Alma had ever acknowledged me as anything other than a nuisance, or something to pray at.

"Come, Josephine." Her voice was surprisingly soft. "I'll explain." And in a stern voice, "Clara, it won't do you any harm to listen too."

Aunt Alma pulled me upon her skinny lap that was not one bit like Aunt Carrie's nice plump one. Ma left her chores, pulled up a straight-backed chair, and sat dutifully down, folding her hands in her lap.

In a voice filled with honey Aunt Alma began: "Now, Josephine, listen carefully. Your Aunt Carrie was one of God's children, and she's been called home to heaven to be with Jesus. Now, to be one of God's children, you must love God with ALL your heart because he gave us his son, Jesus who died on the cross to save us from our sins."

My lower lip came out. "But I don't want 'a love God with ALL my heart, cause I love Aunt Carrie with ALL my heart, and I want 'a be with her."

"Oh dear," gasped Aunt Alma.

Ma said, "Josephine, loving Aunt Carrie is like loving God. It was God's love in Aunt Carrie that made her so nice. She's in heaven now and'll wait for you there."

"Humm, well, yes . . . that's right," Aunt Alma hem-hawed, surprised at Ma's answer, "humm . . . yes, yes . . . now let's see . . . that's right, you must love God like Aunt Carrie, only more, if you want to go to heaven when Jesus calls you."

"Where's heaven?"

"Heaven's God's home way up in the sky where Jesus waits to welcome all believers into God's shining presence." Aunt Alma almost shone too.

"I want'a see if she's up there."

Aunt Alma cooed, "We must wait until we're called home to heaven to see them."

I wasn't about to be fooled. "I didn't like those men who came and took Aunt Carrie away. Which one was Jesus? They wouldn't let me wake her up to say goodbye."

"Oh, my," sniffed Aunt Alma.

Ma said, "They were ambulance helpers, not Jesus. They took Aunt Carrie to the hospital in hopes the doctor could make her better. She couldn't wake up. Her soul had already gone to heaven."

"Where're her shoes? I want 'a see if her soles are gone," I wailed, pushing on Aunt Alma to get away. Heaven must be far away from the Sweet Shop, and it was not easy for Aunt Carrie to walk.

Ma reached out and grabbed me, pulling me against her knees. "Josephine, stop it. You can't see a person's soul. It has nothing to do with your shoes. It's the part of you that talks, and laughs, and cries." There were tears on Ma's cheeks, "Aunt Carrie's gone. We have to accept that, and we must be glad she loved God and is in heaven."

Nothing made any sense, and I put my head in Ma's lap and cried very hard.

Aunt Alma convinced Ma that I should accompany them to the viewing. She thought it was a mistake when children were shielded from the realities of life. There was a righteous flutter in her cheeks as she stated with finality, "Anyway, such a bright child should have a chance to say goodbye."

Bright child? It did solve the problem of what to do with me, because of course, Ma should go to the viewing, and babysitters cost money. Ma's only wages were our room and board.

When I saw Aunt Carrie lying there in her fancy box, I was overwhelmed. "See, she's not in heaven; she's just sleeping!" Overjoyed, I ran to her. "Wake up Aunt Carrie, wake up," I shouted as I started to scramble up to get my chin over the side of the coffin.

Ma was right behind me. "Hush, hush Josephine . . . Come away now and behave yourself."

I was snatched down, but I kept my eyes glued right on Aunt Carrie peacefully sleeping there on her beautiful pink ruffled pillow. Just maybe they were wrong and she'd wake up.

As if Ma read my thoughts, in her sharpest voice, "Now, Josephine, Aunt Carrie's not sleeping. That's only her body. She can't wake up. Her soul's gone to heaven." Ma knew I was not convinced, and kept a firm hold of my hand as we three stood in a row, they studying Aunt Carrie, but of course this close I couldn't see over the side.

In her sugar voice, Aunt Alma said, "She looks more like herself than she has in some time . . . so peaceful . . . didn't they do a marvelous job...she could be sleeping."

That made me angry; I had been harshly scolded for saying the same thing. Aunt Alma cried in her handkerchief, and Ma patted her shoulder.

Aunt Alma sniffled, "If only I could have had her wake at home...but those stairs." Then Ma guided her away to the cloakroom to hang up our coats.

This was my chance. I scurried, unnoticed, back in to Aunt Carrie, and quickly shinnied up over the side of the casket, was kneeling on Aunt Carries' very hard cold lap, not the soft loving lap I expected, and was busy unbuttoning her dress when Aunt Alma exploded back into the room.

She let out a blood curdling cry, "You dreadful child! What are you doing? How awful, you horrible, horrible child." She grabbed me roughly, as if I were vermin.

I beat Aunt Alma with my little fists as hard as I could, but she never flinched and my hands stung. "Let me alone. Let me alone. I want'a see the hole where the soul came out. I want'a see. Let me go."

Ma lifted me, not so gently, out of Aunt Alma's grasp. Why couldn't they understand, all I wanted was to see the hole Aunt Carrie's soul made when it came out.

Ma and I were ushered into a room where we were alone. This is the only time I can remember Ma ever holding me on her lap.

I sobbed, "I only wanted to find the hole Aunt Carrie's soul made when it came out."

"Oh Josephine, Josephine, what're we going to do with you?" She seemed almost loving like Aunt Carrie. "Your soul doesn't need a hole. It's invisible. You can't see it."

"But I want'a see it," not believing Ma, I pushed away from her as if I didn't want to be comforted. How could I ever feel good again? Aunt Carrie had abandoned me.

Ma studied my tear streaked face for a moment. "Put your hand here on my chest." She placed my hand just below the hollow in her neck, "Feel your hand going up and down?"

I nodded.

"Feel the air going in and out of your mouth and nose? Here, feel my breath." She blew softly against my cheek, "You can't see it, can you?"

Reluctantly, I shook my head.

"When Aunt Carrie died her breath left her body. No one could see it, and her soul left with it. That's something we just have to accept."

After that I kept my ears open, listening for any bits of information that might help me understand what was happening to my world. And I shared it all with Aunt Carrie especially at night before sleep came.

Aunt Carrie, when you were in that big fancy box was your soul already in heaven? Are you in two places? Ma and I never saw Luke and Mathew's ma in her fancy box. They wouldn't let us go because of what happened when I climbed into your box. I still can't see why they got so excited. Is Jesus real or is he an imaginary friend? Ma says you can't see a person's soul just like you mostly can't really see an imaginary friend. How can you be in two places? What happened to the part of you in the box? I wish there was some way to know about these things. I pretend you're an imaginary friend here with me, and no ones knows I'm talking to you only you don't ever answer me. I miss you all the time.

***

Aunt Alma made arrangements for the wedding to take place at the Baptist parsonage exactly one week from the day she made the announcement that her tall scary son was to be my step-daddy. The parsonage was around the corner on Elm Street where she and Aunt Carrie had gone to church before Ma came to live with them. Back in those days, after church, Paul Osborn had come every Sunday to take them both out to the country for an afternoon visit. In my early memories, he came early every Sunday to fetch Aunt Alma to attend True Faith Church, and spend the day with her, duly proclaimed, "Perfect little country family."

Sniffing, she'd explain to any who might be curious about the change, "Carrie's poorly . . . dropsy, don't you know . . . such a pity. She just can't go traipsing about anymore." I'm sure everyone knew she didn't trust Ma to be alone in the Sweet Shop, though Aunt Carrie was ill, more ill than anyone knew.

The instant the door closed behind Aunt Alma and her long-faced son, I was up the stairs into Aunt Carrie's arms. She'd squeeze me and tell me we could make as much noise as we wanted while Aunt Alma was away. There'd be no one to shush us up, and we'd not have to listen to her prayers; we'd have a good old time. She'd say, "You're Aunt Carrie's little sweetheart. What'd I do before I had you to love," then she'd add, "and you take such good care of me. You're the tonic I need. I just couldn't get along without you." More hugs and kisses and tickles always followed.

As we grew our beautiful world we never mentioned Ma who slaved away down in the kitchen. How much did she know about Ma? I have no idea what kind of understanding they may have had. I am sure, between Aunt Carrie and me, there was much more than our mutual need for each other. She purposely built a shield of love around me; her love for me exceeded her natural artesian outpouring of goodness. Looking back, I now comfort myself knowing that I was able to fulfill her starved maternal heart. There are so many things I wish I knew about her. I wonder about her youth, and how she came to be in the Sweet Shop, and why she never married? But, I was too young to think about such things. Why didn't I quiz Aunt Alma? Why is it, life moves you along so quickly that the questions you should have asked go unanswered, and haunt you forever? That Aunt Carrie owned the Sweet Shop became evident many years later when Aunt Alma died. Until then, we all thought Aunt Alma was the sole owner and had given Aunt Carrie a home.

***

The week between Aunt Alma's announcement about Ma's impending marriage and the day of the wedding, my life hung in peril. Ma was only in the kitchen long enough to cook dinner for the noon lunch room crowd. She was neglecting her candy making duties altogether, and sat at the sewing machine every spare minute. I expected Aunt Alma to come screeching up the stairs to scold her, and I was amazed Aunt Alma didn't mind at all that Ma had cut up Aunt Carrie's blue dress, but I was horrified.

Since Aunt Carrie's death I had become Ma's little helper. I scurried around, handing her things and putting the dirty pots and pans to soak in the sink. To be something other than a nuisance was a door opening, and I hoped to win Ma's love. Aunt Alma's announcement changed everything, and I was leaving the only security I had ever known, the place where Aunt Carrie had loved me.

I began remembering words, words Ma had spoken the day Aunt Alma went to her daughter-in-law's funeral, words Ma spoke about leaving the city. At the time they were just words that had a friendly feel to them almost as if she were struggling to be a little bit like Aunt Carrie, and I hung on to every hope that might be true.

The funeral had been on a Sunday when the Sweet Shop was closed. Thus, Ma and I were alone for the first time; customers wouldn't even be coming in. Aunt Alma liked to proclaim, "A good Christian never does business on The Lord's Day, even though it'd be our most profitable day."

Ma said, "We're going for a little walk, Josephine."

"Aunt Alma'll be mad."

"It'll be our little secret."

"But who'll make the candy?"

"We'll be back in plenty of time."

A secret with Ma! I was thrilled! Never had I dreamed of anything as wonderful as a secret with Ma. We sauntered along window shopping hand in hand just like Ma was Aunt Carrie. Sometimes, we'd laugh and Ma'd say, "Whatever do people do with that?" Or, Ma would exclaim, "We could use two of those." It was absolutely the best time. Occasionally, a fellow window shopper added texture to the scene; that kept my world real. Otherwise my feet might have floated right up off the sidewalk, I was so happy.

"If I take you by the toy store, promise you won't cry, because you'll want everything you see?"

I had no idea what Ma was talking about, but I promised never anticipating the explosion of desire that overwhelmed me as we stood gazing at all the amazing things in the window, dolls that looked so real they might burst out laughing, cars all hooked together, running around and around on what looked to me like a funny little wire street. This was more magic than my mind could absorb. Ma's hand on my shoulder was the only thing that kept me from bursting into tears.

Unbidden, my mind flew away. *Oh, Aunt Carrie, see that furry little black kitten? Isn't it just like the one in the Chinese school story you read me about Ting Ping? I want it. I want'a feel its fur. I want it; I want it.*

This was when Ma said the surprising friendly words: "You know, Josephine, this is not the life I want for you. I intend to get you out of the city." I wondered what, out of the city was, never dreaming it was going to live with Paul Osborn in the country. At the time I thought, "Ma does love me!" That was a hope bigger than a furry black kitten. Was that the moment Ma saw herself going to the country to take care of Paul Osborn's children? Since Aunt Carrie's death, Ma had been unable to pretend I was Aunt Carrie's child. No longer was Aunt Carrie there to provide me with the love and care she was unable to give me. The Sweet Shop had been her escape from the world, a place of penance and security. But now, Ma was confronted with her maternal responsibility. Did her own life's experience make her feel that responsibility more sharply, and force her to plot a new life for us?

But, Aunt Alma had her own plot. Later, I learned why Aunt Alma wanted Ma married as soon as possible. Plus, she wanted "her perfect little country family," consisting now of three motherless children, held together, and by someone she could control. I wager, unbeknown to either, a two-sided scheme was hatched, solution to their separate dilemmas.

After Paul Osborn's wife died his visits were so rare Aunt Alma walked around the corner to the Baptist Church where she and Aunt Carrie had gone before Ma came to live with them. The rest of the Lord's Day she spent in meditation as all believers should. Nothing was said about Ma leaving the candy making to meditate, but of course, she was a heathen.

During these stressful days, I sought solace wandering in the Sweet Shop mural, pretending I was sitting on the bench, or, I was outside on my rooftop world. Wherever I was, I told my troubles to Aunt Carrie.

Why do we have to leave the city? You said there was a magic carpet that could take me anywhere I wanted to go. I don't want'a go to the country and have a step-daddy, or live with Aunt Alma's perfect grandsons. Aunt Alma doesn't like me and they won't either. And Paul Osborn's even scarier than Aunt Alma. Aunt Alma says, "That poor motherless baby can't do without his daddy." That's why he hasn't been around to visit Aunt Alma. I don't like the way her scary son hurries right past the kitchen door and grunts "hello" to Ma. Funny thing...last Sunday when he was here, Aunt Alma called Ma upstairs from the kitchen. She never did that before. Ma's chin went out as she took off her dirty apron and wiped her sweaty face. She even smoothed her hair before she went up. I followed right behind her and sat on the top step. Why did they have a pen and paper? They all wrote on the paper and gave it to Ma. Ma folded it and put it in her pocket. All their faces looked strange. I was so scared I ran downstairs and crawled way back under the kitchen table so they wouldn't see me. That's when Aunt Alma called me out from under the table and told me Paul Osborn was going to be my step-daddy. "Out of sight, out of mind" didn't work that time! Yes, Aunt Alma still yells that at me all the time, even more without you here because I have to be with Ma more. Why does Paul Osborn have that dark shadow on his face? It looks ugly, and I don't think he has any lips. There's just a line where lips are suppose to be. But he's so tall maybe I just can't see them. I know he's mad at Ma for being a heathen and working on Sunday. Is that the reason we have heathens, to make candy on Sunday? Will Ma make candy for Paul Osborn now? Will he still be mad at her? I know you're never coming back because Ma's cutting up your blue dress. It almost made me cry when I saw what she was doing. Why can't the magic carpet take me to live with you and Jesus? That's where I really want to be, more than anything.

***

Ma must have felt like a modern day mail order bride, one you read about in novels because there had been no courtship or any chance to get acquainted. But, unlike a mail order bride, she had seen the bridegroom, and was confident marriage was the right solution to her problems. She didn't appear to be at all nervous about the bargain she had made for the course our lives would soon take. That course has proven to be a bumpy one full of ups and downs as my Yo nickname suggests. To dangle at the end of the yoyo's string, if you survive, takes you places and teaches you lessons difficult to learn.

My week of peril finally came to an end, and we began to pack. After Aunt Carrie died Ma and I had moved into Aunt Carrie's room. We had her dresser and her metal rack on the back of the door where we hung our extra dress to be worn on wash day.

Ma was impatient. "Don't pack that new dress. Aunt Alma gave it to you for the wedding."

"I don't want'a wear it. I hate it cause it makes me look like Aunt Alma. Can't I wear what I've got on? It's better'n that old thing Aunt Alma gave me."

"It's too short. When you bend over your bloomers'll show."

"I don't care."

"Well, neither do I, but Aunt Alma does."

"Will she still tell us what to do when we're in the country?"

"No."

"Then, I'm not wearing it."

"What's all that stuff you're putting in your bag?" Ma had stopped packing, and was threading her needle. Quickly, she began basting up the hem of the dress Aunt Alma had bought from the Baptist Church Thrift Basement which was so long it hung nearly to my ankles.

Ma asked again, "Well, what're you sneaking into that bag?"

"Aunt Carrie's doll and her book and the paper people we cut out. I need'um, to remember our stories."

"Oh, alright. Now, put this dress on. Aunt Alma meant well; she likes brown; she thought she was doing you a favor."

All our worldly belongings were packed into three shopping bags, one for me and two for Ma. At the time I had no feeling of deprivation at how Spartan our three bags were, and I even think Ma was so confident of her decision, she felt little pain at the meager measure of her life. What more could she hope for than a legitimate family to hide me in and a safe place of escape for herself?

Paul Osborn came at noon to drive us to the parsonage for the wedding. Ma had washed her hair and it was not all plastered down but soft and curly, and she had put on a light touch of lipstick. She looked just like one of those models in the catalog Aunt Carrie and I cut our paper people from. Before I could get used to this change in Ma, we were herded out to Paul Osborn's car, shopping bags in hand, to find the car's trunk was too full of junk to hold our shopping bags.

Aunt Alma said, "Paul, I would 'a thought you'd've cleaned out the trunk."

"There wasn't time. You have no appreciation for a farmer's life."

"Well, I suppose not."

Ma looked hassled as we crowded into the narrow dirty backseat with our three shopping bags, not at all like prim Aunt Alma who sat in the front seat like a queen. As Ma pulled the car door shut, she looked over at me and rolled her eyes. I'm sure it was exasperation but it felt friendly. I wiggled and turned from side to side checking everything. This was one of those wonderful cars I had watched driving by on the street in front of the Sweet Shop. And zip, before my amazement was quelled, we were around the corner, jerking to a stop.

Oh Aunt Carrie, is this the country? This must be the magic carpet you told me about! Maybe this won't be so bad!

The parsonage was not the country, but it was the first house I had ever seen. It had a lovely gleaming white porch with a spindled railing, and beautiful matching baby spindles around the porch ceiling that tickled me. I jumped out of the car, and in a flash, I was upon that railing. What else were railings for?

"Why, I never, get down from there this instant. What has gotten into you, Josephine?" Aunt Alma hissed nearly yanking my arm out of its socket.

I had learned it was better not to answer Aunt Alma. Ma gave me her, "why were you born," stare that said she wished she wasn't my mother.

Right at that moment, a Monarch butterfly hovered, quivering right beside me before it flew jauntily through the porch and on out into the lawn. Both my hands sprung up to my mouth to hold in my squeal. I shut out the world, and retreated into the comfort of my thoughts.

Thank you, Aunt Carrie, for teaching me about butterflies. You'd let me climb on the porch railing wouldn't you? And you'd say, "Be careful now, don't fall and hurt yourself."

More and more I retreated into Aunt Carrie's world.

Aunt Alma knocked and Mrs. Herman opened the door, gushing, "How lovely to see all of you on such a happy day. Come on in. Rev. Herman's gathering his things and will be right with us in the living room."

The living room reached right out and hugged me. All the furniture was rounded and soft. The curtains were perky, white, fluffy and ruffled. The carpet was thick plush with roses all blending together. There were red roses on an oval coffee-table that must have been made especially for people my size. Mrs. Herman took one of the red roses and pinned it on the powder blue dress that had been Aunt Carrie's which made Ma's eyes look like someone had painted them with a piece of the sky. As if the warmth of that room were not enough, a beautiful cat dressed in a furry tuxedo, perfect for the occasion, was curled up in the corner of the sofa. He stretched, yawned and sat up as if to say, "Proceed, I'm ready." I gasped in pure delight, and rushed to take my seat beside him. The cat looked up at me with glittering green eyes, yawned again, curling his whiskers in a circle around his nose, carefully laid two furry white paws that protruded from his furry black jacket sleeves, right in the middle of my lap, and went back to sleep. My heart nearly stopped. I could hardly breathe from my exalted pleasure.

Mrs. Herman said, "There now, Clara, what a lovely bride you make," as she finished pinning the rose on Ma's dress. Ma's cheeks burned pink, and she made no response.

Rev. Herman came through the doorway, and greeted everyone, then said, "I see all is ready. Shall we begin?"

Ma and Paul Osborn stood like statues in front of him. What a contrast the stiff, awkward and disjointed wedding ceremony was in the midst of such a warm loving room. After a long and very funny story about how God took part of man to make a woman, Rev. Herman pronounced, "You are man and wife. You may kiss the bride." Ma's face blushed red as the rose on her dress. An unrumpled, pressed and well shaven Paul Osborn, grunted "humph," and finally managed to peck a thin lipped kiss on Ma's cheek.

Mrs. Herman started giving congratulations in her warm friendly voice. Aunt Alma was profusely polite. Ma was uncomfortable with her tall awkward husband, who looked stern or angry, standing there beside her not at all interested in the proceedings. My eyes were darting around the circle of players, trying to figure out what came next, when Aunt Alma bleared out, "Now, Josephine, you have a new step-daddy;

and you must call him Daddy just as my grandchildren do." Strange, how could this make her son my daddy? I never wanted to leave that lovely house and magnificent cat.

I was too young to realize all the changes that were involved with this new arrangement. Aunt Alma rented the Sweet Shop. Under the usual Sunday CLOSED sign in the window, there was a GOING OUT OF BUSINESS CANDY SALE notice. I was not to see the Sweet Shop again until years later when I went to Phelpsburg High, and by then it was a bakery. Aunt Alma rented an apartment on Elm Street across from the Baptist Church. It was where all her friends were, and she was just around the corner from Phelpsburg's Main Street.

As we left the parsonage that afternoon Aunt Alma came with us for what was to become the resumption of her Sunday visits to the farm with her now "less than perfect little country family." She sat regally stiff in the front seat with DADDY, while Ma and I again rode tag-along in the back seat. This didn't seem at all strange to me at the time, but I wonder what Rev. and Mrs. Herman thought?

The country was mind opening; how big the world was; how many houses there were. Most astonishing, it was amazingly green, so many trees, so much sky above great hills that reached right up and touched the clouds. This world was even stranger and more wonderful than the wallpaper mural in the Sweet Shop lunchroom. Everything was startling. I had no idea the world was shaped like that!

Yes, Aunt Carrie, the car certainly is the magic carpet and this world is not make-believe!

It took forever to get to wherever we were going, and it was all up through those wonderful awe inspiring hills. Eventually, we came to a dirt road, and as we buzzed along it, a huge dusty cloud billowed out behind us. Abruptly, the car swung into a driveway, the dusty balloon engulfed us momentarily, and sailed on by, exposing a huge white house surrounded by a seemingly never ending wonderfully green carpet. We had arrived at the Stanley farm where Daddy worked.

When Ma opened my car door, I burst out. And, in my excitement at feeling the green grass so thick and inviting, I was overcome with joy, and began rolling on the lovely surprisingly cool new phenomenon. Everyone stood shocked, starring at me dumbfounded.

The yoyo I had in the pocket of my dress fell out, and rolled along on the grass. Before I could reach it, Luke, the Billy Sunday grandson, grabbed it. This was one of my three most prized possessions. I had the rag doll Aunt Carrie had made me with black hair like mine, her thick storybook and my yoyo that one of the men who ate in the Sweet Shop had given me. Panic overtook any good judgment a six year old might possess, and I screamed, "Giv'me it. It's mine," and I started clawing at his hand.

"Who's this little skinny, inny wild Gypsy?" He was laughing and dancing around, holding the yoyo up high in the air. Pushing me away, he demanded, "Here, let me show you how it's done." And he snapped the yoyo out the string so hard it flew right off, leaving the string dangling in his hand. I ran after the yoyo, burning with anger, full of confusion about Aunt Alma's perfect grandson.

Luke asked, "Daddy, did you say our new STEP-sister's Josephine? Well Yoyo Jo, come and get your old string."

There were no tears in my eyes as I snatched the string from his fingers, but they stung behind my eyes where no one could see them. Luke was more like a grownup than one of Aunt Alma's perfect grandsons she was always bragging about. He was almost as tall as my new Daddy. His eyes were snapping cinnamon brown and mean. He wore a smirk on his face, and his hair was a springy helmet of cinnamon brown, emphasizing the intensity of his eyes. In time I would learn he was handsome and very clever.

Ma stood in horror, unable to speak, and Aunt Alma smirked as if she thought her Billy Sunday grandson exceptionally gifted. Mrs. Stanley quickly came to my rescue. "Well now, Josephine, I'm so glad to meet you," turning to Ma, "hello, Clara. I'm so pleased to have you both for my new neighbors. I'm May Stanley. This is my husband, Fred, our two children, Abigail and Forrest. And, Josephine, these are your new brothers, Luke, and little Mathew. Baby Mark is asleep in the house."

Mathew was a chubby three year old with a round moon face, clinging fine sandy hair and large gray saucer eyes. He put his warm pudgy hand in mine, and I knew we were going to be friends and a comfort to each other. Abigail and Forrest looked like grownups too even though Forrest was shorter and looked younger than Luke. His eyes were wise and kind behind his glasses. Abigail looked as old as Ma.

Mrs. Stanley announced, "Come everyone. Abbey and I have a reception dinner and wedding cake ready, waiting to be served."

I was right about Forrest being kind. He winked at me as he sat down beside me at the dinner table. I knew I had disgraced myself, and I was feeling all strange about that plus everything was so fancy with a white linen table cloth and napkins to match, not at all like the lunchroom tables in the Sweet Shop, that before that moment, I had thought quite grand.

He turned to me and held out his hand for the yoyo still clenched tightly in my fist. "Let's see it a second . . . I think I can fix it."

Reluctantly, I handed it over.

He managed to retie the string, and smiled at me as he placed it back in my hand. "There you are. Good as new."

Luke glowered at us from across the table.

After dinner Mrs. Stanley pulled me upon her lap that was not as plump as Aunt Carrie's, but friendly and snuggly like hers. "We're going to be great friends, you and I." My heart swelled up so big I thought it might come right out through my ribs. About then, Mark woke up and cried out. Mrs. Stanley took my hand, "Come with me, Josephine, and meet your littlest brother."

The house was so big it was never ending, and I could see rooms even better than Rev. Herman's, if that were possible. At the end of the long hall there was an open stairway.

Aunt Carrie, I'd sure like to slide down that long railing, but not when Aunt Alma's here! Yes, I'd be careful not to fall."

I had never seen a baby up close before, and baby Mark was so cute I wanted to squeeze him. He was all smiles with dimples, blue eyes and sunshine curls. When Mrs. Stanley placed him in Ma's lap I could see Ma thought so too.

She said, "Well now, aren't you the happiest little fellow." She held both of his sweet little hands, patting them together. He squealed and his eyes shone with glee. Ma kissed the end of his nose just like Aunt Carrie used to kiss mine. Before the day was over, I could tell he was going to worm his way into the place in Ma's heart I longed for.

Abigail said, "Come, Josephine, I'll show you the new baby calf down in the barn." She knew just the right way to distract my jealousy.

Mathew danced up and down on his fat little legs. "Me too, me too."

"You silly-willy Matt, of course you too."

"Silly-willy . . . me too."

Abigail had soft hands with long tapered fingers and beautiful red polished nails. There were three gold bracelets on her wrist that clinked together, making musical sounds. She wore saddle shoes and a pleated skirt. I couldn't take my eyes away from her. Everything about her fascinated me because she looked just like the girl on the calendar that hung behind the candy counter in the Sweet Shop. She could be the smiling girl, holding a tray of Coca Cola bottles and glasses, inviting you to take one.

Little Mathew took her hand chanting, "Abbey, Abbey's showing us the baby calf."

"Yes, Matt, we'll see the baby calf." She leaned down and kissed the top of his head. He looked up and gave her a shy grin. I kind'a wanted her to kiss my head too, but I concluded that I must be too old for top of the head kissing.

Luke and Forest sauntered down across the lawn and across the road to the fence in back of the barn. A wonderful big tan and white dog sniffed Forrest's hand as it jauntily bounced along beside him.

"Why's that dog kissing Forrest's hand?"

"That's Forrest's dog, Laddie. He goes everywhere with Forrest because he likes Forrest better than anyone in the world."

"Better'n anyone?"

"Yes, better than anyone."

Forrest and Luke climbed upon the fence, cupped their hands around their mouths, and at the top of their lungs began calling, "Y-oo'll-dee-od-ll yol-de-old-de-oo . . . Carl." From the hill across the valley, ". . . yol-de-old-de-oo . . . Carl" came calling right back.

I pulled Abigail's hand, "Who's over there calling?"

Her laugh was a soft happy sound in my ears. "Why, that's an echo, Josephine. It's their own voice bouncing right back to them from across the hill just like a rubber ball."

I know I looked at her with much wonder and disbelief on my face because she reassured, "Really. You'll learn all about these things in time."

I sure hoped she was right because it was a very different world out here in the country from the one I had overseen from my rooftop. At that moment I caught a glimpse of what Ma had meant when she said she wanted to get me out of the city.

Abigail went on explaining, "The boys are trying to get their friends who live way over there on the hill to call back."

"How do you know it's not them calling back?"

"An echo's the caller's voice and words. Their friends' voices would have different words."

"Would my voice come back?"

"Of course it would. After we see the calf we'll try it."

I wondered how anything you couldn't see, could bounce like a rubber ball, but I thought I'd better not ask. It could be something like a person's soul, and that might get me in trouble.

The barn was still another world. The pungent, moist smell of animal dung stung my nostrils the instant we walked in. In time I learned to love and welcome that smell. My eyes were slow to adjust to how dark it was compared to the dazzling sunlight we had so abruptly left behind as we stepped through the door, and descended narrow stairs down into a brown and very old looking world. One wall, higher than Abigail's head, was laid up with fieldstone. So great was the barn's impression on me that whenever stories include castles and knights, my mind flies back in time, and I am six years old again overwhelmed by the feel of the barn that first day. There were big square posts holding up the ceiling that had dusty, dirty things mystically hanging half attached, giving you the creepy feeling they might fall down on you. The windows were high up so I couldn't see out them, and they were so dusty they muted the sunlight. There was no floor, just the ground, and there were board fences that Abigail called pens. I thought you wrote with pens! But this was the country where things bounced that you couldn't see. Inside one of those pens there was a monstrously big, black and white animal looking out at us. It stretched its neck out toward us, and let out a bellowing, MOO. I couldn't help myself, I grabbed Abigail's arm. Little Mathew didn't seem at all frightened, and I was ashamed. Abigail lowered herself down to my size, and put her arm around me.

"You've never seen a cow before, have you Josephine?" I shook my head with my chin rubbing my chest in shame. "Well, cows are very friendly animals that give us the milk we drink."

At that moment a little bitsy cow got up from the hay where it had been resting out of sight. Its legs were long and shaky as it wobbled over to the cow. That was the baby calf. I was so tickled; I laughed out loud. It butted along its mother's underside until it found what it was looking for.

I gasped, "What's it doing?"

There was that soft laugh again. "The baby calf's nursing. The mother cow has milk in that bag hanging under her. That's what the calf's drinking. My dad and your new daddy squeeze those tits and milk comes out, and that's what we sell to make a living. That's where the milk you drink comes from."

I said nothing because I was so amazed that my mind just couldn't take in all the new information. I watched the little calf butt the mother cow as it wagged its tail to-and-fro, very pleased with its dinner. The mother cow took her big, long tongue and licked her wobbly baby. I don't know why but that pleased me so much, I laughed out loud again.

Abigail still squatted between Mathew and me, and her arm felt just right around me. She said, "You like the little calf, don't you?"

Mathew leaped right upon her knee, "Yes, yes I like the calf, and Abbey, and Yoyo," and she kissed his upturned face.

Luke appeared in the doorway, looking like a cat with cream on its whiskers. "Why don't you show her the bull, Abbey?"

Mathew jumped down, yanking on her arm. "Want'a see the bull, Abbey. Show me the bull."

Luke walked ahead of us, and slid open a very large door that looked like a whole wall moving. Before us was a huge area with two rows I learned were stanchions where the cows were milked with their necks locked in the stanchions. Everything was clean, whitewashed and the floor was not dirt but concrete. In the far corner there was another pen that was a separate room with a heavy door made of bars very close together. The bull was inside. He looked right at us and snorted as he pawed the straw that covered the floor of his pen. In the middle of his pen, hanging on a chain, was a short section of a huge square beam like those that held up the ceiling. The bull butted the beam with his head, making the timber swing like a giant pendulum. The bull let the heavy beam swing back against his head, and this started a butting frenzy. Never had I seen anything so brutal and frightening.

Stammering, I pushed myself against Abbey, "What's the bull doing?"

"Bulls have more energy than they know what to do with, so they like to butt things. He's getting his exercise."

Luke laughed, "You better watch out or he'll butt you, Yoyo Jo."

"He'll butt you Yoyo." Mathew mimicked.

"Luke, that's just plain mean. There's no need to frighten Josephine. Everything's new to her, and you better be a good boy, Matt. It's not nice to tease."

"Well, she'd better be scared of the bull or she'll, BOOTY-WHOO-WHO, be killed." Luke mocked refusing to be silenced. "You never know when the bull might get out." He made a frightening lunge at me. "And if not our bull, then a neighbor's."

I crowded even more tightly against Abigail. "Will the cows kill me too?"

Luke began to laugh, holding his sides.

"Leave her alone, Luke. You're not one bit funny. Isn't it time you got the cows in for milking?"

Luke didn't budge, and continued snickering.

Abigail explained, paying no attention to Luke. "Cows are friendly. But until you get used to them, you shouldn't come to the barn or go into the pasture alone. A grown up should be with you. Luke is right about bulls. Never put your hand through the bars. You can never ever trust one…ever. That's something you must remember."

Concern widened my eyes. "How can I tell a cow from a bull?"

"What a stupid little creep." Luke muttered under his breath.

"Little creep," Mathew mimicked.

"One more word out of you, Luke Osborn, and your father'll hear about it. You'd better be after the cows. I'm sure Forrest and Laddie are, and we're sick of your mouth."

He swaggered past Abigail deliberately bumping her shoulder as he left the barn.

"Josephine, a bull is a daddy cow and doesn't give milk."

This she thought answered all I needed to know, but as I looked at the bull pacing back and forth in front of the gate, looking for a way out of his pen to kill me, I saw a funny looking bag hanging down under him too. I still needed to ask more questions, but Abigail ushered us out of the barn, and I knew that was the cue for no more questions.

She forgot all about having me call to the hill for an echo, and I was too shy to remind her. I could see the cows, following one another up over the pasture toward the barn with Luke, Forrest and Laddie walking behind them, laughing and talking with the sun dancing all around them, lighting up their hair and Laddie, running to and fro, sniffing here and there, always coming back to Forrest's side.

Aunt Carrie, what a wonderful world this country is; I feel all fuzzy inside. I sure wish you were here. I wonder what happens when the cows come in and they do that magical thing, milking?

I was summing up courage to ask Abigail all about it when she said, "Your mother'll be waiting for us. It's time for the men to do the milking chores."

When we came into the house, Mrs. Stanley asked, "Josephine, what'd you think of that little calf?"

"It gets milk out of those things hanging down under its mother, and the bull is a daddy cow and doesn't give milk."

Aunt Alma squawked, "Oh dear."

Mrs. Stanley took no notice of Aunt Alma. "Is that so?"

"And the bull'll kill me if I don't watch out."

"Well, well, now, we'll see that he doesn't do that; there's no need to worry."

In her preachy, screechy voice Aunt Alma's words came like a slap. "Nice little girls DO NOT say 'bull' they say 'critter.'"

Abigail came to my rescue. "My fault Mrs. Osborn . . . Josephine, don't worry . . . I should've told you. It's not your fault." And, she touched the end of my nose with her pointed red fingernail, which was almost as good as a kiss.

Then Ma said something unusual. "Josephine'll be quick to learn all these things," instead of giving me one of her, why were you born, looks.

See, Aunt Carrie, Ma's right. The country is a whole lot better!

Mr. Stanley came downstairs with his barn clothes on, and said to Daddy who sat silently listening with a dark grimace on his face. "Paul, you take your family on down and get them settled. We'll get along without you this evening."

"I appreciate that Fred. Got'a get Mom back to Phelpsburg before it's too late. May, that was mighty good vitals and very thoughtful of you. Clara and I can't thank you enough."

That surprised me; Daddy spoke Ma's name just like he knew her!

The tenant house was small with a side porch, but to my disappointment, there was no pretty railing for me to climb on. Twin windows in the living room stared out at me like eyes with a single window centered above them, making a perfect nose for an upside-down face. I remember thinking that if you turned the house over the pointed roof would make the house smile. On reflection, that summed up life within that little house: We had all the right components for happiness, if everything hadn't been upside down.

Daddy drove the car around to the back of the house where there was another porch with a roof that extended out to a woodshed, enabling wood to be carried into the house under shelter. At that point however, I was unaware of what a convenience that was, having never seen a wood-burning cook-stove that burned quantities of wood, even in summer. Over the porch roof there was a lone window that I learned was in Luke and Mathew's room, and served Luke well more times than anyone would ever know.

Daddy told Aunt Alma, "Sit tight, while I get them unloaded."

I detected a note of disappointment in her reaction, but there was no protest. After having Ma with her for over six years, there was no exchange of good wishes. Merely a, "I'll see you next Sunday, Clara."

"Yes, goodbye, I'll have dinner ready for you."

Luke came running over from the barn to say goodbye. He leaned into the car and kissed his grandmother's cheek. She reached up and stroked his curly head. "Bless you, Luke."

Daddy held Mathew up. "Give Grandma a kiss."

Wriggling to get down, "Don't wan'a."

Luke teased, "I'll kiss Grandma for you, Matt." Coyly, he planted another kiss on Aunt Alma's cheek.

This family scene was very interesting to me. I watched it so closely Luke took advantage of my engrossed concentration, and reached out suddenly, and pinched my nose between the knuckles of his first two fingers so hard tears stung my eyes.

"Got your nose, Yoyo Jo," and he held out his hand with his thumb sticking out between his fingers, proof of my missing nose.

Involuntarily, my hand flew up to find my nose. Luke then showed his thumb to Aunt Alma who gave a hearty laugh, and to Mathew chided, "Go on with you," and in a fake crying voice, "I'll save your kiss for another day. I can see you miss your nap."

I was glad Mathew didn't want to kiss her. I couldn't imagine anyone wanting to kiss Aunt Alma except Luke, and I thought they were "birds of feather," an expression Aunt Alma often used.

Daddy set Mathew on his little, fat legs. "Here, Clara, take this bad boy."

Ma shifted baby Mark to her hip, and took Mathew's hand as they walked up the back steps onto the porch and into the house. Daddy followed with the shopping bags, and we all stood like dummies in the middle of the kitchen floor.

The awkward silence was short lived. Daddy ordered, "You get settled in Clara. Your things go in the big bedroom upstairs. I shan't be gone long. Luke, you go on over to the barn; take my place with the milking. "

This, I could see, was not pleasing to Luke. I'm sure he had his mind set on harassing Ma and me.

"Aw, do I hav'ta. What about Young Peoples?"

"That's not until seven. There's time."

"But Daddy, I still have to learn my verses."

"See that you do then."

Daddy gave no further instructions. Nothing was said about where things were or what time to have supper. I was glad to have him gone. It'd give us a chance to get acquainted with the house that was to be our new home, and his presence was like having Aunt Alma looking at you, only more so.

As soon as the car started backing down the driveway, Luke announced he was going to telephone Woody, his name for Forrest, to see if he'd go to Young Peoples with him.

Telephone? I rushed to the window. He crossed the driveway to a gnarly old apple tree whose branches hung out over the cow-pasture fence that bordered the driveway. Placing his hands on the top wire, he vaulted the fence, and swung up into the apple tree with an ease and beautiful grace that was not at all like that of a clumsy adolescent.

Up at the big house, Laddie was barking his head off as he ran around and around the big old pear tree by the chicken coup. Forrest was barely visible perched among the tree's knurly braches. Then hanging almost upside down, he pointed his hand at Laddie, and with one last little bark, Laddie lay faithfully down at the foot of the tree to wait for his friend.

Luke took a tin can from a crotch in the apple tree and held it up to his ear. When I studied the can very carefully I could see a string coming out the bottom of the can. Forrest had a can held up to his mouth. Luke was scowling; he didn't like what he was hearing. Luke changed the can to his mouth. That was too much; I ran out onto the back porch and peered round the porch post, listening hard. I could hear muffled sounds as Luke talked into his can.

Luke came swaggering in with a smarty smirk pasted on his face as if he were some kind of genius, me right behind him. He looked at Ma and was disappointed she had not been interested in his antics.

"Darn, Woody has to milk, and if I don't help, he won't get done in time for Young Peoples."

Now he had Ma's attention. "Don't you usually help?" Ma jostled Mark who wasn't sure he liked being left with a stranger.

"I only work when I get paid. Tonight I won't get paid. If you call it pay. Daddy hocks it, and puts it toward my schooling."

"I'd say that's good pay."

"Well, I'd say it's not fair."

"Maybe you'd rather be a farmhand like your daddy?"

"Maybe I'd rather be anything other than what my daddy has picked out for me."

Ma left it there. I wanted to know if Daddy had picked out a "Billy Sunday," whatever that was, for Luke like Aunt Alma had. I knew what an ordinary Sunday was; it was the day Ma made candy.

Ma asked, "Do you and Forrest usually go to Young Peoples together?"

"No, Woody's a Methodist. We go to True Faith Church."

"I see," was all Ma said.

"I'm going to the barn. Yoyo Jo, don't you touch my telephone," Luke threatened.

Under my breath, but loud enough so he could hear, "Who'd want your old tin can." But I really did. I was burning with jealousy, and he knew it.

"What about your bible lesson?"

"I already know it. Anyway, who cares?"

"Obviously, your father."

"Don't you try to tell me what to do. You're not my mother. You're not much older'n me." And he stormed out of the house, forehead furled, with the smirk wiped off his face.

I have looked back many times on what Ma managed to accomplish in just the short time Daddy was gone, and I marvel at what an extraordinary person she was. In 1935 electricity had not yet reached all the rural areas of the country. It would be another eight years before the electric company extended service beyond Tate Town, the crossroads village, nestled in the narrow creek valley one mile south of the farm.

She quickly checked the cupboards, and scouted the cellar with Mark in her arms, Mathew and me at her heels. The cupboard was bare except for bread. There were milk, eggs, and a small portion of sowbelly stored down in the cellar in an old boiler that had been dug down into the ground where it would be a little cooler than just sitting on the cellar floor. There were potatoes and onions in a bin.

Mark was restless and began to whimper, so Ma spread a blanket on the living room floor and fed him the bottle Mrs. Stanley had prepared. He made happy little sucking noises, and by the time his bottle was finished Ma had coaxed him to sleep.

My habit of watching everything Ma did in hopes I could hand her something, helped my mind record images of how she prepared that first meal. First she lighted a fire in the big old black woodstove which fascinated me because this was the first time I had ever seen a fire. And, up until then, all Ma had to do was turn a knob to heat up the stove for cooking. Then, she peeled the potatoes, put eggs in the pot with them and covered them with water, not from a faucet, but from the spring out in a corner of the weed patch. While the pot came to a boil, she ran out to the weed patch and found leaf lettuce, again, not from the refrigerator, but from outside. She cut the sowbelly in little pieces, and fried them down until browned crisps. Into the fat drippings, she sautéed chopped onion. Next, the hard boiled eggs were carefully fished from the pot of potatoes and put in cold water. When the potatoes were so done they began to fall apart, she drained most of the water into a funny black sink, and slashed the potatoes into little chunky bits. Into this mixture, she added the sautéed onion and sowbelly crisps, spices and milk.

Ma then dipped a little of the soup into a small pan, into it she beat uncooked egg yolks, some sugar with a little flour, a little vinegar, a generous sprinkle of pepper, a little fat from the drippings jar and cooked it while briskly beating the mixture.   When it became very thick she placed that pan in cold water to hurry its cooling. This was salad dressing made without consulting a recipe. She mashed the hard boiled eggs and mixed them with the dressing. Now, she was ready to make sandwiches. It amazes me at how many "make do" skills Ma learned from the many foster homes she had lived in. No wonder she did so well in the Sweet Shop. Aunt Carrie called Ma, a blessing; Aunt Alma called Ma, answered prayer.

I was sent out to the weed patch to pick wild daisies for the table. Minutes after Daddy walked in, we were ready to sit down to a supper of egg-salad and lettuce sandwiches and a steaming, hearty, big, hot pot of potato soup.

Daddy looked well pleased. "Not quite 'the feeding of five thousand,' nonetheless, 'the feeding of five' is miracle enough." I was proud of Ma, and I softened a little toward Daddy even though I didn't know what, "the feeding of five thousand" was. I did know what, "the feeding of five" was.

At that moment, Luke came hurrying in full of smiles "All finished up in record time, Daddy, and Woody's going to Young Peoples with me."

Luke hadn't been happy to help out! He could fool Daddy but he couldn't fool me!

"Good, son, what about your Bible verses?"

"Finished them too."

"I'm always happy to have Forrest hear the Good News." Daddy's face lost its scary look as he gave Luke's shoulder a squeeze. I could see how extra special Daddy thought Luke was.

Mathew started to bang the table with his spoon handle for some attention. Daddy barked, "Mathew, stop that, this minute, or it's no supper and to bed with you."

My spoon was raised ready too, and I remember the shiver that narrow escape caused. Mathew put his head down, and I wanted to reach over and pat him, and I wanted to tell him that I liked him better than Luke, but I didn't dare.

Before Daddy ladled out our soup he took a long time to thank God for the food on the table. Yet I knew, he knew, it was Ma who had cooked the meal. He talked a lot longer to his imaginary friend than Aunt Alma did though he ended the same way, "in Jesus' name, Amen."

Soon as supper was over Daddy headed for the living room. "Come along Luke. I'll hear your verses before you leave for Young Peoples."

They woke Mark and he began to cry. Ma dried her hands on her apron, and rushed in to check on him. As she knelt, unpinning a very soggy diaper, Daddy barked, "For heaven's sake woman, not in here. There's a little girl present. Don't you know modesty is a virtue? Sin needs no encouragement."

Aunt Carrie, what'd he mean? There's that "sin" word again that Aunt Alma's always talking about. She knows what sin is. Does it have something to do with what's under Mark's diaper?

A look of contempt past over Ma's face, and silently, she dutifully picked Mark up and started upstairs. I ran to her not wanting to be left alone with Daddy and Luke.

"Josephine . . . " Daddy's voice boomed.

Ma halted, placed a hand on my shoulder, "Josephine, go to the kitchen and dry the dishes for me."

"Yes, Ma." I had escaped having to take an order from Daddy.

When Ma came into the kitchen baby Mark had been lulled back to sleep, and was tucked into his crib for the night.

"Dishes all wiped, Josephine?"

"Yes, Ma."

"Good girl."

At this moment, Forrest appeared at the back door, and Luke grabbed up his bible. When his back was to Ma and Daddy he looked at me with leering hate in his cinnamon brown eyes. Then he stuck out a very pointed tongue, wagging it back and forth trying to goad me, into making a response that would get me into trouble, but I was too surprised at his ugly tongue to take the bait.

Ma stayed in the kitchen long after the dishes were put away. Probably she dreaded going into the living room where Daddy was.

Suddenly he rose from his chair. "Clara, let that work be; go fetch Mark. Prayer meeting's at eight. We can still make it if we hurry."

Ma made no move to fetch Mark. "Paul, you go ahead. Mark is all tucked in for the night. It's been a hard day for Josephine and me. We're going on to bed. I'll be glad to keep Mathew for you if you'd like. He's pretty worn out too."

Daddy stopped short, anger radiated from his eyes. Looks that I didn't comprehend passed between them, and to my great surprise Daddy answered, "As you say, it's been a long day. I think it best if I turn in early too. You three go on up to bed."

There were no goodnights. Ma never hesitated. She collected Mathew and up we went. The stairway came up into Mathew and Luke's bedroom. At the top of the stairs, the little window I had looked up at over the back porch roof, gave the little room its only light. Two cots were at opposite sides of the room with a small dresser between them. Mathew ran to the far cot and scrambled upon it.

"This is my bed . . . " He looked up at Ma with a questioning face. "Are you my real Ma now?"

"You only have one real Ma, Mathew. Don't you remember her?" He shook his head "no" with his lips pressed in a tight line between his very pink, round cheeks. "I'd be glad to have you call me Ma. Would you like to do that?" He nodded enthusiastically.

"Do you need help with your pajamas?" There was more head bobbing.

I don't think he really needed help, according to Aunt Alma, but he very much needed reassurance. That, I understood very well.

"Josephine, go to our room and get your pajamas on. Don't wake Mark. I'll be in shortly."

I was disappointed. The last person to help me into my pajamas was Aunt Carrie.

Come, Aunt Carrie. I know where my pajamas are. I'll show you. After I'm in bed I'll tell you the story about the scary bull . . . critter.

Ma's and my room was the front bedroom that looked out the nose to the upside down face. Our bedroom door was opposite the stairway on the far side of Mathew and Luke's portion of the room. A board railing each side of the stairway opening protected anyone from falling down the stairs. There was just enough room at the top of the stairs to crowd by in either direction, depending on whether you were going into their side or along the narrow walkway to our door.

Mark looked like a cherub as he slept curled up in a little ball behind the slats of his crib. Our three sacks stood forlornly in the middle of the bed.

See, Aunt Carrie, I get to sleep with Ma again; isn't that nice? But, I wish I still lived with you. Why did you go live in heaven with Aunt Alma's imaginary friends? Is it because you can't see a person's soul, and that makes it belong to imaginary friends? Souls and imaginary friends are very hard to understand, echoes too. Where is the rest of you? No, I'm not going to cry. Don't let the bull get me. I don't want my soul to come out yet. I think I might like the country.

When Ma came to bed a few minutes later, she shut the door softly behind herself and slid the bolt to the lock. As she climbed into bed, she sighed and turned away from me to sleep. "Good night, Josephine."

"Good night, Ma." I think it was a long time before either of us slept.

That was my first day on the farm, and how I got my nickname, Yo.

Chapter 4

Next morning I awoke suddenly, struggling for air. Luke was straddling my legs with his hand held tightly over my mouth. My thrashing and muffled, "MMMMM's," woke Mark and he began to whimper.

"Ssshh, ssshh, don't you bite, you little creep. I'm taking my hand away. Not one sound, if you know what's good for you. One peep, and I'll throw you in the bull pen."

I nodded my head.

"Not one word."

"I'llll be quieeet, I'llll be quieettt." I was trembling so hard my teeth chattered.

He jumped off me, ran quickly to the crib, grabbed up the now loudly crying Mark, and started down stairs, jostling and cooing to him, "Hey, hey little fellow. What's the matter? Want some breakfast."

Ma met him at the bottom of the stairs. Her look went quickly from Luke to me where I stood on the stairs still trembling. When she started to take Mark from Luke's arms, he protested, "I'll feed him for you. I fed him all the time for Mrs. Stanley when he lived up there after Mom died."

Ma kept her eyes on me as she slowly said, "Why, Luke, how thoughtful of you. Thank you. That's very nice."

I heard Daddy's voice coming from the kitchen, "Your mother'd be pleased with you, son."

"Aw, it's nothing. Mark's my buddy."

Ma continued studying me. I hadn't done anything, but I braced myself for a scolding.

"You seem to be all right," she was hesitant, with some doubt, or maybe surprise, "go upstairs and wake Mathew. Then get yourself dressed." As I turned, she whispered, "Slide the bolt behind you."

I shivered and shook as I put my clothes on even though it was a warm June morning. Visions of the bull butting me like he butted his butting beam terrified me. How I longed for Aunt Carrie's loving arms.

Aunt Carrie, I do want to be in heaven with you, but I don't want Luke to throw me in the bul-critter pen. I wonder how you get dead without being thrown in the critter pen.

For a moment I saw myself in a coffin and wondered if Ma would be sorry I died?

When I came into the kitchen, Luke was feeding Mark corn mush. Ma put a bowl of corn mush on the table for me. Mathew, still in his pajamas, was already eating his. Daddy had finished and was sipping coffee too hot to drink. Between sips, "How was Young Peoples last night?"

Luke's hand stopped midway to Mark's open baby-bird lips, "That Woody...sometimes I don't know about him."

Mark let out a squeal, and Luke stuffed the spoon, not too gently, into his gapping mouth, and he choked, spitting food all over his chin and bib.

There was no reprimand from Daddy. "Does Forrest good to get a taste of the real message once in a while. Those Methodists have a 'watered down' message."

I knew what "watered down" soup was. It was how Aunt Alma wanted Ma to serve the Sweet Shop soup, but Ma didn't listen. If

Forrest went to the "watered down," Methodist Church then, "watered down" was preferable when it came to churches. The notion anything having to do with Luke could be better than Forrest was ludicrous. Therefore, I concluded, I wouldn't like True Faith regardless of what Ma said about thin soup.

"It was so embarrassing; nosey old Mrs. Williams, squawked," Luke's voice became high pitched, "'is your Dad sick? He never misses church and prayer service." And in a natural voice, "Woody piped right up, 'He got married this morning.' You can imagine how surprised everyone was, and curious . . . disgusting. I know what they're thinking. Poor Mom, I explained Grandma thought it wouldn't be right for a woman to come into our house to live unless you married her. So, I explained, we've sort-of-got a permanent baby sitter, nothing more."

Ma looked amused, but Daddy didn't look at all pleased. "I guess you did the best you could under the circumstances, son. I'm sorry it fell to you. I should've been there." And he glowered at Ma meaning it was her fault he wasn't. He hesitated as if to wipe that slate clean, and in a very stern voice continued, looking right at Luke, "Now, this permanent baby sitter is legally my wife, and your step-mother . . . not just a baby sitter, or a 'her' . . . OK."

"I'm not calling her, Ma. She's not my mother."

"You can call her, Mrs. Osborn."

"No way, she's not old enough to be my mother or Mrs. Osborn."

"Luke, you surprise me. You should be praising the Lord for His solution to our problem."

By now my corn mush tasted like chicken mash. Though, at the time, I didn't know what chicken mash was. Ma and I might just as well have been wooden dolls, or not have been there at all, though, Ma seemed undisturbed.

But, Luke surely was and his cinnamon eyes snapped. "How about calling her, MADOM?"

With this Ma's head snapped up. "Listen to me young man. It's nothing to me if you call me, Mrs. Osborn, Ma or even Clara. I'm not your mother, or do I wish to take her place. But, I will not tolerate that kind of insult from you or anyone else. After my hard luck with marriage, the aunts kindly took me in; and I was glad to call the Sweet Shop home for over six years; and during that time I worked every day including Sunday. Why don't you come right out and ask me about Josephine's father?"

Ma looked demandingly from Luke to Daddy. I couldn't believe my ears, and I could see Daddy was shocked. And, she had Luke's full attention.

"I was young and inexperienced, but that's no excuse. It was just after high school when I was out of foster care and on my own. I foolishly married thinking I wouldn't be alone. I should'a known better. He was a crazy kid who was not ready for responsibility anymore than I was. We hadn't been married much more than a month when he was killed in a car crash, a foolish drinking accident. Luke Osborn, you're luckier than I could be in my wildest dreams to have had a good mother, and still have a father who cares deeply about you, and your brothers . . . enough to marry me in order to have someone to look after you."

Ma never blinked, nonchalantly took Mark's bottle from the warming basin of water, tested it on her wrist, and, taking Mark gently from Luke sat down and began giving an eager Mark his bottle.

What did all this mean? There was dead silence except for Mark's sucking sounds. His sweet little hand patted Ma in contentment. It seemed to me his pats were to console. Thinking back she looked the perfect picture of a Madonna.

The realization I had a father suddenly overwhelmed me, one who had died. And, I wondered if he was in heaven with Aunt Carrie. Was he the father in heaven who was supposed to be thanked for everything and loved me? Then a terrible thought popped into my mind: Could there be something wrong with me? Did loving me make people die?

Aunt Carrie, why did I make you die? . . . and my real daddy? I didn't mean to. No wonder Ma doesn't love me!

Interrupting my thoughts, Daddy broke the silence, "His people wouldn't stand by you?"

"No one knew we were married. He said his family would disown him if they knew he married an orphan. And, who'd have believed a welfare orphan anyway? I panicked and ran....you know the rest."

Ma told her story with the saddest most sincere countenance. Daddy appeared to believe her, after all, the story would avoid the inevitable gossip. Thoughtfully, he slowly finished drinking his coffee and left for the barn with a pleased look on his long face.

After chores, Daddy announced, "Think we better go to town and lay in some groceries. The pantry's about as bare as it can get. Luke can sit with the kids."

Fear overwhelmed me; I could see Luke throwing me into the bull...critter pen. Luke's foxy cinnamon brown eyes told me, he had the same thought.

"I'll put the baby down for a nap, and he can watch him. I can manage the other two easy enough."

Now, Luke was scowling, "Jeepers . . . "

"Never mind, I can manage Mark too. He's no trouble."

"Good, that's all settled. Luke, I want to see the weeds in the garden pulled when I get back. Idle hands do the devil's work."

Ma's hands were never idle so she didn't do the devil's work even though she was a heathen and worked on Sunday, but she worked for

Aunt Alma and Daddy, that surely made a difference.

Certain pictures are imprinted on my memory in vivid detail like pictures in a story book. Aunt Carrie and I sat side by side, so happy, shelling peas for the lunchroom. She said, "Some people are like "peas in a pod." Then, she gave me a wink, and said, "You and I are 'peas in a pod'."

I laughed and said, "We'd make a funny looking pod!"

She laughed too, "We still are. Can you figure out why?"

That morning, with Daddy sounding like Aunt Alma, I thought, Daddy and Aunt Alma are "peas in a pod." And, Luke would be in the pod with them!

Mathew was bubbling over with excitement, and started dancing up and down, sing-songing, "Ma, want'a go . . . want'a go to town," over and over.

Daddy threatened, "One more word out of you Master Mathew, and you'll stay home with your big brother."

I caught Matt's hand, "Let's wait outside."

On the back porch Luke hissed at me, "I'll get you yet. Don't think you're so smart with your pinched up witch face and your, madam for a Ma. I should call her M and M." He broke out laughing.

I knew what a witch's face looked like because there was a picture of one in Aunt Carrie's storybook. At that time, I didn't understand what the madam part meant, but I knew it wasn't good.

On the way home, Matt taught me "Pease porridge hot, Pease porridge cold" as we huddled together in the backseat with the groceries taking up most of the room. When the car finally came to a stop in our driveway, it was evident Luke had performed a miracle in the garden. Nice clean rows stood out basking in the sunshine, and he sat on the back porch, innocent as you please, whittling.

"Good job, Luke."

Ma joined in, "Why, what'a beautiful garden. With the weeds gone I can see it won't be long and we'll be having fresh peas. Thank you, Luke."

Luke's halo shone. He looked up at Daddy and asked very humbly, using his good deed as a bargaining lever, "Woody and I thought to make sling shots this afternoon?"

"Well, if you're sure Forest doesn't have to work."

"I'm sure."

"OK then. But use those sling shots in a Christian manner. The fun is in the making, not in killing birds."

As soon as Matt and Mark were down for their naps, Ma set about stirring up a batch of divinity and chocolate covered caramels. The candy was to be a thank you gift for Mrs. Stanley. Daddy said he thought that was very thoughtful of Ma. They were getting on quite amiably, I decided. Maybe Daddy was OK, sort-of.

I was so anxious to go up to the Stanley's, I thought Matt and Mark would never wake up, but finally, we were on our way to deliver the candy. Ma lifted the knocker twice, and Mrs. Stanley opened the door, "Clara, how nice to see you, and how sweet of you to bring us candy." She ruffled Matt's hair, "What's my big boy up to today?" And she took Mark from Ma's arms giving his dimpled cheek a kiss.

"Want'a see Abbey." Matt announced, pushing ahead into the house.

"I don't know where she's got to, Matt."

As she ushered us in, I began to notice things that I had been too excited to see on Sunday in all the excitement and embarrassment. There was a marvelous bay window that stuck right out on the side of the house that let you look in three directions. In the bay there was a window seat with a thick velvet cushion the color of Ma's mint candy. Buttons were all squished down in the velvet, making the cushion puffy and pretty enough to eat. Very thin wispy lace curtains fluttered in the soft summer breeze. There was a piano against one wall, and Matt ran to it and started to pound on the keys, such magic. I wanted to pound the keys too. I had never seen or heard of such a thing before, but Ma ran to Mathew.

"No, no, little man. Gently, like this." She played a few chords of chopsticks, and guided his fingers softly over a few keys then said, "That's enough, Mathew. The piano's not a toy."

The sound Ma made on the piano made me think of Aunt Carrie singing.

I wish you were here to tell me all about what that sound is. Could you hear it up there in heaven? Do you have one up there?

"Mrs. Stanley, we can't stay." Ma had Matt firmly by the hand. "Paul and I just wanted to thank you for such a lovely dinner reception and all your kindness."

"Please call me May. We're to be neighbors and friends." Mrs. Stanley handed me a picture storybook, "Stay a while. Josephine and Matt can look at pictures while we visit."

I was delighted. "Thank you, May, I love books. Aunt Carrie gave me her storybook. Com'on Matt."

"Josephine," Ma was clearly embarrassed, "only grownups can call other grownups by their first names. You must call May, Mrs. Stanley."

I hung my head. "I'm sorry, Mrs. Stanley."

"She patted my head very kindly. "That's true, but you're a good girl. Clara, she's a darling girl. Just like a miniature grown up with her serious little face . . . please don't rush away. I'm dying to tell you something."

I knew I liked Mrs. Stanley. Now, I knew why; she liked me.

Aunt Carrie, isn't it wonderful, what's, "a darling girl"? I hope it's not something that will make Mrs. Stanley go to heaven. Cause I've been so lonely without you. If it's OK with you, I'd like to be Mrs. Stanley's 'little sweetheart'; that is, if it won't make Jesus come get her.

Mathew and I settled ourselves on the window seat out of the way.

Mrs. Stanley was chuckling and smiling as she bounced Mark on her knees. "You weren't out of the driveway this morning when Luke was up here. He's such a handsome charmer. You've already got him wound around your little finger."

"I don't think so."

"Don't be too sure . . . he said, more than anything, he wanted to have a nice surprise for you when you got home because you were working your fingers to the bone and never complained. He just knew you would be out there weeding that garden as soon as you could find a minute...wouldn't Woody and Abbey like to help him really surprise you? He said he nearly cried when you told him about how your husband had been killed in a car crash, and you ran away because your in-laws wouldn't stand by you. Abbey and Forrest were gung-hoe to pitch into that garden."

I looked up from the picture book to see the smile on Ma's lips. "How very kind of Abbey and Forrest. Luke's a clever one. I wouldn't be too sure he had my best interests at heart. Paul ordered him to do the weeding while we were shopping. I must say we were very impressed with his accomplishment!"

"You mean it was Tom Sawyer's fence all over again?"

"I'd say so."

"Don't be too hard on him, Clara. Paul's so strict with him at the same time he spoils him, and in his eyes Luke can do no wrong. Everyone loves him, even though he's spoiled; he's such a clown when his father's not around. And, the girls, they're all ga-ga over him. I worry about that."

"I see what you mean," Ma agreed, but I didn't understand.

"I think he's gone on Abbey, and of course, she thinks he's a kid and won't give him the time of day."

That, I understood, and was glad. My mind was only half on the pictures in the storybook.

Mrs. Stanley turned serious. "He did tell your story with sincere feeling, and I think it's good that you told it. The air needed to be cleared. Imaginations are best put to rest before they take on a life of their own."

"Maybe you're right . . . come children. We mustn't take up May's whole afternoon."

"You're welcome anytime, and if you need someone to baby-sit, keep Abbey and me in mind. And, Clara, your candies are perfect. Alma used to give us candy from the Sweet Shop at Christmas time. You know, if I were you, I'd make some to sell. I'm sure there'd be plenty of people who'd be glad to buy them. Wouldn't your own pocket money be nice?"

"You really think there's a market around here?"

"I'm sure of it."

"I think I might just do that. Thanks for the tip."

For me, that was the beginning of seeing Luke through someone else's eyes. I began to understand what clever meant. Handsome took longer to see, but he was that too.

Just as we were walking out the door Abbey came downstairs. "Mom, you should've called me. I didn't know we had company."

Mathew threw himself into her arms, "Abbey, Abbey, let's play."

"Here's my big boy again. Tickle, tickle who's got you now...hi, Josephine . . . hello, Mrs. Osborn, were you surprised when you saw your garden?"

"Yes, indeed. Thank you very much. I understand it was quite a project Luke had going. He's a real finagler, but a nice one. It's a big load off my list of things to do."

"Luke's a pest."

Mathew wriggled down. "Come, Abbey, show us the calf."

"Not today, Matt." She stood behind me absentmindedly running her fingers down over my hair. "Have you ever seen so much hair?" Gathering it up in a wad off my neck, "Mom, doesn't she look just like a pixie?"

"I suppose she does with her bright little grown-up face."

"Would it be all right with you, Mrs. Osborn, if I sewed Josephine a dress from one of our pretty feed sacks? I'm just learning to sew. It'd be fun."

"I think it'd be more than OK. What do you say, Josephine?"

"Thank you Ma. Thank you Abbey."

Aunt Carrie, I'm not mad at you any more for not taking me to heaven with you. I'm glad you let me stay . . . and that you'll wait for me. I hope Jesus is as much fun for you as Abbey is for me.

At that moment, Abbey plumped my nose just as she was always doing to Matt's. "I'll be down soon to measure you."

On the way home I don't think my feet touched the ground, I felt so light. Across the driveway, out in the pasture, Luke, Forrest and Laddie came into view. Each of the boys was carrying a stick in their hand as they herded the cows in to be milked. Even Laddie had a stick in his mouth.

"Come on, Matt; let's see what they're gonna do."

"Let's see, Yoyo."

We hung over the fence under the apple tree the tin can telephone was in to wait for them. We watched a car stop while the cows, full udders swinging to and fro, hurried across the road, and into the cow-yard at the south end of the barn. Then, the boys turned toward our house and were soon on our back porch, sticks in hand. Laddie laid his stick at Forrest's feet, and plunked down beside him, tongue hanging out like a trough, dripping sweat.

Matt sat down right up close in front of Luke. "Watch out Matt, I might whittle your nose." Matt pushed back just a little. Then Luke threatened me, "Curiosity killed the cat," and I shrunk back even further behind the post, my preferred watching place.

"Don't listen to Luke, Yo, his bark's worse'n his bite." Forrest motioned to me, "Com'ere. This here's hickory wood. It's hard . . . see the nice even Y shape crotches hickory tree branches make. We cut the two Y arms the same length, and leave the handle the right length for my hand to hold on to."

I watched as he skillfully did his measuring and cutting. Then, he picked up an old discarded inner-tube. "We cut a strap that is wider in the middle and tapered to the ends. The wide part holds the pebble we're gonna shoot. We have to make sure each side of the strap is exactly alike so it'll shoot straight. Then we lash its ends to the ends of the Y. That's all there is to it."

He took a nice round pebble out of his pocket, and placed it in the sling. "Want'a see me scare that robin off the fence?"

He took aim, drew back the rubber inner-tube strap and fired. The robin's song stopped; it fell, clunk, to the ground.

Forrest jumped to his feet very disturbed and started muttering, "I killed it . . . how'd I do that? . . . I killed a robin . . . I KILLED A ROBIN . . . " He waved his arms up and down as if he were going to take flight.

Luke whined, "It's just an old bird, for Pete's sake, Woody."

With that, Forrest threw his sling shot on the ground, reached down and held it so that when he stomped on it, it broke the crotch in two. Then he continued stomping right down the driveway, leaving us standing there, our mouths hanging open.

Matt ran into the house hollering, "Daddy, Daddy, Woody kilt a bird."

I ran across the driveway to the fence where the robin lay. I gathered it up in my warm hands and felt it wriggle.

Luke screeched, "Yoyo, put that bird down."

I didn't pay any attention to him, and started running down the driveway. "Forrest, FORREST, the robin's moving."

He stopped suddenly, and I bumped right into him. To keep from falling, I opened my hands, and the robin flew away.

"Well, I'll be." Forrest reached down and picked me right off my feet, and swung me around. "Happy, happy day."

I threw my arms around his neck. Nothing had ever felt as wonderfully exciting as that. On the second day on the farm, I fell in love.

They may say a six year old doesn't know what it is to fall in love, but I know better. In that moment when my arms went around Forrest's neck my world turned upside down. For weeks my most urgent goal was to catch a glimpse of him from the safety of our back porch. Or, sometimes, I'd boldly hang over the fence on the other side of the driveway under the hanging down limbs of the apple tree, hoping no one guessed the reason for my always goggling up across the pasture toward the big house. I'd watched him going in and out of the house doing his household chores, or going out to bring in the cows, or running down across his lawn to the barn. When he came down to the tenant house to play with Luke, my heart stood still. Maybe it was because he was the first boy to show me kindness. It felt a lot like the pair-bonding some species experience. Or, maybe my love for him sprang up to fill the void a father's love should have occupied. Can anyone really explain the chemistry of love between opposite sexes, especially that of a six year old girl? Or, can they describe its sweetness devoid of sexual lust, yet full of attraction that defined me female. From that point on everything that happened to me was measured in some manner against the backdrop of that new depth of feeling. Aunt Carrie's love gave me the soil for love. Knowing and loving Forrest gave love breadth and depth.

***

Tuesday morning I was awakened again from a sound sleep, only this time, it was Ma shaking my shoulder.

"Josephine...Josephine, wake up, and slide the bolt. I'm going down stairs now, and it's too early for you to get up." She made no explanation, but I knew she didn't want Luke coming into our room, even to get Mark, and I was very much relieved.

Later, in the afternoon, Abbey and Mrs. Stanley came down the road with two samples of flowered feed sacks, tape measure, pad and pencil. One sack had bright bold red flowers on a white background. The other was huckleberry blue with little pink flowers sprinkled all over it.

Abbey held up the material, "Which one do you like best, Jo? The red goes so nicely with your black hair and dark brown eyes, but the blue is so pretty, I couldn't decide."

Luke had been in the living room listening. Things were much too interesting; he came and stood in the kitchen doorway where he could check things out. Matt and Mark were napping. Ma was setting out cookies and milk on the kitchen table for everyone. Abbey was busy measuring me.

Mrs. Stanley took a seat at the kitchen table. "I think Josephine has made up her mind, she can't take her eyes away from the blue one . . . Luke, come sit down and join the hen-party....Clara, how do you do it?

Anyone'd think you'd been living here months, not a few days?"

Abbey finished and started to fold her measuring tape. "You're going to be the cutest little pixie."

Luke put his finger up to his cheek in innocent contemplation. "Don't you mean gnome? Or, maybe, gargoyle, with that oversized nose?"

Abbey took her tape measure and started after Luke, hitting him over the head with it. "Get out of here, Luke Osborn."

He danced around the room with his hands over his head. "Or maybe, a witch, with that witch's hair..."

"You have no idea how mean you are...out, out, out..."

Ma stepped to the door and opened the screen. Luke knew that was his cue, and barged through it onto the back porch.

I heard Forrest's voice, "Jeepers, Luke, you don't have to run over a guy."

"Out'a my way, your tyrant sister's up on her high-horse again."

Abbey stuck her head out the door. "How do you stand it to play with such a beast?"

Matt appeared, rubbing his eyes as he went over to Mrs. Stanley and put his sleepy head in her lap. "Now, see what you hyenas have done. We come down here and all havoc breaks loose." She smoothed Matt's sweaty hair. "Pipe down, or you'll have Mark awake too."

I could feel Forrest's presence as he came into the kitchen. His blue eyes smiled at me from behind his glasses. His straight bristle colored hair stood up with a cowlick in the middle of his forehead, and his face was soft with no shadow of hair on it as there was on Luke's. He was carrying a stack of honey pails in his hand which he started separating. "Anyone for straw-berrying?"

Laddie barked impatiently from the back porch to say he was ready.

I didn't know what "straw-berrying" was, but I wanted to do

anything that Forrest wanted to do. "Please, Ma, can I go?"

From the back porch Luke put his two cents in. "She'd be in the way, and probably'd eat more'n she'd pick."

Ma surprised me and said, "We've heard enough of that, Luke. Abbey, are you going?"

"A short cake'd taste awful good. I'll look after Jo."

"You won't mind?"

"It'll be fun, everything's so new to her. I enjoy her excitement."

I wondered a little if she meant I was dumb like Luke implied, but it was plain to see she wanted me to go, and that was enough to make me happy, to say nothing about a chance to be with Forrest.

This excursion was an education to my senses. The sun on my back was so hot that when the breeze brushed over my skin it felt like Aunt Carrie's kisses. At the end of the lane we passed the woodlot, and Abbey explained that when trees were close together they were called, "the woods."

"Why does Luke call Forrest, Woody? He doesn't look like a tree."

Again, her laughter was soft merry tinkling bells down in her throat. "I see. Woods and a forest are different words for the same thing. Forrest's also a name for boys, and usually parents who name their boys, Forrest, like the woods a whole bunch... and you know Luke, he just started calling Forrest, Woody."

Luke couldn't let that pass. "Yeah, right, kind'a like after his wooden head, right Woody, old wooden head. Take Yoyo, now, she's made out of wood all the way through just like Pinocchio, and she's told so many lies her nose's already nearly a foot long. It's growing so fast the rest of her can't grow at all."

He broke out laughing, pretending to almost fall down. Forrest gave him a playful shove, and Luke dropped his honey pail. "Now see what you've gone and made me do!"

Why did I have to be so little and ugly anyway? But, I couldn't let Luke see how I felt. "If Forrest's made of wood, then, I want to be made of wood too. No one wants to be made of what you're made of."

"You tell'um Jo. He's made'a 'rags and tags and puppy dog tails'...that's what he's made of." Abbey grabbed my hand, and we ran into the woods.

The woods were cool, mysterious, enchanted, where dreams and make-believe brushed so close they became real. Right at the edge of the woods, around the gnarled roots of some big old trees and outcroppings of rock, velvety green moss grew lush in such abundance that I could picture Robin Good Fellow with his hand on his hip, leading the fairy dance over them with star dust sprinkling down all around them as they glided over the velvety mounds.

Aunt Carrie, just like in your storybook. Did you know about this place? Oh, I hope so. I'll make up a new story tonight and tell it to you.

Way up high on the top most branch of the tallest tree an orange and black bird sang a lilting song. The sound of it plucked something deep inside me that made me feel light and full of joy. Forrest said, "See that Baltimore Oriole, Josephine? Way up high, they like the top most branches."

Luke piped up, "Josephine! Don't you mean, Yoyo, the witch who brings birds back to life?"

Abbey stuck her tongue out at Luke. "Don't pay any attention to him; he's the mad joker."

I was glad Abbey came to my rescue, but I wished it had been Forrest. Could I be a witch and not know it, flashed through my mind.

On the other side of the woods we climbed over a fence into a neighbor's pasture. "The Blackwell's said we could berry in their pasture," Forrest explained, "their meadows are fallow because they have retired and no longer have cows. Our cows eat the strawberry

110

plants."

"What's 'fallow,' Forrest?"

Luke mimicked, "What's 'fallow,' Forrest. Come on now, tell us."

Forrest paid no attention to Luke. "The Blackwell's meadows are retired just like they are. The meadows are allowed to rest and go back to the plants nature intended."

"Like strawberries."

"Right, like strawberries."

Forrest said he always went out early in spring to find where the strawberry plants were blooming so he'd know just where to find the berries later on. I learned what the plants looked like, and that the flowers they made were little and white. I wondered if anything could be as wonderful as white flowers turning into delicious red berries. I was convinced Forrest knew everything, and best of all he liked explaining things to me.

***

Wednesday evening Daddy announced it was time to get ready for Prayer Meeting. Ma was right quick to say she couldn't possibly go. She had four pints of peas in the canner, and four more were nearly ready. Daddy didn't look very pleased, but he and Luke went on to prayer meeting. Next day, Mrs. Stanley was in the Red and White Grocery over in Tate Town and heard that Daddy had given a glowing prayer, thanking God for providing him with a wife to be helpmate and mother to his children.

One of the main functions of a grocery store in all small country towns was to act as distribution center for local news and gossip. Our Tate Town Red and White was more than happy to oblige. Mrs. Stanley had no idea how welcome her presence was to the gossips that morning. On her way home she stopped at the tenant house happy to report Daddy's glowing prayer. Ma's only comment was, "Well, it seems to be working out, doesn't it?" I wondered what all Mrs. Stanley had heard about the situation, and I wouldn't have minded hearing what Daddy had to say about Ma in his prayer. He sure did look stormy as he and Luke went out the door. But, Luke, on the other hand, looked pleased Ma wasn't going. I was confused about God's providing Ma? I thought it was Ma's way of getting us out of the city.

Prayer meeting had served Daddy well; he was able to say to God the things he wanted the listening people to hear. By saying them to God, the people couldn't contest them; if God approved them, so must they. Was Daddy innocently clever in managing that hurdle, or was it planned?

***

Matt and I were out playing "touched you last" behind the woodshed. We were squealing and running around in circles when suddenly, Luke appeared out of nowhere, and grabbed each of us by the wrist. "I've got'cha both."

I pulled hard to get away. "Let go'a me."

"Shall I drag you over to the bull pen, or are you gonna shut up?"

He pulled us through the back door of the woodshed. I hadn't been in the woodshed because I was too small to carry wood. It was unpainted, weathered, dark and spooky with the sunlight peeking in through knotholes and cracks. Matt didn't seem scared and that helped a little. Luke pushed us up a rickety stairway at the back of the woodshed to a low A shaped loft with a narrow window from the floor to the peak. Luke shoved me roughly toward it. Then he ordered me to take down my bloomers, and I shook my head "no".

"What do you think you've got under there that's so special?"

"Nothing."

"That's exactly right. You've got nothing, and I'll prove it. Now, take'um off, or I'll throw you in the bull pen!"

I quickly pulled my bloomers down around my knees with my heart quaking. I could hear Aunt Alma screech and Daddy thunder, "Sin needs no encouragement," because, I was convinced, sin lurked someplace under your clothes.

Luke was impatient with me and motioned "up" with his hands as he snarled through his teeth, "Up with that dress…we want'a see what you're so fond'a hiding."

It was hot up so close under the roof rafters, and the dusty smell filled my nostrils. Sweat prickled on my scalp underneath my hair and ran down my neck, and tears ran on the inside of my eyes where Luke couldn't see them. I gathered my dress up in a wad at my waist.

Luke unbuckled Matt's bib overalls, and they fell down around his ankles. He was bewildered and began to run his tongue round and around his lips. Not caring, Luke pulled his briefs down exposing Matt's genitals. How very amazing, I didn't have anything like that. Then, Luke unbuttoned his own fly, and pulled out his gigantic genitals, rotating his hips at me in a threatening gesture. I was horrified and terrified. I grabbed up my bloomers, and ran past Luke so fast he couldn't conceal himself and Matt fast enough to stop me. I went straight up to the front bedroom, slide the bolt and crawled under the bed. I felt cold even though our bedroom had no attic and was an oven in the afternoon summer heat.

At the dinner table, I was still in shock. It amazed me that Luke behaved as if it were a normal supper, as if nothing unusual had happened. Matt was another story; out of the blue he announced, "Yoyo doesn't have a 'thingy.'"

My heart stood still, and my eyes flew to Luke. He stopped chewing and glowered back at me with a menacing look that hid the fear I knew he had to have felt. Now, everyone would know what had taken place upstairs in the woodshed. And, on top of that, I was so humiliated not to have a "thingy" because, of course, I supposed I should have had one. I was sure Daddy would spank me as Aunt Alma was always praying to God not to have to do.

Aunt Carrie, I am so bad. Do you still love me? Am I still your Sweetheart? Now, Ma will never love me. Why didn't you take me with you?

Knocking my thoughts asunder, Daddy's voice, in a peculiar disbelieving tone, boomed, "What did you say?"

"Yoyo hasn't got a 'thingy' and Luke has a biiiggg one..." With his eyes down cast in shame, Matt continued, "I've got a little one."

Daddy thumped the table making the dishes rattle. "Clara, I will not have this. Didn't I speak to you about modesty? See what you've started. There was none of this until now. See to that daughter of yours. And see to it she doesn't corrupt this family. And Luke, now that you share a room with Mathew, be more careful."

"I will Daddy. I had no idea."

Ma said to me, "To your room, this minute. I'll be up directly."

What did Luke mean, he had no idea? Everyone was staring at me. I was already so traumatized by what happened that afternoon in the woodshed I didn't want to eat anyway, and was glad to get away from everyone.

I quickly got into my pajamas, crawled into bed and pulled the sheet up over my head. I never wanted to come out, and I'd never understand anything.

Aunt Carrie, I wish I had died too and was in heaven with you. But I'm scared to die if it means getting thrown in the bull...critter pen. What'um-I gonna do? Is Jesus anything like Luke?

I heard the door open softly. I stopped breathing; was it Luke? I had forgotten to slide the bolt. Then Ma whispered, "Josephine?"

I didn't answer, and. she came to the bedside and sat down. Pulling the sheet away from my face, she scolded, "You must always remember to slide the bolt on the door, always."

With my teeth chattering, I nodded my head "yes."

"I'm not going to punish you. Stop your shaking. Luke's the one, wasn't he?"

I shook my head "yes" again.

"What did he do to you?"

"He made us show him our 'thingies' and made us look at his...and it was big and awful. Why don't I have a 'thingy'?"

"Because girls aren't supposed to have one."

I wondered how much more I was going to have to learn. The country was getting more and more complicated all the time. There were so many loose ends in my mind. Aunt Carrie was a girl so I was glad I was a girl too. I was relieved that Ma wasn't mad at me, though, I'd rather have Ma mad than Daddy. He frightened me even when he wasn't mad.

"I know this is going to be hard for you to understand...I'm going to let Daddy think Luke had nothing to do with this. He wouldn't believe you unless Luke was to confess, and forcing the issue would only make matters worse for everyone. You're going to have to watch out for Luke to keep this from happening again. Do you understand?"

"I'm not sure, Ma."

"Don't let him get you alone."

I nodded my head "yes" with doubt sticking out of my eyes.

She cupped my chin with her hand lifting my face, "Can I count on you?"

"Yes, Ma."

Somehow, I knew I had to find a way. Ma was counting on me. How I longed to feel Aunt Carrie's stout arms, hugging me against her ample soft bosom.

Aunt Carrie, why's what's under your clothes so bad? Is it the 'thingy' that boys have, or because girls don't have one? I'm glad I'm a girl like you. I know you're good because Jesus took you to his home with the Heavenly Father. Forest must have a 'thingy', 'cause he's a boy, and I'm sure he's not bad.

Then into my most private thoughts popped the knowledge that I wouldn't mind seeing Forrest's 'thingy' if he didn't know I was peaking. Then, I knew I was very, very bad. And, I hoped Aunt Carrie didn't know all my thoughts.

***

Abbey came knocking on the screen door with my new dress over her arm. She was like sunshine entering the kitchen. Her lipstick was shiny, her nails bright red, and the white on her saddle shoes freshly polished. She was a walking laughing Coca Cola girl, not real at all. Her hair was bristle colored the same as Forrest's only hers was soft and curly, bouncing around her face as she talked. "I've got my needle and thread. All I have to do is hem the skirt."

Abbey had sewn a skirt of the huckleberry blue feed sack and a white blouse trimmed with the feed sack material to match the skirt. I had never had a skirt and blouse before, and it was beautiful beyond anything I could imagine. There were pretty matching suspenders on the skirt that went over my shoulders to keep the skirt from falling down. I hugged it to me like a living thing. "Thank you, thank you, Abbey. I can't believe it's for me."

She sat down with Ma at the kitchen table and hemmed while Ma peeled potatoes for supper. I sat in the corner watching, Abbey with her head bent over her sewing, Ma guiding the knife expertly just under the potato skin. Both were so intent, so companionable, maybe like sisters would be, but, Ma looked real. Her hair, which was only a shade darker than Abbey's, was tied severely back in a knot at the nape of her neck the way Aunt Alma liked it. Abbey's eyes were sunny-day blue like Ma's, not dark and cloudy like mine. Abbey had even called mine dark. Why couldn't I look like Ma? I knew Luke was right; I was ugly. But, I could tell Abbey liked me. I sure hoped she would never find out about what happened in the woodshed. Then she wouldn't like me either. Forrest? Oh, how I hoped Luke wouldn't tell him.

Looking back on that scene, Ma was the star because her face was full of the world's woes yet beautiful and plain. Abbey's was without a care in the world so that her face had the innocent beauty of an adult child. It was comforting to sit and watch them work. Now and again, they exchanged a comment or two about some inconsequential thought.

Abbey bit off her thread. "Finished. Let's try it on."

We went up the stairs to the front bedroom, and I slid the bolt. Abbey looked so surprised I explained, "Ma, said I should never forget to slide the bolt."

Her eyes widened. "You must always follow your mother's wishes."

"I know; Ma's counting on me."

I have to say that when the skirt and blouse were on me, I felt transfixed.

"You're the cutest little pixie." Abbey took the brush from the dresser, and began brushing the snarls out of my hair. When she had finished, I had two braids that reached over my shoulders. "You've the thickest, heaviest hair of anyone I know. These're the fattest pigtails I ever saw."

I didn't like my hair called pigtails! "I thought pigs had curly tails.

Least my hair's one thing about me that's not skinny! But why does it have to be this awful black?"

"Why, Jo, you've got beautiful hair. Braids are most often called pigtails. Look, here, I've brought some blue ribbons just the color of your skirt to tie on your braids."

She tied one on each pigtail, and I could see out the corner of my eyes that they were pretty. I was floating way up in the clouds, and I threw my arms around her waist. "Thank you, Abbey. Oh, thank you...thank you."

"You're welcome, Sweetheart."

Sweetheart! Abbey called me sweetheart, oh happy day.

"Come on; let's go show your mother how pretty you are."

Ma looked up from the hot stove; her face was red and sweaty. "Well now, doesn't she look nice."

***

Unexpectedly, one day I took my first step into the realm of a believer. I felt so excited to wear my new skirt and blouse. That it should be saved for a special occasion never occurred to me. Ma didn't scold me, or suggest I should save it for Sunday. She probably didn't even look at me long enough to realize I had it on.

There was a huge clump of daisies blooming just over the fence in the cow pasture, and I was so pleased with myself, I thought I'd pick a bouquet.

Suddenly, out of nowhere, there was Luke again, running toward me. "I thought you were told never to go in the pasture, you stupid little sinner."

I threw myself on the ground to roll under the fence just as he caught up with me. He put one foot on me and gave a big push, RIP.

118

Luke vaulted the fence and grabbed me by the shoulder, pushing me ahead of him. "We'll see what your Ma has to say about this, you stupid little klutz."

My beautiful skirt was ruined. Panic overwhelmed me, squeezing my throat shut. What would Ma say?

Luke opened the screen door. "Look what your darling daughter's done to her new skirt, and she was in the pasture."

"Get on with you, Luke; I'll take care of this. Get on about your business."

Thank goodness he wouldn't see what Ma was going to do to me. "What have you been told about the pasture? How many times do I have to tell you to keep out of Luke's way? He'll get you in trouble every time."

"Yes, Ma."

"Why do you have that skirt and blouse on today?"

"I thought I should wear it."

"You thought you should wear it. Maybe Aunt Alma's right about you. Now, what will Abbey think? What am I to do with such a careless girl? Trot yourself right up there this minute, and show them what a bad girl you are."

"But, Ma, Luke's up there." I was terrified about what Abbey and Mrs. Stanley were going to think of me.

"Forrest and Luke are after the cows." Ma jammed her fists down hard on her hips. "Right now, go."

My feet were glued to the ground as I pulled myself up the road. My heart was so heavy my chin nearly touched my chest.

Aunt Carrie, what'um I to do? I tore my pixie skirt, and Abbey'll hate me; and Ma's mad at me; and I'll never be happy again. Can't I please come to heaven and live with you? How do you get dead without being thrown in the bull pen? Am I so bad I know God won't let me in heaven to be with you? Do you have to be like

Aunt Alma and Daddy? You're not like them. Is my real daddy up there with you? Have you met him? Did he die because of me? Is that why Ma doesn't like me? Oh, how I wish you could answer me. If you have to be like Aunt Alma for God to like you, I'm not sure I want to be His friend. I'm not even sure there is a God. But I do want to be with you more'n anything in the whole world. If there is a God, will you please tell God that if He keeps Abbey and Mrs. Stanley from hating me, and from dying because of me, I'll know He's real, and I'll never let Luke near me again. Something I can't understand is: why does God like Luke so much when he doesn't seem at all good to me, but don't tell God that, or He'll never like me. And, another thing, does God like True Faith Church better than Methodists? Daddy thinks He does. Oh, Aunt Carrie, I think I'm going to cry.

I never had to knock. Mrs. Stanley opened the door. "What ever is the trouble, Josephine? There, there don't cry. It can't be that bad." She gathered me up and held me tightly in her arms. I sobbed, and she cooed, "Shh-sh-sh-sh, there, there now."

Abbey came into the room, and saw the tear in my skirt. "Jo, Jo, don't worry about an old skirt. You're more important than any old skirt."

"You still like me?"

"Nothing could make me not like you, silly. You're my Pixie, remember?"

I nodded.

Mrs. Stanley covered my tear-streaked face with kisses. I hadn't been kissed since Aunt Carrie died.

"Come, we'll have that skirt good as new in the jerk of a lamb's tail." Abbey lifted me out of Mrs. Stanley's arms. There had to be a God!

That night, as I was settling down to sleep I needed a talk with Aunt Carrie:

There is a God, Aunt Carrie. Thank you for talking to Him for me. I should've known He's real since you're up in heaven. I'm glad He's up there, and please, thank Him for making Abbey and Mrs. Stanley still like me. And, I'll try even harder to be a good girl and stay out of Luke's way.

***

Sunday morning was still another lesson. It started when Daddy told Ma it was time to get ready for Church.

Ma's voice was firm, "Nothing was said about going to church...church was not part of our agreement. I thought you knew I was no church go'er."

"I know my mother had you working every Sunday. That's not my intention . . . get yourself and the children ready."

I didn't like the look on Daddy's long thin face. His eyebrows stuck out too far, and the creases by his mouth stuck in too far. So, I shrank back in the corner under the table just as I had back in the Sweet Shop kitchen.

"Now Paul, it's not my intention to cause trouble, or you any concern, but I am not going to church. I'll be glad to get Mathew ready, and Mark if you wish, though I think he'd be better off staying home with Josephine and me."

"That child of yours is going to grow up to be a heathen. I heard all about her antics at Aunt Carrie's viewing. There's a demon in that child. I fear her soul is already lost."

From under the table I protested, "My soul's not lost...it's still in my body . . . Aunt Carrie wanted me to keep it so I can grow up. I'm not going near the b-critter pen and get dead."

"Listen to that, that child . . . I will not have a heathen growing up in this house with my children . . . do you hear me?"

"Is that a threat?"

"If you want to make it one."

"There's no need to scare a five year old child. She's just never been made to be dishonest; going to church might well teach her that. I swore two things before that God of yours: She'd never go to an orphanage and that once I was on my own, I'd never let anyone ram religion down my throat again. And further more, if that was a threat; let's get this settled right now. I'm sure I could get this marriage annulled, if that's what you want."

"My word's good."

"Good. So's mine. That's settled."

"What am I going to do? Two heathen souls have been entrusted to me. God in heaven, help me. I may not be her birth father, but I am her legal guardian. I'm responsible for her, and I mean to see that she knows her heavenly Father, and that her sins are forgiven. For now, get Mathew ready, we'll continue this some other time."

Daddy looked so distressed I almost felt sorry for him. I stayed under the table until they were out of the house, and I heard the car drive away. Never had my heart been so heavy. Daddy didn't like me. My heavenly daddy didn't like me, and, Ma didn't like me, because, it was my fault he died. On top of everything else, Aunt Alma would be visiting, and I didn't want her to hear about how bad I was, though, I was sure, it would be no surprise to her.

When Daddy came from Phelpsburg with Aunt Alma, dinner was all ready. Ma had made the table look pretty even though all the plates didn't match. Aunt Alma said there was no reason to keep the plates from the Sweet Shop since she no longer needed them; she'd bring a bunch of stuff next Sunday. Then she began making a big fuss over Luke, rumpling his hair amidst much exclaiming on how he was growing so tall, and would make such a handsome minister.

For dinner Ma had roast beef, mashed potatoes and gravy, peas from the garden, deviled eggs, radishes and lettuce. Daddy and Aunt Alma sprinkled vinegar over their lettuce, sifted sugar on the vinegar and then rolled the lettuce up before eating it. For dessert Ma had baked a chocolate cake because it was Aunt Alma's favorite. I think she was pleased because she had no complaints. I was happy no one paid any attention to me. What a relief, I hoped all the bad stuff was forgotten. If only I could forget how bad I was.

After dinner Ma put Matt and Mark down for their naps, and I helped her with the dishes. Aunt Alma and Daddy went into the living room with the Phelpsburg Gazette.

Luke asked, "Daddy, Woody and I are going over to Billy's this afternoon; if you say I can."

"Your Grandma's visiting."

"Let him go, Paul. He's so good to me."

"Go on then if you've studied your lesson for Young Peoples."

When the dishes were finished, instead of going into the living room with Daddy and Aunt Alma, Ma took me out to the garden.

"I thought maybe you'd like to take some lettuce and radishes up to the Stanleys. They'll taste good with their Sunday night sandwiches." Ma knew, like a lot of farmers, they ate a late Sunday dinner and a snack supper of sandwiches.

Nothing could possibly have pleased me more. Now, I could escape and not have to face Aunt Alma. "Are you coming too, Ma?"

"Not this time, the garden needs some work."

Mrs. Stanley made much over the lettuce and radishes, and over me, just as Aunt Carrie had. I thanked Abbey again for fixing my skirt, and I explained it almost made me forget about causing Aunt Carrie and my real daddy, to die and go live with Jesus in heaven. "My real daddy died so he's my heavenly father, and my new Daddy is going to see to it I'm not a heathen forever, and he's going to be sure I know my other

Heavenly Father."

Despite their efforts to conceal their surprise and concern, I could see my revelation was a shocker. Plus, I am sure Abbey had confided to her mother my strange behavior of sliding the bolt on the bedroom door. In seconds they had their countenances well in hand, and began a discourse that managed to coax out of me my fears about how loving me, made people die. Mrs. Stanley gathered me up in her arms, and I could see tears in Abbey's eyes. They convinced me dying had nothing to do with loving me, and that God was the one and only Heavenly Father. This was quite a leap for my reasoning ability because if my real daddy was in heaven then why wasn't he a heavenly father? Something told me it would be better to let it be, and talk it over with Aunt Carrie when I was alone.

"You know, Josephine, your real daddy died before you were born so you couldn't have had anything to do with his dying."

"What's born?"

"Born is the day you come into the world as a little baby. It's sad that your real daddy never knew you."

Born was another puzzle to be talked over with Aunt Carrie sometime. Mrs. Stanley only hesitated an instant and went on. "And, the love you gave Aunt Carrie made her live longer than she would have, I'm sure. She was very sick, and you helped take care of her. That makes you very special. God likes all people to love. That's what God is all about. Our loving each other is a good thing."

My head was full of new ideas, and my heart was full too because Mrs. Stanley and Abbey loved me, and I was free to love them back. How much my world had changed.

Chapter 5

Ma was right when she assured everyone that first day, "Josephine will be quick to learn all these things." Abbey was right too, when she observed, "Everything's new to her." That first summer my life's learning curve accelerated at a rate that made every minute exciting, and no time since has it been equaled.

My days hung suspended in time and were endless. Most of those hours were happy ones enriched by the warp and woof woven of green grass clipped like a "brush cut", blue skies with giant globs of whipped cream floating heavenward for Aunt Carrie, pelting rains perfuming the air with the smell of wet earth, tasseled grain whipped by the wind into a sea of swirling rippling waves, cows grazing in the pasture, then resting as they chewed their cuds. To burst out onto the back porch, screen-door banging shut behind me, to find myself surrounded by that wonderful world, was nourishment for my parched soul. Nature's pervasive lushness, always present, mingling and coloring every moment, was the frosting on life, free for the taking. Ma was also right when she promised the country would be better, and living in a real family was better too. Amidst all the emotional ups-and-downs, a stubborn independence, born of Aunt Carrie's love and enriched by the world expanding all around me, took root and grew. Knowing nature's beauty and soul-healing balm, an awareness germinated that first summer, solidified a kinship with nature that still sustains me.

Washing lamp chimneys and filling the lamps with kerosene oil became part of our daily routine. I rather liked taking my weekly bath in the big tub filled with water Ma heated in buckets on top of the big black kitchen woodstove. The outhouse was a little scary because of Luke, but there was a chamber pot in our bedroom that took care of nightly needs and my daytime emergencies if Luke lurked about. It was my unpleasant task to be in charge of emptying and washing the chamber pots. Looking back, these inconveniences must have been hurtles for Ma, but no one would have guessed by the ease with which she went about her new life.

It wasn't long before my mind was agile enough that I never slipped and said "bull" instead of "critter" even though in my mind I always thought "bull". The difference between the cows and the bull became obvious upon closer scrutiny after my woodshed experience, and Ma's explanation that only boys had, in my vocabulary of the time, thingies. I was glad the cows had bags which balanced the scale for me because girls had to have something boys didn't have. Matt and I called across the hill and listened to the echo to our hearts' content. It soon became hard to remember the innocence I had possessed when I came to the farm.

I was Ma's baby-sitter. Mark would squeal and hold his chubby little arms out to me and slobber a kiss on my cheek. It was more evident everyday that Ma loved her two little stepsons in a way she would never love me. It surprised me that Ma knew how to be so open and loving to them, very much like Aunt Carrie had been to me. I watched with amazed jealousy, and since Mark was "the baby," Ma adored him, but jealous as I was, I loved him too. How could I not love Mark when he so freely loved me? When his care passed between Ma and me, it was almost like a bridge of love between us because Ma's love in him came through to me, and I think, mine traveled back to her. Intuitively, I knew she approved of the love we shared in this way.

Without the affection Mrs. Stanley and Abbey lavished on me, I think my jealousy would have consumed my emotions, and probably interfered with my ability to accept, or love, either Mark or Matt. I was soon to learn Ma's early years lacked the nurturing necessary to awaken the notion love could be freely given. She had learned to purchase the only love she was privileged to know from the arms of the children she had cared for in her many foster homes. I knew I didn't deserve her love, and without realizing it, I began to try to find ways to purchase love just as she had learned to do.

Matt was the playmate of my dreams, and that summer we played house with a real live baby Mark. I suppose in reality, I was looking after them both. Matt and I became "eaches," inseparable and loyal. This served me well against Luke; he knew Matt would run tell on him in the blink of an eye. Whenever Luke managed to grab me and pin me against the back of the house in a suggestive rub, Matt would run up behind him and kick the back of his legs, shouting, "Stop it, Luke, or I'll tell Ma." Matt became such a good boy with Ma's love and guidance that Daddy practically never had to scold him. While he never scolded, neither did he praise him. Rather, the better boy Matt was, the louder Daddy praised Luke.

When Matt and Mark were napping, I was free. Ma trusted me completely and cared nothing about where I was, or what I was doing. If the way was clear of Luke, and Ma didn't yell after me, "Don't be bothering May and Abbey," my legs would propel me up the road. There, I luxuriated in an atmosphere of acceptance. In the midst of all this happiness, out of the blue, Abbey invited me for an overnight. As Ma packed my pajamas in a paper bag, I remember being so happy I thought I could jump right over the moon just like the cow in "The

Cat and the Fiddle." Not only was I to stay overnight, I was to accompany the Stanleys to church and stay for Sunday dinner.

That Saturday night before bedtime, Abbey taught me to play checkers. Mr. and Mrs. Stanley relaxed companionably nearby in their easy chairs. Their conversation distracted my attention, but I tried hard to concentrate so Abbey wouldn't think I was dumb.

Mrs. Stanley sighed. "It's been over a year since Grace died."

"Has it been that long? This year's been a long one for Rev. Grey."

"I'm sure the last TWO years have been long ones." Mrs. Stanley hesitated. "For all of us."

"Leukemia's a bad one." Mr. Stanley laid the Phelpsburg Gusset aside.

"You know, I don't believe Rev. Grey has eaten a single Sunday meal alone."

"That's as it should be. I have to hand it to you gals."

Abbey tweaked my cheek. "You'll help us cheer-up Rev. Grey, won't you, Jo? He'll be having Sunday dinner with us too."

I was greatly disappointed that a stranger was coming to dinner, but I was determined not to show it, and I made up my mind to make Abbey proud of me. So next day, as we were all coming into the house after church, I took Rev. Grey's hand and said, "I'm sad too because Jesus took my Aunt Carrie just like he took your wife. Maybe they can be friends in heaven. I've been worried about Aunt Carrie missing me."

He reached right down and picked me up in his arms and hugged me. "Bless you, I'll bet you're lonely too. They can be friends up in heaven; what'a you say, we can be friends down here." Then he sat me back down on the floor. "Let's see what's for dinner."

He was not gruff and old like Daddy, and to be picked up by a big man was not exactly the same "nice" as when Forrest picked me up and swung me around, but very nice all the same. I decided I liked Rev.

128

Grey, and it was OK with me that he was going to eat dinner with us. I had another friend.

After dinner, I wandered outside hoping to find Forrest, but he was already down on our back porch with Luke. Abbey had given me permission to play with one of her dolls, so I decided to play house underneath a big bush by the front porch that made a sheltered cozy little den. I crawled in, pretending this was my secret hiding place where Luke couldn't find me. As I spread the blanket out to sit on, the front door opened. Thus began the first of countless spying episodes that taught me many interesting things without which, I could not write my story.

"May, I can't thank you enough for such a delicious dinner and pleasant visit. I wonder where Josephine is? I should say goodbye. She's such a strange little mite."

If Rev. Grey hadn't called me little and strange, I'd have rushed right out to say goodbye, and missed this first episode. But, at that moment, I was disappointed in him.

Mrs. Stanley laughed. "She's around here somewhere. We enjoy her so much. I don't think she gets much love at home though Clara's a worker and is doing a splendid job with the Osborn children. It's an odd situation, to say the least."

"Well, Josephine's won my heart. I can tell you that."

"Ours too. Abbey tells me, besides being a very good little singer, she made quite a stir in Sunday School this morning. It was a missionary lesson, 'Go ye into the nations and preach the gospel,' of course, to save the poor heathens' souls."

"I don't know why we can't emphasize the helping hand side of missionary work more."

"Abbey said Josephine was so restless that Mrs. Richards finally asked her if she needed to go to the rest room. Josephine stopped wiggling and asked, 'What's hell?' Mrs. Richards answered, 'It's the place bad people who do not accept Jesus as their savior go when they die.' Josephine spoke right up and said she was sure her Aunt Carrie was in heaven. Her Aunt Alma said so, and Aunt Alma talked about Jesus all the time and would know. Poor little tyke, you can see where she was coming from. Then she asked why God sent all those heathens to hell when it wasn't their fault they didn't have a church to know about Jesus."

"Out of the mouth of babes."

"I should say. That stopped Mrs. Richards in her tracks for a moment; then she stammered, explaining, she thought if they had not heard the word and were truly innocent of knowing about Jesus, God didn't judge them the same as he did people who had heard, and they would go to heaven. Josephine shocked even Abbey then by asking if that meant her Ma would go to hell because Daddy called her a heathen because she knew about Jesus and wouldn't go to church. Mrs. Richards stammered she was sure Josephine's mother was not a heathen and attempted to go on with her lesson, but Josephine said she wished she could be sure because Daddy was a True Faith, as if that explained everything. Then, she said they shouldn't send missionaries because heathens were probably happy and might not believe a stranger, and then they wouldn't get to go to heaven. Mrs. Richards was all shook up and muttered, 'Oh dear!' Josephine continued, saying her Daddy had called her a heathen too, but she believed there was a Jesus because He took her Aunt Carrie to heaven, and Aunt Carrie talked to God for her. By now Mrs. Richards was wringing her hands. Rev. Grey, I think she was glad when that class was over." Mrs. Stanley was laughing a strange laugh, not exactly like it was funny.

Rev. Grey chuckled. "I can just imagine she was. I think we have ourselves a little thinker who's going to keep us on our toes, wouldn't you say?"

Just then Daddy was driving by on his way back from taking Aunt Alma home, and very unlike him, he stopped. I remember thinking, I hoped he wasn't going to get after Rev. Grey for being a "thin soup" Methodist.

He came up to the porch and said, "Rev. Grey, could I have a word with you?"

"Of course."

"It concerns my new wife, Clara. She was a Methodist as a child and refuses to come to True Faith. I fear for her soul. I've prayed for a miracle. I just can't get through to her, and I'm about out of my mind. When I saw you, I thought maybe you're my miracle. Would you mind calling on her from time to time and see what you can do."

"More than glad to. I'm honored you'd ask."

"Much obliged, I'd appreciate it." Daddy drove on, leaving an amazed Mrs. Stanley and Rev. Grey standing on the porch.

For a few moments they were speechless. Finally, Mrs. Stanley broke the silence. "Well, I never. That took a lot of courage. He's a very devout True Faith, and the best hired man we've ever had."

"I give him high marks for his concern and willingness to cross a line that must have been very difficult for him."

These were strange thoughts to be used to describe Daddy! Even then, in the back of my mind there was the reluctant knowledge that there were some good parts to Daddy, and for the first time it occurred to me that maybe I should feel sorry for him because Aunt Alma was his mother.

There was concern in Mrs. Stanley's voice. "I hesitate to tell you this, but last night Abbey had to get a chair for Josephine to use to block her bedroom door. And, Abbey said, when she was down there trying a skirt and blouse on her, Josephine slid the bolt on the bedroom door, and said her Ma told her she must never forget to do that."

"Now, that is definitely a concern. Thank you for telling me. I'll see what I can do."

"I hate being a gossip, but it's a marriage of convenience. Paul needed a mother for his children. I'm sure they don't share a bedroom."

"Now, I'm the one to say, 'oh, dear'. I shan't waste any time in following through on Paul's request. Thank you again."

After he left, I was smart enough to know it would be a mistake to let anyone know I had overheard those conversations. My mind was whirling with new information I didn't know exactly how to process. I was glad to know Rev. Grey thought I was a "thinker", and wished Luke could hear him say that. I decided Daddy had to be very worried about Ma being a heathen because he'd asked a "watered-down Methodist" for help, and I wanted to tell them how Luke was, so they'd know why I slid the bolt on the bedroom door, and why Ma told me to. She was worried that the Stanleys didn't have locks on their doors so I should put a chair under the doorknob. I had tried to tell Ma that Forrest was nothing like Luke, but she insisted.

I slipped quietly around to the side door.

"There you are, Jo." Abbey was on her way out to look for me. "Don't you think it's time I sent you home? The men are on their way to the barn. Your Ma'll be needing you. If you want, you can take that doll home with you."

"I'd really like to keep her up here…in my bedroom."

"It is your room, just as I said it was. That's probably best because Matt might not be too careful with her and Mark surely wouldn't. Her name's Mary Ann because that's what I wished my name was when I was little, but you can name her whatever you like."

"Abbey Ann, because I love you."

***

One afternoon in the middle of the following week, I was about to slip up to play with Abbey Ann, when I realized Rev. Grey had just driven in our driveway. From the back porch, I could hear him greet Ma who was in the garden.

"Hello, Mrs. Osborn. I'm Rev Grey from the Methodist Church. What a fine looking garden you have there."

"Yes, it seems to be keeping up with our needs."

"Looks like you have a good sized mess of beans picked for supper."

"Yes."

"I suppose snapping them is next on the agenda."

"That's right."

"Mr. Osborn tells me you're a Methodist, and invited me to stop by. Mind if I tag along?"

"Suit yourself. If being raised in a Methodist orphanage for your first five years makes you a Methodist, then I am one."

"Here, let me carry those beans."

They started for the house. I wasn't sure Ma would approve of my presence, so I tiptoed quietly up the stairs not to wake Matt, opened the door to our room softly, not to wake Mark, slid the bolt and rolled under the bed. I pressed my face against the register grate that was used, during winter, to allow heat to drift up from the stove in the living room below. Their voices came clearly up to me.

"No. I never snap beans. I find it faster to cut them."

"Can I give you a hand?"

"I think I'd rather tend to them myself. Too many fingers in the pot may get one nipped. "

"As you wish, I don't want to upset the applecart, rather the bean pot."

Ma made no response. I thought it funny but made no sound. I could see them clearly. Ma sat down stiffly in a straight back chair. A relaxed Rev. Grey sat down on the end of the sofa closest to her chair. Ma's nimble fingers flew at their task as if economy of time and motion would keep her protected from the unwelcome intruder.

"How was life in the orphanage?"

Long silence, and Rev. Grey seemed not to mind and just waited patiently.

Aunt Carrie, What's an orphanage? I thought Ma always lived with you and Aunt Alma. Do you think I'll ever learn all the things I need to know? If you were here I could ask you all my questions, couldn't I? You wouldn't keep secrets from me.

"Let's say it wasn't exactly a picnic." Ma never looked up.

"No, I don't suppose it was. You said it was a Methodist orphanage."

Aunt Carrie, does that mean Ma lived in a" watered-down" orphanage?

Ma sing-songed, "Oh, yes, 'Jesus loves me, this I know, for the Bible tells so.'"

Rev Grey murmured sympathetically, "I see, just words, not much chance for, one to one relationships."

"Empty words...stuffed down my throat...year after year, no visitor, no adoption."

Aunt Carrie, maybe it's better to be a "thick soup" True Faith. But, I want'a be what Forrest is. Does that make me bad?

"Very empty words, I'd say. What came after those first five years?"

"Foster homes. Now, I had value. Not only did my foster homes get money for me, I was free labor."

"How many homes?"

"Seven. And, dozens of children."

"Plenty of one to one there."

"Oh, yes, flash card relationships."

"Ah, I get the picture, never long enough in one place for a lasting relationship there either."

There was an extra long silence.

Ma lived in foster homes too? Did you know that, Aunt Carrie? What're they?

"I understand from the Sunday School teacher, Josephine has a beautiful little singing voice."

"Does she? I didn't know that. That's nice."

"Yes, I guess she was very enthusiastic in her singing "This Little Light of Mine". Maybe she'd like to join the children's choir?"

I learned all the motions too, Aunt Carrie. Thank you for teaching me to sing; I'm sorry I forgot about singing after Jesus took you to heaven.

"I don't think so. I'd have to talk it over with Paul."

"Well, we'll put that on hold. You must find her a great blessing, a child of your very own, no flash card relationship there,"

There was a long silence, and I held my breath waiting for Ma to say something nice about me. I was so anxious my thoughts didn't even turn to Aunt Carrie cause Rev. Grey was telling Ma some good things about me. Maybe, some day she'd think they were true.

Ma never answered.

"I fear I'm being too pushy when really, I just want'a be a friend. One who doesn't stuff, push or preach. May I come again?" Another long silence. "I'd love to get to know both you and Josephine better. She's a wonderful little girl."

"It's a free country."

"Good. I see you've about polished off that kettle of beans. Next week then."

I didn't think Ma liked Rev. Grey very much, but I did. And, I wanted her to like him. And, I wanted to know what an orphanage and foster home were. As soon as they left the living room, I was down stairs and out the front door. Before the dust died down behind his car, my feet, as if they had a mind of their own, hurried me up the road to the Stanley's.

Mrs. Stanley called from inside, "No need to knock, come right on in. Here to play with Abbey Ann? Go right on up; she's on your bed. I'm on my way out to the pump."

"Thank you, Mrs. Stanley." I ran up the stairs wishing so much I could come right out and ask her the things I wanted to know. I dressed Abbey Ann in her best dress to play my visiting game with Mrs. Stanley. I paused at the kitchen door and knocked on the door-jam, my signal the game was beginning. Mrs. Stanley was at the sink washing vegetables.

"Come in, Josephine, how's Abbey Ann today?"

"Feeling much better now. She needs fresh air, so we came over to visit you."

"That's the thing. Just keep her out of a draft. I could use a break. How about, I make us some tea?"

"That'd be lovely. Wouldn't it, Abbey Ann?" I chucked Abbey Ann under the chin, sat her on one of Mrs. Stanley's kitchen chairs, and I slipped into the one next to her. "She agrees," I smiled, elbows on the table, as I watched Mrs. Stanley bustling around to put the teakettle over to boil.

She got out three cups and saucers and placed them around on the table. "Sugar with your tea?"

"Oh, yes, please."

Mrs. Stanley made her tea first, very strong, then she poured Abbey Ann's and my tea quickly over the same bag, barely coloring the water.

As if I were a grown up, she said, "Help yourself to the sugar."

I carefully divided one teaspoon between our cups. "See, Abbey Ann, you shouldn't be piggish. When you're older, you can put your own sugar in." I stirred each cup and drank mine quickly then switched my cup with Abbey Ann's.

"Abbey Ann and I sometimes visit Aunt Carrie. She thinks there's no one like Abbey Ann. She says she never knew a baby so smart, even smarter than Aunt Alma's 'country family.' But really Matt and Mark are as smart as Aunt Alma says, but we don't like Luke."

"Why ever not?"

"He doesn't play nice with anyone cept Forrest."

"I guess big brothers always think little kids are a pest."

"Forrest doesn't."

"You've got me there. But, you're having a good time in the country with your new family, aren't you?"

"Oh, yes, better than I ever imagined. Aunt Carrie's magic carpet brought me here. Only I don't think she knew it was for real; she thought in was only in books."

"She'd be very happy that it's real. So am I. Aunt Carrie and I were great friends."

I slid out of my chair and gave Mrs. Stanley a big hug. I almost felt she was Aunt Carrie at that moment and blurted out, "What's an orphanage?"

She held me away from her searching my face as if to find the answer there. "It's a very large home for a whole bunch of children who have no parents to take care of them."

"No mother or father?"

"That's right."

"Are they in heaven with Jesus?"

"Sometimes. Sometimes the parents are sick, or for some other reason, have no way to take care of their children."

"What's a foster home?"

"It's a regular home that agrees to keep children whose parents are unable to look after them. Are you worried about something?"

"No. Ma was in an orphanage and foster homes, and I just wanted to know what it was. What's adopted?"

"That's when a family gives one of those children their name, and the child becomes their own forever and never has to leave."

"I adopted Abbey Ann. Abbey says she's my very own, and this is her foster home. I wish..." I never finished that sentence.

There were tears in Mrs. Stanley's eyes, and I didn't know why. She pulled me upon her lap and held me close as we finished our tea.

***

Another week crept by in snail's fashion, time counted off in minutes and seconds the way a child's lazy summer counts time. I never thought about there being another episode to the ongoing eavesdropping saga even though Rev. Grey had said, "Until next week." What that meant never sunk in until I saw his car backing out of our driveway as I was saying goodbye to Abbey. I was surprised to realize how disappointed I was not to have been home to hear what went on between Ma and Rev. Grey, hard telling what information I'd missed out on. I decided right then and there, I'd not miss the next one even though it would be difficult to stay home because I loved the stories Abbey was reading to me. They introduced me to wonderful new worlds. I hadn't been read to since Aunt Carrie died, and now Abbey was filling that big empty place in my heart.

When I walked in the back door Ma said, "I've told Rev. Grey you can sing in the children's choir."

"Will Daddy let me?"

"He said might as well let you, you live up at the Stanley's anyway."

"Yippee!" I wanted to hug Ma, but I had never done that.

***

I have no way of knowing how many of Rev. Grey's visits I may have missed, but the next time I managed to have my face pressed against the register for my next episode, Ma was more relaxed and sat on the opposite end of the sofa from Rev. Grey. She pulled her mending basket over to her knee and began to thread her needle.

"Never an idle moment for you, is there, Clara?"

He called Ma by her name like Daddy and Mrs. Stanley!

"I suppose not. Don't idle hands do the Devil's work? Seems like I've heard that a few times."

"Bet you have. If that's right, I'd say you're a saint."

Ma's face reddened as she wet her finger to roll the knot in her thread. "You're too clever for me."

"No, just honest observation." Long silence.

What's a saint, Aunt Carrie? I think it's very good. Don't you?

"How does Josephine like singing in the children's choir?"

"Fine…I really don't know."

"I get very good reports." Rev. Grey's lips formed a straight line, and he was silent for a time. Finally he asked, "What about Josephine's father? His death must have been a terrible blow."

"So you've heard that story."

"Everyone in Tate Town has."

"I'd rather skip that one."

"Too painful, I understand."

"How callous of me, I was very sorry to hear about your wife. I don't mean to be unfeeling."

"I know. You're anything but calloused. Grace was very dear to me. Time doesn't heal all, as I'm sure you are all too aware. But, this year has taken the sharp edge from my pain.........how did you survive, how many foster homes did you say?"

"Too many."

"Even one can be too many."

"You're certainly right about that." Ma puzzled a moment before continuing, "You turn off, tune out and become very clever."

"Sounds impossible to me."

"Survival is the best teacher in the world."

"But how does a child learn it?"

"In the orphanage, I became aware that there was a very good reason why I wasn't adopted; someone wouldn't sign off until I was too old to be desirable, excellent motive to turn off."

"Your Mother?"

"I suppose. I never met her. Rather, there was a woman; she came a couple of times, spoke only to the house mother, never to me, but I've wondered if perhaps she was my mother. She could've been anyone's mother. "

"How very sad." And his eyes said how sad he was. I could see that even from my perch. His eyes held Ma's steady without her looking away. They sat quietly, friendly like, sort'a like Abbey and Ma, and I liked that.

Aunt Carrie, I wish Ma could'a had an aunt like you, poor Ma. If that was her mother, I hate her.

Rev. Grey repeated, "Very sad...but not so sad if you turn off. I see."

140

"Well, why not? It was a long time ago, and the edge has gone from that too."

"What about, tuned out?"

After another long pause, with Ma's lips pressed tightly together as if she were weighing the pros and cons of continuing, then in a tight voice she began: "I had moved into my third foster home. I was nine and shared a bedroom with Timothy, their year old baby. One night after I had been there long enough to win all kinds of praise for my care of Timmy, I awoke suddenly in the middle of the night, and screamed because someone was climbing into my bed. Timmy woke up and started to cry. Mr. Finley quickly jumped out of bed and was bending over Timmy when the very pregnant Mrs. Finley came hurrying in. I ran to her and tried to put my arms around her. Her comforting words were, 'you little hussy. I should have known better than to get a pretty one.' All havoc broke loose, and in the blink of an eye, I was in another foster home. Now I was labeled a 'problem child'. This time it was a minister's family with four children, the oldest six. Undoubtedly, they had chosen a minister's home in order to reform the 'problem child'."

Aunt Carrie, so that's how Ma knew about Luke. He's not the only one like that.

"So you, tuned out?"

"Saves a lot of pain."

"Yes, but too high a price. You were a defenseless child. I'm horrified." Now, he gave her a soft smile. "I think we're tuning in! Anyway I feel we are. What about, clever?"

"From that time on, my bedroom door was blocked for safe keeping. Even in the minister's house, even though I'm sure there was no need. What I needed in that house was a way to block out all the 'stuffing' going on every which way I turned. I became very 'saved', very convincingly 'SAVED'."

"Just more words. From where I sit, there's nothing wrong with surviving, and everything right with it. You know what else I see? I see a beautiful woman sitting there, mending, who has given so much to the world, and is long overdue for some real happiness."

There was another long pause with Ma not looking up, and Rev. Grey wanting her to. Anyway I wanted her to.

"And, inside that woman, I think, there's a whole host of talents just waiting for you to acknowledge. Everyone except you is very aware of them."

Yes, Aunt Carrie, everyone in the Sweet Shop knew. So does Mrs. Stanley, and I know, and I'm glad Rev. Grey knows. I wouldn't be surprised if Daddy knows. Aunt Alma doesn't want anyone to know. I can't help but hate her. I try not to.

Ma still didn't answer.

"I hope your silence doesn't mean I've made you, tune out. That's the last thing I want'a do. You're going to have to get used to hearing nice things said about you."

That's right, isn't it, Aunt Carrie?

Ma kept her eyes on her mending, and I could feel Rev. Grey wanting Ma to answer. I think she wanted to say something, but just couldn't let herself go.

"You said not all the foster homes had children."

Reluctantly, "That's right."

"I have a feeling that it's a very long story, and one you're not anxious to share. We'll tackle that one another time...think I'll be on my way. In parting let me say, everyone needs a friend they can talk things out with. I'd like to be that kind of friend. You know, all my friends in Tate Town are in my congregation. It'd be nice to have one who's not. I need you too."

"That's hard to imagine," Ma finally said as she put her mending down with deliberation and rose to walk him to the kitchen door. I slipped down the stairs, out the front door, and ran to the maple tree by the corner of the driveway where I could wave at Rev. Grey when he backed out to the road.

***

The following week, I was running home from the Stanley's when I saw Rev. Grey's car in the drive. I wanted to be upstairs with my face over the grate, but that was impossible. Under the kitchen table was the best I could do. I could hear them very well, and thankfully the oil cloth hung down long enough to hide me. It was definitely not as good as looking through the grate. Rev. Grey was talking about his family, and I sure wished I had heard all of it.

"No, not my Dad, his brother. Dad and my Uncle Simon were no more alike than 'the man in the moon.' But our families were very close, and Dad and Uncle Simon were devoted to each other. My family never bothered with church, and it seemed like Uncle Simon's lived in the church. The parsonage was across the road from the church and right in the middle of town. Summers with Uncle Simon and Aunt Jane were picture-book perfect. Paul was my age, Bobby a year older. Eleanor and Mickey were the little kids who tagged after us everywhere. There was summer Bible School....we made all kinds of crafty things and there were games. It was lots of fun. Those evenings were a rat race getting ready for the next day. Time was jammed full......Aunt Jane was always putting band-aides on our knees or making snacks for all the kids in the neighborhood. Everything was happening at once.......there was never a dull moment, and I was out of the city......I'm sure if Uncle Simon had been a farmer instead of a minister, I'd probably be a farmer."

"I can't imagine that."

"Well, the city was a pretty sad place compared to all that excitement. I was an only child….and doted on too much." Rev. Grey paused for a moment in contemplation before going on. "Grace and I were unable to fulfill that picture I had of the perfect family. Josephine must be a big comfort to you."

Ma managed a hesitant, "I suppose."

"Are you worried about her?"

"No, not really."

"You don't seem all that sure……want'a talk about it? Do you think she is unsafe in some way? Maybe, you're worried because of your experience in that foster home?"

"No, really, I'm not worried. I've talked to Josephine about Luke. I don't trust him, with good reason. I've made it clear to her to never let him get her alone, and to always keep our bedroom door locked."

Rev. Grey let his concern show in his voice. "Josephine sleeps in your room?"

"And Mark."

"That seems like an odd arrangement. Want to talk about it?"

Aunt Carrie, what can be wrong with sleeping with Ma? I've slept with her ever since Jesus took you to heaven. I like sleeping with Ma, and I like knowing we have our door bolted. Another thing, I don't think Ma is glad I'll be singing in the choir. I think she thought Daddy wouldn't let me. I wish I was Mrs. Stanley's little girl.

"I don't want to get into that. Listen, Mathew and Mark will be awaking up. Josephine will be coming home. She practically lives up at the Stanley's"

"They think the world of her. Guess I better be heading on out. Maybe another time."

They came into the kitchen. Their legs were right beside me where I cowered under the table. Ma stepped out onto the back porch.

144

Ma's voice was friendly again. "I enjoyed hearing about your life."

"See, we both need a friend. Goodbye, Clara...Clara's a nice name. I like it."

I could tell that flustered Ma. "Goodbye, Rev. Grey."

I was out from under that table fast and out the front door. By the time Rev. Grey was in his car, I was out of sight.

***

It was on an August day when the cicadas' shrill song filled the air lifting spirits to soaring when I saw Mrs. Stanley walking down the road to our house, carrying a package in her hands. It was late afternoon before the men started milking chores. Excited, I ran to meet her.

"Hello there, Josephine. Today's Matt's birthday. Soon as the men come in from early chores, your Ma says we'll have birthday cake." Her arm went around my shoulder.

There were two presents all wrapped up in colored paper on the kitchen table beside a fluffy white cake with four little red candles.

"Goody, goody. Can I wake up Matt?"

"In a few minutes." Ma sprinkled little colored candies on the cake.

"When's my birthday?"

Ma didn't look up from her task of pouring glasses of Kool Aid, "June 15th."

"When's that?"

Luke had come into the kitchen and made a disgusted snort.

Mrs. Stanley smoothed back my hair. "Just before you came to the country."

"Then I'm six years old!"

Mrs. Stanley planted a kiss on my cheek. "That's right, six years old, and getting to be a big girl."

I slipped out of her arms and went outside to hide my disappointment, as I determined a big girl should.

Aunt Carrie, you used to remember my birthday. You'd've remembered even though I'm dumb and have a witch face, wouldn't you? Matt and Mark get everything. It's not fair. I wish Jesus had taken me to heaven with you.

Across the road, Daddy and Mr. Stanley were coming up out of the barn. Forrest sauntered down the road, whistling as if the day were perfect. At his side, Laddie trotted along, tongue hanging out, flopping up and down in rhythm with his gait.

I wasn't sure I wanted any cake, but when Matt blew out his candles, his face was so happy it brightened up the way I felt. The Stanleys had given him the cutest cuddly brown Teddy bear. Ma and Daddy's gift was a little red tractor, and the third gift was a new pair of overalls from Aunt Alma. I was glad it wasn't Sunday so she was not there to know Ma had forgotten my birthday.

We were finishing up our cake when Mrs. Stanley asked, "Clara, choir practice is tomorrow morning. Might Josephine come home with me? I'll be taking her to practice anyway, and she can spend the weekend."

"Please, Ma."

She looked at me, and the softness was still in her eyes from Matt's excitement. After a second's thought, "Well, I guess that'd be OK. Run along and pack up your things."

I was beyond happy. I made myself think going home with Mrs. Stanley was preferable to birthday cake with candles and presents. Three days was an eternity to a six year old, and it turned out to be one of the most important weekends of my life. The children's choir director surprised me by choosing me to sing the solo part for our Thanksgiving special service. We had an unbirthday party for all of us;

146

and best of all, Forrest gave me a real live kitten, Snooks. I was important.

One of the many books Abbey had read to me was the strange story "Alice in Wonderland" which introduced me to the notion of "unbirthdays". To my great surprise, after church on Sunday the Stanleys surprised me with an "unbirthday" party. They said it was a celebration for all our "unbirthdays", and we had five candles, one for each of us, on the cake. We lit the candles five times, so each one of us could blow them out. Our party was five times better than Matt's.

I was still in the state of mind where Forrest need only look at me to make me happy. Not only did he sit beside me, there was no Luke present to spoil the fun.

Forrest insisted, "You're first, Yo. Make a wish…..come on, Yo; keep blowing…..you can do it," and when the last candle was out he gave me a hug, "now, never tell anyone your wish, and just maybe it'll come true." Of course, I wished he would marry me, and I could live with him and the Stanleys until Jesus took me to live with Aunt Carrie.

Mr. Stanley was the last one to have the candles lighted, and when he blew out the last candle, Forrest jumped to his feet. "I have just the right present for Yo. Wait just a second."

Mrs. Stanley was agitated. "I wish you wouldn't call Josephine, Yo. If you have to use a nickname, Jo's very nice."

"I agree." Abbey was vehement. "Luke started that."

Forrest insisted. "Everyone calls her, Yo. You can't change the whole world."

Luke meant Yo as an insult, but I came to Forrest's defense because to be on his side was of utmost importance. "I don't mind."

Forrest had a big smile on his face, and his hands held behind his back when he came in from the backroom. "Close your eyes, Yo, and hold out your hands."

There was a scared little "meow" as the prickly fur-ball touched my hands. I opened my eyes, and to this day, I can still feel the thrill of that moment, so intense was my joy. In my hands, hanging on for dear life with its needle-sharp claws, was the tiniest little black kitten, wearing a white bib to match its white whiskers. Its soft cries for its mother spoke directly to my heart, and I closed my hands around it, cuddling it next to my chest, and the crying stopped. It was the best present in the whole world, and it was a gift from Forrest. That was the coming together of two loves, sealed together forever, each nurturing the other.

Mrs. Stanley said, "Oh, Forrest, you should've checked with Clara first."

"There's plenty of time, the kitten can't leave its mother yet."

"Suppose.....never mind, we'll see."

***

In my heightened state of euphoria, I failed to recognize the peril that nearly wiped my happiness away. Ma said I couldn't have the kitten. It was an expense and bother she was not going to allow. Invisible hands closed around my throat. My own hands flew up as if to pull those invisible hands away. I closed my eyes to shut the dizzy world out.

Mrs. Stanley must have seen how devastated I was. "Clara, suppose I keep the kitten up here? I'll be needing a chore-girl when school starts up. Abbey'll be so busy getting things lined up for college and keeping her grades up. Maybe Josephine could help out and take care of her kitten at the same time."

My live was saved.

Aunt Carrie, I have a kitten, all my own. I named it Snooks after Baby

Snooks. I almost named it Sissy after the little girl that comes to visit Fiber Magee and Molly, but Snooks is a better name for a kitten, don't you think? Wish we had a battery radio like the Stanley's. I get to turn theirs on and off for Mr. Stanley. He calls me "his girl Friday". I go up every day and when school starts, I'll be stopping at the Stanley's every night to do my chores and take care of Snooks. I'm pretending I live up there because I have a room, and Abbey Ann, and Snooks, all up there, just like I lived there. Now, there's no way Ma can keep me from spending time up there every day cause I'm a real hired-girl. I still love you most of all, then Forrest.

Snooks followed me around, and my work was play. She preferred me to anyone else, and slept on the bed in my room with Abbey Ann, even when I wasn't sleeping up there, so Mrs. Stanley bragged which made everyone, except Luke, smile, even me. Snooks belonged to me, or rather, we belonged to each other. The feel of Aunt Carrie's love was in the softness of her fur. I'd curl up around her purring little body, and felt contented in a way I hadn't since that awful day when Aunt Carrie died.

***

Summer was nearly over, and I was upstairs putting Matt and Mark down for their naps when the next register eavesdropping episode occurred. With all the time I was spending up at the Stanley's, I had regrettably missed many episodes. I pressed my face against the grate in anticipation.

Rev. Grey was apologizing as they came into the living room, "....it's been such a busy time with vacation bible school."

"I haven't expected you."

"I'm disappointed."

Ma blushed as she gestured for Rev. Grey to sit down on the sofa.

"Have you come to a decision about starting a candy business?"

"I have half a notion to give it a try."

"Fall's the perfect time to get things going. May thinks there're quite a few in the church who'll want to place orders. And, I wouldn't be surprised if the Red and White'll want to carry it."

"Some Christmas money of my own would be nice. Maybe I'll make up some samples for May to take to church."

"What about trying the store? I'd be glad to help out in any way."

"Thanks, but we'll manage."

"Good enough.....Josephine is taking to choir like a duck to water. Did you know she'll be singing a little solo part next month when the children sing during church service?"

"Really."

"And she already has one for our Thanksgiving service. Maybe you can talk Paul into coming to hear her then."

"That'll be the day!"

"Don't be too sure, Thanksgiving's a long way off. Strange things do happen."

"I hope I'm wrong; is there a bit of 'stuffing' going on here?"

"Not a bit of it. Have I ever?"

"No, can't say as you have."

He laughed. "Or, I'd not be welcome, I'm sure, and I'd be the loser."

Ma's face blushed again. I never knew Ma to have such a friendly face, even to Mrs. Stanley. Ma started fiddling with the edge of her apron where it crossed her knees.

"Last time you almost decided to share your story with me. Can you trust me yet?"

Ma didn't look up but shrugged her shoulders.

"Clara, it needs out. You couldn't tell me anything that would make me think less of you. You're very special to me."

"If it needs out so much, why's it locked in so tight?" Ma's voice was pinched.

"Maybe, because the door has never been opened; maybe because it's too painful to open it; maybe you just don't know how to get started. Could be the latch-string is trusting me enough to share it. If that's the case, I'll wait; I'll be your friend even if you never share it."

There was such a long silence I wanted to call down and tell her, couldn't she see Rev. Grey was her friend, and I desperately wanted to hear her story. Ma shifted several times on her end of the sofa and made a soft half sound that was almost a word.

He slid over and took both her hands in his. "Only if you're ready."

I could see this made her more reluctant and he released her hands.

Ma's fingers resumed their fidgeting. "The Wallace's were my last foster home, and it was a real home where there was harmony, and I had never been in a house where everything was well kept with really nice things."

Aunt Carrie, does that mean my real Daddy was the Wallace's son? Why would they make Ma run away? Did you know about this?

Ma cleared her throat as if something was choking her. "They were not in the foster parent program. Mr. Wallace had had a heart attack and Mrs. Wallace needed help. They thought it would be nice to have a welfare girl who could go to the high school that was close to where they lived." Ma hesitated. "They were so nice to me, and encouraged me in my studies, and they even bought me nice clothes like all the other girls were wearing. They said I was pretty, and I began to feel pretty, and I began to curl my hair."

"You are more than pretty."

Ma's cheeks flushed again. "I was popular at school."

"I just bet you were."

"Mrs. Wallace encouraged me to do things, go to the games and dances. I even had a few dates."

"I gamble, more than a few."

"It was wonderful. I began to believe the world was a good place." Ma dreamed a bit, eyes downcast, fingers still working the edge of her apron. "When I became too old for the foster program, Mr. and Mrs. Wallace insisted I stay with them while I finished high school even though Mrs. Wallace didn't need me anymore. After I graduated, I went to work for rich friends of the Wallaces that lived close by. I was delighted. It was a good place to work, but I was wrong about the world being a good place."

Ma stopped, unable to go on. Rev. Grey waited quietly.

"Everything went along great until right after college started. The people I worked for had a son in college and he brought a friend home for the weekend. The friend was so polite and nice, I didn't for one minute suspect he had ulterior motives. By now I had been lulled into believing in a fairyland world. I no longer locked my bedroom door even though in that rich house there were locks on all the bedroom doors, no more chairs under doorknobs. In that house everyone was so kind; certainly there was no need to think of such things." Ma was rigid, hands folded still as death, her face was hard, and she stared straight ahead as if she were talking to the wall.

"I had just turned out my light....I had been reading....my door opened softly, and the nice friend stepped into my room. I switched on the light, and told him I couldn't have company in my room. He said he just wanted to get to know me, and I said we could do that on my day off, that this was the wrong time and place. He was stronger than I was.....he made no sweet overtures....he stuffed my mouth with his handkerchief and raped me. After all the locked doors," Ma hesitated and dropped her gaze to her lifeless hands where they lay in her lap.

"I desperately wanted to believe in the good life I'd tasted. I decided to lock my door, to trust no one, absolutely no one. To my surprise, when I turned out my light the following night, my head had barely touched my pillow when a hand covered my mouth, and the horrible scene of the night before repeated itself. He had been under my bed waiting for me. I can't begin to tell you how angry and stupid I felt. I had been exposed to some pretty crude people....nothing like this......this high brow snob obviously had no regard for someone like me....I'm a survivor.....I thought if I were lucky, only my virginity, my self-respect, my faith in a good world would be lost, that I could go on and make a life for myself. He left the next morning, and I've never seen him again."

Rev. Grey said, "It's OK to cry. Let it out," and his arms were around Ma, and she sobbed violently.

I cried too, silently so they couldn't hear me. I just couldn't help it, and I wanted Aunt Carrie more than ever.

Finally, Ma suddenly stopped crying, but her body still shook, making her voice quiver. "End of story," and she pulled away.

"Not the end of story. Please try to finish. You have every right to your whole story. It's OK with me if you sit close enough to me that I can hold your hand. When Grace died I think the only way I was able to get though those first days was by friends holding my hands."

"It's not that I don't want to be touched, I just never have had a chance to get used to it. Except from the kids I took care of."

"It's time you got used to it. If I'm offensive just nudge me, and I'll get the message." Rev. Grey moved over close to Ma, who had retreated against the arm of the sofa, and took her hand. "Now, I'm just going to sit here and hold this hand tightly while you continue."

"I told no one about what had happened. I was so ashamed. The Wallaces were still looking out after me and took me places on my days off. The family I worked for found my work more than satisfactory. I wanted that new world so much, but it was not to be. I was pregnant. I didn't know what to do. There was no way I was going to let the Wallaces know, or the family I worked for. When the family took me along to their cottage, I ran away. The Aunts took me in and I became Clara Wallace and Josephine was born there. It was the perfect place for me. They shut out the world I hated, and Carrie took care of Josephine for me."

Ma paused and my mind had been racing as I listened. I didn't have a heavenly daddy. He was still alive, and he had forced "dirty stuff" on Ma. He was like Luke too!

Oh, Aunt Carrie, what does it mean?

"You pretty much know the rest. I had to get Josephine away from Alma after Carrie died."

"I'm not sure I do. Josephine is such a delight."

Ma blurted out, "But, I can't love her. Is that what you're waiting to hear?"

She began to shake again, and Rev. Grey's arms were around her again, and she sobbed for a long time.

I already knew Ma didn't love me, but it made my throat ache to hear her say it. Did it mean it was my fault? Was there something wrong with me? Would she ever love me? Something was wrong with me; I knew it beyond a doubt. Sobs shook my body too, but I made no sound.

Rev. Grey took out his handkerchief and handed it to Ma. "I know how hard it was for you to say those words."

"Why can't I love her? I'm so ashamed. I want what's best for her, with all my heart."

"Of course you do." Rev. Grey's arms were back around Ma, and she made no protest.

"She shouldn't suffer as I did. I'd rather die than put her in an orphanage as my mother did me. Whatever am I going to do? Aren't you going to be overcome with concern for my soul and plead for my salvation?"

"I suppose I would if I felt there was a need to do that. You're the only one who thinks there's anything wrong with your soul." He held Ma away from himself so he could look into her eyes. "There're many kinds of love. I think you know the love of sacrifice better than anyone I know. You've learned that love too well."

"You're just being a minister."

"No, I'm not just being a minister."

"I thought you were coming because…."

"Because I wanted to rescue you from the fiery pits of hell? Haven't we gotten beyond that? Clara, you've got to start believing in yourself; you're loveable, just as you are. We're friends forever, no matter what."

"But, I'm uncomfortable. I don't…."

"No buts, you do know. When I see you with Mark and Matt, especially Mark, I see you do know."

"I forgot Josephine's birthday. How could a mother do that?"

Yeah, Aunt Carrie, you never forgot. I miss you so much.

Ma rubbed her hands together. "Why can't I love her the same way?"

"Because you couldn't heal fast enough to allow yourself to become attached to that little baby who kept you from stepping into the new world you had glimpsed."

See, Aunt Carrie, I was bad for Ma. I know everything's my fault. I wish I could be someone else or come be your 'little sweetheart' again. Then Ma could be happy.

Finally, Ma turned toward Rev. Grey, as he continued, "Life in that Sweet Shop was grueling. How could you learn love there?" Their faces were very close together. "See how easy it is to be hugged." His arms closed around Ma again. "And it feels good, to me too."

"It's not proper."

"It's not only proper, it's necessary. Don't you worry about Josephine; we all love her so much. May is wonderful with her, and Abbey and Forrest love her like a little sister. Could be you'll learn to love her from the way we love her."

I thought their lips were going to touch. There was a whole different feeling happening. It made me think of how I felt about Forrest. I thought it would be wonderful to be hugged and kissed by Forrest. I could just imagine how it would feel. I began to wish they would kiss.

But, Rev. Grey released Ma. He reached up and took the pins out of her hair, and with his fingers loosened it, letting it fall around her face. "I want you to promise me you'll stop pinning your hair back. You've every right to be pretty. And, you're entitled to love."

"Have I made a wrong choice?"

"It's one you can change. I know a very good counselor I can recommend. With all that you've been through you could benefit from professional counseling."

"What do you call this?"

"We're friends. I don't know the answers."

"Does anyone? No counseling for me. You know what they say, 'I've made my bed. Now I have to lie in it!'"

"I fear it's a very lonely bed." Both of Rev. Grey's hands went up in self condemnation. "I'm sorry. I shouldn't have said that. My baser self got out of hand."

Ma smiled a broad smile, her first. "Then you do have one. I didn't think ministers did."

"I like your tease. It means we're friends." He moved away slightly.

"Good enough friends to talk a little more about why no counselor?"

Ma was quiet, thoughtful. She looked so different with her hair loose, not pulled back so tight it drew on her face skin.

"Yes, good enough friends that I'll state my case, I've given my word in contract to Paul, and as long as he lives up to his side of the bargain, I'll live up to mine."

"Is that fair to you, or Josephine?"

"What's fair? Josephine has a family. We have security. I'm bringing stability to a family badly in need of it. What would it do to those two little boys if I begin to think about what's fair for me? Is life ever fair? Has it been fair to you?"

"You know I can't answer those questions. They're big stumbling blocks you're throwing in the way of logic; it's not selfish to ask for help. Help wouldn't ask you to break your contract. When I, as your friend, say things you may suspect I have ulterior motives and may not be seeing things as objectively as I should, which is, in all honesty, true, but, I can assure you, I'll never lose sight of my responsibility as a minister even though I might like to. I'll never give you those kinds of reasons to shut me out. Anyone who's been abused as you have been should have professional counseling. But, I'll push no more."

"Good, I'm not comfortable with it. Anyway, I'm tougher than you think; ask Josephine. There's where I need the help."

"Where is Josephine?"

A look of horror passed over Ma's face, and she glanced up at the ceiling. "She's upstairs!" She proclaimed as she jumped to her feet.

I rolled out from under the bed very quietly, and quickly stretched out on the bed with my face away from the door as if I were asleep. I hadn't slid the bolt. Ma would be mad about that. She opened the door noiselessly, stood a moment, and shut the door again. I lay still but I could hear their voices.

"She's sound asleep, thank heavens."

"Bless her heart, that'd be no way for her to hear and only half understand …are you comfortable with Luke now?"

"Luke is my one big worry, not only for Josephine, though I think she's learning to be smart about avoiding him. He's a very unhappy boy, and tries to make himself think my being here is the cause of his problems, but I feel sure it's resentment for his father."

"Yes, I think you're right, a father too strict, who favors him too much, is a double problem."

"Exactly, you have that figured out right. I fear one of these days Paul may be forced to see reality, and, that scares me."

"Could you take Rev. Baker into your confidence? You might get some help there."

"Everything's black and white, sin and salvation. I don't think that's what Luke needs. Plus, I've never met Rev. Baker, and from all I gather Luke is something of a prodigy wonder boy minister in the making at church. He wouldn't believe me."

"Maybe we should talk more about this my next visit. I hope the candy business is a great success….."

Their voices faded away as they left the living room. My mind spun as I huddled in my pretend sleep. Rev. Grey was right, I didn't quite understand; why was that awful person my real father? But, I knew he was. My real daddy now had the face of Luke, and I hated him just like Ma hated my father. He was worse than Luke, if that were possible. I began to grasp why Ma didn't love me, but it made me want her to love me all the more. I wanted her to be like Aunt Carrie. Then, I'd be glad I was alive. I wanted to cry some more, but if I did Ma would surely know I wasn't asleep, and that would make her feel bad. I knew how much I loved Ma by how much my insides hurt. She did say she cared very much for me even though she didn't love me. Rev. Grey said maybe she'd learn to love me. Could she? Maybe she wasn't a heathen. Maybe Daddy was wrong. Rev. Grey didn't treat her like a heathen, but he was a "thin soup" Methodist. What would happen to me? I didn't want a real daddy! I liked it better when I thought he was a heavenly daddy with Aunt Carrie, and Jesus, and God.

I was the cause of all Ma's problems. All I had to hang onto was the knowledge that Aunt Carrie had loved me, and was in heaven, waiting for me. I wondered if there were any other ways for Jesus to come take me other than letting Luke throw me in the bull pen.

Chapter 6

In my dream, Luke sing-songed, "Yoyo's got a witch's fa-ace...and she-ee's so du-umb she can't re-e-e-ad." I was surrounded by a ring of strange kids, all dancing, and laughing, and pointing their fingers at me. Their laughter reverberated, louder and louder, suffocating me. Forrest's face appeared in the background, but when I called to him no sound came out of my mouth. I awoke, tossing and turning in panic.

Ma was shaking me. "For heaven's sake, be still. It'll be morning soon enough."

I lay there trembling inside. Right from the start, school had loomed with contradictory feelings in my emotions. I wanted to go, but maybe the kids would make fun of my witch's face. I was anxious to be able to read stories for myself, but suppose I couldn't learn to read. Suppose Luke was right? What if I was dumb? I told myself Forrest was going, and I wanted to go too.

Starting down the driveway to school with Luke that next morning, gave me the strangest feeling. I didn't want to go any place with Luke. How could I keep my promise to Ma? To my relief, we were not to be alone. There at the end of our driveway was the girl I had seen riding her bicycle by our house.

Luke gave an effected flick of his hand to his cheek in contemplation. "Well now, Isabel, don't we look all gussied up this morning?"

Totally ignoring me, Isabel tee-heed and was full of smiles. I could see she was much taken with Luke as we sauntered up the road to where Forrest waited for us.

As he fell into step, Luke gave him a shove. "Gees, Woody, you should just give up. A tub of bear grease won't stick that cowlick down."

Involuntarily, Forrest's hand flew up to check his hair. His clothes were spiffy brand spanking-new khaki pants, plaid shirt and oxford shoes. My heart turned over.

Isabel tee-heed again, "What'a ya put in your hair, Luke, curlers?"

Grinning at her mischievously, he danced around her. "It's all natural beauty. Want'a feel?" Then Luke made some get-cha-get-cha motions with his fingers. "Want me to feel'a your hair?"

It was plain to see Isabel liked Luke much better than she did Forrest, which was the first of many surprises about Luke that day. At school he was king. Everyone, even Miss Brown the teacher, smiled on him. In light of all the clowning and adulation, he seemed less frightening to me, and I saw he was handsome in a way I hadn't been able to comprehend before. It shocked me to realize that if this were all I knew about Luke, I'd like him too, and in my secret heart I wished he liked me.

Miss Brown guided me to a front seat. "Luke, is this new girl your stepsister? I understand your father has remarried."

He cringed. "Sort'a. She's the daughter of the woman who keeps house for us that Dad married."

He was the same old Luke who would always hate me. Miss Brown smiled smugly and made no correction as Daddy had. That made a bad start with Miss Brown.

Billy, the big boy across the hill where the echo came from, had a little brother and sister, Carl and Carol, twins, who were also in the first grade. Twins was an exciting new idea, and I studied them as closely and they studied me.

Carl suddenly poked Carol. "She don't look so awful."

"Sh-sh you're not posed to say that."

My heart sunk. Luke had already told everyone how ugly I was. Carol tried to steer Carl away, but he won't budge. "You really live with Luke?"

"I'd rather live with Forrest."

"You would?"

"Would you want to live with someone who went around saying bad things about you?"

"He said your Ma didn't look anything like you."

"My Ma's pretty."

School was a double-edged learning process. The things that I was supposed to be learning were impossible, but were easy for Carol and Carl. Luke was only too glad to keep Ma and Daddy informed of my stupidity. Daddy said, "Give her a little help, Luke. Learning's not easy for everyone like it is for you. It's a good chance to practice your Christianity."

I thought, I'd rather be dumb than to be like Luke.

Ma never looked up from the stove where she was making grape jelly. "Try harder, Josephine."

Every day Miss Brown humiliated me because I couldn't seem to get past 10 in learning my numbers. After a week of going to the blackboard ashamed, I noticed Carol, who could count to 100 before she came to the first grade, had her lesson paper written neatly with numbers 1 through 10 on the top line, underneath in the second line, the teens and so on down the paper. The secret clicked. I went to the board and wrote my numbers to 100.   A rage began to boil in my mind because I knew Miss Brown knew the secret, and didn't tell me and let me look dumb on purpose. I knew, beyond a doubt, she must hate me too.

Aunt Carrie, What's wrong with me that makes people not like me? Luke must be right about me, cause everybody likes him best, cept me. I like Forrest best, but .he even likes Luke best too. I can't help it that I look like a gypsy and have a witch face. Numbers are easy now. I hate Miss Brown; I hate her; I hate her. I wish I could make her look dumb. If Jesus hadn't taken you to heaven, you'd've told me about numbers, wouldn't you?

School politics were the other side of the learning process. I learned the ins and outs of the pecking order, and hated my place at the bottom of it. I learned to never let anyone know how much it hurt to be teased about being dumb; it was no fun to tease someone who didn't care. Carol was afraid of snakes, and often ran screaming into the schoolhouse, so I never let anyone know what scared me. Carl taught me never to be a tattletale when he was punched in the stomach for telling the teacher who teased Carol about snakes.

To my dismay, I learned what born was, or rather, what came before you were born. This knowledge was thrust upon me by Sally. There were six in her family, and all six were interested in stuff that Daddy and Aunt Alma would have a fit about. Two fits, I know, because Daddy said what was under Mark's dirty diaper was sinful and shouldn't even be looked at or you'd encourage sin.

We were on our way home from school, and Luke, Isabel, Forrest and I stopped at Sally's to see their new puppy. I was shocked when I saw a naked doll lying on the floor in plain sight. The doll had a cloth body, composition head, arms and legs. Not only was the doll without clothes, it had a gaping hole poked into the cloth stuffing between its legs. I shuddered to think what Daddy and Aunt Alma would say about that! I could hardly enjoy the cute little white roly-poly puppy.

Sally must have read my surprised look because she said, "You have a smarty face, know where babies come from?"

"I never thought about it."

"Never thought about 'the birds and the bees'? Gees, a goody two-shoes!" She cupped her hand to her mouth as if the rest of the world shouldn't hear, and thankfully no one was near by. "A guy sticks his pecker in you, and plants a seed, and it grows, making you look like you swallowed a pumpkin; only it's a baby growing in there."

Having seen Luke's thingy, I knew what she meant by a pecker, and I instantly knew what he was threatening to do to me. I was astounded at the idea of a baby growing inside of you and blurted, "How does the baby get out?"

"That's for you to find out." And she ran away laughing.

Worrying about the getting born part of the story caused me many anxious hours. There was absolutely no way for a baby to get out. The "birds and bees" mystery was one I would rather not have learned.

I began to notice the rooster jumping on top of the hens. Dogs were mating in the school yard, and Miss Brown made all us children go in from recess, and there was a lot of snickering and laughing. I saw a heifer and bull mating in the lower pasture where the young stock was kept separated from the milking cows. Even flies were doing it. Everywhere I looked it was going on. I thought about all the living people, animals and bugs that had to have had a seed to start them. My mind whirled, and it made me sick to my stomach to think about all that seed sewing. Most shocking was realizing, that was what my real daddy must have done to Ma, and I knew she'd never love me. Suddenly, I thought, that was what Daddy and Aunt Alma must be preaching about. That was the sin under your clothes! And, it was so bad you shouldn't even look at it.

Always, in the back of my mind I was worried; did knowing about "dirty stuff" make you bad? What if Aunt Carrie thought I was bad?

What if God shut the door to heaven, and I never got to be with Aunt Carrie again? This thought was terrifying, and my mind flew down forbidden lanes. Daddy had to have done "dirty stuff" with his first wife or he'd not have Luke, Matt and Mark. Ma didn't look like she swallowed a pumpkin so she and Daddy didn't do "dirty stuff". Even Aunt Alma had to have done "dirty stuff" once or Daddy wouldn't have been born. I knew Aunt Carrie had no trouble getting into heaven because she never did "dirty stuff". That Daddy and Aunt Alma were sure they were going to heaven was puzzling. All my antennas were primed to receive more information.

The seed sewing mystery, cloaked in half truths, intensified an obsessive fascination and repulsion. The aura of religious Victorianism tore at my heart and security. At school I'd stare out the window when my reading lesson became impossible, and for a few minutes, my mind traveled out amongst the trees and clouds. In my thoughts, Forrest and I ran over the fields; we went berrying, and he told me all kinds of interesting things like how to recognize the bird's song, and where they nested; he showed me where the weasel lived and told me stories about why the weasel turned white like the snow in winter. Then we danced with the Fairies over the mossy mounts at the edge of the woods, and I planned how I'd marry him when I grew up. I wondered; would we do dirty stuff? Then the dark world of fascination and fear descended, unwelcome again, filling my thoughts. It just wasn't fair, thinking about "dirty stuff" just happened even though you tried to force it out of your mind. I knew I wasn't supposed to know about how you got babies, and I continually worried about how they got out, and I was afraid of what Daddy might do if he ever found out what I was thinking about.

Autumn came and the once green leaves changed right before my eyes as if nature colored them with crayons bright scarlet, red, orange and gold. Their brilliance floated and scampered, coloring the restless winds of coming winter. We raked Mother Nature's colorful rustling quilt pieces into piles, jumped in them and covered each other with them. Eventually we ran plowing through them, scattering and freeing them again to the impatient frisky wind. My world was dramatic and surprising on all levels. My emotions ranged from the exalted height of nature's display of color, to the low of her now barren branches left behind.

So many things were happening to me. Every day after school, Forrest and I came into the Stanley's kitchen together where Mrs. Stanley waited with cheery greetings, and Snooks waited to be petted and fed. Forrest was beginning to help me with my reading so I didn't look quite as dumb at school. He couldn't understand why reading was so difficult for me when he said I was the smartest kid he ever knew. I loved it when he said that even though I couldn't understand why he thought I was smart when it was so obvious I was not. I saw little of Abbey except on Sundays when we went to Sunday School and children's choir. Ma was still letting me go, but she wouldn't come to hear the choir sing for our special Thanksgiving service. I think Rev. Grey was as disappointed as I was. It helped a little when during our Thanksgiving dinner up at the Stanley's, Mrs. Stanley said she was proud of the children's choir, and that she was especially proud of my solo, right in front of Ma and Daddy. Luke snorted when Daddy said, "Good for you, Josephine."

Daddy had a bible home study class for Luke and Matt, and I had to sit in on it if Daddy could find me. When I could manage, I'd sneak up to the Stanleys when it was time for class. I suppose Daddy thought my being in on the bible study made up for my going to the watered-down Methodist Church. However, I was learning things that helped me understand what sin was, but my six year old reasoning ability was

166

having a hard time, trying to understand God. I couldn't figure out why God made Adam and Eve blind. If He had just made them so they could see, Eve wouldn't have had to get Adam to eat the forbidden apple. She didn't want them to be blind even though Adam didn't mind. Once Adam could see Eve had no clothes covering sin, he started doing "dirty stuff", and God threw them out of the Garden of Eden, gave Eve babies, and made them wear clothes to hide their sin. Once they were out of the Garden of Eden they had to do hard work to live. I decided I was glad I wasn't blind, and hoped it didn't mean God would be mad at me. I was already in danger because I knew what sin was. Surely Jesus wouldn't take me to heaven to be with Aunt Carrie.

I was comforted in the knowledge that Mrs. Stanley and Abbey liked me, and I hoped with all my heart they would never find out I knew how you got babies because if they knew they'd cross me off their list of friends. I was more and more convinced there was a God even though I didn't quite understand God's reasons for making Adam and Eve blind; I guessed He must have had His reasons. Maybe it was the only way it was possible for Him to make them. That made the most sense because God had to be too smart to do something dumb or He couldn't have been able to make the world.

I'm sure Rev. Grey was still visiting Ma because sometimes he was leaving our house when Forrest and I turned in up at the Stanley's after school. Luke continued on down the road to our house, muttering under his breath, "What's that Charlatan doing at our house again? Daddy should put a stop to that….."

***

In the middle of December, Luke and Forrest went to the woods to cut Christmas trees, their yearly ritual that positively had no room in it for me, so stated Luke. This was my first Christmas tree, and Ma made sure I was home to help trim it, evidence of Rev. Grey's influence, I thought.

Luke said trimming trees was baby stuff and wouldn't help. I knew it was because I was helping, and Ma wasn't his mother. I was surprised to find the Stanleys had also saved the trimming of their tree until I could help. Forrest held me up so I could put the star on the tree's spiky top. I remember I felt warm and fuzzy, unreal like I was living a scene from a storybook.

For the school pageant I was supposed to recite the "The Night Before Christmas" which was unfamiliar to me and much too difficult to learn. Thankfully, Mrs. Stanley came to my rescue and talked Miss Brown into changing my part in the pageant to singing "Away in a Manger" which Mrs. Stanley assured her, I could do very nicely. This change pleased Daddy because he said Santa was a fairy tale and would confuse me about God. I think Miss Brown was impressed that Mrs. Stanley took an interest in me and how I was doing in my studies.

It was a new idea that Christmas was Jesus' birthday. I asked Mrs. Stanley, "Then Jesus isn't an imaginary friend even though he took Aunt Carrie's soul that you can't see to heaven."

"That's right; Jesus was a real person who lived many, many years ago. But because he's God's Son and so special to all Christians, we feel like He's still alive in our hearts. Kind'a like you still feel about Aunt Carrie. I think you do still think a lot about her and miss her, don't you?"

"Oh, yes, Mrs. Stanley."

"I thought so. Does that answer your question?"

"Does God have a birthday like Jesus?"

"No. He was in the beginning; He's the one who made the world.

He sent his son, Jesus, to live among us so we'd know God like a Father and know that He loves us."

"Sort'a like me calling Daddy, Daddy even though he's not my true father?"

"Well…I guess…sort of."

"And Jesus is kind'a like a brother, like Matt and Mark?" I didn't include Luke. I didn't want Luke for a brother!

"I guess…a little bit like that."

I said, "Oh," and went on my way, but thought I wished Aunt Carrie could tell me for sure that God wasn't an imaginary father because He was never born. Maybe Jesus had a different daddy. He might not have had a register to listen and look through to find out who His Father was.

When Daddy read the Christmas story from the bible it said Jesus' mother, Mary, was a virgin. I learned from talk out behind the schoolhouse that a virgin was someone who never did "dirty stuff". God sent an angel down from heaven with God's seed so Jesus could be special and take people to heaven like He did Aunt Carrie. I still wanted to know why God couldn't send a seed down to anyone who wanted a baby, but I knew better than to ask.

Daddy came with Ma, Matt and Mark to see the school program. I figured they came to hear Luke do his reading about Scrooge. Still, I was pleased, they'd have to hear me sing too, and I knew I did a good job because Mr. and Mrs. Stanley, and even Miss Brown, said I did. Ma was proud of me too even though she couldn't quite say so. It was in her eyes. Daddy was surprised at me because he lifted his eyebrows and praised Luke an extra lot. He wasn't used to anyone else getting praise, especially me.

The next afternoon I was disappointed because Ma and Daddy didn't go to the Methodist children's Christmas program, and I heard

Rev. Grey say to Mrs. Stanley that he had been sure Ma would come to hear me sing. He had purposely scheduled the program in the afternoon so it wouldn't conflict with True Faith's evening Christmas program.

I said, "Rev. Grey, Ma already heard me sing at the school program." I didn't want him to give up on trying to get Ma to love me.

That afternoon when our program was over, Daddy heard Matt and me singing "Away in a Manger" together, and was so impressed he said he was going to ask Rev. Baker if we could sing it in their Christmas pageant. Ma asked what I thought about singing in True Faith Church, and Matt and I both clapped our hands. Luke protested, and Daddy asked if he'd like to sing with us. He said, "Not on your life."

To my surprise, at True Faith's Christmas program, Luke stood behind the pulpit and was the reader for the whole program. Right in the middle of it when baby Jesus was in the manger, Matt and I sang, and everyone had smiles on their faces. Luke stood beside Rev. Baker at the end of the service, and people shook his hand just like he was the minister. This was a most important night for Daddy because, not only was he proud of Luke, Matt and me, he had finally succeeded in getting Ma to come to True Faith Church, and he looked exceedingly pleased. I was pleased too, and I hoped it wasn't just so Ma could hear Matt sing.

Ma's candy sales were so successful there weren't presents for everyone on Christmas morning. Daddy had Aunt Alma buy material for Ma a new dress. Ma gave Aunt Alma a shawl and Daddy warm boots for his chores. It was plain to see Luke was pleased with his gift of real dress pants and a sweater to match. He thanked Daddy who started to explain it was from Ma, but Ma motioned him quiet. Matt, Mark and I all got warm snowsuits. In Mark's package there was a pull toy he could learn to walk with; in Matt's package, tiddlywinks; in mine,

"Heidi". Daddy was so happy that Christmas, he didn't notice Luke's sulking. I figured Luke didn't like Ma playing such an important part in the family.

Snow in the country was a far different experience from the snow that fell on my rooftop play-yard in the city. In the warmth of my new snow suit, there were new challenges and beauty to be enjoyed in a white marshmallow world that was very different but just as magical as fall's painted leaves. Ma even laughed at our snowman and gave us buttons for eyes and a carrot for his nose. Daddy parked his barn cap on him while he ate supper!

***

Triumphant over all the seasons, was the thrill of spring's renewal which took the exaltation of my expanding world to new heights. Sometimes it felt as though my heart would burst right open with the wonder of it. I tried to tell Aunt Carrie about the vibrant feel of the frisky warming breezes, the smell of spring's wet earth, its texture, rebirth and color. During April the grass turned screaming green. By the middle of May the trees were wearing their green canopy, and the melodious songs of newly paired birds filled the air.

Snooks was a full grown cat now, and Mrs. Stanley said she never heard a cat purr as loudly as Snooks did for me. Spring meant there were more chores to do, and I stayed longer after school. Mrs. Stanley paid me fifty cents a week. Luke, as always, kept my feet anchored firmly on the ground. He said, "Mrs. Stanley feels sorry for you; you're such a scrawny ugly little brat."

Candy sales slacked off and made time for Ma to do her spring cleaning. Daddy plowed Ma's garden and helped her plant it. Even Mark was excited to see the little green seedlings break through the ground in neat rows. Forrest was so busy helping with spring planting he had little time for helping me with my reading, much to my dismay. Luke, however, was beside himself without anyone to hang around with, and was continually badgering Forrest about his working all the time. He wanted to go up to Stanley's and listen to records on Abbey's new windup Victrola. Sometimes, Abbey would get home, from high school in time to play records for us to listen to as she helped me finish up my chores before I had to go home. I could see why Luke wanted to listen to records. It was like magic, and I could sing all the songs. He'd say to Ma, "Can't you make her shut up that racket?" He was jealous, and it felt good.

After the corn was planted, Luke, Isabel, Forrest and I were on our way home from school when we heard a gun blast. Luke teased, "Is that your Daddy out there, shooting rainbows in the sky again?" And, he laughed and slapped Forrest on the back, too hard.

I wondered what Luke could be talking about. There was no rainbow in the sky. "What's Mr. Stanley doing, Forrest?"

"Scaring the crows away so they don't eat the seed-corn."

Luke said, "Gees, Woody, they're just old crows. They'll be back to eat the corn. Everyone knows that."

"Well, Dad hates killing 'um."

Luke continued on down the road, dejected, muttering how stupid some people were. Part of his problem was that he was jealous because I was stopping at the Stanley's, and he had to go home.

I could see Mr. Stanley out in the side pasture shooting his shotgun up in the air over the freshly planted cornfield. Crows scattered in all directions. Then, I saw Mr. Stanley turn toward the house.

I was in the backroom, feeding Snooks when he came in. "Mr. Stanley, why don't you shoot the crows? Everyone knows they'll come back and eat the corn. Luke said it was stupid to shoot rainbows in the sky."

"Well now, you know, he's right about that." He sat down on a chair next to the outside door and began taking off his work shoes. "Come over here, and I'll tell you a story."

I went over and stood by his knee, and he put his arm around me.

"When I was just about your age, I had a talking crow named Midnight. Ever heard of a talking crow?"

"Really, crows can't talk." I wormed my way right upon his lap.

He gave me a hug. "Now that's better. This one could. My uncle gave me that talking crow. Its tongue had been slit before my uncle got him. That's what made him so he could talk."

"Didn't it hurt?"

"Nah, he was the happiest darn crow you ever did see, and I loved that old bird. I'd ride my bicycle up and down the road right out front here with Midnight on my shoulder. I'd swerve, this way and that, going two forty, trying to spill Midnight off, but he was a crafty old bird, and he'd flap his wings and hang on for dear life."

Mr. Stanley placed his hands on my shoulders and weaved me around from side to side as if I were riding like the wind too.

"Midnight just loved it, because he thought just riding along was too boring. My mother used to sit on the front porch, doing her endless mending, watching the pair of us at our antics. She'd call after me, 'One of these days that crow's gonna get the better of you. Now, you be careful.'"

"Yeah, that's just what Aunt Carrie'd say too." I nodded very intent.

"Well now, of course she would......well, one day, my mother couldn't find her thimble. This was a sterling silver thimble that she prized highly because it had been her mother's. She was after each one of us, did we see her thimble. Of course we had no call to know where her thimble was. Now, right during this time there was stone layers here laying up those big square silos where the ensilage is stored."

"Yeah, it's spooky in that passage. I pretend it's the dungeon."

"You know that's the very thing, I used to pretend that too."

"Really, when you were a boy?"

"Yep. And, those workmen used to watch Midnight and me go flying by as they worked. Mama didn't want to think one of them workmen took her thimble, but where could it have got to? She figured one of them workmen must have sneaked upon the porch, thinking of course to give it to his wife, don't you know, whilst she was in fix'n their dinner. You know, kind'a like, biting the hand that feeds them! But, of course, she really didn't want to think that. She was one who never wanted to think ill of anyone.

"Now, at the time of the missing thimble, that stone silo was pretty tall, and the workmen had to climb up ladders to get to their work, had to carry all those stones up there too. And, you can imagine what a job that was. Well, that afternoon, of course not having the slightest notion what Mama was thinking they had done, well, when they climbed up their ladders, what do you think they saw up there on top of that high up wall?"

"The thimble?"

"That's right, Mama's sterling silver thimble. She was right; someone had stolen it while she was in the house cooking dinner for those workers. Can you guess who?"

"Not, Midnight?"

"You're right, it was Midnight. Midnight taught us, crows love shiny things. We had to be very careful what we left lay'n around. Anything shiny he'd make off with. You never knew what the workmen would find up there. Now, that's why I shoot up in the air, at rainbows, as Luke says, when there ain't no rain. I just have a special fondness for crows. They're very smart birds too. You watch; they'll always post a guard in the top of a tree to watch for trespassers. You can't walk in the woods without that guard sounding the alarm, caw, caw, caw, signaling all the wild creatures there's danger about, beware. They always made me want to fly; they're such good fliers. When I was a shaver like you, to fly was just a dream."

"I'm glad you don't shoot crows, Mr. Stanley. I like crows too."

"Good for you. Now, run along and do your chores."

***

At the end of June, Luke and Forrest would be graduating from the eighth grade. I'd be glad to be rid of Luke, but that Forrest wouldn't be in school with me was a stab in the heart. Aunt Alma always said, "You have to take the bitter with the sweet."

Isabel's family rented the aunt's old Sweet Shop, and they were moving to Phelpsburg as soon as school was out. All day Sally and Isabel hung around each other's neck bemoaning their impending separation. Isabel said, half joking, she doubted Sally would really miss her because she'd have Luke all to herself. He'd be visiting her twice as often. That's when I knew for sure Luke was sneaking out his bedroom window, and I trembled to think what would happen if Daddy ever found out.

I was setting the table for Mrs. Stanley and I began to wonder what Jesus thought about Luke's sneaking out the window to visit Isobel and Sally. Setting the table was my last chore before I ran home to do the same for Ma. Carefully, I placed the knife and spoon to the right of the plate and the fork to the left.

Suddenly, I blurted out, "Mrs. Stanley, Do you ever wonder what Jesus is thinking?"

"Can't say that I do."

I thought maybe a different tack would get me an answer. "Is it true, God made everything?"

Mrs. Stanley went right on chopping cabbage for a salad. "That's right; that's what the bible says."

"Good and bad? Not everything's good."

"Never thought about that."

I pressed on, aware Mrs. Stanley was not exactly pleased with my questions. "And God was testing Adam and Eve with the one tree even though the bible says God knows everything before it happens?"

"Well, I guess that's right."

"You know, Mrs. Stanley, God sounds more like Aunt Alma than he does like Aunt Carrie, and I'm having a hard time figuring that out, because, I don't want Aunt Alma to be right."

"Bless you, child. If I don't miss my guess, you'll straighten this world out by the time you're grown. Run along home before your Ma has to set her own table, and remember, before anything else, God is love. That's the real test."

That sort'a helped put my mind at ease even though it didn't explain things the way I needed them to be explained. At least Mrs. Stanley said God is love, not mean like Aunt Alma.

Finally, it was the last day of school, and I was so happy until at the end of the day when something happened that changed everything. That last day of school is etched in my memory as the horrendous day that barred me from heaven because now I knew I really was a heathen, and the trauma of that day survived into my adulthood to torment me.

On the last day of school, Mr. and Mrs. Stanley and Abbey were at the schoolhouse waiting for Forrest because there was a special service in Phelpsburg for high school seniors and their families. As Forrest climbed into the back seat of their car with Abbey, they called to Luke and me from the window, "Come here a minute."

Mr. Stanley told Luke, "Your father wants you to hurry home to help with the chores because with Forrest and me both gone he'll really be short-handed. Keep track of your time so I'll know what I owe you."

"Jeepers, alright, but I don't see why I couldn't have gone with Forrest. No one would know I wasn't a brother, and they wouldn't care anyway."

Mrs. Stanley said, "Josephine, the backroom is open so you can feed Snooks. Don't worry about the rest of your chores."

Terror froze in my heart. I'd be alone in the backroom, and Luke knew it. I didn't wait for her to finish, I started to run. I desperately hoped Sally would dally along the way to her house and keep Luke from catching up to me.

I thought I had succeeded, but just as I opened the backroom door to run on home, Luke was there.

"Where do you think you're going so fast, witch face?"

I was cornered prey, and I grabbed a shovel that stood nearby. "Don't you touch me, Luke Osborn."

He stepped closer. "Think a little turd like you can scare me?"

I swung the shovel as hard as I could and hit him side of the legs. I knew it hurt, and he grabbed the shovel out of my hands with a grimace.

"So you want to play rough, do you."

He took hold of my arm so hard I thought he'd break it. I bit him on the hand, and he let go. I ran for the door, but he caught me, lifting me right off the floor. I kicked and screamed to no avail.

"You knew I'd get you sooner or later, you unholy little sinner. This is all your fault just like it was Eve's fault Adam sinned. You heathen, you and your Ma are the reason for all the troubles in our family. It's no sin for me because you're a heathen, you're a nothing. Just listen to the sermons, and you'll know I'm right. And, if you breathe one word of this to anyone, I'll see to it the whole world knows how bad you are, and I'll see to it the bull gets you."

What happened next is blocked from my memory. I only remember running home, crying. Ma was in the garden and saw me coming. I ran past her into the kitchen where Luke stood, nonchalantly eating a cookie which made him choke with shock when he saw me. He thought I'd come sneaking home after he'd gone to the barn. He had probably even ordered me to do that, but I was too traumatized to comprehend or remember. The screen door banged shut; Ma was right behind me, spade still clutched in her hand. I must have been a frightful mess.

"Luke Osborn, what's going on here?"

"Nothing, only Josephine's careless tussle with Laddie and that cat of hers. You'd think she'd know better with her school clothes on."

"Why is she not up at the Stanley's doing her chores?"

"Ask her. Not me."

"Oh, yes, I remember. They're all in town at the high school." Ma pushed Luke into a chair, "You know Laddie's always on the line when they're not home. Josephine, come out from under the table."

I was shaking from head to foot.

"Look at her, Luke Osborn. Aren't you proud of yourself?" Ma started the motion to strike him with her spade, but at the last minute, held back. She shook her head. "I don't even know where to begin," she spat her words out through clenched teeth in rage. "This I do know, you had better start trembling too, because you step out of line once more, and I swear, your father..."

"You're threatening me?" Luke asked as if that was an unfathomable thought. "My father wouldn't believe anything you told him about me, madam."

Ma let that slip by as if he had never spoken. There was a look on her face that was terrible to see. She rammed her face within inches of his. "Listen to me carefully; I know exactly what happened, all about it. You're lower than any animal I know. How can you look another human being in the eyes? I went along with your game, hoping you'd grow up. Now, I don't owe you anything, no more chances. Josephine is to tell me if you ever step one inch out of line, one tiny iota. One word from her, and believe me, I'll see to it you get your just desserts even if I have to turn this whole family upside down."

He started to open his mouth, and Ma shook her finger in his face. "Not a word, not one word. Come here, Josephine."

I came and stood beside her. "Step up and spit in Luke's face...come on. He'll never hurt you again." My mouth was dry, but I did spit on him.

Then Ma said, "Tell her you'll never hurt her again."

He clamped his lips together with such an angry fire burning in his cinnamon brown eyes that they made me shrivel to look at them.

"Josephine," Ma's voice was resolute and calm. "Run over to the barn and fetch your Daddy."

"I'll never hurt her again," came spewing out of his mouth.

"Say, I'll never hurt you again, Josephine."

"I'll never hurt you again, Josephine."

"Get to the barn and out of my sight."

The reservoir on the old black woodstove was full of hot water. Ma dipped it into the bathing tub, washed me tenderly from head to foot, carried me upstairs, put my pajamas on me, and tucked me into bed. Surprising me even more, she sat down on the edge of the bed. This saddest of all bonds shared between mother and daughter, for a few moments, melted the barrier between us. I am sure she struggled with her own memories, but at the time I only felt a devastating separation from goodness and God.

"I know this seems like the end of world, Josephine, but it's not. Don't be afraid anymore, and no matter what threat Luke may make, come to me. I meant every word I said, and Luke knows it. You don't have to come down to supper tonight; I'll bring you up something. Slide the bolt after me... always. No matter where you are or how needless it seems, lock the door."

Almost as soon as I slid the bolt, Matt, who had been napping, rattled the latch, and I could hear Ma tell him to come away, that I was not feeling well. I was thankful because I didn't want anyone to know how bad I was, and thankful Ma said I never had to be afraid of Luke again; she had meant every word. It had been wonderful for Ma to be so kind to me and understand. Still, she was a heathen, and in my heart, I thought Luke was right about it being my fault. I reasoned, Ma understood because of what happened to her with my real daddy, and that was why she was a heathen. My mind flew to Aunt Carrie, and in that instant I knew, beyond a doubt, Jesus would never take me to heaven, that I could never talk to Aunt Carrie again. I cried myself to sleep. The next thing I remember, Ma was at our door, waking me to let her in.

"I am so very sorry, Josephine. You'll be alright. It just takes time." She slid the bolt, and we both settled down to sleep.

***

My guilt bothered me so much, all joy left me; I no longer felt like escaping up to the Stanley's. I stayed just long enough to take care of Snooks and do my chores. Snooks started coming down to our house to spend time with me, and surprisingly, Ma never said anything as long as Snooks stayed outside. Mrs. Stanley knew something was bothering me, but I couldn't let anyone know how bad I was, so I said I needed to help Ma more. I lived in constant fear that Mrs. Stanley would find out I was unworthy of her friendship. I thought of Aunt Carrie all the time and missed the therapy of talking to her so much the hurt inside me festered and grew.

Then, in one of Daddy's lessons, I was presented a way out of my dilemma. Instantly my mind flew to heaven.

Aunt Carrie, I've found a way to come to heaven to see you after all. More than anything in the world, I want to be with you. Luke said I was a heathen and heathens didn't count. Daddy said that everyone, even babies, have sinned because Eve passes it on to everyone even if they never did "dirty stuff". And, the reason Luke isn't a heathen, is because he's saved by the blood of Jesus. All I have to do is believe Jesus died for my sins. I'm so happy that I can be with you some day. There are some things that are bothering me that I have to find out about. Maybe I'll ask Daddy when Luke's not around because I don't want him to know that I'm finding out things he doesn't want me to know. I missed you so.

My chance to ask Daddy came one evening right after supper when Luke rushed up to play ball with Forrest. Daddy was enjoying a second piece of Ma's good apple pie.

"Is it really true everyone's a sinner?"

"That's right. Everyone falls short of the glory of God. Jesus came to save us all from sin."

"Is Jesus really God's son?"

"Yes, God's only begotten Son. The Bible says, 'For God so loved the world, that he gave his only begotten Son, that whosoever believeth in him should not perish, but have everlasting life.'"

"Like Aunt Carrie has in heaven?"

"That's right. God sacrificed his son so that all who accept him as their Savior are saved and go to heaven."

Daddy looked extremely pleased with this conversation. Ma got up from the table and went out to the garden. That took some of the pleasure from Daddy's face.

"What's sacrifice?"

"When you give away something that means a lot to you."

"But Jesus is back up in heaven with God all safe and sound with His Father where God wants him to be. God didn't really give him away."

"I see what you mean...God sent His Son so He could take the punishment for our sins, and all we have to do is believe Jesus was crucified and suffered on the cross for our sins."

"If God wanted us to be good, why did He put that tree in the garden in the first place?"

"God wants us to freely choose Him. To love Him with all our heart, soul and mind."

"My Sunday School teacher says it's a sin to be selfish and prideful. Doesn't that mean God is selfish if he wants me to love him more than I do Aunt Carrie, when she was so good to me, and was never selfish?"

"You must learn to fear God and never question the Bible, or the fires of hell will be your reward."

"What's crucified?"

"The people of Jesus time nailed him to a cross and He suffered until He died."

"Did his blood run out?"

"Yes."

"Is that, washed in his blood?"

"That's it, Josephine. You're exactly right."

"Oh!"

I left the table slowly, but as soon as I was in the living room, I ran upstairs, slide the bolt on the bedroom door and flung myself onto the bed.

Aunt Carrie, I don't want anyone to die because of my sins. I don't want to be washed in blood. How could God send His own Son to be killed? I don't think I can like anyone who'd do that. Even Ma, who is still a heathen and doesn't love me, wouldn't do that. She would turn this family upside down to keep Luke from hurting me, and he's saved. Did God really want His Son killed? Didn't God say it was a sin to kill? Are you really in heaven? Did you get a bath in Jesus' blood? I'm not sure I want to go to heaven even if you are there if it means God had to kill His Son because of my sins. I don't want to go to heaven that bad, even if you are there. I'd rather go to hell when I die if Daddy and Aunt Alma are right. I hope you can send me a sign because I don't see any other way out. I wish I was one of the heathens that had never heard of Jesus.

These revelations disturbed me so greatly I refused to go to church with the Stanleys. Ma didn't seem to mind. She put me to work in the garden picking beans to can. Mrs. Stanley was upset and kept asking me if something was troubling me. She must have talked to Rev. Grey because I was playing with Snooks behind the woodshed when Rev. Grey stopped by. Ma was in the garden.

"Hello." He called as he came across the lawn. "How about I give you a hand."

"Hello." Ma stood up and stretched her back.

"Weeding's good for the soul," he said.

Ma laughed. "I'll keep that in mind."

"Now, Clara."

"Couldn't resist." Ma was smiling, pleased that she had goaded him to respond.

"I must say, you certainly know how to coax this garden into producing something other than stones."

"It's a challenge. You know, the more the challenge…" Ma kept up her tease.

"Whoa…we're way past this…you're not a challenge…" He started to laugh too.

"Got you again."

"You sure did."

"Whoosh," Ma said. "The heat's almost got me."

Smiling with his hands extended in an open gesture, he said, "Isn't friendship wonderful?"

After some minutes of weeding in silence, Rev. Grey asked, "What's with Josephine, she hasn't been in church lately. We all miss her and the children's choir isn't the same. Mrs. Stanley says she's not acting herself these days, and she's worried too. Any ideas about what could be bothering her?"

"Not really. I've had it out with Luke. He's been avoiding her…..well, now, maybe it was that talk she had with Paul. It was right after that she started skipping church."

"A talk with Paul? Was she being punished for something?"

"Punished?" Ma laughed, "Maybe she was unknowingly, in a roundabout way. But, she hadn't done anything, only asked about sin and salvation. I don't think she has the stomach for theology. She's too reasonable in her thinking, and has never been taught you can't be reasonable."

"I'm not going to touch that one! Only to say, hell and damnation are not fit for children, to my way of thinking."

"Let's go on in the house…whew…the sun's too hot out here. Could you stay for lunch?"

"No thanks to lunch, but I'd like to talk to Josephine before I leave."

Ma lead the way into the house, and their conversation faded away. Ma knew how to joke! My mind spun. Rev. Grey came to see me. There was too much to think about. Could he help? In a few minutes, he called to me from the back porch.

"I've missed seeing you at church and everyone's asking about you. Is everything alright?"

I wanted to come right out and ask him about what Daddy told me, but I said, "Ma's pretty busy these days, what with canning and everything."

"I'm sure she would be happy to let you go to church. I miss you. Choir's not the same without you. Everyone misses you and asked me to come see how you are. Is there anything about church bothering you? Maybe I can help."

"No. Well, sort'a. Did Jesus die on the cross?"

"Yes, he did, but that's a very complicated story meant for grown ups."

"Not according to Daddy and True Faith."

"That is true. Not everyone agrees on these things. That's why we have more than one church. There's more than one way to worship and learn about God. Each one of us must find the way that helps us understand God. We're all very different with different ideas."

"But there's only one God?"

"That's true."

"That's what I thought." I felt pretty glum because Rev. Grey had no answers.

Later Matt tried to cheer me up with a game of tiddlywinks, but I was so troubled, I couldn't concentrate. I was trying to visualize hell's fiery pit, washed in blood was easy to imagine.

Mark was hanging on the hem of Ma's dress, following every step she took as she prepared lunch. In exasperation she sputtered, "Josephine, could you and Matt take Mark outside, or I'll never get this lunch on the table?"

"Yes, Ma. Come on Matt."

Good. That would get my mind off all the gory things tumbling around in my brain. Mark was always on the move, and watching him outside was a full time job Ma seldom trusted to anyone. I threw the ball and it rolled toward the road. Matt quickly ran and stopped the ball, but Mark kept right on going toward the road, his fat little legs churning. Luke was on his way from the barn and saw me running to catch Mark.

"Witch face creep, you better keep him out'a the road. That's one thing even your Ma will get you for. You remember this, she doesn't write the rules for who gets into heaven. You'll get your punishment, Yo-yo-deee-oo-whooo-whoo, dumbbell."

I hugged Mark's baby beautiful body close in my arms for comfort as I carried him to the safety of the backyard. Matt ran along behind me saying, "Don't pay any tension to Luke. He's a old meany. Yo, don't cry." I knew Luke was right; I'd always be a heathen if I had to be washed in blood. There were tears on my cheeks, but I wasn't crying.

That night, my dreams were so troubled I was restless in my sleep. Ma had to push me to my side of the bed. I was afraid to go back to sleep. Ma heard me crying. "Josephine," she actually stroked my back, "go to sleep. It'll pass in time. You're safe now." I wanted to roll over and hug her, but I knew Ma had crossed a line that only she could cross. Still I was comforted in a way that brought sleep and the strange and wonderful dream that rescued me from torment:

I was sitting beneath the huge old maple at the corner of our driveway when I saw a young boy my age dressed in a mid-calf burlap smock and sandals with wrappings of raw hide around his ankles. His long black hair was blowing in the soft breeze. I was compelled to run to his side, and I started walking up the driveway with him. He turned, looking directly into my eyes, and asked, "Do you know who I am?"

I nodded. "You're Jesus."

"That's right. I wasn't sure you would know me. Look at me. I have hair just like yours. Your eyes are like looking into my own. See, we are very much alike. I don't think we're ugly."

I studied him very closely, and it was true. We did look quite a lot alike.

"Your Aunt Carrie has told me you are her 'little sweetheart.' She told me about you and how much you loved each other. Love IS the true test as Mrs. Stanley said."

"Oh, thank you, thank you. I asked for a sign. Did you die on the cross?"

"Yes, but think hard…what did I say to God?"

We walked, and I thought, and thought. I had to remember. I couldn't believe it, Jesus was right there with me, walking under the apple tree that hung out over the driveway that had Luke's tin can telephone up in its branches.

"I know. You said, 'forgive them, Father, for they know not what they do.'"

"That's right, they do not know…"

I turned to look at him, and he was gone. The driveway was empty. When I awoke in the morning, I felt light as a feather, and I knew, I'd go to heaven. And, Aunt Carrie was right and Mrs. Stanley was right, and not Aunt Alma, and not Daddy, and not Luke.

My dream was a lifeboat in the sea of religiosity that swirled around me. It was the buffer that kept me safe, helped me measure and make allowances for the inconsistencies in the adult world. Now, I was a confirmed believer. Doubt seldom reared its ugly head to confront me. Occasionally, a bible story would trouble me such as Noah and the flood. I was sure there was a great flood, and Noah built an ark. My logic couldn't explain how Noah managed to reach Africa and herd all those big animals back to his ark. How could he carry that much food? Some animals only ate other animals and would have to be kept from eating the ones he was going to save. I decided Noah must have taken only the animals from his valley, because he thought his valley was the whole world, and told the story that way. The rainbow was God's sign to Noah that the flood was over, not that God wouldn't flood the world again because there had been floods since then. I quickly learned it was better not to ask questions because it made grown-ups uncomfortable, and they looked at me strangely. I learned to be very good at mental gymnastics that kept grown-ups happy and me a believer. I knew the answer to the true test right from Jesus. I never told anyone about my dream because I didn't want to be a bragger or too prideful.

***

Without Luke and Forrest, school was a different place. Yo, stuck as my nickname. Mark would run around the house singing, "Pay-O, pay-O, pay-O," with Matt right behind him, "No, Mark. It's, play, Yo…..Yo, Mark," to no avail. At school, no one called me witch face any more, and Luke wasn't there to carry stories home about how stupid I was. I was thrilled and surprised when Forrest still had me bring my reading lesson home.

To my surprise, Luke's marks went down and Forrest's went up. Forrest told Luke he'd better start doing his homework before he came to class, or he'd get way behind and be in trouble. Luke said he'd never had to do schoolwork at home before, and he wasn't going to start. Forrest said he'd better get used to it, that high school required it no matter how smart you were. I'm sure it was a rude awakening for Luke to face competition with so many bright students. Forrest was used to working for his grades, so it was easy for him to make the transition. Luke was popular, as usual, and wanted to have a good time.

He decided copying Forrest's homework was the answer until Mrs. Stanley put a stop to that. I was in the backroom when I heard her say, "Forrest, you better keep Luke from copying your homework, or I will."

"Gees, Mom, a lot of kids do their homework together."

"Which will it be?"

"Aw, all right."

"Enough said."

"Gees, Mom."

Luke's charms may not have worked to pave the way to scholastic excellence, but where the girls were concerned it was a different story. The sheer size of his new arena of pretty girls to impress, despite the added competition from a larger array of smart and talented guys, though none more handsome, must have been like a kid in a toy store. It made him drunk with power, and even more distasteful to me, partly because Forrest still couldn't see past his charms.

He constantly teased Forrest about the new girl, Linda, who lived in Isabel's old house. "Woody, you should hide those cow eyes, or everyone'll think you're jealous cause...Lind-a...sits with me on the bus."

I knew what cow eyes meant and didn't like Forrest seeing Linda that way, but I still didn't want Luke to get the better of Forrest. Neither did I want Forrest sitting with Linda, especially after I saw her. Sometimes Luke would bring Linda by the Stanley's for a visit while I was still up there finishing my chores, and I could see why Forrest was jealous. She was beautiful, not the same kind of pretty Abbey was, all sweet and pure. She was a magnet, radiant and fascinating. Her flame colored hair was wild and wavy like fire licking around her face and shoulder. Her green eyes were large as marbles, and she had pointy breasts that she wiggled around at Luke and Forrest. Her charismatic sparkle drew your eyes to her against your will. She was like flypaper to flies or honey to bees. Of course, I was jealous, because I knew I could never measure up to Linda.

When Linda came walking down the road with her friend, Maryanne, from down in Tate Town, Luke was out our door fast. I'd rushed over to hang over the fence to see if Forrest was going to come out to visit with them.

Once Luke called out to me, "Everyone knows you're a rubberneck pea-green bastard."

"I'm going to tell Daddy what you said."

"I dare you to. Who do you think he'll believe?"

One day when I was finishing up my chores, Mrs. Stanley said, "On your way home, Josephine, tell Forrest supper's on the table."

The three of them were sitting on the stonewall at the foot of the Stanley's side yard. Linda sat in the middle and leaned first on one and then the other as she laughed and flirted.

As I started down the road I called out, "Supper's on, Forrest."

Luke called after me, "Woody's too old for you, jealous jellybean. Earn your quarter this week, super midget?"

Linda laughed and gave Luke a playful jab. "Luke, you're too funny."

Forrest tried to smooth it over with, "Bye, Yo, see you tomorrow."

I clinched my fist and wanted to scream.

I can't help it, Aunt Carrie, I hate Luke. I know you'd say I shouldn't hate a saved person, but I just can't help it. It's not fair for him to be so mean and be saved, and it's not fair for Linda to be so pretty. I don't think God is always fair!

I decided Linda could give Luke a taste of his own medicine, and I couldn't help myself, I hoped she would. "Birds of a feather, flock together" was another Aunt Alma saying. Luke and Linda were definitely of a feather. Except, Aunt Alma or Daddy would never have allowed them in the same nest!

Daddy most decidedly wasn't going to allow it. He said, "You bring Linda to church, or stop hanging around her. If I don't miss my bet, Satan has a firm grip on her. You watch out, son; Satan has his ways."

"I think I have her talked into coming, Daddy. If I can just spend a little extra time with her, I'm sure I can talk her into accepting Jesus as her Savor."

"Good for you, Luke. Wednesday night would be a good start when she can hear all the testimonies."

"Just what I was thinking."

Chapter 7

That following summer of 1938 when I was nine years old, Daddy became panicky about the possibility of not having enough money for Luke's education. In three short years he'd be going off to college.

Daddy emphatically declared, "By George, Luke's not going to be one of those ministers ordained by a congregation. He's going to be college educated...someone to be looked up to...someone with authority."

Consequently, Daddy urged him to accept all the available work Mr. Stanley could give him. That was a rude awakening for Luke.

"But Daddy, you know I don't like farm work."

"Never you mind. You're one in a million. The Lord has laid his hands on you...blessed you with a special calling, and I'll do whatever it takes to see to it you're prepared for the Lord's biding." It pained Daddy to be at cross purposes with Luke, and he bemoaned, "It's a pity, that you have to lower yourself to do manual labor, but what must be borne, must be borne. Remember, the Lord works in mysterious ways, His wonders to behold... His will be done, you know that, son."

Luke made no attempt to hide his aversion to the work necessary to bring the Lord's, or more accurately Daddy's, biding into fruition, but he puffed up like a peacock as he lapped up the praise with a smug smile on his face, not because he wanted the cloistered life Daddy was planning for him, but because he knew how little it made the rest of us feel.

192

My feelings toward Daddy were becoming more and more confusing, and kept me on edge. I still couldn't help being afraid of him because he was so righteously stern. He did care about me, and he worried about my salvation and was never mean to me. Still, his concern failed to be a comfort. What came through to me was, the not so subtle message: I wasn't good enough. My insecurity screamed: how dare I doubt Daddy, who was such a good strong believer, who did such good honest work for the Stanleys, who cared about me, who never bothered Ma with "dirty stuff", and who treated her kindly even though she was a heathen.

Aunt Alma was always harping that no one could compare to the righteousness of a "dyed in the wool" True Faither, and Daddy was definitely a True Faith believer. I wished Jesus had come right out and said Daddy and True Faith were wrong, and the watered-down Methodists and Rev Grey were right. They both couldn't be right, could they? It was crucial that I know because it was my fault Ma and I couldn't go to heaven. I'd never get to see Aunt Carrie again. Jesus did tell me Mrs. Stanley was on the right side because she knew love was the true test, but I didn't love God in the same way True Faithers did. And I didn't love Luke or Aunt Alma.

Aunt Carrie, I just can't love Luke and Aunt Alma even though she is your sister. Can you see how it is? Daddy gives all his love to Luke. Ma gives all her love to Matt and Mark and you're not here. That makes me left out. Does God know what I'm thinking? I hope not because I'm still mad at Him for sending Jesus to take you to heaven. Does that make me a bad person? It's not Matt and Mark's fault Ma loves them, and not me, and I truly do love them even though I'm jealous. It seems to me Jesus shouldn't leave so much up to us to figure out. Bet you know all the answers to everything. I try so hard to keep these thoughts out of my mind. Did you send Jesus down to talk to me in my dream? It was wonderful to see him. Without His help I'd be lost for sure. I think I love God even though I'm mad

He took you away from me, because He made the world so beautiful.

***

Abbey wanted to earn money for college and was hired to work at the cosmetic counter in WOOLWORTH'S. With her Coca Cola pinup beauty, I could see why she was given that job. She would make everyone want to buy something to make themselves as pretty as she was. Now the Stanley's car began to go out the road to Phelpsburg every day except Sunday because, of course, stores were closed on Sunday in honor of the Lord's Day.

Ma said, "See, Luke, Abbey has to work and save money for college too." She thought that would make him feel better.

But he whined, "If you call driving to Phelpsburg everyday to work in a store, work."

He was beginning to thaw a little toward Ma. He could see how the whole family depended on her. The house had never run as smoothly, and her candy money made all the difference. Ma's little kitchen business now reached all the way down to Phelpsburg, via Aunt Alma, who of course, was interested in promoting anything that benefited her "country family". Ma's enterprise was fast turning into more than just a candy business. She made pies and cakes, decorated for special events, and whatever a customer wanted to order. Her hands were never idle, as Rev. Grey had said. Aunt Alma, despite her obvious pleasure, withheld her praise but wore her own arm out patting herself on the back, claiming responsibility for the expansion of the business to Phelpsburg. I suppose, in fairness, without her connections to the old Sweet Shop clientele, and her church friends, taking the business to Phelpsburg would have been much more difficult.

My days were full. With Abbey working in town, I did more and

194

more of her chores, almost like I was part of their family. I now earned a dollar a week, and thought I was rich. Plus, Ma kept me busy every minute I wasn't up at the Stanley's, weeding the garden or picking whatever was ready. I didn't realize how useful all that knowledge and my dollars were going to be in the future. I was like the King in the counting room counting out his money; with that thought, I laughed. Aunt Alma was the Queen in the kitchen eating bread and honey, and I wished a black bird would come along and snip off her nose!

The fire in the big old black cook stove never went out between Ma's canning and the candy business. Candles drooped in the kitchen heat, and Ma continually mopped her face to keep her sweat from dripping into her cooking pots. The shade of the maples out front provided the only relief. But for them, sleeping would have been impossible. We opened the doors and all the windows, letting the ever present hill top westerly breeze blow through the house, carrying a goodly portion of the kitchen heat along with it.

I could see that Forrest was changing. For one thing, he started to shave the fine peachy fuzz from his face, and his voice deepened to a mellow bass. He began to look almost as grown up as Luke, only much shorter.

I have to admit, Luke did work hard that summer. He wanted to out-shine Forrest because he was bigger and, he thought, stronger. Stronger though, was definitely debatable. Forrest had always worked hard, and was steadier and could outdistance him in endurance. Unaware of the contest, Forrest was right there to say how great Luke was. I wished I could think that it was Forrest's way of tricking Luke into working hard, but it wasn't. He was blind where his friend was concerned, and he was too well adjusted to be threatened. Yes, I was jealous.

At nine, I was old enough to see that Luke had real charm, and I could see why everyone liked him and had a good time when he was around; everyone except me. There was no doubt that he still hated me, maybe even more, now that Ma had laid the law down and I was out of his reach. I was becoming more self confident, but I still never let my guard down which aggravated him. His insults stung as much as ever, but I hoped he couldn't tell, because I'd fling right back at him, "Whatever you say I am, you are."

I studied Luke as he watched Ma's outpouring of love to both his little brothers who were thriving, and it was obvious he wished he had played his cards differently, but Ma would never be a real friend to him. There was no way he could fool her. On the surface, she was friendly and treated him fairly. Underneath she kept their relationship guarded, warding off his attempts to test her resolve.

I was glad Matt was crowding Luke with his good marks. He would be starting the second grade when school started in the fall. Aunt Alma bragged he was taking to school like "a duck to water."

Ma had been so proud when Matt brought his final first grade report card home that she gave him a dollar to spend any old way he pleased. "Now, go show that report card to your daddy."

Daddy had ruffed-up Matt's hair. "Looks like you're following in your big brother's footsteps with these marks, little man."

Luke had given Matt a push. "Don't get too big for your britches, little squirt."

At that moment, Matt must have remembered that day in the woodshed, just as I did. That's what Luke wanted him to remember and feel belittled. He couldn't let Matt have one little slice of Daddy's approval. That bugged me because Luke would always be daddy's favorite, no matter what.

***

When one of the women from True Faith came to pick up a birthday cake she had ordered, she asked Ma if she would consider helping with their harvest dinner.

Ma was caught off guard, and answered, "Well, I guess I could do that."

With all her experience in the Sweet Shop, her abilities were obvious and much appreciated, and True Faith worshipers began to speculate, "Sooner or later, Paul's going to convince Clara to convert. Mark my words."

They had taken note and appreciated how devoted she was to Matt and Mark. They no longer thought her good looks had had undo influence on Daddy's judgment, though there were still whispers about the dark-complexioned daughter she and Daddy allowed to go to the Methodist Church. Behind Daddy's back, Luke whispered, "Daddy's too naive to know how people gossip." Even at that age I knew he was laughing at Daddy.

Now that Ma had helped with the harvest dinner, Daddy was more hopeful than ever that Ma would see the light, and accept Jesus as her personal savior. What if she didn't? Jesus said Mrs. Stanley had the right idea, but could I be saved if Ma wasn't? Rev. Grey was Ma's special friend and a minister too, even if he was a watered-down Methodist, and he didn't think Ma needed saving. He didn't think she would be shut out of heaven. I was still haunted about who was right, Daddy or Rev. Grey? There still lingered the nagging suspicion, that maybe, due to my real daddy and Luke, that somehow, there was something wrong with Ma and me.

All the many hours I spent with the Stanleys slowly wore away my doubts. Their love gradually filled the void left by Aunt Carrie's death and the loss of the unconditional love she had lavished on me. My immediate need to join Aunt Carrie in heaven faded into obscurity. I tucked my doubts away in my subconscious, and I kept my talk with Jesus ever present in my mind and a secret where it was safe.

My snug little world with my new found security continued all that next school year and all through the next summer. Abbey worked again at WOOLWORTH'S in Phelpsburg. Luke continued to work on the farm, with the renewed protest about the unfairness of working and not being allowed to spend any of his earnings.

Forrest tried to make light of it. "Heck, Luke, aren't you too tired to spend it?"

"You know me, Woody, old man. I'm never too tired for some things."

"Yeah, yeah."

But the guys were too tired to walk down to Tate Town, so Linda and Mary Ann often ventured up in the evening to listen to records and dance. Seeing Forrest socialize with girls his own age tormented me with jealousy. To make matters worse, it was obvious Forrest really didn't care for Mary Ann in "that way"; he liked Linda too. Despite my jealousy, it burned me to see Forrest play second fiddle to Luke, and Luke's obvious pleasure in lording it over him. Even Mary Ann only pretended to like Forrest. She really wanted Luke. This was a mystery beyond my comprehension. Forrest was far superior to Luke in every way unless not wearing glasses, being six feet tall with curly cinnamon brown hair and cinnamon brown eyes made you superior. I preferred the cut of Forrest's strong jaw tanned all bronze in contrast to his sun-bleached almost white hair and blue eyes. He was solid with an air of sincerity about him that made people seek his opinion. No one sought Luke's, though everyone congregated around him because they knew he was the life of the party and would show them a good time which was in sharp contrast to the way Daddy saw Luke. Daddy was just never going to tumble to Luke's duplicity.

I heard it whispered many times, "When Luke's a minister, he's going to charm them right down to the altar instead of scaring folks to death. What'll his daddy think about that?"

Poor Sally was left out altogether except for the slips that clued me in that it was not Linda who Luke sneaked out his bedroom window to visit; it was Sally. Linda was too smart to be easy, and had been clever enough to start attending True Faith.

Daddy praised, "Look what Luke's done for Linda. She's a True Faith believer." Then he turned to Luke and warned, "Don't you go tempting Satan. There's no time in the Lord's plans for you to marry for some years."

"Don't worry, Daddy, she's not the girl for me. Marriage is the last thing on my mind."

Linda was on his mind though. She was the girl he couldn't seduce, plus she was the girl Forrest was crazy about. I couldn't tell which of these facts had the greater allure for Luke. She was the prettiest girl I had ever seen, and she knew just how to make every boy think, maybe, just maybe he could win her love, but she held them all at bay to wonder. I figured it was only a matter of time until she gave in to Luke. Marriage might not have been in Luke's mind, but I think it was very much in Linda's plans.

***

It was hard for me to remember those days when I was cooped-up in the Sweet Shop apartment with no clue that there were other worlds out there, waiting to be discovered. The country and its embracing beauty was so much a part of me that it felt as though it always had been.

Ma had also gone through a gradual transformation. It was not only that her sandy-blonde hair was always loose and curly around her face. Matt and Mark had kissed away all her worry lines, and Rev. Grey's friendship had made her eyes shine. Occasionally, his car still turned into our driveway, but there were so many other things taking up my time and thoughts, I was never lucky enough to be upstairs with my face pressed over the grate.

As Thanksgiving approached, Ma decided we should spend the day with just our family because the Stanleys were having Mr. Stanley's brothers and their families for a visit. Daddy said he thought it would be nice to spend the day by ourselves. We didn't do that often enough.

Luke protested, "Why can't Clara cook for everyone? It'd be nothing for her. Now I won't get to see Forrest's cousins."

Daddy lifted his eyebrows. "Luke, I'm surprised at you. Clara has her hands full enough. You know that. Besides, they need time to enjoy family they don't see all that often."

Hurray! I thought, for once, Daddy corrected Luke in favor of Ma. Maybe there was hope!

Monday Mrs. Stanley began cooking up a storm, and after school I dug into the cleaning. She wanted everything to be just so for Mr. Stanley's family. Tuesday I hurried home to help open-up the dining room table, but Mrs. Stanley was feeling so poorly, she said, "Abbey'll be home from college tomorrow. It'll keep til then." Wednesday shortly after my arrival, Mrs. Stanley became so ill, that while I was feeding Snooks, always my first task before I started my chores, Abbey called to me.

"Jo, come quick! Go to the barn and find Daddy. Tell him to drop everything; Mom needs a doctor! Hurry, hurry. Tell him to just go. Tell him her pulse is all funny; she's sweaty and has pain up her arm and up her neck; I've given her an aspirin, and she's in bed propped up on pillows. Can you remember all that....should I write it down?"

"I'll remember."

Mr. Stanley ran to the car and raced the mile down to Tate Town where the central telephone switchboard was located in the Spencer residence. This was the only way outlying farms near picturesque small farming towns had access to a telephone.

It took forever before the doctor, black bag in hand, stepped into the front hall. Mr. Stanley hurried Dr. Miller upstairs while Abbey, Forrest and I sat long-faced down in the kitchen afraid to voice our concerns. Finally we heard Dr. Miller's and Mr. Stanley's footsteps on the stairs.

"Fred, your wife has had a heart attack. Abbey, you used excellent judgment and did all the right things. Maybe you should change your mind and become a nurse....I've written out thorough instructions and left medication. I'll be around tomorrow morning after hospital rounds. Plan a quiet Thanksgiving, no excitement."

***

Luke got his wish, Ma cooked Thanksgiving dinner. Mr. Stanley's family postponed their visit until spring when Mrs. Stanley would be feeling better. Everyone kept their voices low and tiptoed around. Ma fixed two trays so Mr. Stanley could share Thanksgiving dinner with Mrs. Stanley in their bedroom. No one was allowed to visit her until late in the afternoon while Daddy was driving Aunt Alma home. Ma was clever. She knew Aunt Alma would be the wrong kind of visitor. Abbey went in first, then Forrest, then Ma and I went in together. I was only allowed to stay long enough to say, "I hope you'll feel better soon, Mrs. Stanley." That sad Thanksgiving we all prayed the same prayer as Mrs. Stanley's life hung in the balance.

Sunday, on the doctor's fifth visit, he announced that Mrs. Stanley's condition was stable; her heart would mend with bed rest. Six months was advised, which he said would take patience and cooperation from the whole family.

Mrs. Stanley insisted it would be too stressful to her if her illness interfered with Abbey's education. Reluctantly, Abbey gave in with the understanding she would come home at a moment's notice if her mother's condition worsened. Before Abbey left, I moved in up at the Stanley's.

"After all," Daddy said, "she practically lives up there anyway."

Ma thought I was more than capable of getting breakfast before I left for school, and with a little help from her with planning, I'd be able to prepare supper.

Mr. Stanley said, "I don't know, that seems like a lot to put on a child."

"I can do it. Please, Mr. Stanley, let me try."

Mrs. Stanley said, "I think Josephine can do it, but only if I move downstairs. I can't have everyone running up and down. I need to be down in the guestroom."

"Simple enough, I'll carry you." Mr. Stanley never hesitated. "It'll be a little bit hard to pretend we're newlyweds," he kidded as he gently picked her up in his arms. "That's the last time I carried you."

"Don't you go hurting yourself; there's a little more of me to carry now."

"You feel just right in my arms. You're 25 years sweeter, and I'm 25 years stronger." Mr. Stanley winked at Abbey and me as we followed along with our arms full of pillows and blankets.

I was so proud of Ma's trust in my abilities that it felt as if I had captured a piece of her in the skills she had taught me. I rationalized that feeling as Ma's love. There were times that her love felt quite real, and other times when no matter how hard I tried, reality won.

Because winter was the slack time on the farm, Mr. Stanley was able to stay in the house after breakfast and take care of Mrs. Stanley until I returned from school. I was able to look after her as I prepared supper. After supper, Forrest helped me with the dishes, and insisted I practice my spelling as we worked. In my imagination I was not a little sister. We were in a foreign country, blissfully married, looking after the kidnapped queen until she could be rescued and put back on her rightful throne. After dishes he did his homework in Mrs. Stanley's room.

Luke was pressured into helping out with the evening barn chores in Forrest's place, again with a loud protest at how unfair it was. He was so upset Daddy soothed, "I know, Luke. Gosh a'mighty, think of the money you can save for your calling, your preparation for the Lord's work. But have no fear; never has anyone been more of a natural talent, my boy. You're a wonder." At this point Daddy resorted to another one of Aunt Alma's sayings, "'There's never a loss but what there's a gain.' With all this extra money coming in and another year to go, you'll have plenty for college."

Matt said, "Then we can start saving for me."

Ma answered, "Of course we will, Matt. Then for Mark."

Mark bobbed his head in an emphatic, yes, "I'll be smarter'n Luke."

Daddy scowled; Ma laughed, "That's right, we have three smarty-pants in this family."

I was not included. This was one of those times when reality rushed in. It was better to feel nothing. I took the bag of groceries Ma had purchased for the Stanleys and walked up the road. I guessed Ma figured I'd not be going to college; I wasn't smart. I'd become another homemaker-caregiver like her. I tried to make that feel like something, but couldn't.

To salve my bruised soul, I pretended I was a long lost cousin of the Stanleys and was welcomed into their family with open arms. Sometimes, I was bold enough to imagine it would soon be discovered that I was in reality the rightful heir to their farm. I would play out in great detail the scene in which I gave the farm to Forrest, who would then recognize how much I loved him, and how much he loved me. In my less favorite imaginings, I was an orphan like Ma, and the Stanleys adopted me. I knew these were fantasies, but they gave me great comfort.

***

That spring, just as Mrs. Stanley was finally allowed to leave her bed and join the family, our lives changed in an unexpected way. Rev. Grey announced that he would be transferred to a new parish. I cried and Mrs. Stanley had tears in her eyes as she explained, "That's the way Methodists do it. The minister has to go where he's sent."

I wished I could talk to Ma about it because I knew she must be very sad. Something inside me had to see them together one more time. I wanted to know if Rev. Grey had been Daddy's miracle. I had to know if Ma was saved. My slumbering doubt continually reared its ugly head. It was crucial I be upstairs looking through the grate when he came to say goodbye.

Aunt Carrie, I need to know if Rev. Grey has been Ma's miracle as Daddy hoped. I need to know if Ma's saved .because I want her to go to heaven even though she doesn't love me. I'll feel like it's my fault if she doesn't. I'm really sorry my being born ruined her life. You can see how looking through the grate is important. It's the only way I ever get to know anything about Ma. So would you ask Jesus to help me because I'm never down at Ma's when Rev. Grey comes? If God lets Jesus help me, I'll know it's a sign from God that it's Ok because I know looking through the grate is stealing their privacy. Matt and Mark don't have to be nosey. They have all of Ma, all the time. I feel you watching over me. I still love you.

God's sign came when I saw Rev. Grey's car turn into Ma's driveway. I was on my way to the barn to get milk, one of my daily chores. Ma and Matt waved to Rev. Grey from the garden.

I quickly ran into the barn and left my milk pail, ran on out the south end of the barn and up to the front porch. Ma was on the back porch telling Matt to keep on weeding; she'd be back out in a few minutes. I hurried up the stairs where Mark was sleeping soundly. I was under the bed with my face over the grate by the time they reached the living room. They sat down next to each other on the sofa.

"I can see Matt's your right-hand helper these days now that Josephine's up at the Stanley's. I don't know what they'd have done without the two of you."

"It did work out quite well. Josephine's a good little worker and very responsible."

Rev. Grey finished, "And loving, and kind."

"Yes. I know she is. I'm proud of her. The Stanleys would like her to stay with them permanently. May's health's going to be fragile for some time, and she's happier up there than she is here. They've made her one of the family. I've about decided it's best."

Aunt Carrie, Ma's proud of me. That makes me so happy. Is that why God let Jesus help me be up here so I could know that? I'll bet you knew it. If only you could tell me what you know.

"Clara, is it best for you?"

"Probably not. But, I haven't been able to make love happen. She deserves more than I can give her. I want so much for her to be whole....in the way I'm unable to be."

When I heard Ma say that, I knew she would never love me, and my need for her love was so strong it obliterated the knowledge that she wanted more for me. As much as I had always wanted to live with the Stanleys, I wanted Ma's love more. Tears sprung out from beneath my eyelids and streamed down my cheeks. The sobs, that I couldn't give vent to, shook my soul and nearly strangled me.

Aunt Carrie, I need you; I need you. Ma is proud of me, but I want her love… like she does Matt and Mark. Why, why are things the way they are?

I had to get hold of myself and listen; Rev. Grey was continuing. "Clara, Clara, is anyone totally whole? Everyone is continually growing and changing. You've come such a long way. You're one of the most special people in my world."

There was a long pause while Ma fiddled with the doily on the arm of the sofa, and Rev. Grey kept twisting the wedding ring he still wore.

"Marshall, you don't have to search any longer for a way to tell me. I know why you've come."

Rev. Grey stood up and took Ma's hand. "Yes, I've come to say goodbye."

Ma stood up.

"Oh, Clara," his arms opened.

To my surprise, Ma walked right into them, pressed her face against his shoulder, but I was able to see her expression clearly. Her face was dreamy and registered the nearness of him as if she needed to drink in his essence to store it for future reference. She closed her eyes. His cheek rested on her hair.

He asked, "How long have you known?"

"A week."

They stood this way for some moments, swaying slightly almost as if dancing to music audible only to them. Then they pulled apart and studied each other intently for a few more seconds.

"Oh, Marshall, you don't need to say a word."

I could barely hear his answer. "This is very hard for me."

"I'll be all right.....Has there been talk? Is that why they're reassigning you to another parish?"

"No way. I'd know, believe me, I'd know. Some parishioners would be only too happy to inform me of such gossip, and the D.S. would be rabid......Are you sure you'll be all right? Can I count on that?"

"Yes, as much as we can count on anything. I'm content."

"Is happy too much to hope for?"

"Contentment is the bigger part of happy. I feel secure, really secure. Think, you've been my friend for four years....May, for four years, and Paul too. I haven't known, or been known, by anyone that long that I can call friend, except for the aunts, and they don't count."

"Clara, how sad that sounds. But yes, it has been four years. We're soul mates."

"Yeah, for me it's kind'a like finding out who I am, how can you know if there's no one to show you?"

"Just believe me. I know who you are. You're a wonderful friend."

They fell back into each other's arms. Their lips never touched, but between them vibrated a look of pure love, better than a kiss.

They stood facing each other still holding hands. Ma said, "How can I tell you how much I'll miss you? I owe you so much. I'm actually going to special events at True Faith. Think of that. Paul is so pleased."

"Who knows what might be next?"

"That's it, on all scores."

He hesitated, letting that pass. "You'd be surprised at how many people sit in church and are only there in body. They're someplace else, holding their own service."

"I can't believe you said that."

"I'm a realist. Not a complete dreamer."

"That could never be the answer for me. Who'd I be then?"

"Well, Clara, I'd never want you to be other than who you are.

Never doubt that."

"I do know that."

"It'd be a whole lot better world if there were more as honest as you; then, maybe those of us behind the pulpit would have to be more honest too. You've made me grow in my faith. Very much, in new ways that makes me a better pastor."

Ma threw her arms around Rev. Grey's neck. That really shocked me! She pressed her cheek against his. "Without you, I don't know where I'd be. Thank you, for being you."

He returned the hug and they stepped apart, "We'll keep in touch. I'll always let you know where I am."

"Yes, we'll write and send cards, all special holidays. That's what friends do."

They held hands for an instant longer, he kissed her forehead; and then, he was gone.

Even though I didn't understand all the subtle nuances of their conversation, there were fresh tears running down my cheeks. Ma stood at the door for some minutes, watching his car until it disappeared up the road in a cloud of dust. I waited until I heard her banging pots and pans in the kitchen as if noise would drive her sadness away, then I slipped down the stairs and out the front door.

***

Rev. Grey's transfer was the incident that earmarked the time there was a big turn-around in my life. One emotional hurtle piled on top of another. His impending move tore at our hearts. A member of our church family was being taken from us. And now with Mrs. Stanley well again, Ma had to decide whether to let me continue living with the Stanleys. Moving back to the tenant house, to an atmosphere where I would always be in the periphery of Ma's love, left me with a terrible dread. If only…if only I could hope she would love me, I knew where my first choice would be.

I didn't have to wait long before I had my answer. Mrs. Stanley said, "Clara, thank you so very much for seeing your way clear to let Josephine stay. Fred'll be so relieved; I have a hired girl." Snooks was always at my feet, rubbing around my ankles, making it known she thought that I was right where I belonged. When Abbey wrote she called me "little sister". Sometimes Forrest did too, which wasn't exactly the relationship I had in mind, but I belonged.

I now lived with the family that employed Luke's father, and Luke was, as Aunt Alma would say, "green with envy." It really showed when Mrs. Stanley bragged about what a wonderful addition I was to their family. She even added, "And what a splendid addition she makes to the adult church choir. Her voice is so pure and strong she's even able to sing the solo part."

I could see Luke didn't like it one bit because Daddy was impressed. He said, "Well now, I can see I should never have let those Methodists steal Josephine away."

Ma said, "That's lovely, Josephine."

The first time I sang the solo, I was so scared I didn't think I'd be able to sing a note, but when it was time, my mouth opened, and I heard my voice filling up the church, and all I could see was Mr. and Mrs. Stanley, smiling at me.

I felt very important and grown up in my new dress and grownup style baby-doll patent leather shoes. Mrs. Stanley braided my hair and pinned it up in big loops. That made it look neat and took away the awfulness of its being black and so thick.

I supposed my wonderful new life with the Stanleys was the way Ma felt when she went to live with the Wallaces before I was born and ruined her life. I knew I wasn't ever going to be pretty like Ma, but it still felt like a wonderful new life beginning anyway.

Mark, bless his heart, said, "Why can't Matt and I go to the Methodist Church and sing with Yo? We like singing together."

There was something special about Mark. He sparkled and had an appealing intelligence that won your heart. He had kept his dimples and curly blonde hair and was clearly Ma's favorite, partly because she had raised him up from a baby, but mostly because he was irresistible.

Mrs. Stanley quickly suggested, "Clara, how about I talk Miss Brown into letting the three of them sing together in the school Christmas program? They can practice at my house with the piano. Of course, they won't have one at school, but by then they won't need one."

Ma said, "Christmas's a long ways away. We'll see."

Mrs. Stanley had saved Ma the unpleasant task of telling Mark his daddy would never let him go to the watered-down Methodist Church.

It was wonderful to live in a house where there was love and respect, where no one was left out, even me. I didn't have to listen to Aunt Alma bragging about her perfect grandchildren; where I didn't have to listen to talk about hell and damnation; dire warnings, you never knew at what moment the reckoning would happen. Those not saved by the blood would be left behind. God would turn his face from them, and they would forever burn in the fiery pit of hell. Up at the Stanley's no one ever talked about religion even though they went to church every Sunday. Was that what being watered-down meant? I thought a lot about that question, because as far as I could see, the Stanleys practiced their religion all week without a lot of scare talking during the week. They didn't do any evil stuff, like cuss and swear and drink and smoke. I did suppose dancing after grange cut them a little short in God's eyes because True Faith said dancing was evil, and those members from True Faith left as soon as the grange meeting was over.

I couldn't figure out what was wrong with dancing, so I asked Sally. She knew everything about such things. She said it stirred up carnal desires. I guessed that meant it made the boys think about doing "dirty stuff". But, Luke was the only one I knew of, thinking about that. When Daddy wasn't at the grange meeting, Luke did dance, and very well. Probably that was part of Luke's problem. However, I wondered about that too because dancing didn't have that effect on Forrest.

Christmas finally came and Matt, Mark and I did sing "Jolly Old Saint Nicholas" in the school Christmas program, and Mark stole the show. He was so pleased with himself that everyone, except Daddy, had an extra good time. He didn't like anything that had to do with Santa Claus because it confused children about God. Forrest came, but Luke said he was through with baby things. Daddy gave him permission to go down and visit Linda. That was great, because he didn't dominate the school party with everyone hanging on his every word. We all got to shine.

***

As the school year neared its close, everyone was excited because Abbey would be graduating from Geneseo. It was hard to realize four years had gone by. I was growing up, and Abbey was ready to assume an independent adult life. She had secured a teaching position in Phelpsburg which was perfect. During the summer, she planned to continue working at the cosmetic counter in WOOLWORTH'S and live at home until she could find a room to rent in Phelpsburg.

Plans were made for Mrs. Stanley and me to drive up to Geneseo a couple of days before graduation, a girls' only adventure with Abbey joining us at the Guest House. Mr. Stanley and Forrest were to drive the truck up early graduation day. That way Mr. Stanley and Forrest wouldn't miss as many chores, and Abbey would have the truck to bring all her things home from the dorm.

The afternoon Mrs. Stanley and I were packing, Luke appeared, anxious to listen to records, but he had to stand around and watch Forrest while he finished cleaning the car for our trip.

"Come on, Woody. You work like a snail."

"Grab a rag and give me a hand."

"Only if I get to go too," Luke quipped half joking. As the boys were growing up he had been included in many of the Stanley outings.

Forrest snapped his rag at Luke. "It's going to be a hen's only trip. Mom, Yo and Abbey are going to spend some girl's time together. Dad and I'll drive the truck up later."

When they finally came in, Mrs. Stanley and I were getting our suitcases out, and I don't think Luke liked seeing me packing up to go on a trip with Mrs. Stanley. It made me too much a part of the family. Luke had only one ear tuned in to the music. The other one was listening to Mrs. Stanley.

"Be sure to pack your new dress, and don't forget to put in your patent leather shoes. You'll need your best school dress when we go out to eat."

In a way, I felt sorry for Luke because I knew just how it felt to be left out. He was definitely not used to that. But mostly, I was glad he was the one left out and not me for a change. I supposed, because I lived with the owner of the farm where his father was the hired-man, that it gave me status that was a thorn to his ego, but that meant nothing to me. If Ma had wanted me, I'd have been glad to live anywhere, and I'd even have given up talking to Aunt Carrie for Ma's love. But, I wasn't dumb enough to let Luke know how I felt about any of that.

At first, the drive was exciting. I found my thoughts returning to that first trip up to the country on Ma's wedding day. The car certainly was the magic carpet to new worlds. We saw country, big beautiful farms, and towns filled with people I'd never meet. It made my head swim, trying to cram it all in. I was almost sorry when we finally arrived at the guest house. Before we could get checked in, a young man drove up out front with Abbey in the car, and as they came up the walk they were holding hands.

She looked up at him coyly. "Mom, Jo, I want you to meet Allen Bennett, my special beau."

Allen Bennett was slim and tall with gray eyes and thick straight dish-water blonde hair. He hung back and was a little retiring, not bashful, just really nice.

After a lot of hugging and kissing and catching up on the news, we decided to eat early to miss the crowds. It was the first time I had ever eaten in a restaurant other than the aunts' Sweet Shop.

Abbey put her arm around me. "We won't have to do the dishes, Jo."

"Or cook it!"

"That's right. You sure know about that."

Then Mrs. Stanley told Allen all about my cooking dinner and taking care of her. Allen made out like he couldn't believe how great that was for someone my age. Of course, needless to say, I liked Allen Bennett right off, and Mrs. Stanley did too.

Forrest and Mr. Stanley arrived so early graduation morning they must have started before the chickens were up. Abbey was trying on her cap and gown. Mr. Stanley said, "My little girl, all grown up ready to take on the world." With those sentiments, Mrs. Stanley wiped away a tear.

Allen came in during this exchange. I could see love shining in

Abbey's eyes as she introduced him to Mr. Stanley and Forrest. You would have thought Forrest and Allen had been friends forever the way they hit it off, and Abbey's face shown with pleasure. Mr. Stanley wore his usual happy "I know secrets face," just like he always did, and he hugged Abbey extra long.

As the pomp and ceremony got under way, I felt lonely and isolated because I knew I would never be standing up there receiving a college diploma. Suddenly it occurred to me I would need a college education to belong to Forrest's world. He would want his wife to be a college graduate. Matt and Mark would belong to that special world because they would both go to college. I would be the only one left out. Why was life so unfair? I wished Jesus could make a miracle.

When Abbey walked across the platform to receive her diploma, unhappy thoughts vanished, and we clapped for joy. Soon after, because the name Stanley was near the end of the alphabet, there was a shower of caps filling the air and the ceremony was over.

Plans had already been made to have dinner with Allen's family who were also farmers so it was as if they had known each other forever. To my surprise after dinner they left without Allen. Everyone else knew he was coming home with Abbey for a visit. What else didn't I know?

As Abbey said a tearful goodbye to the last of her friends, Allen's arm went protectively around her shoulder. Mr. Stanley said, "Mom and I'll lead the way. Allen, you and Abbey follow. Forrest and Josephine can be the caboose."

Was I excited, Forrest all to myself for that nice long ride home in the truck. It didn't take me long to decide it was a date. I was glad I still had on my new dress and patent leather shoes. Forrest took off his suit jacket and tie, and laid them over the back of the car-seat, but he still looked sharp in his dress pants and white shirt. If only I were in high school!

Aunt Carrie, aren't I lucky! I hope it's not too sinful to pretend Forrest likes me in the same way I like him when I know he only thinks of me as a little sister. I hope God can tell I know the difference. I don't want Him to think I'm a liar cause it's only make-believe. OK?

Forrest started humming, "'….you could be better than you are……'." I listened quietly, not pleased. "'…….if you hate to go to school, you could grow up to be a mule…….'"

Why was he humming that song? I hated it. Everyone wanted to "carry moonbeams home in jar." I thought he was the only one who thought I was smart. I couldn't help it that I didn't like school. I did wish I could go to college. I knew it was the only way to belong. He probably wondered why I didn't sing along. Anger made my lips clamp together. When they opened what came out was not a sing along.

"Why do you let Luke get the best of you? You're smarter'n Luke, and you know it!"

Forrest's humming stopped; he was irritated. "I don't know it. Where do you get these crazy notions?"

"Your marks are better'n his now he's away from prissy Miss Brown, and he copies your homework."

"That's because he's smarter and doesn't have to cram to pass."

"Come on, Forrest."

"Luke's a special case. He's, well, he's Luke."

"Yeah, you said it."

"Come on now. Don't be hard on Luke. He has it tough at home."

"Yeah, like he can do no wrong. Like, he always gets his way. Like, I feel sorry for Matt. And, you let him walk all over you."

"Come on, Yo. I do no such thing. You know his daddy expects him to be perfect… won't let him out of his sight. How'd you like him for a dad?"

"Well, he is my stepfather, and I did live with him. Isn't he the best hired man you ever had?"

"That's not fair. That has nothing to do with Luke."

"Well, for another thing, Linda's his girl."

"Don't you think I know that?"

"Then why do you want her for your girl too? Mary Ann's nicer."

"I like Mary Ann. She's a good friend. What's got into you anyway?"

"Luke likes to make you jealous, and you don't even know it. And Linda fools around with every guy, trying to make Luke jealous, and you're blind with your eyes open."

"Where do you get these ideas?"

"I've got eyes. I'm not blind."

"Don't you think maybe you're just a little bit prejudiced?"

"If prejudice means I'm on your side, yes. If it means I don't know what I'm talking about, no."

"When you're older you'll understand. I don't expect Linda to like me. Heck, Luke's my best friend. You just can't help noticing Linda. It doesn't mean anything. OK?"

Dancing popped into my mind. "Why does dancing stir up carnal desires in some and not in others?"

Forrest snapped his head around and looked right at me even though he should have had his eyes on the road. "Where in heaven's name do you come up with this nonsense?"

"True Faith says it's evil to dance, so I asked Sally why. She said it stirs up carnal desires. And, she knows."

"What makes you think Sally knows?"

"Don't pretend with me, Forrest Stanley. Everyone knows about Sally, especially your best friend."

"Luke?"

"Yeah, Luke. He dances sometimes when his daddy isn't around, and he sneaks out the bedroom window, and he doesn't go to Linda's; he goes to Sally's."

"That's not true."

"Is to."

"I'd know."

"You do now."

The wind had gone right out of my pretend date. Forrest had a disturbed look on his face. It wasn't my fault his old friend had carnal desires. It was time he knew it, but I wished he'd say something even if he was mad at me for telling him.

"You better ask your Ma about things like that, not Sally."

"I don't live with Ma. I don't want'a talk to her. She doesn't want me." I almost started crying because now Forrest wouldn't want me in his family either. If the Stanleys didn't want me, where would I go?

He reached out his arm and pulled me over next to him. "Yo, your ma was just doing us a favor because we need you. We like you. You're the best little sister in the world. I'm sure your ma would want to talk to you. So would Mom and Abbey, and you know you can talk to me, just like you are now."

He put both hands back on the stirring wheel, and I wished even harder it was a girlfriend hug, but it wasn't. I moved over to my side of the seat and didn't answer. I knew he was wrong about Ma, but I wished it were me who was wrong. Not only that, he never answered my question about carnal desire, and I thought he probably didn't know either.

He started singing, "Oh, Susannah." "Come on, Yo, sing too."

That was something I knew I could do as well as anyone.

***

All that summer it felt strange when I walked down the road to visit Ma and my stepbrothers. Ma slept downstairs in the room that had been Daddy's. Daddy, Matt and Mark slept in the big room Ma and I had shared with Mark. To see three beds, crowded into our old room, made it look so much smaller. Luke had the room at the top of the stairs all to himself. I couldn't help thinking how convenient that was for his night activities. Seeing the changes made me realize there was no longer a place in the house for me because Ma's downstairs bedroom was only big enough for a single bed. I had to struggle to keep Ma from seeing how much that hurt. My only defense was to turn away and pretend I didn't care; I must try hard not to care. It looked as though Ma meant for me to always take care of the Stanleys just the same way she was taking care of the Osborns. I also began to realize that I must be very careful to please the Stanleys. What in the world would become of me, if they didn't want me? I'd have no place to go.

Maybe it was for the best. I liked the Stanleys, and my greatest hope was that Forrest would wait for me to grow up and love me in the way that I loved him. Then, he'd marry me and life would be grand.

I poured my heart out to Aunt Carrie in a way that I hadn't since Rev. Grey left.

Aunt Carrie, can God make things like that happen? Will my ugliness disappear when I grow up and have breasts? I guess I'll always have this awful black hair and all these black lashes and eyebrows. My real daddy must have been from someplace different because no one around here looks like me. I did see people that looked like me at Abbey's graduation. I even saw two black people getting their diplomas. I'll bet they have a harder time than me. I tried not to stare at them because I know how that feels, but I was curious. I figure that's why everyone stared at me when I moved to the country. You didn't even notice so I didn't know I was different until I moved to the country, and Luke told me I looked like a Gypsy. Maybe, that's why Aunt Alma doesn't like me. Don't you think that to marry

Forrest is the best thing that could happen to me since I have to live with the Stanleys? I suppose I could marry someone else but I can't love anyone but Forrest. And I want to be like Mr. and Mrs. Stanley who love each other, not like Ma and Daddy. I pray to God everyday to send me a sign telling me my plan is OK? I know you want me to be happy, and for me, Forrest is the only way.

***

During that summer Allen's frequent weekend visits to the farm taught me an important lesson about romance. I liked the way Abbey and Allen looked at each other even when they were lending a helping hand in the kitchen, and they were always holding hands. One night when I was going up to bed, they were on the front steps with their arms around each other, and they were kissing and it looked nice. It helped me realize that what I felt for Forrest, which had been confusing on account of Luke, was alright. The time I saw Luke kissing Sally out behind the school house when I was in the first grade, looked rough, like it was "dirty stuff". I ran away because I didn't want to see anymore, and I didn't want them to see me.

Before the summer was over they announced their engagement and set their wedding date for next summer in July after the school year was over. I was thrilled because Abbey asked me to be her bridesmaid just like I was her real sister.

I thought about Ma's marriage and began to understand that she had made a big mistake by not marrying for love. It helped me see how my real daddy and I had ruined her life. No wonder she didn't want me around. Unbidden, my thoughts turned to Rev. Grey. I wondered if she felt about him the way Abbey felt about Allen and I felt about Forrest. They had been very friendly when I watched them through the grate. A picture of Rev. Grey as my stepfather filled my mind. I would

219

have liked to have him for my stepfather. I didn't let myself dwell on that because there was no way it could happen, but Rev. Grey would have helped Ma see me in a different light. It made me want Ma's love all the more.

By the time school started, Abbey had found a room in Phelpsburg, and Allen came for the weekend to help with her move. He considered himself fortunate because he could live at home and save rent-money by lending a hand on his family's farm. Luckily, Clayton, where he would be teaching social studies, was only thirty five miles south of Phelpsburg.

Life was settling into a new rhythm. Mrs. Stanley was happy because Abbey came home weekends. Once in a while, Allen came too, and sometimes he took Abbey to spend the weekend with his parents. There was a little sadness under all the happiness because, much as everyone loved Allen and was pleased about how Abbey's life was turning out, everything was changing too fast. Soon Abbey and Allen would be married and Forrest would be away to college. Often, Mrs. Stanley hugged me, declaring she'd be lost without me.

There were so many complicated new emotions surfacing that summer, I think I was growing up to a whole new plateau of understanding. One day right after school started, Mrs. Stanley and I were getting my winter clothes ready for the changing season, and out of the blue she started a conversation that made me realize she too was aware of my new plateau.

"You're going to be noticing changes in some of your girl friends this year, and maybe soon in yourself, and I don't want you worrying about what's happening. It's normal for girls between eleven and fourteen to develop breasts."

"I've been wondering when that would happen. I'd like to be grown up."

"I guess that's about as normal as you can get. I remember wishing the same thing. Only now, I think childhood is all too short. My mother never told me anything about what to expect when this change took place, and I don't want you to have the same concerns and misinformation. When your breasts start to develop, your body is getting ready for the time when you'll start your period. Have your friends talked about that?"

"No."

I think she was surprised and maybe didn't believe me. Much to my disappointment, I didn't have a "bosom friend or kindred spirit" as Anne Shirley did in "ANNE OF GREEN GABLES". I longed to have one, but decided you had to be the smartest girl in school and I'd never be that.

Mrs. Stanley set aside the sweater she was mending and motioned for me to sit beside her. "I don't know how good I am at explaining...living on a farm I'm sure you have some idea where babies come from."

"Yes, Sally told me a boy plants a seed in you and a baby grows."

"That's right." Mrs. Stanley wasn't surprised or concerned.

That was the chance I'd been waiting for. "How's the baby get out? That's worried me."

"I'm sorry you've had to worry. You can ask me anything...I thought you knew that. If I don't know the answer, I'll try to find out...You've seen a chicken lay an egg, I'm sure?" I nodded. "In humans the egg stays inside a woman's body, and the baby develops in a special organ called the uterus. When the baby's ready to be born, the mother's body sends a signal to the uterus, and the uterus pushes the baby out a special channel just like the chicken pushes her egg out. So, when young girls grow up this special organ also begins to change. A special lining develops in the uterus that would nourish a baby if sperm, that's the boy's seed, is planted. If no sperm is planted the lining sloughs off once a month in a bloody discharge called menstruation. We girls call it our period. We have special pads to wear when that happens. Those blue boxes of Kotex you see around are those special pads."

"Then a seed can't grow in little girls." This was very surprising. My brain just couldn't process all that information. Troubling things in the back of my mind tried to surface, but were lost, yet I knew they were important.

"No it can't. Josephine, why do you ask? Are you troubled about something? I'm here; you can ask me anything."

Mrs. Stanley was troubled and looked at me expectantly. My mind shuffled fleeting scenes. I remembered Ma's washing me from head to foot and promising me if Luke ever bothered me again, she'd protect me even if she had to turn the family upside down. After that, I knew I was safe. Yet, there was something awful down deep inside where no one could see it, even me. If it got out no one would like me, but Jesus came in my dream and walked with me and said I was OK.

I had to say something. "I was worried about how babies got out because Sally wouldn't tell me." I could see Mrs. Stanley was still troubled. But, it was true; I spent a lot of time worrying about how babies were born.

Concern and compassion were overflowing in Mrs. Stanley's voice, "Josephine, there are many more things you'll be wondering about as you grow up. When questions come up, please don't be shy about asking me. And if anything ever bothers, no matter what it might be, I hope you know you can come to me. I don't want you to be worried about anything."

"I will, Mrs. Stanley. I really like it here with you."

Mrs. Stanley seemed to be weighing something for a few minutes, then began again, "There are many kinds of love connected to life....new kinds of love that go along with choosing a mate for life. Right now that seems like a long way off, but it's part of growing up."

I thought I knew what she was talking about, and I knew I wanted Forrest for my mate. I was resigned to wait for my body to catch up with my emotions. Maybe by then he would be able to grow a new kind of love for me. "I already know who my mate will be but it's a secret."

Mrs. Stanley smiled, "You know when I was your age I had picked out my mate too. It was my older cousin who was so kind and smart he just left no room in my heart for anyone else for a long time."

"And it wasn't Mr. Stanley?"

"No. My cousin married when I was in grade school and broke my heart. I had forgotten all about how I felt about that cousin until now."

That told me she guessed it was Forrest, and she was trying to tell me I would get hurt, that I'd change my mind. But I'd never love anyone except Forrest. I knew that for sure.

***

These days, Forrest had very little time for me. He needed good grades his senior year because he was applying to Cornell's engineering program. He wanted to design farm machinery and anything that had to do with farming. It was hard for me to see him growing away from me even though I knew he still liked me just as much, as a little sister, of course. There was never time to help me with my homework, and our talks were a thing of the past. I began to worry that I might not catch up to him in time. Even Luke, Linda and Mary Ann never came anymore unless it was on a Saturday afternoon. Once they all went to the movies and Luke really caught it from Daddy because he hadn't given him permission to go. He said movies were the work of the devil. Mr. Stanley scolded Forrest, saying he should have known how Paul felt.

Forrest looked grumpy. "I feel sorry for Luke."

"I know, son, but we have to respect other folks' views."

"I'm afraid he'll be doing a lot of things his father's not going to like next year when he goes to college."

"Well, let's hope not. He's a good kid at heart; it'd break Paul's heart."

Matt had turned out to be a hard worker and an excellent student. It was as if he wanted to be all the things Daddy expected Luke to be. He even studied his Sunday School lesson without being reminded. His chubby roundness had turned lanky, and it was plain to see he was going to be tall like Luke, only his hair was straight, sandy brown and stuck out in an ornery fashion, defying all attempts to stick it down. Often he was too busy with his studies to come up for a visit, and Mark trudged up alone. Despite all this studious hard work, Daddy never recognized his efforts to please. One time when I was down there, Matt said, "Daddy, hear my bible verses?"

Daddy never looked up, "Later, Matt."

I'd have thought Daddy, the dyed in the wool True Faither, would have jumped at the chance to hear anyone's bible verses, anytime. He was only reading the paper. I put that bit of information on the Methodist's side of "the who's right scale."

Ma was cutting ribbon candy on the kitchen table. "Come, Matt, I'll hear your verses." She was only too glad to sooth his hurt feelings.

"Guess I'll go on home," I said to my own mother so she could mother someone who was not her child.

"Kin I go with Yo?" Mark jumped up and down. "Please, please."

Ma looked at me for the first time. "Let him come, Ma."

"Not for supper, young man. I want you home for supper." She didn't invite me, but I wouldn't have accepted anyway even though Mrs. Stanley thought I should spend more time with Ma. She knew, down deep, how I felt, and would have been happy to let me skip my chores.

***

With Forrest all tied up in his studies, I found myself studying Mr. Stanley. Something that fascinated me about him was how few words he actually spoke, and yet, how much information he managed to convey. "Is that so," "Seems like," "Got me," "If you say so," "Not on your life," "Golly," "That's dandy," "Well, I never," and so on. He always had an under the surface smile on his face, as if he knew something he wasn't about to tell you. I got to wondering what it could be, and how I could find out. Or maybe he was just exceedingly pleased with life.

One day in March, I caught him sitting on the banking of hay he put up around the house foundation every fall to keep the cellar from freezing and the house easier to heat. I also liked the banking these last days of winter when the sun shining on the protected south side of the house made the boards on top of the banking feel like summer.

"Sunning yourself, Mr. Stanley?" I squeezed up next to him. "Feels good, doesn't it?"

True to form he answered, "Indeedy." It did say everything.

"How come you don't say much?"

"Now, isn't enough said, enough?"

"I suppose, but it's not like other people talk."

His under the surface smile was on the surface now. "How is it other people talk?"

"You know, in long sentences."

"Come to that, I know what's in my head without hearing my voice."

"You're funning me, Mr. Stanley."

"Could be most use too many words."

"Mrs. Stanley uses lots of words."

"Now, there's someone I can listen to and never get tired of."

"How come?"

"Because I love her, and her voice is like velvet in my ears, never harsh. But, I really do know what you're aiming at, Josephine. I'm what you call an introvert. That's kind of a fancy way to say I'd rather listen. My thoughts are pretty much my own unless it has to do with farming. I talk a lot to Paul and Forrest. You just don't happen to hear me."

"Do you talk to Abbey?"

"Just looking at Abbey makes me happy."

"How come?"

"Don't know…the way she's sunny in the kitchen, helping her mother and chattering away…and she's like sunshine."

"I know. She looks like the Coca Cola girl."

"I'll be! So she does."

"I wish I made someone happy to look at me."

"Just looking into your bewitching brown eyes makes me happy, just wondering what's going on in that curious head of yours."

"Luke says I look like a witch. I don't want bewitching eyes." My eyes felt watery.

"Bewitching eyes are one of the very best kind." He gave me a hug. "Luke's unhappy. Making you feel bad makes him think he's not the only one down in the dumps, you know, 'misery likes company'. And, believe it or not, I might add, witches are very misunderstood and quite the opposite of what Luke thinks."

226

"But he acts happy."

"You said just the right word, he 'acts' happy, not 'is'. If he shouts he's happy loud enough, long enough, maybe he'll believe it. He's convinced just about everyone, except the person that really matters, himself. If you study, really see people, you can learn a lot about life."

"You sure know a lot. How'd you get so smart and happy? You're always smiling even when there's no one to see."

"Just lucky."

"How'd ya get so lucky?"

"Farmin's the best life there is, to my way of think'n. Plus, May's the love of my life, and I have Forrest and Abbey, and now, you too."

That put a buzz in my heart. "I'm lucky too cause I live with you, and I like farming."

"It seemed to me my three older brothers had the best of everything which, of course, was first dibs on this farm. All I ever wanted was to farm from the time I can remember. To my surprise, one by one they left the farm."

"How could they do that?"

"Don't rightly know. Couldn't imagine anyone would want'a do that. Just plain lucky, I guess. Here I am with the farm and everything I dreamed about, and more."

"I like your dream. Tell me, why are witches misunderstood?"

"In ancient times people knew very little about science, medicine, nature and the likes, but there was those few special people who knew about herbs and their healing powers. Those old time folks thought the healers had magic powers, and was in awe of them, and at the same time they was kind'a scared of them because they didn't understand where their powers came from. Of course folks was drawn to them for cures, for their ailments, all the same. When disasters, epidemics, such like came, folks most often turned on them...blamed them and called them witches. But really, they was the smart ones who, in time, poked holes in the people's superstitions. I don't believe there's any such thing as witches. In a way, don't you see, we owe those healers a lot. They was the ones on the right path. It's just too bad the history of witches isn't better understood, and they'd not have such a bad name. Sometimes, all through history, people have been called witches, for selfish purposes, sort'a like Luke calling you a witch. If I was you, I'd think of it as a compliment, and Luke kind'a dumb to hand one out not knowing it."

I thought about that for a minute and decided that wasn't a bad idea. I might even tell Luke a thing or two he didn't know. Then I thought aloud, "What about gypsies? Luke calls me a gypsy sometimes."

"Ah, now, at one time, I thought I might become a gypsy myself."

"Really?"

"Indeedy."

"How come?"

"When I was a little shaver, younger'n you, I got my first look at a gypsy. I was sent over to the back pasture to pick blackberries for a pie for supper. I was daydreaming as usual and not much interested in berry-picking when I saw her, a little gypsy girl about my age. My Pa always let the gypsies camp on our farm. He said they had to camp somewhere. Mama wasn't too happy about that, but Pa said it was good insurance. The reason being, it was thought they were thieves, and Pa decided they probably wouldn't steal from someone who befriended them. Worst of all, it was thought they sometimes even stole little children. I was forbidden to ever go near their camp. As you can imagine, I was not about to disobey. Of course that was no more true than all the people in Tate Town are saints. Truth be told, over the years I got to thinking about it and figured probably some folks, who had a tendency to be light-fingered, waited for the gypsies to come so's they'd be blamed for their own thievery. You never know what to believe as I'm sure you've guessed. No kids were ever kidnapped that I heard of, and nothing was ever stolen from my pa.

"Anyway, so, I froze in my tracks and sneaked behind some bushes where I could watch her. There was butterflies flying all around her, like magic, as she picked. She was mighty cute and hummed as she picked, and that was probably the reason she didn't hear me. All at once she stopped her humming." He snapped his fingers. "Just like that, a butterfly lit right on her finger, and she lifted it up to her face. I suppose the butterfly was licking berry juice off her finger. Now, that seemed very special to me. It's one of the prettiest pictures in my memory, and it's true, she did look a lot like you and from that moment, I belonged to her. I spied on her until she had her bucket full. Then, as she left, she turned and smiled, a very winning blackberry smile, at the bush I was behind, and said, 'Catch me, if you can.' Well, I was too startled to move, and beside that, I still had to pick my berries. Did I catch it when I got home for taking so long, but I offered no explanation because they didn't know the gypsies were back, and I wanted to go and look for her again."

"Did you find her?"

"No, they must have left very soon after that. I found where their camp had been way over on the other side of the woods. They came and left from Mill Run. That's why no one knew they were back."

"Did they ever come back? Did you see her again?"

"Yes, a few times. They didn't always come our way, or did I always know when they came."

"Didn't you ever talk to her?"

"Once. She came to the house with her father to ask the way to a doctor. Her baby brother was sick. My pa took Althea's father, that was her name, to the doctor with our horse and buggy, and I walked Althea back to their camp. Mama plainly didn't like it that Pa said I should, and whispered to me not to go near their camp and catch their fever."

"Were you scared?"

"Not in the least. I should've been. The baby had scarlet fever and might have died if Pa hadn't helped out, and if I'd disobeyed, I might have brought the fever home to our family."

"What'd she say?"

"Althea was no more of a talker than I was. We told our names. She told her father she knew me…that's why she came with him. I told her I found their camp sometimes. She said she knew that. I asked, did she think I'd found it this time, and she said, yes. I hadn't and was disappointed because I thought she had magic powers. She said, I had found it, and ran from me. By then we was nearly there, and I stood a little way off and watched her run into their wagon-house. There was four of the most beautifully painted wagons…pretty as circus wagons, forming somewhat of a circle with a fire burning in the center. People sat outside on their wagon-house steps. One man played the accordion very softly. I was mesmerized. Their big horses grazed nearby on pickets, everything was peaceful, inviting and quiet. There was no singing or dancing. I'm sure everyone was worried about the sick baby."

"Why did you say you almost joined the gypsies?"

"That picture of Althea picking berries stayed in my head, and she was so mysterious. I watched her grow into a beautiful young lady. I was convinced the farm would never be mine, their world looked very inviting and exciting…always on the move…seeing new places…always singing and dancing. I wanted to run away and never look back. They came and made camp in our cow pasture not far from the barn…down on the flat by the pond. They'd never camped in plain sight before. I wondered how I could escape...with them so visible...everyone would know. I waited until dark when the singing began. I had sneaked up to the hay mow to watch and plan. The music began and Althea came out to dance with her long flowing jet black hair, whirling around her face...her body swaying, and the music swelled around her as if she was the music. My heart was leaping in my chest. Just when I decided I must go and declare my intentions, one of the young gypsy men came out of his wagon and began dancing with her. They moved in unison...like one person, and I knew they were in love. My heart was broken, and I crept back to the house never to see her again."

"But you said Mrs. Stanley was the love of your life."

"Yes, we was made for each other. I hope Althea and her dancing beau are as happy as May and I. My brother, Ben, left the farm the next year. Had I run away, I'd've lost my true dream. That's why I'm so lucky."

"Life is sure strange," I managed to say as my mind swam in confusion.

"That it is," was his final comment.

"I sure hope I'm lucky like you," was my final comment, but my mind kept right on trying to fathom the new concept about witches and gypsies. Forrest filled my thoughts, as ever he did, only now, Forrest and the farm merged in my dream.

Mrs. Stanley told me she had loved her cousin when she was little and had forgotten all about it. Mr. Stanley fell in love with the little gypsy girl, and he said Mrs. Stanley was the love of his life. This was troubling because no one would ever be the love of my life except Forrest. I wanted my life to be like Mr. and Mrs. Stanley's and not like Ma's and Daddy's.

Aunt Carrie, will I ever figure things out? Did you have a love of your life? I wish I knew. You think Forrest's the right one for me, don't you? I think Mr. and Mrs. Stanley are trying to tell me that they don't think Forrest's right for me. They could be wrong couldn't they, even though I love them and they're not at all like Aunt Alma? I wonder what Ma thinks. She probably hasn't even thought about it. I wish you could tell me what I should do to make Forrest love me. I miss you.

Chapter 8

When life changing events happen, our memory couches them in the framework of the weather. June had wafted in with the sweetness of full-blown summer, and on a perfect Saturday early in the month, just such an earthshaking event took place. Ma asked Mrs. Stanley if we'd watch Matt and Mark while she went to Phelpsburg to deliver her baked goods and do a little grocery shopping.

"It's so nice out I hate to make the boys go along. They'll look after themselves, but I don't want to leave them down home on their own."

Daddy had taught Ma to drive because he said there was no need to keep her business waiting on him. It seemed strange to see her drive by with the boys neatly tucked in the back seat. Sometimes, I asked myself if she were really my mother, she had changed so much. I think it had a lot to do with Rev. Grey, though Daddy never let on he noticed that Rev. Grey had had any effect on Ma. It was true Daddy did deserve a lot of the credit. He was the one who asked Rev. Grey to visit Ma. He was the one who gave her a home, security and two little boys to love, but he definitely got the better part of that bargain. My peeks through the bedroom grate told me Rev. Grey's friendship was important too and a whole lot more interesting. Though, if it weren't for Daddy, we'd never have come to the country.

It was the middle of the afternoon when we saw Ma drive back in down at the tenant house. Mrs. Stanley shook her head. "Don't know how she does it. She'll be plum tuckered out. When you go for milk, run on over and invite her to tea. The boys aren't ready to go home yet."

Going to the milk-house for our daily supply of fresh milk was necessary because with no refrigeration milk soured quickly. Consequently, there was always a pan of sour milk simmering on the back of the big black woodstove for cottage cheese. When the cheese was ready, Mrs. Stanley strained the curds from the whey, and I took the whey out to the big hollow Indian stone. I'd call, "Chick, chick, here chick, chick," as the stampeding flock of eager chickens swarmed around my ankles in anticipation.

How much I had changed from the frightened little girl those years ago when Abbey first took Matt and me to the barn to see the new calf. I now loved the musky smell of the animals, the sent of hay and feed, and the muted light in the barn Today the big doors were opened at each end of the barn and between the dirt floor part and the milking end, letting in light and the fresh breeze. For an instant, my mind returned to last winter when I happened into the barn as one of the cows was getting ready to freshen. Luck would have it, that the only other person in the barn was Forrest. I pleaded, "Let me stay. I want'a see how the calf is born, what really happens."

He wasn't happy with the idea, but I insisted Ma could care less, and his mother was open-minded. The only ones who would think it a sin were Aunt Alma and Daddy, and they didn't count. So, I stayed and saw the little hoofs as they came pushing their way out with the calf's head neatly tucked down between its front legs. A few more contractions and the rest of the slippery little body followed with an amazing plop. There squeezed out of the mother cow, lying on the straw, was a brand new life. Forrest explained the umbilical cord and afterbirth, and how the mother cow ate the afterbirth which gave her the nutrients that helped prevent milk fever. I was convinced Forrest knew everything. At long last I saw how a fetus got out, putting to rest all those ponderings and frightening pictures tumbling around in my mind. Best of all, Forrest, my most special friend, had shared with me one of the most sacred experiences in the whole world, birth. I now knew exactly how you got born!

When I entered the milk-house, Daddy was in there finishing up the morning chores, and as he dipped the milk for me he asked, "Luke by chance up at your house with the little kids?"

"No. I think Forrest's studying."

Daddy walked out the end of the barn with me in search of Luke. As we neared the end of their driveway, we heard a clattering racket. Something toppled inside the house, and then a muffled, "No...no... no...NO."

Daddy began to sprint with me right behind him. Something inside me froze. Intuition clicked in my brain, and a picture of Luke flashed though my head.

Ma cowered in the corner of the sofa with her blouse torn and her bra straps broken, exposing her breasts. Luke stood over her unfastening his pants, unaware Daddy had burst into the room.

Luke snarled, "Bitch, I knew if I waited long enough I'd get my chance."

In the heat of Luke's lust, his guard was down, and Ma was able to deliver a foot to his groin. All the air passed out of Luke's lungs in a hateful groan as he bent over in excruciating pain. Daddy struck Luke a blow that knocked him on down to the floor, something I never thought I'd see. Ma's groceries lay strewn over the kitchen table and onto the floor, evidence of their struggle. I watched from just inside the kitchen door unnoticed by Ma and out of Daddy's mind in his anger.

Luke whimpered, "It's her fault, the whore."

Daddy shook with anger. "Why'er her clothes torn? Why'd she kick you? Because she was inviting you?"

"Always shaking her tits at me. Here I am, get me if you can."

Daddy was so angry he couldn't answer, and he took his foot and pushed Luke so hard he rolled over.

Luke's eyes burned with hatred. "You're crazy. If you were half a man you'd be in her bed, and I wouldn't be faced with temptation."

Ma slunk off to her little cubbyhole bedroom and shut the door.

"Down on your knees before you disgrace yourself beyond redemption."

"I hate you and your redemption. I like the flesh."

"What you need's a good thrash'n. Get upstairs, before I do something I'll regret. I've some praying to do. I'll deal with you later, and I better find you down on your knees."

I ran from the house as fast as I could. Once on the road, my feet slowed to a snail's pace as I struggled with my emotions. Fate had a strangle hold on me and Ma. We were doomed. My chest heaved as I fought to stifle my sobs. How could I face Mrs. Stanley? Nausea swept over me, and I swallowed hard to keep from throwing up. I was at the door, and somehow I had to put on a straight face.

Mustering all my willpower, I managed to calmly say, "Ma's got a headache. Could Matt and Mark have dinner with us?"

"Of course. Will Luke be coming up?"

"Daddy has a job for him."

For all outward appearances, dinner was normal as apple pie, which indeed we did have, apple pie being both Matt and Mark's favorite. Mrs. Stanley always canned plenty of apples so she could whip up a pie at a moment's notice. During dinner preparations, and after dinner, I made no explanation about anything that had happened to Ma. My emotions and ability to form the words were in total shut-down. I couldn't even articulate what was going on inside my mind to Aunt Carrie. There were strange feelings stirring below the surface, out of reach, choking me. Plus, I was so worried about what was going on down at the tenant house. It felt like nettles under my skin. Despite this, my body carried on without conscious instruction, and I was able to keep Matt and Mark busy playing hide and seek until it began to grow dark. I hoped I had kept them long enough for Daddy to deal with Luke, and for Ma to get her equilibrium so she could take care of getting Matt and Mark off to bed without upsetting them.

During the evening the radio played as if everything were normal. I tried to listen but couldn't concentrate. It's chattering annoyed me so much I finally said goodnight to Mr. and Mrs. Stanley.

"It's early, Josephine, you alright?"

"Matt and Mark tired me out. Might as well give up and go to bed." I had to get away where I could be by myself, where I didn't have to keep a straight face.

Mrs. Stanley chuckled as Snooks roused up from her nap on the window seat. "Snooks is ready too."

Snooks shot past me like a streak of grease-lightning. "Snooks says goodnight too." She loped up the stairs, skidded into my room and gave a gliding leap upon the foot of my bed. My soul cried out for comfort. I curled around her furry little body, and I cried myself to sleep.

***

Ma and I were running, running, running in the far pasture and Mrs. Stanley was calling after me, "The well...the well...don't fall down the old well." Luke was laughing, his laughter growing louder in hot pursuit. Just ahead of us, I could see the dark well-hole that Mrs. Stanley always warned me never to go near. I grabbed hold of Ma's arm, "NO, MA, the well!" Luke gave a shove. "Too bad you heathen whores had to go and slip in." Ma and I tumbled bumping into each other as we fell, down, down into the black pit. I looked up, and for an instant Aunt Carrie's face was looking down from above. "AUNT CARRIE, AUNT CARRIE," I screamed. Luke's laughter echoed down the well-hole reverberating all around us.

"Josephine, wake up . . . wake up. Everything's alright . . . she . . . sssh . . . there . . . there." Mrs. Stanley was gently shaking me. I opened my eyes, relieved to be rescued from the horror of my dream, and I threw my arms around her neck.

She smoothed back my hair. "It's just a bad dream. You were calling for Aunt Carrie as I was coming up the stairs to bed."

"I dreamed me and Ma fell in the old well."

"Well now, we're not going to let that happen. Isn't that right Snoops? She must have lulled you to sleep. Put your jimmies on. We covered that hole with a new cover last year, remember? Nighty-nite."

Next morning on our way to church, to my great surprise, Matt and Mark were in their yard, in their play clothes, which meant they were not going to church. The only time I could remember that ever happening was on Ma and Daddy's wedding day when Ma and I moved to the farm. Of course, there were times when someone was sick and stayed home with Ma but never everyone at the same time. I shivered and there was a sick lump in my stomach.

At church the feeling of foreboding still hung over me. I dared not think of all the possibilities. Would Daddy make Ma move out? What did he do to Luke? My nerves were so frayed that when the choir rose to sing the anthem, my lips moved, but not a note passed through them.

On the way home, as we approached the tenant house, Matt and Mark came running out to the road and Mr. Stanley stopped the car.

"Ma's sick. Yo, kin you stay and cook our dinner?"

Daddy appeared on the front porch and gave a wave to us, then said, "Come, boys. We're on our way to Phelpsburg to visit Grandma. Let's give Clara some peace and quiet."

Fear gripped my heart and broke the lock on my tongue. "Luke going with you?" Ma would be alone. Would Daddy let that happen after yesterday?

Matt started to say something and Daddy cut in, "No, Josephine, Luke's not home."

Mrs. Stanley spoke up, "I'll look in on Clara later?"

"I'm sure all she needs is a good rest. But thanks."

We drove on home, and as soon as the table was set for dinner, and Mrs. Stanley was busy putting cornbread in the oven, I slipped down the road to the tenant house. That Luke was not home didn't mean he might not come back as soon as Daddy was out of sight, and I had to know if Ma had remembered to lock the doors. I quietly tested both the front door and the back door. Then I looked up at the window over the back porch and wondered if Ma knew that was Luke's way in and out of the house at night. I looked about trying to figure out how Luke climbed back up to the porch roof. The woodshed must hold the answer. I stood at the door and fought to overcome my fear to go in. Was Luke hiding in there at that moment? My scalp prickled and my mouth was dry. No way could I go in the woodshed. In desperation, my eyes sought out the bedroom window again. Almost concealed, there in the window was a stick, locking the window shut. Satisfied, I hurried up the road, half expecting Luke to jump out and grab me, and all of a sudden I knew Ma could no longer protect me from him, and I was petrified.

As I came into the kitchen, Mrs. Stanley was bent over the oven door, checking the macaroni casserole and cornbread. "There you are, Josephine. Clara all right? Call Fred. It's ready."

"Yeah, she'll be OK."

Next morning on the way to school, Matt told me Luke had not slept at home for two nights, and Ma was still sickly looking as she cooked breakfast. He said his grandma fussed and fussed because she had to cook their Sunday dinner even though Daddy had taken leftover pot-roast and one of Ma's blueberry pies. Matt was clearly more upset than I had ever seen him. His grandma said, Luke had slept there, but had gone out to visit a friend. Matt wanted to know, why did Luke stay with his Grandma? He'd never done that before. Daddy was glad to know where Luke had slept, and said to send him home. Why didn't Daddy know where Luke was? What was going on? Grandma had scolded Daddy in such a mad voice about whatever it was that ailed Ma, that in a huff they had left. Then daddy stopped at the park like he didn't want to go home. They'd never done that before. Matt said Ma didn't come out of her room until breakfast time. He wanted to know couldn't I come home with him and fix everything. I told him that the best tonic for Ma would be for him and Mark to be extra good boys and help her out all they could, that she didn't need me. I felt a little bit ashamed after I said that because I knew it wasn't his fault Ma preferred him and Mark to me, and at that moment he just needed to reach out to someone. But, I had no one to reach out to. I didn't even have Forrest anymore.

How I wished he wasn't so tied up in his studies. He didn't even notice how upset I was. How I missed him. This was not the kind of thing I could share with Mrs. Stanley. Upon pondering what I'd say to Forrest, I knew I couldn't talk to him about it either.

That night as Snooks and I snuggled, waiting for sleep, I poured my heart out as I hadn't done in some time.

Aunt Carrie, what's going to happen? Will Ma be all right? Will Daddy think it's her fault and blame her for how Luke is? How will I be able to keep away from him when he comes home? I can't think about what might have happened if Daddy hadn't been with me. Is there something wrong with Ma? Is it her fault? Is it my fault? I feel like it is. Something inside me won't stop shaking, and I can't let myself think about that because if I do, I'll shake myself into little pieces. Could I be like Ma? Part of me wants her to resist Daddy's pleas for her to be saved while part of me hates her being called a heathen. I want to believe Rev. Grey. He doesn't think she's a heathen. But somehow, I don't think Daddy would approve of Rev. Grey if he'd been watching through the grate. I hate Luke so much it scares me. My Jesus dream does count, doesn't it? Like Joseph's dream and Jacob's ladder in the bible. I wish Jesus would tell me again that I'm OK. I'll never be able to face Ma again because there is something way down inside of me all tied up in a tight knot. I don't think she knows I saw what happened. I'd die if she did. Does Daddy know I saw? If he does, he'll know for sure I'm a heathen just like Ma, because it's a sin to know and see stuff like that. What will he do to me if he finds out? I just can't pray to God about this. Why is that? Do you mind me talking to you? I still remember your arms around me. Sometimes, I have to work at it to keep that feeling from fading. Don't ever let that happen. I still love you.

Matt and I were always home from school long before Forrest and Luke because they had to ride the school bus from Phelpsburg and still walk the mile from Tate Town up to the farm. I hurried through my chores so I could watch for them. Surely Luke would be on the bus. I hadn't seen him since Daddy rolled him over on the floor, and I wondered if Ma was down there trembling as much as I was, wondering what would happen when he came home. My trembling was for naught. Forrest was alone and hurried up the road as if someone had chastised him for being late. He strode right past me into the kitchen, and I followed, where Mrs. Stanley was starting supper.

"Mom, did you know Luke's run away from home and's living with his grandmother?"

"NO, so that's what's going on."

Forrest looked at me, and held back what he would have said if I hadn't been present. "I guess there was a big blow up and Luke walked out."

Mrs. Stanley sat down as if she were very tired. "Come here, Josephine. Do you know anything about what's going on?"

She put her arms around me and pulled me right upon her lap even though, despite how small I was for my age, I was still too big to be held on her lap. It had been ages since she had held me thus. Still, I was reluctant to say anything.

"Well, come on, Yoyo, tell us." I didn't like Forrest speaking to me like that. He made it seem as if I had done something wrong. Very unlike me, I started to cry, and once I started the dam broke. I couldn't stop, and I buried my face in Mrs. Stanley's shoulder.

She motioned for Forrest to leave. "Isn't it time you changed your clothes?"

"Aw, all right." Forrest left reluctantly.

"Just cry it out. Something's made you very unhappy, and that makes me very sad too." Mrs. Stanley stroked my back soothingly, and my sobbing shook my body and my tears flowed like a river wetting a big spot on her black and white polka dot dress.

After some time, I sniffled, "Life...w-will...nev...never...be...the...same...a-a-again."

"Life's always changing, we can't stop that. This too, will pass. You're safe here with us."

Half crying, I stuttered, "La...La...uk..ke...was go...going to hu...h..urt Ma, and Daddy ca..caught him just in t...time...and stopped him, and Luke said it was M...Ma's fault and it wasn't. I know

242

it wasn't. What will happen if Daddy believes Luke?"

"There, there, tell me about it."

"When I went to the barn to get milk on Saturday, and you told me to go invite Ma up to tea. Daddy dipped the milk and walked over to the tenant house to get Luke. And Luke'd torn Ma's blouse 'n bra, and Daddy hit Luke." I started to cry again.

Mrs. Stanley's arms hugged me even closer as she said, "You poor, poor child…there-there…your mother's going to be alright." Her voice cracked with emotion as she continued, "Thank heavens Paul arrived in time. If he were going to believe Luke, Luke'd be at home. Don't worry your pretty little head about that. We'll figure something out. The world's sure upside down, but it'll come right again. Let's put our heads together and figure out how we're going to help your mother feel better. Poor Paul, he must be beside himself. He's put such store in Luke. For now, let's just carry on. Time to get the table set for supper."

Mrs. Stanley did make me feel some better, and I was able to eat my supper for the first time without it sticking in my throat, though Forrest's cloudy face didn't help any. He stormed off to his room early to study. No one else noticed his curt motions, but I felt them in my heart. I did the dishes while Mrs. Stanley took the clothes basket out to the back yard to take the washing down from the clotheslines. She sorted out the mending, leaving the ironing for me. Then she went into the living room with her mending basket. While the flat irons were heating on the stove, I sprinkled and rolled the clothes. Work was the best tonic so while the sprinkled clothes set a while, to even their dampness, I decided to start ironing the pile of things that didn't need to be sprinkled. I got out the ironing board Mr. Stanley had made when they were newlyweds, and put it across the back of two chairs. Taking a pot-holder, I lifted one of the irons. Then I licked my finger and tested the iron. It hissed just right, and I began carefully smoothing out the fabric ahead of the hot iron.

I think Mr. and Mrs. Stanley forgot I was in the kitchen.

"May, have you talked to Forrest?"

"No, Josephine was in the kitchen."

"From what Forrest says, Luke's left home for good, and it's all Clara's doing."

"Bosh!"

"Now, you haven't heard. Luke says she teased him to the point of no return, and his dad walked in and found them in the act."

"Not true. Josephine was there and saw everything, and Paul walked in before anything happened and knocked Luke down."

"What can a child tell? Clara's a very fetching, very young woman."

"Fred, you disappoint me. Don't be a typical male. That's not like you."

"Luke's got Forrest convinced."

"When do we make up our minds before we've heard all sides?"

"Now, May, don't tell me you believe that cock-and-bull story about her being married and no one knowing it? And, that trumped-up accident?" Mr. Stanley had that figured out.

"Of course not. But it's as good as any story. Whatever happened is in the past and so painful it drove a young girl to run away, and painful enough to seek refuge with two old women who took terrible advantage of her. Yes, two. Carrie let it happen even though I think she was just desperate for someone to love. No hussy would've put up with them and the way they worked her, or would one have accepted a loveless marriage and three stepsons, if that were her nature." Mrs. Stanley had that figured out too.

"I suppose not."

"Suppose not! I should think most definitely not! Can you honestly, in your wildest dreams, see Clara in that light?"

"Not really."

"Can you see Luke ever telling the truth?"

"Not really."

"Enough said, until we get this sorted out. If indeed it be our place to sort it out at all. But, we do have a very upset young girl on the verge of womanhood, in our care. That is our business."

I had heard enough to know it wouldn't be a good idea to let them know I was in the kitchen, so I left the ironing board up, not to make noise, and sneaked up the stairs quietly. Forrest was coming out of his bedroom, probably to go downstairs to tell Mrs. Stanley Luke's lies. I grabbed his arm and pulled him into my room.

I gave him a push toward my bed. "Sit down, traitor." I climbed up and sat cross-legged on the foot of my bed as far away from him as I could get. "I know about the lies you told your father. How can you trust someone like Luke without even questioning? He's the liar and the worst person I know, meaner'n mean." Tears welled up in my eyes despite the fact that I thought I was cried out. "I was there. I saw what happened."

"Well?"

"Well, Daddy and I were going up the driveway when we heard things falling. Luke had knocked Ma onto the sofa and had torn her blouse, and her bra off, and was undoing his pants when me and Daddy got there. Ma kicked Luke hard, and Daddy finished knocking him down, and Luke said he hated Daddy and Daddy's way of thinking. It was terrible. And, you believe a liar. How can you do a thing like that? I thought you liked me and Ma."

"I do. But you know Luke and how he can make you believe anything."

"No, I don't. He never's done one nice thing to me and hated me

245

from the minute he saw me, and I thought you knew that, when you made me feel better that first day by sitting beside me instead of by Luke, and you fixed my yoyo."

"That's true; I was mad at Luke. But, you have no idea what a different little girl you were to what we expected. You looked just like one of those old time dolls made with a little girl's body and a grownup's face…with all your black hair and dark eyes and lashes and eyebrows…you looked like you had make-up on. Luke's been jealous of you ever since."

"Of me? With no father, and a mother who doesn't want me. That's ridiculous."

"I think he saw you as someone who'd steal some of his attention. After all, you sure had all the attention that day as you rolled around on the grass as if that was the normal way to greet new people."

I moved over and hit Forest on the shoulder.

"That's better, Yo."

"Was I really that awful?"

"Awful nice, and cute."

I gave him a "yeah really" look. "You're just saying that, but that's OK."

"We'd never seen a little girl who looked like a miniature adult before. And Luke, he never had anyone challenge his place before."

"That I just can't see. Me, who had nothing."

"You have more'n you know. Plus, to Luke being free from a parent mightn't have looked like such a bad idea. Mr. Osborn's never given him room to breathe with all his plans and rules."

"Yeah, but he always takes room and makes life miserable for the rest of us. And, Daddy never sees it…poor Matt and Mark, and me when I was there, and Ma. And he got away with it…'til now."

"You can't see it but Luke's not all bad. In fact, for most of us he's great to be around. He knows people. He can see right through you. Not many people can do that. That's how he charms everyone."

"Or hurts them." I couldn't let that pass. "If you know all that, how come you always let him get the best of you?"

"I don't."

"Do to. You believed him when you should know better. You're a grown up now."

"That's true, but I don't let him get the best of me. Some things are just not important to me, that're very important to him; I just don't make an issue."

"Then he gets the best of you…in his mind. Maybe if people didn't let him get away with everything, he wouldn't be where he is today."

"See what I mean, you've got more sense than rest of us put together."

"Do you think Luke'll ever come home?"

"Don't know. His grandmother'll never doubt his word. I'm sure he's got her wrapped round his little finger. He'll probably like it there and'll want'a stay. He's in town where he's always wanted to be."

Later, with Snooks curled up at my feet, my eyes refused to shut as the evening conversations played over and over in my mind. What Mrs. Stanley said about Aunt Carrie was a thorn in my heart. Aunt Carrie who had no faults, took advantage of Ma? Aunt Alma is the one who took advantage of Ma? Did Aunt Carrie let it happen? I decided Mrs. Stanley couldn't be exactly right about everything, but a tiny crack opened up in Aunt Carrie's perfection. I thought about Luke and how he and Forrest had been friends almost from the beginning of their lives. It must be hard on Forrest to think badly of his best friend who was like a brother to him. That realization made me feel guilty for not being more understanding. Forrest wasn't the only one taken in by Luke. Most everyone thought highly of Luke. That was the normal thing to do. Forrest was right. Everyone couldn't be completely wrong, could they? At that moment, I realized if Luke had been nice to me, I would have gladly joined his fan club. I knew that it was because he didn't like me, that I was left out, and I knew he did it on purpose. Way down deep, I wanted to be a member of the inner circle.

It was hard to believe in a couple months Forrest would be gone far away to Cornell. I couldn't imagine life on the farm without him even though we had grown apart. Hopefully when graduation was over and all the pressure over good grades for college was behind him, we could get back together the way we used to be. If only that happened, his going away would be much easier to bear.

It had been rewardingly sweet to hear Mrs. Stanley put Mr. Stanley straight. She knew Luke. It surprised me that Mr. Stanley was taken in because I thought he had Luke figured out better than anyone. Hearing the lies from Forrest was probably what made the lies believable. Both Forrest and Abbey meant the world to him. With that thought I began to think about Abbey and how much I missed her. Could I have confided in her? I finally drifted off to sleep with pleasant thoughts about Abbey's having asked me to be her bridesmaid.

**

In reward for all his hard work, Forrest was one of seven tapped for the National Honor Society. We didn't tell Daddy because there was no point in rubbing salt into his broken heart because Luke had not come home and was not tapped. It pleased me greatly that Forrest had finally managed to outshine Luke, though underneath my glee I knew Luke could have made the National Honor Society if he had wanted to. He just wanted to have fun more. It was like a breath of fresh air to have Luke gone. Only now I was always looking over my shoulder, thinking he might appear suddenly and grab me.

Daddy had made it clear that he had no intention of going to the graduation where he was not wanted. When Aunt Alma heard, she got after him in a big way with her screechy voice. Mr. Stanley quietly began urging Daddy to go, because he said, if he didn't he'd regret it and feel badly about it in the future. Eventually, Luke would be glad he came.

Mrs. Stanley said, "Anyway, the rest of us will be disappointed if you're not there."

Graduation weekend, Abbey and Allen came to the farm Friday night after school instead of waiting until Saturday morning as they usually did. We were all in the kitchen cleaning up the supper dishes.

"It's just like old times seeing the two of you doing up the dishes," Mrs. Stanley cooed as she scooped the last of her steaming chocolate pudding into serving dishes. Handing the cooking pot to them she added, "Here you go," and like old times, Abbey and I shared licking the pudding-pan clean before we washed and dried it.

Allen went to the barn with Mr. Stanley. Laddie was at Forrest's heels, barking and teasing him to hurry and go for the cows. I disappeared out to the backroom to feed Snooks who had been rubbing around my ankles all the while I was drying the dishes. Without a thought about my being within earshot, Abbey and Mrs. Stanley kept right on talking.

"All this business with Luke has thrown Clara for a loop. I just don't know what's to become of her. She won't snap out of it. It's as if she blames herself for what happened. I don't know what she thinks she could have done differently. If anyone's to blame, it's Paul, for never seeing any of Luke's faults and keeping too tight a rein on'im in some things and not tight enough in others. And, Paul's acting so pigheaded about not going to the graduation it's not helping anything.

Though, I do think your dad's finally turned him around on that score. Maybe that'll help."

"I sure hope so, Mom. After all these years, it wouldn't seem right without them at the graduation. I never did trust Luke as far as I could throw him, but it's hard to believe he's really that depraved."

"I know. Keep in mind he was always sweet on you. Now he's in Phelpsburg, don't you let him in if he comes knocking on your door."

"Now, Mom, Luke's not going to try anything with me."

"See what I mean. Promise me, or I'll not sleep."

"Alright. If Luke comes, which he won't, I won't let him in. Satisfied?"

"I'm not so sure we know everything. Josephine has this dark cloud hanging over her head, and she jumps at her own shadow."

"If I ever found out he's harmed her, well, I don't think I'd be responsible for what I'd do. I love her like a sister."

"Forrest does too."

"Mom, you must know how Jo feels about him?"

"She'll get over that in time."

"I'm not so sure. She's way old for her years. I hope you're right."

Abbey was right. I knew that without a doubt. I'd always love Forrest. To hear Abbey say how much she loved me was nice, but I didn't like hearing Mrs. Stanley say I'd get over Forrest. I wished they hadn't guessed how I feel about Forrest.

I heard the cupboard doors bang shut and knew Mrs. Stanley had finished putting the dishes away.

"Getting back to Clara," she continued, "I'm going to write Rev. Grey and invite him to come stay with us for the wedding."

"Oh, Mom that'd be perfect. I'll write and ask him to take part in the ceremony. I should've thought of that. I can't wait to tell Allen....... Ah, I see...Mom, you're a crafty one. Clara, right?"

"Clara needs him. This is the perfect excuse to get him here. Monday I'll get my letter off."

"And, I'll put mine in with it."

***

Graduation night our two families took up nearly a whole row in the auditorium. Imagine, me belonging to such a big family. The wonder of it thrilled me.

There had to be one fly in the ointment. When Aunt Alma came down the aisle at the last minute to join us, she forced Ma to give up her seat beside Mark, and before Aunt Alma's bottom touched the seat she leaned over Mark, and started haranguing Daddy. "Did you bring the money, Paul?"

Daddy's face didn't look at all happy. It was the cloudy face I remembered when I was a little girl. He thrust an envelope into her hand. "It's all documented. Every cent, not one penny more'n his due."

She hissed, spewing saliva. "That's just like you, skinflint."

"Mother, that's beneath you, a good Christian."

Her face was beet-red with anger. "He's your son, and she's…"

"My wife. Enough. I knew it was a mistake to come here."

Mark squirmed. "Move over, Grandma, you're squishing me."

Aunt Alma made a huffy grunt, but moved over and was quiet. Matt looked at me, and I took his hand. I knew we were not intended to hear all that, but it was impossible not to. The heated exchange added steam to the already hot and humid late June evening. Daddy ran his finger around the tight collar of his shirt. I could feel his frustration. He was a private man who didn't want his business aired in public. Hard telling who might have heard bits and pieces of the conversation despite all the chatter and confusion. I was embarrassed for Ma because I knew she must have guessed what the whispering was about.

All of us, except Aunt Alma, were on edge because we were going to see Luke for the first time since that terrible day. Poor Daddy must be suffering in ways none of us could comprehend except possibly Ma. He'd lived his life through Luke. He must be asking himself if his life's purpose was as big a mistake as Luke's transgressions. His loyalty and faith were challenged. Matt told me Daddy prayed continually for the day the prodigal repented and came home to open arms. If that happened Daddy would be exonerated and his plan, his purpose in life, would have only suffered a glitch. What if Daddy's prayers were not answered? What if Luke didn't repent? No wonder Ma was having such a hard time.

Suddenly, the auditorium became quiet as all eyes turned to watch the graduates come marching across the front of the auditorium to take their seats. Forrest and Luke walked side by side as they had done all their school days. There were too many speeches and awards given. I suppose I thought that because my mind was busy thinking about other things, and I knew I'd be lucky if I ever managed to get a diploma.

As soon as the last graduate received his diploma, their recessional began. Instantly, the auditorium was a-buzz, and again, Aunt Alma started to harass Daddy. "How could you bring that woman here?"

He never answered her but gathered Matt and Mark by their hands. "Come, Clara." They left Aunt Alma standing with her mouth open and no one to scold.

Forrest and Luke made their way over to us and all bedlam broke loose. Forrest was hugging and kissing everyone. Aunt Alma threw her arms around Luke's neck and kissed his cheek. "There you are, my handsome grandson. Congratulations."

Luke was impatient to be on his way. "Grandma, I'll be home late.

Some of the guys want'a celebrate. Daddy bring it?"

"Later, Luke. Go have your fun."

Out of the other ear, I could here Forrest saying to Mr. Stanley. "I have to ask him, don't I?"

"Of course you do, son."

Forrest darted a couple of steps and caught Luke by the arm, "Next Saturday, seven, a graduation party with the old gang, at my house."

"Swell, wouldn't miss it for the world, old man."

"See you then."

***

I was given the option of either going down to visit Matt and Mark or stay in my room the night of Forrest's graduation party. Mr. and Mrs. Stanley said they would keep to the kitchen, and tend to the treats. I didn't see why I couldn't help them, but they said they were actually chaperones, and needless to say, I didn't fall into that category. Even Abbey wasn't invited which made me feel a little less shut out. I wanted to be as close to the action as possible, so I chose to stay in my room.

Fortunately, my room was on the front of the house where I could watch everyone coming to the party, and if I left my door open a crack, I'd be able to hear a lot of what went on downstairs. I decided to test my strategy ahead of time and gave a listen. I heard Mr. and Mrs. Stanley talking about Abbey moving back home in a week now that she had finished up all the loose ends after her first year teaching school. Of course, that would mean moving all her things back home because next year she would be living with Allen. Mr. Stanley said he was afraid Allen would be called-up in the draft before school started in the fall. He said he didn't like the war news. Mrs. Stanley said that was on her mind too because one group of draftees had already left for Fort

Niagara, and she hesitated to say anything about it in front of Abbey. These were new thoughts that had never occurred to me, and jarred me to the core, and started me thinking in ways that were really scary. People died in war. Why hadn't I thought about the war before?

I learned Rev. Grey had written and was coming. He was very concerned about Ma and was so pleased to be invited to take part in Abbey's wedding. Now, Ma would be all right. Rev. Grey would know what to say to her.

Also, Mr. and Mrs. Stanley were worried about Luke's coming to the party. Maybe they should have told Forrest not to invite him. What he had attempted to do to Ma was not easily forgiven, if it could be forgiven at all. It was just that he had been like a brother to Forrest. Should they have offered to give him a ride? Aunt Alma didn't have a car. They wondered if he'd even want to come. They hoped he'd be too embarrassed to show his face.

I decided listening at the crack of my bedroom door was almost as good as the upstairs grate over the living room down at the tenant house! Saturday night though, I knew I'd want to see as well as hear, what was going on in the worst kind of way. For my trial, it hadn't mattered. In my mind I could see the living room. Mr. Stanley was looking over his newspaper at Mrs. Stanley. She was nodding to him, never missing a stitch in her knitting which was a red sweater for me. I hopped into bed and tried to turn my thoughts off, but they were so troubled about the war I had a hard time getting to sleep, and Snooks was out hunting, so I had no furry friend to comfort me.

I had never known a week to be so long, but Saturday night finally came. After supper, I squeezed the lemons and pumped the water for the lemonade last thing, so it'd be as cool as possible. I carried up the coca cola from the cellar where Mrs. Stanley was keeping it cool. Some of Forrest's friends from down in Tate Town, where they had electricity, were bringing ice cubes. I hoped I'd get to have a coke with ice. Mrs. Stanley had planned to have everything as modern as if we were living in town. Lights would still have to be oil lamps though, which would be romantic. With all my tasks done, I quickly did up the last few dishes and went dutifully up to my room.

I had worried that I might have to hide behind the curtains, but no one looked up at the face peering down from behind the screen in my open window. The girls looked all pretty and happy in their party dresses, hair all brushed and bouncy in the breeze, and on their feet, dress pumps had replaced their usual saddle shoes, and the guys had shiny grease on their slicked down hair. Their greetings and laughter filled the air. I knew just about everyone that crossed the lawn or sauntered up the walk.

Music floated up the stairway and out the windows across the lawn. The victrola never wound down. I knew couples were dancing, and some drifted out onto the front porch. By pressing my cheek tightly against the screen I could see the corner of the porch, and I caught a glimpse of Forrest dancing with Mary Ann. In the mix of voices, someone asked, "Where's Luke? Is it true he lives with his grandmother? Why?" Forrest avoided answering by just saying, "You know Luke and town."

At that very moment, a magnificent midnight blue convertible came charging down the road, past the tenant house. Matt and Mark were in their yard playing catch and started jumping up and down, waving and shouting. Sitting in the passenger seat, I recognized Linda with her beautiful red hair whipping in the wind, and it was clearly Luke driving, his dark cinnamon brown hair standing on end. They were beautiful and the car! What a car!

It was a 1937 Cord with cream-colored leather seats. There wasn't a spot on the wide whitewall tires and the bulging chrome hubcaps shone like mirrors. The radiator fins wrapped around the sides past the fenders like wings. It yelled speed and class. Luke hopped over the side and came around and opened the car door for Linda. No one could doubt he was king, and that he owned the world and everything in it.

I boiled with jealousy and hatred. How dare he show his face? It wasn't fair. Now he'd take over Forrest's party as he always did. What kind of God always let Luke win? Hopefully, no one but our two families knew what had happened and why Luke really lived in Phelpsburg, but if Luke had told any version of the story, you can be sure he was as innocent as a baby, and Ma was a whore.

Everyone poured out through the front door and surrounded Luke and Linda and his Cord. Luke ran his fingers through his disheveled hair, bringing his curls back into shape. "My graduation present to myself. What'a ya think? Pretty swell! Wouldn't you say? Got it for a song. This old couple Grandma knows had it in their garage and was letting it gather dust. What'a perfect shame. Hadn't been out of the garage in three years. You can be sure its dust gathering days are OVER!"

Amidst the chatter, the girls finally broke and made their way toward the house, Mary Ann's arm looped through Linda's with the guys soon following. Luke and Forrest were last and walked in together. As they came into the front-hall, they stopped.

"Listen, Woody, old man, you're not beginning to believe any of that stuff that whore next door is spreading around?"

"Just a darn minute, Luke. No one's spreading any rumors. You know darn well Clara's no whore. What's gotten into you anyway?"

"You can't believe the way that woman . . . take your hands off me, Woody. I saw that nasty little lying turd standing in the doorway. She's more of a . . . ouch, Woody, stop shoving me . . . that's enough . . . I'm leaving."

A few minutes later I saw him, in a huff, firm grip on Linda's wrist, pulling her stumbling along over the lawn toward that beautiful car, and away they flew out the road, leaving a dust cloud behind them.

Luke was talking about me standing in the doorway, and Forrest wouldn't let him call me names even though they had been friends forever, and he didn't blame Ma. Maybe this summer would be a turning point. Oh, how I hoped so.

***

The week following Forrest's party, Abbey moved back home, but it was not the happy occasion I had been anticipating. Abbey cried continually. Allen had received his draft notice and would be leaving for the army two weeks after their wedding. She kept saying why hadn't they gotten married right after graduation? There was no good reason to wait. "We thought we'd save some money toward a house and all the things we'd need to set up housekeeping." Then, she'd cry some more. Finally, Mr. Stanley spoke up and told her she must get hold of herself, or she'd spoil the joy of preparing for her wedding, and spoil the short time the two of them had before Allen had to leave.

This emotional upheaval stunned me because it was so unlike our sunshine Abbey. Again, I asked myself why I hadn't thought about the war until I had overheard Mr. and Mrs. Stanley talking about it. I was vaguely aware of the cloud Pearl Harbor had cast over Christmas, but I was just too wrapped up with my own importance, singing with Matt and Mark in the school program. How callus that was stung my conscience. June 15th I had turned thirteen, old enough not to be thinking like a child. Why hadn't I taken more notice that Mr. Stanley always had his ear glued to the radio? Now I realized he was listening for the latest war news. But on the farm, everything seemed the same with the fighting far away for other people to worry about. No getting around its ugly finger was pointing right at us, and suddenly, I knew there was no escape.

Mrs. Stanley said, "Luke'll be called up soon, I should think."

My heart was in my throat. "What about Forrest?"

Mr. Stanley was visibly peevish. "He's mule-headed. He could've applied for a farm deferment, but no, he wants to design farm machinery. He can't do that and live on the farm."

My ears couldn't believe what I heard. Forrest, leave the farm! My world was falling apart.

Mrs. Stanley smiled her smile that said her thoughts were in the past. "Thank heavens; he's younger than the other graduates. He wanted to go to school with Luke so bad we just didn't have the heart to separate them. Maybe the war'll be over by the time he has to register."

I could see the two little boys going out the road that first day, Forrest so proud, tagging along after Luke. I heaved a sigh of relief. Surely, the war would be over by the time Forrest was old enough for the draft. Luke in the army! Somehow, I couldn't make that picture real. Soldiers had to obey orders. There'd be no bedroom window or grandma to come to the rescue.

Now, when the news came on the radio, I listened. I had stepped into the reality of the adult world with a suddenness that hurt. In my heart I felt as old as Abbey, and thought I understood her pain. I hated the war all the more for casting such an ominous sadness over her wedding. That was simply not fair. Ah, but there was one way around this sad situation.

I knocked and slipped into her bedroom where she had escaped after Mr. Stanley's chastisement to tell her my plan. "I think you and Allen should run away and elope. Then you could live together right now." An image of Abbey melodramatically climbing out onto the front porch roof passed through my mind.

She opened her reddened blue eyes wide and stared at me. Then she burst into tears again, sniffling, "But the wedding plans."

"I don't know. I just think you should get married right now."

Despairingly she cried, "What about your dress, and, and, my dress, and all the invitations?" Tears slid down her cheeks.

"Have two weddings. I don't know. You could just let people come anyway...you could have the reception and wear your dress....I'd wear mine too...run away to Rev. Grey. He'd be so happy to be the one to marry you."

"Oh, Jo, you have more sense than the rest of us put together." I'd heard that before. "Don't tell anyone. I might just talk it over with Allen when he comes tomorrow. If we do, I'll never tell it was your idea. I love you, Jo."

She went to her dressing table and started brushing her hair that was matted and tangled with all her crying. I lay across her bed and watched her eyes turn to a shiny crystal blue. A smile grew around her lips, and I thought how beautiful she was, and how lucky I was, and how much I loved her.

Next day when Allen arrived, everyone walked around on egg shells, not to set Abbey off on another crying jag, but to everyone's surprise, she had her emotions under control.

After supper I said, "You guys go on. Go for your walk, I'll do the dishes."

Allen gave me a hug. "Thanks, Jo." I liked him, and knew Abbey was lucky, and I knew what they would be talking about.

Next morning there was a letter waiting for us on the kitchen table.

My dearest Mom, Dad, Forrest and Jo,

My heart tells me you'll understand and forgive our selfishness when I explain what Allen and I have done. By the time you read this we will be at Rev. Grey's house and married soon after. I know your disappointment in not seeing me walk down the aisle on Dad's arm and taking our vows in front of you and all the relatives and friends. We will be married in Rev .Grey's church, and I promise we'll come home so Dad can walk Allen and me down the aisle on our planned wedding day, in our wedding clothes. He can introduce us as man and wife. Allen and I can give an explanation and both ministers can send us off with their good wishes and prayers. We'll go ahead with the reception just as planned. The invitations won't have to be changed or anything. We'll be home in plenty of time to make any last minute changes. I feel we have your blessings, good wishes and love that you have always so freely given. Our hearts are so full of love for all of you and for each other they nearly burst.

We love you so much, Abbey and Allen

Mrs. Stanley cried and Mr. Stanley took her in his arms.

Forrest said, "Perfect solution."

I felt pretty smug and not at all surprised.

Mrs. Stanley moaned, "My little girl married."

Mr. Stanley soothed, "Only a little sooner. Abbey's right and Forrest too."

"I suppose."

"That's more like it, May."

I wanted to say it was my idea, but of course I knew better. I hoped my thinking of "the plan" somehow made up for my callus and late coming to the realization the world was at war and what that meant.

***

Excitement erupted when Mrs. Stanley spotted Allen's car coming down the road, and we all made a mad dash for the back driveway. There was a lot of hugging, kissing and tears. Suitcases were carried in with everyone talking at once. I quickly put two more plates on the table and served up supper. We lingered around the dinner table while Abbey and Allen explained how Rev. Grey let them work out their own service. How they held hands, looking into each other's eyes as they exchanged their vows like a love poem! They said it was meaningful in ways they had never anticipated, and their eyes melted together as they told their story. Dinner became our own private little wedding celebration as their stories and love filled our hearts and minds with pictures.

They told how they had called ahead to Rev. Grey so he was all prepared. He had made reservations for their dinner and first night's lodging at an exclusive inn on the little lake near by. I was enthralled with all the romance and became very aware of Forrest who was sitting next to me, so much so that I only half heard the details about their travels. My imagination was busy picturing exactly what it was all about which only revved up my strange new sensations. My body was waking up to sexual feelings I had witnessed happening between others, and I had wondered how they allowed themselves to behave so foolishly. The feelings were very pleasant. I could see how easily one could fall into the giddy trap of making a fool of one's self, but I vowed I'd never let my body trick me into behaving thus.

Clearing up and doing the dishes took place well after bedtime and was incorporated into the party mood. As we all made our way up the stairs together, Abbey and Allen turned into Abbey's bedroom together, and I watched Forrest go into his room and shut the door. The overwhelming desire I had to run in after him scared me. In my mind I saw Abbey and Allen snuggling, arms wrapped around each other, and the loneliest feeling I had ever experienced swept over me. I cried and for what I didn't know, maybe for the innocence of childhood.

***

For the wedding, Mrs. Stanley had bought me my first bra to wear under my heavenly pink dress. Abbey braided pink fabric through my hair, and wound the braids around my head, making it look like a matching tiara. I couldn't believe how grownup I looked. Abbey seemed to float like a princess dressed in a wispy cloud of white. Over a stain chemise and floor-length skirt, her dress had a sheer long-sleeved over-blouse and over-skirt. The over-skirt trailed out behind her in a long train, and because she was already married, her veil was turned back, flowing around her shoulders down to her waist.

As I waited at the front of the church for Mr. Stanley to walk Abbey and Allen down the aisle, a hundred thoughts raced around in my head. I was thrilled that Forrest, who stood opposite me, was to be my escort for the whole affair. I hoped he would notice how grown up I looked. How good it was to see Rev. Grey standing beside Rev. Alderman. This was the first time Ma had ever seen Rev. Grey in his official role as a minister. What was she thinking? Her mood was still so somber. I knew if anyone could snap her out of her depression it would be Rev. Grey. For the first time since that awful day, Ma had curled her hair, and it softened her cloudy face. She had taken to pulling it back in a tight knot again. Rev. Grey must have talked her out of that. I saw him walking down the road to visit her shortly after dinner the night he arrived. How I wished I could have been upstairs with my face pressed over the grate. I'd never know what he said to her, or what he said to Daddy, Matt and Mark when they came in from the barn.

Even Matt looked so much older today. Mark shone like a new penny where he sat as a buffer between Ma and Daddy as always. They existed in insolated spheres living a dance, never touching.   Luke's draft notice had come yesterday, and earlier, Daddy had given it to Aunt Alma, and her eyes were red from all her crying. Both their faces looked as if they had pulled the shades and were some place else in their thoughts. Luke had been Daddy's whole world and should be sitting with them. I knew he was worried to have Luke go off to war because he had not repented. Daddy had his arms crossed, pressed in tightly against his body. I figured so as not to be defiled by sitting in the Methodist Church! He looked so forbidding like when Ma and I first came to the country. What troubling thoughts Luke's behavior must have stirred up in Daddy's mind. Luke told him he was not a normal man. If he were an ordinary husband would he be jealous of Rev. Grey's visits with Ma? How could Ma and Daddy help comparing their marriage to Abbey's and Allen's? It would take some deep digging to unearth the thoughts and questions sealed deep down in their subconscious minds. With Daddy's and Ma's blank faces it was impossible to know what they were thinking.

Allen's family and friends didn't fill his side of the church. I could see a touch of sadness in their eyes. Allen was an only child and a midlife baby. It was plain to see he was the apple of their eyes, and it must be very hard for them to think about him going off to war. They were probably like Mr. Stanley and had wanted Allen to be a farmer. If he were a farmer, he wouldn't have to go off to war.

Back in the doorway, Abbey and Allen were smiling one on either side of Mr. Stanley. My breath caught, they were so picture-book beautiful. I swallowed the lump in my throat; the organ began to play and they started their walk down the aisle. I took a deep breath and from where I stood began to sing. "I'll be loving you always….." When the music stopped, they turned and Mr. Stanley introduced them as Mr. and Mrs. Allen Bennett, hugged them both, and kissed Abbey on the cheek. He joined their hands together then took his place beside Mrs. Stanley.

Rev. Grey stepped forward and Mr. and Mrs. Bennett turned to face him. Taking their hands in his, he told the story of how they came to him to be married in order to have time to be together before Allen had to report for duty. He told about how privileged he was to have had the pleasure of watching Abbey grow into the serious, capable and happy young lady she had become, and how lucky the two of them were to have found each other. In ending his story, he said God had created all of nature and especially the call for two lovers to be united in marriage. That marriage was the Holiest of all the institutions created by man, and sanctified with God's most special blessing. He challenged them to be strong in the face of their impending separation and to pray for each other. Only, he was eloquent and all I could think about was Ma out there listening, and I wished I could turn around and look at her face. I could see Forrest out the corner of my eye, standing beside Allen so serious, and wondered if I'd ever be standing by his side at this rail. It'd be my dream come true, and I wanted Rev. Grey to marry us.

Rev. Alderman gave a short sermon on the duties of forming a good Christian home, and the pleasures it insured, and a long prayer asking God's blessing on the newlyweds.

At the reception, I received a number of compliments for my singing and was glad Forrest had to listen to them. However, the thrill I expected at his being my escort failed to happen. Was it the war, or the idea his big sister was married, or the absences of Luke? Ever since the night of the party whenever there was a lull in activities, Forrest acted like the light had gone out of him. I tried hard to make it anything but Luke, but down deep I knew Luke had been there beside him all of his growing up years, setting the pace and tone for, not only him, but for all those in the encompassing sphere of their social world. Suddenly, I realized Forrest was watching me.

"Penny for your thoughts." He flicked his napkin absently.

"I'm feeling sorry for you without your chum to liven things up."

"Who needs Luke when I have the prettiest little sister to keep me company?"

I made a face at him and hit him on the shoulder as any good little sister should. "Glad you see the light. You never did need him. He needs you."

"He doesn't need anyone with that magnificent Cord to go racing around in and with no daddy to say no."

"I suppose." Now, I knew what was bothering him, Luke racing around in that beautiful car with Linda by his side. The world would never come right.

Chapter 9

Before any of us could come to grips with the intrusive nature of war, its undiscriminating long arm reached out into our world, and left us all standing at the train depot dejected and forlorn as Allen's troop-train disappeared down the tracks. His parents had come and spent the weekend at the farm so our group at the depot was large enough to attract the attention of the Phelpsburg Gazette, and they chose Abbey for an interview. She fit their criteria for an emotional article perfectly. She was a pretty newlywed saying a brave goodbye to her husband. We stood like statues fighting for control as Abbey's blue eyes filled with tears that finally broke free and slipped down her cheeks. Forrest stepped forward, put his arm protectively around his sister and politely answered a few additional questions before he led her safely away.

My love for Forrest soared; my hero had the presence of mind to rescue his sister. How could I not love him? It struck me poignantly that he had truly become a man, mature and thoughtful in ways beyond the count of years. He was leaving me behind. I must grow up very fast before it was too late. Because my emotions were being bombarded from so many different angles, I felt as though it was Forrest who was leaving, and all too soon, summer would be over and he'd be off to college. In one sense, he had already left me. I could only imagine what Abbey must be going through. She and Allen had shared a married life;

she was saying goodbye to her husband, and war posed horrific dangers impossible to allow our minds to contemplate.

There were more tearful goodbyes as Allen's parents departed, with Abbey promising to visit them often. Suddenly everything felt empty and awkward as we five turned toward Mr. Stanley's car. In a moment's time, our lives had turned an earthshaking corner yet the sun still shone brightly; up in the country the oats were peacefully growing in that same sun, and cows were probably at the gate waiting to be milked like any normal day. The pages on the calendar would continue to turn, but now life must center around Allen and all our GIs, and we must devote our energies to finding ways to help win the war. It was up to us to give our troops a world worth fighting for. We tucked our fears away in secret places hidden from each other.

***

In the silence of my room that night I began to ponder my fate. What would become of me? Abbey would be living at home during the war. Would the Stanleys still need me? Should I ask Ma if I could move back in with them? Now that Luke had been called up, there was no chance he would be coming home. With him gone Daddy could move back into his old room downstairs. Mark would be with Matt in Luke's room, and Ma and I could have our old room back. It seemed simple as pie until I saw myself asking Ma. It had been so long since she and I had passed baby Mark back and forth between us and shared love in that roundabout way that those feelings had now faded. Mark was no longer a baby to rekindle that love. Instead he was now only an avenue usurping Ma's love.

How tenuous my position was came thundering home to me with a vengeance. I didn't belong anywhere or to anyone. I knew without asking, that the Stanleys didn't need me, and if I did ask, they'd feel duty bound to say they did. That's the kind of people they were. I'd have to ask Ma.

I didn't sleep well, and as the sun rose the following morning I asked myself: was I being too hasty? Could I wait and see? But, no amount of wishful thinking on my part could change the facts and the decision facing me. This was the last time I'd be waking up in this room. A wave of nausea swept over me. I must ask Ma if I could move back, but NO way could I ask Ma. I decided to pack my bag and simply walk on down the road as if I were going home after a weekend visit at the Stanley's.

My immediate hurdle was also daunting. I had to find just the right way to tell the Stanleys. The world was pressing in on me. Snooks was on the foot of my bed. I gathered her up in my arms and let her soft warm fur dry my tears. How could I leave this house where there was love, more than enough love to go around?

To my surprise, Ma was at our door as I came downstairs. I should have known Ma by now. Mrs. Stanley opened the door. "Come in, Clara. Everything all right?"

"Not to alarm you. I just came up to help Josephine gather her things to move her back home since you won't be needing her anymore."

Obviously, she thought that I would be willing to take advantage of the Stanleys, and my feelings were hurt. Why couldn't she trust me a little, give me a chance? Never was I as relieved and gratified to be able to unequivocally prove myself to her, and also to the Stanleys, as I was when I proudly announced, "My bag's all packed. I've come down to say goodbye."

To my surprise, in a chorus, all the Stanleys gave a great protest, proclaiming that I was not only needed, but they'd be lost without me.

That was, unless Ma was in special need of my help. Abbey would be teaching in the Tate Town one room school, and her evenings would be spent correcting school papers. Forrest would be gone and there would be all his chores around the house that would make more work for someone. Mr. Stanley would be busier than ever with Forrest gone. Though of course, I wouldn't be expected to work in the barn.

Mr. Stanley spook up. "With the war and all, we have'ta have a Victory Garden, and I'll be needing Josephine's help there too."

Mrs. Stanley added, "Indeed he will. My back's the reason we gave up having a garden."

And Abbey ended the spiel with, "She's my little sister, and we can't get along without her!"

Never was I so relieved. I felt proud to have Ma hearing all this. I did belong somewhere, and if not to her, then there was no place I wanted to belong as much as I wanted to belong to the Stanleys.

We invited Ma to sit down and have some breakfast.

"Thanks. That'd be nice. I left just as Paul and the boys were getting started."

It wasn't long before Matt and Mark came marching up the road looking for her, and I got out the cookie jar and milk. I thought, why not have a little party, celebrating my evolution onto the next plateau of life? I felt secure. I had a family, and I was fast becoming an adult. Perhaps I was already there, if only my body would be a little quicker to catch up.

Matt and Mark reinforced my elation. "But we want Yo to come home and live with us."

Ma took a little of the wind out of my sails. "We'll just have to make-do without her boys. You may have to come up here and give her a helping hand. That'd make you feel better wouldn't it?"

Why couldn't she have just accepted the idea that they wanted me instead of only worrying about how to comfort them?

"Can we stay today?"

"Today's not the day."

Mrs. Stanley came to their rescue. "Let'em stay, Clara. The kids can have a picnic lunch and check for blackberries. Abbey needs a break, Josephine too. It'll do them all good."

We packed egg salad sandwiches on homemade bread, cheese, bananas, and more cookies in our berry-pails and headed out the lane to the back pasture. Abbey began to tell stories reminiscing about the first time she brought me over to pick strawberries when everything was shockingly new to me.

"Can you believe Jo had never been out of the city, hardly out of her upstairs apartment home?"

"Yo had never even seen a strawberry plant." Forrest explained as he started to share his knowledge of nature just as he had with me those many years ago, only Matt and Mark were two jumps ahead of him.

Mark insisted, "Well, Yo's the one who told us all about how to check for strawberry blooms in spring so we'd know where to pick."

We laughed about that and Forest told me it was obvious I had done a good job passing on the tradition. It had been a long time since he had been berrying with me, but it felt great to be tagging after him like old times. I half expected him to pat me on the head like a good little sister. Laddie also thought life had finally returned to normal the way it should have been all along. He eagerly ran sniffing around each bush, selectively lifting his leg to mark his territory. Now and then he paused to quickly slurp up the stream of spittle that ran dripping off the end of his tongue that was flopping out the side of his mouth. Proud as a prancing horse, he'd circle back for Forrest's approval.

Matt said, "If you weren't here, Woody, Laddie'd come to me."

"That's a good smart dog…Good boy, Laddie…Thanks for looking after him for me, Matt."

By the time we had eaten our berry-pail lunches, Abbey had shed her gloomy patina just as Mrs. Stanley had planned when she suggested our outing, and we headed home with empty pails, but bright-eyed and refreshed.

Matt said, "Mrs. Stanley, the blackberries need a few more days to ripen."

"Yeah." Mark's face shone with radiant self confidence. "We'll be back in a few days and pick you a whole big bunch."

Next time, we did come home with our pails full. Mrs. Stanley baked our first-of-season blackberry pie, and Abbey taught me to make jam. When we carried the jars into the pantry, seeing them lined up on the shelf beautifully waiting for the long cold winter ahead, something inside me was set on fire. That fall I was consumed with a passion to see our larder grow. The smell and feel of mature August with her bounty filled me up. Mother Earth became the blooming woman inside of me, growing and reaching out. I could hardly wait for next year when I'd have all the produce from our victory garden to can. I was like a squirrel hoarding nuts. The Stanleys laughed at me as they sang my praises.

***

At the end of August Luke left for the army without going home to say goodbye to his father which must have bothered Ma almost as much as it did Daddy. She knew it was her presence in the family that caused Luke to leave home. Daddy's loyalties were pulled in two directions because Ma had actually rescued the family for him, and at the same time, maybe Luke wouldn't have succumbed to temptation if Ma hadn't been there. Underneath, did he realize Luke had been deceiving him all along? How easy it is to see only what you want to see, and Daddy was a pro in that department when it came to Luke. But, his unchanged attitude toward Ma made it obvious that he was not totally blind.

Forrest talked Abbey and me into going with him to the train station to see Luke off. I thought it was wrong to give Luke even the slightest hint that what he had done was acceptable or forgiven. Forrest said that he agreed, it wasn't acceptable, but Luke was going to be fighting for our country. He could be killed.

"He was like a brother to me. No matter what a brother does, you still owe him a good bye."

"You mean like he should've said goodbye to his father?" Luke had taught me how to be a brat!

"Yo, I'm not even going to answer that."

Luke's leaving was a big plus in my mind. I could stop worrying about him suddenly appearing if I let my guard down, and I'd seen all of him I ever cared to see, but I went to please Forrest.

There was a big crowd surrounding the inductees, but it was not hard to spot Linda's wild radiant hair. She hung around Luke's neck, hardly giving the weeping Aunt Alma a chance to kiss him goodbye, and Linda's kisses were often and long as if no one else were present. I felt sorry for poor Forrest who I felt sure was green with envy.

When the conductor hung out the door, calling, "all aboard," Forrest said, "I'll be joining you before you know it. Take it easy, Luke."

"You can be sure I won't do that, Woody, old man. Don't let Linda get lonesome."

Abbey said, "We'll pray for your safe return."

272

I didn't say anything. I couldn't even manage a "good luck." To my surprise he ignored me too without an insult.

Soon as the train pulled out, taking Luke at his word, Linda started right in. "What ever could Luke have meant by that, Woody?" And, she rolled her eyes at Forrest as if two minutes before she hadn't been hanging around Luke's neck. It made me sick to my stomach because I could see how it was going to be from now on.

Aunt Alma said, "Just come right out and ask Forrest if he'll give you a lift home. Don't make a fool of yourself." I could see she didn't like Linda, but she didn't want Luke's girl flirting with Forrest.

"Sure thing, Linda, I'll be glad to give you a ride. Won't be much out of our way."

I thought, yeah, he'll be right there to wait on Linda hand and foot and keep her safe for Luke while he dies inside wanting her for himself.

I know, Aunt Carrie, I try to be a good person but sometimes it's impossible not to think the obvious. I pray this war will be over soon. Please, God, let this war be over soon and bring Allen and Luke home safe. Yes, Luke, I don't want anyone to die. See, Aunt Carrie, I'm growing up!

Now that Luke was off to the army our attention was totally on Forrest's impending departure. Every day we had been checking the early apple tree. How our mouth's watered for that first-end-of-summer fresh apple pie before Forrest had to leave.

He said, "By jinx, I'd miss going to college sooner I'd miss Mom's first apple pie."

That pleased Mrs. Stanley and she assured him there'd still be plenty of apples at Thanksgiving time when he came home.

"But not fresh picked apples from the early apple tree."

I climbed the tree and managed to get a generous pan full for a pie, but canning them would have to wait a little longer.

During that last morning, I watched as Forrest gathered his things together. "You know, Yo, I can never thank you enough for all you do around here. Makes my leaving much easier."

My heart swelled up. I wanted to cry, but I would have plenty of time for that after he left.

The good-byes from the back door were an anticlimax compared to sending Allen and Luke off to war at the train station, but for me it was devastating. I was saying goodbye to my childhood hero. Try as I might, our old closeness had managed to elude us. There were times it was close, but there was a curtain between us, and my heart wept fearing I would never be able to grow up fast enough to open it. Now he would grow in new ways, in strange places I'd never see with new people I'd never know.

Mrs. Stanley said, "We're off. We'll be late coming home. Don't worry."

Laddie knew something was amiss and had been glued to Forrest for days. Now he ran barking after the car, something he never did. Forrest turned and waved at us through the back window of the car, and tears welled up in my eyes. As Abbey and I turned to go back into the house, I heard the lonesome call of a straggler robin also left behind. I wondered what its story was and wished it good luck in its solo flight. This was the first year I could remember being so obsessed with their migration that had started in August with flocks stopping to feed before they flew on southward. Their strut was nervous and worried as they picked at the dry grass, cocking their heads as they listened and looked for worms. Their call had an urgent timber accompanied by the rustling few early fallen leaves and bluer skies.

The wonderfully pungent smell of overripe autumn filled me with longing for the old days when Forrest and I gathered the earth's bounty together. In years past, we had almost made ourselves sick,

274

tasting every kind of fruit we picked. Gratefully, now it had become the task that helped fill the hollow place in my heart. Good work that was making me a new kind of proud. Our pantry was lined with rows of colorful jars. Jars I had canned, food for the long days of winter that would soon descend upon us, another isolating threat.

"Come on, Jo. Let's dig into some job we've been dreading and get our minds off sad thoughts…let's clean the back room…that should do it."

"I don't know…that might be just a little too dreaded. Don't you have papers to correct?"

Abbey found teaching in the one room school a challenge that held a rewarding sweetness for her that teaching in the city had lacked. It was like coming home to her roots. However the high point in her day was returning home from school and mail time. She had rejoiced as she danced around the house with her letter pressed against her heart when she received the news that Allen was training to be an instructor in the Army's radio repair school. Now he would never have to see action.

I also had an interest in the mail that I kept secret, and could hardly believe it when Forrest's first letter finally arrived. A weight was lifted from me because it was not written to a little sister, but to a person he truly missed. He said he especially looked forward to my letters because I told him about the things he missed most. I wrote about the fall colors being brighter than usual, some years are like that, about the harvest, how much Abbey and I canned, and about how I dreaded it being my last year in the one-room school. I even wrote about Matt being in the sixth grade and determined to be the minister Luke was supposed to have been. About how slow Daddy was in waking up to how good Matt was, and how hard he worked. He had taken over so many of the barn chores, with Laddie at his heels, that Mr. Stanley was paying him, and how unlike Luke, he voluntarily saved his money for college. I explained how Mark was a charmer like Luke only he wasn't stuck on himself. Even though he was only in first grade, second grade work was a snap for him, and he'd probably turn out to be a genius.

Of course, I wrote about the farm and everything going on around the house. I kept track of the songs that made the Hit Parade. I told him Abbey and I went to the movies now and again, and asked him if he'd seen "Woman of the Year" with Spencer Tracy and Katherine Hepburn. I told him I wished I were smarter so I could write stories. Forrest was the only one I could tell things like that to.

I drew him a diagram of the Victory Garden I was planning. I told how I planned to let more hens set come spring to increase our flock, how many calves were heifers, and about all the cute things Snooks did, everything.

In Forrest's answers, I could see he was a farmer at heart, and that he loved my letters. Mr. Stanley was right in wanting to pass the farm on to him one day. In my opinion and everyone else's, he should have stayed on the farm and requested a farm deferment from the draft. What could be more important to the war effort than feeding people? These were things I did not write about, not even a hint.

***

It seemed to take forever for Thanksgiving to finally arrive. Laddie knew the instant Forrest stepped out of the car, and he came bounding up the road from the tenant house. He yipped happily and nearly wiggled himself right out of his skin. Forrest scrubbed his fingers through Laddie's side-fur and scratched his ears in an enthusiastic greeting. I couldn't help thinking dogs had the advantage in being able to openly display their affection, but to my surprise, even before

Forrest took his suitcase into the house, he wanted to see where I planned to put the garden.

"Excellent, Yo. I'm sure Dad has more calf-pens to muck out. Suppose I spread manure on your plot; then it'll be aged compost by spring and won't burn your plants."

It was late, and Abbey and I had prepared a light supper, so all we had to do was put it on the table. After the dishes were done, Matt and Mark came up, and we all listened to records for a while. They complained, "Ma's busy, busy baking pies. There's nothing to do down home."

Mrs. Stanley told them, "Clara's busy today. We'll be busy tomorrow!"

It was true. We four farm women put on a Thanksgiving feast fit for kings. Mrs. Stanley, Abbey and I scurried around, made the dressing and put the turkey in to roast, peeled potatoes and broke up a huge winter squash with a maul, peeled and cooked it. Ma brought her good home-canned green beans and beets. She had baked apple, mince, pumpkin and pecan pies, plus fancy breads and cranberry sauce. The smell of roasting turkey and homemade rolls teased and sharpened our appetites.

We put all the leaves in the table and made a centerpiece of gourds, pressed leaves and a pumpkin with Mr. Stanley's World War I army hat jauntily set at an angle on top of it to pay tribute to our soldiers. Abbey was all smiles but there was a drawn look around her eyes, and I knew she was thinking what it would be like if only Allen were there and the world were normal. She wasn't the only one thinking those thoughts. Aunt Alma was teary-eyed. Her attitude made an unhappy strain on the whole day. She went on and on about how wonderfully Luke was doing in the army. Poor Daddy wore his long stern face of old. Undoubtedly, penance until the lost sheep came home. Then he could allow himself to be happy again. Ma kept to the kitchen out of Aunt Alma's sight and hearing.

She had resumed her weekly visits despite how she felt about Ma. The first time I saw her getting out of Daddy's car down at the tenant house, I smiled.

Aunt Carrie, Aunt Alma must like Ma's cooking more than she dislikes her!

Then, I felt guilty because Aunt Alma did love her grandchildren and Daddy. But I'm sure I wasn't the only one who wondered how they managed to get through their Sunday dinners.

Friday was an almost perfect day. Forrest and I worked side by side joking and laughing just like old times as we mucked out manure for my garden, and my head was fuzzy with happiness. Almost perfect! Right on cue, Linda and Mary Ann showed up as we were coming up out of the barn stinky and dirty, our task finished. Like air out of a balloon, the fuzzy feeling in my head fizzled out.

After gushing "hellos" they said, "Forrest, a little bird told us you were home. Let's listen to records. Life's boring."

Without Luke, I silently added to myself, but it was plain, Forrest was happy to see them. He set the records out for them while we cleaned up. I said, "Guess I'll wash my hair." I didn't want to be hurt because I knew I wouldn't be invited to join them.

Mrs. Stanley said, "There's plenty of hot water, Jo. Just fill the reservoir when you're finished so there'll be hot water for dishes, and put a stick of wood in the stove while you're there."

My hair always took a ton of hot water, and I was always cutting our supply short.

Abbey said, "Come on Linda, let's dance. Uncle Sam's stolen our guys, but we can still shake a leg."

When Forrest joined them I could hear him say, "Come on, Mary Ann."

I wound my hair up tightly in a towel on top of my head, filled the reservoir and added wood to the stove. The victrola was winding down so I stopped on my way upstairs to wind it up for the dancers.

"Gees, Yo," Linda said, "you look just like a princess out of 'The Arabian Knights.'"

Forrest snapped his head around to give me another look as he swung Mary Ann, making her skirt wind up around her legs.

Mary Ann was breathless. "She does. Those eyes!"

I never thought I'd get that kind of compliment from Linda. I blushed and didn't know what to say. Abbey caught my eye and winked.

Then Linda spoiled her compliment and put me back into the real world. "We have the wrong music for belly dancing."

Belly dancing! She meant that as an insult. She gave her jitterbug step an extra twist to show off as I escaped upstairs. There was a mean streak in Linda that was just like Luke. My jealous heart wanted to think that being beautiful made people mean, but I knew that wasn't true because Abbey was pretty, and she didn't have a mean bone in her body. I thought: this is my house not Linda's; I'm not going to be a scaredy cat; I don't need an invitation; I live here. I bravely left my hair loose to dry around my shoulders like a sleek black rag-mop and went down stairs.

Linda was flinging her flaming hair around and shaking her hips, teasing Forrest, trying to coax him away from Mary Ann. I stood by the victrola to keep it wound and the records changed. Mr. Stanley came in and stood in the doorway to watch the dancers. As usual, he was smiling that smile of his that made you want to know his secrets, and his stocking feet kept time to the music.

He danced over to me. "Come on, Jo, let's have us a dance." He took my hand in his huge rough callused one, bowed regally in his bib overalls and looking at his feet, continued, "I don't think I can do too much damage if I step on your feet." And he wiggled his toes at me.

Mr. Stanley was the best substitute father in the whole world, and I loved him. "But, I don't know how to dance."

"Well, we'll fix that quick enough." He explained the two-step and the uneven foxtrot. "From there it's a short leap to jitterbugging."

Since singing was my talent, I had a good sense of rhythm, and it wasn't long before Mr. Stanley broke through my inhibitions, and we were cutting-up, laughing, stepping all over each other's feet and having a better time than anyone. He said, "Now, if we accent our rhythm with a swag of the hips, zing of knees and a howdy dip of the shoulders, I think we'll have the jitterbug." Mr. Stanley kept my thick jet mop swinging and slapping my cheeks. I'm sure we were the funniest looking couple in the world, but everyone was laughing and having a better time because of us.

Later, after Mr. Stanley had gone back to work and I was busy setting the table for supper, I tried to figure out, was I part of the gang? Did Luke's absence make that much difference? Had I crossed an invisible barrier when I stepped onto that new plateau? Had Forrest adjusted to losing Luke? Had he turned a corner without Luke around setting the pace? Surprisingly, he had let Linda fend for herself and hadn't shown any sign of annoyance that Mary Ann was openly possessive. Linda pretended to be satisfied to dance with Abbey, but I could see through her innocent act cutely cutting up, calling attention to herself, but when didn't she do that? She disgusted me but that wasn't new either. Member of the gang or not, something was different. Everything was opening up for me. I enjoyed my place in the scheme of things, yes my place!

Saturday Forrest helped Mr. Stanley finish cleaning the calf pens. Saturday night Forrest, Abbey and I went to the movies and saw

"Yankee Doodle Dandy" with Jimmy Cagney. After the show, Mr. and Mrs. Stanley had hot spiced cider and doughnuts waiting for us, and we sat around the kitchen table with a wood fire burning in the big old black cook stove. Its warmth matched the glow in our hearts as we enjoyed our oasis in the midst of a world at war. Snooks jumped upon my lap and purred contentedly. Laddie slept under the table on Forrest's feet. I was part of a real family. Little sister was good enough for now.

Sunday, Mr. and Mrs. Stanley drove Forrest back to Ithaca.

Chapter 10

During the following summer the expanse of my spirit was reflected in the bounty of my garden. The garden was the center of my world. Even my hero worship for Forrest took second place, and to my surprise our friendship flourished as if it too were a seed in moist soil. The bursting forth of all those little plants filled me up with an abundance of creative joy. It showed in my countenance. I was at home with myself, who I was, and everyone was pleased with me. Whenever anyone wanted me they'd say, "Look in the garden. Jo lives in that garden!" It was the focus of all that was happening to me.

That summer my recorded memories were couched around what was growing in my garden, and it was a summer of homecomings and departures. Allen came home on furlough when the string beans were budding. Abbey had finished her school year, and was flitting around the house like a nesting bird hardly able to contain herself in anticipation. Allen was to be stationed in New Jersey for the foreseeable future. He had rented a small apartment near the army base for her. After a short visit with both sets of parents, they planned to drive back to New Jersey. Even though the drive back would take longer than by train, they reasoned Allen's car would make life easier for Abbey. If Uncle Sam's plans changed and Allen was shipped overseas, she'd have the car for her trip home.

There were tears, but as usual Forrest became the philosopher. "Think how great it'll be for Abbey and Allen to be together. How many couples get that chance these days? It's something to be happy about in the middle of this war."

Mrs. Stanley told me over and over again how fortunate they were to have me with them. I was their one comfort in all the upheaval and sadness. To be able to repay them, however little it might be for the home and love they had given me, was a gift, a joy and a seal to my security.

It was when the shiny little green tomatoes appeared on the vines that Sgt. Luke Osborn drove into the Stanley's driveway early one evening. Linda was with him; her radiant green eyes shown out from her perfect unfreckled face. She was that rare redhead whose creamy skin was flawless down to the flirting shapely legs in her daring very short, shorts. The drive in Luke's speed demon midnight-blue Cord, top down, had whipped her dazzling red hair into a scorching sun goddess' halo that flowed out over Luke's arm where it rested around her shoulder. Luke was handsome beyond words in his immaculate uniform with his dark cinnamon-brown hair peeking out from under his Garrison cap. If ever there was perfection, it was the two of them standing there beside that magnificent car.

As Forrest walked toward them, he said, "Gees, Luke, Sgt. already. Congratulations."

"Darn right." He immediately started bragging about the soft touch he had managed to secure chauffeuring the "big brass" around. When he had exhausted that topic he started a new one. "I tell ya, it couldn't get any better...that is unless...well, I'm getting ready to ship overseas...got'a check out those foreign girls." He made figure suggesting motions. "See how they stack up to our good old American girls."

It had been a beautiful, but hot summer day, the kind of day when the cool of the evening was especially sweet, and Forrest had joined me in the garden.

Luke coaxed, "Hop in Woody. We'll pick-up Mary Anne and go for a spin."

"I'm beat. Been haying it all day."

Luke hit Forrest on the shoulder, a little too enthusiastically. "Come on old man, all work and no play makes Woody a dull blade."

"I guess, only I promised Yo I'd help sucker the tomatoes plants."

Luke called to me. "No, that can't be Yo? By darn, it is Yo. Still a runt, but she has shape. Forget Mary Anne. Bring Yo along. She'll forget those tomatoes soon enough. Isn't that right, Gypsy face?"

I stayed bent over pretending to be absorbed in my task, not hearing.

Forest said, "Great to have him home, eh, Linda. You two go on…I'm sure you'd rather be alone anyway. Good to see you looking great, Luke."

I wanted to believe it was calling me "Gypsy face" that turned Forrest away from them, back to me and the tomato patch, but I was not that foolish. Seeing Linda so radiant and happy with the now SGT renegade was hard to swallow. As he rejoined me in the garden, his jaw was set, and our relaxed happy atmosphere had vanished with the cloud of dust behind Luke's Cord.

It was evident that Luke could no longer cast his spell over Forrest despite their past brother-like relationship. Now dissolved, the loss of that relationship left a gaping hole in Forrest's life leaving room for our new budding friendship. In reality, I was doing what I had always done ever since the day long ago when Forrest stunned the robin with his sling shot. I was trying to fill the gaping hole in my own soul.

At the end of August when the rows in the garden had been transformed into rows of vegetables peeking out of cans on the pantry shelves, Mr. Stanley drove Forrest back to Cornell for his sophomore year of college. Every time I turned around I expect to see him. I missed him so much. There were potatoes, rutabagas, horseradishes, beets and carrots to be dug, and there were apples and pears to be picked. It wouldn't be fun without him.

When the pumpkins began to turn dark gold, I started my freshmen year in high school. Going from our one-room school to Phelpsburg High where there were more kids my own age than I had imagined existed in the world, was a shock. Plus the long commute carried me far away from the farm and time I needed to spend in the garden.

My spirits were pulled up by the enthusiasm of the echo twins, Carol and Carl, from across the hill. They loved high school. It was nice to have friends to sit with on the bus and familiar faces in the sea of strangers. Our being newcomers where clicks were already established, drew us closer together reinforcing our waning friendship.

Carol and Carl started coming by to visit and usually found me in the garden. We'd end up listening to records just like Forrest and Luke used to. They always went to the Grange dances and starting coaxing me to join them.

"Come on, Yo. There's a live band. It'll be fun."

Mrs. Stanley was on their side. "Yes. Go. It'll do you good to have some fun."

Due to Mr. Stanley's dancing lesson, it was fun. To my great surprise, Carl acted like he wanted me, with my Gypsy face, to be his girlfriend. That was so confusing I stopped going, and turned my attention back to putting my garden to bed for the winter.

On a blustery day in October when bare branches etched the bluest of blue skies, Linda came walking out to the garden where I was mulching the asparagus bed I had started in spring. That shocked me because I knew she shared Luke's dislike for me, and with Forrest at Cornell and Abbey moved away to Allen's Base, there was no reason for her to be stopping by. At first she tried to make small talk as if we were friends.

That was so awkward she gave up. "Yo, I really came to ask a big favor. Could you get Luke's address for me?"

I was surprised and dumbfounded. They were obviously not writing to each other. "How can I get it? He never writes to the Stanleys or to Daddy." I wanted nothing to do with Luke, and I thought she'd be better off without him too.

"Please, Yo."

I shrugged my shoulders.

"Couldn't you ask Luke's grandma? She comes out to visit Mr. Osborn…..and your mother, and the boys every Sunday, doesn't she?"

"Aunt Alma? She tells lies about Ma. She'd never give it to me. Anyway, she'd think it was fishy if I asked her."

"Ask Mrs. Stanley. She'd give it to her."

"Why don't you ask her yourself?"

"I thought you'd be glad to."

"I'm not."

Linda burst into tears. "Please, Yo. I can't ask, and I have to have it."

"Give him up; he's a no good liar. You'd be better off without him. There're other fish in the pond."

"I can't….I'm….I'm…pregnant. I love him, and I'm so scared. My dad'll throw me out as soon as he finds out. He's been after me to go to work. He can't understand why I haven't got a job. I don't know what to do."

I wasn't all that surprised that she was pregnant, knowing how Luke was, and here he was messing up another life. I doubted writing to him would do any good, but I knew she had to try. "OK, I'll get it, and I hope it works out for you."

"Please don't tell anyone, please, please."

"I won't."

"If my dad ever finds out..... I haven't told anyone."

I wanted to say he'll have to know sooner or later, but at that point I was feeling really sorry for her. As much as I didn't like her, she was too good for Luke.

Getting Luke's address was easier than I had thought. Ma invited Mrs. Stanley and me down on Sunday afternoon to taste a new recipe for pumpkin-pecan pie. While we were there Mrs. Stanley commented that it'd be Thanksgiving before we knew it; we should start making plans.

Aunt Alma said, "Pretty soon we'll have to be thinking about overseas Christmas packages and cards. May, I'll give you Luke's address. It'd mean a lot to him to get a card from you and Fred. He practically lived up there."

Later I copied it off and walked it down to Linda who was so happy to see me you'd have thought I was her best friend.

***

With my gardening chores completed, I wanted my freedom to tramp in the woods, to listen to the rustling leaves underfoot, to smell their pungent declaration of autumn, to enjoy those last days before the howling winds of winter stung our noses pink and carpeted the ground white. I caught myself sympathizing with Luke's avoidance of school homework. It occurred to me that had I been smart enough to get away with it, I'd have coasted along on my laurels too. But I wanted Forrest's approval, so I worked hard all the while knowing I would never measure up to his standard of academic achievement, though he had always said he thought I was smart. In truth, I was the one not satisfied with my mediocre grades.

I was so busy I was forced to substitute my walks home from the school bus stop in Tate Town for hiking in the woods. Instead, I kicked the rustling leaves caught in the dried grass along the edge of the dirt road.

Lined up on shelves in the pantry, I counted five hundred and some gleaming multicolored canned jars of produce. Plus there was plenty of root-cellar-food stored in the basement.

I gathered black walnuts and hickory nuts with the frisky late October breezes tugging at my braids. The days were glorious, and my woods tromping needs and my hoarding instincts were well satisfied. We were ready for the long winter ahead.

Ma's praises had been noticeably missing from the chorus of gardening compliments everyone else had given me. Instead now, gardener to gardener, she applauded my success by sharing her select garden seeds that had taken her years to develop by only saving the seeds from her best plants. Seed gathering was one of the ultimate tests of a true gardener. It would have taken me years of collecting seeds to equal them. I basked in that ray of sunshine, hoping it might be soil for a new relationship.

I continued to write everything to Forrest except, of course, Linda's predicament. I knew that news would be very upsetting to him, and I was in truth, a little scared of what his reaction might be. With our relationship on a new and hopeful plain I didn't want him worrying about Linda. I hadn't heard from her to know what Luke's response had been. However I didn't see how Luke could be of much help to

288

her with an ocean between them. And I wondered if her dad was still in the dark? Had he thrown her out?

In the second week of November, an impatient old man winter surprised us with a preview of what he had in store for us. Poor Snooks was caught in the barn and was near exhaustion when Mr. Stanley rescued her as she plowed her way through the deep snow trying to reach the house.

"Never you wonder if this little cat loves you, Jo. I think she'd have died trying to get to you if I hadn't come along and rescued her. Her little heart's about to leap right out'a her body."

"Thank you, thank you, Mr. Stanley. I couldn't stand it if anything happened to Snooks."

Her fur was wet and cold from the snow. I gathered her up into my arms and warmed her by the big old black potbellied stove in the living-room.

Mrs. Stanley always said you couldn't have Indian Summer until you saw snow in the air. This year it seemed she couldn't have been more wrong. All that beautiful weather in October had to have been Indian Summer, and it came without the appearance of a single snow flake. This snow was definitely after the fact and more than a shake of Mother Hulda's feather bed!

But the snow quickly melted and fall-like weather did return for Thanksgiving. Neither Linda nor Mary Anne showed their faces, making it a Hallmark-fairytale Thanksgiving for me. I had Forrest all to myself which sharpened all my senses. The kitchen woodstove with its warming oven kept the teakettle steaming all day, and the potbellied stove in the living room was kept banked-down day and night, keeping our cocooned world cozy. The world and its war were far away, shut out of my mind. We played monopoly and went for long walks. He never asked about either Mary Anne or Linda, and I kept silent about

Linda's pregnancy. When we were coming over the lane, he put his arm around my shoulder. I wanted to think there was more to it than a brotherly gesture, but I had seen him put his arm around Abbey many times. So I made little of it even though it felt as though his arm was right where it belonged.

Even Forrest's goodbye was special as he and Mr. Stanley left for the trip back to Cornell. He hugged and kissed Mrs. Stanley, then turned to me with another tight hug and a kiss on the forehead. I thought I saw a hint of disapproval on Mrs. Stanley's face, but couldn't face the prospect that she might not approve, and I chalked it up to a look of sadness at his departure.

When Christmas came, Forrest greeted me with not only a hug, but twirled me tight right off the floor as he had that first time long ago, only this time his cheek was pressed against mine, and the ruff of his whiskers set my heart on fire. Now there was no doubt about Mrs. Stanley's feelings. She had a look on her face that was plainly worried. I chose, worried look, rather than one of disapproval, because I never doubted she loved me. There was my age, the war and many things to happen before I would be old enough for Forrest. I knew that, but my heart and body were ready. That could be a reason to worry.

For Christmas, Forrest gave me a charm bracelet with three charms, a cat for Snooks, a cluster of gardening tools for my latest obsession, and a bird. He had remembered the robin he stunned with his slingshot, and that my warm hands had brought it back to life!

My eyes shone, and he was very pleased with himself. I threw my arms around his neck and added a loud sisterly kiss on his cheek. "Thank you, Forrest. It's, it's perfect....perfect." He took the bracelet out of its box and fastened it around my wrist.

I danced around the room, showing it to Mr. and Mrs. Stanley. They asked, "Well, Jo, there's just one gift left under the tree. Could that be your gift for Forrest?"

I handed the gift to Forrest, and he quickly tore away the wrappings. "A leather shaving kit. Just what I've needed. It'll be just the ticket when my draft notice comes......and, what's this inside....your knot. You raided your treasure box? I don't believe it."

"Yes. Remember, I found it in the hay mow?"

"Yep."

"And you told that big long yarn about your Dad buying this farm from the great-grandson of the man who cleared the land and built the barn from trees that were growing when George Washington was president, and that very knot was a limb on one of those trees. Remember, we found the round hole the knot fit. You're to leave it in your shaving kit so every time you shave, no matter where you are, you'll think about home and all the good times you had growing up on this farm."

"I don't know what to say.....as always, you know just the right thing. Thank you. I know what your treasure box means to you, and I'll think about my very special little sister too, every time I shave."

Mr. Stanley cleared his throat, and with tears in her eyes, Mrs. Stanley said, "Come, Jo. Put the sticky-buns in the oven. In the shake of a lamb's tail, we'll have a breakfast fit for kings on the table, and we'll not have to eat 'til tonight when the Osborns'll all be up for another round of presents and dinner."

***

Matt was eleven now and looked the part of a budding minister with his hair neatly slicked down. His stack of gifts was arranged in tidy order according to size. Mark was eight and full of confidence, enthusiasm and curiosity. He could hardly see over his haphazard arm load of gifts.

Ma was scolding. "Mark, where's your coat? You'll catch your death running up here in your sweater. And tuck in your shirt tail."

They were all stomping the snow from their boots, laughing and wishing everyone a Merry Christmas. It was well into the supper hour because the milking had been done and chores finished before they could join the party.   So Ma and Daddy carried their food contributions right out to the kitchen, and we began to serve up dinner. Aunt Alma followed the boys into the living room bossing the distribution of presents under the tree. "Now boys, don't just throw the gifts under the tree. Arrange them nicely so each person's gifts are scattered around and not all clumped together." Then she began to lament Luke's and Abbey's absence without a thought about how it made the rest of us feel. We were trying to keep our chins up on our first Christmas without Abbey and Allen, and Daddy had never received even one letter from Luke. Though Ma appeared to have put the trauma of Luke's attack behind her, with things the way they were, on Christmas day it had to be very near the surface of her emotions.

As we gathered around the table, sad thoughts were put to rest with exclamations about the beautiful display of harvest's bounty. We joined hands around the table and Mr. Stanley prayed: "We give thanks for this family, near and far. We pray for their safety and for a speedy end to this war. We give thanks for an abundant harvest, for the tenders of that harvest, and for the loving hands that set it before us on this Christmas Day. Amen." Then he added, "If only everyone could be sitting down to a meal like this."

Laddie, who had come in with Matt and had settled under the table at his feet, gave an appropriate little bark. We all laughed, and I got up and mixed a little turkey in some dog food. That brought Snooks scurrying to the kitchen, so I fixed her supper with turkey too.

When I sat back down at the table, Aunt Alma had already begun a new spiel. "Have you heard? Mary Anne's working in Newberry's. I have to say, she's a really nice girl. Always friendly and asks, 'Hasn't Forrest been called up yet? Does he like college? Say 'hello', to him for me'. She hopes to see you, Forrest, during Christmas. Why don't you stop by Newberry's? It'd make her day. She's trying to get in the factory where she can make more money. She rides to work with Linda's mother."

That speech was a thunder bolt to me. If Forrest saw Mary Anne, she'd certainly tell him about Linda. She had to know. If he heard it from her and found out I knew and hadn't told him, I'd have a hard time explaining that. But, how could I tell him?

Forrest asked, "Where's Linda working?"

Aunt Alma didn't look pleased with that question. "She went to visit her cousin in Philadelphia. She thought she could do better down there, so Mary Anne says. Luke's not writing to her, and I'm just as well pleased. Never thought she was good enough for him…..definitely not a good influence. I wish she'd stay right down there, but I think she's due back soon."

Forrest pretended casual interest. "Tell Mary Anne I'll look her up."

My heart sunk. He was probably hoping Linda and Luke had broken up. His interest was anything but casual. Here was his chance! I had to think of something, and soon. I could see Forrest blazing a trail right down to Mary Anne to find out.

When the Osborns were packing up to go home, Forrest and I put on our barn-boots and coats to help carry all their gifts down to the tenant house. It was a beautiful still and cold winter evening with the crunch of snow underfoot and a half moon over our shoulders.

Coming back, I wanted it to be as romantic as the scene mandated, but with these new circumstances that was impossible to even imagine, and this might be my only chance to dig myself out of a deep hole.

"I...I don't know...just how to tell you...Linda isn't looking for a job. It's true, Luke's not writing her. I know because she came up here wanting me to get his address. Forrest...she's pregnant. I should have written it to you...but I just couldn't say that in a letter. It's hard now. Luke spoils everything. I know you're not going to like this...but...I really hate him...really hate...and always have."

His shoulders visibly slumped, and I knew him so well I didn't have to see his face to know the set of his jaw. "You should've told me."

"I didn't want to spoil Christmas...just like now. Anyway, I promised not to tell. She said her father'd throw her out, and she was scared. That's probably why she went to visit her cousin. I hadn't heard that 'til tonight."

"I'll write to Luke. Maybe I can talk some sense into him. If he were here, I'd punch him in the mouth."

"He needs it...but so does she. It takes two. She looked pretty pleased with herself the day they stopped in that beautiful car of his." I shouldn't have said that. I knew he felt badly, but so did I. "What good could writing to Luke do?"

He never answered.

Forrest deliberately found things to do all the next day that took him to the barn where he could sulk privately. I could only guess at what was going through his mind. One thing, I knew he didn't write to Luke because the flag was never put up on the mail box.

The following day, he took the car and headed out. When he returned, he was ready to talk. We dressed warmly, with new matching red plaid scarves, Christmas gifts from Mark, wrapped around our faces. Our feet took us down the lane toward the woods. How different this walk was from our Thanksgiving walks. Why, oh why, did my luck always turn on me? I felt a foreboding. My world was going to fall apart.

When we reached the embracing enclosure of the woods that sheltered us from the wind, we pulled the scarves from our mouths. Forrest said, "I nearly spilled the beans. Mary Anne doesn't know."

"What?"

"She doesn't know, and she hasn't heard from Linda. She doesn't even know her cousin's address."

My heart perked up a little bit because this could mean Linda had gone down there to have her baby and that's the last we'd hear of her. "Maybe it's for the best."

"Well, I went over to the sewing counter where Linda's mother works and asked her when Linda was coming home, and she said she thought soon."

"That's where Mary Anne gets her information."

"I have her cousin's address, and I'm going to write and ask her if she's heard from Luke, and offer to help her find a place if she wants to keep the baby for when Luke gets home."

At that moment I knew if I hadn't told him, he wouldn't have found out. He would have been spared the agonizing responsibility he now felt for her. Why was I so dumb, and why did everything end up my fault?

Our walk was totally ruined. Luke would never agree to that. Forrest was going to be sucked right in over his head, and there was not one thing I could do about it

He left for Cornell New Year's Day, and with him went all the strides we had made in our relationship, or so it seemed to me as he said his subdued "goodbyes". He walked head down, suitcase in hand, out to the car where Mr. Stanley waited. Mr. Stanley had also looked pretty glum as he walked out the door, and Mrs. Stanley made no attempt to hide her tears.

There was a letter for me at the end of the week which went a little way toward putting things right again. Forrest said he didn't mean to take it out on me. I had nothing to do with the problem. He'd be forever grateful to me for cluing him in, especially since he knew how hard anything to do with Luke was for me, and he wished he had listened to me about him long ago.

***

Forrest's draft notice arrived the middle of January, and it became clear to me that Mr. and Mrs. Stanley had been expecting it. That was why they were so openly sad when Forrest left. I just couldn't seem to keep up with the rhythm of war events, so it hit me hard in light of everything that was going on. It would have been devastating even without Linda's predicament coming between Forrest and me. The only good thing about Forrest's notice was that it might get him away from the impending Linda entanglement. My heart was hurting so much it swelled up so big it was choking me.

We were disappointed when Forrest's letter came saying he wouldn't be ready to come home for another week. The mail arrived just in time or Mr. Stanley would have been on his way to Ithaca. We couldn't figure out what was taking Forrest so long to tie up the formalities at Cornell. His time at home was going to be cut short. "Tied up" was too mild a term for what was going on in Ithaca. "Hogtied" would be more accurate. All my foreboding was to come true beyond my worst nightmare.

When Forrest came through the back door, Linda was with him. Our mouths fell open and Mrs. Stanley was speechless. Linda's

296

pregnancy was very apparent. The thoughts that must have been flying through Mrs. Stanley's mind! Mr. Stanley was the last person in the procession and wore the saddest face I had ever seen. That pleased-with-the-world look of his had completely vanished. The secrets he knew now were not of the pleasant variety.

He said, "Let's take off our coats and go in the living-room and sit down. Forrest has something he wants to say."

No greetings were exchanged, and as Mr. Stanley hung his coat on the hall tree in the little entrance hall to the cellar, Mrs. Stanley hovered at his elbow. He whispered, "Be strong, May," and putting a comforting arm around her, guided her to the sofa where he protectively sat down beside her.

Forrest and Linda remained standing and Forrest said, "I'll take Linda on upstairs....."

Mr. Stanley didn't wait for him to finish his sentence. "....Sit down Linda. You should be present."

Forrest was noticeably taken aback and uneasy. "Mom....Jo... Linda has no place to go. Her father has thrown her out. Luke wants no part of this and says the baby's not his. Linda needs a home and a name for her baby. We were married yesterday."

I felt a thunderbolt had hit!

Disbelief flooded Mrs. Stanley's face and quickly turned to anger. "No, Forrest. You can't marry without our signature. Fred, we'll get this annulled...immediately....What was you thinking, Forrest? Absolutely not. Today, we're getting this marriage annulled...today...this very day."

She bristled like a wet hen, shaking out her feathers. I could feel her outrage where I sat across the room tucked way back in the corner of the window seat. My world had come to an end. I was in shock and the room weaved in and out of focus. My arms were wrapped tightly around my body, and I squeezed them tighter, with all my might, to hold myself together. The conversation went into my ears and was recorded to be translated later when I was alone.

Now Forrest was more than uneasy. He was agitated. "If I'm old enough to go to war, I'm old enough to get married. We went across the state line. Mom, I've thought this through….."

"No, you haven't. We'll see that Linda has a place to go, and is looked after. You are not required to do this. There's no need for you to get involved in Luke's debacle. She should be knocking on Paul Osborn's door."

Mr. Stanley's attention was on Mrs. Stanley, and he was plainly beside himself with concern. "Calm yourself, May. We can't have you getting sick. Let Forrest talk. We've been all through this. We're going to have to go along."

"Yes, Mom. Please, don't make yourself sick. Everything'll work out all right. Linda can have Abbey's room 'til I leave, then she can move into my room. When the war's over, we'll work it out. In the meantime Linda'll have a home. She won't be any trouble. You'll have another helper."

Mrs. Stanley looked right at Linda for the first time and snidely asked, "And what do you have to say for yourself?"

This was a Mrs. Stanley I had never seen before. She was a mother protecting her child. Only due to the war and circumstances, Forrest was no long a child. In reality in most ways, he had always been mature beyond his years.

Linda looked the part of the poor helpless, pregnant girl who had just been slapped. "I promised Forrest I'd never be a problem, and I'll be forever grateful. Forrest's the best person in the world, and you're the family that made him that way."

Mrs. Stanley started to say something, but Mr. Stanley didn't give her a chance. "Enough said, May. We're all going to be living together...the less said, the less mended. Forrest, take Linda on upstairs and get her settled."

I escaped out through the kitchen to the backroom where I grabbed my barn coat. My mind flew to Aunt Carrie, and I longed for her stout arms to enfold me, but I didn't cry to her. I cried out to God. "Help me, please God...help me...help me hold on. What's the matter with Forrest? Why, why? Hold me together. Oh, please, God...hold me together." It was bitterly cold, and my tears felt frozen on my cheeks as I ran toward the warmth of the barn. The thought of the tenant house, and a warm and cozy scene popped into my head. Matt and Mark would be in the kitchen doing their homework while Ma baked her goodies to sell next day. Daddy would be in the living room, contentedly reading the paper. But there was no warmth there for me. With that thought, sobs came wrenching from my chest before I reached the barn door.

I ran down the stairs, slid the door to the milking part of the barn where the milking herd stood placidly with their heads in the stanchions, munching hay or chewing their cuds oblivious to the world collapsing around me. I threw myself down on the hay in front of the stanchions, just out of the cow's reach and wept.

Ugly thoughts ran one on top of the other through my mind. Linda would never love Forrest, and she'd never let him go. I hated her with a frightening passion. I couldn't imagine living in the same house with her, and poor Mr. and Mrs. Stanley. How could I bear it? Whatever in the world would become of us? So tenuous was my sense of wellbeing, that my shattered heart plunged me into a despair where death suddenly loomed up as the only avenue of escape. I was no longer the little girl who thought the only way to die was to be thrown into the bullpen by Luke, Luke who thought only of himself and caused so much pain. I hated him even more than Linda. Every mean act he had ever visited upon me marched though my emotions. How could God allow people like him go through life, leaving destroyed lives in his wake? And seemingly shine on him. With those hateful thoughts, I knew I was evil, Ma too, just like Luke said. I was the cause of everything bad.

There was a clouded area in my mind, just beyond my memory, out of reach, and I felt myself being bathed in warm soothing water and put to bed. Oblivion beckoned. My mind began to plot my revenge on the world. I'd write it all out so Linda would know it was hers and Luke's fault, and when Forrest saw my body lying in the coffin, he'd see the light, and know what Linda was, and be saved from her trap. That would be a fitting end for me.

As I sat up to right myself before tackling the first phase of my plan, Forrest appeared and heaving a big sigh of relief, sat down beside me. "Here you are. Have you any idea what a scare you've given us? I've looked everywhere. Supper's on. Mom's frantic."

"So eat without me. How could you dump her on us like this, then go marching off to war?" I turned on him and beat him on the chest with both my fists. "How could you...how could you?" He took me in his arms, holding me so tightly my arms were pinned down, but I still thrashed about.

"Yo, please...Yo, settle down. Talk to me."

I collapsed against his chest and wept. "Don't cry, Yo. I can't stand it for you to cry. Everything'll work out. Think how Linda must feel, she knows she's not wanted here. She's in love with Luke who doesn't want her or the baby. Her father's thrown her out and disowned her."

How could he talk to me like that? Of course I knew what it was like to be unwanted. Why in the world wasn't I with Ma, for crying out loud? Linda could have done anything. She was smart and beautiful. She should have thought about what could happen and known Luke would never stand by her, especially when he wasn't even going to be around.

Forrest gave up on my answering and continued, "She said he forced her." Maybe he thought I'd buy that, knowing what he tried to do to Ma. I wondered if even he believed it. "I've explained to Mom that when the war's over, maybe Luke'll see things differently. War does change people. We can annul the marriage then. If not, we'll go from there."

"How dumb can you get? He won't want to be tied to a ready made family, even if it's his own. You still don't know Luke. You must love her a lot. She'll need you even more when the war's over and you come home."

"Is love such a bad thing?"

"Love's everything. Look at Ma and Daddy. Do you want a marriage like theirs? They don't sleep in the same room. Daddy gave Ma a name, and she's his babysitter just like Luke said. Looks very similar to me."

"There're some things you're just not old enough to understand."

"There're some things you're just too blind to let sink in. How're your folks gonna face people who think you're the father...that you two-timed Luke while he was off fighting a war...wonderful Luke...who terrible Ma drove away. What'a ya think Daddy'll think? How about Aunt Alma's tongue? Please.....can't you see it's wrong?"

"I couldn't live with myself if I turned my back on her. How could I go off to war with that on my conscious? She's so helpless and alone."

He waited for me to say something, but I just couldn't because I could never see Linda as helpless, and the proof of that was right in front of him. Look what she had managed to manipulate.

He continued, hoping my silence was surrender. "Yo, you're the best little sister a guy could ever have. You've made me love you in all those protective ways big brothers feel. Nothing can come between us. No one can take your place." He had no idea what I was really going through, and how my world had come to a crashing end. "Yo, I'm depending on you to be the one that helps Mom through this. She loves you so much. You've helped her through Abbey's leaving. Think how much more she'll need you now.....can't we go up and ease her mind?"

Underneath my crushing hurt was the realization that the last thing in the world I wanted to do was to hurt Mr. and Mrs. Stanley. Forrest was being pig-headedly selfish, blinded by his love for Linda, but that didn't give me permission to do the same. Yet in that last way down deep place in my shattered heart, there was a tumbling turmoil of love for Forrest mixed with the desire to strike back at him so he could feel my pain.

He got up and pulled me to my feet. Brushing the hay off me, he said, "Let's go on up to supper. Yo, you must know you mean the world to me. More'n there are words to say how much."

My heart melted. I wanted to cry out to him about how sorry he was going to be, that someday he'd be as brokenhearted as I was, but I couldn't. Fate was going to punish him. I didn't need to. Such a tender love for him welled up in my heart that it sent fresh tears sliding silently down my cheeks.

I dreaded to face Mr. and Mrs. Stanley. Forrest knew and took charge. "I should've known Yo'd be in the barn communing with the cows. I have to agree with her. They're good listeners."

"I'm sorry. I forgot about helping with supper. I didn't mean to worry you."

Supper was dismal and as soon as the dishes were finished, I slipped out into the hall and up to my room. I thought unnoticed, but instantly Mrs. Stanley was at my bedroom door. "Jo, it's too cold up here." She sat down on my bed and patted the spot beside her. "Come, sit by me." We were both shivering, and she gathered me up in her arms for comfort and warmth, but nothing could thaw the winter that had settled in our hearts. She continued, "I think I know what you feel for Forrest, and there's nothing I can say to take the hurt away. I can only assure you, young hearts do mend. We've got to stick together to get through this. My heart is broken too." We looked into each others reddened eyes that were filling anew with tears. "I may never stop crying, but I must, and you must too, Josephine. Forrest is going off to war with all the awful things he'll be facing. We must do this for him and, Josephine, pray for a miracle."

We cried some more, and I finally said, "Forrest says everything'll be all right. Mr. Stanley always says don't borrow trouble. Somewhere there's a silver lining. We'll send Forrest off with our blessings."

She hugged me again, extra long and hard, and said, "Goodnight, Josephine. What a blessing you are to all of us."

As I waited for sleep, "young hearts do mend," played over and over in my mind. Did Mrs. Stanley imply that her heart was too old and sick to mend? A new fear for her wellbeing sprung up in my heart. I resolved to ease her burden as Forrest asked, and to help ease Forrest's burden as he headed off to war, as Mrs. Stanley asked.

Thinking back on that traumatic time, I was caught in the middle of two unsolvable heart-wrenching dilemmas. What a heavy burden for one so young to carry, especially one whose world had also suffered a shattering blow.

***

The very next day a representative from the REA (Rural Electrification Administration) came to the farm. They were notifying the outlying residents of Tate Town that they were ready to set electric poles as soon as the ground thawed. Thanks to President Roosevelt's New Deal we were going to join the twentieth century.

Mercifully, workmen followed, invading the Stanley's house to map out a wiring plan in preparation for work to begin. Ordinarily this intrusion would have been unwelcome during these special days before Forrest had to report, but under the circumstances it served a useful purpose. Everyone had to be calm and polite, and it gave us a neutral topic of conversation. There were hundreds of decisions to be made, where to have the outlets and switches etc. that kept our minds busy.

When Forrest wasn't busy helping with these decisions in the barn, he took Linda for a walk. I tried not to let my jealousy show, but I don't think I fooled anyone except Forrest, and he was the only one who counted at that point.

Linda was thoughtful enough in those few remaining days to act contrite. She read and stayed out of the way when Forrest wasn't around. I'm sure she didn't want any unnecessary waves until her presence was firmly implanted in the family. Forrest was on his toes every minute playing the part of conciliator. I wanted to cry out, "Why does it have to be like this, why can't he just enjoy these last days?" But, it was not to be, and I wondered if it was a role he was doomed to play for the rest of his life. He was cheerful, and I could see hope and love burning in his eyes every time he looked at Linda.

At breakfast, the morning of Forrest's departure, Linda announced she would stay home and let the rest of us see Forrest off. She said while we were gone, she'd move her things into Forrest's room. I had to admit that it was kind of her to see how uncomfortable it would be for us if she were there, but I couldn't make myself believe it was us she was thinking about.

At eleven o'clock the train pulled out with Forrest on board. There were only the three of us there to see him off, and as the train lurched forward Mrs. Stanley gave in to her tears as Mr. Stanley guided her away. I stayed and waved to Forrest as he hung out the train window, and I felt empty and sorrier than I thought I was capable of enduring. What must he have been suffering to love someone so much he was willing to put his mother and dad, to say nothing about me, through what lay ahead?

Chapter 11

Linda and I got off to a bad start. When we arrived home from Forrest's unnatural sad departure gloom hung palpably in the air as we hung our coats on the hall tree in the little connecting hallway. I was irritated because Linda was nowhere to be seen. The electricians were just leaving the house. She should have been downstairs taking responsibility for seeing them out, and she should have started supper.

Mr. and Mrs. Stanley made no derogatory comments, and I held my tongue. Mr. Stanley changed into his work clothes and went to the barn. Mrs. Stanley and I set about cooking supper.

Even with the noise in the kitchen, Linda didn't appear. When Mr. Stanley came in from chores, Mrs. Stanley said, "Jo, I suppose Linda has to be told supper's on."

"I suppose." How were we ever going to survive this intolerable situation? She'd be no trouble. In my eye! This was no way to win points.

I knocked lightly on Forrest's door and opened it. She lay on the bed with a comforter thrown over her.

"Linda, supper's on."

"In the future, don't open my door unless I invite you in."

"OK, but you better learn how things are done around here. Let's try to get along."

"I know how you feel about Forrest and what you're hoping. Remember this, I'm the daughter-in-law. You're the hired girl."

So much for her promise to Forrest. "Well, if that's the way you want it." I turned on my heels and left.

At the supper table I had never seen sorrier looking faces. Mr. Stanley tried to be casual, but his habit of playing the part of quipped reframes, didn't serve him very well. The best he could do was, "Good, hash-browns. Anyone for cabbage salad?" And so on. Mrs. Stanley was still teary-eyed and picked at her food. Linda looked as though she had a sour taste in her mouth, but she was the only one with generous helpings on her plate. She was eating for two, I told myself.

I served the cake, and as I finished eating mine, I nonchalantly asked, "If it's OK, I'd like to go to the barn with Mr. Stanley. I'm sure Matt and I together can manage Forrest's chores. Linda'll be in the kitchen to help Mrs. Stanley."

Mr. Stanley eagerly agreed. "Good idea, Jo. It'll give Linda a chance to get to know the kitchen and May. Good idea."

Battle lines were drawn. I was past lying down to be walked on, but at the same time I really didn't want a fight either. It was a fight I was ill-equipped to win even though I knew in my heart where I stood with Mr. and Mrs. Stanley, but Linda would always hold the trump card, Forrest. I just wanted to be away from her. Let the daughter-in-law help in the kitchen!

When Matt and I were watering the calves he wanted to know, "Is it true Linda's going to live with you?"

"Yes."

"Is she really married to Forrest and going to have Luke's baby?"

"Sorry to say, yes." What else could I say? Might as well get it right out and over with.

"Ma's acting funny, and Daddy's so upset." Matt stopped and poured a little more milk into the calf feeding pail and went to the next eager calf that nearly butted the pail out of his hands. "Hold on, you little rascal, or you'll have no supper." The calf guzzled the milk, and Matt reluctantly continued. "I overheard Grandma talking to Daddy and she said Luke'd written to her and said Linda's blaming him when it wasn't his baby. She said Linda'd try anything to snare him and it was Forrest who married her so it must be his. Later Ma said to Daddy that he knew that it wasn't Forrest's, and Daddy cried. I never knew Daddy to cry before. He thought Mark and I were doing our homework and didn't know what was going on. We both pretended we didn't."

"Yeah, things are pretty strained up at the Stanley's too. It's done, there's nothing we can do about it; no point in worrying. Everything'll work out."

"The baby'll be my nephew, or niece. Are you sure it's Luke's?"

"Linda said it is."

"Why'd Forrest marry her? Can you imagine how Daddy and us feel?"

"Yeah, I can...her father disowned her and she had no place to go. Forrest said the baby needed to have a name."

"She should'a waited for Luke to come home."

"Forrest's sure it'll work out all right. Linda had to have someplace to go. Forrest says it's just a marriage in name, and they'll annul it when Luke comes home."

"Oh, really. That's good." He let it go with that. I was more than willing to do the same.

Matt had been my special friend since those first days on the farm, and despite how little he was, we became each other's protector. Now he was inches taller than I was, had grown so responsible and hard working it was difficult to think of him as needing protection, but he did. He was such a tender spirit. He was worried about its affect on Ma and Daddy. What was it going to do to the relationship between our two families? He saw himself as peacemaker, protector destined to look after all those around him. He was a clergyman in the making. Hopefully Ma's selfless unconditional love, even though she was not religious, was softening the strictured theology he had inherited from his father.

As Mr. Stanley and I left the barn for the house, chores done and Matt on his way to the tenant house, Mr. Stanley started a conversation that by his tone weighted heavily on his mind. "You know, Jo, Forrest has no idea about what you're feeling. He said to me, 'Pay more attention to Yo until she gets used to my leaving.' And he's some vague notion about your dislike for Linda. He hasn't a clue. You're a kid sister....and he needs you now, more'n ever...unfair as that is....and it's unfair to all of us. I expect even to Linda even though it looks like she's the only winner. 'Nothing's fair in love or war,' so they say. They're sure right in this case. There's plenty of grief to go round. I'm count'n on you to help me hold this family together."

"I'll try...." I threw my arms around his waist and buried my face in his barn coat. I barely came to his armpits, and he held my head tenderly against his chest.

"There's just no way to know what we may have to endure." His voice was hoarse with emotion.

I knew exactly what he was saying. In war people can be killed, or maimed, or we could be stuck with Linda and Luke's baby forever. Of course I was just a kid sister, but I wasn't; I wasn't. I was years older than my height and age. A desperate feeling of isolation swept over me. Where was God? How could I be so selfish to only think about my own hurt? The centering place inside me, the core of my being, was empty. There was no one to help hold me together. God and His Goodness had abandoned me. I drank in the familiar musky barn smells emanating from Mr. Stanley's coat. I must hold on to what the farm had come to mean to me. Could I ever separate it from my love for Forrest, Forrest who loved Linda? Would she learn to love the farm? Would she learn to love Forrest?

When we came into the house Jack Benny was on the radio. Mrs. Stanley's mending basket was at her knee, and a very pregnant Linda was stretched out on the sofa. Taking up the Sunday Telegram, Mr. Stanley made his way to the chair next to Mrs. Stanley. I gathered Snooks into my arms, and together we curled up on the window seat to listen. We looked like a typical cozy family, but it was a lie. Four hearts were breaking, each for its own reasons. Somewhere Forrest was chugging along, off to war and unknown dangers; what was his heart feeling? Perhaps it was better I didn't know.

In the morning Mr. Stanley heard me stirring around getting dressed and knocked on my bedroom door. "Jo, don't come to the barn. There's no need. Just get yourself ready for school."

For once I was glad to go to school and away from the farm. I would be away from Linda.

By the time I reached home that evening the sun was touching the horizon. The electricians were gone and had left a mess. "Mrs. Stanley, I'll clean this mess up for you before I go to the barn. You and Linda have enough on your hands with supper."

On my way downstairs after changing my clothes, I carried Mrs. Stanley's slop-pail to empty it before I set about sweeping up the plaster and wood shavings.

Linda waddled after me. "Yo, didn't you forget something? What about my slop-pail?"

"What about it?"

"Well, empty it."

"What! Empty your own."

"You're the hired girl. You're empting Mrs. Stanley's."

310

"You had all day. You should've already emptied yours and hers. I haven't criticized you. Figure it out."

"Barbarians. I can't even take a decent bath." And she stomped out, nose in the air.

***

At the end of the second week, Mrs. Stanley took me aside. "Make an effort, Jo. I'm beginning to feel sorry for Linda. She hasn't been out of this house since Forrest left. I'm going for groceries this afternoon and I'd like you to offer to go with her to get some baby supplies. That baby's going to be here before we know it."

I felt like she was asking water to flow uphill! I rolled my eyes. "Sure, I'll give it a try." We couldn't avoid each other forever.

This was our first attempt at a truce. The minute we walked into JC Penney's baby department with all those adorable little clothes and soft squishy toys my heart melted. I bought a soft cuddly kitten like the one I wanted when Ma took me window shopping on my first outing back when we lived over the Sweet Shop. Linda bought diapers and receiving blankets. Then I suggested nightgowns with drawstring bottoms. She stopped to look at a tiny frilly pink dress, and I caught a wistful look in her eyes. Then she said, "It'll probably be a boy." And I said, "Look at this cute yellow sleeper set either could wear." I had to concede, it was a little bit fun, and we had made a good first step toward a truce.

Mrs. Stanley was all smiles when she joined us. While she was in the grocery store she had used the pay phone to make an appointment for Linda with their family physician, Dr. Miller. Linda was genuinely appreciative, and thanked Mrs. Stanley for not only making the appointment but especially for offering to go with her.

She had no one. I began to realize how scared and alone she must feel. Mr. Stanley was right. Linda was not a winner. I couldn't begin to put myself in her place. When I tried it was a nightmare that had so many undercurrents racing around inside of me I had to turn it off before it tore me apart. My thoughts were full of Ma and her pregnancy, the Aunts, my real father and an unwanted black-haired baby. A whirlpool of overlapping images chased each other.

As soon as we were back at the farm and groceries were put away, I grabbed my barn coat and headed out the door.   I had to turn off my emotions.

A smiling Matt ran toward me and met me at the barn door. "Yo, goodie, I like working with you."

Tears slipped out and ran silently down my cheeks.

"Don't cry, Yo. God has a plan….it'll be all right. Please, don't cry. You're the one that makes everything all right." He put his arm around my shoulder, hugging me tightly.

"You're the one, Matt. You're the special one…I can always count on you. Linda and I bought baby clothes today. I'm OK now."

"That's my Yo."

By the time Matt and I had finished chores, he had managed to turn my emotions around. I did have to meet Linda halfway. Mrs. Stanley had wisely put me on a shaky path to a new beginning with Linda.

***

The key event that set the stage for how the war years would play out for me happened while I was in church. Over and over I had wanted to take my troubles to Aunt Carrie as I had when I was little, but I had outgrown the picture-book ideas about death that had sufficed in my childhood. My heart searched for a substitute avenue to seek council for my frustrated emotions. I continually implored God to send me a sign, something to show me the way.

Then one Sunday morning we sang, "What a friend we have in Jesus, all our sins and grieves to bear! What a privilege to carry, everything to God in prayer!" That song had never particularly appealed to me before. But that Sunday the feeling it stirred up in my heart felt comforting, as if maybe I should talk my troubles over with Jesus instead of Aunt Carrie. It occurred to me that the feeling could be a message from God; Matt would sure think so. This was a new notion, not at all like my usual train of thought.

Ironically, as soon as the service was over, a beautiful lady came up to me and introduced herself. "I'm Mrs. Miller, Matt and Mark's new teacher. I've been anxious to meet you."

Matt and Mark had been overjoyed with their new teacher and hadn't been able to say enough good things about her, and insisted, "...and, Yo, she looks just like a movie star."

"I'm glad to meet you too, Mrs. Miller. Your father-in-law is the Stanley's physician."

"My husband is trying to follow in his father's footsteps, but right now he's doctoring soldiers for Uncle Sam, which brings me to why I'm so anxious to meet you. Do you know anything about 4-H?"

"Just that it's a kid's club."

"Well, I'd like to get one started. I've been hearing about your gardening skills, and a Victory Garden would make a great 4-H project. Would you consider being my assistant, my junior leader?"

"Me, a leader?"

"Yes, Josephine, you have the skills I'm looking for."

"I'll try. Thank you for asking me."

"I thank you. And with that voice of yours, you'll be a tremendous help pepping up the music."

Mrs. Miller's persona was one of grace and sophistication. Her clothes were coordinated in a manner that said she came from some place other than Phelpsburg, and there she was in Tate Town teaching Matt and Mark, the wife of a doctor, and she had singled me out to help her start a 4-H club. Just talking to her made me feel special. That Sunday morning I had two messages from on high. God had not abandoned me. He had a new direction for my life.

I was still excited when we arrived back at the farm. As Mr. and Mrs. Stanley and I were taking off our coats in the little connecting hall, I said, "Did you see the clothes she was wearing? Weren't they just like what Betty Davis or Joan Crawford would wear?"

That grabbed Linda's attention, "Who're you talking about?"

"Mrs. Miller, Matt and Mark's new teacher. And her make-up was like a movie star's. She had on a black pin-stripe suit with white piping around the lapels and those square shoulder pads are what really made her stand out like a star. Her hat was black and a little bit like a man's felt hat, only hers had a flat crown, and the brim turned down and was lined with white feathers."

"La-tee-da."

Mrs. Stanley said, "She's asked Jo to help her get a 4-H club started."

"Really. Well aren't you somebody." I think Linda was genuinely impressed though her comment was ho-hum. With hardly a pause, she proudly announced, "Leftovers are on the table."

Mrs. Stanley looked well pleased. "That's nice, Linda, thank you."

Mr. Stanley said, "Yes, Linda, but you should come to church. It's not good to be cooped up like this. The sooner braved, the better."

Mrs. Stanley added, "That's true, you should come."

That Sunday was the start of my beginning to pray much as I used to talk things over with Aunt Carrie. I prayed to Jesus to give me

God's' guidance to help me overcome my broken heart and my hatred of Linda. After all, I concluded, Jesus had come to me in a dream and saved me when I was little. Now it was time to broaden that relationship, take it to a more adult level.

What Aunt Carrie and I had was a secret that everyone would have called make-believe. This new avenue of prayer was legitimate, one everyone would recognize, and it put me right in step with a world at war. A world very definitely engaged in prayer. I desperately needed to fit in, to find a way to fill the emptiness in my soul, lest I fold in on myself, shrivel up and cease to exist.

***

At our first 4-H meeting, Mrs. Miller reviewed the 4-H organization's structure and history. She had a poster of the four-leaf clover emblem with the 4-H pledge: "I PLEDGE MY HEAD TO CLEARER THINKING, MY HEART TO GREATER LOYALTY, MY HANDS TO LARGER SERVICE, AND MY HEALTH TO BETTER LIVING FOR MY CLUB, MY COMMUNITY AND MY COUNTRY." Under the pledge, the 4-H club motto: "TO MAKE THE BEST BETTER." The 4-H club colors: "GREEN AND WHITE." She introduced me as her junior leader.

With our twenty members, we decided to lend our efforts to winning the war. Our first project was to have a war-bond drive. We distributed saving-bond stamp books to each child in the one-room schools in our district, and encouraged them to buy war-bonds stamps to fill it. We told the students Uncle Sam needed funds to fight the war, and it was a wonderful way to save money for the future. Then we canvassed all the residents of Tate Town, and collected pledges for $6,000.00 worth of war bonds. As we canvassed we encouraged the residents, especially farmers, to help with our scrap metal drive. That turned into an ongoing effort and Tate Town contributed many pick-up truck loads to the Phelpsburg area organization. We had all our members collecting cooking fat from their mothers and from their neighbors. We also started saving aluminum foil, and we decided to have a milkweed pod gathering party in late summer. These items were needed for the war effort. We could hardly wait for spring when we could concentrate on getting our Victory Gardens started. There was great enthusiasm about our mission and much admiration for our 4H club and Mrs. Miller.

Something wonderful was happening in spite of my broken heart. I felt privileged and important. I had something unique to give. I was accepted, integrated socially in a way that I had never known before.

Linda's presence in the house was less important. Forrest wrote to me often, making Linda jealous. She said, "Whatever do you and Forrest find so interesting to write about?"

"Stuff on the farm and 4-H."

"You get twice as many letters as I do."

"I write twice as many as you do."

"I can't think of anything to say."

"That'll change when the baby comes."

She gave me a pleading look. "I can't even imagine that. Yo, I'm scared."

That touched my heart because I knew I'd be more than scared; I'd be terrified. "You'll be fine...you'll have a beautiful baby just like you."

"You know, I miss my mother....I wonder what she thinks...and if she misses me." There were tears in her eyes. "I appreciate being here, but I miss home."

At that moment she must have thought about the fact that her living here made the Osborns so uncomfortable that my mother never

316

came up, because she said, "I'm sorry my being here makes things hard on everyone."

She was softening me up, but I couldn't quite make myself say it didn't matter because it did matter. Ma and Mrs. Stanley never visited each other anymore, and I hadn't seen Ma since Linda came to live with us. Once in a while Matt and Mark came up to play board games. Time works magic in rounding off the corners of hard feelings. Linda and I had found a surface truce, and she had worked her way into the household routine, slop-pail detail and all. Now and then she'd sigh and say, "I hope those electric poles are all set in time!"

I knew life without the conveniences she was used to must be unbearable. At first I felt like it served her right to have to put up with our primitive ways, as she put it, because she had forced her way into our lives. She deserved to suffer. Now I could see how hard it would be to have a baby with no running water, diapers to wash and all the extra work that would make.

Mr. Stanley had already arranged to have a well drilled, and a carpenter was coming to put in a bathroom. Forrest sent money demanding it be used to make life easier for everyone. I knew he meant for Linda and the baby, but when I prayed to Jesus about it, it became clear to me that Forrest would have sent the money to his mom and dad even if Linda were not there. I was trying very hard to change my attitude.

By the end of April, we had electric lights and running water to the kitchen, and in another week we had a working bathroom. There was much jubilation and taking of baths. We ceremonially washed, and carried to the attic, all the chamber pails and all but one oil lamp, saved for emergencies. Mrs. Stanley and Linda went shopping and bought an electric stove, refrigerator, washing machine and an electric flatiron. The farm had come of age in the twentieth century and none too soon.

The middle of May I wrote Forrest my shortest letter ever, and I wrote about Linda for the first time:

Dear Forrest,

May Day has come and gone. Remember how we always went in search of wild strawberry blossoms? Yesterday, I went over beyond the woods to see the apple orchard in bloom and it looks like a bumper yield if we don't get a late killing frost. Everywhere I look the earth is coming alive. At 4-H we're in full speed ahead with our Victory Gardens. Yesterday I finished putting in peas, the moon was right, ha, ha, so the old timers would say. And Linda went into labor; again the moon was right, as the old timers would say, right! As I said, new life is blooming all over the place...Jeffery Lynn Stanley, 7 lbs. 6 ozs. Born 11: PM, Sunday, May 11, 1943. I went to the hospital to see him this afternoon and he has a lusty cry and very red-orange peach-fuzz hair. Your mom says Linda came through in flying colors, and I'm sure she's relieved to have it over. Jeffery's arrival will put a whole new dimension in life around here. Legally, you're a father. Congratulations, I guess. Write you what he looks like when I see him up close. As always, I pray the war will be over soon and you'll be home safe, Yo

My first thought when I saw Jeffery up close was, Luke'll never want'a claim him! Linda saw my look, and accused, "I thought you said I'd have a beautiful baby. This creature looks like a hairless mouse or an old emaciated toothless man. I can't be its mother." I knew she meant, how could Luke be the father?

Mrs. Stanley cooed over Jeffery. "Don't talk about your Jeffery like that. He's a little pinker than usual because he's going to be a redhead. What did you expect? Jeffery's a beautiful baby."

Linda said, "I didn't want a redhead. I wanted his hair to be the color of freshly shelled horse chestnuts, rich brown like Luke's."

I added, "I hope you'd keep Jeffy's beautiful blue eyes that are uniquely his." I wanted to say I'm glad they're not mean wily cinnamony-fox-colored eyes like Luke's or green cat eyes like yours.

The reference to Luke must have been a slip because it surprised all three of us. It told me Linda was still obsessed with Luke. I wished with all my heart that Luke would claim his family for everyone's sake.

Linda chose not to nurse Jeffery. Good thing because she avoided him as much as possible, pawning him off on Mrs. Stanley whenever she could get away with it. I'd hear her say, "Wouldn't you like to feed him while I help Yo with the dishes?" Or, "I'll mop the floor for you if you'll rock Jeffery to sleep," and so on. It put me in mind of how it must have been when I was born. Only something told me that in my case not only was Ma glad to be relieved of my care, Aunt Alma had planned it that way so she could make a slave of Ma. In any case, I began to feel a certain kinship with Jeffy, and I hoped he'd not grow up with the same stigma that I had. But he wouldn't because of Forrest, would he?

Mr. and Mrs. Stanley made a big fuss over the baby, and I wondered if Linda knew how lucky she was. Probably not. Life had been pretty much her way up until she found herself pregnant and cloistered, now her friends were out working, making money, buying pretty clothes and dating service men on leave. That must be a bitter pill, but it didn't excuse her. She should make more of an effort to put her selfish interests aside for Jeffy's sake.

I ran into Mary Ann at the Red & White when I got off the school bus over in Tate Town. We said our hellos and nice to see you. Then Mary Ann said, "I hear Linda's had a boy."

"Yes, Jeffery Lynn." I didn't say Stanley. I just couldn't bring myself to. "You should come see him. Linda'd be pleased. I'm sure she gets lonely."

"After what she did to Forrest, no thank you. They're married, aren't they?"

"Yes." I had to say it.

Mary Ann spit her words out. "She cares nothing for what she does to other people. I knew Forrest didn't really want me for his girl, but he might've if she'd left him alone. She was always teasing and flirting, especially with Forrest. Luke was jealous of Forrest, and he couldn't stand it to be jealous of anyone....and Linda knew it....and cared nothing about my feelings or Forrest's. I could never figure out why Luke was jealous of Forrest."

"That's easy, Forrest's worth two of Luke and there's nothing Luke could do about that. He fooled everyone but himself...even Forrest thought Luke was great.....but no more.....he didn't fool me and he hated me."

Mary Ann studied me with a look of revelation on her face. "Yeah, you're right. Wait and see; she'll ditch Forrest the minute Luke comes marching home, and she'll run off without as much as a thank you. Forrest.....he's such a chump, letting Linda hoodwink him like that. I'm not sure I'll feel sorry for him."

I wanted to say I already felt sorry for him because she only knew the half of it, but I said, "Yeah, you're probably right. Anyway, Forrest's in for a rough ride, but so is Linda."

I was sorry I ran into Mary Ann, and sorry I invited her over. Linda was going to have a big job ahead of her if she ever managed to be accepted back into her group of friends. I was glad it wasn't me, but that wasn't exactly the truth because I would have been in seventh heaven if I were married to Forrest.

***

The first weekend in June was glorious, a day for romance. Everywhere nature was smiling and singing her song of growth, a budding promise of fulfillment begging you to go outside to taste her elixir. Linda felt its wiles and was listless with unfilled energies. Finally she said, "Jeffery's napping on the side porch. Yo, if you'll watch him, I'm going for a walk. He won't wake up. I'll be back in time for 4-H."

"OK but be sure you are, because I have to leave, back or not."

"Alright, already, I'll be back."

Before Linda had time to be out of sight, Mrs. Stanley said to me, "This has gone on long enough. Leave the lunch dishes. We're going calling. Paul'll be resting after lunch. It's time he met his grandson."

Mr. Stanley raised his eyebrows but said nothing. Mrs. Stanley and I walked out to the side porch and proceeded to push the sleeping Jeffy down the road in the old yellow wicker carriage that had been stored in the attic since Forrest was a baby. There had been a faraway look in Mrs. Stanley's eyes the day Mr. Stanley brought it down. I could only imagine what she was feeling, and my heart was squeezed tight again and was in my throat. Every which way we turned there were new hurts. When would it ever stop?

There was surprise plainly showing on Ma's face as she answered my knock on the screen door. Mrs. Stanley gathered the sleeping Jeffery up in her arms, didn't wait to be invited in, but stepped right on into the kitchen saying, "Is Paul still resting after lunch?" And she barged right on into the living room where Daddy was stretched out on the sofa. "This foolishness has gone on long enough. Paul, meet Jeffery Lynn," and she placed Jeffy in Daddy's arms. "We've been friends many years. There's no reason to change that, and this baby is someone you should get to know."

I looked from Daddy to Ma, and there was a look of relief and wonder on their faces that said it all. The ice was broken. This was the beginning of a new relationship between our two families. I felt the muscles between my shoulder blades relax. Until that moment I hadn't realized they were in a knot. Matt and Mark came rushing into the room from somewhere and stood on either side of me. My arms went out and drew them close. One truce accomplished. What would happen when the other armistice was signed and the war was over, what then?

The summer sped by with Matt and Mark out of school. They reveled in their role as uncles now that Mrs. Stanley had made the first step in reconciling relations. They no longer had to pretend they wanted to play board games, and Linda was more than happy to let them relieve her of Jeffy's care.

My new maturity "in the faith" must have shown because in September as the Sunday School classes were formed for the coming year I was asked to be a teacher's helper for the first and second grade. I did look older because I no longer wore my hair in pigtails but braided it loosely in one braid down my back. On Sunday I wound it around my head like a grownup. I never left my heavy black hair loose because Luke's many chidings about my witch hair was still inhibiting. At school I was still the shortest pupil and the only one who looked like a Gypsy.

In mid October we had a few crystal snowflakes on a frosty morning, and Mrs. Stanley's rule for Indian Summer played out perfectly. By midday a warm south wind chased the clouds away, making way for the beginning of a perfect Indian Summer with the warm sun drawing the pungent overripe aroma from Mother Earth.

By the end of November a wet snow fell overnight, creating a sparkling world edged in white lace. Mrs. Stanley called it apple pie weather. The apple bins were full, and there were plenty of apples canned to make pies until next year's harvest. She stood in front of her

Hoosier cabinet, apron smeared with flour, cutting a piecrust as she rotated the pie tin on the tips of her fingers. "Didn't think I'd ever hear myself say this, but I miss my old woodstove. Things're almost too easy. Or, maybe it's the 'home-fire' feeling, I'm missing."

Linda answered, "I sure don't miss any of it. The 'home-fires' are for the movies. Give me a knob to turn any day."

Jeffy was in his highchair. One hand was holding the teething ring he chewed while with his other hand he smeared spittle enthusiastically around on his highchair tray, all the while rhythmically keeping his chubby little legs churning. His round face put you in mind of a jack-o-lantern due to his pumpkin colored hair and pale phantom eyebrows and curling eyelashes.

I had just decided to change into my barn clothes, when I saw a soldier pass the kitchen window.

"Forrest's home!"

Before anyone could react Forrest opened the kitchen door, and Mrs. Stanley was in his arms. The man who stood before us was not the Forrest we had said goodbye to. He was older, a totally mature man. There was no sign of the boy. He grabbed his cap off and a bristle colored brush-cut still had the familiar cowlick. That was comforting to me.

Surprisingly, Linda held back, unsure of just how to greet her husband. Jeffy squealed, sensing the excitement, and Forrest turned to him. "So this is my new little buddy." Jeffy immediately threw his teething ring on the floor as both his arms shot up into the air. "Well, big guy, sure I'll take you. Just how heavy are you anyway?"

Linda rushed forward. "Wait, wait…he'll mess up your uniform."

"So be it." And Forrest lifted him up into his arms, slobber and all. "You did good, Linda. He's a fine little boy." Jeffy started picking at the strips on Forrest's sleeve. "Yep, Tech. Sgt. Me and my mechanics'll keep those planes in the air, won't we little buddy." He shifted Jeffy, supporting him with both hands as he flew him around, Jeffy squealing and kicking. Forrest accompanied the airplane ride with the proper sound-effects, then back into his high-chair. "Safe and sound. Good landing."

Mrs. Stanley asked, "Does this mean you'll be going overseas?"

"Fraid so, Mom."

"Oh dear, but I'm glad you'll be fix'n'um instead'a flying'um."

In the course of this exchange, Forrest had reached me, and placing his hands on my shoulders exclaimed, "Yo, my faithful letter writer. I've been picturing you as 'little sister'. You've grown up. I'm going to have to get used to that." And he hugged me tightly, kissing the top of my head. "Not so very far up though," he added as his hand measured my height to his chin.

Then he turned and looked around at all of us and asked, "Is it working out OK? Am I sending enough money? My gosh, can this be our old kitchen all modern like this?"

At that moment, Mr. Stanley came though the kitchen door. "Good to see you, son." They threw their arms around each other. "How long're you home for?"

"'Til Friday."

"Then, it's overseas?"

"Fraid so, Dad…..that's hello to everyone except the 'little mother.' Linda, let me stuff my duffel bag in the guest room while you and Jeffy get into some coats, and we'll go for a walk. Do my heart good to have a look around."

Linda didn't look very enthused about a walk, and my heart jumped right up in my throat because it was me he should have asked. I was the one who always walked the fields with Forrest, checking everything over; was the hay dry enough; the ground's ready to plow; there'll be plenty of blackberries if we get rain; wormy apples this year, or maybe just a walk for the fun of it. I was the one who wrote everything to him. I found refuge in my room and prayed:

God, (thought with the energy of a cuss word) *how am I going to get through these next few days? Forrest is someone I don't know. On paper, in letters, we're still kindred spirits, but as long as Linda's in the picture he's lost to me. I know it. Help me, Jesus, accept it. Oh, please help me, I'm desperate.*

At that exact moment it occurred to me that Linda had lost her love too. Why did that suddenly pop into my mind? I saw the box she was in with an unwanted baby and an unwanted husband. A husband I wished were mine, and a baby I had come to genuinely love. Jeffy was such a good little fellow, affectionate and smart. He was a ruddy carrot top with chubby cheeks that made him look like his head was a ball set on his shoulders, not at all what Linda could equate with a baby she and Luke had produced. But he was so full of joyful wonder, always reaching out to all the world had to offer. He was not handsome, but he was an appealing heart stealer, cuter than cute.

Why couldn't Linda see it? I knew in my heart why. She knew Luke would never accept Jeffy, and Luke was her passion just as Forest was mine. She was desperate and brokenhearted too. She felt trapped and alone even in the midst of the Stanley's loving family.

Jesus, are you putting these thoughts in my head to show me the way….to see Linda differently? It's a hard road to follow even though it may be the right one. I'm not sure I can travel it. Is it true you know our every thought? It pains me to have you know what an awful person I am. Especially after coming to me in my dream and telling me I was OK. It's just that my life has always been on the fringe, outside looking in. Only with Forrest I was my true self; now who am I? With him I was inside the circle, and now I've lost that one real place. Are you telling me to count on you? Thank you for the new life you've lead me into through Mrs. Miller and the 4-H. You can see what a success we've made of it, and how it has boosted me up especially in my own eyes. And it's nice to have friends. That's what Forrest saw in my face when he said I had grown up. I really do know that even if Linda wasn't here, Forrest has grown away from me in maturity. I never have been his girlfriend. It was such a shock to see him look so much older. I know that's not Linda's fault. Maybe it was the uniform. Maybe when he puts on his work clothes he'll be more natural, less a stranger. Please, Jesus, put a shield around my heart to protect me from my own bad thoughts that I can be pleasing to you and those around me. Amen.

Thankfully, I was off to school the next day, and that evening after Jeffy was put down to sleep, I suggested, "Forrest, why don't you take Linda to the movies? I'll listen for Jeffy while I do my homework."

Linda brightened. "Thanks, Yo. I don't know when I've been to the movies."

Spending another uncomfortable evening with Forrest and Linda in the same room was too much for me. Better to get them out of the house. Everyday except Thursday, Forrest was in his barn clothes when I came home from school so I presumed he spent his days with Mr. Stanley.

Thursday it was obvious he and Linda had spent the day on an outing of some kind with Jeffy because he wouldn't let Forrest out of his sight, and Forrest loved it. Linda took my place on the window seat with a book; I escaped upstairs with Snooks at my heels. I didn't want to know anything about where they went or what they had done.

Thursday evening turned into a family game of Monopoly, and I played too because it was Forrest's last night before he had to leave. No one mentioned it, but we were all very much aware of it

Friday morning as I was about to go out the door for my walk to catch the school bus, Forrest hurried into the kitchen from the barn.

"Hey there not so fast, little sister, I can't let you leave without saying goodbye."

326

The musky scent wafted out to greet my nostrils, and he was in need of a shave. It wasn't that long ago that the two of us ran through the barn playing tag until Mr. Stanley'd say, chores are waiting, Forrest. My heart was breaking. It was a stranger who stood before me not knowing if he should hug me or not. Yet if I closed my eyes he was the person I knew better than anyone else in the world.

He said, "Keep those letters coming, Yo. Yours are the best, the ones I look forward to."

I threw myself against him in a bear hug. "I love you, Forrest. Be safe and come home to us." I ran out the door with tears streaming down my cheeks. When I came home from school he was gone, and it felt as though he had never been home.

***

Our flagging spirits were given a boost a few days later when a letter arrived from Abbey. She would be home for Christmas. Allen was going to be shipped overseas and was due for a furlough. She was pregnant and her excitement fairly jumped off the page.

Mrs. Stanley was ecstatic. "My little girl. A baby! Home for Christmas. Oh, Josephine, let's start our plans."

December first we had another letter from Abbey saying they had arrived at Allen's parents and would soon follow on up to the farm so Allen could have a short visit before he took the train to Seymour Johnson Field, Over Sea's Replacement Depot, Goldsboro, North Carolina.

During the war train schedules were impossible. Consequently the trip to North Carolina involved difficult changes. Allen's visit with the Stanleys turned out to be a hurried overnight. They arrived in the late afternoon, and Allen left early the next morning.

When I was little and lived in the tenant house with Ma and Daddy, I felt that whenever Abbey entered the room, the sun came out. Nothing had changed. The minute she walked into the house the clouds of tension lifted. She treated Linda as if it were the most natural thing in the world for her to be there. How she could be like that was a mystery to me. She knew as well as any of us that Linda had taken terrible advantage of Forrest's blinding love, and how devastated her mother and dad were, me too, and of course Ma and Daddy.

There is something to be said about a Pollyanna. I'm not sure it's the easy way out that most of us think. It must take great courage and insight to be able to put aside your own misgivings and cleverly influence the mood of so many people.

"Just think," Abbey cooed. "Our baby could be born on Jeffy's birthday. Wouldn't that be swell? We could celebrate their birthdays together."

She was enthralled with Jeffy, and the affect on Linda was amazing. She began to wonder if maybe Jeffy was loveable. Was it due to Abbey's ability to be nonjudgmental? Was it because she was pregnant? I wanted to think it was because Abbey's goodness shamed Linda into a different frame of mind. Thinking like that shamed me! Abbey had the same affect on all of us.

Forgive me, Jesus. I pray, give me a pure heart like Abbey's.

Abbey and Linda made their doctor appointments together, and it became their special day for shopping and lunch out. All three of us went to the movies Saturday night when Abbey had gas stamps left over. Mrs. Stanley's eyes brightened and Mr. Stanley began to whistle as he did chores. A better attitude was sneaking up on me despite the war going on inside my heart and the larger more menacing one going on the other sides of both oceans.

There had been little visiting between the Stanleys and Osborns, even after Mrs. Stanley had taken the initiative to introduce Jeffy to his true grandfather. Aunt Alma kept the waters muddy by insisting to anyone she could corner that Jeffy was not Luke's child. She should know. He had been living with her because he was forced out of his own home. Luke had written to her and said it couldn't possibly be his child, and it didn't have his name, meaning it was Forrest's. Legally she was right, but it made my blood boil. I wanted to, just once in my life, make Aunt Alma see the truth.

Jesus, is there no justice? There has to be some justice! I can't be all bad for just recognizing the truth and wanting it accepted. Can I? Does all Aunt Alma's praying make her right? If that's true I'm lost forever.

Aunt Alma's attitude had spoiled our having Thanksgiving with the Osborn's as we usually did. No one dared think of putting her in the same room with Linda and Jeffy. It was the loneliest Thanksgiving ever. It felt as if everyone had deserted us, and nothing would ever be right again. With Abbey's magic everything changed. She paid no attention to Aunt Alma. She just took it for granted that we'd all be together for Christmas and just started planning it. Mrs. Stanley and Ma fell in step, and Aunt Alma had no choice but to go along.

On Christmas Day our two families were together all afternoon for a festive Christmas dinner celebration. Aunt Alma was very quiet, nice change. When she did speak, after studying Jeffy closely for some time, I heard her mutter under her breath, "That child does not look one thing like Luke, as I expected." That was the first time she had actually seen him. Jeffy took that moment to pound his highchair tray and squeal.

In the evening, each family was off to our separate churches for Christmas evening services. Abbey coaxed Linda into going to church with us for the first time. Abbey insisted she must go because it was to include a Christmas prayer vigil for our service men. Abbey said, "Everyone has to go. Jeffy'll be a good boy." She made it seem as though it had been Jeffy who kept Linda home. It did simplify the issue!

Even I could be generous on Christmas night! I loved it that Jesus was born in a lowly stable visited by shepherds and wise men. I was too much of a nonconformist to believe there were actual angels visible in the sky, but I liked the idea, especially this Christmas, when we needed peace on earth so very much. I was one of those angels in the pageant, singing praises to the new born King, and at that moment it didn't seem at all inconsistent with my belief system.

Abbey and Linda sat side by side in the pew, Jeffy happily asleep in Abbey's lap. How natural and normal. No one lifted an eyebrow; a new page had been turned. And I knew in my heart that Abbey and Linda sitting there like chums, Jeffy on Abbey's lap obviously completely integrated into the family, was subliminally responsible for the ease with which that new page had turned. The spirit of Christmas so filled the hearts of all with prayers for those so far from home in harm's way, that it left no room for petty thoughts. It was the season of goodwill to all.

***

Now that the holidays were over my life settled into a busy litany of activities. My first chore was school and homework. Choir practice was a breeze and we met the same night as 4-H. Both meetings were at the Methodist Church which worked out very well. Mrs. Miller met me at the school bus stop with bag lunches for the two of us, so we could go directly to the church to prepare for our meeting. Our 4-H was part of the big home front machine helping to move the war effort forward. At our meetings we rolled bandages, learned to knit warm socks, and we wrote letters to all the soldiers from Tate Town.

My letters to Forrest were not part of the ones I wrote at 4-H meetings. I wrote to him at night after I finished the homework I was unable to complete in homeroom or in the library after lunch. In our letters our relationship remained as close as it had ever been. I kept them coming as Forrest's last words commanded. I still relayed every nuance of the farm operation, everything going on in our 4-H war effort and of course town and family news. I noticed that Linda was doing better at writing to Forrest since Abbey's arrival. I tried not to think about Linda belonging to Forrest, or to let it interfere with how I felt about writing. In my mind Forrest and I were pals like we had been after Luke left and before Linda entered his life.

Sometimes I invited Mrs. Miller for Sunday dinner, and sometimes she joined Abbey, Linda and me for our Saturday night movie. I knew she was lonely and missed the social life she had known before Uncle Sam called on Dr. Miller to serve his country. It was nice for her because Abbey and Linda were close to her age and were friends who could call her Annette. My being a lowly school girl forbade that even though I knew her best. She was always praising my contribution to 4-H in front of them, which of course, did my ego a world of good. She loved to look in our pantry at all the canned fruits and vegetables. It made me feel good all over to see the colors shining out through the glass jars. We opened something from our larder every day, and for the most part I was the one responsible for our pantry. What a wonderful feeling that was. Thanks to Mrs. Miller and her 4-H there had been many Victory Gardens and now many full pantries in Tate Town.

With March just around the corner the choir began to practice for Easter which in 1944 was April ninth. I wished Rev. Gray were still here so I could talk to him about the meaning of the crucifixion. Those terrible images of washed in blood still bothered me. I easily accepted that Jesus died on the cross, and his life's lessons were mankind's "Good News" as Jesus said, and you better follow them if you wanted a righteous happy life. That his death was necessary for our salvation was still a problem. Most of the time these troubling thoughts were far from my mind, but with the Easter music I couldn't avoid my unorthodox misgivings. A loving God could not require the death of His own Son, or any living creature to die because we were born in sin. No one chose to be born. And wasn't it God who designed how a new life got started? It was totally more reasonable to be held accountable for the behavior you were responsible for. I was so conflicted about the nature of God. There had to be an explanation, but I just didn't know how to find it. Our new pastor, Rev. Rankin, was an older man very set in traditional theology, and I couldn't imagine talking to him. I wondered if all my doubts about theology were because of Ma like Daddy said. Were we both bad? But if I were so bad that someone had to be killed to make me acceptable I guessed I would rather be unacceptable! I decided not to think about it, to set it aside as unsolvable. Jesus lived so long ago something must have been lost in the translation.

Easter Sunday dawned foggy in the valleys, but on top of the hill our sunrise service was spectacular. The sun broke up over the rim of the horizon with the splendor of an illustration in a child's storybook. Jesus was as real to me in that moment as if He were walking with me as he had in my dream when I was a troubled child. In the choir I sang HALLELUJAH as a believer with a full heart.

It was again the season for the magic of spring and rebirth. Our 4-H Victory Garden preparations were getting underway which was right in step with the pervasive excitement surrounding Abbey's approaching due date. As I made the soil ready for planting, Abbey and Linda put up a crib in Abbey's room. My prayers for a better attitude had made something wonderful happen because it was OK with me that Linda, not me, was helping Abbey get ready for the baby. What a relief to have a more tranquil heart. The good vibes swept all of us along.

Mrs. Stanley tried her best to slow Abbey down, but she waddled around insisting exercise was the best thing for her, and insisted that it made time pass more quickly. One afternoon I came into the kitchen as Abbey took the last tin of chocolate chip cookies from the oven. I had just finished planting the peas and was famished. The smell of the cookies elicited an instant filling of my mouth with juicy anticipation.

Abbey pulled out a chair at the kitchen table. "Sit yourself down right here, Jo, and we'll have ourselves a treat."

"You sit. I'll pour the milk." Abbey looked like she needed the break more than I did. "Where is everyone?....MMMM, these hit the spot."

"Mom's resting. Jeffy's napping so Linda's probably sleeping too."

"Why aren't you? You should be. Boy you make the best chocolate chippers of anyone. They're so soft and chewy."

"Just take'um out before they look done. With an electric stove who couldn't make good cookies?"

"Me!....Linda. You take after your mom."

"Thank you."

"What're you going to name the baby?"

"If it's a boy, for Allen. A girl, we haven't decided. I wouldn't want her named for me. Allen wants me to pick. I think, May for Mom as a middle name. I've thought some of picking Laura for you. What would you say to that?"

I was overcome with pleasure that Abbey even thought of such a thing. She really did think of me as a sister. Sometimes the world was just too perfect. "Oh, Abbey, I love you so, thank you, thank you." Tears formed in my eyes, then in hers too. "Laura May…I don't know. I always liked my middle name, but it doesn't sound quite right. How about Louisa May? It rolls off the tongue….after one of our favorite authors."

"Perfect, Yo. If it's a girl, you named her, and Louisa is especially for you. I like it."

Jeffy was taking his first faltering steps as each of us cheered him on with outstretched arms. By his birthday he was a marathon walker and into everything. We had a party with all the Osborns present. Life was certainly strange. Jeffy was so innocent and unaware of the strange mix of relatives surrounding him. He called Linda, Da, instead of Ma, Mrs. Stanley, Gan, Mr. Stanley, Pa, and Abbey, Bea. We couldn't get him to try Matt or Mark, but he loved them. He'd run to them and tap them on their knee. He hid his face if Daddy talked to him. That I understood very well from days gone by. It was plain, Daddy truly loved him despite the fact that the situation still made him noticeably uncomfortable. And Jeffy called me, "O", loud and often.

Linda confided she had been sure Abbey's baby would be born on Jeffy's birthday. Abbey said it would have been nice, but now Jeffy would have a day of his own. The babies could have twice as much fun with two parties.

Five days later on May 15, 1944, Louisa May Bennett, 8lbs 8ozs, was born early in the morning after a difficult labor. Mr. and Mrs.

Stanley were barely home in time for Mr. Stanley to help with the milking. Both looked worn out as if it had been them who had labored all day and night. Five days later a still weak Abbey came home with a fat little Louisa May who had already gained two ounces.

Linda said, "That's what a baby should look like, a doll ready to put under the Christmas tree."

Abbey said, "Oh, Linda, isn't it wonderful? Now, we're both mothers. Jeffy'll soon have a little playmate. Come here Jeffy and meet Louisa."

Jeffy stood upon his very tippy-toes and pulled at the blanket and said, "Eee-za," with a gleeful smile showing his perfect eight little white teeth.

The camera was busy flashing pictures to send off to Allen and Forrest. I'm afraid my running farm report letters were relegated to the back burner, but the babies were so much fun I didn't care all that much. I did keep my letters going out, but growing babies were as much a part of them as my garden and farm news.

Louisa was a beautiful baby with blond curls and blue eyes like Abbey's and Forrest's. She was good in every way and much adored. It was a joy to see Abbey with the two babies. Jeffy was so responsive to Louisa and so cute with her that he stole the show. I could see Linda would have liked to trade babies, and Abbey would have been happy to adopt Jeffy.

These days Linda was clever at disguising her feelings about Jeffy. Much more than she had been in the beginning, Abbey's influence, but I could see through her plain as day. She saw Jeffy as the impediment that kept Luke from her. She knew he would be much more attracted to a frilly beautiful dimpled-knees little girl with sunshine curls than he would be to a clever little boy who would be competition. She was right about that, and I had as much to lose with that scenario as she did.

One day as I was coming in from the garden, I came up to the side porch just as Linda was lifting Louisa out of the carriage from an outdoor afternoon nap. Jeffy was at her heels anxious to help as Abbey allowed him to do, but Linda pushed him away, and then saw that I had witnessed her unmotherly act.

"You can wipe that look off your face, Yo. You'd like to think I'm some kind of monster, but you know better than that. I'll be out of your hair soon enough."

"I doubt that, knowing Luke."

"You only think you know him."

That made me mad. "Don't forget I lived with him."

"And I know you...too well. You and all your poison letters."

"Poison letters!"

"Yes, poison letters, writing about what an awful person I am."

"You flatter yourself. I never write about you. Jeffy, yes. And it's all good. I know the game you're playing, down deep you know you need Forrest because you're pretty well convinced you've lost Luke, and you have an escape route. And Forrest, unfortunately, loves you so much he's willing to give it to you, no questions asked. You're free to choose when the war's over. How can you be so cruel to someone like Forrest?"

"You're so smart, you can answer that. He loves me and wants me to be happy." She pushed Jeffy ahead of her, rather roughly, into the house.

So much for all the progress I had made with my attitude. I ran to the barn and cried. I should never have allowed such ugliness to be put into words. She was right! I should love Forrest equally as well as he loved Linda! Through my tears I prayed:

336

Jesus, I should know that when you reach out and hurt someone, they'll hurt you back. But, Linda started it. I didn't hurt first. How can anyone treat Jeffy like that? But I know....it feels like it's me...and I'm really asking why doesn't Ma love me? Things are never what they seem. The thing is, I know I have to learn God's love...love that wants what's best for those we love, even if it it's not what we want. How can I do that? I try. I'm not convinced Linda will make Forrest happy. Is that my selfishness talking? More than anything, I need to know what's right in your eyes. Help me accept whatever happens. Please help me accept it as your will. Show me the path I should take. I want to be a good person. I pray the war is over soon, and please, please, above all else, keep Forrest and Allen safe...and Luke too. Amen.

***

During every summer True Faith sponsored an old-fashioned Revival meeting with guest evangelists. Matt and Mark always teased me to go because they said it wouldn't be so boring if I went. They never let Daddy know they thought that! This year was the same. Matt came running up the road so excited I thought something wonderful was about to happen.

"Yo, you've got to come to the Revival with us this time. We've got this young singer who's really great. You should hear him. With your voice you'll love it. I mean it. He's really good."

"I don't think so. You know how I feel about blood and thunder preaching. Sorry."

"You won't even notice the preaching."

"I would. I'm not used to it like you are."

The next day Matt came walking out to the garden with the young singing evangelist. "Yo, this is Porter Kent. Porter this is Josephine. I've told him about your voice and he insisted on meeting you."

337

"Hello, Porter. Matt's been barraging about your singing." My first thought was that he should've been in the army. He made me think of Forrest because he was almost as blonde, only Porter was taller and as handsome as Luke.

"Nice to meet you, Josephine. How do you get Yo out of Josephine?"

"Luke, one of my step-brothers, gave it to me because he thought I was too fond of my yoyo."

"So there are three step-brothers."

Matt said, "Luke's in the service."

Porter was defensive. "I regret to say I'm 4F."

I wanted to say you look fit to me, but of course I didn't. Instead I said, "Come on in the house. We don't have to stand out here."

"Yeah, Porter, Yo lives in her garden."

"VICTORY Garden . . . " I did that for Porter's ears. *Sorry, Jesus. I know Porter can't help it if he's 4F.*

We walked to the house and I stopped in the backroom to wash up. "Matt, take Porter on into the house to meet Mr. and Mrs. Stanley. I'll be along in a second."

When I came into the living room, Mrs. Stanley was at the piano and Porter was singing the Lord's Prayer, and I have to say he was good. I was impressed. Before I knew what was happening Matt had us singing together. Our voices blended as if we had been singing together all our lives. Mr. Stanley put his newspaper down wide-eyed. Abbey and Linda came rushing down from upstairs where they had been putting the babies to bed.

Matt was beside himself with pleasure. "I knew it! I knew it. Your voices were made for each other."

Abbey said, "They do sound professional."

Linda was open-mouthed in amazement. I guess she was surprised I could do anything but dig in the dirt. Everyone started talking at once. Porter was very pleased with himself, and I have to admit it was hard not to be affected by all that adulation.

Finally I consented to sing with Porter the following evening which would be their final Revival service. Mr. and Mrs. Stanley and Linda came, but Abbey stayed home and babysat because it was nursing time for Louisa May. To my great surprise Ma came with Daddy, Matt and Mark. Even Aunt Alma stayed late so she could come to hear us sing.

It was Ma who made singing worthwhile when she said, "Josephine, very well done, beautiful really." I had been waiting for that praise ever since those days long ago when I helped her with the cleanup in the Sweet Shop kitchen after Aunt Carrie died. She looked at me, really saw me and heard me. Wondrous day!

Aunt Alma said, "Josephine, you should think about a singing career."

Porter Kent and I stood side by side at the back of the church receiving praises and handshakes just as Luke had done in the past. I couldn't help being aware of the irony in my standing in Luke's cherished spot with a young man as handsome as Luke who was destined to become the minister everyone thought Luke would become. And I wondered what the people thought about the black haired step-daughter who chose to go to the Methodist Church.

It wasn't until I was alone in my room away from all the flattery and excitement that Porter's testimony rang in my ears: "Praise the lord! Praise the Lord for my salvation. Praises be to my good friend Pastor Fillmore who led me to the cross and salvation. Romans 5:12 'Wherefore, as by one man sin entered into the world, and death by sin; and so death passed upon all men, for that all have sinned.' Yes my friends, you do not have to live the life of corruption as I have to be in need of salvation. Open your hearts and let the Lord in. John 3:16 'For God so loved the world, that he gave his only begotten Son, that whosoever believeth in him should not perish, but have everlasting life.' Thank you Lord Jesus. Praise God, I'm saved, saved at last."

I put my pillow over my head to try and shut out Rev. Fillmore's frequent brow mopping, and brow beating condemnation, declaring our unworthiness to even gather the crumbs under God's table as dogs do, and imploring us to come forward to the altar, the only way to escape a fire and brimstone eternity in hell.

I had stayed glued to the pew as did all the Stanleys and Osborns. Why did I ever consent to go to a revival meeting? How different my life might have been had I never stood at the back of True Faith Church with the handsome Porter Kent receiving handshakes and praise.

Chapter 12

On May 8, 1945, news the Germans had surrendered came gloriously over the radio. Mrs. Stanley threw her arms up into the air. "Happy day, oh happy day!"

Mr. Stanley grabbed Louisa May up into his arms and started dancing around the radio. "Happy, happy day."

Soon we were all dancing as Jeffy clapped his hands and sang, "Happy day, happy day," over and over.

Suddenly Abbey stopped her singing and exclaimed, "That'll mean Allen'll be deployed to the Pacific. All those jungles and suicide bombers scare me to death."

Mr. Stanley put his free arm around her and drew her close. "Don't you go borrowing trouble."

Louisa May, still on his other arm, leaned away from Mr. Stanley, placing her head on Abbey's shoulder and soothed, "Mommy, Mommy."

"Let's just think about the wing-dinger party you gals'll be cooking up….a birthday for the babies, and an end of the war in Europe bash."

"That's right, Dad….we've plenty to celebrate...good idea, huh, Linda...huh, Jo? We'll do it up right."

"By jingle, that's the ticket, Abbey!"

The air was filled with good cheer. The pear and apple trees trumpeted spring's arrival with an explosion of blossoms. Louisa May left her first faltering steps behind as she wobbled after Jeffy, arms outstretched, squealing. Jeffy kept just out of reach ahead of her, very pleased with his superior two-year-old command of upright mobility.

"That's right, Jeffy, keep her coming…that's a good boy. Come on Louisa May; what a big girl you are."

My mind was divided between Abbey's coaxing voice and her comment about Allen's possible deployment to the Pacific. In a strange coincidence, Forrest, Allen and Luke were all stationed in England. Forrest was on a combat air base, keeping the airplanes flying over Germany. Allen was doing something top secret, and Luke was driving the big brass around. But happy as we all were with the surrender of Germany, the war was not over. Japan still had to surrender. Forrest would certainly be transferred to the Pacific Theater. As I contemplated these thoughts, it scared me because, as Abbey said, there were all those jungles and suicide bombers. How could we win against men like that? The Japanese would fight to the last man. My spirits sunk down to the bottom of my shoes.

All summer I lived in fear, anticipating word that Forrest or Allen had been transferred. The summer wore on with no change. August sixth, my second planting of beans were just coming on strong, and I was cutting a mess for canning when the news came blaring over the radio that the first atomic bomb had been dropped on Hiroshima.

The news commentator said, "Between seventy and eighty thousand were killed in a burst of light brighter than a thousand suns."

Mrs. Stanley wrung her hands. "Oh dear. What can it mean?"

Linda said, "It means the war can't last much longer."

I put my beans aside and ran to the barn to tell Mr. Stanley, Daddy and Matt. In shock, they abruptly left their chores. Daddy and Matt ran toward the tenant house, and I jogged after Mr. Stanley as he hurried up to the house.

He listened and shook his head in disbelief. "Those poor buggers can't hold out much longer…such waste; war's hell."

We all knew something terrible had been unleashed. My insides trembled and my nerves were on edge not knowing what to think or expect next. Three days later the world had not recovered from the shock of the first atomic bomb, when a second bomb was dropped on Nagasaki, killing between thirty five and forty thousand.

The news continued: "The carnage was held down by the mountains surrounding Nagasaki. And as we reported with the terrible death toll in Hiroshima, in each horrific instance an equal number of casualties were maimed…."

We all knew Linda and Mr. Stanley had to be right. Even the Japanese couldn't hold out against such devastation. Our anxious anticipation ended on August 14, 1945 when President Truman announced the Japanese had surrendered. The war was finally over.

Abbey and Linda grabbed each other and began jumping up and down in the middle of the kitchen floor while Mr. and Mrs. Stanley stayed huddled beside the radio. Forrest, Allen and Luke would be coming home! What would Luke do? Linda's exuberance told me it wasn't Forrest she was thinking about as her hopes were very tellingly running wild.

I dared not let mine. Only time would tell that story. I went out to the garden to pick corn for canning. There was a new tightness between my shoulders that I didn't want to confront. Better to can corn while its kernels were newly mature and not tough.

A few days passed and my low spirits must have shown because Abbey said, "Leave that garden…come on, Jo, let's go for a walk."

Most all our walks headed out the lane to the pasture and woods where moss grew on the fairy stones of my childhood imaginings. No matter how down I was, the sight of them always stirred up the nostalgia of all the wonderful stories I had made up for my talks with Aunt Carrie in heaven, and of all my ramblings at Forrest's elbow as he taught me the mysteries of nature. The busy world of the insects filled my ears, proclaiming the fullness of summer and the bounty of August's harvest. A sensual soft breeze dried the perspiration from our brows, and birds twittered happily in the depths of the woods. The war was over and the beauty of the day invaded my heart and soul, and yet, there was no lightness in my step.

Abbey stopped and climbed up to sit on the top rail of the fence that bordered the woods. Way back at the farm's beginning those rails had been split of chestnut wood, the old timer's choice due to their toughness and ability to withstand the ravages of nature. They were sturdy still, aged gray and weather-checked with wisdom. Despite the chestnut tree's toughness, fungus bark disease had claimed the chestnut tree and they were no more. How appropriate for my mood. I climbed up and sat beside Abbey.

"This's been a difficult two years, Jo, and I don't know any other person your age who could've contributed the way you have. You've practically fed us with your garden."

"You all helped, don't forget."

"Not that much...plus, the way you've helped Annett with 4H...you don't realize how talented you are...you don't give yourself enough credit...and with everything changing...Yo, I'm worried about you."

I shrugged and made some protestations.

Abbey continued. "I came home with fear and trembling at how we were all going to live together in harmony."

"But you seemed so accepting and natural. You calmed the troubled waters...for all of us."

"Somehow, I had to find a way. I was so worried about Mom's health. I didn't see how she could stand the tension. She loves Forrest so, and to see him taken advantage of that way, and I never saw Dad so drawn."

"I never dreamed you felt like that. You acted as though everything was OK with you."

"It had to be OK. Everyone had to get along. You certainly helped make it easier for me the way you moved over to make room for Linda, and the way you love Jeffy."

Right then my mind was racing. The reason I had gone to the barn to work was to get away from Linda, not to help Abbey. "I do love Jeffy, but Linda should never have come here. You and the babies are what kept us all sane. "

"She did have choices, but....."

"But, that's right," I interrupted. "She should have gone away and had her baby, and either kept it for Luke, or given it up for adoption and never involved us."

"Oh, Jo, you're forgetting how Forrest figures into the equation. Who knows the way of the heart? He must love her with a purity of unselfish love that is beyond reason. He's the reason she's here."

Again, my mind went wild, beyond reason, indeed! Linda always flaunted her beautiful sexy self in his face, driving him crazy. He wanted her at any cost, without any thought about how it affected anyone, especially his parents. In my book that wasn't unselfish. What was I thinking; wasn't I just as selfish?

Neither of us spoke for some minutes before she continued. "None of us know how things are going to turn out."

"I know what you're saying. Luke won't want Linda and a ready-made family, even though it's his own."

"I know how you feel about Forrest, and I'm so worried about you."

"She'll never make him happy. She doesn't like the farm, and she's a terrible mother."

"Don't allow things to develop into hatreds that can't be mended." She put her arms around me as we balanced precariously on the top rail. "You're so young, Jo. Time heals. I love you so, and I know Forrest does too."

My ears heard the words, but my heart asked if anyone could really love me? Ma didn't love me; I was a total reject. My old thought patterns overwhelmed me. The tightness between my shoulders became a knotting pain, and I knew I could never live in the same house with Forrest and Linda. What would become of me?

"Say something, Jo. Please talk to me."

I got down from the fence and started back over the pasture. The insect world was now a suffocating ringing in my ears, and the bird songs rancorous and territorial. My mind blocked out all thought.

"Jo, oh Jo, please. I know you're upset. Let me help. I want to help. Wait for me."

I turned and waited for her. "Come on. I've got'a pick chard for supper." We hurried on in silence.

I stopped in the backroom for a market basket and knife to cut chard. Then I sought solace in the garden. The chard stalks were beautiful, plump and pinkish-red. I cut the huge leaves from the stalks and neatly layered them in my market basket. I chose six full ears of corn with dried brown silk, walked over to the compost pile and husked them. Lastly, I went to the early tomato patch, picked five shiny red tomatoes and placed them on top the golden corn. The market basket was brim full. Even in my withdrawn state of mind, the beauty of those vegetables touched me. I was the one who planted the seeds

346

in the soil and hovered over them as they grew. I was feeding the family.

I knew, at that exact moment, that I had reached the plateau in life that belonged to adults. I had turned sixteen that summer; I had a woman's heart and a woman's shapely physique. True, I was still only four feet eleven inches tall, but inside that little frame beat a woman's heart. In a moment's time I had left my childhood behind as surely as Louisa May had left her first faltering steps behind. Everything in my life up to that point had been framed retrospectively through the mind of a child, through her many stages of development, in many ways a precocious and astute child, but through a child's mind none the less.

I was so certain of my adulthood that I failed to see the developmental split in my maturity. One side of my development, the side I now recognized and accepted as adult, had flourished and bloomed in ways beyond my years. But an equally important side of my development had been neglected. It was the part of my development that required my relationship to Ma, and with Ma's marriage to Daddy, and their relationship to each other, to be worked through and put into realistic perspective. That lopsided development left me unprepared for what lay ahead.

***

We began to anticipate Allen's homecoming. Abbey hummed and her eyes shown. Everyday, Mrs. Stanley baked as if she were expecting company. Mr. Stanley scanned the newspapers checking for the first arrival of returning GIs. When news of the first one appeared, he announced, "Paper says Bill Thomson's home. He left in the same group as Allen."

That morning Matt must have been thinking similar thoughts as we busily fed and watered the calves because he said, "I'll bet Allen's on his way home right now. He must have lots of points since he was drafted first…that newest calf still has to have milk."

"I'll do it."

"Ok, I've got'a help with milking when I'm finished here. Bet Luke has almost enough points too. He went in right after Allen…and gees…I don't know how to feel. He's my brother and I pray for him but not like Daddy does. Our lives have been so much better without him around that it makes me feel guilty. That's what I pray about and for his safety. And I'm worried about what he'll do about Linda. It'll break Daddy's heart if he doesn't want'a claim Jeffy. Yo, how'd things ever get so mixed up? I pray about that too. What do you think'll happen?"

"I don't see any happy endings. So, don't ask, Matt. I don't want'a think about it. The only thing I'm sure about is that you shouldn't feel guilty. You and Mark'll go right on as you always have. You shouldn't worry about Daddy either cause he has his cut-and-dried, right-and-wrong set of beliefs that'll come to his rescue. And you couldn't be a better son."

"Ya really think so?"

"I really do."

In my new adult heart, I knew how things got so mixed up. Luke never learned the lesson about consequences and responsibility, and Forrest has never completely separated himself from Luke's influence; Luke who made the sun shine on life in ways no one else could. When he chose a girl she was automatically the best girl in the world, and the same was true of almost anything he singled out. This false truth had been imprinted in Forrest's brain since he was a little boy. I dreaded to think of what it would take to erase that blinding imprint. In some ways Forrest was behaving not so very differently from Luke, much as it pained me to think that. But it didn't change my love for him. He was still all the other wonderful things that had made my childhood full of special experiences. Plus without him, I would never have learned to read. One of these days he'd wake up. That is unless Linda changed a great deal and became a devoted wife. Was I adult enough to wish for that? Dare I contemplate the slim chance that when Luke came home he would have changed, and he'd rescue Linda and Jeffy? I would not count on either of these improbable events, but if only one were possible so much unhappiness could be avoided.

I still couldn't pray, "Our Father who art in heaven"; would I ever be able to? I prayed: *Jesus, I still cannot call God my Father. It would be insulting with all my hateful feelings about my real father. Even the idea of us all being brothers and sisters is a little bit troubling right now because I know two people I don't want to be related to. And you know who they are. I suppose Daddy's right and I should pray for them. Even that bothers me because Daddy thinks saying a few words will wipe the slate clean. Does it? Can a few words change me into a new good person? Luke is saved by those words, and he said Linda was too. That makes me the odd one out! But I can't lie about how I feel about 'saved'. I know I have a lot of faults to overcome, and if I could overcome them with a few words, it'd be easy to say them. I sure don't have anything against easy. Why can't I believe that? Is it because the people who talk about being saved are no different from lots of people who don't even go to church? Or is there something wrong with me? I wish you would send Jesus to me again. I feel I can trust what Jesus told me more than I can trust what people say. But I was so little maybe I didn't understand. Help me to know your will. I am ready to be responsible, and I'm willing to work hard. If only I could be more like Matt, I'd be a missionary, but you understand the trouble I'd have telling someone their god was no good. It seems to me that if you wanted everyone to have the same faith you'd have sent Jesus to live with them too. I may be mixed up about taking your gospel to the corners of the world, but Jesus hadn't died on the cross yet when He preached the "good news" and gave that commandment. So to me, it was about taking the "good news" of love…and healing….and of freedom from the Pharisee's laws to the people. Isn't that what Jesus meant about putting new wine in old skins? If I was smarter, I'd be a nurse and go and help heal the sick. Then again, if you wanted me to do that, school would be easier for me. I could never pass Latin and algebra, and they say a nurse needs them. You have always given me a sign to show me the way, and I'm on the lookout for one. Something'll come along, and I'll know it when it does. And if worse comes to worse, I'll do like Ma and take care of someone else's family. I can see what a difference she's made in Matt and Mark's lives, Daddy's too. So, guide me in these days of decision on my new journey into adulthood. Bring Allen and Forrest, and Luke too, home soon. Amen*

***

It was in the middle of October, when Mother Nature had finished her portrait in reds and gold, that a taxi pulled up out front, and Allen came up the stone walk, duffel bag over his shoulder, and Abbey's scream hung suspended in autumn's warm dusky air.

"Allen's home!" She flew into his arms before he reached the porch. "Allen, oh Allen, you're home." They kissed, and then she turned toward the house. "Where's Louisa May? There you are. Come meet your Daddy, Sweetheart."

Louisa May stood on the side porch clutching my leg. She was not about to greet this strange man who caused her mother to scream, and who held her captive in his arms. Jeffy, on the other hand, went boldly forward tugging Louisa May's hand.

"Hello, Daddy. Weesa May's scared cause she's a girl. Com'on, Weesa May. I want'a see Daddy."

I swooped Louisa May up into my arms and delivered them both to Abbey and Allen. Allen gathered them into his arms, and the four of them walked into the house where the rest of the family waited to greet him.

Allen and Abbey stayed with us several days before they left for Allen's parents and to check in with the school where he would be reclaiming his old position. During those days Indian summer smiled on them with dazzling blue skies. They scuffed the rustling leaves underfoot and raked them into piles for Louisa May and Jeffy to jump in. They took the kids on walks to the woods, and I'm sure, to the mossy stones where the fairies danced. Their arms were always around each other, and it was beautiful to see. During those days Jeffy insisted on calling Allen, Daddy, and he seemed not to mind at all.

The mood was so happy it made life brighter and lighter for me, but it made Linda uncommonly quiet. Probably she was thinking about Luke's return at any moment, wishing it could be as happy as the one she was witnessing.

I heard from Aunt Alma soon after Allen, Abbey and Louisa May left, that Luke was home. She made sure I knew he had no intention of seeing Linda without coming right out and saying so, and I'm sure she wanted me to run right up and tell Linda.

Aunt Alma bragged. "Luke's never looked better. Landed a wonderful job at Morrison's GM auto dealership. Soon as the new cars start coming in, he'll be on top of the world."

The last thing I would be party to, was Aunt Alma's poison tongue. I didn't run right up and tell Linda. I wasn't going to be the one to dash her hopes. Linda and Luke could settle that themselves. Who could say what would happen when they saw each other for the first time.

Aunt Alma's devious intention of making me into a mean gossip prepared me for what would have been even more upsetting had I not known Luke was home. There was a commercial four corner intersection near the high school in Phelpsburg where, in the noon-hour break, I sometimes ran errands for Mrs. Stanley at the Rexall Drugstore. While I was at the counter paying for a bottle of aspirin, Luke stepped up beside me, handsomer than ever, just as Aunt Alma said.

"Can this be Yo all shapely and grown up?"

"Hello, Luke. How long've you been home?"

"Bout two weeks. Forrest say when he'll be home?"

"Doesn't know."

"Let me give you a lift back to school."

"NO, thanks. I'll walk."

"Same little spitfire, hey? I like a little fight. We'll get together for a date one of these times. Wait and see." He smirked as he ran his fingers along the single braid that hung down my back. "Same jet gypsy hair."

The feel of his fingers made me squirm. "Never." I turned my back on him and walked away.

"Say hello to Forrest's wife and kid for me."

Inside I burned with all the old hatred, and I couldn't get out of there fast enough.

Linda didn't learn about Luke's return home until a few weeks later when Abbey and Louisa May came home for the weekend while Allen painted the apartment they had rented. Allen insisted he didn't want Louisa May breathing the paint fumes. At first they had wanted to buy a house right away with their combined savings, but it was too much pressure. They decided to take their time to pick the right house because it would be the most important purchase of their lives.

352

It was wonderful to have them with us again. And just like old times, when Jeffy and Louise May were tucked in for the night, Linda suggested, "Yo and I haven't been to the movies since you left. How about it, Abbey? MILDRED PIERCE is playing with Zachary Scott and Joan Crawford. The paper says, 'a blistering performance.'"

Mrs. Stanley offered, "I'll listen for the babies."

"Not babies anymore, Mom."

"They're babies 'til they go to school."

Abbey looked at me. "Got your homework done?"

"Near enough. Let's go."

It was a little early for the nine o'clock showing so we gals decided to get a coke in CATHY'S DINER next door to the theater. We took the back corner booth, and I sat alone with my back to the door. As we joked with the waitress about being out on the town, I didn't have to turn around to know who walked in. Linda's face lit up with a radiance only Luke could turn on.

He slid into the seat next to me, and Linda exclaimed, "Luke, you're home!"

"It would seem." He looked up at his friends who had followed him. "OK you guys; get us a booth and order me a burger and coke. I'll be right there."

One of his friends gave him a, not on your life, jab on the shoulder. "Come on, share and share alike, and how!"

"Buzz off. Two are married old friends and the runt is underage."

Reluctantly, they left.

Abbey said, "Your looking great, Luke."

"And you, never better. You know, Abbey, I'm still in love with you." Same old joking Luke.

"Yeah, I'll bet. I'm the big sister who was always chewing you out."

Linda was animated. "Aren't you going to say hello to me, Luke?" She looked secure in her ability to win the attention she had always commanded.

"Why not. Hello, Forrest's wife." There was no edge in his voice, only a conciliatory sweetness. "Congratulations to you both. I always knew he had the hots for you. You deserve each other."

Abbey's mouth fell open in disbelief. I shuddered in rage.

Tears brimmed Linda's eyes. "That's not fair, Luke. You got my letters. What was I supposed to do, fall off the earth?"

"I don't know what you're talking about. Don't you have the prize? You're on the Stanley farm surrounded by all that goodness and love."

"Don't you want to see Jeffy?" The light had gone out of Linda, replaced with a horror-stricken pallor. Her eyes swam glossy and watery streaks slipped down her colorless cheeks.

"Forrest's freckled kid? I suppose I should after growing up like brothers, but, no thank you. He should've finished college before saddling himself with a wife and kid. Me now, I'm going places. I'm no where's near ready to be burdened with all that responsibility. Not 'til I've made my mark, and I very definitely will do that."

"Can't we go some place and talk?"

"With a married woman? No way."

He reached out and touched my hair that hung loose nearly to my waist. "Now if this bewitching little gypsy…"

"Take your filthy hand off…" I never let my hair loose and at that moment, I hated that I had broken my rule.

Before I finished my sentence, which was just as well, Abbey said, "Get out, Luke, before I strangle you. And don't you come near us again."

"Ok, I'm on my way but first, Yo, has that pretty ma of yours managed to get my dad in bed yet?"

354

How did he know how to hurt so thoroughly, in so few words, smiling all the time with that perfect smile, cinnamon eyes that matched the shine on his crisp neatly cut cinnamon waves? I boiled with hatred, willing myself not to fly at him, scratching and clawing. "Not everyone's a beast, but you wouldn't know that."

Linda was shaking and weeping now, and Abbey guided her out of the restaurant. I paid for our cokes, and as I passed Luke's booth, he said, "It's just a matter of time."

I knew what he meant. I turned, and with all my might, swung and slapped his face. Due to my gardening and barn chores, little as I was, I packed a powerful wallop. In a quick reflex action, he grabbed my arm. Just as quickly, I doubled my free fist and popped him squarely on the chin, and he let go.

Abbey had come back in and quickly pulled me away. "Jo, come on before you're thrown out or arrested. I saw that through the window; good for you."

Needless to say, there was no movie that night. Abbey drove in silence while Linda cried and I sulked. Abbey had her arm around Linda as we entered the house, and she rushed Linda upstairs as she explained to Mr. and Mrs. Stanley, who were listening to Tin Can Alley on the radio, that Linda had taken suddenly too ill to go to the movies.

Mrs. Stanley said, "Oh dear, that's too bad. How about a hot cup of milk?"

Abbey didn't want any more questions. "I don't think so, Mom, she'll feel better in the morning."

Things were still a little iffy Monday morning as I was leaving to catch the school bus. Abbey said, "Things are gonna be tense around here. I hate to leave, but Allen's expecting me. Linda's a survivor if ever there was one. She'll come around, but I'm worried about the rest of you, especially Mom."

"I'm worried about your mom too…no need to worry about me."

She hugged me hard. "I don't know what our family'd do without you. Hurry now. Don't miss your bus, and keep me posted. Especially let me know if you need me."

My heart was heavy as I hurried the mile to Tate Town to catch the school bus. I knew it wouldn't be long before Forrest came home. Could Mr. and Mrs. Stanley accept the inevitable: Forrest and Linda taking up a married life together? They already loved Jeffy as a grandson. I knew I couldn't accept it. It was clear to me there was no place for me in that picture, and I determined to keep my sensors tuned in for new opportunities.

Please Jesus, Take care of Mr. and Mrs. Stanley, and Ma and Daddy, Matt and Mark. Help them, and me, accept whatever happens. I'm desperate for a sign. Please show me the way you want me to go.

***

As we turned the calendar page to December, Mrs. Stanley began making plans for Christmas in hopes Forrest would be home in time, but it was not to be. It was on a mild day with a warm wind out of the south when the January thaw gurgled and splashed in roadside ditches, that Forrest passed the kitchen window. We were just getting ready to sit down to our midday dinner, and the aroma of roast beef and apple pie filled the kitchen. Mrs. Stanley was turning from the oven with a casserole of scalloped corn in her hands when she saw him and let out a joyful exclamation. "Forrest's home!"

In another instant, he stood in the doorway, hat in hand, filling my heart with his presence. The war had aged the face I had once known so well. His cowlick was the only indication of the boy who roamed the fields with me. Would I ever know the man behind that war-worn smiling face?

He let his duffel bag fall to the floor, eyes glistening, voice a controlled quiet, "Humm, does it ever smell like home. Know how I've dreamed of this kitchen and all of you."

Mrs. Stanley quickly set the scalloped corn on the table, and was in Forrest's arms, next Mr. Stanley and then he took both my hands in his. "Your letters were my lifeline. Thank you, thank you. "

An awkward moment of silence followed before he turned around and said, "Hello, Linda. Luke must be home. Have you heard from him?"

We were all surprised with his out and out directness, at least I was. Even Linda was taken off balance.

"Err...hello, Forrest, good to have you home."

"Double good to be here."

"Err...let's just enjoy our dinner." Linda pushed Jeffy toward his highchair. "We'll talk later."

"Good idea." Forrest bent down to Jeffy. "And who's this big boy?"

Without an instant's hesitation, "Jeffy, and you're Forrest."

"Right." Forrest held his hand out. "Put it right there, partner."

Jeffy snapped his little hand right into Forrest's. "Yeah, part'er." His eyes danced a peacock-blue and a smile lit up his freckle spattered face.

Forrest swung Jeffy up into his highchair, pushed him up to the table and sat down beside Linda. Grinning from ear to ear, "The returning GI is hungry."

Jeffy thumped his spoon on the table. "Me too."

Taking the cue, I quickly added another place setting to the table.

He rambled on about the food, and how good it was to have home cooking. You'd have thought the family was as normal as the apple pie he praised, but it rang false. We were actors, and I waited with dread for the curtain to go up for act two.

Obviously, Linda wasn't ready to confront reality because just as soon as we finished eating, she began clearing the table. So much for act two. I couldn't blame her for not wanting to describe her meeting with Luke.

Forrest turned to me. "Come on, Yo, give me a hand. Half these clothes in my duffel bag are dirty. Talk to me while I sort them out."

I followed him into the guest room. For one second I thought that maybe time and distance had given him some clear-headed perspective; that things might work out after all. But he began asking about how things had been while he was away, and had I seen Luke? He just wanted a chance to quiz me. It was obvious, true to form, what he really wanted to know was what I thought Luke's intentions were. What to say? I didn't want to get in the middle of that debacle.

"Really, Forrest, you should get your information from Linda."

It was the strangest feeling. Wonderful as it was to have Forrest safely home and be in the same room with him, he had moved out of my life with a finality that separated him from me more sharply than when he was across the ocean. Now I could no longer keep his friendship through our letters. And he wouldn't even miss those letters now that he was home on the farm he loved. In no time he'd know Luke was out of the picture, and his world would be taken up with trying to win Linda's love. I was calm in spite of the pain I felt. That had to be evidence of my new maturity.

For the rest of the day without Abbey around to guide us, it was again eggshell walking time. No one knew what to say. Was the curtain ever going to go up on the second act? Jeffy's role was that of the neutral buffer. Without him, there would have been an explosion. He was like an eager happy puppy, running to each of us lapping up all the attention.

Mrs. Stanley said, "We're spoiling him."

Linda made no comment because I think she was more than happy to let Jeffy have center stage.

Forrest said, "Come'er big guy. Settle down. Let's see how many animals you know….what's the cow say?"

Linda said, "MOOO. It's to bed! No more spoiling him!" And she disappeared upstairs to her bedroom without a goodnight to Forrest, or anyone.

Next morning, I heard Forrest say to Linda, "This pussy-foot'n around has gone on long enough. I'm going to visit Luke and have it out with him."

At last, ACT TWO: It'd be settled one way or the other. I went off to school not knowing what I'd come home to. It wasn't until we were finishing supper that Forrest made his announcement. "After dishes, let's all get together in the living room before we scatter. I have something I want to say to everyone."

I thought: The plot thickens! Be strong.

Forrest explained that Luke had no intention of marrying Linda or claiming his son. "Luke knew all about my plan to have our marriage annulled when he came home. He just laughed at me…I've offered to help Linda get an apartment in town if that's what she'd like, or I've told her I'd be happy to have her stay on long enough to see how things work out between us." He reached over where Linda sat beside him on the sofa and took her hand. "I'm glad she's decided to stay and give us a chance to see how things go."

I guess he assumed that after all this time with Linda and Jeffy settled in, there would be no objection. The reaction was a stunned silence. I guess when you're well loved you take a lot for granted. Mr.

and Mrs. Stanley were far too quiet, stunned, or was I imagining it? Was it me? I had good reason. Linda would never stop loving Luke, and she would make Forrest miserable. His folks must know that too. Or maybe I was afraid she would change and would make him very happy. *Dear God, I can't be that bad. I want Forrest to be happy.*

I had to get out of there. It was too cold to spend time in my unheated bedroom. So I put on my hat and coat to go for a walk, but my feet turned toward the barn. I thought I had slipped away quietly, but before I reached the barn door Forrest was beside me.

"Mom said I better follow you, that I needed to talk to you. What'd she mean? It's a bit hard to get used to your being so grown up. All the while I was away I kept picturing you as my little sister with pigtails."

We stepped inside the horse and calf side of the barn where it was out of the wind, and was warmed by the heat of the animals. I climbed upon the old well-worn and well-chewed-on feedbox, and sat down, letting my legs dangle over the edge. Forrest joined me with the feedbox hasp separating our dangling legs. I began to finger the gnawed edge of the lid as I kicked my heels against the box, letting my disgruntled feelings show.

Forrest crossed the hasp with his leg and stopped my kicking. "Come on, Yo, talk."

"I still wear a braid down my back, and I've always been more grownup than you thought." I liked the feel of his foot over mine.

"Not so, I've always known you were way grownup from the time you took care of Mom when she had her heart attack. Why are you running away to the barn? What did Mom mean? Yo, talk to me."

"I'll miss chores now that you're home. Anyways, cows are better company than some humans."

"Me, obviously."

"What was the war like? Was it awful? Do we seem petty and small to you?"

"You could never be petty or small, never....Yes, it was awful. So many pilots never came back. I hardly knew most of'um. They were there one day and gone forever the next, while I was safe, keeping their planes in the air. I felt so guilty. Yet...I thanked my lucky stars daily that I was born on a farm and had worked around machinery all my life, and had some engineering courses that made me a perfect fit for my mechanics job. I don't think I would've survived the war if I had been in the infantry and been in combat."

"How'll we heal all the grief?

"Maybe it's best if we have some scars. Maybe it'll help us remember not to let it happen again. We do the best we can, and keep putting one foot in front of other....no more procrastinating...why did Mom send me after you?"

"How would I know? Your guess is as good as mine."

"I'd guess it has something to do with my little talk in the living room just now."

"You'd be right about that.....you don't have to do this. Linda still loves Luke no matter how worthless he is.....and you might as well know she's not a good mother. Abbey mothered Louisa May and Jeffy. Also your mom and dad did....and me too. We all love Jeffy more'n she does."

"Wait just a minute, Yo...."

"Open your eyes. Take off the rose-colored glasses. You don't owe her anything."

"But, don't you understand....I love her. You're right about Luke. I couldn't believe anyone could be as crass. He was all polished and polite, in a new suit, dressed like Rockefeller, and greeted me as if we had just parted on the best of terms. That is, until I asked him what he intended to do about Linda and his son. He looked me right in the eye and asked what on earth was I talking about? All innocence, congratulated me on my marriage and son. Can you believe that?"

"He tried to pick me up. Can you believe that?"

He gave me a much appreciated grin. "Yeah, I can."

"You better believe I put Luke in his place fast enough....But, Forrest, how can you be so sure you love Linda when you haven't been home long enough to really know her?"

"When you love someone, you won't have to ask."

He was right about that. I did know that, but I also knew he didn't know Linda, and if he did he might think differently. "What can I say? I hope you won't regret it. I hope it works out the way you want it to."

He said he had to try; he had to give it a chance. He felt in his bones that she would come to love him. He thanked me again for all my letters to him. They had brought home to him all the way across the ocean in a way no other letters had. I wanted to tell him that was because I loved him in a way no one else did, but of course, I said nothing.

He said, "You mean more to me than words can express." And he went on about how thankful he was for all the work I had done while he was away. Abbey had written him glowing reports about all the things I did for the family, for 4H and raved about my many talents.

Then, he began to expound about all his great plans for the future. His head was way up in the clouds. "Yo, Jeffy's so wonderful...like a son already. And you know how Mom and Dad love him...it's so great...and you too." Everything was superlatives, all difficult to hear. My heart was breaking. By the euphoria in Forrest's voice I knew his mind was made up, and it was only a matter of time until Linda opened his own bedroom door to him even though I was sure she would never love him the way a wife should love her husband.

362

My prediction was accurate. Linda opened her bedroom door to Forrest almost immediately. I was shocked at how quickly, and I wondered why she hadn't prolonged the courting stage. After all, that was the kind of attention she craved. Maybe she was afraid Forrest would find out her true nature and send her packing. There was no mention of his going back to Cornell. I knew that made Mr. Stanley happy. But all through high school all Forrest wanted to do was design farm equipment. People do change; it was the farm that Forrest wanted to hear about in my letters, and never once did he say anything about going back to college. If Linda were smart she'd encourage him to go to college because she'd be much happier with an engineer than a farmer. Not me, I'd prefer a farmer.

***

The asking guidance praying Josephine, that I had struggled to be all during the war, was emotionally bankrupt. Dr. and Mrs. Miller had purchased a house in Phelpsburg. Without her and with the war over, 4H had lost its flavor. Our new projects seemed juvenile to me. I continued singing in the choir, but that outlet felt flat also. I think the pressure of winning the war held my everyday world together. Now that the pressure was gone my life was empty, except for the undercover tug of war going on between Linda and me. She tried to make herself look good, and I tried to make her do her share of the work without it being obvious. That was difficult because I had to prevent Mrs. Stanley from taking up the slack. I could see Linda was counting the time until I graduated and was out of her hair. She'd change her mind soon enough when she had to do my share of the work. I couldn't wait to accommodate her wish. I had to get out of there, and soon, hopefully before I graduated.

Jesus, you came to me once. I desperately need a sign. Help me to have eyes to see it and be guided by it. And please take care of Mrs. Stanley after I'm gone. Show Linda how to be a helpful daughter-in-law. I'm not so sure being an adult is all that it's cracked up to be. Help me put away selfish thoughts. I put my whole trust in you.

***

The week before Easter, Matt, full of enthusiastic smiles, came running up to the Stanley's. "Yo, guess who's coming to True Faith for Good Friday and Easter Sunday, Porter Kent."

"Thought you didn't like Revival meetings. I sure don't. Why all the excitement?"

"He wants me to get you to sing with him…Mark and me too. Everyone's still talking about last year. You'll do it won't you?"

"I have a choir solo on Easter."

"But it's for four days ending on Easter Sunday. Say you'll do it. They're counting on us."

I was so bored that against my better judgment, I said, "OK, but not on Easter."

Rev. Fillmore and Porter came Thursday morning, and that evening, with no rehearsal, the four of us sang amazing harmony, but sitting through Rev. Fillmore's fire scorching sermon only added to my feeling of desolation. How could I make myself go back and subject myself to more punishment? Plus I hated having everyone staring at that strange girl Daddy let go to the Methodist Church, staring with their minds spinning, trying to figure out that strange arrangement. Even Daddy was probably wishing he had never let me go to the watered-down Methodist Church. I wanted to curl up and die.

Both Carol and Carl from across the hill came and sat with me. They were excited; they had never been to a Revival meeting before. I wished with all my might they had stayed at home because they accepted the altar call. Of course I couldn't! Daddy would say that's proof I'm a heathen just like Ma.

Rev. Fillmore raved on and on about the lustful and sinful nature of man. So grievous was our sin that it was impossible to escape hell's fiery pit on our own. Our punishment was an eternity in hell. Even the most pious man could not erase the sin of his birth. There was only one way to avoid burning in hell for an eternity. He implored, "Accept Jesus as your personal Savior. The price has been paid. God's loving gift of His Son, Jesus Christ, has paid the price for our sins. Christ's death on the cross is your passport to heaven. Come on down, brothers and sisters, claim eternal life. Salvation is yours. You're among friends. Your brothers and sisters in Christ wait with open arms to embrace you and welcome you into the body of believers."

Carol and Carl whispered, "Come on, Yo."

I shook my head as they stood up and proceeded down front to kneel at the raised platform in front of the pulpit.

Rev. Fillmore looked right at me, and with the whole congregation staring at me, held out his arms and said, "Come, join your friends and receive salvation."

I'm sure my face burned as red as one of my hot peppers. I couldn't let him get away with insulting and embarrassing me like that. "I'm a Methodist just here to help out with the singing. That invitation is unnecessary. No, thank you."

There was a stunned silence, and I had to fight the urge to run out of there as fast as my legs could accommodate, but I couldn't embarrass Matt anymore than I already had. I didn't care about how

Daddy felt, and Mark was tongue-in-cheek about the whole religion thing. He went along only to keep Daddy happy. He was Ma's darling.

But I had to go back. And it would be Good Friday! Rev. Fillmore's sermon was bound to be even more scorching and would be aimed right at me. It'd be his chance to get even with me for my refusal to go down front.

I know that's not true, God. Forgive me. Sometimes thoughts just pop into my head uninvited. How am going to go back and face everyone staring at me?

I should have known Matt would guess how I felt and come to my rescue. He was at the door as I was putting my coat on to walk down to his house to catch my ride to church.

He said, "I was ready early so I thought I'd come up to kill time."

Bless his heart! I knew he wanted to reassure me, and help me in that last minute when I wanted to turn and run and hide where no one would ever see me again.

"Don't look so glum, Yo. We sing great. People love us."

I was right. Everyone did stare at me, but Matt was right beside me, talking to me as if we were the only ones in the church who mattered.

Rev. Fillmore did rail on, but if the people were open to all he said they'd have had to realize they should not shun me. The Good Samaritan didn't. The rest of his sermon was just what I expected. When he started pacing back and forth across the platform vigorously mopping his brow as he described the horrors of dying on the cross, I shut my mind off. I decided I'd sing my utmost best to shame everyone who was staring at me.

No, Jesus, I don't mean that. Then I'd be doing something for a hurtful reason just like them. I'll sing only to Your glory.

To my surprise, as we were leaving the church, Porter asked if he could walk me home. "It'll be a chance for us to talk."

After that sermon I needed a walk. Only he better not talk about salvation, or he'd hear an earful. I said, "Sure. It's a good night for a walk." Mark rolled his eyes at me, and I instantly wished I had said no.

It was a balmy bare arm evening with the peepers peeping their lungs out. The earth smelled sweet and ready to be tilled for planting the garden. It was a romantic nest-building night. Too bad it was Porter walking beside me stiff and formal, though, he was very handsome. Even I was aware of how all the girls twitter around him. He was older than Forrest, handsomer in a too perfect way, very blond but no cowlick in the front like Forrest's. Porter's hair lay obediently in place as I was sure everything in his life did. I smiled at that thought, because after this walk his perfectly polished shoes would be all muddy.

We hadn't walked far when he said, "When I leave here, I've been asked to pastor a little Free Baptist Church in Jackson Junction, down in the Pennsylvania mountains."

"I didn't know you were a minister. Bet it's beautiful down there."

"I wasn't a minister the last time you saw me. I've been helping their pastor, Rev Burk, who's nearly blind, and had been waiting patiently for someone to come along so he could retire. He's convinced God sent me to him, that I'm the answer to his prayer. That confirmed it for me because I felt the call even before he made his offer. The congregation was very much in favor and had me ordained."

Immediately, I thought about how Daddy had placed so much stock in Luke having a college education. But I said, "Congratulations. You must be anxious to get started."

"That's an understatement." He let some minutes go by with the peepers filling the void with their seductive mating call. "I'm the one who convinced Rev. Fillmore we should come back here to Tate Town. I wanted to see you again. I have an idea our two voices should be together permanently. And by the way, you sang like an angel tonight."

I was surprised, sang like angel, an unsaved angel! "Thank you."

"I think we could make some extra money singing in Williamsport, and I need a wife now that I'm taking on all this responsibility. And, I've heard nothing but praises about you."

Even after last night? I doubted that. Then I realized: he was asking me to marry him! Was this my sign? My heart stood still. Our muffled footfalls on the damp dirt road sounded a soft drumbeat in my ears.

"Are you asking me to marry you?"

"Yes, I am. Will you marry me, Josephine?" His arms hung straight down at his sides. Our hands never touched.

"Just like that?"

"I know what I want and I go after it, simple as that."

"Simple as that?" My teeth nearly fell out of my mouth. You could have pushed me over with a feather. Here was my passport to another life. I had prayed for a sign; this must be God's answer for me! Porter was religious like Daddy, and Ma had found her place with him. Was I supposed to do the same? Did God want me to follow in Ma's footsteps? Was I strong enough to?

"I can't give you my answer tonight. I have to think about it, and pray about it. I'll tell you tomorrow, or Easter Sunday evening at the latest."

We walked in silence. At the Stanley's door, he said, "'Til tomorrow then. Good night, Josephine. I'm just down the road at your parent's."

"Good night, Porter."

There was no whispered endearments, no kiss. My mind was in a dizzying whirl. Tomorrow I had to have an answer. I turned and watched him walk down the smooth slate stone walk, stones smooth as the blackboards in the one room school, stones that I had played hopscotch on only a couple of summers ago, old stones, comforting familiar friends.

I couldn't go in just yet. So on impulse, I stepped around the corner of the house and peeked in the bay window at the living room scene. Mr. Stanley, chin on chest, was asleep with the newspaper in his lap. Mrs. Stanley yawned and rose from her chair and went out to the kitchen. Forrest was sitting in the corner of the sofa with Linda tucked under his arm. She looked bored and listless until Forrest cupped his hand and whispered something in her ear. Then she popped up all perky and smiles. Taking his hands, she pulled him up and led him toward the stairs.

They met Mrs. Stanley in the doorway. She said, "You two off to bed?"

"Yeah, good night, Mom."

"Us too…nite you two…..Fred, Fred, wake up."

I ran fast as I could to the front porch where I could peek in the windows either side of the heavy deep-paneled Greek Revival front door that reeked of history and security. Forrest had his arm around Linda's waist as they mounted the stairs. I could hear her laugh as he kissed her hair, then he turned her face to kiss her lips. Tears I hadn't realized had formed, wet my cheeks. A cry caught in my throat and the peepers mocked me.

Mr. and Mrs. Stanley followed in a few minutes. "You didn't forget and lock Josephine out?"

"No, Fred. And the light's on."

He put his hand under her elbow, and she looked up at him and smiled.

I waited a few more minutes before I went into the familiar house that had been home and a sanctuary where love abided, but I felt cold. I shivered, locked up and turned out the lights. As I passed Forrest's and Linda's door, I could hear them bounce on the bed and begin to make love.

Snooks waited for me, curled up on my bed, and I buried my face in her fur.

Jesus, do you know if God wants me to marry Porter? I know I couldn't if I had to sleep with him. It seems to me that he has no interest in sex. He didn't hold my hand or put his arm around me. I know I could never love him like that. I guess God thinks it would be better if I didn't have children because I probably wouldn't love them just like Ma doesn't love me. You know, I wonder if you put a man and woman to sleep like they were going to have surgery, and you took the man's seed and planted it in the woman, if that baby would be free of sin. I wish I dared to ask Rev. Fillmore that! What seems funny to me is that I thought God was more like Rev. Grey and the Methodists than like Aunt Alma and True Faith. I've about come to the conclusion that the only prayers that work are the ones that try to find out God's will and seeks God's help to become a better person. Any other prayer can run into problems because someone is praying for no rain while someone else is praying for rain. I think maybe God has his laws and we better find ways of working with them. I guess I think like that because I'm a gardener. Maybe I shouldn't talk about things like this because I know what most Christians, especially True Faith Christians, would think if they knew I had these kinds of thoughts. But I really believe that you know my thoughts whether I admit them or not, and I believe God has a plan for me and has given me a sign. Maybe I shouldn't admit my doubts by asking for courage to carry it out. I should just say thank you for your sign.

Snooks reached out with her paw and touched my face. I gathered her up into my arms, and she put her purring motor into high gear. "Puss, oh puss, you sweetheart. Am I to lose you too? Am I going to lose everything I love? Is this sad ACT going to be ACT THREE? Is it the start of a whole new life with new players? I don't think I'll be in

English class to finish our study of Shakespeare. Sans, Snooks, to all my loves."

Chapter 13

In my dream, Aunt Alma stood in the middle of the church frantically waving her bible in the air. "I warned you, Josephine. You were always in need of a spanking, and that sister of mine couldn't see it. Now look at you. You're a heathen just like your Ma."

Everyone had left. I had to get out of there. "Let me by; let me by. I'm not like Ma."

Her cackling laugh rang out, echoing in my head as she ran out the door.

Rev. Fillmore slammed the door shut and bolted the lock with a loud resounding clang. "You will repent." He blocked my passage and grabbing my hands, he pulled me down, down the aisle that got narrower and narrower, but the once low-raised platform where the pulpit stood had grown higher than my head.

"Now see what you've done!" He forced me to kneel on the floor with the platform towering over me. "See how low you've sunk. SIINNNERR, repent before it's too late....accept the Loorrrddd Jeessssus as your Savior...." The words came to me through the ether.

With every last ounce of strength, I struggled to stand up, and I shouted, "No, no, never," but I wasn't sure any sound came out of my mouth. Then I sang in a low squeaky voice. "Jesus loves me this I know because He told me so." My feet tried to run, but they were glued to the floor.

There was a loud knocking at the door. I could hear Forrest's voice far, far away. "Yo, can you hear me? Yo, come. I need you. Help me muck out the calf pens...mulch your garden."

My feet broke free, and as I started to run, I stumbled and fell face down in the aisle.

Rev. Fillmore grabbed me by the foot. "You can't escape. You've received your sign."

I awoke suddenly with Snooks' wet nose bunting my cheek. "Hey, hey, Snooks, my wonderful sweet puss, thank you for rescuing me." I gave her some loving strokes and pulled her under the covers to snuggle. Her furry little body vibrated with her happy purring, soothing my rattled nerves. I slipped out of bed still troubled by my dream and slowly dressed to go downstairs for breakfast.

Mrs. Stanley was in the kitchen making oatmeal. I could hear Forrest and Mr. Stanley in the backroom, already up from chores. I quickly buttered the toast and we all sat down to eat.

I was still so shaken my breakfast refused to go down, but to my great relief, no one seemed to notice. Mrs. Stanley said, "Any more orange juice in that pitcher, Jo?"

"No, I'll fill it." As I got up from the table, I glanced out the window, and saw Porter come out of the tenant house and start up the road.

Panic filled my heart. I didn't think I'd have to have my answer ready so early in the morning. I quickly put the refilled pitcher of orange juice on the table, and said, "I'll be back shortly," and scooted out the backdoor before anyone could ask me where I was going in such a hurry, or should they save my oatmeal.

The warmth of April's early taste of summer washed over me like an endorsement to the monumental change about to happen in my life. The earth smelled sweet, ready to be tilled, but in spite of nature's vote, my empty stomach churned. I met him on the smooth stone walk before he reached the door.

He greeted me with a simple, "Good morning, Josephine."

"It is a nice morning. Let's sit out here."

So Porter and I sat down on the front steps where I had seen Abbey and Allen sit with their arms around each other. We sat as strangers unaffected by the warmth of early morning's dewy caress.

He wasted no time. "Do you have an answer for me, Josephine?"

I hesitated. My mind was caught in a current that swirled my thoughts in all directions at once. Ma had married Daddy without so much as a walk home from the church with the peepers buoying her up, though she did have me to provide for, to give her courage. In a round about way, didn't it still come down to providing for me? As an adult, I must provide for myself. Suddenly it occurred to me that as far as Ma was concerned, I had been doing that for some time. I had received so much from the Stanleys. How could I ever repay them? I knew the answer: by not becoming a burden.

Suddenly, an overpowering sadness overwhelmed me. I was about to leave everything familiar behind. The sun splayed yellow fingers everywhere, turning the world golden. How could I store the sight of it as it grazed the newly greening lawn? Soon the pastures would be lush and the cows would be out to graze for the first time, and I'd miss the way they kicked up their heels with joy to be out of the barn again. Mrs. Stanley always stopped her work to go out on the side porch to watch them.

Matt came out of the tenant house and headed toward the barn with its musky smells. How could I get along without Matt's friendship? I'd miss Mark too with his enthusiasm for life. He was probably upstairs doing some extra project for school. Daddy came out and followed Matt to the barn. It surprised me to realize I'd even miss him and his steady dependable ways, and how good he was to Ma. Would I miss her? Would I be done with needing and wanting her love? Would she miss me? There was an empty place where there should have been an answer. I must love her, or I wouldn't ask those questions.

Most of all, I'd miss living in this house with the love Mr. and Mrs. Stanley so freely gave me. Forrest came into my mind last for the first time. It must be because our separation was complete. Still, I knew I would love him forever. The loss of his special friendship, which had vanished with his return home, was a knife in my heart. I had to get away.

"Hey, hey, Josephine...do you have an answer for me? Will you marry me?"

I had prayed for a sign, and God had clearly given it to me. All I had to do was accept it. I must not let my dream shake me. "Yes, Porter, I'll marry you, sing with you and keep house for you." There were no ringing bells, no confirming flash of light.

Porter said, "Praise God."

There were no endearments exchanged, no holding of hands or embrace. Praise God was just right! At the time anything more would have scared me.

As we rose from the steps, he said, "Before we tell anyone, we need to get your mother's permission."

I had been on my own for so long, that to need permission was a surprise. Why would Ma have anything to say about what happened to me, the Stanley's possibly. But, I followed dutifully on down to the tenant house.

Daddy came out of the barn. "You two going to do some practicing for tonight?'

"No, Mr. Osborn. Josephine and I have something we need to discuss. I'm glad you've come back to the house."

"I forgot my work gloves."

Ma was clearing up breakfast dishes. "Oh, Paul, your gloves are on the chair. And what can I do for the two of you?"

"Josephine and I have something we need to ask you."

Not sensing the seriousness of the occasion, very flippantly she said, "Ask away."

"Well, Mrs. Osborn, as you know, I have taken on the responsibility of ministering to a small church down in Jackson Junction, probably never heard of it. It's smaller than Tate Town because it only has one church. And with all this responsibility I'm very much in need of a helpmate. Josephine has very graciously consented to be my wife. We're begging your blessing and permission to marry."

"Josephine's still in school."

"Ma, you know I have no future here. Porter says we can have a singing career, and he needs a housekeeper."

To my great surprise Daddy said, "She's too young, Clara. I say no." I never thought Daddy cared two beans about me, and would be in favor of my marrying a religious man like himself, someone who could be my salvation. That he might be putting my personal welfare above what appeared to be his religious duty stunned me.

"Hear them out, Paul."

"Our singing voices are a perfect match." Porter was animated. "And my church is close enough to Williamsport that with any luck I think we can get on the radio. You know, a testimony in inspirational song type program. I've heard they're looking in that direction."

"It'll be an arrangement sort'a like yours and Daddy's."

Daddy very quickly said, "I say no, Clara."

"It's worked for us. Why are you against it?"

"She's too young. She's only half way through high school. We were older."

"If that's all. If you're sure it's what you want, Josephine, I'll sign."

Porter didn't give me a chance to respond. "Thank you Mrs. Osborn. Now, on up to tell the Stanleys."

Before we were out of hearing range, we heard Daddy say again, "She's too young, Clara."

"But, Paul, it may be her only chance...."their voices faded. I cringed, was hurt, and embarrassed to have Porter hear that. Soon, I'd be far away where she couldn't hurt me any more.

At the Stanley's there was an explosion. Mrs. Stanley stood up and plumped her fists down hard on her hips. "No, Josephine. You can not marry without permission. You're way too young to even know your own mind."

"Ma gave her permission."

Things deteriorated with everyone talking at once in high pitched voices. The only quiet person was Linda who still sat at the breakfast table with a smug look on her face. Thoughtlessly, with one hand she pushed my cold oatmeal aside, and the thought of oatmeal started my stomach churning again.

Forrest raised his hands, pumping them up and down in the air to command silence. "What do you mean; you have your mother's permission?"

By this time, Mrs. Stanley was red-faced and near tears. "Clara, gave her consent? I don't believe it."

"Believe it." With tears in my own eyes, I took Porter's hand, and strangely, this was the first time we had touched each other. "I'll walk you to the door. I think you'd better leave now."

He held back. "First, I must lay out my plan." Continuing to hold my hand, which was more upsetting than comforting, he barged ahead with no thought of how upset everyone was. "I've been assisting Rev. Burk pretty much ever since I was here at the end of last summer. He's nearly blind...you know, macular degeneration...he still has a little side vision. Anyway, his daughter's here now to take him home with her. So, it's imperative that I return Monday to take over. To save myself the trip back up here, I plan to take Josephine with me. So I need to get this settled to give her time to pack. I have arranged for her to stay with my neighbor who is more than willing for the company. Her husband died this winter and she's lonely. The women of Jackson Junction Free Methodist Church are planning the wedding for next Saturday."

That was so shocking I was numb, beyond responding. How egotistical, he made all those plans without consulting me! How could he be so sure of himself? What should I do? I was in a current that was completely out my control. Did he deliberately trick me so I'd be humiliated if I changed my mind?

Mr. Stanley doubled his fist. For a moment I thought he was going to hit Porter, and I found that a pleasing notion. But instead, he thumped his fist down on the kitchen table so hard it made the breakfast dishes rattle. "This is where I put my foot down. Josephine is not leaving this house this weekend. She's lived with us long enough for us to have some say in this matter."

Other than a surprised blink, even that didn't faze Porter. "There's very little room for compromise. The wedding must go on as planned otherwise it'll interfere with the singing engagements that are already in the works."

How dare he? As if he owned me. His spiel went on without a pause.

378

"I've been keeping our audition secret. It's not quite a sure thing. Rev. Fillmore has waggled a try-out with the radio station in Williamsport. He's planning to come to Jackson Junction to marry us and accompany us to the audition."

"There better be room for some compromise or I'll call the authorities." I had never seen Mr. Stanley angry before. I wanted to run to him and slip under his arm.

With that, Porter was visibly taken aback. The wind was out of his sails, but he was not backing down. "The best I can do is to drive back up here on Friday to pick her up. The wedding can't be postponed."

I thought Forrest was going to explode, and I wished he would be my knight in shining armor, but how could he be with Linda right there beside him, looking very amused.

He asked, "Doesn't Josephine get a vote here? We don't know you from Adam. The bride plans the wedding."

Until that moment, I might as well not been present. Was it the singing ministry God had planned for His glory? Was I going to wreck it with my pride? "Ugh, er, well...anything's Ok with me." It wasn't, but I hurt so deep down I couldn't think or begin to articulate anything coherently.

Mrs. Stanley left the kitchen in despair.

Mr. Stanley said, "Suppose, we work out a plan for us to drive Josephine down next Saturday in time for the wedding. Give her a little chance to get used to the idea and there's people she'll want to say goodbye to." He rubbed his chin thoughtfully.

Forrest said, "If she doesn't change her mind."

"I won't change my mind."

With frayed feelings on edge, plans were finalized around my deaf ears. My emotions were in such a deep trough of despair, to turn off, and retreat into oblivion was my well learned defense. My body let circumstances, like a puppeteer, pull my strings.

***

At dinner that noon, we sat stiff like strangers; we who had lived together so long. Our sad faces were greatly out of step with the kitchen that still looked so friendly. The red gingham curtains cheerfully hung at the two south windows that looked always down across the lawn toward the tenant house. The shiny new stove and refrigerator heralded our step into the modern world. The old Hoosier kitchen cabinet invited someone to stir up a cake. The pantry was just behind the closed door where there were still canned fruits and vegetables waiting to be eaten. I was leaving all this, my haven, and because of that, we were already separating even though there were five full days before my departure.

I got up from the table and started upstairs. Mr. Stanley began to speak. I stopped to listen.

"May, get hold of yourself or you'll make yourself sick. Though I can't say I blame you. I'm sick too. Think you should invite Porter to dinner tomorrow so we can get to know him a little bit. In fact, I'm going down there right now and have a few words with him."

"Yes, Fred. You invite him."

This was a side of Mr. Stanley I hadn't seen before.

He continued: "Linda, you stay in the kitchen and give May a hand. There'll be baking to do for dinner tomorrow. Forrest, if you can coax Jo into a walk, I think it'd do her a world of good, maybe you some too."

I ran on up the stairs for a good cry. I loved Mr. Stanley so much. He always got it right.

In half an hour there was a knock on my door. "Yo, I need a walk. We haven't been on a hike since I got home. This may be our only chance. How about it?"

I wanted that walk, but at the same time I wanted to be snide, and ask whose fault was that, but I said, "Give me a few minutes."

"I'll be in the back room getting my boots on."

Forrest and I walked side by side as we always had. Except that, now it was a man and woman who walked toward the woods, past the fairy stones, and the apple orchard just coming to life. The Yo of years past would have been making up a story about the how the fairies were planning their spring dance. All that came to mind was that the fairies would have to dance forever without me, and I'd not be around to see the apple trees burst into bloom or to harvest and can the apples.

"A penny for your thoughts, Yo."

"I'll miss all of this...but, I suppose there're other places with walking lanes, but it won't be this walking lane."

He grabbed my arm. "Don't go through with it. It's not too late."

"Seems like I said something similar to you not so many days ago. I've made my decision."

"Listen to me, Yo. You don't love each other. You can't do this."

"Did you listen to me? You were only too anxious to jump right in where there was no turning back."

"That's different. It sounds to me more like a business arrangement than a marriage."

"Really! Who're you to talk? If you asked me, it seems sort'a like an arrangement on Linda's side too, and that was OK with you." I sensed that ruffled his feathers.

We walked on in silence until we reached the woods where the trees embraced us. The sentinel crow of Mr. Stanley's story announced our arrival, and the protesting flock flew on to other places to scavenge food. We found a fallen tree trunk, remnant of a strong easterly wind, that the reinforced root system designed for west winds, could not withstand. Forrest brushed the dirt away, and we took our places side by side, arms touching. In the stillness under the twig canopy, barren branches swayed above our heads, clicking softly in the gentle breeze that played in the treetops.

I wanted to sit and let this wonderful peace fill my troubled soul. I wanted to feel the brush of our coat sleeves as if we were still the friends of yesterday. I wanted to turn and study the face of the man I'd never know to see if I could find traces of the boy I knew so well.

But Forrest was not as intuitive as his father. "Let's talk this over and see if we can't make some sense of it."

So much for all my longings…my longings that would never cease. "There's nothing to say."

"I'm afraid for you, Yo."

"As I am for you."

"How has it come to this?" He looked at me as if he'd like to take me in his arms to protect me from all harm.

My broken heart turned over as it always did, and always would as long as I was near him. I wanted to cry, but I said, "A fine kettle of fish, but you have no right to moralize."

"Maybe so, but I don't think you know what you're getting yourself into."

"There's where you're wrong, wrong, wrong. Hear me, wrong. I'm going to sing and I'm going to keep house, the two things I can do really well. It's good enough for Ma, and it's good enough for me."

"There'll be more to it than that; don't kid yourself. And, you're way too young."

"Stop right there. You're way off base. That's strictly none of your business, but you're wrong. Ma and Daddy….."

"Porter's not Paul...."

I jumped to my feet. "This conversation is over." And I started back toward the lane and home.

"Wait a sec, Yo. Let's not part like this. Don't you understand? I care so much about what happens to you; you're breaking my heart."

"I'm sorry, Forrest...I truly am, but I am going to marry Porter." I truly was sorry; my broken heart understood. I turned and waited. He came up to me, and held me tightly in his arms for a moment. Then we walked back to the house with his arm around my shoulder, as he played the part of the worried big brother, the role he had cut out for himself. We were still strangers.

***

Saturday evening, everyone came to hear us sing, but I no longer cared. I was numb.

Linda said, "Porter's divine. You must be pleased as a peacock."

Forrest was somber and withdrawn, unreadable. Mr. Stanley's attention was totally on Mrs. Stanley who could not hide her tears.

At the end of the service, again, I stood at the back of the church in the lineup: Rev. Fillmore, Porter, myself, Matt and Mark. Many people added their congratulations to Porter and me on our engagement along with their praises for our singing. "We can see you were made for each other. It's a match made in heaven."

It did tend to make me a little easier in my emotions because that was the way I wanted to see it. Porter knew just how to respond and was in his element.

When it was time to part and go our separate ways home, Porter pulled me aside and said, "I'll be accompanying you to the Methodist Church tomorrow. Mr. Stanley has ordered me, in no uncertain terms, to be there when your pastor announces our plans to marry, and on thinking about it, he's right. I should have thought of that myself." It did help to know Porter would be there. I felt a little less like an unfeeling commodity. I should have wanted to hug Porter, but the person I wanted to hug was Mr. Stanley.

Next morning, Forrest lingered at the breakfast table. Linda had all ready taken Jeffy upstairs to get him ready for church.

Mr. Stanley said, "Forrest, Rev. Burk will be announcing Josephine's and Porter's engagement this morning. You should be there."

I spoke up. "It's OK, Mr. Stanley." I was hoping he'd stay home.

"It's not OK, Son," emphatically, and he left the room.

I didn't think my spirits could sink any lower until I realized I would be saying goodbye to the church that had been so welcoming to me and had nurtured my faith.

Porter was there, as he promised, sitting along side all the Stanleys down front in the second pew where they nearly always sat. From my place in the choir, I tried to read Porter's thoughts, but his face was a blank sheet. That should have scared me, but I thought it was probably just as well I couldn't read it, because I'm sure our Easter service was quite different from True Faith's. Rev. Burk wouldn't be offering him an altar call!

Forrest was there with Jeffy on his lap, Linda next to him, perfectly groomed and the prettiest face in the congregation. I could see Mr. Stanley squeezing Mrs. Stanley's hand. I knew his concern, and her eyes were still swollen and red.

Rev. Burk ended his announcements with our engagement. There was a shocked silence that turned to audible surprise as Rev. Burk requested the very handsome Rev. Porter Kent stand up so the congregation could welcome him. I should have been proud. Instead, I thought people were probably asking, "What can he possibly see in her?"

I managed to sing my solo. Miraculously, a different self stepped forward whenever I stood up to sing. She was a mystery to me. The world vanished and there was only the music and my voice, filling the air.

After the service, Porter stood beside me accepting congratulations on our engagement. Again, he was right at home, and used the opportunity to invite everyone to the last Revival Meeting at seven that evening. "Come and hear us sing together." It made me feel shy, until I began to realize, if they did come they'd understand the future we had together!

Porter's invitation was rewarded. Every pew in True Faith Church was filled and chairs were brought in and lined the back of the church to accommodate the overflow. Rev. Fillmore was set on fire by the crowd! This was his chance to shine for Jesus. He exploded into a tumult of preaching. He pounded the pulpit with zeal, paced back and forth and mopped the sweat from his brow in torment, as he railed against man's sinful nature. When exhaustion overcame him, he sunk down onto the chair behind the pulpit. Porter and I rose and sang "The Old Rugged Cross" as Rev. Fillmore listened, eyes closed in prayer.

Revived, he stepped forward, past the pulpit, down to the pews, arms spread wide in welcoming embrace. "Listen, my fellow sinner, no one knows the hour of Jesus' return. Many will cry, Lord, Lord, and it will be too late. There will be wailing and crying and some will be left behind. Now is the time to prepare for His coming."

Porter, Matt, Mark and I stood and softly sang, "Amazing Grace", as Rev. Fillmore continued fervently pleading for all who had not accepted the Lord Jesus as their personal savior to come forward and receive salvation. He called on backsliders to come forward and renew their commitment to their Lord and savior.

I had the feeling Porter was willing me to break ranks with the singers and kneel with the others at the raised platform. I was committed to sing and keep his house. He would never own my soul. Jesus had all ready accepted me long ago.

After the service Porter and I said a formal stiff good by. He and Rev. Fillmore would be on their way very early the next morning. Porter's last words to me were, "They're going to try to talk you out of marrying me. Think of what a success we're going to be. I feel the Lord's blessing is on my plans. Something wonderful is going to happen."

He should have said our plans. "I hope so. I'll be there."

***

Monday morning everything felt strange, and I couldn't get my mind to focus. I stumbled over Snooks with my hands full of plates as I hurried around, setting the table for breakfast.

Mrs. Stanley said, "Josephine, that cat is always underfoot. She senses your reluctance to leave us. She wants you to stay. Listen to her plea. There's still time to change your mind."

Mrs. Stanley put the plate of pancakes she just finished making into the oven to keep warm, and I ran into her arms. She held me tightly against her bosom. I thought of Aunt Carrie's arms and started to cry. Soon we were both weeping, and the kitchen reeked with grief when Linda walked in.

"Oops." And she turned on her heels and left.

"Mrs. Stanley, will you keep Snooks for me? She wouldn't be happy any place but here."

386

"I'm afraid you won't be happy away from here either, and we won't be happy without you. You're only engaged. Engagements can be broken."

That was right. I began to see why Porter was worried, and why Mr. Stanley had announced nothing about our wedding day. They were all hoping to talk me out of my marriage before next Saturday. A bolt of reality hit me. At this time next week I'd be waking up as a married woman, getting breakfast for a husband I didn't really know.

I sniffed and blew my nose and before I could say anything Mr. Stanley walked in. "Did I hear someone say engagements can be broken?"

"Yes you did, Fred. Jo'll listen to you."

He put his arms around both of us. "You know, Jo, it'd be an easy thing to say you decided to finish high school before you take the big step. You'd have time to get to know each other...just postpone it a bit."

"Porter needs me now. He has it all planned out. And I may never have a chance like this again even though I can hardly bring myself to leave both of you. I know your arguments, and I'm glad you want me to stay, but I can't. Don't you see; this opportunity was tailor-made for me." I had to say the words to give them some credibility.

"Better we not answer that."

Mrs. Stanley sniffled, "Oh, Fred, you give up too easily."

"This is not the time to argue."

Mr. Stanley unwrapped his arms from around us and Mrs. Stanley said, "Getting back to Snooks, I'll be happy to keep her for you, forever or until you say differently."

"Thank you, thank you. That's a load off my mind. She's so used to being here where she's free."

My emotions needed to be free to store all the things I was going to miss. These five days would be full of feelings that must be held at bay to make room, also held at bay if I were to keep my resolve to go through with Porter's plans.

Forrest came in with the fresh smell of the barn on his clothes just as Linda reappeared with Jeffy still in his PJs. She glanced from Forrest to Mr. Stanley, and wrinkled her nose. "We should put the two of you at the other end of the table."

Forrest winked at Jeffy and sat down next to him. "You don't mind if I stink. Soon you'll be going to the barn with me…Yum, pancakes this morning, big guy."

That wonderful barn aroma was something I'd definitely store; I drank it in.

Mrs. Stanley said, "I called Abbey on the church phone yesterday. She and Allen and Louisa May will be here Friday evening. Abbey's meeting Allen at school, all packed, and they're leaving right from there."

I swallowed hard. I should have listened to Porter and insisted on leaving with him. This was going to be more difficult than I had imagined. I had thought it would make it easier for everyone if I waited, but I could see I was wrong. However, at least now I had something to think about and plan for.

I cleaned Abbey's room and made the bed with fresh sheets. Everyone tiptoed around me expecting me to falter, watching for me to give way. Tuesday was the same. On Wednesday Mrs. Stanley insisted on taking me shopping for a new dress, hat and shoes. It took a lot of persuading on her part, but finally I remembered Ma painstakingly remaking Aunt Carrie's blue dress for her wedding and that she curled her hair for a man she had never had a private conversation with, and I consented.

By Thursday morning I began to wonder if Ma was going to miss me at all. It needled me that she hadn't been up to see how I faired, or to offer a helping hand. Low and behold, before the morning was over, she and Mark came carrying a huge package so large it was gift wrapped in newspaper and tied with a red ribbon.

Ma said, "Of all the things I could think of to get you, my mind always came back to this." They slid the package onto the kitchen table, covering it completely.

Mark's grin was even wider than usual. "You're going to like it, Yo. And guess what? I saw the telephone trucks, and they're getting ready to set the telephone poles. You're going to miss the new phones."

"No I won't. They'll have them in Jackson Junction, and it'll mean you'll only be a phone call away."

That thought was comforting. I appreciated the government's mandate that The Bell Telephone Company provide phone service to rural areas. Now, a doctor would only be a phone call away for Mrs. Stanley, another happy thought to store in my hollow place.

"Open it, Yo."

With trembling hands, I tore the wrapping away. Inside was a wooden box, beautifully crafted with multiple compartments to hold bags of garden seeds. Some compartments were already filled with labeled bags of her favorite flower and vegetable seeds. The box was designed to hang on the wall or to lie flat on a bench. It was perfect.

"Thank you, thank you, Ma." My heart swelled; she was thinking about me.

"You're always in the garden or canning up a storm. You can fill the other compartments with your best seeds. Matt and Paul made the box. One compartment contains money for gardening tools in case the parsonage doesn't have any."

Mark said, "I put my own money in for you, Yo, and Ma did too, besides the seeds. I'm not much of a builder."

"Thank you Mark. I know how much money for college means to you."

"Ma thinks I'd make a good lawyer, but I'm thinking doctor."

"Good for you." It must be wonderful to have plans like that.

Ma said, "It's so big we're going to have to tie it on top of the car. Paul said he'd see to it."

"It's perfect, Ma. Nothing could please me more." I could see Matt and Daddy with their heads together, planning and making the box. I wanted to hug her, but I had never done that. My eyes filled with tears as they often did these days. "I get my love of gardening from you, Ma, and it's the part of me I like best."

That afternoon Mrs. Stanley said she had some banking to do, didn't I want to go along which was just exactly what I needed to do, as I'm sure she surmised.

I had been saving my money ever since I took care of Mrs. Stanley. I had three hundred dollars, and I wanted to ask Mrs. Stanley if she'd let me put her name on my savings account in case of an unanticipated emergency.

"Of course, Jo, good idea." Then, to my surprise she had two hundred dollars transferred from their savings into mine to bring my account up to an even five hundred dollars. "That's for a rainy day. We'll keep this account just between the two of us."

I wondered how she knew I didn't want Porter to know. "I can't accept that money unless you promise me that it'll still be your money that you can take out and use any time. I'll let you leave it in my savings account if it makes you feel better, but when you see that I don't need it you'll reclaim it."

"If you promise that you'll use it if things don't turn out according to plan."

There was great concern and worry in her eyes. And again, I was acutely aware of how much she was against my marriage and apprehensive about my future. They couldn't afford to give me two hundred dollars. My resolve was being attacked from all sides. Would all the tattered feelings eventually heal, turn to confetti and blow away?

Try as I might, doom followed me all the rest of the day and up the stairs to bed. I had been neglecting my prayers. Was I afraid God had other plans for me? Was I arranging the signs to suit my purposes? Ask!

Dear God and Jesus, is this Your plan for me? It seemed very clear to me, but now everything's getting mixed up. I hate to leave the Stanleys. I'm making them unhappy when they've been so good to me. My heart is breaking. I pray Linda will change and make Forrest happy. I know it's sinful to have the feelings toward her that I do, but it's so hard to see how blind Forrest is. He wants her to love him, and since she is his wife, I want that too. And, Forrest and Linda will have children. There won't be room for me. Ma has made a meaningful life for herself, and I'm willing to do the same. Please comfort and give strength to each of us as we work our way through what lies ahead. It's not fair that I'm making Mr. and Mrs. Stanley so unhappy. Make my choices unselfish and true to Your plan. I shall look for a sign; if you want me to stay, show me.

***

Friday night before Abbey would leave my room, she insisted she was going to roll my hair up on rags. Just as I hadn't been able to win the argument with Mrs. Stanley about buying me a new dress for my wedding, I was afraid I wasn't going to win this argument either.

"I'd really rather you didn't, Abbey. Porter doesn't care a thing about appearances, and he might get the wrong idea. This is not a romance marriage."

We had just put a very tired reluctant Louisa May to bed. She had wanted to stay up and play with Yo. After all, wasn't that the reason they came? She hadn't seen me forever! And, it pained me to know I wouldn't be here next time she came, and I had to fight back tears. Abbey was just as aware of this as I was, but neither of us wanted to give our tears permission to start.

Instead, she asked, "No romance? Don't kid yourself. Anyway, the bride must be beautiful."

In my mind, I saw Ma on her wedding day with her hair down and fluffy for the first time. How beautiful she had been with her sky blue eyes that matched Aunt Carrie's dress. Maybe it was alright. Still, what would Porter think? I was definitely not romantic about our wedding, and romance was far from my thoughts, and I was equally sure it was not in Porter's mind.

I said, "This is a marriage like Ma's. I'm just going to sing with Porter, maybe even on the radio, and keep his house. That'll be good because they're the things I can do really well."

"Suppose you're wrong?"

"I'm not. Porter's never made even one romantic gesture."

"You really don't know each other. Given that any thought? Given any thought to being a mother?"

"I don't think Porter would want a baby. It'd be in the way of his plans, and I don't want his baby."

"You haven't talked to him about your understanding of the relationship?"

"No."

"You're scaring me, Jo. It's not too late to call it off. Don't marry without love. You lose even if you're right.   And, I doubt Porter sees things the way you think he does. Men are just not like that. "

"Daddy is. He never sleeps with Ma. They have an understanding."

"But Mr. Osborn had a marriage and kids before your Ma."

I hadn't thought about that, and it did poke a hole in my logic, but I closed that peephole of light with no hesitation. "Porter is just as religious as Daddy, maybe more so because he's a minister. Besides, I prayed for God to send me a sign about what I should do with my life. I know things would be better around here if I was out of the way. And, God has given me my answer."

"You could never be in the way."

"I doubt Linda would agree, and I put my trust in God and prayer."

For a moment I thought she was going to protest, but she couldn't argue with prayer and God, and I was right about Linda. The Pollyanna Abbey, whose wisdom and strength had guided us through the troubled war years, took over. Only the worried look around her eyes remained as she picked up the comb and started to wind my hair.

"This will just put some waves in your hair." She went on explaining how she planned my hair style to compliment the little half-moon hat Mrs. Stanley bought for me to match my dress. She chattered on, but it sailed right over my head because it took all my concentration to calm the restlessness our talk had stirred up in my already vulnerable emotions. Vaguely, I saw her check and lay out the things Mrs. Stanley had bought for my wedding.

As she left she said, "Jo, are you listening? I said, I'm leaving now. Remember, don't set your alarm. The kids might hear it. I'll wake you and help you dress."

With the unfamiliar lumpy rag curlers poking my head, it was impossible for me to turn off my churning troubles. So, I had only nicely drifted off to sleep when Abbey came tip-toeing into my room.

She sang softly, "Here comes the bride, tiny and not very wide. Wake up, Jo. It's your wedding day."

Abbey could make the absurd, seem normal. We were sisters and chums, getting ready on this, my wedding day, my special day just as if it really was a real wedding, and legally, I would be married. That realization ruffled my emotions even deeper down under my calm.

"Come, here's your robe…the bride must eat."

***

"Abbey, no nail polish."

"This is just clear, just a hint of pink," and she applied it fast and skillfully. Then she touched my cheeks lightly with rouge.

I hated stockings and garter belts, but I put them on. "I know I'll fall flat on my face with these high heels. Why in the world can't I wear my regular shoes?"

"Anyone who can run around over these fields the way you do will find high heels a breeze. Stop your complaining. Now, we're ready for that beautiful dress."

Mrs. Stanley had chosen a fine white eyelet over pink satin. The oval neckline and three quarter sleeves were also bound in pink satin. At my waist there was a narrow belt also of the pink satin with a flat tailored bow in the back. The skirt was cut on the bias, smooth over the hips, but hung in full folds half way to my ankles. I knew it was beautiful and flattered my figure very well, but I'd have felt more comfortable if it hadn't.

Now it was time to comb out my hair. She carefully unwound the curler-rags, and combed the front of my hair up and away from my face with the back falling in waves down my back almost to the pink bow at my waist. My wonderful little half-moon hat was white covered with pink satin rose buds, and it clipped over the top of my head and was perfect to hold my hair in place.

Abbey fluffed out the puffy veil that surrounded my head to just below my chin. "There, Jo, that's perfect. You look absolutely beautiful. Now, we'll turn the front of the veil back until we get to the church."

I closed my eyes and I was a little girl again. I could hear Abbey say, "You're the cutest little pixie." I had never seen anything as beautiful as that feed sack skirt and blouse she made for me that first week I was on the farm. Remembering the thrill I felt that day made my heartache. I could even feel the summer heat as I bolted Ma's and my bedroom door behind us as we prepared to try it on. There was no hat and veil, but she tied blue ribbons on my pigtails. Here we were, many years later, in a different bedroom, my very own, and we were saying goodbye.

"I don't trust myself to say anything, Jo, and don't you say anything either." She hugged me close, kissed my cheek and as she turned to go, added, "I'll give you a few minutes alone to gather up the last few things to put in your bag."

***

Regardless, rain or shine, birth or death, marriage or world events, the farm work must go on. Forrest said he and Paul should be the ones to stay home for chores; his father could walk Yo down the aisle. Jeffy and Louisa May were too young for such a long trip, and naturally

Linda would stay home to look after them. No one protested the plan though I thought Linda would have liked to go, but she was Jeffy's mother so what could she say? That meant Forrest would not be at the wedding, and for that I was thankful.

From my bedroom window, I watched Mr. Stanley load my bags into the trunk of his car. My worldly goods fit easily into one medium sized suitcase and a traveling bag instead of one paper shopping bag. My real treasure I couldn't pack to take with me. Some of it I had stored in that hollow place in my heart.

Snooks was curled up on my bed. How could I manage without her? The minute I walked out the door, this would no longer be my room or my home. Even my well-groomed body in high heels was unfamiliar to me. Without this place, this view of the barn, these fields, my garden, Snooks, this family around me, who would I be? The barn door flew open and Forrest burst though it on the run. I turned and left my haven to say goodbye to the one who felt like half of my soul.

We meet at the bottom of the stairs. "Is this my Yo? You're so beautiful, lucky, lucky Porter. But, I like you best in your bib overalls. I don't know how I can ever get along without you."

I threw my arms around Forrest's neck just as I had that day long ago when the robin he had stunned flew out of my hands. He became my love that day, and this day my heart was breaking. He swung me around as easily as he had that long ago day.

"Be happy, Yo. I need you to be happy."

I slipped out of his arms and ran out to where everyone had gathered by Mr. Stanley's car.

Linda's mouth dropped open when she saw me. "Wow, Yo, you look terrific. I envy you your exciting life with a singing career and everything. I wish I was going."

396

Ironically, I would have ten times rather traded places with her. "Thanks, kiss Jeffy and Louisa May for me and tell them I'll write."

At this point, Daddy joined the group. "Josephine, I still wish you had finished high school but since that's not to be, God's blessing to you and Porter and on your marriage."

***

As I started down the church aisle on Mr. Stanley's arm, the white New Testament with a single white rose tied to it with a white ribbon, Porter's gift, felt strange in my hands. Panic pulsed through my veins and my legs wanted to take flight, making my knees tremble. The groom's side of the aisle was an army of strange faces ready to interrogate me while on the other side of the church, the bride's defense, didn't completely fill one pew. Then, my eye caught sight of a lone figure, an older woman, sitting by herself, smiling at me, lighting up those empty pews. Her gray streaked hair refused to be tucked under her black pillbox hat; one I was sure had seen much of life. There were wistful curls that matched friendly eyes with welcome written plainly in them. An ally, a friend, I was sure. She had chosen the bride's side of the church to let me know. Hadn't a friend always miraculously been there to rescue me? With a friend I could face anything.

Porter looked almost as austere in his black preaching suit as Daddy did on Ma's wedding day. There was no hint of surprise or displeasure in his eyes as they caught mine. What relief. After Abbey's make-over, I had dreaded to see his reaction. Mr. Stanley squeezed my elbow as he guided me down the aisle. At Porter's side, he kissed my forehead, turned and took his place beside Mrs. Stanley.

The words of the ceremony stung my conscience, and Abbey's words, "Even if you're right, you lose," rang louder than Rev. Fillmore's voice. Way down under my desire to escape the pain of Forrest's love for Linda, I knew a loveless marriage was wrong, and that knowledge was desperately trying to break through my stubborn resolve. I wanted to bury my face in Snooks' soft fur. I almost burst into tears. The memory of the wonderful comforting tuxedo cat at Ma's wedding flashed through my mind.

Porter turned back my veil and planted a kiss solidly on my unsuspecting lips. Not a peck on the cheek as Daddy had reluctantly managed to place on Ma's cheek. Before I could control my reflex, my hand came up between us, but I stopped short of pushing him away. I was Mrs. Porter Kent, married! His hand was on my elbow and all eyes were on us as we made our way up the aisle.

Porter and I stood at the back of the church. I was Rev. Kent's wife to the strangers taking my hand or kissing my cheek. "How lucky you are, Mrs. Kent, to be Pastor Kent's wife. He's such a dear, dear man. We love him so," was repeated over and over.

One of the young women, wet hankie in hand, averted my eyes as she quickly said her hello to me, then raised lovesick eyes to Porter and with a solemn, sniffing crackly voice said, "Congratulations, Rev. Kent. I look forward to hearing the two of you sing."

Apparently, only for my voice, she would probably have been his choice. Right behind her, the lone little lady in the black pillbox hat put her arms around me for my first hug.

"We're to be friends. I'm Mildred Comb, call me Millie. You can see the corner of my barn from the parsonage porch. My house is out of sight against the mountain. If you need anything, call on me. When you don't need anything, call on me."

"Thank you. I will, Millie. Call me Jo."

We gathered in the basement for an ice cream and wedding cake reception. The strangers comprising the lopsided groom's side of the church rearranged themselves throughout the dining area, and I realized how small the congregation was, and what a proud hardworking community Jackson Junction appeared to be. At that moment, I felt surprisingly akin to them, and at the same time an alien unequipped to deal with my new role in their lives.

It never occurred to me that there would be gifts. Ma had had no gifts at her wedding. Not even the Stanley's dinner reception had gifts. I was overcome with shyness. This was far too much like a real wedding, not a working arrangement. I had thought the seeds and seed shelf were the best gift ever, but Ma, Daddy and the boys also gave us sheets and pillowcases; from Mr. and Mrs. Stanley beautiful lush towels, more than it seemed we'd need, this plus the clothes Mrs. Stanley had bought for me. Abbey and Allen gave us a tablecloth and napkins in bright large checked red gingham like Mrs. Stanley's so I wouldn't be homesick. Porter's parishioners gave us gifts that were especially touching personal things that I'm sure they made with loving thoughts of their handsome inspiring young pastor who was bringing excitement and fresh new hope into the Jackson Junction Free Methodist Church. There were crocheted doilies, a knit sofa scarf set, a teapot cozy, woven hot pads, sofa pillows, etc, and from Millie a big flower pot full of geraniums and petunias.

"For the front porch, Jo. I used to be a gardener."

"Me too, Millie." I was right, a kindred spirit, thank God.

Too soon, painful awkward goodbyes were said. Should I have invited Mr. and Mrs. Stanley, Abbey and Allen, Ma and the boys over to see the parsonage? I thought it was strange Porter didn't suggest it. I was unable to control the foreboding quiver that raised goose-bumps though the April day was warm and beautiful. Everyone said, "Happy the bride the sun shines on."

The Stanley and Bennett cars disappeared down the narrow road, all that was familiar and dear disappeared. Even the "me" that I was used to who wore braids, flat shoes and overalls was gone. Matt had held me close and whispered, "You'll win them over. Look how you've won all of us." At that moment Ma had impatiently motioned to Matt.

"Not everyone, not the one I needed to win most."

"Don't be so sure. It's just harder to see. And these people need you. Anyone can see that."

"But, I'm not good like you, Matt."

"You're better."

How I would miss him!

Chapter 14

When the wedding reception was finally over, the clean-up crew hastily began to put the church kitchen back in order. My natural response was to grab a dish towel.

"No, no, Mrs. Kent, not on your wedding day." Millie took me by the arm and ushered me out to where Porter was loading the car with our gifts. "Rev. Kent, take this little lady home and get her settled. The kitchen's not for her today." And she laughed as she gently pushed me toward the car.

Porter said, "Thanks, Millie, we're all loaded. Thanks again for a lovely reception. You ladies are miracle workers."

"Go on with the both of you!" She waited and closed the car door behind me.

The mountains rose up steeply behind the church, crowding it. I could see the parsonage across the road partially hidden by a grove of beautiful mature sugar maples. Behind and high above the house and trees more mountains loomed, leaving only a small patch of sky overhead. Nature had me caged in! I was used to open meadows and fields atop the rolling hills of central New York. There was no village here like Tate Town back home. On the road up ahead, only Millie's barn peeked around the bend. I now realized Jackson Junction was a few houses strung out along the road that snaked its way through the narrow valley. Later, I learned that teenage classmates in nearby Maplehurst, city of ten thousand, called it Jack's Junkyard.

Out of the isolating silence, Porter spoke. "I'm afraid the parsonage is in quite a mess. Rev. Burk's daughter was late getting here, and they only left yesterday. Keep in mind, he was nearly blind." The car stopped. "Well, Josephine, this is it."

The parsonage was in a dilapidated state of repair, but at one time had been a lovely house. We entered the porch where last fall's leaves had managed to find their way in through rusty holes in the screen, but those leaves came from the wonderful maples that I knew I would come to love, maples that would make the porch cool and inviting in summer, and next spring, I'd tap them and make maple syrup. My suitcases and Ma's seed shelf waited in the midst of the porch debris where Mr. Stanley and the boys had left them. What could they have thought? No wonder they had worried eyes. They must have thought this a poor welcome and judgment of my worth?

I swallowed hard and said, "I'll put this right soon enough."

He put his foot on my seed shelf. "Good heavens...what is this beast all about?"

"Daddy and the boys made it for me." His equating my seed shelf with the word "beast" won him no points.

"What'n the world am I going to do with that? Maybe I can put it to some use over in the church,"

"No way, that's mine."

He raised his eyebrows with an "excuse me look", and opened the door.

"Where should I put my things?"

"The bedroom's off the dining room. You'll see the upstairs is beyond hope, hasn't been used in years."

Alarm bells rang. I was not to have a room of my own! What should I do? I said nothing as I put my armload of gifts down on a dirty wicker sofa in the living room. Porter went out for the rest of the gifts, and I brought in my suitcases and added them to the things in the living room.

"Could I get you something to eat before I get settled?"

"The lady's tea was plenty for me. I have some work to do on my sermon. You'll need to change the sheets on the bed. Not one of Rev. Burke's priorities, I'm sure. Millie's been putting me up."

He disappeared into the tiny room off the living room. Mrs. Stanley told me that in the past those tiny rooms were common and played an important role in a family's life. They were just big enough to hold the birthing bed or a coffin. For a second, I saw myself climbing up and over the side into Aunt Carrie's casket, and immediately shook myself free of that vision.

I appreciated time to evaluate and get used to my surroundings. The dining room was large with water stained wallpaper that at one time had been a beautiful small Provencal floral print. The table had massive rope legs with a matching massive buffet. There were two closed doors adjacent to each other, and I opened the first one. I could see at one time it had been the pantry, but had been converted into a bathroom, barren, filthy but functional. I avoided the bedroom and opened the other door. It led up steep stairs to a narrow hall and three bedrooms. The smell of ancient dust, age-yellowed peeling wallpaper, and neglect filled my nostrils. Last summer's mummified honey flies clung to light-switch-strings, holding time captive as if at any moment they would be set free and take flight. They crunched under foot and blackened the window sills. My heart thundered; what to do? There was no bed for me to claim. God, stop time! could I take flight?

I ran downstairs, closed my eyes and went into the bedroom. My eyes snapped opened; the headboard to the old oak three-quarter-sized bed nearly reached the ceiling, and was a threatening presence to any who dared sleep so close in such a narrow bed. I recovered my eyes. I'd sleep on the wicker sofa in the living room. It was an unusually large one, and I was, for the first time in my life, thankful for being so small. Once that decision was made, I felt better.

The kitchen had a skirted sink; a refrigerator with the coil on top; a stove one half electric and one half wood-burning; an old dark pine armoire for dishes and dry foods; and in the middle of the floor a long narrow work table.

It was time to get to work! I quickly changed into overalls and hung my new dress in the closet. To my surprise, Porter's clothes nearly filled the closet, and didn't fit my picture of a struggling young minister. My high school wardrobe was not going to do. Mrs. Stanley knew what she was doing when she chose my wedding dress.

I made Porter's bed with our new sheets, and found some rather yellowed ones on the shelf in the bathroom for the wicker sofa. Then I dug into some general very tough cleaning.

Darkness descended swiftly down the narrow valley, barricading the parsonage from all around it, the church with its eerie little hillside cemetery, Millie's barn and the road that led the long way home. I was scrubbing the bathroom floor on my hands and knees when Porter finally emerged from his study. He hung his suit coat and tie in the closet, then came and stood in the bathroom doorway, hand above his head nonchalantly propped against the door-jam as he studied my progress.

"Bedtime, Josephine."

"I'll be finished in a few minutes."

"Tomorrow's another day."

My thought was that Porter needed to use the bathroom, and I quickly rescued my mop-pail and retreated to the kitchen to empty the dirty water and take care of my cleaning things. When I finished, Porter was in the bedroom undressing so I did the same in the kitchen, and was settling myself on the wicker sofa when he reappeared.

Leering down at me, he asked, "And what do you think you're doing, Mrs. Kent?"

"Really, it's no problem; I'll be quite comfortable here."

"A wife's place is in her husband's bed."

I was desperate. "But, I only agreed to sing and keep house...."

"The wedding ceremony says you are a wife....to have and to hold...so, it's to bed, NOW."

I hugged the sheets around me in panic. "But we don't love each other."

"Didn't Paul say in 1 Corinthians that a married man would care about worldly things, and an unmarried man about things of the spirit? With our kind of marriage, I can concentrate on the Lord's work and keep the spirit of the law if not the letter, the best of both worlds. I have a husband's right to your body which will take care of my lustful nature in an acceptable way, while being aloof from the temptations of wanting to serve your worldly ways."

"But I don't have a lustful nature, and the only worldly things I like are keeping house and gardening." I wanted to make a comment about the clothes in his closet and worldliness, but I held my temper.

"Honor and obey." He gathered me up off the wicker sofa, sheets pulling out and dragging the floor as he stomped across the dining room.

"I don't want your baby. I'm too young to be a mother. Put me down." I began to beat on his chest.

"Don't be so naive. Only in novels do you get pregnant the first time."

He threw me on the bed, and I began to kick and scream.

***

Next morning I was startled awake with Porter loudly demanding, "Don't play coy with me. Get up and get ready for church. And, I don't ever want to hear any screaming out of you again; you were no virgin. Who do you think you're fooling?"

"What do you mean? And I'll scream all I want."

"Alma said you were a sheltered innocent with a voice like an angel. Little did she know!"

The Stanley's back room whirled around in my brain. Screaming sounded in my memory. Suddenly, the screaming was in my throat and reached my ears. It was not Luke, but Porter, who came around the bed and began shaking me.

"Stop it, Josephine....stop it, this instant. You and I are singing a duet this morning, like or not. You will play the part."

I stopped screaming. Luke was the lurking figment in the back of my memory, the element in the Stanley's backroom that haunted me, the erased memory that still couldn't break through. But I knew, and Porter was another Luke. I whispered, "Oh Ma, why did you give your permission? Oh to be tenderly washed as you did that awful day when I was a child."

"I mean it, Josephine. Get yourself ready. I'll see you repent on your knees, asking for forgiveness and God's mercy."

"Never." How was I to endure? Life was a charade, a great big farce, a fractured existence with only parts to be played. I braided my hair so tight it pulled my skin until it made my face shiny. In robot motions, I dressed and came out of the bedroom.

"For heavens sake, Josephine, you look like a little kid. Go back in there and put on grown up clothes. People'll think I married a child."

"These are my clothes. I was a high school student."

"Get back in that bedroom and take off those ankle socks and put on stockings and heels. And, wind that awful braid around your head. And, hurry up about it or we'll be late. There's no time for breakfast as it is."

Good, I couldn't eat anyway, and I sure didn't want to cook for him! Dutifully, I put on my garter-belt and hose, but I put my penny-loafers back on and wound my braid around my head. He would have to beat me before I'd wear heels.

When I stood to sing with Porter I looked out at all the strange faces intently studying me. They, like Abbey, knew what the wedding night was all about. I couldn't feel my legs under me, how could I possibly sing? No sound would come out of my mouth, but then I saw Millie smiling at me, my voice joined Porter's. As I returned to my seat, Porter announced, "Tune your radios in to EROH Williamsport next Friday and hopefully you'll hear Josephine and me sing right after the noon news." Everyone clapped.

When the service was over, I refused to stand with Porter at the back of the church to greet his parishioners. He didn't want to make a scene, and let me slink away to sit in the last pew where hopefully I'd be ignored. I listened to Porter receiving many compliments on our singing, and an interesting conversation he had with Erma, the cow-eyed young woman he should have married.

"Rev. Kent, she's soooo young and shy. She can't be more than sixteen."

"She's older than she looks. She's so small."

"I see. She must make you feel very masterful. Such a big voice for such a little person… and for one so shy."

"I knew the first time I heard her voice that we were meant for the air. Rev Fillmore saw it too."

"You're going to be a big hit. I'll be listening."

I'm sure there were looks of understanding compassion exchanged, and I wished with all my heart she had my voice and was his wife. Self loathing and pity filled my heart. How had I been so stupid as to have allowed myself to be manipulated, duped into this impossible situation?

Millie greeted Porter with, "Rev. Kent, you and Jo are invited to share chicken and biscuits with me. The bride shouldn't have to cook today."

"Your famous biscuits baked on top of chicken stew?"

"None other."

"We'll be right along, thank you."

How grateful I felt to be temporarily rescued. I needed a friend to give me courage. Even her gravelly driveway underfoot felt like home. Chickens rested under the quince bushes that bordered the driveway. They sang happily and scratched clouds of dust through their feathers. Millie's quince bushes were so thick the ground beneath them was powdery dry, perfect remedy for chicken lice. With contented half-closed eyes, the chickens ran their beaks along the oil gland that grew on top of their tails, and combed the oil through their feathers.

Millie's place was a small farm with a weathered house and barn that had been well maintained though in need of paint. The table was set with white ironstone dishes that had probably been Millie's grandmother's. Everything in the house had stood the test of time and told me to relax, that the world was a stable safe place you could depend on.

Obviously, Porter felt at home because he picked up the newspaper and disappeared into the living room. Millie motioned me to the kitchen which was of the same vintage as the one in the parsonage, except here there was a friendliness that jumped out to welcome you. Everything was sparkling clean. The wallpaper was a blue handkerchief print, and all kinds of cooking pots and pans hung on the wall by the stove. A long pine work table took up the whole center of the kitchen, and on it all the ingredients were laid out ready for mixing the biscuits.

"Millie, what a wonderful house and kitchen." Before I had time to note all the details, she was putting her casserole into the oven.

"We'll be eating in half an hour."

"You're a wonder, Millie. This is so nice of you. I don't think there's one thing in the cupboard next door to fix a proper meal."

"We'll shop together. Maplehurst's the closest grocery store."

While our dinner baked I learned that Millie needed someone to help with barn chores. This winter had taken its toll on her with the sudden death of her husband.

I saw a place for me. Maybe God brought me here to help Mille. Maybe God had a plan for me after all. Maybe God had not abandoned me. Maybe Matt was right.

Millie went on explaining. "Herbert was such a good kind man. I miss him so much . . . his death has been hard for me to accept. He'd hardly been sick a day in his life and was as strong as when he was young. Here one day and gone the next."

"I'm so sorry, Millie. How awful, but how wonderful he had such a healthy life. Mr. Stanley, he walked me down the aisle...he owns the farm I lived on and sounds just like your husband. He'd say that's the way to go."

"Having you two next door's going to help. We all love Rev. Kent. If I can just hold out this year, Jimmy Henderson, he'll be graduating from high school next spring, is going to take over the farm for me. Herbert and I had only one child, a son Bill, and he wants no part of the farm. He's an engineer and is so relieved and happy Jimmy wants the farm."

"Mr. Stanley's son, Forrest, wanted to be an engineer too, but he gave it up and is on the farm."

The conversation turned to domestic things and Millie said, "I apologize for the condition of the parsonage. Rev. Burk didn't leave until it was so late we had no time to get in there and clean things up. It was in pretty bad shape last time I took food over."

"I understand, but it's no problem for me. I'll have it ship-shape in a few days."

"It'll take more than a few days and a miracle. Come on out to my backroom. I've been saving feed sacks for you."

Those words put a buzz in my heart because it had been feed sacks when I was a little girl that had made all the difference. Millie had a huge pile, enough to work wonders in the gloomy rooms next door.

"How absolutely wonderful. These are the miracle you mentioned. Thank you, thank you. You know, do you by chance happen to have a Robinson's wallpaper catalog? That'd make the miracle complete."

"Sure do.   And I have the tools you can borrow."

I thought I'd cry. Millie saw my look and held out her arms, and I ran into them. "Do you have any idea how much it meant to me to see your smiling face sitting on the bride's side of the church? And how much all of this means to me?"

"I do, Honey, and it gives me even more pleasure."

Millie's timer rang, and we three sat down to dinner.

Before Porter and I left for the parsonage, Millie's feed sacks, portable Singer sewing machine, Robinson's wallpaper catalog and wallpapering tools were in Porter's car.

410

Again, Millie waited to close the car door. "I'll let you know when I go shopping."

Porter said, "Easy on the shopping, money's tight."

Millie winked at me and closed the car door, and I knew I'd survive.

***

Next morning at daybreak, I was at Millie's backdoor in my barn clothes ready for work. I needed to help her more than she needed my help. That day new life flowed into my veins. I was needed. I could be of help, and I was learning a whole new business. Millie had seventy five chickens and sold her eggs in Maplehurst. Her delivery days were Tuesdays and Fridays, so on this Monday morning she was busy cleaning and candling the eggs over a special light that checked for blood. She rejected bloody and cracked eggs and packed the rest in crates ready for her Tuesday route.

She explained, "I don't weigh for size. I charge one price for all. I lose money that way, but I don't have time to hand weigh every egg. Someday Jimmy'll buy one of those fancy machines that do it automatically."

I worked until the middle of the afternoon, and as we worked, we made plans. I agreed to do the early morning barn chores. Jimmy already did the evening barn chores and the last egg gathering. Now Millie could devote her time to getting the eggs ready for market.

Millie said she and Herbert had always grown their own vegetables, and she didn't see how she could manage a garden alone. That was music to my ears because there was no place for a garden at the parsonage. She had no more than got the words out of her mouth, and we looked at each other and knew the answer to that problem. She'd have Jimmy plow our garden plot that very evening.

***

It was hard to know just where to start; the parsonage was so needy; did it matter? Literally everything needed attention. I quickly decided the poor porch was the place to start. I put my seed shelf on a throw-rug and pulled it into the kitchen. Later I'd have Millie help me hang it, it'd give the kitchen a little character. Next I removed all the old rusty screening, and took a stout pancake turner and scrapped the loose pealing paint from the wood. Already it looked one hundred percent better! Then I got rid of all the leaves and crud and scrubbed the floor with a broom and soapy water.

There was a wonderful door with a full length beveled glass leading into the dining room with a window on each side of it. I washed them inside and out, and lastly, I put Millie's huge pot of red geraniums in the protected corner until I could be sure of the weather. What a difference! The house smiled a thank you.

Now my thoughts turned to supper even though the idea of cooking for Porter was unappetizing. Before I left for Millie's that morning I woke him for breakfast. His response was, "Don't ever wake me again at this ungodly hour." He explained he didn't eat breakfast. He got a late bite at the Maplehurst Memorial Hospital when he made rounds, and it served as breakfast and lunch. I had no idea what time he might be home for supper, and the only thing I could think of to fix was pancakes and scrambled eggs. Millie said she had more rejects than she and Jimmy's family could use so I'd have a good supply of free eggs.

When Porter arrived, his greeting was, "I can see that you didn't spend all of your time over at Millie's though you still look like a farmer."

412

I thought it wouldn't have hurt him to say the porch looked nice. I knew the farmer part was not meant as a compliment, but for me it was.

I said, "I'm sorry...but all I can fix for supper is pancakes and scrambled eggs. It'll only be a few minutes."

"That's fine. Food means very little to me at this point. I eat to live, not the other way around. My total focus is on building up church attendance. You might better put your efforts there rather than at Millie's, much as I love her."

"She's supplying us with free eggs and I'll make some money for groceries. I'll be going to town with her tomorrow. I need a way to shop."

"That's good. I've no money this week."

I didn't tell him about my money from Ma and Mark. Thank heavens Millie had garden tools. I didn't tell him about the garden either.

***

Tuesday morning as Millie and I were finishing up her egg deliveries, I asked, "Would you know of a place that sells secondhand clothes?"

"Sure do...the bargain basement at the Episcopal Church. The rich church people in Williamsport send their clothes over to Maplehurst to help keep that little church afloat. They're real nice. Just right for a classy little lady like you...here we go."

Once there, Millie took me straight to the petite rack. Her eyes were much quicker than mine. "Jo, look at this. You said you needed something toned down, but dressy, for your audition Friday. Look at

413

this. I think it'd fit. And by the way, I'm not planning on you doing chores Friday morning."

"I'll just get up a little earlier."

She held up a light gray pin-strip tailored dress with shiny black buttons and a patent leather belt.

"Try it on."

"Can I do that?"

"There's a bathroom over there in the corner."

While I was changing she asked the volunteer if she had accessories to match, and she had a little gray conductor style hat to match and a pair of black patent leather shoes that were undoubtedly part of the original outfit.

"Look at yourself, Jo. You look beautiful, right in style."

"What am I going to do with this braid?"

She quickly wound it into a coil on the back of my head. "Wear it like a bun. It looks stylish."

Porter wouldn't call the woman who stared back at me from the mirror, a little kid. I wasn't exactly happy with the idea of pleasing him, but I did want our audition to be a success. I felt as if my life depended on it.

Millie pulled out another dress. "Every minister's wife should own an all-purpose basic black dress, and I have it right here, and I think the same little lady had owned this one too." And to our attendant she asked, "Do you have the hat to go with this one?"

"We do...a black straw sailor, perfect for summer, though the black linen dress can also be worn in winter. If you would like, I have a red, gray and black patterned scarf that would go very nicely with the black dress for winter, and then the Gray felt hat would be a perfect match...would you like the boxy little jacket that matches the black dress? It could be worn with both outfits. It'd be all you need for warmth in spring and fall."

When we left the bargain basement I had a whole new wardrobe for fourteen dollars. Now, not only was I an adult, I would be dressing like one!

Chapter 15

The wind blew the snow up our little valley with a vengeance so fierce my flashlight was useless, and I had to feel my way along the edge of the road to Millie's barn. Last week's snow had lain quietly until the morning of February 12, 1947, a day that was soon to become one of the most important of my life.   There was the feel of a storm brewing. The wind drove the cold through my coat, and the snow stung my face as I made my way.

Today was Porter's and my scheduled day to go to Williamsport for our very successful "Gospel in Song" broadcast. I had crept out of bed quietly though Porter seldom woke when I rose for my chores at Millie's. I was afraid, with my luck, this morning would be the exception, and I didn't feel up to dealing with another confrontation.

Once chores were done, I made my way from the barn up to Millie's back door. There was no need to go back to the parsonage and give Porter a chance to force me into going.

Millie was in the backroom packing eggs for market. "Come in out of that wind. I declare it's time you let Jimmy do your chores. You know his mom said she can make-do without him for a few weeks...said she'd have to soon enough anyway...and he can catch the school bus from here. You shouldn't be out in that barn...by the looks of you it could be any time." She led the way into the kitchen, and taking the teakettle from the back of the stove, continued, "Get yourself over here to the stove and warm up. A cup of tea'll help."

We had just begun to drink our tea when there was a knock on the front door, and when Millie opened it a gust of wind blew all the way out to the kitchen before she could close the door. "Good morning, Rev. Kent…burrr…that wind. Come on in out of the cold."

"Good morning, neighbor. Is Josephine here, or is she still in the barn?"

"Just came in and is chilled to the bone." She led him out to the kitchen.

"Josephine," Porter voice was controlled but impatient. "Have you forgotten what day it is? We need to leave early with this storm brewing."

"I told you last week, I wouldn't be able to make it until after the baby comes."

"Nonsense. Come on home and get ready." He turned to Millie. "Keeping busy is the best thing for her, isn't that right? If she can do chores, she can certainly sing."

"Afraid I see it her way…I've been telling her she's working too hard. Jimmy Henderson's coming to do the chores, starting tomorrow morning. By the looks, the baby has dropped and it could come anytime. I think she'd do well to take it easy today…have a cup of tea with us before you go?"

Millie's invitation was a proclamation that the issue was settled. How thankful I was to have this scene playing out with Millie to fight my battle. If it were between just Porter and me, he would force me into submission. In front of Millie he couldn't get away with that.

"Come on, Josephine, one more week won't hurt."

"You'll have to go without me…"

Millie said, "The little mother has spoken. I think you're right to get an early start. I feel a storm in the air." She made no further mention of tea, but rather guided him back to the front door. "I'll look after Jo until you get back from Williamsport. I'm sure your radio fans will enjoy your solos when you tell them there'll soon be another little Kent in your household."

The door shut behind him.

"Thank you, Millie. I just couldn't go today. I have such a stomach ache."

"Where?"

"From my back right around my belly."

Millie ran out of the house calling to Porter. "Rev. Kent, wait...I think the baby's on its way!"

He was already in his car. "She'll be alright. She's just being dramatic." And he slammed the car door shut and drove away.

Millie looked pale when she came back into the kitchen. "He's gone, and he should know you're not the dramatic type!"

"It's just as well. I'm sure he's right. And he'd have to go anyway. The show must go on."

"Nonsense. The world wouldn't come to an end. The station could fill in. They have to have a back- up."

"Maybe you're right, but that's not what Porter thinks. Anyway, Millie, I'm glad he's gone. This tea is making me feel a lot better."

"Pain all gone?"

"Just about."

"I don't want you over there alone today. You're going to stay put until Rev. Kent gets back home."

I don't know what came over me, but as Millie settled me on her sofa and was tucking the blanket around me, I grabbed hold of her hand and said, "Talk to me. I'm so scared."

418

"Everyone's scared with the first baby. You're young and healthy. You're the strongest young lady I ever saw." She sat down on the sofa at my knees. "I'll never forget that first Monday morning when you appeared at my door in your bib overalls and asked if I was sincere in wanting a chore-girl."

"Pretty bold, wasn't I?"

"I thought so for anyone as shy as you were the day before at church and at my dinner table, but it didn't take you long to show me you were the chore-girl of all chore-girls. Before I knew it I was ordering extra chicks, and now we have one hundred twenty five laying hens."

"And increased your egg route. You're so lucky Jimmy wants to be a farmer. Think I'll have him start my morning chores tomorrow. I'll give him a ring tonight."

"Know what, we're both dummies. Today's Lincoln's birthday…there's no school…Jimmie's home. Lay still…I'll give him a call right now. "

While Millie was talking to Jimmy my stomach grumbled again, but when she came back I said nothing about it, and she resumed her position at my knees.

"Stomach still quiet?"

I nodded and took her hand back in mine. "I know I could die, but, Millie, what really scares me is: I'm not sure I'll love it."

"Of course you'll love it. All mothers love their babies."

"I'm too young to be a mother, and Porter's not happy about a baby." I started to cry, and Millie gathered me up in her arms with my bulging abdomen between us.

"Sh-sh-sh, calm and easy, don't upset yourself. Look at what you've done for the church with your nursery. I ask you, could anyone who didn't love babies do that? I can't decide if it's Rev. Kent they come to hear or a chance to be free of their babies and toddlers for an hour. What you two have done for that church in these short months. I'll never forget that first broadcast. You two made shivers go up my spine and people began to come. Now look at our church, busting at the seams...and the money coming in from listeners! It's a miracle."

"Porter says it's God blessing his ministry."

"No doubt that's true...but look at what you've done! No one would know it's the same parsonage. What elbow grease and some of my old flowered feed sacks and a little wallpapering'll do. So, dry those tears. You're going to be the best little mother in the world."

I wanted to tell her everything. The reason I started the nursery was so I wouldn't have to listen to Porter preach. It turned out to be a wonderful idea, and I loved the children and way the parents were so appreciative. I wanted to tell her why I had her pay me the same day we went shopping. That way Porter never saw the money. I wanted to tell her how important sharing her garden plot was to me. We both had all the vegetables we'd need until the garden came on in the spring. I knew how important it was to have a good diet when you're pregnant. Abbey's letters kept insisting I go for prenatal care, and the only way was to make my appointments so I could go with Millie on her egg route. If only I could bring myself to write to Forrest. He was the person I wanted to unburden my heart to. But I knew he was the last person I could confide in. We had not exchanged even one letter since I left. I wondered if he read the letters I wrote to Mrs. Stanley, and what he thought about the baby. I had no idea whether he was happy, or if Linda had become accustomed to being a farmer's wife. Mrs. Stanley wrote volumes about Jeffy and Louisa May, but never confided the personal details I wondered about.

Millie was waiting for my answer. "I wish...if only I could believe that. Ma didn't want me, and didn't love me. Her idea of love was not to put me in an orphanage; that's where her mother put her. She still farmed me out for someone else to raise. Maybe I'm just like her."

"Never. And I think you're wrong about your mother. Some people have an odd way of showing love."

"She had no trouble loving my stepbrothers. She lavished love on them, and I went next door to the Stanleys to get mine."

"Oh, Jo, that sounds so awful. I don't know who I feel sorrier for, you or your mother. Anyone would love to have you for a daughter, and what a tortured life she must have had at that orphanage. Do you want to talk about it…your father?"

I felt a tightening in my belly and in my heart. "I'm not supposed to know, but I'm the product of rape, and I'm a constant reminder of him. Please don't tell anyone…Porter doesn't know. Oh, Millie, I'm sorry…I shouldn't have blurted that out." I almost said, and this baby too, but I stopped myself. Porter was their hero. "I have no idea who my father was, nor do I want to know." She waited, thinking I would say more. My mind switched to Daddy. "My stepfather is very good to Ma even though he thinks she's a lost soul." I waited a minute weighing my next question. "Did you ever, you know, go down front and accept Jesus as your personal savior?"

"Well, not exactly. I suppose every Christian is continually in a state of repentance, since none of us are perfect. But, no, I never went down front."

I knew by the puzzled quality in her voice I should have stopped my questions, but I couldn't. "And you're still saved?"

"Well, yes I am."

"How?"

"I suppose it's because I've never known a time when I wasn't a Christian."

"Kind'a like you knew God and Jesus before you knew about going down front?"

"I guess so. Why all these strange questions?"

"Porter says Ma's not saved and that I'm just like her because I've never gone down front, and he can't stand it to have his child born to a heathen." What had come over me to say such a thing?

"We both know you're not a heathen. But, if it means so much to him why don't you humor him and go down front? What's the harm?"

"It'd be a lie to God. It'd be saying to God I didn't know Him. I think He'd turn his back on me if I did that. He wouldn't know me anymore, and I wouldn't know myself, and the more Porter pushes on me the harder it is to keep sight of God. If I lose my faith what will I have left?"

"You're too deep for me, Jo. Maybe you're just misreading an innocent remark. I can't imagine Rev. Kent thinking such a thing. Wait until the baby comes and see if that doesn't put a different light on things. How's the tummy?"

"Just a little grumpy." I felt so alone; I needed someone to understand. I wasn't just being temperamental due to my pregnancy. "I didn't mean that as anything bad about Porter. I know how much everyone loves him, but I should never have married him. I didn't know what marriage was all about. I thought it was just singing on the radio and keeping house. Ma and Daddy have a marriage of convenience so Ma could be mother to my stepbrothers." That came out all wrong too.

"What you're trying to tell me is that you and Rev. Kent are incompatible. Oh, Jo, you shouldn't tell me these things. Maybe this baby'll make things better for both of you."

I had to let Millie think that maybe she was right, but if she could have heard Porter when he found out I had conceived the first month, she would never think that. He ranted and raved and said it was my fault that I was pregnant. He said, "If you were a virgin this wouldn't have happened so soon. Now everyone's going to think we had to get married. You better have a boy is all I've got to say. And before this baby is born you better repent your wicked ways. I will not have my baby born to an unrepenting sinner."

I was so mad I couldn't answer him. Yes, I suppose technically I was not a virgin, that is, if I guessed right and Luke did rape me, but I was just a child. As if I could control the sex of the baby. And even I knew you can get pregnant the first time.

I shook myself back to the present. "Millie, I know now I did wrong to marry. I prayed...honestly I did, but I think I must have jumped to the wrong conclusion about what God wanted me to do. What if I am unsaved? I feel like Jesus is abandoning me. And, I know I'm not being fair to Porter." I wanted to tell her I was afraid to let anyone know, that I couldn't pray anymore. And I was worried sick about that.

"Let me tell you something that I want you to think hard about and take to heart. About your radio broadcast...Rev. Kent sounds good because you make him sound good. You sing like an angel; your voice is the real talent. The way you always defer to Rev. Kent, you make him look invincible. No one would ever guess you have all these doubts. You're exactly what he needs, and what's more, I think, down deep, he knows it."

"Oh, I'm sure you're wrong about that. It's not that I can't understand how wonderful he is to his congregation. I can see how he's always there when someone needs him, and how helpful he is to lend a hand. And the way the church is growing! Now he's talking about the possibility of adding on after the roof's paid for."

"All true, and he looks wonderful up there behind the pulpit. He's a handsome man and your tiny little frame makes him look even more powerful and handsome. Everyone can see that, and how good you are to him."

Those words went straight to my middle and caused a cramp so painful, I grabbed hold of my abdomen. "I've got'a get to the bathroom...fast."

When I stood up Millie said, "Oh dear, there's blood on the back of your jeans. We've got to get you to the hospital. This baby's on its way."

***

Millie was with me when they put Carrie May, 6 lbs. 9oz. all bathed and wrapped in a pink blanket, into my arms. I had told Millie I was carrying a girl, and she had said that it was just my wishful thinking that was talking, but I knew it wasn't. It made no difference to me; one sex was no more appealing than the other, and I was sure I wouldn't love her. But the minute I saw that little pink face, those tiny little fingers stretching as they peeked out of her oversized shirt, and saw that tiny little mouth pucker into a perfect O as if she were trying to say "hello", there was a quaking in my heart, and my arms tightened around that little bundle, and I said to Millie, "Meet Carrie May."

"She's beautiful, Jo, and I like her name...a good old-fashioned name."

"Yes. And, Millie, I love her."

"Didn't I tell you, you would? When did you decided on a girl's name?"

"This very minute."

"What if Rev. Kent doesn't like it?"

424

"A mother should name her daughter. That seems fair to me."

"Maybe you're right. Especially one whose eyes shine so brightly with love."

"Oh, Millie, I'm happy. At this moment, I'm truly happy."

"So am I, Jo."

When the nurse came in and took Carrie May away, Millie said, "Try to get some sleep, Jo. I'm going to call Rev. Kent."

Later, when I awoke, the nurse was bringing Carrie May back into my room, and as she placed her in my arms, Porter appeared in the doorway.

Millie rose from her chair. "Meet your daughter, Rev. Kent. She's beautiful and perfect."

"Babies are babies, they all look alike." I pulled the blanket back so he could see Carrie May, and he scowled. "She has rather a lot of hair. Is that normal? But at least it's sandy-brown."

Meaning it wasn't black like mine. If Millie noticed she didn't let on. Why couldn't he be accepting on this one day and appreciate what we had made together, a perfect little person, ready to make her way in the world?

Carrie May opened brown eyes and looked accusingly right at her father!

Millie laughed. "Very normal, Rev. Kent...want to hold her?"

"Aw...a...it's too scary. Sorry I left you with the burden of getting Josephine to the hospital. Who'd think someone would go out and do chores the morning labor started."

"Well, it worked out OK."

"We can always depend on you, Millie, to solve a problem...yes, glad it worked out...the show must go on. Josephine, if you had gotten word to me sooner, I could have announced it over the radio. The listeners would have loved it."

Always the opportunist, fatherhood and the baby could be exploited; something I doubted he had thought about until that moment. That would make both acceptable, but never the unsaved mother. A voice inside me said: "just as I would never accept him." If it were put to a jury of The Jackson Junction Free Methodist Church parishioners as to who was in the right, I was sure I'd lose. They thought I was the luckiest wife alive. I was doing my best. Our broadcast ministry was important to me too, and it was the money from our radio broadcast that was turning the church finances around.

Millie gave a snorting cackle. "Jo was a little too busy providing the news to pass it on...I'm the one who flubbed up. I should've been smart enough to report sooner. It would've been a wonderful chance to let your listeners share in the thrill of getting the news hot off the press, as they say. By next week it'll be old news. Darn it anyway."

Porter said, "Oh well, the baby's here safe and sound; that's what counts."

Millie said, "Amen."

"Amen...yes indeed...let's have a word of prayer and be on our way. It's really getting nasty out there......Let's bow our heads: Lord Jesus, we give praise and thanks for a safe delivery, and we ask your blessings on this child that she grow up in the fear of God and in righteousness. Make us mindful of your plan for us. 'All things work together for good to them that love God.' Make us worthy of your trust in us for giving this infant into our care. May this be the turning point in Josephine's journey to the Lord. In Jesus name we pray, Amen."

I couldn't believe Porter said that in front of Millie. At least now she'd know! And it seemed I was not the only one saying unexpected things that day.

Four days later Millie's truck bucked the snow drifts along Church Hill Road as we made our way to Jackson Junction, but with her skill at the wheel I felt perfectly safe even with tiny Carrie peacefully asleep in my arms. Because everyone called Louisa May by both her given names, I decided to stick with just Carrie though I didn't think it would matter that much since we lived so far away. When Porter called the Stanleys to report Carrie May's arrival, Mrs. Stanley told him how pleased she was to have two grand daughters named for her. And she took special pains to tell him again that I was like a daughter to her and was part of the Stanley family.

Porter had not been happy that I named Carrie without consulting him. He said she should have a biblical name like Mary Ruth. I told him, "Why, it never crossed my mind that you cared. You only asked that we name a boy for you. Other than that, you've shown no interest in planning for the baby." That had settled that.

We were almost home and Millie glanced over at Carrie sleeping in my arms. "You two make a beautiful picture."

"How can I ever repay you? Carrie has to belong to you in some special way since you were there when she came into the world, and here you are delivering us back home.....whoops, you went right by our driveway."

"You're staying with me...four days are just not long enough to be ready to take on a new baby and a household. The doctor asked me if I was the one who was going to be looking after you when you got home. I knew right then you had talked him into letting you go home early. I know you and how frugal you are. It wouldn't hurt the church to give Rev. Kent a raise. The money the two of you are bringing into the church these days!"

"Are you sure it'll be OK with Porter? How'll he know where we'll be?"

"When I get the two of you settled I'll run a note over and leave it on the front porch."

I felt the muscles between my shoulders relax, and the tension under my breastbone dissolve. "Thank you, Millie. I have to admit, it's a relief." Now, I'd have a few days to get my strength back before I confronted Porter with my ultimatum.

***

Thankfully, Porter said it would be easier for him to sleep at the parsonage where he wouldn't disturb Carrie with his comings and goings, and not to hold supper as he hardly ever ate at home anyway. If he needed something, he'd fix a sandwich for himself. He was just so thankful to Millie who was always coming to his rescue.

Winter raged away outside, shutting out the world, closing us in a cloistered burrow of safety and warmth where mother and daughter bonded under the watchful eye and loving care Millie lavished on us. Sometimes, the wind stopped and gentle, fat snowflakes drifted down as if fairytale Mother Hulda, in the upper world, shook out her featherbed. At other times the fierce wind drove the snow in sheets of white fury past the window. I felt snug, as if in a cocoon, as I wrapped my love around this new little person who would one day immerge, run about, and have a voice. Everyday Millie made her way through the snow to the bird feeder with the winter-world framed beautifully around her by the window. I loved the farm atmosphere; it felt right for the beginning of this special, once in a life time experience. Never again would I be a mother for the first time, and as my marriage stood, hopefully, never a mother again.

In quiet times, eyes closed, I could have been back at the Stanley's. Farm noises are all the same. Sometimes, when Jimmy came stomping the snow from his feet, there was a fleeting moment when I thought it was Forrest or Mr. Stanley coming in from the barn, and I'd smile, thankful for that extra moment of happiness. Then I'd look at Carrie's little face and know I couldn't possibly love her more than I did. But, there was an empty pain in my heart, and I wondered what Forrest thought. I wondered how I'd feel if I received a letter saying he and Linda were expecting. Why hadn't it already happened?

Porter checked in on us every evening in a whirl of excitement as he flattered Millie, praised her kindness, and shared with her the day's activities. Like so much of my life, I listened on the fringe though I was glad he showed his appreciation to Millie, who like all his parishioners, were charmed into blindness where his faults were concerned.

He asked, "Millie, when do you think I can ask people to stop by? Everone's anxious to see Carrie."

I spoke up. "Not until we're settled in at the parsonage. I'll not have people traipsing through making more work for Millie, or bringing Carrie a cold."

Porter's interest in Carrie grew in direct proportion to all the outside adulation over his blessed baby girl. He chucked her under the chin and placed his finger in her little fist. I was pleased by this change in his attitude. Carrie needed a father. There were moments when he was bending over Carrie, that for an instant, I saw Forrest and not Porter. Then I'd quickly shake myself, knowing that was a dangerous place to tarry. It was so easy; they were both very blonde though Porter was taller and would easily have won a photo contest for who was handsomer, but I preferred Forrest's looks.

Aunt Alma always said, "Beauty is in the eye of the beholder," a truism. She also said, "Pretty is as pretty does," for sure another truism that didn't necessarily prove the first. I could never agree with Aunt Alma on what constituted beauty. In that fleeting moment when I shook Forrest out of my imagination, I wondered what constituted the real truth. Porter was loved by a great many people with good reason. He worked hard and long at his pastoral duties, and he had wit, charm and good looks. Certainly, this fit all the correct criteria for "Pretty is as pretty does," and "Beauty is in the eye of the beholder." I was greatly envied by those same people, not for who I was, but because I was married to Rev. Kent.

Forrest also worked equally hard at farming, and was a giving, generous person who had the admiration of many people also qualifying him with the correct criteria. I decided that it all depended on the scales measuring the person's actions, the eye of the beholder, me or whoever. Forrest hadn't forced himself on Linda as much as he desired her. Porter continually claimed his conjugal rights without the tenderness of love. Then again, was that so different from the love that existed between Forrest and Linda when I knew she still loved Luke? Hopefully by now, Forrest had won her love. Those were things I needed to know, and no one dared write about. By contrast the people in Forrest's world loved me for who I was even though Ma didn't want me. Many thoughts tumbled about in my head, had done so all my short life, but my marriage to Porter cast a different light on old thoughts. And, with the birth of Carrie, I had an urgent need to find a new way to survive.

***

After two weeks with Millie, Porter moved Carrie and me back home to the parsonage. During my convalescence I had gained singleness of purpose, a mother's protective love. At Millie's, surrounded by the quiet embrace of the farm and nurtured by her loving kindness, I had gained physical and emotional strength. I was ready to give Porter my ultimatum.

As we came into the parsonage, Porter said, "I've moved the little basket-bed into our bedroom. It'll be a while before Carrie can sleep upstairs."

"Yes, that'll be good for now, but I have a few things I need to get settled right now so there's no misunderstanding. That cot up in the nursery is one I bought at a garage sale, and I bought it for myself. It's not for Carrie to grow into. I will be sleeping upstairs. With all the work I have to do, I can't be pregnant and take care of Carrie and make ends meet...."

He held up a hand to stop me from continuing, and I could see fire behind his eyes. "You expect me to believe all this prattle about no sex. Don't kid me. You were no virgin when we got married. Where do you plan to get your nookie, with Jimmy?"

"WHAT?" I had never heard that word, but I knew what it implied, and with Jimmy! Given his warped thinking, I supposed he could think that. Jimmy was nice and a high school student just as I should be. Impossible as that seemed to me now. I felt years older than Jimmy, and I had my wonderful, perfect baby Carrie to love and care for...and plan for.

"I know your type." He ranted as if he were behind the pulpit. "Your father was never killed in any car crash. Your mother was never married; she just got caught up with...daughter like mother."

"Nookie? Is that the vocabulary of a minister? If you really want the truth, I'll give it to you...right between the eyes. You're right about my mother not being married...she was raped. I'm not supposed to know that, but I overheard her wrenching confession to Rev. Grey. For all your bad thoughts about her, she and my stepfather don't even share a bed. That was part of the agreement between them. I thought because you never made any overtures of love, you wanted the same kind of relationship, and also because you're religious like Daddy. Had I known what you are, I'd never have married you. The way you treat me, sex is a sin!"

Here, he stopped me again. "That doesn't explain why you were no virgin."

"I was so little, and it was so awful my mind has blocked it out. But, something happened to me, and I was bloody, and Ma threatened Luke she'd tell Daddy, and he was so scared he apologized."

"What about the others? What about Forrest? I understand you were at his heels all the time, and he got a girl pregnant and tried to pass the baby off as Luke's."

"Honestly, Porter, you amaze me. How can you be so dense? This is the same Luke that abused me when I was a child, and tried to rape Ma. Everyone's not sex crazy like you and Luke. Linda freely admits the baby is Luke's."

"Because she tried to trap him into marriage. I know all about it."

"You may think you do. When Linda got pregnant Forrest wasn't any where near Linda. It must have been one of your immaculate conceptions! Forrest married her to give the baby a name, and Linda a place to stay during her pregnancy and during the war. When the war was over, Forrest took a different bedroom and gave Linda every chance to make up with Luke and get an annulment. Very different from the way you've treated me, but no more."

"We'll see. The bible says...."

"I don't care what the bible says. If you don't agree, I'll never sing another note. If necessary, I'll leave. Agree and I'll be a dutiful wife in every other way. I'll do the nursery as usual; I'll sing with you on the radio and be cooperative in all ways except, there will be no more sex."

"In your wedding vows you said, 'honor and obey'. The wife is supposed to call her husband lord even as Sarah called Abraham lord."

"Yeah, husbands are supposed to love their wives as Christ loved the church. If that's the case, I pity your church."

"It's my duty to save you, and you just refuse to listen and mock the Word. Sin entered the world by woman. Don't forget that."

"Now you've crossed the line and made me mad! If sex is the sin, you're the aggressor. Eve didn't run around with some forbidden fruit corrupting man. A man wrote that story to cover up his own sinful aggression that he felt guilty about."

"Blasphemy! Be quiet, or God will strike you down. Be careful, you're committing the unforgivable sin. I knew you were a heretic. Our poor baby. What shall I do?"

"Go read your bible. Doesn't it say in 1 Corinthians 7:14, an unbelieving wife is sanctified by her husband or else their children would be unclean? So if you're going to throw scripture at me, take that one to heart yourself." Porter stood with his mouth open because he thought I knew nothing about the bible and before he could answer, I continued. "It also says: judge not. Only God can say who's saved. You know nothing about what I believe........No one need know I'm sleeping upstairs. I will not argue about this anymore."

***

By April first, tender little blades of grass were breaking through winter's bondage, thrusting boldly up in protected places, screaming green to a world reborn, and the peepers stretched their tiny throats in a confirming chorus. Maybe it was the exaltation of motherhood that heightened the sights and sounds of spring because I was in love with the world. I had learned to rationalize the fact that I lived in two worlds. Dominant in my heart was my preferred world, the one that revolved around Carrie and my work at Millie's. In my other world, Porter had accepted my ultimatum, and we had achieved a working peace. I rose at five and nursed Carrie; then I carried her down to Porter's bedroom where she slept while I tended to Millie's early morning chores. I was back at the parsonage in plenty of time before Porter left for his pastoral duties.

Millie thought of everything. She had bought a playpen to have at her house. She said it'd be handy when we had tea together, and useful to have in case I needed a babysitter. It was wonderful. I was able to put Carrie down for her morning and afternoon naps while I candled, cleaned and packed eggs. Life was full and purposeful.

On the day Porter and I went to Williamsport to sing on the radio, Jimmy tended to my farming tasks even though this was the end of his busy senior school year. Everyone at EROH radio loved Carrie and quarreled over who would hold her while we did the show.

The station did a phenomenal promotional photo of Rev. & Mrs. Kent with their blessed baby, Carrie May. Porter insisted I wear my wedding dress and hat and curl my hair, something that I finally had to ask Millie to help me with. The picture didn't look at all like me, but was a big success which made Porter happy. Of course Carrie was the real attraction. She was a beautiful baby and adorably sweet tempered. That was the consensus of everyone, not just her prejudiced parents. The way people warmed to her made all the difference to Porter, and he had become a doting father which softened my feelings toward him.

As we sat down to breakfast on that April morning, I said, "Remember, Mr. and Mrs. Stanley and Ma are coming to see Carrie. Shall I plan dinner for you too? They'd like to see you." I had no idea what Porter did all day, but he was seldom home, though since Carrie's arrival he was home for supper much of the time.

"Sure. What time should I be here? Of course I probably won't be able to stay, but it'll give me a chance to say hello."

***

I planned a farmer's dinner to be ready right at noon because they would be hungry after such an early start, and farmers were used to eating a big meal in the middle of the day. Plus unfortunately, they'd have to leave by the middle of the afternoon in order to get back home at a decent hour. They had been planning this trip ever since Carrie's birth, but had to wait for the threat of a winter blizzard to pass.

At three months Carrie had been exposed to so many different people she was responsive to anyone willing to make a fuss over her. Her abundant light brown hair had turned to ringlets, and there was a glowing light behind her soft brown eyes that sparkled with the thrill to be alive. At last the Stanleys and Ma would see this wonderful little person born to me. Anticipation vibrated in every fiber of my being.

I had saved a portion of my egg money for several weeks in order to buy a ham and sweet potatoes. I had my own navy beans for baked beans; my canned corn for scalloped corn which I made in soufflé style because I had an unlimited supply of eggs; my own tasty canned green beans smothered in coarsely chopped hickory nutmeats scrounged last fall from the tree in Millie's back field; cabbage salad; deviled eggs to dress up my ham plate; homemade rolls; and pie made with my canned peaches.

Despite the shade of the porch, the bright spring sunshine gave the dining room a rosy glow. The windows on either side of the dining room door had perky white tie-back curtains trimmed with ruffles made from Millie's red calico feed sacks. The tablecloth was Abbey's red and white checkered-plaid wedding gift. I had wintered-over Millie's big pot of red geraniums, and they filled a corner of the dining room, waiting for the weather to welcome them back out to the porch. To accent my setting, the delicious aroma of baking ham wafted through the house.

I heard tires on the gravel driveway and ran to the window as the Stanley's car came to a halt. Across the road, Porter came out of the church with four very important looking men dressed in suits. Who were they? They shook hands with Porter and made their way to the parking lot.

I rushed out to the Stanley's car and was greeted with a long anticipated round of hugs. Porter, who enjoyed playing the role of the perfect host, hurried across the road and ushered everyone though the newly screened-in porch, screen purchased with my garden tool money, and on into the house. Carrie lay nestled in her basket-bed beside my work table in the kitchen, babbling and cooing at her kicking feet.

Porter lifted her from her basket-bed. "Come on, you little sweetheart. That's right, just keep on cooing and smiling and meet your grandma." He placed her in Ma's arms, then shepherded them all into the living room.

I stood in the doorway basking in the wonder of such a comely scene, one that could have been painted by Norman Rockwell. Mrs. Stanley and Ma sat on the newly slip-covered wicker sofa, admiring Carrie as she charmed them with her nonstop smiles. Porter and Mr. Stanley looked on with the usual polite exchanges. Today I'd pretend I lived in that idealized world, the world that was centered around Carrie. That world overshadowed and made my role in Porter's world tolerable. I turned to the kitchen, and in short order, called them to dinner.

Porter said grace, thanking almighty God for Josephine's family safely delivered to them for a visit, for His grace in the gift of this blessed child whose family now came to pay homage. He entreated the Lord Jesus to guide the life of this child as she grew in stature, in grace and in the ways of the Lord. Lastly, he gave thanks for a bountiful table, blessed the food and those who partook of it, and admonished them to the service of Lord Jesus in whose name he prayed.

As the meal progressed Mr. Stanley said, "You haven't lost your touch, Josephine. This dinner is superb. We sure do miss you. Linda doesn't have your knack. Now, May, don't you let on I said that."

Mrs. Stanley just smiled and made no reply. I had been waiting for an opening to ask, "How are Linda and Forrest? I hear a lot about Jeffy."

Mr. Stanley answered. "There's not much to tell. Busy, you know farm life. Grange is not Linda's idea of a night out so Saturday nights May and I baby-sit, and they go out to the movies. Forrest planted a small garden last year but most of it went to waste. Don't think he'll plant one this year. To be eating your home- canned vegetables taste mighty good to us."

Mrs. Stanley added, "They sure do!"

Ma said, "Linda has taken to helping me when I take my baked goods to town. She likes dealing with people and being in town."

I bet Linda would worm her way into Ma's heart as I never could. What would Aunt Alma think of that? I thought I could feel undercurrents of discontent though I wasn't sure, and I sincerely hoped I was wrong because I wanted Forrest to be happy. I knew from

Mrs. Stanley's letters that he had a great relationship with Jeffy, and I hoped Linda appreciated how lucky she was.

As I was cutting the peach pie, Mrs. Stanley explained she had left the best news until last. "Abbey said I should tell you: they're expecting in October. I think they're hoping for a boy but they'll be happy no matter…and, she said be sure and invite you to come home for your birthday…twist your arm if necessary. June would be a perfect time for a visit. What'a you think? Let's start making plans now."

Porter cleared his throat, "Umm, I hate throwing a wet blanket on your invitation but, I haven't had a chance to tell Josephine how plans for the church have escalated. They've been tentative until this morning. We just a few minutes ago, finalized plans for building a new church. Josephine and I will be doing singing tours all summer to help raise money….."

My ears shut off. So that's who those men were. My preferred world receded into obscurity. There was no way I could live in both worlds. What should I do? What about Carrie? What would Millie do? I said nothing in protest. Always in the presence of others, I never questioned or confronted Porter in any way. In the long run, it was the policy that won. I never became the center of discourse. However, this put my two worlds on a collision course. My mind was in a panic as I went through the motions of hosting the people I had so longed to see.

To my surprise and dismay, Porter stayed and shared the afternoon with us. I think he didn't want to give Mr. and Mrs. Stanley or Ma a chance to influence me to rebel against his plans, not that they would have, but of course, he didn't know them.

I think they guessed how I felt because they hugged me extra hard and lingered as if they hated to take leave of me. Ma said, "Your seed shelf looks wonderful in the kitchen, and is perfect for your spices and odds and ends."

"I love it. Millie has everything we need for our garden, and the kitchen was so bare. It's perfect."

Mrs. Stanley took one last look at Carrie. "She's a beautiful baby and such a charmer. I know how much you love her. You always loved Jeffy and Louisa May so much."

As we were saying our final goodbyes on the porch, I said, "Ma, hug Matt and Mark for me and tell Daddy hello. Mrs. Stanley, tell Abbey and Allen I think their news is wonderful and I'll write."

Mr. Stanley was the last in line, and as Porter was seeing Ma and Mrs. Stanley to the car, he whispered to me, "I was worried, Jo, but I should've known you could do it. You're quite a little lady. We're always here for you. Forrest anxiously awaits our report and sends his love."

Tears slipped down my cheeks and Mr. Stanley took his finger and wiped them away, then kissed each cheek. At that moment, he gave the love I needed, and I loved him right back as the father I should have had. In my turmoil, his love was the rock I clung to. The stories he told me as a child came flooding back to me for comfort. I knew he understood as no one else did, and he knew how, in a few words, to reach out and let me know.

Instead of going across the road to the church which was his usual preference, Porter followed me back into the parsonage. I wanted to scream and cry out in protest, but Carrie slept peacefully in her basket-bed beside the wicker sofa where Ma and Mrs. Stanley had left her. Now, his campaign to wear me down would begin, and he wasn't about to give me time to fuel my arguments.

Escape! I fought for control. "Since you're in the house to watch Carrie, I'll go on over to Millie's and do my chores."

"You know Jimmy's over there. We might as well settle this right now. And, that's another thing; Millie hasn't increased her pledge since her increase in income."

"Just a darn minute! Hold it right there. First off, she increased her flock so she could afford to pay Jimmy and me. Any increase from now on will go to give Jimmy a fulltime wage. She gets little or nothing to compensate for all the extra work hauling more eggs to market and extra overhead expenses. Don't you dare say one word to Millie. Further more, I can't go gallivanting all over creation. I'm getting our garden ready to plant. We need those vegetables and so does Millie. I'm committed to help. To say nothing about caring for Carrie."

"If these building plans are to succeed, everyone has to be willing to sacrifice. Wait until you hear what we've planned. We're going to build the new church in that open area just this side of Maplehurst. It'll be strategically located to draw people from a very large and growing area. Our plans are for growth, but we'll start out modestly."

Talk about shock; move the church out of Jackson Junction! These were country people. They wouldn't want a big church where they'd lose their identity and be controlled by outsiders. How could Porter care so little about them? "I can't believe the trusties agreed to this grandiose plan."

"We're presenting it to them tonight."

"In other words, they have no choice."

"That's about the size of it, but I think they'll see the merit in our plan and what it will mean for the Lord's work. With or without them the church will be built."

"Whether it's good for them or not?"

"The church will be built for the glory of God. How could it not be good for them? Josephine, you have got to get in step. You have everyone fooled into thinking you're a born-again Christian with an angel's voice. One day you'll see the light, confess your sins, repent your ways and accept Jesus as your savior. Until then, you will keep on fooling them. You will cooperate and you will lead the way by setting an example by publicly announcing your tithe."

"Never. I will not. We'd starve if I gave a tithe to the church out of my earnings. Are you proposing to buy the groceries?"

"People will feed us. They've always feed me. Didn't Jesus say have no care where you sleep or eat?"

"They may feed you...I haven't seen them feeding me. I say, charity starts at home. That doesn't mean just Carrie and me. It means Jackson Junction. These people can barely make ends meet. They can't even do things for their kids. They don't have money for a doctor. Who do you think pays Carrie's doctor bills? My work at Millie's."

"The Lord will provide. Think of what this will mean to our area!"

"Yeah, look what Rev. Porter Kent has wrought. It's all about ego and you cover it up with your glory to God pitch...and to heck with people and their feelings. You know what I think? I'll announce that in bible times it was a church state and the tithe was a person's tax to the government because the church was the government, and everyone should figure their taxes into their tithe. How'd you like that? And, it's true. People are more important than bricks and wood."

Porter looked unmoved, handsome in his smug way, sure of himself. "Nobody said they weren't. You ask them if they're happy with me. See what they say. You watch; they'll get on board with my plans. Even your Millie's going to think it's wonderful. You're all alone, Josephine, alone. You'll be glad to come along. These people you're so fond of will fall down at the feet of the singers who made it all possible. You're going to be a star, like it or not, take your choice."

Chapter 16

I looked up to see Carrie standing in my bedroom doorway, threadbare cuddle-blanket tucked under her nose, eyes downcast. "Sweetheart, you come to help Mommy pack?"

"I want'a go too."

I held out my arms to her. "Come here. I know you do, and I'd like for you to come too. But remember," I hesitated, "Grandpa's very, very sick and they don't let little girls visit Grandpas in the hospital." I gathered her up into my arms and sat down on the edge of my bed. "Mommy's so sorry. I know Grandpa wants to see you, and I'll tell him how much you wanted to see him."

"Is Grandpa going to die, and will he go to Daddy's heaven?"

"I hope Grandpa'll be better soon, but we'll have to wait and see. And, it's not Daddy's heaven. Heaven belongs to all the people. Don't you worry about that."

"Daddy says only good people who know Jesus go to heaven. Is Grandpa a good people? He's awful quiet and a little scary."

"Grandpa's very good indeed. When I was a little girl I thought he was scary too. But, I don't think so any more."

"I prayed Grandpa won't die."

"I'm sure God heard your prayer, but God knows what's best for Grandpa, and it's not always what we pray for."

442

"When will you come home?"

"Several days."

Carrie held up three fingers. "This many?"

"How many fingers is that?"

"One, two, Three."

"How old are you?"

"Four."

"And how many more fingers is that?"

"One."

"Right. You're my very big girl. Maybe one more than four."

"Five?"

"I think so. But you're going to have a good time with Auntie Erma. Remember, Aunt Millie's going to take you to the new church after the two of you drop me off at the bus station. Auntie Erma loves to have you stay with her."

During the four grueling years it took to build The Good Shepherd Evangelical Church, Erma Wetherby, the wet-hankie friend who should have married Porter, and I had formed a close symbiotic friendship that served each of us very well. She traveled with us on all our fund-raising tours to help with Carrie, keep us packed and on schedule. It hadn't been difficult to convince Porter of the wisdom and merit in that plan. I flatly refused to go on tour unless Carrie traveled with us. Erma was happy for any excuse to be of service to Porter. She genuinely loved Carrie, and Carrie loved her; that was what I cared about.

"I don't think Daddy wants you to go." Carrie's worried eyes were wide set, soft brown speckled with flecks of gold, heavily lashed and her hair was the color of buckwheat honey. She was the perfect poster child for the stylized cherubs painted on calendars right after the turn of the century.

I loved her so; I thought my heart would break. "I know, Sweetheart, but Mommy'll be back in plenty of time for Daddy's big celebration when everyone's invited to come see his new church. Don't worry. Mommy wouldn't miss that."

"I still want'a go with you. You promised to show me where the fairies dance by the woods on Mr. Stanley's farm, and where you and Forrest picked strawberries."

"I know…remember, you're going to visit the farm this summer with Aunt Abbey and Uncle Allen. You and Louisa May'll have lots of fun. And…I'll just bet you'll get to see the fairy mounds. And…just think, Jeffy's eight years old now." I held up both hands with my thumbs folded back.

With her finger she touched each of mine, "One, two, three, four, five, six, seven, EIGHT."

"Yes."

"I can count far."

"I know you can. You're my very big girl who's going visiting this summer too."

"Will Louisa May be in school?"

"No, and Jenny's three now. You can help look after her like Louisa May looked after you last year."

Carrie's little hands had been busy patting every piece of clothing I put into my suitcase. I was about to close the lid when Millie was at the bottom of the stairs.

"You up there? I knocked, and knocked. There was no answer so I came on in."

"Hello, Millie. Just a couple more things for Carrie." I gently pushed Carrie toward the door. "Be a good little helper; run down and show Aunt Millie where the banana-nut bread is that we baked for her and

Auntie Erma......and tell Aunt Millie, there's time for tea if she'll put the teakettle on."

No one knew Porter and I had separate bedrooms, and I wanted to keep it that way. I really did have a few more things to put in Carrie's suitcase. When I came downstairs, I was careful to place our suitcases by Porter's bedroom door before joining them in the kitchen.

"Jo, you look stunning. Every time I look at you, I can't believe you're the same scared little bride that I met that first day."

"Frankly, neither can I." We laughed. "Porter said he was going to make me a star. He's made a very reluctant one. I prefer chicken farming and gardening any day."

"You can't mean that?"

"I do." My clothes were sleek like our 4 H leader, Mrs. Miller's, except I was not tall and stately even though I wore very high heels at Porter's insistence. My hair was styled with smooth wings pulled up in front of my ears and curly bangs. It did make me look a little taller. The back of my hair was curly just above the shoulders, framing my neck from the front. Porter said it made me look older and like a star. Fortunately, it was an easy hairdo I could manage. I hated going to the beauty shop. He insisted I have my eyebrows shaped, and I now used rouge and lipstick. My eyelashes were long and sooty so I talked him out of mascara. After all, I argued, you don't want a hymn-singing wife to look like a hussy! I laughed out loud as I thought Luke wouldn't call me a witch anymore, but rather, something that rhymed with it!

Millie picked up on that, "What's so funny?"

"Nothing, just how surprised my oldest stepbrother would be to see me now."

"You never talk about him. Will you be seeing him?"

"I shouldn't think so. He's never made up with my stepfather though he's remained close to Daddy's meddling controlling mother. I shouldn't say that, poor Aunt Alma; she means well. But did she ever give me a hard time when I was little."

"At any rate, it's past time you went home. Anxious to see the farm you talk so much about?"

I was torn. My soul cried out for home, but it would mean facing Forrest. We still hadn't exchanged even one letter since that last morning on my wedding day five years ago. I longed for the cheery kitchen in the morning with cornmeal pancakes sizzling on the griddle while Mrs. Stanley hummed and bustled about. I closed my eyes and I could almost smell the faint musky barn odor on Mr. Stanley's clothes. How I missed them, and my heart was still full of Forrest. There were times my mind persisted in torturing me with replays of all the troubling things we said to each other those last few days. Other times, comforting memories flooded my mind, and again I roamed the familiar meadows and woods with him.

I longed for my room and Snooks. It was probably Jeffy's room now. Would Snooks curl up with him as she did with me? I'd most likely be in the guestroom downstairs. I hoped so because it would be too painful to be near Forrest and Linda as they prepared for bed. What about Linda? She, Forrest and Daddy always stayed behind on the farm when the rest of the family came on their rare visits. What would she be like after five years with Forrest and life as a farm wife? Was she happy? Did she love Forrest? Was he still blindly in love with her? If he had found happiness, the news of it had not spilled over to me through Abbey. She did say Linda was working in Phelpsburg.

"Mommy, Mommy, come." Carrie pulled on my hand. "The tea's ready." She had been busily playing her favorite role as hostess, putting cups and napkins around the kitchen table.

"Very nice, you're the best little helper in the whole world. Thank you. Come, Millie…sit… I'll pour." I filled cups for Millie and me, a squirt for Carrie and finished her cup with milk just as Mrs. Stanley used to do for me.

Millie took a sip. "Any idea when you'll be back?"

"Depends, I'll have to see. I've got'a get back to help prepare for Good Shepherd's dedication. Porter's having a fit about my going at all, and I hate not being able to take Carrie."

"Yeah, Mommy promised, but they don't let little girls in the hospital, but Mommy's going to tell Grandpa I prayed just like my Daddy."

I wanted to explain to Millie that I just hoped I'd get there in time to say goodbye, but I didn't want to upset Carrie. Mrs. Stanley had called early that morning before Porter left for his new office. In a fit of tears she explained Daddy was in the hospital, and they didn't expect him to live through another night. He was asking for me, and I should come home immediately; she'd have a room ready for me. She was sure Ma was trying to call me at that very moment to urge me to come. Thoughts of Ma came flooding in and were confusing. Why hadn't she called me?

As I hung up the phone, Porter came out of his bedroom ready to leave. "What's all the fuss about?"

"Daddy's in the hospital and I have to go home. He's not expected to live."

"And why should you go running home to someone who was never a father to you? You lived with the Stanleys."

"They don't expect him to live another night. After all he took Ma and me in and gave us a home. He is my stepfather. He's asking for me, and I should be there for Ma."

"You can't possibly leave right now with all there is to do for the dedication."

The phone rang. "Yes, Ma, I'm coming....I know, there's not much time....it's important to me too." She said Daddy pleaded with her to call me. I explained Mrs. Stanley had invited me to stay with them, and there was no invitation to change my plans and stay with her. Some things never changed. I supposed Matt would be home from Alfred University. It was hard to think of my little brother off to college. He had decided to become a teacher before going on to seminary. Mark was now a senior in high school, and had a good chance for a scholarship to Cornell's pre-med program. Life on the farm would be so different now. My psyche found it hard to emotionally visualize it.

I turned to Porter. "You heard me, I'm going and that's all there is to it."

He left in huff, but I didn't care. I had to see Daddy before he died.

Millie and Carrie had been chatting away when suddenly, Carrie became impatient. "Mommy, Mommy, you're not paying any 'tention."

"Yes I am. You told Aunt Millie you prayed for Grandpa just like Daddy."

Millie said, "You're the sweetest, pray'n'est little girl I know. And, Jo, I don't see why she can't stay with me instead of at Erma's."

"Yes, Mommy, I can help Jimmy feed the chickens." Carrie's little face was so hopeful and earnest.

"Sure you could. Mommy knows what a helper you are." Then I turned to Millie. "You know full well why. How'd you get your chores done and the eggs delivered? You're always my first choice in everything. It's you and your farm that's my retreat, my haven. It's a second home to me. I should be helping you get the garden ready to plant right now."

"Jo, you forget; Jimmy's here...he'll do that. Maybe you better give up on the garden with all the new responsibilities of two churches."

"Not on your life. And there better be two churches. I tremble to think of what it would have been like if you good people of Jackson Junction hadn't insisted Porter keep our little church open. I never want to move from this parsonage next to you, and I wish I was still doing chores for you."

"Everything's worked out just right. It makes my son so happy not to have to feel guilty anymore about not wanting the farm...."

"Jimmy's wonderful and puts me in mind of Matt so much. It's working out even better than you expected. He'll soon have to hire someone to help out. I wish it could be me. He's a real farmer."

By now Carrie's eyes were full of tears. "I'm a real farmer too...aren't I, Mommy?"

I took her up into my arms and gave her a flubbering loud kiss on the neck. "You are the best real farmer in the whole world. But, you'll have fun with Auntie Erma, and you'll see Daddy every day."

"Hey now, we better get a move on or you'll miss the bus."

***

When the bus stopped in Phelpsburg, my high school days came flooding back to me. At the time I hated school, and cared very little that I was leaving it when I married Porter. Now I yearned to be in school learning all things that would open doors to the world I glimpsed beyond Jackson Junction. I'd never know what choices I might have had.

There was no need to waste money on a taxi. A walk would steel my nerves for what lay ahead. Phelpsburg felt as foreign as my artificial looks; a stranger walked down a strange street as if an artist's painting had suddenly become animated. I shook myself and concentrated on the rhythmic click of my high heels on the sidewalk as I hurried the four blocks to Phelpsburg Hospital. Hopefully, Daddy had rallied and I'd be on my way home tomorrow. There was no way I could miss the radio program leading up to the dedication. I had promised Porter. But I did need to see Daddy. Perhaps, even more than he needed to see me. My childhood fear of him had been much more unfair to him than he had ever been to me, and in my heart I knew he would never have farmed me out to the Stanleys as Ma had. Or let me marry so young.

Once inside the hospital, my high heels echoed up and down the hall, and I raised them off the floor. The nurse had said Daddy's room was at the end of the hall. Now that I was so close, I slowed, holding back, dreading what I might find.

Daddy was speaking, voice weak but clear. "No, Clara, we have to be honest. I'm not going to make it, and there're things we have to talk about."

My eavesdropping days of the past kicked in as if I were lying on my stomach looking down through the register in Ma's and my bedroom in the tenant house. I had to hear. Would they answer the questions that had plagued me ever since the day I cowered under the table in the Sweet Shop kitchen, and Aunt Alma announced I was to have a new daddy; that Ma and I were going to be part of her "country family"? The door was ajar and Ma leaned forward so Daddy wouldn't have to strain his voice to make her hear.

She answered. "After all these years we don't need words."

"I do. Where will you go? You can't stay on after I'm gone."

"Don't upset yourself, Paul; I'll be fine. Alma needs me...I'll live with her. She loves the boys, and it'll be convenient for my baking business."

"I don't want you living with my mother. I put up with the way she's treated you because she's my mother. I know your sense of loyalty. You don't owe her."

"Alma and I understand each other."

"Rev. Grey, what about Rev. Grey? Yes, I was in denial, but underneath I knew how you felt about each other, and was too selfish to set you free from your promise."

"Paul, there's no need…."

"Yes, there is. You'll never know how I feared you'd leave. And, when you didn't, I knew the depth of your honor."

"How could you think I'd leave? I was safe."

"Clara, Clara, what a fool I've been……"

"Sh, sh, now don't waste your strength."

"No, hear me out. Way back when I came down to get my mother while Emily was still alive, I knew the kind of woman you were, lonely, tortured with guilt, and above all else hard-working. It was true, at first I had thought it was a mistake for them to take you in, young wayward tramp, and I told them so. Then, when I saw the way you turned away from your baby, and the way you made no effort to escape, the way you allowed yourself to be taken advantage of…and finally after our marriage, making up that story about your husband being killed was never necessary for me." There was a pause here and a weak laugh. "But, I'm glad you told it; it was ridiculous enough that the people who needed it, believed it……I think I fell in love with you way back then. Yes, it's true I told myself I only wanted to save your soul. My narrow ways kept me from knowing the truth."

"Please Paul, this is not necessary. Save your strength."

"When I think of what my stubborn ways have denied me. Don't deprive yourself; go to Rev. Grey. It would relieve my guilt if I thought you would."

"Please, please Paul. There's no need. Rev. Grey has been happily married for three years and has a son. He was a special friend. I wouldn't have left even if you had opened the way. Your so-called

451

stubbornness gave me the protection I need. I thank you from the bottom of my heart. Yes, Paul, I cherish your friendship. My lips can't speak of love. And, how can I ever thank you for Matt and Mark."

"That leads to Josephine. You did for Matt and Mark what I should have done for Josephine, what you should have done for Josephine. That weighs heavy on my heart as I prepare to meet my Maker."

"What can I say? You're right. She's such a stout heart and so deserving of the love I have never been able to give. Her father....."

"Don't Clara. Don't put yourself through that. There's no need in this short time we have to be together, together in this new honesty."

"I see his face every time I look at her. Josephine's done nothing to deserve the way I've treated her. I ...I should be able to love her. I knew I was doing wrong at the same time I couldn't make my heart feel what wasn't there. But I did care deeply, and I wanted her to have real love and acceptance. May and Fred loved her in the way I couldn't....and she wanted to be up there...it was easy to tell myself that...even when I knew what she wanted more, and I still couldn't give it. Nothing can free me from that guilt. "

There was a burst of understanding for Ma at that moment. It wasn't my fault! Ma couldn't help how she felt anymore than I could help the way I felt about Forrest, or that I couldn't go down front and pretend to be saved just to please Porter. Ma wanted me to have love, even wanted to give it to me herself. We can pretend to be what we are not; it would be a lie.

Daddy reached out and touched Ma's cheek. "Listen, there's guilt to go around, and as for your salvation, the salvation I so wrongly worried about. You have more of God's grace than anyone I know. Who am I to think you ever needed to be saved? It's you who have taught me the ways of true love. All those sermons I've sat through on 'the sinful ways of the flesh' and thought I needed to save you when you have no corruption of the flesh, and me, all that time I wanted you. Oh yes, Luke was right about me. If there is guilt, look what I've done to Luke. Look what your love has made of Matt and Mark. And could have made of Luke had you had a chance. But, that's the past. Maybe, some day, Luke'll have a rebirth of faith. I pray for it daily. I knew that day he tried to force you that I too wanted you and had for a long, long time. It was also the day I knew in my heart your true story. You'll never know the soul searching I've done . . . and the discipline it's taken me to live up to our bargain, feeling for you the way I do. I hope that's not too distressful to you. I only speak of it because this is the end of the road for me, and there can be no pressure for you to return those feelings, that I need to speak of it." . . . Ma stirred on her chair. "No, Clara . . . please don't try to answer. The reason I speak is because you're young. It's not too late for you to find someone who can bring you the happiness you deserve . . . No, no, don't protest. Give my thoughts time. Know how lovely you are, and know how much you have to give . . . and to receive. Just let it germinate like your seeds in the garden you love and tend so diligently."

"Oh, Paul, I . . . "

"Now, do as I ask, don't answer. No answer is the best answer." He was quiet for some seconds. "You said Josephine was coming. I can't go yet; I'm hanging on until I see her."

"Yes, any minute. She's so busy. I just don't know the exact time."

I tip-toed down the hall to the restroom to dry my tears.

***

In a whisper I said, "Hello, Ma. Is Daddy sleeping?"

His eyes were closed, maybe their talk had exhausted him though he looked peaceful, and I thought: confession is good for the soul, without applying it to my own.

"Josephine, you're here. Paul…Josephine is here…good…come in…he's been waiting for you."

He opened his eyes.

"Hello, Daddy, if you're too tired, rest, and I'll come back in a bit."

"I can always rest; come close so I can see you….better pull up a chair."

"It's so good to see you, Daddy, but this feels so strange. You should be in the field, or doing chores, or reading the paper, or at devotions after supper."

"I'm afraid those days are gone, and before I depart this world and stand before my God, I have some amends to attend to."

I let that thought rest for a moment. "Not you who've been so true and faithful."

"True and faithful…" he mimicked me, and plunged ahead. "That doesn't excuse me for abandoning my duties as a father. I have no excuse except ignorance, and it was the easy way out. I'm so sorry, and sorrier for what I've missed."

"Listen, I came to say I was sorry for thinking you were a scary mean man when you're really a kind loving man. What a kettle of fish! Know what…things have a way of working out the best they can. I think your God will be pleased with you; I am."

"I need to know whether you're happy, and with your new sophistication, I can't tell. Are you happy, Josephine?"

In that moment I knew the secret of how love and happiness were linked. Forrest had also said he needed me to be happy. He must wonder why I had backed away. He must wonder why my love seemed

454

to change so abruptly. I must learn how to let my love show just as Daddy had learned to do.

Ma spoke up. "Of course she's happy, Paul. Look how far she's come."

Plainly, there it was: Love is concerned for your happiness. Others only see the mask you wear.

"Clara, you know that kind of success isn't necessarily happy. I see Josephine running over these fields like a tomboy, not caring a thing about religion like her mother."

That brought a smile to Ma's face and to mine.

"Yes, Daddy, there you have it! But I have my garden and Millie's farm right next door; and above everything else, I have Carrie. She's the joy of my life. You have me pretty well figured out and, Daddy, after all these years, I think I come close to understanding you; and I'm not one bit scared of you, and I love you. Thank you for the home you've given Ma, and for two wonderful brothers I love more than words can say. Things have worked out just right."

There were tears in his eyes as he reached out, brought my face to his and planted a tender kiss on my forehead. In a flash I saw the miserly thin-lipped kiss he had placed on Ma's cheek on their wedding day, and I realized how much he had changed, changed in ways I had thought impossible. I was happy for him, and at the same time sad. Because I knew it was the only kiss he had ever been able to give Ma. Through tears, I glanced back at Ma, and there were tears in her eyes. My heart was breaking for all three of us. Was it possible, that maybe, even I had changed!

***

Matt and Mark arrived, adding to our companionable setting. Ma jumped up and embraced Matt. "I'm so glad you've come. Your father needs you."

Both of my stepbrothers took their turn hugging me, exclaiming how wonderful I looked, and how great it was to finally have me back in home territory. Then they greeted their father with love and concern. We were, at long last, just another loving family gathered to say good-bye to a cherished member.

Matt exchanged a few remarks about college. He could stay a bit longer because spring break would start in a couple days. Mark told Matt he was waiting to see if Cornell had accepted him. Mark told us he had stopped in the hospital office on his way home yesterday, and he had a summer job as an errand boy in Central Supply.

Mostly we were just there, surrounding Daddy with love. Finally he asked, "Sing for me, Josephine."

"I'd love to if Matt and Mark will help me. Which hymn would you like?"

"'In The Garden.'"

It had been a long time since the three of us had sung together. We softly hummed until we had control of our emotions and were able to sing the words without our voices cracking.

Daddy looked worn out as he whispered in a raspy voice, "Josephine, you sing like an angel, and are a blessing to all who hear you. Now, Matt, say a prayer, and then I'd like to rest."

"Give me your hand, Daddy. Our Father who art in heaven, bless and keep this man, our earthy father whom we love and cherish. Bless and give strength to this family, his family, gathered around, and also to those family and friends in other places. We pray in the name of the One who taught us how to pray and how to love. Amen."

"Well said, Matt, thank you. Now, Clara, take the children home and have supper together."

"You three go on home, and thank Fred and May for their thoughtfulness in giving you the use of their car. They told me they were going to do that when they came down earlier. Paul, I'd just like to sit here quietly while you nap. Maybe I'll close my eyes too."

The boys draped their arms across my shoulders, and mine went round their waists. We needed comfort and support as we made our way out of the hospital.

On the steps we met Linda. "Why, hello, Yo. I'm surprised you could get away. Matt, when did you get here? How's Paul?"

"Slipping away. We're leaving to let him sleep."

"I won't disturb him then. I came over to say 'hello' to Paul and to send word home to Forrest that I'll be working late. He's never in the house; will you tell him?"

Matt said, "We'll pass the word."

Linda said, "Thanks. You look terrific, Yo."

"So do you, Linda. You've cut your beautiful hair, but it looks really nice short too." Her make-up was perfect, and her clothes were expensive. Obviously, her money didn't go to help out on the farm.

"I envy your exciting life."

"Not so exciting. Just a lot of hard work."

"That's the kind of hard work I'd love. It's bores-ville around here."

"Where do you work?"

"'Gallagers'. I sell clothes to all the rich ladies in the area. One of these days I'm going to be buyer. At least then I'll get to go to New York. Still nothing compared to being a star."

"I'm far from a star. Mostly I'm a mother, same as you."

"Not quite the same. Tuttle-lu. See ya later." And she was gone.

There was a gleeful roar when we walked into the Stanley kitchen. "Jo, let me dry my hands....come over here and let me hug you...and hug you." Mrs. Stanley had just finished cutting up two frying chickens.

"How wonderful your arms feel. Especially when they're around me in your kitchen. Fried chicken, good...let me do the honors."

Matt and Mark gave Mrs. Stanley hugs and thanked her for the use of her car.

She said, "And boys, you're to stay for supper."

Matt said, "I'm away to change clothes and go to the barn. I'm sure they could use some help."

Mrs. Stanley had tears in her eyes. "It's so special to see the three of you together. I wish it could be like old times. I'm so sad and concerned for all of you. Let us help in any way."

"You already are. Thanks."

Mrs. Stanley reached for an apron for me. "Let's tackle supper, Jo. Mark, how about digging us a mess of dandelion greens. A spring tonic's just what we need."

The kitchen became a beehive of activity and was soon filled with the aroma of fried chicken. Mark washed and cooked the dandelion greens. Mrs. Stanley set the table in the dining room, while I mashed the potatoes. When the biscuits were about ready to come out of the oven, I heard the men in the backroom. Chores were all done-up for the day, and the dreaded moment had arrived. I must face Forrest. As they came in, the welcome musky smell of the barn proceeded them and mingled with the aroma of supper; I knew I was home.

Forrest looked tired and was in need of a haircut. Unlike the person I knew, he hesitated. "I'm too smelly, Yo. I daren't give you a hug.

Without your bib-overalls, you're definitely not a little sister anymore, but it's good to see you looking so well. "

"I've missed you and that wonderful cow-barn smell…and who's this big farmer? Can it be Jeffy practically all grown up?"

"Yep, and I'm going to take Grandpa's place until he gets well."

Jeffy obviously called Daddy, Grandpa. Mr. Stanley noted my surprise, and took that as his cue to initiate his greeting.

"Yes, Jeffy knows Fred's his grandpa, and he knows who his blood father is. But, Josephine, this kitchen has never been the same since you left it. What a pleasure it is to see you in it again." He turned to Forrest. "'Never judge a book by its cover.'" Then to me he said, "Isn't that right?" Smelly clothes and all, he gathered me into his strong loving arms in the best bear hug I had had since the Stanleys last visit to Jackson Junction.

Jeffy said, "Yeah, Aunt Yo, I have two grandpas, but Forrest's my true Dad. I never saw my other dad. I don't remember you, but I know you. You're the little sister my dad gave Snooks to. Now she's kind'a mine because she sleeps with me."

Forrest ruffed Jeffy's hair. "You betcha. I'm your true dad." He hesitated only a second more then folded his arms around me as if it were the most natural thing in the world, held me close and whispered next to my ear, "It's so good to see you, Yo, so good."

Jeffy was anxious to say something more. "My Dad told me I should let you have your old room back so Snooks wouldn't be confused. I get to sleep in the guest room." Then he went to the stairs and called, "Here, kitty, here Snooks."

And there she was trotting into the kitchen, tail straight up like a flagpole. She stopped, wondering why she had been called. Then without further hesitation, she was at my ankles, marking me with her cheeks once again as her very own possession. I gathered her up into my arms, and tears ran shamelessly down my cheeks.

***

It was wonderful to sleep in my old room again with the now very old lazy Snooks. I was thrilled that she remembered me. I needn't have worried about sleeping too close to Linda and Forrest even though their room was next to mine, because I'm sure Forrest was sound asleep when Linda came tip-toeing in.

In the morning I donned my bib-overalls, tied my hair up in a curly ponytail, and crept past the guestroom not to wake Jeffy. Linda should be up and in the kitchen getting breakfast, but I knew she wouldn't be. She should be an at-home farm wife, taking the load off Mrs. Stanley who was clearly worn out. I couldn't help but wish Ma would change her mind and move up to the Stanley's to take over. I didn't want her living with Aunt Alma either. As I pondered the irony of life, I knew Ma would move to the city because she was right when she told Daddy, she and Aunt Alma understand each other. That's exactly why things worked out as they did years ago. Now, they both wanted the same thing again. Ma's baking business would pay for Matt's and Mark's college. Giving the Stanleys a hand didn't figure in that equation.

It wasn't long and Mrs. Stanley came into the kitchen all apologies because she had overslept.

"Good…I'm glad. You must have needed it, too much excitement last night. Pancakes and sausage are all set, just waiting for the men to appear."

Jeffy joined us all sleepy-eyed and looked in the skillet. "Yummy, Aunt Yo, gravy."

"Nothing like gravy on pancakes to stick to the ribs." Snooks was rubbing around my ankles. "You're next little friend. I think I'll give her a little sausage. It can't hurt her one time. How I've missed her. Where're the boys? Must be Ma's home. I planned on them for breakfast too."

Jeffy was eyeing the table. "Oh boy. Cinnamon applesauce!"

Mr. Stanley opened the door. "Did I hear someone ask, 'where's the boys?'" Hesitantly, he continued, "They came over as we were going into the barn to say Clara had called and asked them to come down...Paul died at four this morning. They have our car, and Matt's so capable I'm sure he can handle everything."

Mrs. Stanley started to cry, and Mr. Stanley shook his head. "I shouldn't have said anything until after breakfast. I've spoiled Josephine's pancakes."

"Yeah, Gramps, you shouldn't 'a. But, I think I'll eat mine anyway."

Mrs. Stanley dried her tears. "I think I will too, Jeffy. I haven't had Josephine's pancakes since, well...before she married."

Mr. Stanley said, "This is going to be a hard few days. We best eat-up to give us the strength to get through them. And, soon as breakfast's over, Jeffy, you take Jo for a nice walk. This'll be the only chance she'll have to visit her old haunts. Jo, I'll help May with the dishes."

"I can't go. I should start preparing food so Ma won't have to. There'll be a ton of people around."

Forrest quickly answered. "There'll be time for that, Yo. I'd like to come too. Jeffy, run up and wake your mother. She'll want to know, and she needs breakfast before she goes to work. "

***

The ground under my feet felt so familiar, so right, but the Forrest who walked beside me was not familiar. There was a sad withdrawnness about his demeanor that was not at all the Forrest I remembered. Jeffy was as bright and enthusiastic as his unruly red hair prophesied. He enthusiastically ran to and fro asking, "Remember this is where the best blackberry bushes are?" And, "Want'a stop and get some birch-bark to chew?" and, on and on. It was wonderful to see how happy he was, and how much Forrest loved him.

Memories danced all around us healing the rift of time, bringing Forrest's and my spirits back into communion. We passed the mossy rocks and mounds by the end of the woods where the ground was damp, and I longed to see the fairies as plainly as I did as a child.

"Forrest, Abbey's invited Carrie to stay for a couple of weeks this summer, and she plans to bring her to the farm when you're haying-it. I've told Carrie so many stories about Robin Goodfellow and the fairies, and I don't know if I'll ever get a chance to bring her here. It'd mean an awful lot to me if you showed her this place. I'll never forget the first time you brought us all over here, and I discovered these beautiful mossy-green fairy mounds, and I saw strawberries growing for the first time. What a miracle."

"You know I will. Carrie captured my heart last summer. I had to twist Abbey's arm a little bit because they had just gone home after haying, and she wasn't keen on coming back so soon, but I convinced her it was probably the only way I'd ever get to see Carrie."

"Did it mean that much to you?"

"Yes…you know it did…and she's a beautiful wonderful little girl just as I knew she would be. I sure will bring her over here. We'll make it a party. I'll bring the whole crew just as we did that first time with you. Maybe we'll get to pick some strawberries. With Paul gone I know

Allen's going to help out even more. And with Abbey here it won't be too much for Mom."

Tears welled up in my eyes. "Carrie'll be so happy. Though I don't know how I can spare her for that long. I love her so. I hope I don't spoil her too much."

"There wasn't a spoiled bone in her body that I could see."

Over and over in my mind, I framed and reframed the question, "Why hadn't he written?" The words just wouldn't come out of my mouth because I couldn't answer why I hadn't written to him. Did both questions hide two broken hearts?

I told Forrest about my talk with Daddy, and how we both had wanted to clear our conscience. "I felt as though I hadn't given Daddy enough credit for what he's done for Ma and me. Isn't it funny how we get things figured out when it's too late? At least we were able to square things and say goodbye."

"Hindsight's a good thing if you don't let it ruin the present." Same old Forrest with the right answers! He went right on without a pause. "Paul was the best farmhand anywhere around. Don't know how we're going to manage without him."

At this point Jeffy had begun to pay close attention and quickly said, "Pretty soon I'll be big enough to help with the milking. Won't I Daddy?"

"You sure will, son."

How strange it was to hear Forrest called Daddy, and for him to call Jeffy, son. Luke would always play a prominent role in Forrest's life. It occurred to me how fitting it was that such a special gift, Jeffy, had come from that boyhood friendship. The world suddenly seemed brighter. There was rhyme and reason in the scheme of things.

Jeffy was now walking backward staring up at me. "Where's heaven, Aunt Yo? You should know because you're married to a minister."

I could have been mistaken, but I thought I sensed Forrest stiffen at the mention of my being married to a minister.

"Well, Jeffy, when I was younger than you, my Aunt Carrie died. I was very, very unhappy and lonely. I tried and tried to figure out where heaven was, and I'm still trying to figure it out. I've decided if we knew it'd take all the fun out of imagining it."

He looked at me for a long moment. "Yeah, Aunt Yo." And away he ran ahead of us.

Forrest's arm went momentarily around my shoulder in his familiar sisterly hug. "How I miss you, Yo."

I dared not look too long into his eyes. "Me too."

***

Back at the house I repacked my bag, and I moved down to the tenant house and into Daddy's room without asking Ma. The next four days were an emotional rollercoaster. Matt and Mark were wonderful to Ma and to me. All four of us worked together as a real family. We comforted each other as we attended to the many details of Daddy's funeral, and I had a glimpse of what I had missed. You can never go back, and to dwell on what might have been would have put the present in jeopardy just as Forrest said.

Aunt Alma was devastated and uncharacteristically docile. She had become frail and a little forgetful. She did need watching over, and her spirit brightened considerably when Ma broached the idea of living with her.

"Why, Clara, that's a wonderful idea. You'd be so much closer to your business market. And I won't charge you rent. I'll be pleased to have company. Luke's so busy he never has time to come around." Then to me she bragged, "Luke has a place of his own...you know...a really swank apartment. He's such an ambitious man…he works all the time, and makes big money."

Then Ma wouldn't have to deal with him. Another problem solved. Somehow for Luke life always came up roses.

Mark said, "Grandma, and it'll be only a short walk to my summer job at the hospital. That'll be a big help."

"Bless you, my smart boy. It'll be so nice to have two of my wonderful grandsons with me for the summer."

Matt announced, "Maybe not me, Grandma. Forrest said he, Linda and Jeffy'll be moving into the tenant house, and he said I could live with them if I wanted to work on the farm this summer. And I'd really like to do that."

I happened to have been present when Forrest broached the idea of moving into the tenant house to Mr. Stanley. He quickly replied, "That's the ticket, Forrest. It'll be good for the three of you to be alone. We'll miss you, but you'll be just down the road."

What a relief it was to me to hear that! Mrs. Stanley looked so pale and exhausted. Forrest, as usual, had that situation sized up. Linda would have to look after her own family.

On the fourth day of my visit we laid Daddy to rest in the little cemetery behind True Faith Church. To my surprise Aunt Carrie's grave was next to where Daddy was being buried. I had never thought about where her grave might be, and I was overwhelmed with emotion as I read her headstone: CARRIE ELIZABETH CRANE, BORN 1875, DIED 1933; GENTLE SOUL AND BELOVED SISTER. Aunt Carrie's body lay underneath that newly green grass in the casket with the frilly pink pillow, the casket I had climbed into to see where her soul came out. It was too much and I began to sob. Matt put his arm around me and I wept on his shoulder.

The ladies of True Faith had a luncheon after the Committal Service for family and friends to honor Paul Osborn, their faithful brother in Christ. It was just what Daddy would have wanted, old and new friends and family mingling and consoling each other. For me it was an opportunity to see Tate Town people who had played an important role in my life that I would seldom if ever see again.

Dr. and Mrs. Miller were there, and as I started to greet them, Mrs. Miller said, "I think it should be Annette, don't you?"

"Yes, Annette. I was quite jealous of Abbey and Linda back in our 4H days for being able to use your given name."

It was wonderful to see them, but it felt very artificial because to them I was the person Porter had shaped. I wanted to shout: I'm still the same old Jo, as inappropriate as that would have been.

I received many compliments on the success of our record business. I was surprised at how many said they had our records. Thanks to Daddy and boys, I'm sure.

As the luncheon was breaking up, I found and opportunity to tell Aunt Alma I hadn't known Aunt Carrie was buried in Tate Town Cemetery.

She answered some of the questions I had wondered about. "Carrie and I grew up in Tate Town. I moved to Phelpsburg when I married. Carrie never married and moved to Rochester and lived with a rich family for many years...was general housekeeper and cook. They loved her and I think they left her some money."

I found that curious and very interesting. Then Aunt Carrie didn't have to depend on Aunt Alma.

***

The next day each sad goodbye tore at my heart. After being away for five years it had still felt like home. They were the people who had nurtured me, and those were the fields and lanes I knew and loved. Yet there was a part of me even in that loved place that knew I was an interloper. Where did I belong? Had it not been for Carrie, I could never have forced myself to leave. In the deepest place in my being it came through to me clearly that my true home was as mother of Carrie, and in that heart-of-hearts there was only one accord; I was a homing pigeon. I had no choice but to return to Jackson Junction and face my increasingly complicated life.

At least Porter would be relieved that my estimated five day trip had proved to be exactly right, and preparations for the dedication and radio broadcast would remain on schedule. However, that schedule allowed very little time for my world that revolved around Carrie, Millie and her farm.

But even more pressing was Porter's increasing possessiveness. I didn't like the way he looked at the person I had become, the so-called star he had fashioned. He was beginning to think he owned his creation. Hopefully, it was only dollar signs he saw when he looked at me because he loved the money; the money that had allowed him to build his new church; the money that gave him new prestige and power. Perhaps, if it were only money he saw when he looked at me, I could deal with that. I had to find a way to do something about the tension that was building between us. I had to find a way to let him know, that I had not changed; that under my artificial façade survived the same Josephine who wore flat shoes, wore her hair in a braid down her back and slept alone in her own bedroom.

***

As the bus sped along toward Maplehurst and Jackson Junction, away from the life I had known as a child, I was overcome with an overpowering sense of sadness and loss. Daddy was gone, forever gone, and I mourned the chance we had missed to develop a father-daughter relationship. Our understanding of each other came too late. The daddy I said goodbye to no longer resembled the scary man with the dark shadow on his face who had come into the Sweet Shop, begrudgingly grunting hello to Ma as she slaved away at the candy-making table while I cowered underneath. Seeing Aunt Carrie's grave renewed old wounds and hurts complicated by Aunt Alma's revelations. Too many details were missing. Was Aunt Carrie unfair to Ma? Would I ever know?

The most tender, heartfelt goodbye was to the Stanley Farm. It was ever as much in my heart and blood as Mr. Stanley predicted. It was my center, my honing place. Being there kindled anew the realization that there was still something special between Forrest and me. I felt it clearly, and I'm certain he felt it too. Could I write him? Would he write me? Even as I wondered, I knew the answer.

Into this troubling mix was the knowledge that a new battle with Porter was brewing, and would confront me the minute I stepped off the bus in Maplehurst. It was a mounting burden. How was I going to maneuver the twists and turns facing my life? I must not lose the freedom I had managed to secure for Carrie and me. I must control Porter's creeping control over my time, my life.

That collage of conflicting emotions tore at my heart as the tires droned their monotonous rhythm on the road.

Chapter 17

It was Millie who rushed out to meet me instead of Erma and Carrie as I had expected. She threw her arms around me.

"Jo, wonderful to have you home…nothing's been right. But it must have been a frightful time for you. I'm so sorry."

Panic gripped me. "Where's Carrie? Is she all right? Why isn't she here? Where's Erma?"

"She's fine, everything's fine. I'm to drop you at Good Shepard. Rev. Kent's in a tizzy because you're not here to see to things. That man simply can't do without you."

"Oh, Millie, you always come to the rescue. A big chunk of my heart belongs to you…but where is Carrie? How'd you ever get away without her?"

"Rev. Kent and Erma are teaching her a song for the dedication. And, I might add, with great difficulty."

"We'll see about that."

Carrie was not going to be one of Porter's projects to exploit. I would nip that in the bud. My heart raced with anger as we drove the mile to the edge of Maplehurst and the grand shiny-new brick church with the big shiny-new paved parking lot.

The minute Carrie saw me she started running up the length of the sanctuary's central aisle, her little feet urgently beating a rhythm on the beautiful peacock-blue carpeting. Either side of her loomed polished oak pews with matching well-padded peacock-blue cushions. Her arms went around my neck as I bent to bring her up into my arms.

"Mommy, Mommy, you were gone too long. Can we go home now?"

"Yes, yes, Sweetheart, we can go home now."

I hugged her close as I planted multiple kisses around her face. Porter came and put his arms around both of us, and kissed my cheek for the benefit of Millie and Erma.

Porter looked frazzled. "Sorry about your step-father. Things are out of hand here. And you can't leave until we get things under control. This child is spoiled and impossible to teach."

"It'll have to wait, Porter. I'm much too tired for anything right now."

Carrie was impatient and started to pat my face for attention. "I don't want'a sing. Jimmy said he'd show me his setting hen, and Daddy said that wasn't fit for little girls. And, Jimmy's sister wants to have a garden too."

Porter thrust his arms up in the air. "See, you're making a hick farmer out of her just like your precious Stanleys. And, hatching chicks is unseemly."

Carrie burst into tears. "I want'a see the little chicks come out of the egg."

"Of course you do. Everyone likes fluffy little yellow chicks."

"Daddy doesn't." She put her little hands either side of my cheeks as she implored, "How come there isn't a chick in the eggs for breakfast?"

Porter covered his face. "See what you've done."

"Hush, Porter. We'll talk about this tonight." I shifted Carrie to my hip as I smoothed back her disheveled hair. "Carrie, when I bake a

470

cake...first I have to have a recipe...then I put the ingredients in a bowl...but it's not a cake. Even when I mix it all together it's still not a cake. It takes just the right temperature and the right amount of time in the oven before it turns into a cake. Eggs can't make little chicks until the egg has the right recipe, and the mother hen keeps the eggs warm, like the oven, until the chick is ready to hatch."

"Where's the recipe?"

Porter's eyes were bugging out. "Seeee!"

"There are two parts to the recipe, and both have to be there to make a chick."

"Where's the parts?"

Porter turned and walked away shaking his head.

"Why the mother hen has half and the daddy rooster has half. That's God's wonderful plan so even a little chick has a mommy and daddy."

"So it's OK to eat eggs."

"Very much OK. Eggs are good for you. You've heard the chickens over at Millie's cackling to let everyone know how happy they are when they lay an egg."

I turned and saw Erma's tired haggard face. Maybe Carrie had been too much for her.

To Carrie I said, "Tell Auntie Erma, thank you."

Carrie was reluctant, but managed a soft pouty, "Thank you, Auntie Erma."

I placed a grateful hand on Erma's arm. "Thank you so much. I can see we're both beat. We'll talk tomorrow."

Then I turned to a smiling Millie who was already holding her arms out to take Carrie from me.

"Come, Carrie. Your mommy's too tired to carry you, and you're such a big girl...you can walk...come. I'll drive you and your mommy home."

As we settled into Millie's truck, Carrie clung to me, and Millie tried to brighten her spirits. "Carrie, is it true you're going to sing a song for your Daddy's big celebration?"

"I don't want'a sing. Daddy's mean."

"But, your Mommy sings so nice. Don't you want'a sing like her?"

"I don't want my Mommy to sing. She'd rather take care of the chickens. Wouldn't you, Mommy?"

Millie threw me a glance. "Woops, wrong question." Then to Carrie added, "I know helping Jimmy and me with chores is more fun than learning a song, but think how important that would make you feel, and how proud your Daddy and Mommy will be."

"Mommy's more proud of my garden...aren't you, Mommy?"

"Well, yes, in a way because everyone has to have food to eat, but it's pretty important to have singing too. Think what a funny world we'd have if the birds stopped singing...the cats stopped purring...and the chickens stopped their crook-crook-crooking song as they lazy in the sun...and the music in church is the best part of the church service. So, you see, I sing to brighten up church. But you shouldn't have to sing if you don't want to...so forget all that...soon we'll plan our garden."

She snuggled into my shoulder, fell fast to sleep, and an overpowering protective love welled up in my heart, a love that fueled my determination to stand my ground with Porter.

***

Home at last. How strange it was to think of the parsonage as home. My mixed-up childhood had mixed-up the meaning of home. My first, and only real home, was Aunt Carrie's loving arms around me. The tenant house was Ma's, Matt's, Mark's and Daddy's home; I felt that clearly. The Stanley's farm was the home that nurtured me and made a nice picture in my mind, but it really didn't belong to me. What would Carrie's idea of home be---my arms, yes, and Porter's, this house and Millie's farm. At that moment I realized Carrie's feelings about home depended on me. I was determined the word "home" have clarity and spell security. And her feelings about home would be vibrantly colored with love, a home made real with love and acceptance.

"Mommy's tired, Carrie. What'a you say we have a sandwich and a glass of milk? Then, off to bed."

"Fried egg? Auntie Erma never makes fried egg sandwiches."

Carrie rushed to the refrigerator and got out two eggs and the bottle of milk, as I hung our coats and placed my suitcase by the stairway. I loved it that she liked to help. She pulled a chair over and watched the eggs drop into the sizzling hot butter.

"Does the yellow yolk turn into a yellow chick if the recipe is right?"

"Sort'a."

By the time the sandwiches were ready she had the table set. We ate slowly, enjoying our fried egg sandwiches made with eggs generously given to us by Millie and Jimmy. As we ate we talked of my visit to the Stanley's farm and of the plans for her visit with them this summer. All her troubles had melted away.

"And now, it's off to bed with you, my chick."

She scampered up the stairs happily patting each step ahead of her. "Tomorrow we see the setting hen. Don't we?"

473

"Oh, I can't promise tomorrow, but soon."

As she nestled down between the covers, she said, "Don't go away again, Mommy. I missed you. Auntie Erma's not fun when you're away." Her lower lip came out. "Daddy either. Read me 'The Little Red Hen,' please."

"OK. You and your chickens."

When the story was finished, and as I bent to kiss her goodnight, she said, "I love you Mommy. You're the little red hen only you plant a garden, not wheat, and I'm the chick. Let's wish on a star."

We went to the window and looked out at the dark starry night. You could barely make out the mountains that formed our beautiful little valley. This was the countryside Carrie would love and always think of as home. Even though the Stanley farm vistas had stolen my heart, as I looked at this view with the freshness of Carrie's eyes, I clearly saw that this snug little valley and the mountains were the most beautiful place in the world. An impartial judge might even deem it so.

As we snuggled close, deep in thought, making our wish, Porter's car lights turned into the driveway. Carrie slipped out of my arms, and ran down the stairs to meet her father.

"Daddy, Daddy come up and help us wish on a star."

He swung her up into his arms, and carried her up the stairs where I waited by the window. Still in Porter's arms, her other arm went around my neck, as she drew the three of us together.

And together, we sang, "Starlight, star-bright, first star we see tonight. We wish we may, we wish we might…grant us the wish we wish tonight."

There were tears on my cheeks as I contemplated our incompatible wishes.

Porter said, "See, Carrie, you can sing very nicely when you want to."

"Not now, Porter, we're all too tired. Kisses and you're off to dreamland, my little one."

I shut Carrie's bedroom door, and the door at the bottom of the stairs, our voices must not reach her ears.

***

I felt Porter bristle as we stood facing each other. "Josephine, it's time we talked."

I braced myself for an onslaught of all Carrie's misdeeds and to be ordered to teach her the song, but Porter threw me a curve.

"It's past time you were a proper wife. I've given you plenty of time to grow up. Everyone thinks you're the perfect wife; it's time you were one. Anyway, Carrie needs a brother or sister. Hopefully, a brother, before she's spoiled beyond hope."

I was too stunned to reply. He stepped toward me, and my hands went up to say stop.

"Josephine, be reasonable. Look what I've made of you, a star. You're actually glamorous, loved by everyone."

"NO, Porter, no."

"It's your wifely duty. The Bible says....."

"I know what the Bible says, and I've heard your tirades on the evils of lust. Apply them to yourself."

"Now, Josephine...God made sex and said, multiply."

"Well, I don't want'a multiply. To bring more children into a loveless marriage would be a sin."

"You twist everything around to suit yourself. There are plenty who think I'm a good specimen. It's not a sin if you're married." He took one more step toward me.

I backed away. "If you're married? What's married anyway? You think saying a few words make a marriage…just like saying a few words gets you a passport to heaven."

"It's the blood of Jesus that's the way to salvation…we're talking about wives obeying their husbands as the bible commands"

"The bible commands a lot of things. In one sentence it says multiply and in the next it says sex is a sin. I accept Apostle Paul's idea on that subject. 'It is good for a man not to touch a woman.'"

"OK, be fair…it also says, 'to avoid fornication, let every man have his own wife.' You're in the wrong and you know it. I only have to look at your background to know where you're coming from."

"Yeah, in your warped mind, I suppose I was born in double sin because Ma wasn't married. But Ma was raped. She had nothing to do with that. For that matter, how come everyone has original sin if it's not sinful if you're married? Don't answer, I've heard it a million times, Eve lead Adam into sin so everyone is sinful. How fair is that? Even I'm fairer than your God. Yet I'm a heretic because I won't say a few words that you say are the only way to be saved. No matter whether they mean anything to me or not, just say them for show. Forget that I had a good relationship with God long before I met you. You and your contradictions drive me away from God."

Porter's face was so red it almost scared me. "Now, you listen to me. I've heard enough of your blasphemy. Be quiet, before God strikes you down. I'm head of this house, and you will submit, and Carrie will sing at the dedication."

"If you ever touch me, I'll never sing another note for your precious church, and I mean it. It's true that I was an immature naive teenager when I thought you were too pure to be interested in sex. You thought it OK to force yourself on me; we were legally married. Had I known what you expected, I'd never have considered marrying you. You led me to believe you wanted to marry me solely because you thought you could make money on my voice. And, I'll never allow you to exploit Carrie."

His eyes flashed anger. "Stop switching and twisting everything."

"Twisting? You're the twister. You want me to climb into your bed out of pure lust. You don't even know me. What little of me comes through to you, you hate and ridicule. For me that kind of sex is a sin, and I won't have it. And, if you ever give Carrie a hard time about singing in church, the same rule goes, I'll stop singing."

"When do you come off so pure? I haven't forgotten; you were no virgin. Alma warned me you were a wayward child, but she thought you'd straighten out away from the Stanley's influence, especially away from Forrest, but Abbey too. She said you needed a place to go because you couldn't stand it to see your precious Forrest married. Admit it; you needed a place to go. And out of the goodness of my heart, I took you in. Now, I'm beat over the head with it. How's that fair?"

The room spun around, I was so angry I began to shake. I could see his egotistical reasoning plainly. In his mind with his pat dogmatic theology, he would always be right no matter what I said.

In anger, I flung back at him, "Think whatever you wish. I will never ever share your bed, EVER. As I promised before, I will be a good wife in other ways. I will sing providing the schedule allows me time for the things I think are important...like being a mother. Also, money! You will start paying me! You've never provided one cent toward household expenses. I've had to do that. No more. I know how the money is made, and I play a big role in that.

I turned, mounted the stairs, leaving him standing there in the middle of our friendly country dining room as shaken as I was.

Porter left quietly next morning without waking me. It was a new experience for him not to find me in the kitchen, coffee made and breakfast on the table. I was thankful that he had let me sleep as I was exhausted. Was it a peace offering, had he accepted my ultimatum? One could hope.

When Carrie and I finally came down to breakfast there was a note from Porter. Erma would be around to pick me up at ten for rehearsal as I expected, but I knew Carrie would be disappointed. She had her heart set on spending the day at Millie's planning our garden.

"Daddy says Auntie Erma is coming this morning to take me to rehearsal for our broadcast tomorrow. Let's call Aunt Millie and see if you can stay with her."

"Yeah, cause I don't want'a stay with Auntie Erma."

Millie never let me down. "Of course she can stay. Thought I said so yesterday. Been expecting your call."

Carrie was happy, and came home from Millie's both Thursday and Friday with glowing tales of the wonderful things happening with Jimmy and the chickens.

"Mommy, Jimmy said he'd take me to his house Saturday to see the setting hen. Did you know chicken farmers can't let their chickens run around outside because they hide their nests? Mother hens lay their eggs in secret places so you can't find the eggs. Isn't that very smart?"

"Very smart. So you're learning a lot of new things from Jimmy. You know, when I first came here to live Aunt Millie had a very small chicken farm, and her chickens ran around outside in the summer."

"Did she have a hard time finding the eggs?"

"You'll have to ask her."

"I told Aunt Millie stories while she packed eggs."

My mind flashed back to Aunt Carrie, and how she and I made up stories, and how even after her death, I still made up stories for her. I gathered Carrie into my arms and hugged and hugged her. "You're the best little storyteller in the whole world."

***

On Saturday, the May morning was more summer than spring, but my mood was definitely spring. I needed to put my hands in the soil, to start growing something, and Carrie and I planned to spend the whole day with Millie and Jimmy.

Carrie was bubbling over with chatter. "Let's have cornflakes, Mommy. We don't have time for oatmeal. Aunt Millie and Jimmy are waiting for us."

"OK. Cornflakes and one of our hardboiled eggs."

When breakfast was over, we gathered up paper, pencil and crayons for making a lay-out chart for planting our garden. Then joining hands, we hurried along our narrow well-worn path that skirted the base of our mountain ridge as it tapered to a gentle mound in Millie's backyard. A pair of robins heralded the beautiful morning, claiming their territory with exuberance. As we scrambled through the small washed-out gully, a phoebe called to its mate. Usually, we stopped there for a few minutes to look for fossils, but today Carrie implored, "Let's not look for fossils today, Mommy."

"Right, no time for fossils today."

The valley widened at Millie's backyard, as if the mountains had been pushed apart to make room for her farm. The house and barn were on opposite sides of the road, and behind the barn stretched a narrow long teardrop-shaped ten acre field. On the far side of the field, Jimmy had setup four beehives he had bargained from his neighbor for a dozen eggs each week for two years. The beehives were just the ticket, as Jimmy put it, for the seed clover he planned to plant for a cash crop. The bees would be happy, and there'd be plenty of pollination going on as they produced a second cash product, honey!

Millie declared over and over: "How'd I ever get so lucky to be blessed with the likes of Jimmy?"

Jimmy just as emphatically declared: "I'm the lucky one. College's not for me."

As we crossed Millie's lawn she was shaking a dust-mop out her back door. "Hey there, you two."

"Hey there yourself. Think we dare start planting this early?"

"Aunt Millie, can we see the setting hen first?"

"Come here, you little rascal. I need a big hug. Did you tell your mommy what a big helper you were?"

"Yep. Can I stay with you every week while Mommy sings? She's not going away again. Are you, Mommy?"

"No, Sweetheart. I'm going to be right here." I crossed my fingers. "Let's hope everyone stays well." Aunt Alma's obvious decline and Mrs. Stanley's exhaustion still troubled me. Mr. Stanley would tell me not to cross that bridge unless I have to.

Under her breath, to me, Millie assured, "It's OK, let her stay."

"Oh, Millie, thank you. We'll see." I'd have to work it out with Porter. "Just look at your tulips. You get better sun than I do. Your red emperors are gorgeous, as always. Mine are a washout. Maybe if I took-up my bulbs, but where would I put them to get any better sun?"

Our hardest task of the morning was convincing Carrie we had to wait for Jimmy to finish his chores before he could take us around to his house to have a peek at his mom's setting hen. We passed the time sorting the seeds, raking and smoothing the garden Jimmy had plowed and dragged for us. No more waiting for Millie's son to do it.

480

After lunch we were finally on our way to see the setting hen, and Sandy was coming to Millie's for the first time. Carrie's excitement was at the bursting point like a balloon inflated with all the air it could hold.

Sandy was a year older than Carrie and went to kindergarten in the one-room schoolhouse. As we pulled into their driveway, she was anxiously waiting in the yard for us. The instant the car stopped, Carrie hopped out of the car, and they grabbed each other's hands and began to dance up and down.

"Come on, Sandy. Jimmy's going to show me the setting hen. Please, now can I see it? "

"It's just an old chicken sitting on a nest."

"But I never saw one. Jimmy promised."

"Aw, all right." Sandy consented even though going to Millie's to work in the garden would be much more fun.

However, the intrigue of showing Carrie something new was a little exciting. She took Carrie's hand. "You have to be very quiet when we peek around the corner at the hen."

The mother hen's nest was hidden under the stairway to the loft. Sandy put her finger up to her lips, motioning to be quiet. Then they flung their arms around each other in pure joy.

"Mommy, I wish I could have a setting hen like Sandy's."

"It's not mine; it's Ma's," Sandy said. "I wouldn't want an old chicken."

"Mommy, Mommy, please, please, could I have it."

Before I could answer, Jimmy came to my rescue. "It would never due to disturb a setting hen. See how quiet we have to be not to scare her off the nest. Those eggs have to stay warm. I'll ask Ma to let me take the mother hen and her chicks over to Millie's once they've hatched so you can watch them grow. How'd that be?"

"But I want'a see them hatch."

Sandy was all smiles, nodding her head. "Yeah, that's fun. Show her, Jimmy."

"We'll try. I'll keep an eye on the setting hen. If I catch the eggs when they start hatching, it takes a quite awhile before they all get hatched, I'll come and get you and your mommy so you can see the chicks come out of the egg. Keep your fingers crossed and hope for the best. I can't promise."

***

That evening, Carrie was garden dirt from tip of her nose down to her toes, and it was pure joy to put her in the tub for a bath. We decided on PJs even though it was only supper time. As we both went laughing into the kitchen, Porter's car appeared in the drive, a rare thing these days with all there was to do at the new church. Carrie went running out to greet him, wide pajama legs flapping around her ankles.

"Daddy, Daddy, I saw the setting hen." She told him all about our wonderful day as I quickly threw together a supper of macaroni and cheese, home-canned green beans and a salad. Had I known he'd be home, I would have planned a nice meal to encourage him to be at home more often. Carrie needed her father's attention.

Like any normal family, Porter tucked Carrie in as I did-up the dishes. In her eyes we were a loving family enjoying the promise of summer's loving warmth to follow the new beginnings of spring. However, loving warmth was a fantasy; this was the evening we both put our cards on the table, though of course, Porter would never have used that analogy because cards were the devil's toys. I smiled to myself because it suddenly occurred to me how appropriate the analogy really was, because to Porter, I was the devil's disciple, and would deal the devil's hand. That was my last smile of the evening.

482

"Josephine, I've grown tired of your threats to leave. You have no place to go; you'd never leave Carrie, and I'd fight you to keep her. I can not have my child grow up a heretic. If you were a real wife, and had another child, you'd see things differently. The bible says of women: (Titus 2:5) 'To be discreet, chaste, keepers at home, good, obedient to their husbands, that the word of God be not blasphemed.'"

"And which word are you talking about? The one that says multiply, or the one that says not to?"

"Honestly, Josephine, I'm afraid for your soul. Stop blaspheming the Word. God will punish you... You're impossible to talk to. You better learn to fear God if you know what's good for you."

"If your God's the true God I want no part of Him. I'm fairer than He is. I need a God better than I am....."

"Don't say such things. (First John 1:9) 'If we confess our sins, he is faithful and just to forgive us our sins, and to cleanse us from all unrighteousness.' Nothing could be fairer than that."

Near tears, I stuck to my guns. "You do have me in a trap because, you're right, I'd never leave Carrie; that's true. But there is no way you can make me sing. And starting this minute I will not sing a note if you persist."

"You can't do that...."

"Don't try me unless you want to explain that to your church members."

Once our positions were hammered out, he agreed: there would be no sex; Carrie would not be forced to sing; I would continue to give four mornings to the record business; no car for me; I was to go in to the studio with Porter in the mornings; Erma would drive me home; Carrie would stay with Millie; I'd continue to fulfill all the social duties of the devoted wife; and I'd have an allowance of twenty dollars a week.

Porter concluded, "I'm paying a prostitute's wage, and for what?" He shook his head, deeply troubled. (Mark 3:29) "'But he that shall blaspheme against the Holy Ghost hath never forgiveness, but is in danger of eternal damnation.'"

"And who gets to say what constitutes blaspheme?"

"The bible. I promise; God will deal with you. I can't."

***

Plans for Good Shepherd Evangelical's dedication continued on schedule, as did our plans for the garden. When the garden planting day finally arrived, there was much jubilation. Millie, Jimmy, Sandy, Carrie and I were all decked out in our clean but frayed jeans. We consulted our planting charts and began marking nice straight rows on our beautifully prepared garden plot that was as smooth and delicious looking as chocolate frosting on one of Millie's cakes.

Even Carrie and Sandy had made a diagram for their corner plot. With pink cheeks streaked with mud, they put their heads together over the sketch they had carefully made with crayons: red circles for their tomato plants; a row of dark green dots, three in each hill, for string beans; a squiggly light green line for lettuce; and orange circles for their pumpkin seeds.

At the end of the day, though we were tired, an impromptu picnic developed. Jimmy had fortuitously brought some hotdogs, just in case. I ran home along our path to my backdoor to get potato salad I had put together that morning, and I grabbed a bag of marshmallows to toast for dessert. Millie provided carrot and celery sticks, apple slices and peanut butter to dip them in.

484

Selecting just the right willow-shoots for skewers was a big production of utmost importance. The skewers must be green to keep from catching on fire and sturdy enough to hold the weight of a hotdog.

Jimmy, Sandy and Carrie collected the downed limbs from under the hickory tree that grew at the edge of Millie's lawn near our path at the foot of the mountain. With Jimmy's expert guidance, Sandy and Carrie learned how to properly lay a campfire, and he explained that you must be patient and wait for the fire to burn down until the coals were red-hot before toasting hotdogs if you wanted them to be yummy well roasted.

We skewered our hotdogs securely through the long way on our green willow-shoots. When we were all ready, we held them over the glowing coals that had only a slight flicker of flame left, carefully turning them until they were a rich bubbly brown that set our taste buds juicing.

Sandy said, "Catsup and mustard on mine, please."

"Mine too, Mommy, like Sandy's."

Jimmy laughed. "It's not a hotdog until you add onion. Right, Jo?"

Both little girls held their noses.

Millie lined her hotdog with pickles. "Now there's a feast!"

The waxing moon was a lopsided milky saucer rising over the mountain as dusk began to settle.

Carrie exclaimed, "See, when the cow jumped over the moon her hoof chipped the moon."

Everyone laughed, and Jimmy said, "I think I'll get me a dog so we can laugh at the moon. What do you say to that?"

In chorus, the girls chanted, "We want a dog…we want a dog!"

We sang songs around the fire, as we toasted our marshmallows. Sometimes our marshmallows caught fire and fell off our sticks, and we laughed. Sometimes we burned our fingers taking them off the sticks, and still laughed.

The day was too perfect to end, and Jimmy, mesmerized by the glowing embers, launched into a yarn: "Once upon a time far away on the other side of our mountain in a little valley, kind'a like ours, there was a beautiful oak forest. It was midmorning on a day when everyone should have been hard at work, but a lazy woodcutter napped in the shade of one of those big old oak trees.

"Not far away a clever little elf sang merrily as he dug a hole under the roots of one of those big old oak trees. The elf was a tiny little man with a round belly and skinny little legs. On his tiny little feet he wore black leather boots with turned-up pointed toes. Around his fat little belly he wore a black belt with a shiny gold buckle. Atop his head sat a jaunty little black leather hat with a brightly striped turkey feather stuck in its band. Beside the little elf sat a pot full of glittering gold coins.

"Now all that singing and digging woke the lazy woodcutter from his nap. 'Ah, ah,'" said the lazy woodcutter. 'I wonder what could be making all that racket?' And he crept quietly through the big old oak tree forest. You can imagine his amazement when he saw the elf with his pot of gold coins. "'Mummm,' he said to himself, 'gold! This is my lucky day.' And the lazy woodcutter watched the little elf as he dug a hole under the roots of that big old oak tree, and low and behold, the little elf buried his treasure.

"Once the pot of glittering gold coins was safely buried, the little elf swung his shovel over his tiny little shoulder, very pleased with himself, and went off through the forest.

"The lazy woodcutter thought, 'How am I going to dig up the pot of gold coins without a shovel? If I go home for one, how will I know which big old oak tree roots the gold is under?' He gave a hearty laugh

486

and took the yellow scarf from around his neck and tied it on the oak tree. Then he hurried away home to fetch a shovel.

"Now the clever little elf thought, 'Maybe I best check on my hiding place just to be sure there's no one in the forest spying on me.' And when he saw the yellow scarf tied on the old oak tree, he pondered what he should do. Elves are not only clever, they're tricksters. He scratched his head as he walked around that big old oak tree, thinking and grinning, deciding what trick to play on the lazy woodcutter.....Can you girls guess what the clever little trickster-elf did to the lazy woodcutter to teach him a lesson?"

Sandy said, "He set a trap with a pail of pig-slop over the gold, and when the mean woodcutter came back the elf pulled a string, and it dumped on the woodcutter's head."

Everyone said that would sure be a big surprise.

But Jimmy said, "No. You'll have to guess again."

Carrie's excitement spilled over. "Tell us, Jimmy...tell us what the little elf did."

"Well, when the thieving, lazy woodcutter came back with his shovel, all the old oak trees in the forest had yellow scarves tied on them, every last tree!"

Sandy and Carrie clapped their hands. "What'a smart trickster-elf!"

Then, Carrie cocked her head quizzically. "Do you think the pot of glittering gold coins is still under the old oak tree?"

Sandy shook her head. "There are no real elves; are there, Jimmy?"

"Well, I never saw one, but who can say."

Carrie closed her eyes. "I can see a forest full of old oak trees all tied with pretty yellow scarves very close to the ground, because elves are very short people...so maybe there are elves!" Then she threw her arms around Jimmy's neck. "That was a gooood story."

Even a perfect day must end. We said our goodbyes, and hand in hand, Carrie and I made our way slowly along the worn path at the foot of our mountain with the moon now a bright gold coin from the elf's treasure, lighting our way.

Carrie stopped suddenly and pointed up at the lopsided moon. "Mommy, the face on the elf's coin is laughing at us because the elf's never gonna to tell where he hid his gold!"

***

When Memorial Day and the dedication of Good Shepherd Evangelical Church arrived, delicate little plants began poking their heads up in our garden, marking neat rows in startling green as if they were decoration on chocolate frosting..

Carrie danced up and down. "I can't wait to show Jeffy and Louisa May and Jenny my garden, and the mother hen, and her chicks."

Just days before, we had arrived at Millie's just in time for Jimmy to rush us over to his house. The chicks were hatching. Luck was with us and Carrie was able to catch one of the little chicks pecking his way out through its egg shell. First the shell cracked and a hole briefly appeared; then the shell broke apart. There, all wet with bugging black eyes, was a scrawny, wet little chick ready to greet the world. I was glad it was not the first chick to hatch so Carrie easily saw that the rather ugly newborn would soon dry out and turn into an adorable fuzzy yellow little baby. However, if the wet bug-eyed chick offended her sensibilities, there was no sign of it for she clapped her hands with glee.

"Mommy, Mommy, it's one of Daddy's miracles."

"Yes it is, sweetheart."

Jimmy had kept his promise, and the mother hen and her chicks were moved over to Millie's for Carrie to feed and watch until the chicks feathered out. Then the brood would be taken back to rejoin his mother's flock.

Witnessing Carrie's wonder and delight as she tagged along after the clucking mother hen kindled anew the wonder and magic of new life. The chicks scampered around as they faithfully followed the metronome clucking of their mother in her endless search for food. When a tasty morsel was found, mother hen sounded a frenzy of clucking, and the chicks spread their tiny fluffy yellow wings, and sped to their mother's beak to claim their treat. When it was nap time for her chicks, mother hen nestled down on the ground, and fluffed out her feathers to make a nice cozy place for her chicks to sleep underneath her. Amid the chick's soft contented peeping, now and then, a little yellow head with sleepy eyes would appear, poking out from under mother hen's wing. Then Carrie would squeal with delight.

Waiting for the arrival of everyone on this much anticipated morning was proving to be too much for Carrie. "When will they get here, Mommy? I can't eat any more breakfast. I wish we didn't have to go to church."

"Don't let your father hear you say that. You know how much this means to him. Calm yourself. There'll be time to play after church."

Hearing Carrie put my own wish into words, sent waves of guilt washing over me. Was I turning her away from God as Porter accused? Ever since Porter's and my last confrontation, self doubt festered anew. It was a cancer growing in my heart. Had Jesus really come to me in a dream and saved me when I was a child? Where was He now? The Jesus that Porter knew was a stranger, not at all like the Jesus I thought I knew. When Porter delivered his sermon Sunday mornings, my mind turned off just as it had when I was a child and life became too painful to bear. I sang even more fervently, as if my life depended on it because, in a way, it did. When we sang a duet and I looked up at

Porter, people thought it was with love and admiration, but I was pleading for peace and a safe place to rest. The words I sang had nothing to do with that place and time. I was lost? Was I a heretic as Porter claimed? Could I ever escape Ma's stigma? I only knew I must endure for Carrie. Porter was her father, and I had no place to go.

"Come; hurry, Carrie; Daddy's ready to leave."

***

To my surprise, Ma came driving up into the Good Shepherd Evangelical Church parking lot in her old gray Ford accompanied by Aunt Alma. Though hunched over with age, Aunt Alma was still bright-eyed. Ma explained, "Alma was determined to come." That meant Ma must drive to make room in the Stanley's car for Linda and Jeffy. Mr. and Mrs. Stanley's car pulled in right behind Ma and Aunt Alma. Abbey and Allen's car soon followed with Louisa May and Jenny still babbling and jabbering about coming to see where Carrie lived.

Carrie jumped up and down and around with excitement.

I had to remind her, "Remember, in the church, you must be quiet, and be a good hostess. There'll be time to see the setting hen after the service and banquet."

"Do we have to stay and eat? I wish we could eat at home."

"Think how much fun it'll be to show Jeffy, Louisa May and Jenny all around Daddy's new church. And you'll still get to eat with them, even though it's here; and there'll be no dishes to do."

Once everyone was seated, the service was ready to begin, and I had to leave to prepare for Porter's and my duet.

I was wearing a white summer suit Porter had chosen for me with a frilly black blouse that framed the jacket and sleeve openings. He insisted I have my hair styled, and my well manicured and painted nails looked as though they had never worked in the garden. Porter was right about pearls; they were the perfect elegant accent. He wore a black suit, white shirt with French cuffs and a black tie. I knew we made a stunning couple. Even my eyes could see how handsome the very blonde Porter was in his black suit, and how perfectly we contrasted each other.

I could read Linda's thoughts as her admiring eyes appraised Porter's impeccable taste. The person I had become was as much a fake as Linda. That knowledge hit me with cruel force and tore at my heart. Exactly who had I become? Who was I? On the heels of this self condemnation, came the realization: I was the only fake; Linda was being true to who she was, and made no bones about it.

The dedication service was flawless. There were welcoming words and a responsive reading commemorating Memorial Day. As Porter and I sang our duet an aurora of awe and admiration shone on the attentive upturned faces. A tangible feeling of wonder lingered as the scripture lesson, Jesus the Good Shepherd, was read. And, in a booming voice that surely reached the heavens, Porter prayed for God's blessing on Good Shepherd Evangelical Church. In return, Good Shepherd Evangelical would honor its name as it endeavored to take the message of salvation out into a sinful world. All of God's sheep would be sought out as far as the radio could carry his voice, not one sheep would be left unattended. The lost would be brought into the fold. He prayed, "In the name and for the sake of Jesus Christ, Lord and Shepherd of us all. Amen."

The prayer ended and the choir, in immaculate new white robes, lined up and entered the choir box. My solo was part of the choir anthem, and as I sang, a hush fell over the people as if a Living Presence had entered the sanctuary. That I could have that much effect on an audience amazed me. Was my ability to win acceptance through my talent enough to salvage the rift between the real me and the stranger I had become? Could, and would, it sustain me?

After the anthem, Porter rose and began his sermon, expounding in great detail on the lesson of the lost sheep, sheep lost in the briers of lust and societies' temptations. Good Shepherd Evangelical's mission was to search out the lost and turn them from the sinful world; a world cast out of the Garden of Eden; a world that had turned its back on the Word of the Lord. The Congregation hung on Porter's every word as if God had written the script. He bellowed: all were sinners, and fell short of the glory of God, and must be brought into the fold, saved to life everlasting, saved from eternal damnation and hellfire. The mission must start now, in that place, and carry forth as Jesus commanded.

I concentrated my eyes on Mr. Stanley's face, and let my mind close around the two of us. We were sitting in the sun, warming ourselves on the banking that skirted the Stanley farmhouse in winter. I became a child, lost to time. My mind tried to wander in that long ago peace, but nagging thoughts persisted. My Jesus was patient, not harsh. He'd never send anyone to hell. But why was there no prayer left in my heart? I desperately fought to stay on the banking with Mr. Stanley, but hard as I tried, I couldn't feel the warmth of the sun.

***

For the banquet, Porter joined Carrie and me, the Stanleys, the Bennetts, Ma and Aunt Alma. He was ever attentive and thoughtful, and assured us that it would be fine for us to leave as soon as we had finished eating in order that we have a nice family visit before they had to leave for the long drive back to their homes. As we dined, the air in the fellowship room was abuzz with compliments for our duet, the choir and my solo, the dedication service, and for the wonderful roast beef dinner.

Finally, Porter pushed back from the table. "Much as I'd like to join you back at the parsonage, my duty is here, attending to my hosting duties, but everyone will understand and be glad to excuse Josephine."

In her most seductive voice Linda said, "What a pity you can't come too. You did make the message of the Good Shepherd come alive. It makes me wonder if I might be a lost sheep."

Porter blushed, and I expected he'd say all were lost, but he was noticeably flustered and brushed it off with, "Thank you all for coming to share this most happy occasion. It's been a whole lot of work, by a lot'a folks, including Josephine, but it's the Lord's work, and that makes it all worthwhile. I'll be along as soon as I can."

Louisa May and Jenny insisted Carrie ride with them, and I crowded into Ma's coupe beside Aunt Alma. Ma had been noticeably quiet throughout the banquet, but now in the car, away from the crowd, she said, "Josephine, what an amazingly talented singer you really are, truly extraordinary."

I had won Ma's attention and praise! Her amazement surprised me because she had heard me sing before, but it was sweet praise.

Frail wizened-up Aunt Alma added, in her most benevolent voice of old, "Everything's turned out just right for you; hasn't it, Josephine, just as I predicted? Porter....er...Rev. Kent has done marvels for you. I told him you'd be a perfect compliment for his superior voice...that you'd make a good partner with his spiritual guidance."

How did she always know your tender spot and proceed to tromp all over it?

The parsonage was cozy, comfortable and friendly, and I was proud of the home I had made. It was obvious everyone felt relaxed, and ready to just sit back for some news gathering, and catching up on the events in each of our lives.

Carrie couldn't wait to take Jeffy, Louisa May and Jenny to see the garden and the mother hen and her chicks.

Mr. Stanley said, "Carrie, you sweet little imp; so you have a garden, do you?"

Allen suggested, "I have to see this garden. What'a you say, Fred? Hadn't we better stretch our legs before the drive home?"

So it was decided, and they trudged along with the kids. I watched them as they started down the path at the foot of our mountain. Jeffy, red hair shining in the sun, took Carrie's hand and led the way. My heart turned over because I saw Forrest taking my hand as he had done so many times long ago.

Linda insisted I explain all the ins-and-outs of the recording business. That was the last thing I wanted to talk about. I'd miss sharing the excitement with Mr. Stanley, Allen and the kids. And I'd miss my chance to find out what was happening back on the Stanley farm. That was definitely the last thing Linda wanted to talk about. She didn't appear to know anything about the farm, and said her life was impossibly tedious.

"Forget about the farm. Tell me, are you going to make a recording of the songs you did this morning? I'd love a record."

"You're in luck." I went into Porter's office and brought out records we had cut of our dedication music, and gave one to Linda, Ma and Mrs. Stanley. On the jacket cover there was a photograph of Porter and me in our dedication outfits. My profile showed my styled jet black hair as I looked admiringly up into Porter's eyes, his handsome face turned to the camera. "Here you are....compliments of the singers. Ma, you can share with Aunt Alma."

494

In the midst of the thank you exclamations, the gang came bustling into the kitchen, everyone talking at once, cheeks pink and eyes shining. With them came life and a breath of fresh air.

Carrie came rushing up to me, bursting with excitement. "Did you know our mountains are named Apple-ace-ins, and have bears in them?"

"Appalachians. Yes I did."

"Why didn't you tell me? Are you afraid of the bears?"

"I never saw one, but I think if I did see a bear, he might be as scared of me, as I would be of him!"

Aunt Alma sniffed. "If that child's not just like her mother."

I'm sure she didn't mean her remark as a compliment, but for me, it was the nicest response she could have given.

Mr. Stanley confirmed it. "Yes, indeedy, just like her mother."

Mrs. Stanley patted Mr. Stanley's hand. "Yes, Fred. Jo, life is just not the same without you."

Abbey finished with, "Amen to that."

Linda and Ma made no comment. I rose and hastily went to the kitchen to make a pot of strong coffee.

Abbey followed me. "Jo, here it is almost time to go and this will be our only chance for a sisterly chat."

We talked the talk of young mothers and confidants as we put out a plate of fresh fruit, cheese and crackers, and little finger sandwiches. I was able to read between the lines and decided the farm was having a hard time financially, and Forrest was having an increasingly difficult struggle to keep his household together with Linda's schedule. I wanted to quiz for more particulars, but knew I shouldn't. Allen was thinking of going to night school for a master's degree so he could move up in the school system. She confirmed my worry about Mrs.

Stanley's health. And she said her dad was doing fine; he just needed to slow down a little.

"This is just right, Jo. A light supper snack after Good Shepherd's feast."

"I thought you would need a little bit to tide you over for the trip home."

Carrie had played hostess too, and had the kitchen table set for the kids. They had their own plate of fruit, no finger sandwiches but peanut butter and jelly sandwiches, milk and chocolate chip cookies she had helped me make especially for this occasion.

All too soon the three cars were pulling out of our driveway, and Carrie started to cry. I took her hand in mine. "Come now, clean up time."

Her sniffles stopped immediately, and her chatter never stopped as we cleared the tables. Mr. Stanley told her that the garden was the best he'd seen since her mother left the farm. Louisa May and Jenny loved the setting hen and her chicks. Carrie told them all about chickens oiling their feathers and taking dust baths, and how they had laughed at that. Jeffy had talked to Jimmy like a grown up about the egg business. He thought maybe he could start a chicken business to help his dad with expenses. It was Jeffy this, and Jeffy that. Jeffy knew all about the fairy mounds, Jeffy knew all the best places where the berries grew, and he couldn't wait for her visit.

By the time I was tucking her in bed, she looked up at me, and with her most serious countenance said, "Mommy, when I grow up, I'm going to marry Jeffy and live on his farm."

Memories of the day I fell in love with Forrest filled me with nostalgia, and made me dizzy with homesickness. Love is beautiful, but little girl love is especially sweet. Oh, what turns life can take. What if she were to actually marry Jeffy?

***

I look back on that summer, after the dedication, before Carrie started kindergarten, as the happiest time of my married life. My schedule, while not perfect, worked out well. I had four afternoons free for gardening, canning and keeping up with housework. Fridays were broadcast day and I was gone all day. Carrie was thrilled to be on the farm with Millie where she could watch the chicks and be a part of all the farm's daily activities. When I came home from the four mornings I worked at the record company, Carrie and I ate lunch with Millie and Jimmy. That was fun for Carrie because she helped plan the food to take to Millie's, and she was Millie's helper just as I had been Ma's in the Sweet Shop kitchen after Aunt Carrie died.

I left with Porter in the morning. Erma, who had become a salaried, fulltime secretary and general schedule-keeper for Good Shepherd Evangelical Church and the recording company, drove me home. Saturdays belonged to Carrie and me to do whatever took our fancy.

Porter had readily agreed to pay Millie for baby sitting. She protested. "What are friends for?"

I reassured her. "We take care of each other, and you give us so much."

Porter increased my weekly allowance to thirty five dollars with no more accusations about there being no service rendered. But, he did say now that I had money there was no need for me to be grubbing in the dirt. He wanted me to give up all that nonsense about growing a garden. It was beneath my station, appearances mattered. People had a high regard for me, and well they should as his wife and star of the recording business.

The recording company was making money hand over fist, as Mr. Stanley would have put it. I'm sure that was the reason Porter no longer dared say there was no service rendered. Even though at the time, I only half realized the leverage and power I had. I began to feel the glamour of my talent. Why not let it buoy me up? Not everyone had my gift. Maybe there was something special about me after all. Those thoughts were a new experience, and felt good. But, I never lost sight of the reason I sang. It was my guarantee to some semblance of freedom. Without that freedom, I'd smother and die.

And Carrie, that summer, was pure joy. She was so eager to learn what made flowers turn into tomatoes or beans; what made plants green; how did the bees know how to fly home? She was enthralled with life, and her enthusiasm was contagious. Millie and Jimmy were caught up in Carrie's exuberance too, and Millie even went out and bought a child's nature encyclopedia so we could answer her questions.

Porter was rarely home. The growing congregation at Good Shepherd Evangelical Church, plus the little Free Methodist Church in Jackson Junction, was so much responsibility, he was busy every minute. Had I been more in tune with his needs, I would have been worried about his health with the schedule he kept. Instead, I was just glad to have him too busy and tired to pay any attention to us. If Carrie missed her father, it was not evident. We went merrily on our way.

The chicks feathered out and Jimmy took them back to his mother's flock. Millie, Jimmy, Carrie and I often planned picnics in Millie's back yard. Jimmy had moved in and boarded at Millie's. He loved the farm and knowing he'd never have to worry about looking for a job he knew he'd hate. That summer Jimmy was a substitute father for Carrie. He paid attention to her garden, took her berrying while I was working at the studio, taught her about chicken farming, bees and honey gathering. She hung on his every word as if it were law!

498

Her trip to the Stanley farm had to be canceled because Allen was in charge of the summer-school program where he taught. Thus, Carrie spent only one week with the Bennetts. I was glad I only had to part with her for a week; while at the same time I was disappointed because I wanted her to know and experience all the things that had meant so much to me when I was her age. I wanted Forrest and Carrie to have time together. I couldn't help being disappointed that Forrest hadn't written, asking her to come anyway, but even as I wished it, I knew he couldn't. With Linda working it would have been impossible. The summer farm work must have been overwhelming with Allen unable to help with the haying. Plus, Mr. Stanley was slowing down. Jeffy was a big help but he couldn't take the place of a hired man, and as far as I knew, they had never attempted to replace Daddy.

At the end of summer, Carrie and Millie counted the jars we had canned; some were quarts, some pints. She learned how many cups in a pint and how many pints in a quart. Millie taught her we'd need to have 365 jars to have one for each day in one year. She felt so grown-up and special when she reported all the things she was learning to me.

We danced in a circle holding hands as we sang, "First we work and then we play. That's the way to be happy and gay." Mr. Stanley used to sing that to me when I was Mrs. Stanley's hired girl. Then he'd say, "Now, don't you forget to play!" When I said that to Carrie she replied, "I was playing, Mommy. Work is Sunday School day." Then I'd feel a bit guilty about that because I didn't know how to answer truthfully.

When September arrived, Carrie started kindergarten in the one-room Jackson Junction School. She loved it, but Porter grumbled: "There's no reason she couldn't be going to the Maplehurst elementary school kindergarten where she'd have more suitable companions. She could ride in to Maplehurst with us, and you'd be free to spend a little extra time at the studio."

It was a reasonable argument. Our records were selling so fast, four mornings were not enough, especially with my choir work. Porter said I couldn't expect to have the world revolve around my whims all the time. But I persisted; Carrie loved the one-room school where Sandy was also a student, and to my way of thinking, was a very suitable companion! But I knew, come next year, everything would be different because the way things were shaping up, I knew Porter would prevail, and Carrie would have to go to Maplehurst to school.

Chapter 18

When school started that following fall, Carrie did indeed start first grade in Maplehurst to outbursts of temper and tears. She had pleaded with Porter to no avail.

"Just please visit my school. You'll see how wonderful it is...Please, please, Daddy."

It broke my heart to see her pleading so fervently.

"I know what a one room school is like...and it's not for a child of mine."

"But, Daddy, I'll never get to see Sandy."

"You don't go to school to see Sandy and play games. You go to learn your lessons."

"Mommy says I'm very smart."

"Of course you're smart. All the more reason to go to Maplehurst where you'll have more advantages to learn, and I dare say, more suitable playmates."

In October nature began her promised splash of brilliant colors everywhere you looked. Again, our senses were shocked into heightened awareness of the world outside ourselves, and Carrie began to adjust. Her horizons widened with her new school experiences. There was always something amazing for her to tell me. Saturdays were still our special day. We mulched the garden for winter, which made our compost pile disappear. Jimmy mucked out the chicken coops and spread some of that manure on our garden to mulch over the winter.

"Mommy, Jimmy says that's food for the soil, and our plants will eat it next summer. Isn't that another one of Daddy's miracles?"

We took long walks in the warmth of Indian summer, kicking the rustling leaves underfoot. Millie often joined us, Jimmy too when he could.

But as the leaves fell and the blackbirds gathered to fly south, there was a restless wind stirring. Porter said the little Free Methodist Church should close its doors, that all the new members had followed him to Good Shepherd. It was too expensive to keep the church open for the few old timers who were stuck in the past. There was no reason they couldn't come on in to Good Shepherd. Plus, there wasn't time enough in his schedule to minister to them in a meaningful way.

Then there was the problem of the parsonage. It was not convenient for the minister of a big growing church like Good Shepherd Evangelical to live way out in the boonies. And it was not suitable for the entertaining necessary for someone in his position. It was common sense that the parsonage should be moved to Maplehurst. The board was considering hiring an associate minister to lighten his schedule. These problems were to be resolved before Easter.

That was a crushing blow to me. My world was again tumbling down around my ears. If we moved to Maplehurst, Porter would be in control of my whole life. It wouldn't be my home anymore; it would be his. There would be no garden; no time for Mille or Jimmy; Carrie would have to give up her interest in the farm, and Porter would try to make her his puppet with all the proper answers.

The Jackson Junction parishioners rose up in protest. They were not about to give up their church; the church of their forefathers; the church where they were married; where their children were baptized; and where they wanted to be eulogized when they died. Rev. Kent, who could do no wrong, was unable to persuade them; they would not budge. Both sides dug in their heels.

I repeatedly reminded Porter that it was the Jackson Junction Free Methodist Church that took him in, loved, revered and ordained him; that he owed them in many ways for the success he now cherished. Millie was very much aware of my feelings. She felt the whole controversy was driving a wedge between Porter and me, and that our close friendship was in some way responsible for my position against Porter's plan. I couldn't tell her the truth about Porter's and my true relationship, that without her friendship I couldn't endure. She began to see he was not a saint, the best husband, or even the best father. He was slipping from his pedestal. I had to walk a delicate line because I couldn't afford to do anything that might encourage his fall. I had to keep playing my role with Porter, to endure. No matter what, I could not share his bed!

A truce of sorts developed on the surface between the two factions because the Thanksgiving and Christmas holidays took temporary precedence over the wrangling. As it turned out, behind closed doors, there was plenty of plotting going on with the protesting voices silenced by the camouflaging season of goodwill. The plotting even escaped me because music was so much a part of both celebrations that I had no choice but let those plans dominate my life.

Much to my dismay, poor little Carrie had to take second place in my time. I even had to give up my cherished Saturdays with her. It grieved me to be spending so much of my time at the church. However, it delighted Porter to be dominating most of my life, which aggravated me immensely, making life even more unpleasant. I tried my hardest not to let him have the satisfaction of showing my irritation.

Both holiday services were such huge successes, many people had to be turned away. Good Shepherd's fame was reaching over the mountains of northern mid-western Pennsylvania, and Porter was thrilled. His master plan for merging Good Shepherd Evangelical Church with his broadcast ministry was increasing his outreach capabilities beyond his wildest dreams. Suddenly it occurred to me, that all too soon, enlarging the sanctuary would be next on his agenda. A new fear loomed up before me; where would it end? I felt a noose slipping around my neck.

***

With the holiday season over, tension again filled the air; it was decision time. The behind closed door plotting emerged when the deacons informed the congregation they had already started interviewing candidates for the associate pastor position. Tensions ratcheted up even further when a house near Good Shepherd Evangelical Church came on the market that would be perfect for the parsonage, and it would be available by the end of March. Porter suggested they should put the decision before the Lord in prayer, keeping in mind one solution to the Free Methodist Church dilemma could be to have the new associate minister live in the Jackson Junction parsonage, take over the ministry there as well as the educational duties of Good Shepherd Evangelical. The associate minister could preach at the Free Methodist Church early Sunday morning, and be in Maplehurst in time to oversee the youth program at Good Shepherd Evangelical. A special prayer meeting was held. All on the board of deacons agreed to go ahead with the plan, and surface tensions moderated.

Now, I knew when the big change would occur, turning my world upside down. Mounting pressure from the recording business was overwhelming. They were demanding more and more from me. Plus, church politics had become unbearable. I was exhausted, and had become so thin Millie exclaimed, "You got'a slow down, gal, or the wind'll blow you away!" I jumped at every noise; everything was an effort. There would be no garden in the spring, no impromptu lunches or tea with Millie. Carrie cried and pleaded with her Daddy not to move. That was when I decided I had to buck-up and make the move work for her sake.

Carrie and I started to plan her new room. "Let's look through my new wallpaper catalog. You can choose the pattern you like best. Saturday we'll go pick out new bunk beds for your room so Sandy can come and stay for sleep-overs."

"Oh, goodie. Sandy'll like that cause she doesn't like the farm and chickens much."

"And I'll bet you, 'a bushel and a peck, and a hug around the neck' that Millie'll have you sleep-over with her sometimes so you can keep up with what's going on with Jimmy and the chickens."

She threw her arms around my neck. "Here's my 'hug around the neck', Mommy."

We found a box to make a miniature copy of her room. We cut windows and a door where they would be. We made wallpaper for the walls, curtains, cardboard furniture and even rugs for the floor. The crisis for Carrie was much improved, but it did nothing for the one mounting inside me. As I began to pack, Millie and I both cried when Carrie was out of the house at school. The move was hard for her too.

***

March first roared in like a lion the day when everything changed. The wind drove the snow in a whiteout blizzard. Porter was up early because we would have to get an early start.

I called up the stairs to Carrie. "Come on, sweetheart…time to get up."

Breakfast was on and no Carrie, so I went upstairs to wake her. "Time to get up, sleepyhead."

"I can't, Mommy. My head hurts."

Porter was impatient and called, "Hurry it up, Josephine. We've got to get going with this weather."

It was unlike Carrie not to be eager. I felt of her forehead, and she was burning up. I put my hand behind her head to smooth her damp hair away, and when I lifted her head she cried out, "Oow, Mommy, don't touch my head; it hurts."

I ran downstairs and got some cold water and a washcloth, and I hurried back up to sponge her hot face. Porter was right behind me.

"Listen, you spoil her. There's nothing wrong with her only she doesn't want to go to school. Get her ready to go as quick as you can. We're already late for an early start."

"Look at her; can't you see…she's burning up. She can't fake that."

"No. I can't see it. Both of you…get a move on."

"Please, Porter, please, I'm begging you, please take her to the emergency room."

"No way…what she needs is a good spanking."

My nerves were frayed to the breaking point. All my pent up fury burned inside me. "Porter, get out of here, this minute before I say things we'll both be sorry for. Go to your precious studio. Go, I don't want Carrie upset with anymore angry words."

506

He turned on his heels. "Have it your way; it always is."

He wasn't out of the driveway when I was on the phone to Millie. "Come quick. Carrie's burning up with fever...Porter's not here, and I have to get her to the emergency room."

I was at the door, Carrie wrapped in a blanket, when Millie pulled into the driveway. We exchanged only brief words of greetings, but our eyes confirmed volumes of panicked concern, and as we drove, the only voice we heard was Carrie's whimpering over and over, "Woo, woo, my head hurts....Mommy, Mommy." Her cries were splinters piercing my heart with fear. Just before we reached the hospital, she lapsed into a deep sleep more frightening than her cries.

One look at Carrie and the nurse took us right into a curtained area and started her evaluation. In less than an hour, the doctor had Carrie admitted to ICU, still unconscious.

Millie said, "I'm going out and call Rev. Kent."

I knew he'd be angry to be disturbed, but I answered, "Yes, maybe you should."

Millie looked upset when she came back, but tried not to show it. "He'll be along at lunch time."

I should have been furious, but all I felt was concern for Carrie. She had never had a sick day before this, nothing more serious than the sniffles.

They let me stay with her, but directed Millie to the waiting room. "I'll be right outside. I won't leave. They'll let me come in for a few minutes every hour. And Jo, I'll be praying every minute."

Carrie lay all uncovered except for her blue faded hospital gown. Her little hand was so hot in mine. Her beautiful, always on the move legs that had been so smeared with dirt from the garden last spring and summer, lay still and helpless on the white sheet.

Despite the nurses tending her every minute, before Millie came in at the end of that first hour, Carrie was gone. The nurses struggled to keep their composure as they smoothed Carrie's hair and covered her with a blanket to make it look as though she were sleeping.

"Should we send your friend in now, Mrs. Kent, or would you like to be alone for a few minutes? We'll call Rev. Kent for you."

"Thank you, yes, please call him. And, yes, I'd like a few minutes alone with Carrie before you send Millie in, thank you."

I smoothed my dearest Carrie's cheek with the back of my hand and kissed both cheeks, knowing that in a short while they would be cold forever. I traced her face from her hairline over the tip of her nose, mouth and chin. I gathered her up in my arms, and was surprised I didn't break into little pieces. I thought no time had gone by when Millie came in, and yet it was an eternity.

"Millie, what are we going to do without our Carrie?"

Millie took Carrie out of my arms, and placed her back in the covers as if she were tucking her in to sleep.

"She was too sweet and good for this world, Jo. No child has ever stolen my heart so completely. We have to be strong. There are so many who loved her. Rev. Kent is on his way."

I could tell Porter was upset and agitated when he came into the room, and he had every right to be. Our precious Carrie was dead. And he was probably upset because he had been so obviously wrong. But I was not prepared for what he said.

"Did you think to pray? What good did it do to bring her to the hospital? You let her die. Prayer rather than an emergency room could have saved her."

"Porter, please, this is no time for this…Carrie's gone, gone forever."

"I warned you…this is God's punishment. I told you God would take His revenge on you."

Millie gasped. "Rev. Kent, surely you're too distraught to know what you're saying. We're all overcome with grief."

"Yes, yes, you're right, Millie. Come, Josephine, we have formalities to attend."

That final blow nearly destroyed me. Hatred for Porter welled up in me, choking me. Would my legs hold me up? How in the world would I get through the next minute? I told my heart to freeze. My old escape mechanism took over, and numbness controlled my emotions and voice. "You go tend to formalities, Porter. Millie will drive me home."

In my state of withdrawal, I can't remember Millie's attempts to comfort me, or what excuses she may have made to soften Porter's outburst. My mind was in another place. I possessed a calm coolness on the surface that surprised me when inside my emotions raged with a furiousness that was frightening. I must never see Porter again, never. This hate could not be contained.

I clearly saw the production I knew he was already planning for Carrie's funeral. There would be an altar call directed at me. If only I could direct my mind to explode and end the pain! Make it a double funeral; death was a perfect escape. Aunt Carrie, Daddy and now sweet precious Carrie, my heart, they were all dead. Was there a heaven? Porter had the comfort of that assurance. Damn Porter and his God; I wanted no part of them.

Ma had it right, never succumb. I needed Ma. I needed to know the answer to where she came from. The Wallaces nearly saved her. Could they save me? Wallace was my surname. My tormented thoughts began to flow through a crack in the compelling surge to my own destruction.

Suddenly, we were at my driveway, and Millie was saying, "Jo, I don't think you should be alone right now. Come on home with me and have some hot tea. You're much too quiet."

"Thanks, Millie, thanks...You're always there for me, how can I ever thank you enough. I'll be OK. I just need some time alone right now."

Reluctantly, she let me out. I thanked her again for her never-failing support. I saw her hesitate before she backed out the drive. I waited until I was sure she had left, then I set about my task with all speed. Time was the key to success.

I ran upstairs and rummaged through my closet until I found one of my high school pleated skirts, a school blouse, sweater and underwear. Next, My old school penny loafers and ankle socks. I stuffed them into a paper shopping bag along with tooth brush, hairbrush and comb. They were things no one would miss. I went into Carrie's room and got barrettes and rubber bands; then I took all the paper money out of her piggybank. No one knew about how much money was in her piggybank but the two of us. Then hurriedly, I took the money I had saved from my allowance and from gifts the Stanleys and Ma had sent at Christmas from where I had hidden it in the tie-backs to my curtains. Next, I went into Porter's office and found the money he had put out for my March allowance. On second thought, I left it; if I took it, it would give me away, and I wanted no part of Porter. I had four hundred and fifty five dollars without it. I ran back upstairs and got my old purse from the closet to put the money in along with a few snapshots of Carrie. I left my shoulder bag with my wallet and all my personal identification just as it was on the kitchen table.

I had to hurry because I knew Jimmy would be ready to leave soon. I didn't feel the wind and snow as I ran along the path at the foot of our mountain for the last time. I was busy planning what I'd say to

510

Jimmy; he mustn't become suspicious. Millie would have had time to tell him about Carrie. I'd say the shopping bag was the clothes for her.

When I got to Millie's yard, luck was with me. Jimmy had just finished loading the egg cartons and had disappeared into the backroom. I climbed over the tailgate into the back of the truck and hid. It was risky; if Jimmy saw me, it would spoil my plan, but if I could get into town without anyone knowing about it, it would guarantee a successful escape.

I could hear Jimmy and Millie. They were both crying, and to my amazement, I was dry-eyed, but I felt every hair on my head, and my nostrils stung with fear.

Jimmy was saying, "What should I do? I've got'a deliver these eggs when I know she needs me now...and you do too."

"Go...and be careful. Stop your crying or you'll have an accident. Then where will we all be?"

I knew they were embracing, and in a moment the truck door slammed shut, and Jimmy was starting the engine. The ride to town happened in only an instant because my mind was dead.

I was jolted back to consciousness when Jimmy came to a sudden halt at Cathy's Diner for his first delivery stop. I was quickly over the tailgate, and across the street. Jimmy never looked my way as he disappeared into the diner before unloading. When he came out to unload the egg cartons, I was out of sight, hurrying to the bus station a short walk around the corner.

I checked the bus schedule and bought a ticket to Binghamton, the first bus north to a large city.

"Hurry lady. The bus is ready to pull out."

The door sucked closed behind me, and I made my way to an empty seat in the back of the bus. Suddenly I could breathe; I had pulled it off. It was a perfect get-away; better than ever I could have planned. No one had seen me. I had escaped! I had left everything behind as if I had just vanished into thin air. Was it a sign? I drew deeper into myself, and began to plot my next move.

I end my journal to await what the future holds for me.

Chapter 19

At work that day I was jittery; nerves on edge; had Rebecca started reading my journal? Was she reading it at that very moment? What would she think? Would her perception of Mary Louise change after seeing her through my eyes? I was terrified. She loved Mary Louise. What would she think of Clara; Clara who stole her name, and gave it to the baby she couldn't love? Would they now be two separate people? It was hard for me to see them as the same person. Had I made an unkind mistake by sharing my story with her? Could my need for her to read my journal be vindictive? Not consciously, I was sure.

Dread overwhelmed me as I drove home from work. I opened the door and called out, "Hello, I'm home."

"Hello, Rachel, I'm out here."

Her answer came from the sunroom. She had read it! The sunroom was the place we migrated to for our serious talks. I took my time getting out of my jacket and hanging it up.

My story lay on the wicker coffee table in front of her. She motioned for me to sit down beside her. And as I did, she placed one hand on my journal, the other on my lifeless one that lay between us.

She squeezed it with reaffirming warmth. "Jo, I've read your journal. Thank you. Thank you from the bottom of my heart for sharing it with me. You've given me a piece of yourself that I'll always treasure. In sharing it with me, especially knowing my relationship with

Mary Louise, I think you've taken possession of your own story for yourself. You've written so candidly...with depth of feeling and accuracy."

I fought to hold back my tears as my arms went around her; my tension dissolved, and tears finally brimmed over. "I was so afraid. Your opinion and acceptance mean so much to me."

"You have both a hundredfold. How lucky I am to know you."

"I'm the lucky one. And it's because of Ma that I've found you."

"And thank you for bringing her back to me. I love Mary Louise as if she were my daughter."

I had to ask, "Do you love Clara too?"

"They're the same person...just as Rachel, Josephine and Yo are the same person. Life has beaten you both up pretty badly, but miraculously, you've both managed to survive...though painfully, and both of you have managed to live useful rewarding good lives...and with much happiness too. Your awareness of life's wonder...your quest for its meaning, is evident all through your journal. You've hung onto beauty with great tenacity, and you managed to do it without Mary Louise's motherly support...yes, she gave all she had to give...and yes, you've had some very wonderful substitute mothers along the way. You're a very strong person...but I asked myself over and over, how did you ever survive Porter?"

"I'm not sure I have. It hasn't been long enough to know the depth of the scars and how I'll deal with them."

***

I gave Hilda the go-ahead to arrange to introduce me to Attorney Abner Baruch, as Rev. Grey had suggested. On the day of my appointment, there were butterflies in my stomach and I was unsure of myself. I had only to close my eyes and Porter's letter replayed in my mind:

You must come home and repent and accept Jesus as your savior, at once. People here are very attached to you and will forgive you anything if you are contrite and pray for their forgiveness for the wrong you thrust upon them. That is to say nothing about the wrong you visited upon me. How could you run out on your daughter's funeral, leaving me to grieve alone and tend to all the formalities? How could you put us all through thinking you had taken your own life?

That echo strengthened my determination to free myself from him. I wished I had never met him, never married him. Life would have been much easier. But, Forrest was right when in his letter he said he was sure I could never envision my life without Carrie having been part of it.

When we arrived at Attorney Baruch's office, his greeting was that of a relaxed friend. "Good to see you, Hilda."

He was a tall angular man, quite handsome with laughing brown eyes and heavy black eyebrows.

She responded in similar manner. "Hello, Abe. Is Martha feeling better? She thought she might be getting the summer sniffles at our bridge luncheon."

"Just her allergies flaring up. Thanks for asking."

"I want you to meet my new friend Rachel Rubin. Rachel, my good friend Atty. Abner Baruch."

He saw my puzzled look. "With a name like Abner Baruch my classmates started calling me A.B. Then when I decided on the law, and with my looks, it became Abe after super lawyer Abe Lincoln…What can I do for you, Rachel?"

I couldn't help but smile. He had already put me at ease. "Hello, Mr. Baruch. I want to dissolve my marriage."

Hilda said, "Rachel, I'll be in the waiting room."

The door closed behind her, and Mr. Baruch motioned me to a chair, then took his place behind the largest desk I had ever seen. He said, "Rachel, start wherever you're comfortable."

"Do you know anything about me, Mr. Baruch?"

"Only that you're a friend of Hilda's and in need of my help."

After hearing my story Atty. Baruch shook his head in disbelief. "This is an age old story with a twist I've never heard before. Clearly you were too young to understand what was going on. You have a perfect case of a marriage contract that's fraudulent. Annulment's the way to go. Rev. Kent clearly married you with ulterior motives. You understood you were to be a singing partner, housekeeper and probably someone to tend to his social obligations. Though it appears he didn't make that clear either. The marriage was basically for financial gain only. It's a case of his refusal to abide by a premarital understanding."

I left his office assured that my nightmare would soon be over. How light and easy it was to breathe, what wonderful relief!

A broad smile spread across Hilda's face. "I can tell things went well."

From his office door, Atty. Baruch said, "Very well, I think we can settle this quickly."

I said, "Thank you again, Mr. Baruch."

"You're welcome, Josephine. I'd like to see you use your real name soon. You have nothing to fear from Rev. Kent. I'll arrange to have a restraining order served immediately."

"I will as soon as I can figure out how to take care of changing my name at work."

Atty. Baruch said, "I can take care of that for you, if you wish."

"I'm to be transferred to a day shift July first. Maybe you could arrange it so I start my new shift as Josephine, I guess Kent, until the annulment's final."

"Done."

"Thank you, thank you…and to you too, Hilda. When you recognized me, I was ready to run again, and here you are the key to my freedom."

***

Hilda and I walked around to the back of Rebecca's house and came in through the slider-door into the sunroom. Rebecca was waiting with lemonade ready for us as we entered.

"I timed you and got it just right," she said. "Sit down and help yourself to a cool drink, and tell me all about it."

I was so excited that before I took my first swallow, I blurted out, "Hooray, it's going to be over soon. Atty. Baruch says I have grounds for an annulment, and he's going to put a restraining order on Porter. You can start calling me Josephine or Jo…soon as I drink my lemonade, I'm going to call Rev. Grey."

Rebecca clapped her hands. "I knew it, I just knew it. That's so great, Josephine…Jo. I think I'll call you Jo."

Before we had finished our drinks, the phone rang, and Rebecca hurried inside to answer it. When she returned her face was full of concern.

"It's for you, Jo. It's Rev. Grey with some distressing news. Aunt Alma has died of a stroke."

"Oh, my goodness…what will Ma do?" I rushed in to the phone, my mind spinning. "Hello, Rev. Grey."

"Hello, Rachel. I hate to be the bearer of bad news on top of everything that's happened to you."

"Rebecca told me; is Ma all right?"

"Yes, she was calm. Mark was with her."

"What happened? Was Aunt Alma ill?"

"She'd been talking to her lawyer on the phone and as she hung up the receiver, she collapsed on the floor in what turned out to be a massive stroke. She never regained conscious."

"How sad. I think you know she wasn't one of my favorite people, but she meant well. Ma must be very upset. What should I do?"

"I told Clara, I'd call you and explain. Alma's lawyer needs to get in contact with you immediately. Something to do with, of all things, Carrie's will."

"That's strange, don't you think? She's been gone so long. And what could it have to do with me? Life is sure hard to figure out. Would you believe, I was about to call you? My attorney is arranging to put a restraining order on Porter. Our marriage is going to be annulled soon so there's no need for me to hide anymore. My mail can come directly to me now, and you can call me Josephine again."

"That's wonderful news. Josephine sounds very nice. Do you think you could handle the stress of going back to Phelpsburg? Or should I insist on being a buffer. That could be arranged."

"I think I can. When I left the lawyer's office this very morning, a terrible burden was lifted. I was about to call you to explain what had transpired. I think I should call Ma, don't you?"

"I was hoping you'd say that."

"You've been a lifesaver Rev. Grey. Not only for what you've done for me in this crisis, but for helping me through a difficult childhood. Whatever would I do without you? From the bottom of my heart, thank you…and another thank you for sending the letters. Except for

Porter's, they've been a great comfort, though I have to say, his letter made talking to Atty. Baruch much easier."

"I'm not surprised to hear that."

"Oh well, I don't think he's any idea how hurtful he is. In his world, he's right. After all…the Bible and his followers say so. My only word is…ouch!!!"

"I know…But words shouldn't be more important than people, or we risk being a tyrant. That's all I better say. Never doubt you're taking the right course of action."

"It's a comfort to hear you say that because I have to get away from Porter. And it's nice to be reassured by you that it's the right path to take. Daddy used to call the Methodist Church watered-down Christianity. That puzzled me because "watered down" meant Aunt Alma's way of making soup when I liked thick soup much better. Porter's thick soup religion's sure not for me! You just explained in one short sentence something I've struggled with for a long time: when words become more important than people, we become tyrants. In the end though, I realized Daddy wasn't a tyrant after all."

"No, he certainly wasn't."

"I'll call Ma and start making plans according to what she tells me."

"I'm quite sure you'll be traveling to Phelpsburg very soon, and it sounds to me as if you're going to handle it well. And, Josephine, if you need me for any reason, I'm just a phone call away. You're one of my most favorite people, and I'm honored that you chose me to lend a helping hand."

"If all ministers were like you, Rev. Grey, it would be a very different world."

"Thank you, but I'm sure that's not true. However, I echo you: it's reassuring to me to hear you say that. We need many different voices as we grow in our spiritual life. What I admire most about you, Josephine, is that you're a seeker. It's nice to use your rightful name."

"Nice to hear it too. Thank you for the precious gift of loving-care and friendship. I'll keep you informed."

"Goodbye, Josephine. You know you're always in my prayers."

"Yes I do. Goodbye, Rev. Grey."

I went back out to the sunroom and relayed Rev. Grey's news to Rebecca and Hilda who were eagerly waiting, and they were stunned by the suggested legal implications of Aunt Carrie's will.

Hilda said, "I think you're going to inherit some money."

My mouth fell open. "That couldn't be. Aunt Alma would never allow that."

Rebecca said, "Sounds fishy to me. You'd better call your mother right now, and if you really have to go, I'll drive you. You're not going alone. Anyway, I'm anxious to see Mary Louise."

Hilda added, "I should go too. I can help with the driving, and I want to see Mary Louise too."

I took a quick swallow of lemonade, and left them to hash that out as I went back inside to phone Ma.

The phone stopped ringing. "Clara's Candy and Bake Goods. What can I do for you?"

"Hello, Ma." I felt lightheaded.

"Josephine! Thank you for calling right away."

"How are you doing, Ma? I'm sorry about Aunt Alma. What's going on with the lawyer?"

"It's a real mess, but it's good to hear your voice. You've been through so much. I hate all this commotion."

"It's good to hear you too. What happened?"

"Well, knowing what I know now, looking back, Alma did act funny when she heard you had disappeared. Then when we got word from

Rev. Grey that you were alive, she immediately called her lawyer. I could see her getting more and more upset, and as she hung up, she just collapsed down on the floor. She's been in the hospital and in a coma. She died last night."

"How awful; what'll you do? I'm worried about you."

"No need to worry. I'll be OK. I'm worried about you. I can keep right on renting this apartment if I want to. The lawyer says you should come at once. I think it has to do with some mix-up about Carrie's will and I can't believe, your inheritance."

"I'm dumbfounded, Ma; what can it mean? Yes, I can come. I'm getting an annulment and I'll explain everything when I get there."

"Good. How far away are you?"

"Not that far. I'm in Bardo."

"Bardo! Of all places, why Bardo?"

"You know why, Ma. I've known since I was a little girl. I wasn't asleep that day when you and Rev. Grey were talking."

"Oh, Josephine, I'm sorry. How awful for you to find out so much when I'm sure you were too young to understand what it meant."

"That's behind us now. I've moved on, and so have you. I'm living with Rebecca Wallace now, and your telling Rev. Grey about living here and tasting the 'good life' was the beacon that saved my life. It's true; Rebecca does have the secret to the 'good life'. We can talk this all out when I get there. Rebecca and Hilda are driving me. Yes, I've met Hilda Burns too, and she's equally wonderful."

"I'm not sure I want to revisit my past. As you said, we've moved on. It's much better for me to let the past be."

"Sometimes we can't do that. They're so happy to know what happened to you, and are anxious to see you again."

"I don't know."

"I do. You'd be forever sorry if you don't see them. Besides, now they know where you are, you couldn't keep them away even if you tried. You'll be glad, Ma....for now, good bye."

"Well, I guess; we'll see. Goodbye, Josephine."

***

"You know, Josephine," Hilda said as the three of us sped along toward the place of my childhood, "I've been driving through Phelpsburg for many years and here Mary Louise was living close by up in the hills. I've stopped there for gas many times."

Her voice came to me through the fog of my musings: Weird...Aunt Alma dead...Aunt Carrie had no money to leave...she lived so poorly...what would it be like to have Ma in town...would it still feel like home? Would anyplace be home without my precious little Carrie? Time was supposed to make the hurt lessen and allow memories to become comforting. My new identity in a new world had allowed me the illusion that I had stepped into another separate world. After all, in my prior life, I had left Carrie's still warm body in the hospital. I hadn't witnessed her cold lifeless one lying in a coffin. In my separate world there were new, loving and understanding friends who had never known Carrie, had never been in her world. Now as I traveled toward the familiar, my arms ached for her cuddly little body that fit so perfectly in my arms. I could almost feel the softness of her little-girl fine curls against my cheek. All my maternal fires burned hot in an empty heart.

Rebecca turned around to me from where she sat beside Hilda, who was driving. "Take heart," she knew me so well. "We'll go directly to the motel and freshen up before we call Mary Louise to say we've arrived."

522

What a comforting thought. It would give me time to ease into my past life gradually. It would give me time to get ready to greet everyone, time for anticipation to germinate. I hadn't seen Matt and Mark since Daddy's funeral. Letters didn't let you see the maturing. Snapshots helped visualize the changes but nothing could inform except seeing their smiling faces, seeing their lips move in greeting, feeling the warmth of their hugs.

Hilda had taken over making all the arrangements for our trip which was a huge stress reliever. No questions, she just knew exactly what to do. Fortunately thoughtful Millie had collected all my personal affects from Porter when they thought I was dead, and as soon as she received word that I was alive, she boxed them up and sent them to Rev. Grey. The transition from a teenager back into an adult in her twenties was as simple as opening the box that had conveniently arrived just in time for this trip.

Enclosed was a smaller box labeled MEMENTOS OF CARRIE. For a moment, I had hesitated with dread before I eagerly opened the little box, knowing it would bring that painful world crashing into my safe haven. Enclosed were a few of Carrie's choice baby clothes. There were pictures Carrie had drawn that I had taped to the refrigerator: one of the chicks trailing behind a fluffy mother hen; a bonfire with Millie, Jimmy, Carrie and me gathered around it with our hotdogs on sticks; a picture of the little Jackson Junction Church she loved. Missing was the picture of Porter waving his arms as he stood behind the pulpit. Millie must have left that one for him. I unfolded the diagram Carrie had made of her little garden; and in an envelope Millie had enclosed copies of the snapshots she had taken all through Carrie's life.

After I had cried myself dry, I shared my treasures with Rebecca. We had poured over each item. She listened with eager interest to the ramblings of a heartbroken mother.

Softly, she said, "Thank you. What wonderful memories. Sharing them is healing because for a little while you're not quite so lonely…and how wonderful, now I can picture just how Carrie looked."

It was comforting to talk about Carrie. It did help. How thankful I was Ma had given me the Wallace name, and that it had led me to find Rebecca. Why hadn't Ma understood that Rebecca and John, and Hilda too, would have stood by her? She should never have run away. But Ma never had an Aunt Carrie to teach her to trust love. Would going back to my beginnings fuse all my worlds into one, one where I'd find peace?

***

At the motel I called Ma. "Why don't we meet at a restaurant for dinner?"

"Diner's nearly ready. In fact, Mark's setting the table right now. He's home from Cornell and's working at Phelpsburg Hospital again this summer."

It was hard to visualize playful charming Mark taking over the role of man-of-the-house. I felt a few trepidations thinking about that domestic scene in the formidable, now deceased, Aunt Alma's home.

Ma prevailed. "Dinner's at six, but why don't you give us some time to get acquainted and arrive fiveish?"

I needed a complete makeover. I shampooed-out the waves my braid had made in my hair, and there was enough curl left from my last perm for the ends of my hair to curl behind my shoulders. I pulled the front of my hair up loosely and secured it with an antique Art Nouveau silver comb Millie had given me. She had explained, "It was made for beautiful black hair like yours, not flyaway white hair like mine. I've always treasured it because Herbert gave it to me. Now it'll give me equal pleasure to know you have it. Someday you can give it to Carrie." With those thoughts I nearly burst into tears. It was gestures of love and acceptance like that that made her so dear to my heart.

I slipped into my basic navy dress with the V-neck, and I felt as though I had stepped through the mirror back into my true identity. That was the first time Rebecca and Hilda had ever seen me as Josephine Kent, a few months ago reluctant wife of a minister, star of a record company and mother of an adorable six-year-old.

They both drew in their breath in approval. Hilda said, "Where did little Rachel hide this amazing young woman, Jo?"

I quipped, "Soon to be Josephine Wallace again."

Rebecca said, "There's no one I'd rather share my name with."

That precipitated an affectionate hug. "Wasn't it prophetic of Ma to take your name?"

"Very, and I wish John and I had legally adopted Mary Louise. Surely that would have changed everything."

$$***$$

As we walked up to the apartment door, Rebecca and Hilda briefly joined hands, and with an uneasy laugh, chorused, "I'm a little nervous. How about you?"

Before we could knock, the door burst open. There stood Mark, smiling broadly, as surprised as we were. He was as tall as Daddy, dressed in pressed suntans and a bright blue polo shirt the color of his eyes. Despite his attempt to stick down his sun-bleached curls, they were springing up in a most handsome way. I was instantly in his arms, and he lifted me off the floor and swished me back and forth like a little girl.

"Yo, my wonderful big-little-bitty sister...it's extra wonderful to have you here."

"You're still a tease, Mark, but very reassuring." With that he kissed me on each cheek. "Put me down this minute! Let me introduce my new friends....This is Rebecca Wallace and Hilda Burns...My step-brother, Mark."

Wearing her apron, Ma hovered in the background. Self-consciously she intoned, "Come in Josephine. Come in Rebecca and Hilda.... I, I...don't know what to say."

Rebecca never hesitated. "I know what to say. I am so happy to see you again, Mary Louise. It's wonderful to know you're all right. Thank you for inviting us to dinner at this busy, and I'm sure, upsetting time."

Hilda added, "Hello, Mary Louise. Rebecca speaks for both of us."

Mark guided everyone into the living room as he explained, "I'm glad to meet you both. I confess I have a million questions, and for Ma. However, I was on my way out the door to drive up to the Stanleys' to pick up Matt. Sometimes I think he should'a been a farmer instead of a preacher. He spends every summer on the farm helping with the," he flounced his polo shirt in a mocked sweat, "disgustingly hot, dirty haying...couldn't catch me doing that. How about it, Yo, want'a ride along? Fill your lungs with that good old country air?"

I looked at Ma. She said, "Go Josephine. We'll have plenty of time to talk later. May and Fred are anxious to see you. I told them you were coming for Alma's funeral."

She was probably asking for privacy to hide the awkward moments about to happen. For an instant I weighed whether to stay. It would be nice to know what was about to happen, what was said, but that was not for me, the proverbial eavesdropper, to know. They needed that time alone to reconnect.

How could it be? Baby Mark was at the wheel of Ma's new Ford station wagon, Ma the now very successful business woman...time...time...fleeting time. There had been way too little of it for precious Carrie. My emotions vacillated between my flight response and the exciting butterfly feeling of going home.

Mark interrupted my trepidations. "I hear you're a nurse-aide...me too. Can you believe that?"

"I can...and I'll just bet the little old ladies love you."

"They're not all that keen about a young whippersnapper specimen of the opposite sex giving them a bath." He glanced at me sideways with his mischievous grin. "I just tell them I'm getting hands on experience! I have to have that before I put on my doctor's hat. Agreed?"

"Mark, you're too much. But you'll make a wonderful doctor."

"I'm sure going to give it my best effort... I did get to take care of Grandma. She just faded away."

"I'm sorry, Mark. I know you loved her... she was a good grandma."

"Too bad she couldn't have spread it around a little more."

"It's OK...it was long time ago. None of us can see our own faults. That's what I've decided."

"Maybe so, Yo, but I think Grandma's faults may have been a little more serious than that. I've talked to the lawyer...haven't told Ma, but I think Grandma tampered with your inheritance from Aunt Carrie...kept it away from you, and from Ma too...a little forewarning to get you prepared."

That was exactly what Hilda had hinted at. I couldn't believe it!

"Yo!" Mark laughed. "Close your mouth. That's good news. Not so good for Grandma's reputation, but hey, you could use a break about now...." We were turning into the Stanley's driveway. "I'll drop you here and drive on down to the tenant house and get Matt."

I slid over on the car seat and gave Mark a kiss on his handsome cheek. "Thanks, Mark. See you in a jiffy."

Mrs. Stanley was in the kitchen setting the table. Everything was exactly the same. It was as if no time had passed.

She dropped everything, and I was in her arms. "My dear, welcome home."

"Home feels very good, Mrs. Stanley." I could see by the number of plates on the table that she was expecting two more for supper.

Mr. Stanley came striding out to the kitchen, newspaper still in his hand. "May, no monopoly...my turn." And I passed into his arms, was given his unique bear-hug; then he thrust me away at arm's length. "Let me feast my eyes on you. I'm so darned happy you're here."

"Yes, Jo, and your room's lonely as all-get-out for you."

At that moment my peripheral vision told me there was a movement in the Boston rocker that always stood by the kitchen window. "Snooks! Oh, Snooks, you little sweetheart." I gathered her up in my arms, hugging her close as she tuned up her purring motor to high gear.

Mrs. Stanley's eyes watered. "She remembers you, Jo."

Mr. Stanley hugged us both. "Indeedy, she does. How could she forget one who loved her so well?"

My eyes filled with tears too. "You can't know how much it means to me to be standing in this kitchen where so many good memories were made."

Mrs. Stanley dried her eyes on the bottom of her apron. "Almost as much as having you here."

The door opened and a very grimy, sweaty Matt stood in the doorway. No longer was he the gawky student, but rather a sturdy

528

muscular man not at all the image of the minister he was soon to become. He looked to be a farmer through and through.

"Hello, favorite playmate, favorite sister of mine..." I quickly stepped toward him, and he held up his hands. "Whoa, hold the hugs, Yo. I'm too smelly."

"I don't care how smelly you are." I stood on tiptoe, reached my arms up and around his neck, and gave him a kiss on the cheek.

"Best kiss I've ever had....Hello Mr. and Mrs. Stanley. Sorry to hurry Yo away. Mark's in the car...says Ma's dinner'll spoil if we keep it waiting."

I turned and said, "Mr. and Mrs. Stanley, I'll see you tomorrow at the funeral."

Matt shifted his weigh restlessly. "Yes, Mr. and Mrs. Stanley, you know Ma's dinners, and you can see it's going to take a little doing to make me presentable. Forrest and Jeffy'll be up soon as they get cleaned-up."

I noted who the two extra place-settings were for.

Matt insisted on riding in the back seat. "Yes, please do, Bro, and kindly open the window." Mark held his nose, joking as always, but Matt did roll his window down.

I turned around to Matt. "Where's Linda? Shouldn't she be taking the load off Mrs. Stanley?"

"She's in New York. Spends a lot of time there...she's the buyer now. Forrest said she'd be home in time for the funeral. I don't know about those two."

"How is Mrs. Stanley?"

"She seems to have gotten a second wind, wouldn't you say, Mark?"

Mark grinned at me sideways. "We all have since we know you're OK...kind 'a puts things in perspective."

Matt finished with, "Oddly, having Forrest and Jeffy around more seems to help. Mrs. Stanley likes a full nest...especially when it's a tranquil one."

Caution, I had best not quiz or try to read between those lines!

***

There was a different, more relaxed, atmosphere when the three of us walked into the apartment. Ma overlooked the fact that Mark had already met Rebecca and Hilda. Putting her hand on Rebecca's arm, calmly said, "Boys, this is Rebecca Wallace. I knew her many years ago when I was in high school. She and her husband graciously shared their home with me, and when I ran away, I stole her name and gave it to Josephine." She paused and taking Hilda's hand, said: "And this is Hilda Burns. I was working for her right after high school...My two step-sons, Matt and Mark...I know you two have a ton of questions, but please, not now." She stepped forward to me and actually put her arm around me as she continued. "Josephine, I'm so thankful you knew where to find hope and protection...had I been as wise...but that's in the past. I'm just so grateful you've brought them both back to me."

As the apartment exploded in a frenzy of greetings and exchanges, Matt excused himself. "Got'a make myself fit for polite company."

Ma held up her hands. "Hurry along. It's almost time to serve it up."

Before we knew it, each of us was carrying a serving bowl filled with Ma's bountiful feast as we gathered around the table. Menu: chicken with Ma's own special barbeque sauce; potato salad; baked beans from scratch and only as Ma could do them; buttered baby beets, beet greens, carrot salad, several different home made pickles, plus home made rolls and cake.

I couldn't stop the flashback of us all gathered around the Stanley holiday dinner table: the laughter, solemn Daddy, complaining Aunt Alma corralling Matt and Mark, Ma and Mrs. Stanley bustling to and fro, Luke teasing Abbey about her painted nails, and Forrest, stubborn cowlick sticking up, catching my eye and winking at me. I felt a heart stab; if only Carrie, but I must not spoil this reunion thinking about the impossible.

In the middle of our dinner conversation Ma said, "Josephine, why don't you move your things into Alma's room? Then you'll get a chance to visit with your brothers."

Ma had actually invited me to stay! She had put me in the same sibling category with Matt and Mark!

Rebecca sat beside me and putting her hand on my arm gently squeezed it. "Why don't you, Jo? Hilda and I'll bring your things over. It's been such a long time since the three of you've had a chance to catch up with each other."

Matt and Mark both gave a cheer. "It's past time, Yo."

It took only a second for me to say, "OK, Ma, I will."

All around me the conversation flowed with solicitous attempts to talk about everything except what was in Aunt Carrie's will? What did Aunt Alma have to do with it? Her viewing was scheduled for that evening from seven until nine, and her funeral service tomorrow. How could I go when I had been absent from my precious Carrie's? Sadness overwhelmed me.

I had to say something or burst into tears. "Listen, everyone. I hate to interrupt but…the viewing tonight is more than I can handle today. I'm fine…but I'm just emotionally done-up tonight…Ma, you, Matt and Mark go on over to the funeral home and let Rebecca, Hilda and me clean-up the kitchen and dishes. Then we'll go on over to the motel and get my suitcase."

Matt spoke up. "Sounds like a good plan to me. This funeral must be extremely difficult for Yo with Carrie's death so recent. You're a trooper, to be here, Yo. We're all aware of what you must be going through, and we're going to play by your rules."

Bless Matt's heart for his wisdom and courage in bravely bringing my feelings out into the open where I could deal with them. "Thanks, Matt. Ma sure did a fabulous job picking brothers for me."

Mark the joker, lightening the mood, tapped Matt's shoulder with a mock blow. "She said BROTHERS...don't go getting a big head."

Matt took the cue. "Yeah, little brother, but she was my playmate when you were running around in diapers."

"But I was so cute and adorable."

Ma said, "Anyone for a slice of rainbow cake?"

We three looked at each other, "Rainbow cake! Yumm."

To Rebecca and Hilda I explained, "Ma layers three different fruits, corresponding Jell-o sprinkled over cubed angel food cake and vanilla ice cream...freezes it and serves it with fresh strawberries and whipped cream on top. It's an irresistible dream."

***

I forced myself to hide the dread I felt as I walked into the funeral home the following day for the customary viewing hour that preceded the funeral service. I couldn't help wondering how Porter had been able to survive Carrie's funeral. Contemplating that scene nearly me sent into a tailspin, and I closed my eyes in an attempt to shut out my thoughts. Every fiber of my being wanted to flee again. I could never have stood beside Carrie's casket next to Porter as he uttered his scripted phrases all aimed at my unrepentant heart.

I found a chair in an out-of-the-way place where hopefully only a few would spot me. Not to be, surprisingly, many of the folks from Tate Town came. They were so happy to see that I had recovered enough to come to my grandmother's funeral. Yes, she was technically my step-grandmother. To me she had always been Aunt Alma. To think of her as grandmother made me feel a little less strange at being present, though I felt my only purpose was to offer support to Ma, Matt and Mark. My well-wishers were also oh-so-sorry about Carrie's death. They understood my devastation. Could anyone? They hoped it wouldn't be long before I'd be back making more wonderful records, and they marveled at my exceptional talent.

Matt had a concerned look on his face every time he glanced my way. In his suit, he looked the part of the consoling pastor. Very soon he would be the minister officiating at funerals. Mark was ever at ease and could easily maneuver through any situation. Now and then he gave me a wink. Ma was the proper retiring daughter-in-law. I thought about Daddy, and I'm sure she did too.

Luke and his new wife slipped in without fanfare. I had forgotten he'd be there, but I should have been prepared, because of course, he had been Aunt Alma's favorite. She had stood by him when he left home. A couple of weeks ago Matt had written to tell me Luke was married to the daughter of the owner of the Morrison GM dealership where he was now assistant manager. She looked wholesome, the very opposite of Linda, fresh scrubbed and hardly old enough to be dating. It was obvious she worshipped the ground Luke walked on and was glued to his side. He was dressed and looked the part of the typical successful business tycoon. His boyish charm had tuned into mature polish, and if anything, he was even more handsome. I would like to have disappeared because I knew eventually he'd find his way over to me.

"Why, Yo, woman with the voice of an angel. I have your records. Who'd ever have thought it?" Luke paused for a moment. "My heartfelt sympathy on your daughter's death. I remember how you loved Mark when he was a baby."

"Hello, Luke. Thank you. Accept mine for Aunt Alma's death. You were her favorite."

"I married this summer. Meet my wife, Cindy. Cindy, my step-sister, little Yoyo Jo."

"Hello, Cindy."

Unexpectedly, he leaned down to my face. "I'll see you at the lawyer's tomorrow. We'll see about you."

Unexpectedly pity welled up in my heart for Cindy. She stood there looking so innocent, so in love and so unaware. I was a vulnerable child again, and my old hatred for Luke made my eyes sting and I mumbled, "Yes, Luke, see you tomorrow," then, bravely added, "yes, we'll see."

At that moment Matt appeared beside Luke. "Rev. Wayland's looking for you."

"Thanks, Matt." And without another word to me, he took Cindy's arm and walked away wearing the persona of conquering warrior.

Matt sat down and took my hand. "You OK, Yo?"

"Yeah, Matt, thanks."

When I looked up, Forrest, Linda and Jeffy had just walked in, and Jeffy came running over as Matt left me to greet them.

"Hello, Aunt Yo. Jeepers, it's good to see ya. Are you gonna come home and live with Grandma and Grandpa? It'd make'um awful happy. Me too."

"Bless your heart, Jeffy. I'm afraid not. I've a job I have to go back to, but I'd love living next door to you."

As Jeffy talked on about the farm and how much hay they had gotten in, my eyes followed Linda. She was sensational. She was poised as if she had gone to finishing school. Her high heels accented her beautiful legs, and her expensive clothes fit her perfect body perfectly. Her hair was no longer the wild mane of a sun goddess but was carefully styled in a French twist, accenting her green eyes and movie star features. She had Luke's full attention and his eyes never left her as she moved about the room. I could see Cindy tighten her grip on his arm.

Once Forrest had greeted Ma, he came directly over to me, and taking both my hands, "Hello, Yo. I can't tell you how good it is to see you. I hope we get a chance to talk."

"Me to. Thanks for your letter…it meant a lot. Jeffy's been keeping me good company, updating me on farm news."

"Good for you, son."

Luke managed to free himself from clinging Cindy and made his way over to us. He didn't want his young innocent wife, daughter of his boss and owner of the GM dealership, to witness this first meeting with his nine year old son.

Jeffy was all smiles with his hand extended. "Hello, Luke, I'm Jeffy."

Luke never changed expressions. "Hello, Jeffy. So this is your son, Forrest."

A look of hurt and disbelief passed over Jeffy's face. But without blinking, straightening his shoulders, confirmed, "Yes, Forrest's my dad." Love shone, replacing hurt. "Aren't you, Forrest?"

"You betcha. As your grandpa would say, indeedy; I am, Jeffy."

Without a moment's hesitation, Jeffy surprised us by declaring, "And he's the best dad in the whole world even though he's not my blood dad. I don't think I like you much, Luke."

If Luke felt anything he didn't show it. "Well, it's a good thing you don't know me then, isn't it?" He never gave Jeffy a chance to answer, turned and walked away. The only indication that the encounter had affected him in any way was his abrupt withdrawal. If Jeffy was hurt he didn't show it.

Forrest said, "Come-on, Jeffy, Grandma and Grandpa just came in. Let's go say hello to them." And to me he added, "Some things are beyond understanding." Then placing his hand on Jeffy's shoulder, they made their way across the room with Jeffy looking up intent on Forrest's every word.

Breaking free, Jeffy ran to Mrs. Stanley, gave her a big hug, then turned to Mr. Stanley who gave him a hearty handshake, and taking each of them by the hand, he led them over to Ma. Luke had watched that display with intent, very intent interest. I hoped he felt the outsider he was, something he was not used to. In years past he would have been controlling this whole affair. He quickly recovered, put a confident smile on his face and turned toward Linda, who was completely unaware of him.

She kept glancing my way, and summoning her courage, walked over to me. "Hello, Jo."

Luke walked away as if he hadn't intended to speak to her at all.

My antennas went up, Jo, and not Yo! "Hello, Linda."

"Could we talk? The owner of the funeral home has graciously given me permission to use his office. Would you kindly come with me?"

"Well…yes…of course." There was a knot in the pit of my stomach. I couldn't help but distrust her motives.

536

We entered the office and each of us took one of the conference chairs in front of the desk.

"Jean Overton, the proprietor's wife…I buy her clothes…she's very nice and we've become friends…she said I could use her husband's office. I wanted a chance to tell you how terribly sorry I am about Carrie's death."

"Thank you, Linda. It's been a struggle to hold it together, but I've had some good help along the way."

"I remember how much you loved Jeffy and Louisa May. I want to tell you how I envied you. I'll never be the maternal type, but I do want you to know I've at long last managed to have a somewhat better relationship with Jeffy. I do understand what a special boy he is…due to Forrest and all the Stanleys…you too in those early days."

"I'm glad, Linda." Could this be what it was all about? They were now a happy little family. For Jeffy's and Forrest's sake, I hoped so.

She continued what turned out to be a long story: "I haven't said anything to Forrest yet, but as soon as this funeral is behind us, I'm going to ask him for a divorce. We should never have married in the first place. We both knew that early on. It's taken a long time, but Forrest and I have become good friends… after we stopped trying to be lovers. I can never thank him enough for what he's done for Jeffy, and what I've learned from him about life and love." She stopped a moment to collect her thoughts before going on. She certainly had my attention, and I sat calmly waiting. "Forrest won't be surprised…probably relieved. I'll always want to be involved in Jeffy's life, but I want him to remain with Forrest. He wouldn't be happy with me, and I'm sure Forrest would fight me and win custody. I've finally discovered where I belong, and it never would have been with Luke. Strange as that seems. I don't think he can ever love anyone but himself. Hopefully, I've been able to outgrow that teenage mentality.

Yes, I realize I was just like him, probably always would have been if it hadn't been for Forrest."

She stopped again and I volunteered, "Maybe things could work out. Are you sure? I know Forrest loves you."

"He only thought he did. It wasn't long and he realized he'd made a terrible mistake. What about you, Jo? Are you going on with your singing career?"

"No. It was just something I had to do…would you believe we have something in common? My marriage was an even bigger mistake and is about to be annulled."

"Really? I am surprised, yet I'm not. I wish I could take back what I did to you when we were teenagers. I knew how you felt about Forrest. Maybe if I hadn't selfishly used everyone for my own purpose things would have worked out for you and Forrest. In those days, as you know all too well, Luke decided who was 'in' and who was 'out' and set the standard for everything. Forrest had a will of his own, even though he was tied to Luke just like the rest of us, maybe more so. The only way I could win Luke was to make Forrest want me; because, I don't know if you realize it but, Luke was jealous of Forrest, and to win Luke was everything to me…enough that I tricked Forrest into rescuing me. I didn't care…Forrest was fulfilling his fantasy…both of us excusing ourselves thinking Luke would change. Maybe Forrest even secretly hoped I'd fall for him and not want Luke. When he came home from the service and Luke wanted no part of me or Jeffy, it didn't take Forrest long to find out that I wasn't the person he thought I was…that he could never love me. Anyone else would have thrown me out."

"We sure messed up our lives didn't we? This is almost too much for me to take in. What are your plans?"

"Well, I'm really good at what I do, and I've a job offer in New York. Jo, I can't begin to tell you how great it is to finally find my niche…to be happy. I've made so many people miserable along the way. At last, I hope to clear some of that up. When we all thought you had taken your life, I felt partially to blame. That's why I wanted you to know my plans before you made plans for the rest of your life. Everyone loves and misses you so much. I hope you'll move back here."

"I don't know what to say, Linda. Thank you for telling me all this…I'm still trying to recover from Carrie's death, and this is a lot to digest. For the moment I have commitments in Bardo."

"I'm so hoping you and Forrest can get together."

There it was, put into words. Now that it was, I didn't know how to feel about it because it had been forbidden territory for so long. "So much has happened. We're different people now. Just as you said, that was teenage mentality. But I'm sure we'll always be friends. It probably wouldn't have worked out even if you hadn't been in the picture. I do hope you're right about Forrest and that he's not going to be thrown for a loop by all of this."

"Believe me, everyone's happier now that I'm not around that much, and when I am, I'm a different person, one they'll be glad to accept as a visitor and mother to Jeffy. That's about the way it is now."

I looked at her, sitting there so beautiful and poised. She could have been a movie star playing a part, but somehow I thought she was sincere, and I wished her good luck in her new life. I didn't allow myself to think about Forrest or her wishes for the two of us. I had to concentrate on getting through Aunt Alma's funeral. And there was the lawyer and Luke to face tomorrow.

When we rejoined those gathering for the funeral service, Rebecca and Hilda had arrived. Rebecca took my hand and I knew with them beside me I'd be able to face the service that was about to begin.

Chapter 20

I awoke early next morning in a cold sweat. Luke had implied a fight when he spoke to me at the funeral home, "We'll see about you." Shake it off; yes, we would see. Everyone was still sleeping because the only sounds were street noises and the robin's melodious greeting to a new day. What irony, waking up in Aunt Alma's room! It didn't feel like home, Ma in Phelpsburg and not on the Stanley farm, and it was strange to have Daddy gone. This was the first time I had slept in Ma's house with Matt and Mark in the next room since I was little girl. I'm sure part of the strangeness was having Matt and Mark grown men, but it was special knowing the three of us were under the same roof, and at Ma's invitation.

For breakfast, we met Rebecca and Hilda at a little restaurant not far from the Sweet Shop. It could have been yesterday that I studied the street from the upstairs apartment window except the sign no longer read THE SWEET SHOP but rather GRANNY'S ATTIC GOODIES.

As we were finishing blueberry pancakes that tasted almost as good as Ma's, Rebecca announced, "Hilda and I have decided to take a walking tour of Phelpsburg while the rest of you are at the lawyer's. We'll see you back at the motel."

Attorney Ferguson's office was off Main Street in the first block on Park in an old house that had been converted into offices. Luke had already arrived and was waiting for us in his new Cadillac. Matt put his arm around me. "Don't let Luke scare you. If I don't miss my bet, he's going to be very unhappy when this meeting's over. I'm right here beside you. Mark and I are with you all the way."

"You bet your boots, Yo." And Mark put his arm around me too.

Attorney Ferguson was short, a little on the stout side, making ample space to display the heavy gold watch-chain that draped across his tweed vest. Introductions were made, and we all sat down around a polished mahogany conference table that looked out of place in the shabby room.

Attorney Ferguson put on his glasses and looking over the top of them, directed his vision around the table at each of us. "Let me begin by reading Carrie Elizabeth Crane's handwritten will: *January 20, 1932. I, Carrie Elizabeth Crane, am of sound mind, owner of the property known as THE SWEET SHOP at 95 Main Street, Phelpsburg, New York in the county of Steuben. This will revokes all previous wills. My first directive is for the prompt payment of my burial expenses, debts and taxes due to be paid. My sister, Alma Jane Osborn is the named beneficiary of my term life insurance policy of $50,000.00 (fifty thousand dollars). Upon my death, two-thirds of the proceeds from the property at 95 Main Street in Phelpsburg are to be paid to Clara Louise Wallace so she can make a proper home for her daughter Josephine Louise Wallace out of the downtown area. When Josephine has finished high school, Clara Louise Wallace is to inherit the property at 95 Main Street in Phelpsburg. All my remaining assets (savings accounts, stocks and bonds) are to be inherited by Josephine Louise Wallace when she is ready to go to college or at the age of twenty one. Should my sister Alma Osborn precede me in death my term life insurance policy is to be divided equally between my nephews: Luke and Mathew Osborn (and* *any future nephews or nieces.) I designate Attorney Ferguson SR. my executor. This will is dully notarized and legal*

Luke began to speak, but Attorney Ferguson held up his hand. "There is more. Miss Crane encloses a notarized statement: *To whomever it may be of interest. My sister, Alma Osborn, has been informed of my wishes. She understands my desire is to not only look after her, but to do the same for Josephine Wallace, who I have come to love as if she were my own child. Josephine's mother, Clara Wallace, has worked for me without wages. My will settles that debt to her.*"

Attorney Ferguson heaved a big regretful sigh before continuing. "There is no question, Mrs. Osborn knew her sister's wishes and deliberately chose to ignore them. Let me make a few observations and apologies. This will was buried in my father's files until Mrs. Osborn came to my office and informed me of Mrs. Kent's suicide, asking for my advice. It took me several days to locate the will and consequently discovered how Clara and Josephine have been cheated. Before I could contact Mrs. Osborn, I was in a dilemma as to how I should handle this most unusual situation, Mrs. Osborn called in quite a state of agitation with the news that Josephine had resurfaced. You all know what happened. I most humbly apologize for my ineptness for not having gone more thoroughly through my father's papers. And, I apologize for my father letting his friendship with his client, Alma Osborn, interfere with what he had to have known were Miss Crane's wishes. There is no excuse for the wrong that has been done to you, Josephine Kent, and to you, Clara Osborn."

Luke could not hold his anger any longer. "I plan to contest this will on a couple of grounds. Blood relatives should override the wishes of a demented old lady and the fact that the so named Clara Wallace is a fictitious person...."

Attorney Ferguson became red in the face as he thumped the flat of his hand down on the table. "Enough, sir. These two women can sue the estate for damages, if they so desire, and you better pray they don't."

Matt and Mark spoke up saying they were completely in accord with their Aunt Carrie's wishes.

Attorney Ferguson continued. "Thank you Matthew and Mark. And staring wide-eyed at Luke, continued, "As for you, Luke Osborn, you should be pleading with these two ladies not to sue the estate for damages, as should I. After Carrie Crane's death, Alma Osborn opened a savings account with the $50,000 term life insurance policy she inherited, and over the intervening years it has accrued a good deal of interest. Obviously even though Alma Osborn was well provided for, she still chose to live on money that should have gone to Clara Osborn and Josephine Kent." Attorney Ferguson paused again, and Luke was steaming but silent.

All eyes turned to Ma and me. Together we quickly confirmed: "We have no wish to sue anyone."

Attorney Ferguson stared over his glasses. "That's as I expected." He turned his gaze to look directly at Luke. "You grandsons can be very thankful for that," and to everyone, "Alma left no will. By law her estate is to be divided among you grandsons: Luke, Matthew and Mark Osborn. All expenses, including mine, will be taken from Alma's estate," turning his glare back to look directly at Luke, "have I made myself clear? Now to the dollar amount of Miss Crane's other assets: She obviously was a very astute investor, because added up, as nearly as we can figure, her combined assets are in the neighborhood of $800,000 dollars."

I was flabbergasted!

As he stood up, dismissing us, he asked, "Mrs. Kent, would it be possible for you to remain in town for a few more days? I'd like to expedite the settling of Carrie Crane's estate to help alleviate my conscience in regard to my responsibility, and my father's, for allowing this injustice to occur to both you and your mother."

***

Back at the motel we were bubbling over with our good news. Rebecca clasped my hands in hers. "Now you're really free, free to do whatever you wish. Are you going to go ahead with your plans to get your high school diploma? From there the sky's the limit."

Hilda said, "Mary Louise, no one deserves this piece of good luck more than you do. Now that you know about the car accident that happened not so very long after you left Bardo, an old chapter has closed. What a wonderful way to move on." And she pulled Ma into her arms.

When the good news had been chewed on and at least partially digested, Rebecca turned the conversation to their walking tour of Phelpsburg. "Mary Louise, your newly acquired property is in excellent repair."

"Yes, Alma was very fussy about that. I can't believe it wasn't hers."

"She thought it was, Ma. That's the whole point."

Hilda took her purchase from its wrapping. "What do you think of this beautiful antique box I found in GRANDMA'S ATTIC GOODIES?"

Rebecca offered, "I told her she should buy it. I've never seen more intricate wood inlay."

Ma surprised us with, "I remember dusting your beautiful collection."

Mark rolled his eyes, "Beautiful," and rubbing his stomach, "anyone for lunch?"

"Come on over to the apartment and I'll fix some sandwiches."

Hilda said, "Thanks. That's very tempting but I have appointments that can't wait. Rebecca and I have to leave this afternoon. How about we go back to the little restaurant where we had breakfast?"

My head swam with murky thoughts as the conversation flowed around me during our lunch. I had to put my emotions on autopilot. There were too many decisions, ramifications of all that was happening to me. Rebecca knew and leaned close as she very softly said, "Don't shut down, Jo. Meet life head on. You can do it. This is wonderful news. I'll take care of calling the Bardo Hospital for you as soon as we get home…one step at time."

Ma allowed herself to be hugged and kissed by both Rebecca and Hilda. When all the good-byes had been said, I closed the car door. "Call, see you soon."

***

Matt drove us back to the apartment. $800,000.00 mine! That was impossible to grasp. *Aunt Carrie, Aunt Carrie why did you live so poorly?* Get with it, Rebecca had said, "Meet life head on." How?

Ma unlocked the door to the apartment. Once inside, a clear thought finally surfaced, and I announced, "I'm going to pay for Matt's and Mark's college."

Ma stopped dead in her tracks. "No, you are not! That money is yours. The money they'll be getting from Alma'll be a big help. Matt's about to take on a church full time. Mark should want his education enough to help work for it. Both boys have had it pretty easy. It's time you did!"

Matt said, "Amen."

Mark said, "Well, I don't know about Amen but a big yea, go Yo, go get 'um."

I couldn't believe Ma! I burst into tears. I never thought I'd hear Ma stick up for me. I cried for Ma, and I cried for Aunt Carrie because she loved me so much. And every tear was in one way or another for my precious little Carrie.

Matt put his arm around me. "Don't cry, Yo. We all want you to have what's rightfully yours....I know...both Carries are gone and there'll always be tears for them."

How did he always know? What a wonderful brother, brothers. They were both so very special! And Ma! Was something new happening? I had to wonder. Still she was her practical self. She strode over and stuffed her purse into the closet, cleared her throat as if say, humph, enough of this talk, and ordered, "Mark, you better drive your brother back to the farm. It's a perfect haying day. They're short-handed."

"Better hurry up, buddy boy, I've got'a be at the hospital by three."

I was hoping Ma would suggest I ride along, but she didn't. Instead, she was setting the stage for the next scene because the kitchen screen-door had hardly banged shut behind Matt and Mark when she started what was to be one of the most important conversations of my life.

"You know, Josephine, seeing Rebecca and Hilda after all these years, seeing how much older they are, all the changes in them, yet still the very same caring people...from them I knew love for a short time...from them I got a glimpse of the good life...seeing them did something to me." Ma paused and fussed with the belt on her dress, giving herself time to summon up courage to go on. "As you know, Hilda also told me the story about...your father...the man responsible for ruining my dream world...it must have shocked you as much as it did me to learn his sad fate. When she told me...the monster...as I thought of him... became human like the rest of us... and a sense of futility...of waste...swept over me. Society had somehow wronged him too. How awful it must be, to be so warped. Seeing him as human doesn't make what he did any less hurtful or wrong, but I feel kind'a different...kind'a like I've hated a sick person...like I wasted my energy hating him when I should've been trying to heal the harm he did to me...like, maybe I should've faced what happened and not let him get away with it...if I had, he might've had a different fate." She heaved a sigh. "And I surely haven't been fair to you."

I was so choked up, I could hardly speak. "Oh, Ma, it's OK...you always made sure I was with someone who loved me." A million things swept through my mind in a split second: she had let Luke get away with what he did to me...if Daddy hadn't caught Luke in time with Ma...would she have let him get away with that...should I have run for help when Porter forced me...where could I have gone...would Millie have believed me...should I expose Porter now? Ma was waiting for me to continue. "Would you have told on Luke if Daddy and I hadn't come running in when we did?"

"You were there too! I didn't know that. It must have been terrible for you. Oh, Josephine, is there no end to what you have gone through?"

"When I was little, why did you let Luke get away with what he did to me that time when he caught me alone in the backroom at the Stanleys'? You know that's all a blank except for coming home and finding Luke in the kitchen, innocent as you please...and you making Luke apologize...washing me and putting me to bed."

"There is no good reason." Ma hung her head. "I was scared. Sometimes fear makes us cowards; sometimes it saves our lives. Even today, I'm not sure which it was, but I'm sorrier than sorry. In a way I'm glad you can't remember, though I'm not sure that's best."

"What is it they say…sins are visited to the seventh generation…I want it to stop with me…you and I have had enough." We were both pretty badly shaken up, and I trembled with emotion. "I'm letting Kent get away with it…he forced himself on me. Are Porter and Luke both sick too? Am I spending my time hating when I should be trying to think of a way to stop them…at least Porter…should I expose him? Would anyone believe a demented mother who ran away rather than face the death of her child? That's what they'd think."

"I don't know the answer…I suppose they are sick…in a way…"

"It's all right. I don't expect an answer. Maybe there's no answer."

We were both silent for some minutes as we tried to get our emotions back on track. Finally Ma said, "I don't see anything clearly, except, being in Rebecca's and Hilda's loving presence, no judging…and forgiving in a way that felt like there was nothing to forgive…seeing you through their eyes, made me realize how important you are to me, and how much I've missed by not being part of your life…"

"I'm overwhelmed, Ma…I don't…."

She plowed right ahead. "There's one more thing I want to say. When you were born, I named you Josephine for Jo in LITTLE WOMEN. I read LITTLE WOMEN when I was eleven, and I so wanted to be in a family like that. I spent hours imagining what it would be like. And I wanted to be the free spirited rebellious sister who loved the family so much she wanted to keep it together forever. Louise is after my middle name. I wanted you to have a name that was part of me. I gave you the Wallace's name because they were the best people I had ever known and for a brief time they had loved me freely."

I wanted to hug Ma but was unsure if it were now permissible. "I think, I'm going to cry again, and I don't want to. I've cried too many tears....Oh, Ma...."

"And there's more. Josephine, could you see yourself coming to live with me? You could get your high school diploma here."

Those were more words I thought I'd never hear, but as elated as I felt my emotional brakes go on. "I don't know. I've my job in the Bardo hospital. Rebecca's depending on me." Hesitantly, I continued, "I suppose I'd be a big help with your baking business."

"No, no, NO, Josephine, put that notion right out of your head...that your only worth is to serve. I'm so sorry I've made you feel that way. You have to start a new life. You have money now. You can do whatever you want with your life."

That was true. It hadn't really sunk in. Wasn't that what Rebecca tried to tell me? I could do whatever I set my heart on. Money sure complicated life. Questions welled up in my mind. Why do we think and do the things we do? Why did one person react one way and someone else another?

I blurted out, "Why in the world did you marry Daddy?"

"Can't you guess? The same reason you married Porter; because I thought I had no other choice."

"But I married Porter because I thought God was telling me that was what I should do."

"Why did you think that? Did God really tell you to?"

I was taken aback. In that instant I knew God never told me anything! "Not unless He's an awful dumb God."

"One of the most important lessons I've learned, is that choices are not what we think they are. Bring God into the decision-making and the decision gets reinforced with absolute authority."

"How do we make decisions? How did you dare marry Daddy, feeling about religion the way you do? And how did you manage to get along with him? I've wondered about that."

"I was lucky. Paul was an honest, decent man."

"And he did change, didn't he?"

"Not really all that much. He always was the same man, with the same basic beliefs. But he did approach his beliefs differently…I think with more insight…more compassion. I changed as much as he did. We're all changing little by little. Hopefully, I'll get a little better at directing that change."

"Did Daddy still think you were a heathen? His thinking you were lost was a big problem for me when I was little."

"I think he was able to stop judging. He accepted me as I am, saved or not…enough of this. Think about my offer. You could have Alma's room, or you could get an apartment of your own. When you're ready, you could even buy a house. You can get a car right away….you could come and go as you please. You've so many things to get used to. I've some things to get used to too…new feelings.…"

"We both need time."

"I wanted you to know how I feel."

"Thanks, Ma. I've got'a go back to Bardo on account of my annulment, and I need to be with Rebecca for a little awhile longer…then there's my job. But I'll definitely be thinking about what you've said. I'm so overwhelmed by it, I don't know what to say or think. I've wanted to hear those words for a long time."

***

As tempting as Ma's offer was it didn't feel right. For my peace of mind I had to come to grips with my annulment and inheritance before

I could make such a monumental decision that would affect the course my life would take. Rebecca called and told me the Bardo Hospital agreed to hold my nurse-aide position open for me if I could be back on the job Monday.

It was strange, but comforting, to be part of Ma's, Matt's and Mark's busy lives. It was a small taste of what life would be like if I decided to move back. Of course Matt would have the responsibilities of an ordained minister. Mark would be coming and going to college for a long time. But for this welcomed short time it felt good, healing, to be reconnecting with the family I had so longed to be a part of. Ma was still her busy brusque self, tending to her baking business efficiently. I was taken into the flow of daily life as if I had always been part of it. There were no gushing unnatural attempts to makeup for lost time, just acceptance in a way that made the transition into this new relationship possible.

I was swept along in a stampede. My brain was running full throttle to keep up. Attorney Ferguson kept his promise to expedite Aunt Carrie's will. I would be financially independent by Sunday when I had to leave Phelpsburg.

Attorney Baruch reported that the annulment was moving along nicely even though Porter was contesting it. Porter was worried about any claims I might make on the recording business. He was sure no one would willingly give up the stardom I had attained with the money it represented. I assured Attorney Baruch that I was not interested in the recording business or any of its assets past or present. I wanted no part of that life. Those phone conversations were long and detailed. Attorney Baruch instructed me to report any effort on Porter's part to contact me by phone, or letter. And he assured me that in the end Porter would co-operate when he realized what a scandal would do to his reputation.

It was Friday before I found the courage to call Millie. As the phone rang, I closed my eyes and felt the warmth of her friendly kitchen I knew so well. I could see her wiping her hands on her apron as she hurried to answer the phone. "Hello...hold on one second...." She was probably turning the stove off. "OK, I'm back."

Her voice sounded so close I should've been looking out the window at the mountain behind the church across the road from the parsonage.

"Hello, Millie, it's Jo."

"Of course it is. I'd know your sweet voice any day and it's so good to hear it."

"Oh, Millie, I've needed one of your hugs so many times these past months. But I'm OK...I've found the best place in the world to help me. I've so much to tell you. How's your schedule? Do you have time for a break?"

"Of course I do. Nothing's as important as talking to you."

"Better pull up a chair...because: this is going to take a while." I explained finding my way to Bardo, why I chose Bardo, the part Rebecca and Hilda played in Ma's life and now in mine. I told her about my work as a nurse-aide, about Hilda figuring out who I was.

"Jo, I'm so glad you ran away. I'm not going to burden you with all the commotion that took place around here...except to say it was pretty awful... Jimmy never lost faith that you were alive. He tried to keep my spirits up, but to be truthful I feared the worst even while I prayed Jimmy was right."

"How is Jimmy?"

"We're all good ever since Rev. Grey called and said you were with friends. He's doing marvels with the farm. Wait until he hears I've talked to you. Can I share your story with him?"

"Please do."

"Where do you go from here?"

"Oh, there's more to my story…Aunt Alma died…I'm calling from Phelpsburg." I loved telling her about my belated inheritance from Aunt Carrie.

"You're taking my breath away, Jo, how wonderful…just the good luck you need and deserve."

"Would you believe, Ma's had a change of heart. Seeing Rebecca and Hilda and hearing about what happened to my biological father has made her see things differently. She really wants me to come back here to live…with her! Or even in an apartment of my own. Can you imagine that?"

"Yes I can, and it's about time things turned around for you. Have you made up your mind?"

"Only that I'm going back to Bardo for a while. I've got'a take care of things there, and it'll give me time to figure out what's best."

"That's wise. I can't wait to tell Jimmy about your inheritance…and I can't believe how conniving Aunt Alma was to trick your mother the way she did…and stealing your money…and her, the pious one?"

Leave it to Millie. She had it all figured out. "She didn't spend it; she just kept it from us."

"Same thing."

"Mr. Stanley'd say, no sense cry'n over spilt milk."

"I'd say that too if I wasn't so peeved. She plotted to get you and your mother a home out of the apartment as your Aunt Carrie's will stipulated at the same time she solved the problem of her motherless grandchildren that she should'a been look'n after herself…to say nothing of the nerve to keep up her Sunday dinners. Unbelievable!" Leave it to Millie not to mince words! "Then when the time was drawing near to when you might go to college, another pitfall for her and your inheritance, she married you off to Rev. Kent."

554

"I don't think she had anything to do with that."

"I just bet she did. Remember, you told me...Rev. Fillmore and Rev. Kent... that they'd been to Alma's church first so she knew them...and I just bet when she thought about the two of you singing together she hatched a plan. And I remember Rev. Kent talking about it too. Remember he lived with me for a while."

"You're right. One time Porter told me in one of his tirades, that Aunt Alma had advised him I'd be a good match...that is, when he got me away from the Stanley's bad influence."

"See. I should 'a seen through him."

"I'll bet you're the only one, except Jimmy, who does yet."

"Well, I don't know. The Jackson Junction Church has completely separated from Good Shepherd and hired their assistant preacher, Rev. Vance, out from under them. Things aren't going so well with Good Shepherd. I'll betcha they wished they hadn't bought that big parsonage. Rev. Vance's wife's really nice and loves the way you fixed-up the parsonage. He's a little shy; a relief after Rev Kent. Erma's about the only one who's left our church. Two beans she never snags him. He's looking for another you."

"I doubt that. He was never happy with me. Erma's just what he needs. She was good to me."

"Yeah, so she could get around Rev. Kent! We all saw through that. Once you were gone nothing went right for him. And he saw how everyone loved you, and he began to act like a lovelorn puppy."

"That was for show...in his letter he sure wasn't lovesick! Oh, well...I don't wish him bad luck. Plenty of people love him."

"I think he found out too late that he did love you. And found out what he'd lost. Anyway, we can always hope he grows up!"

"I can't believe you said that."

"You've changed me, Jo! I'm not as easily fooled these days!"

From there our conversation turned to Jimmy's plans for the farm.

***

My bag was all packed to spend Saturday night with the Stanleys. "Ma, I don't feel right about this. I wish we were having dinner here like I wanted."

"Saturday's my busiest day."

"If I didn't have to stay all night."

"You know how disappointed May and Fred would be if you didn't spend the night."

"I know, I know. You're coming to the bus to see me off tomorrow?"

"Of course I am. This isn't good bye."

"This'll mean the Stanleys'll have to drive me to the bus station."

"They'd want'a be there anyway. I don't know why you're acting like this. You should be excited to sleep in your old room. I know you loved living with them."

"Yes, I really did. But…"

"I know, but we're gonna have plenty of time to get to know each other. I'm not even sure I know myself…..Here's Fred now…..Off with you."

I did a very bold thing, something I'd never done before; I kissed Ma on the cheek, and wonders, Ma kissed mine. I felt lightheaded. My world turned upside down. It was 1952; I was 23 years old and something monumental happened!

***

We buzzed up through those familiar awe-inspiring hills in the Stanley farm truck that rode more like a lumber wagon than the magic carpet I imagined that first time Ma and I rode in the crowded back seat of Daddy's car. I felt a quickening of my pulse, and my heart was jumping nearly up into my mouth. So much had happened since the last time I had slept upstairs in the Stanley farmhouse, soothed by the rhythmic chorus of night creatures, the best night creatures in the world; the best because they lived on the farm I loved so dearly. Tonight, just down the road in the tenant house, Forrest my hero, who filled the pages of my childhood fantasies would also be sleeping, perhaps not so peacefully, lulled by the same night chorus, sleeping beside a wife who was going to divorce him. But I no longer dwelled in a land of fantasies.

Mr. Stanley reached over and patted my knee. "I know, everything's too much the same when nothings the same."

"You could always say it in so few words. I'm glad you're the same. But…"

"But, this is a hurdle. Life on the farm has a way of remaining comfortingly the same underneath the turmoil we humans manage to stir up on top of it. We all love you, Jo, and you're as much a part of the farm as anyone of us. You'll see."

I was greeted with hugs and kisses, and was swept into the flurry of picnic preparations. Then suddenly, Jeffy burst through the back door hollering, "She's here, Forrest…," and turning to his mother, in a softer voice, "Good-bye, Linda. See you next Sunday."

I was surprised Jeffy called Linda by her given name, but I shouldn't have been.

Her reply was quick. "Come back here, young man. Give your mother a proper kiss."

He obeyed, pulling Linda's face down to his.

"That's better. Now, hold yourself in check, give Jo a little peace. Let everyone have a chance to have a piece of her...Hello, Jo. I'm off to New York on the commuter plane." She came over to me, and pressing her cheek to mine, whispered, "Don't forget what I told you."

Forrest came in behind her and gave me a quick hug. "I'll be back soon as I drop Linda at the airport....Mom, can the picnic hold for forty-five minutes?"

"Sure it can. Have a good week, Linda."

What'a relief, I'd have a few minutes to collect myself. Had Linda asked Forrest for the divorce? Did Jeffy know? Did Mr. and Mrs. Stanley know? I'd have to face Forrest not knowing the answer to all those questions.

Mrs. Stanley broke the spell. "Jo, the funniest thing happened this morning when I made your bed. Snooks followed me upstairs and is curled up on the foot of your bed. She hasn't slept up there in a long time. It's just as if she knows you'll be sleeping up there tonight."

Jeffy grabbed my hand. "Come on, Aunt Yo, let's go up and see her." He took my hand and pulled me along up the wonderful staircase with the railing I had wanted desperately to slide down that first day when Mrs. Stanley took me up to meet my littlest stepbrother, baby Mark. That was the beginning of a whole new life for me. Now I felt I was in a new struggle to hang on to the remnants of that life I had loved so much while at the same time I must embark on yet another.

"There she is, Aunt Yo, just like Grandma said."

Because Snooks was nearly deaf, she never moved until she felt the vibrations of the bed jiggling. She gave her half-purr, half-meow greeting, stood, arched her back and came directly over to me. Forgetting all about Jeffy, I gathered her up in my arms and crept upon the bed to curl up around her furry little body as I had done so many times in the past.

Jeffy leaned over the footboard of the bed looking at us. "Aunt Yo, I can hear Snooks purring way up here."

"Come on, Jeffy, you can curl up with us too. Your Grandma says Snooks loves you best of anyone when I'm not here."

"Yeah, she does, and I love her too. You know I have a new puppy, and I'm naming him Laddie after Forrest's dog that he had when he was my age."

So many pictures of Forrest with Laddie at his side filled my mind with longing for the innocence of those wonderful sunny summer days I thought would never end.

By the time Forrest came back from the airport we had the picnic table all set under the big old ash tree in the back yard. Forrest had told me when I was Jeffy's age, and was always following at his heels, that the old ash tree had been growing there ever since the land was cleared to make the farm. Now, Jeffy retold the story to me and Forrest ruffed his hair. "I think Yo's heard that story before."

"But it's a good story that should be told over and over," I flipped the last hamburger. "Someday, Jeffy, you'll be telling it to your children."

"Aw, I'm never gonna get married now that Carrie's gone."

There was a moment of startled silence, then Mr. Stanley said, "Chow's on. The burgers and hot dogs are ready."

At the end of the meal, as I was serving the strawberry shortcake, Forrest ventured, "Mom tells me you're going to finish high school. That's wonderful. You always were the smartest kid I ever knew."

"I'll bet. Remember, you were my reading tutor."

"That kind of smarts just takes some time and only counts when you're a kid. I've been thinking, with your talent and all that money, you should go to college and study music. You really do have a special gift to give to the world."

Mrs. Stanley agreed, "Yes, Jo. I never thought of that. You really should."

My answer was quick. "I don't think so. I don't want any part of that life."

Forrest was adamant. "You'll change your mind."

Mr. Stanley had the final word. "Jo has plenty of time to decide."

Jeffy piped up with, "This is boring. Come on, Aunt Yo. You haven't gone for a walk yet."

Forrest settled that. "Good idea, son. Go on, Yo, I'll help Mom with the clean up."

I got the message that Forrest didn't want to walk with me. This would have been our chance to talk. Mr. Stanley looked as if he wanted to say something, then thought better of it, stood up and started helping with the clean up. Jeffy took my hand and we were away over the lane.

The richness of my memories and the feel of my feet treading the familiar path, brought the farm's soil right up to surge and fuse with my blood. This farm was part of my soul; I did belong to the soil and always would. Mr. Stanley was a wise sage. How very much I loved him.

I was so caught up in my own thoughts it never occurred to me that Jeffy was unusually quiet until he began to unburden his heart. "Yo, Forrest would'a come but he has a lot on his mind. He and Linda are gonna get unmarried."

"I see. How do you feel about that?"

"Well, Forrest says he'll still be my dad. I was worried but...Linda says she wants me to stay on the farm with Forrest."

"I'm glad of that."

"Me too. Linda says she'll still come and see me, and...if ever I want to, I can come to New York and she'll show me the sights. I don't think I'll ever want'a do that. But Forrest says you never know, maybe I'll wanna some time."

I kept quiet waiting for Jeffy to continue. To my relief, he didn't seem all that upset about the divorce. But he was too quiet. Finally, after a long puzzled silence he said, "You know, Aunt Yo, if you weren't still married you could come and be my ma. Forrest's not my real dad; Luke is and I've only seen him once, and I don't even like him. I do like Linda better than I used to, and I'll still see her, but I'd like a real ma, not a blood mother, to match Forrest. Do you suppose Forrest'll marry again? That's what I worry about. Suppose she doesn't like me."

"Jeffy, I can't imagine anyone not liking and loving you."

"Luke doesn't and Linda didn't used to."

"Well, I'm sure Forrest would never marry anyone who didn't like you."

"He married Linda."

"But that was very different. He married Linda before you were born." That was too complicated to explain. "Look at how much you and Forrest love each other. I think you can trust Forrest to always do what's best for you."

"Yeah, and I love him too."

"What'a you say, we go check the apple crop, then head on back?"

One of my questions was answered, and I gambled that by the time Jeffy and I got back to the house Mr. and Mrs. Stanley would know all about Forrest's pending divorce. I was glad Jeffy didn't know about my annulment, and I was equally troubled that Forrest and Mr. and Mrs. Stanley did know. That probably explained why Forrest didn't want to go walking with me. It was making my stay awkward.

However, it turned out not to be awkward in the least. Forrest had the monopoly game all set up in the middle of the living room floor when Jeffy and I walked in. Mr. Stanley put the evening paper aside. "How're the apples looking?"

"Lots of 'um, wouldn't you say, Aunt Yo?

Mrs. Stanley was busy knitting mittens. "Come over here, Jeffy, before you get started on your game and let me see just how big I need to make these mittens."

"Grandma makes the best mittens, Aunt Yo. She says she used ta make your mittens too."

"That's right and they were the best mittens ever."

Forrest said, "Time's wasting. Come, you two." As the three of us stretched out on our stomachs he continued, "And, no matter who's ahead, at nine o'clock the game's over. OK, Jeffy?"

He gave Forrest a reluctant nod, shook the dice and our game was underway. We laughed at each other's bad luck and feigned crying when we were ordered: Go directly to jail. Do not collect $200.00.

Sometimes, Mr. Stanley gave Jeffy little clues. "Yes, I'd buy any utility. They're always a good investment."

The click of Mrs. Stanley's knitting needles stopped, and soon the smell of popcorn filled the air. It was like old times. Playing and being part of Jeffy's good time, I was a kid again.

As the big hand on the grandfather clock neared twelve, getting ready to strike nine, Snook came down the stairs, sauntered over and laid down right in the middle of our game, purring to beat the band. We all began to laugh.

Mr. Stanley said, "Wouldn't that beat all?"

Mrs. Stanley put her knitting down, and retold her story about making the bed that morning. Tears formed in my eyes. Jeffy gave Snooks some stroking pats; she squirmed, rolled over on her back, then took off like a young cat up the stairs.

That set us all to laughing, and Forrest began to pick up the strewn-around pieces of the monopoly game. "Jeffy, Snooks is telling us it's time to go home."

***

Snooks and I were awakened with the smell of sizzling bacon wafting up the stairs. I hurried and was downstairs in time to take over tending the hash-browns, and was setting the table as Mr. Stanley, Forrest and Jeffy came in from early chores. I left the hash-browns to Mrs. Stanley, and immediately began frying eggs-over-easy for the top of the hash-browns.   Apple-fritter cake made with canned apples from the early apple tree filled the air with the delicious aroma of cinnamon and butter.

Mrs. Stanley opened the oven door. "Not as good as fresh picked apples, but a good second best!"

As we were finishing up breakfast the atmosphere became somber. Soon we'd be saying goodbye. Mrs. Stanley took that moment to make an announcement: "I've thought this over, and, I'm here to say I've learned something new from Rebecca and Hilda. It's taken a few days to germinate, but here it is: from now on, Jo, you're to call Fred and me by our given names. After all, you're no longer a child and most importantly, you're family."

We both rose from the table and I was in her arms. My tears began to shamelessly slide down my cheeks. Seems I was always crying. "Oh, Mrs. Stanley, May. Here I am making a fool of myself when I'm so happy."

Mr. Stanley took me in his arms. "Fred." And it felt so funny but so just right!

Jeffy was impatiently waiting for his turn. "Yeah, Aunt Yo, you're family, just like me."

With that everyone blinked their tears away as Forrest took me in his arms and held me tightly and long. "That's right, Yo, just like Jeffy."

***

After breakfast Fred, it was so strange to think of Mr. Stanley as Fred, drove me to the bus station. Forrest and Jeffy stayed behind to do the chores. May decided good-bye was better said at home where her tears were her own. Ma, Matt and Mark were at the bus station waiting to see me off.

Ma hugged me and said, "Why don't you come, for the Labor Day holiday?" just like it was the most natural thing in the world, when in reality it was an enigma. Emotionally in many ways, it was a foreign place that I was leaving behind. It felt so unreal to be invited. She continued, "We've always gone up to the farm and helped Fred and Forrest with the apple harvest; it's fun and they share the apples."

Passengers began embarking. Mark gave me a kiss. "Yeah, Yo, they even used to get reluctant me to go along. This year I'll be at Cornell."

With a hug, Matt added, "Without me too, I'm afraid. Just think; I'll be finishing up at seminary."

Mark teased, "They'll need you all the more, Yo. Go, help'um storm the orchard and conquer the wily beast."

Fred hugged last. "Maybe we'll be seeing you," and he sang, "'in apple-picking time.'"

The bus pulled out of the station with smiles all around, misty eyes and waving hands. I was caught between two worlds, both beckoning, both incomplete. I must finish the one that had rescued me from disaster first. Would I find my place there, someplace other than the familiar world I was at that moment leaving behind? Time would tell. Before I could decide, my annulment must be completed, and it wasn't time to leave Rebecca just yet. I'd know when it was time for me to leave, as I knew I must, and in the not too distant future, no matter what direction my life was to take. In the meantime I'd buy a car. That would give me all kinds of new freedom, and no matter how difficult, I would get my high school diploma.

As the bus sped along, scenes persistently flashed though my mind of Ma and me playing out our new relationship, and it took conscious effort to tamp down my runaway anticipation. Too many times my hopes had been dashed. This time had to be different.

My mind refused to travel any further into the future. There was a roadblock I dare not explore too deeply. I clearly felt a new and different kind of distance between Forrest and me. We were both entering uncharted territory, life after divorce and annulment. Would I always be his little sister? Was Linda right when she said he didn't love her anymore? I tried to contemplate our worlds coming together, changing my childhood fantasies into an adult reality, but could not.

Chapter 21

By apple picking time, I was driving myself to work in my new Ford. Every time I pulled the car door shut, I shook my head in disbelief, my own car, my own name. Gone were all the outward traces of Rachel Rubin; thank you Atty. Baruch, and thank you Aunt Carrie for my new car.

I loved the last days of summer when the earth smelled warm and ripe, when the sun began to slip lower in the sky toward its winter-time position making shadows grow longer. The farmer and gardener in me always savored rewarding lazy days when the growing season was over, and nature had generously provided us her most precious of all gifts, the harvest.

I was in quandary, should I go home to pick apples? Rebecca and I were in the kitchen fixing supper, only in Bardo it was dinner. "I can't decide if I should go or not. Come with me, Rebecca."

"I'm tempted, but not this time. I'm not up to picking apples. Spring would be better for me. Anyway, it's time you had a real chance to be on your own...just think; you can get in that car of yours and take off."

"That is an exciting thought, but...."

"It'll never get easier. You'll be so busy picking apples you won't have time to worry about how to fill the gaps." She stopped, and took lettuce from the refrigerator to make a salad. "It's really entirely up to how you feel."

"That's the trouble. I've conflicting emotions…I'm really not ready to go, but when I close my eyes …..umm, I can almost smell the orchard…bees buzzing around the bruised, overripe apples that have fallen to the ground, filling the air with the sweet aroma of cider…the apple tree branches hanging low with their abundance…all around the orchard, berry bushes beginning to turn their brilliant scarlet-red…the birds sounding differently…flighty, getting ready for migration."

"I love the way you say things. It makes a beautiful picture."

That night as I climbed into bed, I was still wrestling with my decision. Many times I'd heard Mr. Stanley…Fred, say, "If in doubt, don't." I had plenty of doubts.

I was nervous about starting my GED course. What if all my old fears about being a slow learner, were true. My annulment was in limbo. When Porter found out I had inherited all that money, his effort to stop the annulment escalated to a frantic tempo. He came to Bardo demanding to talk to me in person. Atty. Baruch alerted the police, and he was apprehended as he was walking up to Rebecca's front door. Thankfully, I was completely unaware of that frightening scenario. Poor Porter! How frustrated he must feel to not only lose his singing partner, but to have my inheritance, all that money, slip through his fingers.

Attorney Baruch chuckled: "I don't think he'll try that again. He had to pay a hefty fine, and I think he has finally come to the understanding that he has no grounds to contest the annulment, and that he cannot break the restraining order without severe consequences. When the judge got through with him, I think Rev. Kent was just glad to say good-bye to Bardo!" His rugged face lit up with a smile. "Poetic justice, hmm?"

Remembering, I smiled to myself; it'd soon be over; could it ever be truly over?

Yes Fred, if in doubt, don't! My decision not to go home was made. I called Ma. "I can't get away...I've got'a work Labor Day weekend, plus my annulment's at a critical point...I'd be worried." I felt a little dishonest because I had volunteered to work for one of my coworkers who wanted the long weekend to attend a wedding, but it gave me the perfect excuse. "So, Ma, the apples'll have'ta get picked without me this year, darn."

In my rationalization to Rebecca, I explained, "I needed an excuse not to go because I couldn't just say to Ma I didn't want'a go, could I?"

"I think you've already answered that. I am surprised by your decision because I thought you were all primed to go."

"Everything's so up in the air. I want my annulment final. It'll be easier then...and I'm just getting started with my GED course. I can't wait until I have my diploma in my hand." Rebecca waited patiently, knowing there was more on my mind. "Ma told me something just before I left to come home after Aunt Alma's funeral that is causing me to question if I should confront Porter legally in some way with what he did to me. I thought that because he's loved by so many, and his ministry depends on his reputation, that it would be wrong and mean-spirited to challenge his behavior. Ma explained that when Hilda told her the fate of my biological father he became human...and she realized she had wasted her time hating a sick person, when she should've been thinking about healing the harm he'd done to her...and maybe if she hadn't let him get away with it, perhaps he'd have had a different fate. Now, I'm wondering if I should confront Porter in some way. I certainly don't want him thinking his treatment of me is normal. It's hard to take action because I still feel...that in someway...it's my fault...that I'm unworthy...that there's something wrong with me...and Ma too. I don't think I'll ever go to church again...just like Ma."

"Jo, I can tell you that's the abused person's typical response. You're wonderfully worthy and acceptable just as you are, as is Mary Louise. You write like a spiritual person. For me, there're as many ways to the truth as there are people in the world."

"Ma said you made her feel like there was nothing to forgive. I can see what she meant. Now that I think about it, when I asked Ma if Daddy had changed, her answer was that he hadn't changed his faith; he just practiced it more compassionately...without judging. How can I do that when it comes to Porter?"

"I think you'll be able to figure that out. Maybe you should mention your concerns to Attorney Baruch."

We were both absorbed in our own musings for some minutes. I decided I would talk it over with Atty. Baruch. He must have dealt with marriage rape before. Maybe he could tie Porter receiving therapy to my giving up my claim to the recording business.

I looked at Rebecca who was looking at me with love radiating from her eyes. "If you love Ma like a daughter, that makes me your granddaughter!"

"It most certainly does." She kissed both of my cheeks and gave me an extra tight hug.

I looked lovingly back into the depth of her accepting eyes. "What grandmotherly thoughts do you have?"

We settled back companionably. "A grandmotherly thought...I think, your thinking of Porter with concern, and I must say, with some element of compassion is the first step in freeing yourself from his ability to continue to harm you." She hesitated, and then ventured, "Forrest has played such a prominent role in your life, yet you never talk about him."

Again, Rebecca had put her finger on the most troubling aspect of my feelings about going home and of the future. "Forrest's going through a big transition in his life too. Linda told me at the funeral she was going to ask him for a divorce, which amazed me....I don't know how he feels about it...we haven't corresponded. Linda's had a real turn-around. She actually apologized to me for the way she treated me when we were teenagers. I was thunderstruck.....when I spent the night at the Stanleys, Forrest avoided spending any time alone with me. It was Jeffy who took me for a walk, and he confided to me that his parents, as he put it, 'were going to get unmarried'."

"Jeffy's a winner. Was he upset about it?"

"I think he's OK because Linda wants him to stay on the farm with Forrest. She's promised to come and visit him often....Jeffy's so...I don't know...direct. He told me he'd like a mother that wasn't a blood mother, to match Forrest who wasn't his blood father."

"I'm surprised he didn't ask you to come and fulfill that role."

Why was Rebecca pushing? She was so intuitive; she had to know she was pushing. "Jeffy thinks I'm married. He doesn't know about my annulment. Thank goodness. I wouldn't want to face explaining that. In the conversation around the picnic table, Forrest told me he thought I should go to college and study music...now that I had money."

"You do have a very special gift. What did you say?"

"I want no part of that world. I don't want to be a star. Forrest's sure I'll change my mind."

"I read in your journal that to Forrest you were his little sister. But you never quite saw him as a brother. I don't think he sees you as a sister anymore, or he'd have accompanied you and Jeffy on your walk. Maybe he's having trouble with a Yo who's not a sister...especially one who has money and doesn't need him. I think he's giving you room to make your decisions. He's playing his traditional role of the hero."

Two months later as Thanksgiving neared, Ma called and insisted Rebecca and I drive down to Phelpsburg and celebrate Thanksgiving.

"Come Thursday. We'll celebrate on Friday. Can you believe, Matt now Rev. Osborn, has his Thanksgiving church service to think about and can't come on Thanksgiving Day. Mark'll be home all weekend and cramming as always; either day's fine with him.

"I should be studying too, Ma. Seems to me school hasn't gotten any easier. How about we drive down Thanksgiving Day after work and leave Saturday after breakfast?"

"If that's the best you can do. It'll be good to see you both. Don't bring anything. You know me; I love do'n the fix'uns."

What a meal it was! She prepared all the favorite familiar dishes we used to enjoy when the Osborns and Stanleys were together for Thanksgiving: turkey and dressing, the dressing made with Ma's good homemade breads; mashed potatoes and gravy; squash; candied sweet potatoes with pineapple and pecans; scalloped corn and scalloped oysters, home-canned green beans; coleslaw with Ma's homemade dressing; Ma's pickled beets, her famous dills and pickled watermelon rind; apple, pecan, and pumpkin pie.

We ate slowly all afternoon. The air was full of shared memories of past Thanksgivings from each of us. Rebecca and Ma told of going over to Hilda's mansion for Thanksgiving because, for Hilda, Thanksgiving was the one holiday all faiths could enjoy equally together.

I said, "The one I remember best is the unhappy one when May had her heart attack...because we were all so scared...and because it was the event that changed everything for me."

Mark feigned heartbreak with both hands over his heart. "Yeah, it was devastating...we lost Yo to the Stanleys, plus being scared out of our wits."

Matt said, "Yes, and Yo was just a little kid, and overnight she became a caregiver and has never strayed from that path, and we love her all the more for it."

I winked at Ma. "'Do'n the what comes naturally.' No big deal."

Rebecca had been quiet, listening with great interest. "It would seem the apple doesn't fall far from the tree, as they say. Am I going to get to see the farm I hear so much about?"

I thought, not this visit; you said spring would suit you better, but I said, "Maybe in spring when it's coming back to life after its winter sleep."

"I'll look forward to that, Jo...Now...I have a surprise for all of you. Give me one minute." Rebecca left the table and came back with her tote-bag. "I have a photo album of snapshots John and I took when Mary Louise was a teenager living with us."

Ma and I cleared away all the serving dishes and plates from the table, and we all crowded together, hovering over the album.

I exclaimed, "Ma, you were a Coca Cola girl just like Abbey!"

"I suppose...in another life...not this me."

Mark said, "It looks like the ma I know. She's not a stranger to me."

Matt's face snapped up from the album and his eyes embraced me, telling me he understood.

Ma put her hands over her face, and her voice was muffled. "She's a stranger to Josephine."

We were all too stunned to speak for a few seconds. Rebecca closed her album. "Thanksgiving's a time to be thankful, and I am so very thankful to have found Mary Louise. So much as happened since the days of this album...I can't reclaim those lost years with Mary Louise, but now we have a new starting place for a new relationship...and one that includes Jo, whom I've come to love as I did her mother...two fine young men," she indicated Matt and Mark, "and in spring, I'll add the Stanleys."

Ma took her hands from her face. "I'm thankful too, Rebecca...thankful for the life that you and John gave to me as a teenager. I had forgotten just how wonderful those years were until we looked at your album. These last years have shaped the person I've become...and not a very nice one from Josephine's perspective. I can never be the mother to her that Carrie and May were...I can't expect to magically fill that place in her life...but I think we have a new starting place too."

Those were sacred words to me. "Ma, we've already taken our first steps......we just need to let each other in." No more holding back. My anticipation soared skyward!

The day ended as we enjoyed small pieces of each of the pies. Ma took care of the left-overs as the rest of us worked on the clean-up slowly, groaning with our gluttony.

Rebecca said, "All that turkey is telling me it's bedtime. I'll say, goodnight all."

Matt said, "I'll say goodnight also. This, ah-er, hard working clergymen, has some finishing touches to do on my sermon. I have to be on my way tomorrow too."

"Me three, for bed," I quickly added, "goodnight, Rebecca, goodnight brothers and goodnight, Ma."

Mark grimaced, "I'll be burning the midnight oil; it's study, study and more study."

Ma laughed, "Sounds wonderful to me, all my children with busy lives, but under my roof one more night...and, Rebecca, you in my life again...what a wonderful Thanksgiving...goodnight, sleep tight."

We slept late next morning and before Ma and I could manage to put together an omelet, it was midmorning. Late as it was, the chorus all around was, "Just a little for me," to compensate for our over-indulgence the day before.

After breakfast, Ma quickly packed an insulated picnic cooler full of iced-down leftovers for us to enjoy in the following days. As we said our good-byes the air was full of love and Thanksgiving and our hugs were filled with promises to visit again for Christmas.

***

May, with Ma's help, planned a big Christmas reunion; how could I refuse? But I hadn't heard one word from Forrest. It was obvious he was avoiding me. I didn't want to just barge in; what would I say? Plus, I wasn't ready to face Louisa May and Jenny. My heart was too vulnerable.

On top of my reluctance, Rebecca declined to go. "Jo, I'd love seeing everyone again, but we agreed spring would be a better time for me to get acquainted with the farm."

My bags were packed when the weather turned nasty with roads too treacherous for travel. Whew, the Christmas reunion took place without me. What an immense relief swept over me. I just wanted to snuggle in a cozy corner, not to have to smile and be sociable, to be allowed to wallow in the melancholy of my memories. I curled up in a big wing-back chair in the library where I knew John had spent much of his time. With an afghan around my legs and an unopened book on my lap, pages from the past flickered before me.

Millie opened her back door and scooped Carrie up into her arms. "MMM, such sweet kisses. Come see what I've made for you."

Spread out on the kitchen work-table was a red velvet pinafore with a white blouse nearly finished beside her sewing basket.

"Oh, goody, goody, just what I wanted. Thank you Aunt Millie." She flung her coat, hat and mittens on a chair and began to dance around the table holding the pinafore up in front of her. "Isn't it beautiful, Mommy. Can I wear it to our Christmas party here at Millie's church? Daddy says I can go."

"Sure you can baby." Millie and I exchanged looks. She knew the fight I'd had with Porter to get him to let us steal the time away from this first Good Shepherd Christmas. My heart ached because I had wanted to make the pinafore, but with the holiday music taking so much of my time Millie had come to my rescue.

I closed my eyes against smarting tears. At least I had been able to make Carrie's last Christmas her happiest. She danced around Millie's Christmas tree with popcorn and cranberry garlands we had strung on the one Saturday afternoon I had demanded to have at Millie's. Jimmy had taken the afternoon off from farm duties and the four of us had a party. Jimmy popped the corn as I made hot chocolate with marshmallows. We all sat around the kitchen table drinking hot chocolate, singing Christmas carols as we fished our cranberries and popcorn through our needles onto the string with half of the popcorn ending up in our tummies. Finally, we tied all our strings together.

Carrie jumped down from her chair. "Look, Jimmy, it goes all the way around the table into the living room."

"Yep, it'll go round and round the tree from the pointy top to its bottom." Jimmy took Millie's hand, "Point me to where you keep the ornaments; it's time to trim the tree."

Carrie's buckwheat curls danced around her shining face as she clapped her hands unable to contain her excitement. "Mommy, Aunt Millie had these when she was a little girl."

"Yes she did, Sweetheart. Be careful of that little cat, it's glass. Make sure it's fastened securely."

Millie unwrapped the Silver Star. "Here Jimmy, better put the star on before we get so many ornaments on or you'll be knocking them off."

I quickly suggested, "Hold Carrie up, Jimmy, and let Carrie put the star on."

Tears streamed down my cheeks. I must not think of her darling little body cold in the ground. I forced my mind back to my first Christmas tree and Forrest holding me up to put the star on the Stanley's Christmas tree.

"Aunt Millie, after Christmas can we put the popcorn strings out for the squirrels and birds? Mommy says that's what Jeffy and the Stanleys do."

"Sure, you can. And I'll save taking the tree down so you can help me pack all these things away for next year."

Sadness lay so heavily on my heart it was crushing me, but in the depth of my despair, my thoughts turned to Porter who would be delivering his Christmas sermon, demanding adherence to the literal truth of every detail of the Christmas story with recrimination for doubters, ending with an altar call, ruining the beautiful meaning of the story.

***

Christmas day, Rebecca said, "You're all geared up to go someplace, let's do our celebrating by going to the movies. 'It's A Wonderful Life' is playing. A happy ending is just what we need."

"Let's go. That is, if you're sure you don't mind seeing it again. "

"I enjoy it every time."

It did take the edge off my jangled nerves. "I can see why it's a classic. Thanks for suggesting it." Of course, movies were off limits for the wife of Rev. Kent, so it was new and engrossing to me.

Hilda interrupted the dismal days between Christmas and the New Year with an invitation to her annual New Year's Eve party that I had heard so much about. I was excited about going to a party in the first true mansion I had ever been in, and it was exactly like in the movies.

The opulence was unreal, and Ma had worked here! Ma had been used to this! I could easily see the beautiful bright young maid circulating among the wealthy guests. It was not hard to picture the handsome, very polite young man giving the pretty maid flattering attention. I imagined the bedroom up the wide circular staircase where Ma's assault had taken place. The image of Ma's life just prior to my birth was complete, making me all the more anxious to move on, to explore our new relationship.

It was the middle of January as Rebecca and I were eating breakfast that Attorney Baruch called. My annulment was final. With the threat of public exposure and the loss of exclusive rights to the recording company, Porter, with great protest, had given in to accepting counseling. I was Josephine Louise Wallace again.

Rebecca said, "I'm so happy to share my name with you, Granddaughter."

I held up my glass of orange juice. "Here's to Ma for picking the right name."

"To Mary Louise Wallace Osborn."

***

Rebecca and I settled in for the long winter. I watched the snow cover the flowerbeds with a feeling of loneliness that threatened to consume me. Even Rebecca seemed distracted. She said, "What's gotten into us? What can we do to shake ourselves out of the dumps?"

"When I was little I used to curl up around Snooks-----she'd purr my sadness away. Maybe that's part of why I'm sad…May wrote that Snooks died just before Christmas."

"You wrote about Snooks very touchingly in your journal. I'm sorry I'm not going to get to meet her. Are you still writing?"

"No."

"It might help."

"Maybe…writing my journal did help…it helped me see the good times, and the not so good times with an adult's mind. Putting my thoughts on paper took them out of myself…they become solid where I could look at them."

"Well said. Maybe you should consider being a writer."

"Not me…I like growing things; writing's not for me. To me nothing's as satisfying as planting a bean seed…and only a little bean seedling pushes up out through the soil… and in due time will nourish anyone who eats it."

The dumps still plagued me as a wintry March, the anniversary of Carrie's death, came howling in. Wasn't it supposed to get easier after that first year? Supposedly you stop measuring time by what you were doing the previous year with the loved one now gone from you forever. I knew that however long I should live, or how much happiness might come my way, Carrie would always be present in my heart. No arbitrary date would change that.

I heard randomly all winter from those I loved most in Jackson Junction, words of tender love and encouragement. I did think of Porter because I knew he was remembering and feeling pain too. I wished circumstances were different so I could visit Carrie's grave. Perhaps there would come a time in the future when that would be possible. However, it wasn't necessary because I carried her in my heart.

Spring must follow March. April was just around the corner, and the snow was slowly disappearing. Decision time was approaching. I said to Rebecca, "Pretty soon the crocus will be blooming, telling me it's time to make up my mind."

"Jo, don't give the garden work a thought. Hilda told me about a retired custodian who's looking for work to supplement his retirement income, and I've decided to employ him."

"That's a good choice." I was standing at the kitchen window washing our breakfast dishes. "Oh look, redpolls, under the feeder. The first sign that spring's really coming."

"What a wonderful sight. They're making their way back up to the Arctic Tundra."

We stopped our conversation, mesmerized as they swept in chirping and twittering, not minding the little patches of snow still lingering here and there around the back yard. I said, "I've only seen them once before. Mr. Stanley...I mean Fred...it's hard to get used to calling them May and Fred...told me they were redpolls."

"Fred's a pretty special person, I must say." She turned to leave. "I've lived long enough to have seen redpolls a few times."

"Rebecca, what should I do? I've set Easter as my deadline. All my excuses are used up. I have my GED and my annulment. In my heart I know I have to give Ma and me a chance to work on our new relationship...but...."

"But, you're worried about Forrest."

"Why hasn't he written? I'd be an intruder. How can I barge in without knowing how he feels?"

"You could write to him. Maybe he's wondering why you haven't written."

"I should...I really should."

But I didn't, and April came bringing cleansing showers, feeding the earth's hunger, and little green shoots began poking their tiny heads up everywhere. Daffodils danced in the warm breeze, calling me out to the garden. The aroma of wet soil rose up, filling my nostrils with the smell of rebirth and hope.

That very day a letter came from Abbey:

Dear Jo,

It's been a while since I've heard from you, and I'm afraid you're having a difficult time now that it's been a year since Carrie's death, and you must be feeling pressure to make some hard decisions. Louisa May and Jenny asked who I was writing to, and said, "Goodie, tell Aunt Jo hello and come see us soon." That would be nice.

Allen is ready for the school year to be over. He has to take some mandated refresher courses this summer. Maybe we can get together while he's away.

I'm very pleased at how well Mom and Dad are doing. Forrest and Jeffy have moved back in with them, and you know how much that pleases Mom. I can't believe the change in Linda. She's sending Forrest money to help with Jeffy's expenses. She even sends Jeffy a small weekly allowance of his own. She writes him regularly and comes up from NYC once a month to visit him. I'm so glad she's found happiness. That's what life's all about, finding our niche.

Forrest and Dad have finally hired a full time hired man, now that the tenant house is available. His name is Harry Turner. His wife's name is Carol. They're expecting their first baby this summer, and Jeffy's all excited about that. He and his dog, Laddie, put me so much in mind of Forrest when we were kids. The girls just love going to the farm to see Grandma and Grandpa, and Uncle Forrest and Jeffy. They think the sun, moon and stars all revolve around him just like a little girl did for Forrest not so many years ago.

That's one of the reasons I'm going out on a limb to offer some observations. Forrest is so openly relieved to have the divorce behind him, to have that chapter in his life put right. But he doesn't look happy. I know the two of you haven't written to each other. I think he's holding back because he thinks you should go on to school, and is reluctant to make any gesture that might interfere. That tells me he doesn't trust his feelings. Excuse me for saying it, but I think he is too ashamed and too blind to see past his nose. I have the feeling that there is much to be settled between the two of you. At the very least you should revisit and cherish the friendship you two used to enjoy. I hate to see this stand-off go on. Jeffy pushes to no avail. Forrest just replies, "We'll see what Aunt Yo decides. She has the chance to do really big things now." I've tried to talk to him, and he pretends to listen, but nothing changes in his attitude. His last comment is always, "What would I say to her?" I said hello is a good place to start!

I hope I haven't overstepped the bounds of a sister's concern, one who loves you both so very much. I hope to see you soon.

My love as always, Abbey

Wasn't that exactly what Rebecca had said? Hearing it again from Abbey clarified my feelings, made them tangible, the impasse manageable. A simple hello was the beginning place. Would we find a new friendship, love? Forrest told Jeff "we'll see". There was one thing for sure; I wanted no part of "bigger and better things".

Rebecca came out to the sun porch. My letter still lay in my lap. "It must be good news. There's a smile on your face."

"From Abbey. She always has a way of calming the waters."

"It's good to see you smiling."

"It feels good too. I've made my decision. I'm going home to stay as soon as I can give my notice at work."

"Good decision, the best…what I've been hoping for. Home is a wonderful place…the best place in the world to start any journey."

"I'm go'n in and call Ma right now."

As I walked to the phone, I thought: soon the apple orchard will be in full bloom. I'll be home when the delicate green veil floats among winter's barren branches.

I longed to run my hand along the old split-rail fence and ask Robin Goodfellow if the fairies still danced on the mossy stones in the moonlight. On second thought, he probably wouldn't hear me. A new page was turning. Life never looked more inviting.

EPILOGUE

My reflections as I face my big five-o birthday. Ma and Lou (Lou thinks Louisa May is too old fashioned.) are planning a big family reunion/fiftieth birthday party for me. Everyone will be here from Dr. Mark Osborn, Mindy and their children, Anna and Bob from way out in Illinois; to even include Linda who has her own dress shop in NYC. I haven't written in my journal since the day I left Rebecca's for my pilgrimage back home. Fifty years gives me pause to look back over my life, and I reread my journal. Perseverance wins! It's a story with a happy ending.

Absent from my journal are the sweet scenes of Forrest's and my struggle to overcome the "impasse". The scenes of the lovely long walks over the much traveled paths of our youth, and yes, arguments with a different magnetism demanding we resolve them. I should have written them but time will not dim them in my memory. Forrest and I have three daughters, Emma, Tansy and Clara. Jeffy married Louisa May, and they are the future of the farm. Forrest and I think that is poetic justice since Daddy, Jeffy's true grandfather, contributed his life's work to the farm and Louisa May carries on the family tradition. Jeffy and Lou have two sons, Little Forrest and Freddie. Emma gave us some anxious moments during her college years with the youth rebellion, but she is now married to a down-to-earth ceramic engineer, Clarence Madison, and she works in the library. Tansy is in college, studying journalism. Clara is in high school, and is so idealistic she is sure to pioneer some good cause.

The hardest to deal with has been the cruelty well-meaning people visited upon me in the name of religion. By the same token some of the kindest, most loved people in my life are: Rev. Grey, who is now in his eighties; Matt, who is pastor of a church near Binghamton, and his wife Beth, and their children, Paul, Mary and Ruth; Abbey and Allen; of course May and Fred who lived long enough to enjoy seeing Jeffy and Louisa May married, the birth of our Emma, Tansy and Clara, and to enjoy life with the Stanley farmhouse full of love and laughter; and Millie, who died many years ago. Thankfully, through my struggle with religion I have been liberated from the torments of believing in the supernatural with its inconsistencies. We can't know what we don't know. I have confidence in our ability to travel toward the continuing revelation of truth, and I am willing to accept the responsibility for my part in that journey.